Jacket design 2025 by Alice G. Bjornstedt

Image design by EAH Creative

Map © 2023 Alice G. Bjornstedt

ISBN: 979-8-9891034-6-1

Also in the Orlell Chronicles

Book 1 - Guardians of Gayrile

Book 2 - The Jewel of Power

Book 3 - The Quest for Drisilas

Book 4 - The Shard and the Shadow

Book 5 - The Curse of the Compass

Book 6 - The Prophecy of Three

Book 7 - The Song of the Stars

THE ORLELL CHRONICLES

Book 7

The Song of the Stars

Alice G. Bjornstedt

This, dear reader,

if you have followed the adventure all this way,

is for you, and I hope you enjoy it as much as I have.

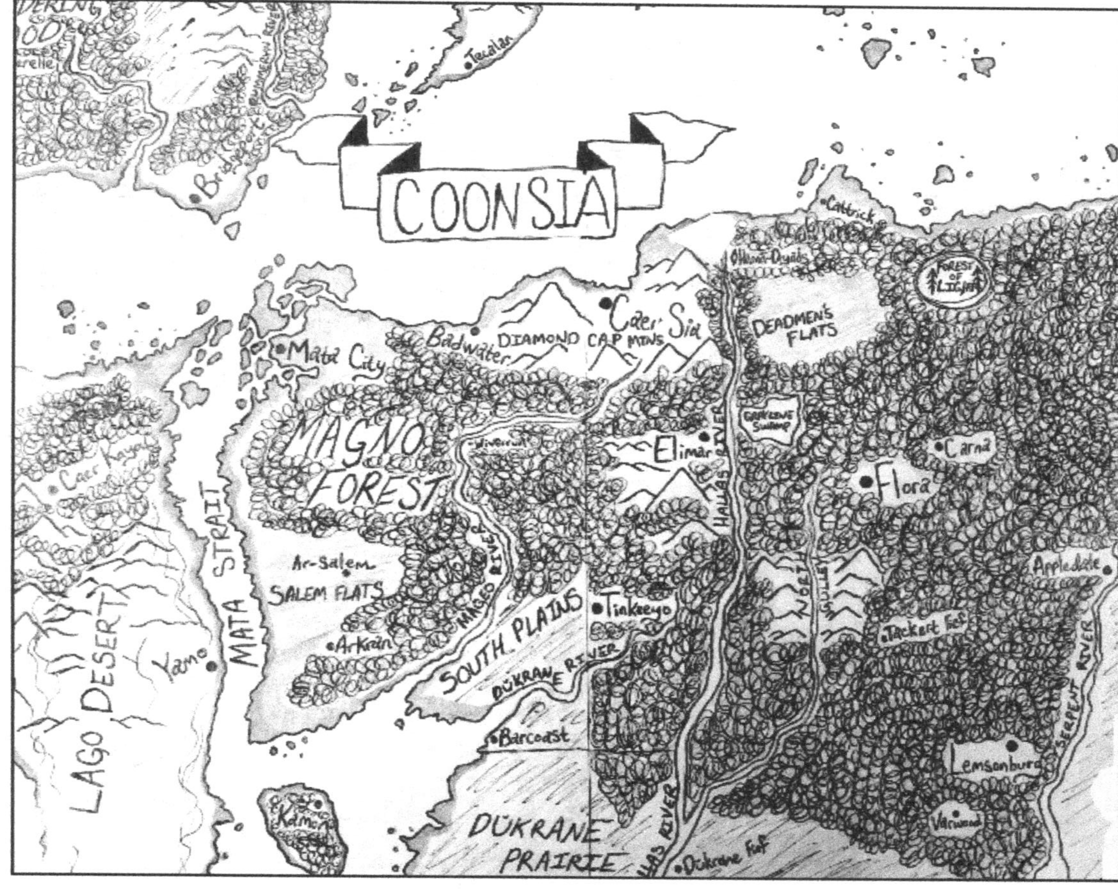

COONSIA
LAGO DESERT
MATA STRAIT
MAGNO FOREST
SALEM FLATS
SOUTH PLAINS
DUKRANE PRAIRIE
DUKRANE RIVER
MAGED RIVER
WAS RIVER
HALLAS RIVER
SERPENT RIVER
NORTH VALLEY
DIAMOND CAP MTNS
DEADMEN'S FLATS
DARKENE SWAMP
FOREST OF LIGHT
Caer Sia
Mata City
Badwater
Tecalan
Caer Layon
Ar-Salem
Arkan
Tinkeeyo
Barcoast
Kalmon
Yamo
Elimar
Flora
Carna
Appledale
Tackert Fort
Lemsonburg
Varwood
Cabrick
Ottoni-Dryads
Dukrane Fort
Riverent

Table of Contents

PART 1

The Waking of the Woods

Prologue

Forty years prior...

Silence.

It filled the desolate village with waiting expectancy as the black gateway opened on a winter night.

The tall figure that stepped through the doorway seemed as much a part of the mortal world as the shadows beneath the skeletal trees. Yet in the glint of his purple-red eyes and the ghostly swirl of his black garments was another power, far darker than the night which he had just entered.

Oh, it was good to be back.

Ahead, a cluster of huts was just visible through the gray light. Snow blanketed the thatched roofs and spindly fences, which bore the scars of a recent storm. No signs marked the road winding through the meager township. It was barely a blotch in Orlell's lonesome wilds, simple farms planted between the wind-strewn wastes of the Salem Flats to the south and the dense Magno Forest to the north.

The shadow inhaled a deep breath of the icy air. The village's location was of less importance than its inhabitants.

With an abrupt motion, he drew a glittering Star-Stone from its concealment and, with a brief flash of pale light, allowed it to seal the gateway it had opened. Its power would be needed again soon, he had no doubt. But not yet.

Wraith-like, he moved toward the decrepit huts. Yes, this place would do. Dead land, all of it. But the few mortals had disregarded the obvious disadvantages and dangers of sheltering here, guided by pride and foolish hope. And so they had come, eleven mortal farmers, transplanting their families to this place that withered the roots and crushed the spirit.

How could they have known their wretched future? They had thought only of their desires, hoping to transform these desolate flats into fertile land, not knowing that rot and disease were imbued in the very soil. They had learned it soon, as the graves beyond the fence showed. Women and children succumbed the quickest to such sicknesses.

The name bestowed upon the cluster of huts was the only remnant of that first hope the eleven farmers had held. The word was Elvish, a name for new life and fresh growth—Tiravale.

Wind moaned over the moors as the dark stranger strode down the frozen path, so that his robes billowed and joined the shadows. The cold breeze sang upon his skin, and he smiled beneath his hood. New life. That was exactly what he had come to offer.

A lone farmer stood on the road before him, bent beneath the freezing wind, leaning heavily upon an ash rod. The man raised his head, as though sensing the lingering chill from the void to another world. Fear crossed his face as he beheld the tall shadow before him. Slowly, he raised the rod, his voice tense. "Halt. What is your business here?"

Liznaeic. Such a barbaric tongue.

The shadow raised his head and exhaled a breath into the wind. "Good evening."

How long it had been since he had heard his own voice in the mortal world. Time had not lessened its effects, he was pleased to hear. His soft, rich tone seemed to call the very ice around him to attention. "Fear me not. I have come with an offer, one for every inhabitant of this village."

The mortal bowed his head, his weary eyes cast upon the parched ground. "We haven't much to give you. There are but eleven of us left."

"I know." There was no surprise in the words.

A new voice called from one of the tumble-down huts. "Who is there?"

How different this man's voice was from the first's, the shadow noted. The tone was smooth, sly, wearing a mask of confidence and strength. The shadow had no doubt that it was this man who had led the others to bring their families here, who had sustained them on false hopes and futile promises even as death had claimed their families. This mortal and his silken voice he relied upon.

"Someone to meet us, sir," the farmer called back, glancing again at the shadow. "Says we ought to gather the others."

The second man moved forward, muffled in a dark cloak. Despite his cool tone, his eyes held the same sadness, the same helplessness, as the first man showed. Only this mortal was better at hiding it. "How might we help you, sir?"

"This is Tiravale, is it not?" the shadow inquired.

At the elegant voice, the village leader hesitated, clearly aware his own tone held no weight or influence compared to the shadow's. "Yes, it is," he said at last. "Though its name, I fear, was wrongly given. There has been no growth here, no life." His voice turned bitter, his worn fingers lingering for a moment on the wedding band he still wore. The graves beyond were the only other reminder of his past life of hope and love.

Yet hope and love could be fickle things. The shadow's offer promised something more.

"Let us speak, then," the shadow said. He raised a hand from the depths of his cloak, ice crystallizing on his fingers. At his motion, the wind ceased, and the snow hung suspended in the air as though time itself had frozen.

The village leader looked at the silenced snow, then back at the stranger with undisguised awe. "We—we are listening."

"I know of your toils here. I know of your grief, your anger, your… fear." He breathed the last word into the night. "You came thus for new life, life you now believe to be unattainable. But life is what I offer."

The other nine farmers had emerged from their homes, stepping through the snow-stilled air as though called forward by the shadow's voice. They listened in silence, interest on their worn faces. But their leader bowed his head. "If you know our toils, then you will know that there is little left for us to live for. What then do you offer?"

"Power."

The whispered word seemed to echo off Tiravale's stones.

"Power," the shadow repeated, studying each face in turn. "Power over sorrow, over mortal kingdoms, over life itself. Power, one day, over all Orlell." He raised a lean hand, allowing ice to play over his dark fingers. "Swear to me, and the darkness shall call you master, the ice will stir your hearts, and the very fear of the mortals shall be as the blood in your veins. My strength shall become your Essence. You shall stand with me in the centuries to come, following where I guide. Vessels of my kingdom. The chosen cards in my game." The Jewel's pale light reflected in his eyes as he looked down upon his captive audience. "The choice is yours."

His words faded away into the snow-scarred village. Before the echoes had gone, the eleven mortals bowed as one before him.

"We will serve," the leader whispered, his face bent to the ground. "I pledge upon my name."

"I ask for no such pledge," the shadow told him. "Your names, your pasts, all must pass away. I give you a new name befitting your task." His hand rested on the leader's bowed head, white ice crystallizing his fingers. "You shall be called by none other, my Deputy in what is to come." His eyes flicked to the first man. "And you, my Messenger. Until another task is given, so shall you remain."

"We will remain," the eleven answered, their murmured voices growing stronger with their certainty. "So we choose."

"Please," the Deputy whispered, his face bent to the ground, "what may we call you, great one?"

The shadow removed his hood, casting his gaze down upon the mortals before him. Night-gray skin stretched over a face chiseled as though from stone, and purple-red eyes glinted from the depths of the sockets. Soon they would all share his face, just as they would share in his purpose, his power, his darkness.

"You may call me Lord."

1

The Exiled
Present day

Shadows filled the sleeping forest as Mel hurried after Iriam.

These woods were vaguely familiar to him. The oaks and elms, leaves green with late spring, grew in Appledale too. Everything around him brought his thoughts back to his home town, which was only a few miles to the southeast. The relief force was headed there now, and Mel would rejoin them as soon as he and Iriam finished their task.

Whatever that task could be, he had no idea. But by now he was used to the Neutral's vagueness.

He and his companions had departed from Caer Sia a little less than a week ago, accompanying fifty Red Dawn warriors to deliver relief supplies to Appledale's civilians. The rocky mountain passes were still dusted in snow, but they'd crossed the border with relative ease, reaching Flora yesterday evening. From Flora they'd headed due east, through the quiet woods towards the prairies where Appledale lay.

What might await them there, Mel did not yet know. He hadn't been there when the Aces had attacked Appledale, only heard the devastating report from Dusty. What he did know was that the Aces and their forces had never intended to claim the tiny village. The attack had been a warning—punishing Mel's friends and neighbors because of his actions.

And there'd been nothing Mel could do to help.

A familiar guilt filled his chest as he continued down the forest trail. No matter how many times his parents reassured him, no matter Iriam's promises that there was little he could have done, Mel still felt responsible for the devastation of his hometown. Whether or not he'd been there, Appledale had suffered, innocent people had died, homes had been leveled, because of him.

He shook his head shortly, eyes on the trail before him. Dawn was still a ways off, and the uneven trail made travel perilous. But Mel was used to the dark of early morning, the crisp air and the silence of the sleeping forest. He'd walked trails like this in the blue hours of dawn more times than he could count, tracking game, pursuing outlaws, or simply because Aryion wanted to get an early start.

Aryion.

The only thought that hurt worse than what the Aces had done to Appledale.

Ahead, Iriam slowed his pace and glanced back at him, his purple-red eyes softening. "Forgive my haste," he said, his deep, quiet voice filling the silence. "But we must continue moving if we are to arrive on time. We are not far."

Mel nodded. He'd long abandoned asking Iriam where they were going or who they were to meet with. The Neutral had given him no answers at all, only shaken him awake a few hours ago. They'd left the rest of the relief force and marched into the chilly moon-lit forest. The only thing Mel had gathered so far was that they were going due north, having left the main road behind and taking this dwindling, overgrown path.

The path reminded him of the way he and Aryion had taken on their way to Wiverrun, crossing the border and entering the foothills of the

Magno Forest. That, of course, had been before they'd learned the message that had called them there was false, before they'd realized they'd been lured into the Ace-Lord's trap.

He still saw the blanched white towers of Castle Droco in his dreams, like the skeleton of some ancient beast. Still felt the icy cold as he fell into the infinite darkness of the Patch. Still heard Aryion's desperate scream as he watched Mel fall.

Heart suddenly racing, he slipped a hand into his pocket and gripped the Blue Stone so hard it hurt. The pain, along with the comforting warmth, helped steady his racing thoughts. The thin cut on his palm had healed by now, but he could still sense the Blood Oath binding him to his promise. He felt it every time he was tempted to leave the war behind, to wander the wilderness, to march up to Ar-Salem itself, if needed, until he found his mentor or died in the attempt.

But the Blood Oath kept him from that. Kept him from the fight he'd thrown himself into ever since the quest for Drisilas. His mother should be happy for that, Mel thought with a wry smile—she'd never liked how often he put himself in danger. But she had been just as worried and sorrowful as everyone else when he'd explained his choice to swear the Oath.

They had good reason to hesitate, of course. For centuries, the Blood Oath had been sworn only for the darkest reasons—vengeance, war, more bloodshed. It had been a long time since someone had sworn it for the reasons Mel had. The Star Queen herself, Cahadras, had told him that when he'd sworn it: *"You redeem the Blood Oath, and so let this redeem the hour."*

Swearing the Oath meant he had given up the rest of his desires, giving his life to protect the Star-Stone. He knew, without an ounce of hesitation, that it had been the right choice. He felt that with unexplainable clarity, as though the High Light Himself had laid hands upon him and spoken the truth into his grieving mind.

No, his hesitation now did not come from the Oath itself, more for his own actions. The world was at war—since he'd sworn to keep himself from the fight, there was not much he could help with. If he was to protect the Stone, did that mean he was to sit uselessly on the sidelines, while friends and comrades gave their lives to rid Orlell of the Aces? If not… then what now was his call?

The New Blood's part in the Prophecy seemed to have ended after he'd joined the Shards, and the ancient words gave no clues as to his future.

The trail dipped down before a wide glade. Mel's boots splashed into cold water, and he drew back with a shudder. In the dim gray light, he could make out a wide stretch of marsh, spanning away before him as far as he could see. Soft mist rose from the dark water, and he hoped Iriam did not intend to cross it.

Thankfully, the Neutral beckoned him to the right, along the bank. "This way. Mind your footing." He strode confidently forward, keen eyes scanning the edge intensely as though searching for something.

Mel trudged after him, splashing through ankle-deep water. "Where are we?" he asked.

"We have reached Grayline Swamp," Iriam replied. "Keep clear of the water. I requested our passage to be unhindered, but one can never be too cautious when dealing with the Sirens." A faint smile crossed his face at the words.

Mel stepped over a fallen log, frowning. "The Sirens? There's Sirens here?" He knew very little of the Sirens. Salamander-like, their cunning intelligence and powers of shape-shifting made them both dangerous opponents and valuable allies, depending on whose side they were fighting for.

"Indeed." Iriam moved forward with an ease that made Mel certain he had been here many times before. At last he stopped, stepping down inside a tunnel carved into the bank, half-hidden by trailing ivy and marsh weed. "Here we are. Stay close."

Mel followed earthen steps down into the tunnel, which seemed to follow the swamp edge for several paces before turning sharply left and slanting steeply down. It was pitch black. Mel kept a hand on the dirt wall, holding the Stone in his other hand and allowing the blue light to illuminate the way.

They must be going underneath Grayline Swamp, he guessed, and glanced uneasily at the ceiling. He noticed it was not carved of soil, but was fortified by stone. This tunnel, as he'd begun to realize, was no mere digging of animals—it had been carved with purpose, leading somewhere.

Abruptly, the tunnel ended before a stone wall. They stood in a small cavern not much bigger than Mel's room at home. Tracks covered the dirt floor, but he saw no sign of life.

"They should be here at their post," Iriam murmured, sounding displeased. He rapped sharply on the stone wall.

"Who…?" Mel began, but stopped as a flat stone slid aside near the base of the wall, and a crafty, lizard-like face peered out.

"So you came after all," the Siren said. His wary voice bore a strong accent.

"I have come as requested by the Council," Iriam answered. "The Council, I might remind you, that your people have sworn to guard. Where then are the guards by this entrance?"

The Siren hesitated, but a new voice, deeper and in clear Coonsian, answered behind them down the tunnel. "It is as I commanded, Iriam. Speak not harshly of my guards."

A second Siren padded down the tunnel into the light of the Blue Stone. His smooth-scaled skin was deep green, and a golden crown glinted on his head. His yellow eyes regarded Iriam and Mel carefully.

"I had thought you would not come," he said. "I had thought the border roads would be cut off. Nonetheless it is good to see you."

"And you, King Sashan," Iriam replied, inclining his head in a slight bow. "The border is well-protected by the forces of Elimar. I must ask why your domain is not similarly guarded."

Sashan gave a quiet order to the guard, who disappeared from the opening. After a pause, the wall gave a shifting thump before rolling slowly to the side. This tunnel was much larger than the last, wide enough for three men to walk side-by-side, and tall enough even Iriam could walk upright.

A wide, circular cavern opened before them. Stone steps led up to a finely fashioned limestone throne, and the remains of a large fire trailed smoke from the center of the room. Usually, Mel guessed, this place would be full of Sirens, come to gather and meet and bring their matters to their king. But there was no one here now, only the dim moonlight sifting through the wide hole in the ceiling.

Sashan's yellow eyes scanned the silent chamber briefly before turning to Iriam. "I have waited for you as you asked. Once more, Iriam—once more only shall I open the passage for you. Then the way shall be closed. My people are leaving this place."

"Leaving?" Iriam repeated, frowning deeply. "To what end?"

"This war is not one we wish to fight," Sashan answered. "We are going east. For too long my people have been driven from our lands by bloodshed—first by Safacon, now by the Aces. The Mainland, I fear, holds no security for us."

"Nowhere will be secure if the Ace-Lord wins," Mel broke in, unable to keep quiet. "We can't just run away—we hardly have a choice whether or not to join the war."

Sashan turned to him, looking him up and down. "So you are the New Blood," he mused thoughtfully. "You are quite young for such responsibility."

"I'm old enough to understand why we need to fight," Mel answered shortly. Iriam threw him a swift, disapproving glance, but Sashan only nodded slowly.

"So I have heard. Understand this, then, child—no bloodshed, no matter its value or plenty, will end this war. The Prophecy alone will see the Dark Ones returned to the land of death."

He padded toward the back wall of the chamber, placing his webbed hand in a slot. As before, the wall rumbled and shifted before rolling to the side. A second stone tunnel gaped before them, letting in a breath of cold air.

"Go, and be swift," Sashan said, turning again to Iriam. "My people have guarded the way for years. Now, the Council must find a new place of exile, as must we."

Iriam's face was grim, but he did not argue the point further. "Know that we are grateful for your service thus far," he said. "But know also that the time of retreat has passed. Protect your people as you will, and beware the Aces."

Sashan gave him a slight nod, then turned away, back through the silent chamber and down the tunnel to follow the few guards. The soft pad of retreating Sirens echoed in the earthen caverns beneath Grayline Swamp, then all was still.

"You would do well to speak less harshly of Sashan's people," Iriam said. His voice held a quiet reprimand. "This war must be fought, in that you speak true. But so, too, are the Sirens right to say we must follow the Prophecy's words. They have stood guard here for many years, at times with great risk to their people."

Mel nodded, though his mind had fixed on Iriam's words. "The Sirens… why were they guarding this place?"

Iriam took a step toward the yawning stone tunnel before them. "Come, and you shall see."

Mel followed. This tunnel was much taller than the one that had led them below ground. Its arching roof reminded him of the marble halls of Castle Droco, but there was no cold fear or foreboding here. Cool air wafted up to his face as they descended slowly. He became aware of a faint pale light far ahead, and chills ran across his skin. But he did not feel afraid. Only invasive, as though he were venturing somewhere he did not belong, into a place outside of time, outside of mortality.

The tunnel ended in a balcony. Stone stairs traced down the side of a massive cavern to an outcrop of stone far below. Silver-blue light rose from a massive pool, clearer than glass and reflecting the moonlight like a great mirror. Tree roots stretched down from the ceiling, trailing delicate fingers in the water.

All was still, yet there was an ever-present sound Mel could not place, lingering on the very fringes of his hearing. A soft whispering rush, like the slow breaths of a resting giant.

He kept close to Iriam as they descended the stairs and reached the stone outcrop beside the pool. It was only when his boots reached the stone that he noticed the figure waiting for them.

An old man knelt beside the pool, back bent with age. He stood as they approached. His skin was pale mossy green, dark eyes keen as a hawk's, despite the lines the years had left upon his face. His hair and beard were gray and wiry like lichen, and his voice soft as he spoke.

"It has been some time since we last met, child."

Mel stared at him for a long moment as memories stirred in the back of his mind. Memories of the quest for Drisilas, of Dandio badly injured, of the companions sheltering with a tribe of hama-dryads in a grove of willows.

How long it had been. Yet Mel remembered. "Chief Munben," he said at last, bowing slightly. "It's—good to see you, sir. I—I didn't know you were the one I was meant to meet," he added, glancing back at Iriam.

"I am not," Munben-Lia answered. "They will be here shortly. We wished to speak with you first, of another matter."

"We?" Mel echoed.

There was a rustle of movement behind him, and another figure emerged from the shadows beyond the stairs, walking along the edge of the pool. A Dwarve, standing a few inches shorter than Mel, stocky and clad in the earthen tones of a healer. His eyes were kind as he studied Mel's face.

"We have not met before, New Blood," he said, his voice quiet and calm. "My name is Larkin Sitka. I served with the Guardians of Gayrile."

"I've heard of you," Mel said, as the memories stirred again. "Rygal told me about you—he said you helped them during the quest for the Jewel." He looked between the three men in total confusion. "What are you all doing here?" he asked at last, gesturing at the moonlit cavern.

"We desired to speak with you," Larkin answered. "Your actions, some quite recent, have become a subject of interest to us."

Mel tightened his grip on the Stone, feeling it dig into the fresh scar on his palm. "I made a promise," he said finally. "All this time I've thought my calling was on the battlefield, but that's not the purpose of the Stone. My role now, my call now, is to keep the Stone safe. I don't know how I can help in this war yet… but I can't go back on the Oath."

He paused, not sure he'd explained himself well. But the others seemed to understand. "It was a wise choice," Munben said thoughtfully. "To redeem the Blood Oath, to use it in protection of the last uncorrupted Star-Stone—that is a noble act, one that must not be taken lightly."

"And yet I sense you hesitate, child," Larkin said gently.

Mel stared at the floor in silence for a moment, seeking the right words. His hesitation, his fear, did not come from his choice to take the Blood Oath. It stemmed from something else, from the abandoned sword beside the battered ranger packs, from the memories that filled his every waking moment, from the stabbing grief and the guilt he could not be rid of.

"My mentor," he whispered at last, choking over the words. "He's… gone. I don't know if he's dead or captured—but I can't do anything to help, not without putting the Stone in danger."

"Do you believe he lives?" Larkin asked.

Mel took a deep breath. When Dusty had first brought the news of the devastating attack on Appledale some three weeks ago, he'd been so convinced that she was wrong, that Aryion had been captured, not killed. He'd clung so stubbornly to that, even beginning to plan how to save him. A plan to track down Bryn with the Dricaster pin she'd given him, and let her and her comrades find and rescue Aryion.

But as the days had passed, his determination had begun to fade, and the sheer impossibility of the task had reared its head. Bryn might be able to help—her skill as a bounty hunter meant she'd at least have some experience in getting in and out of dangerous places—but first Mel would have to find her, which would be incredibly difficult. After they'd parted ways in Esile City, Aryion's sister could have sailed anywhere to the north. In fact, who was to say she was still in the north? It had been months. She and the *Burman Marie* might be anywhere on the far seas.

Besides, even if he found Bryn, how could he convince her to help? Asking her and her crew to risk their lives on a chance—he couldn't ask that of her. Aryion wouldn't want that. And so Mel soothed his uncertainty with grief. Aryion was dead. Mel couldn't help him.

But deep down, in the depths of his heart, Mel knew that wasn't true. The unshakable possibility whispered in his mind in the middle of the night, searing his heart with guilt. *He's alive, Mel. He's alive, and you're doing nothing to help him.*

His throat was dry, and he could not answer Larkin's question.

"I understand your pain," the Dwarve said after a pause. "To be unable to help one's friends, to be unsure if they yet live—I too recall a time where I felt the same."

Iriam spoke, his deep voice holding a rare note of gentleness. "It is a great burden to bear a Blood Oath, an even greater burden to surrender one's desires. But the reward of such a choice is even greater."

"So I just have to… forget about him," Mel guessed. The thought had filled his mind several times, but hearing it aloud pierced his heart like a blade of ice.

But Iriam shook his head. "Not forget. Set aside the task, perhaps. If you believe him to be alive, there are those willing to seek him on your behalf while you guard the Stone, if you will ask for aid."

Mel raised his head, startled, as he finally understood what they offered. The three faces stared back at him, waiting for his answer. At last he managed to speak. "I—I can't ask you to do that. I mean—I don't even know where to start—if Aryion's alive, he's probably in Ar-Salem, but—I don't know how someone would figure that out."

To his surprise, Munben laughed softly. "Ah, that will be seen to. If you wish our aid, know we will give it."

"There are ways of finding those lost," Iriam said. "Whether you wish us to seek your mentor directly, or to contact Bryn as you had planned, the Scribes will do so."

Mel stared at them, overwhelmed with gratitude for a moment. "Why?" he asked finally, choked with emotion. "Why would you help me?"

Larkin chuckled and shook his head. "If you have done half the things Iriam has told us you have, then you have earned our thanks."

"Allow us to help you," Munben said. "Your quest to protect the Stone might be better accomplished if your heart is at ease."

Mel swallowed hard. The questions that had plagued him for so long lingered in his mind, but the knowledge that he might soon have answers filled his heart with hope. "Thank you," he managed finally. "I—I do have this." He reached into his pocket, producing the little red pin. Bryn had given it to Aryion after their mission in Esile. Her words echoed afresh in Mel's mind: *If you ever have need of me, show that to any pirate in the north. They'll find me.*

"Bryn gave us a promise," he said aloud. "I don't know where she is, or how much she can do, but—I think she might be able to help."

He set the pin in Larkin's hand. The Dwarve studied the red bear insignia, impressed. "A Dricaster badge—it has been quite a while since

I have seen one under positive circumstances."

"Asking aid of a bounty hunter may be unorthodox," Munben mused with a smile, "but I suppose the times require it."

"I am sure Lammar can handle it," Larkin said absently, tucking the pin away. "Now, you had better call the Council, Iriam, before they grow weary of our chatter."

Mel had assumed "the Council" consisted of Munben and Larkin, with Iriam and Lammar playing some role as well. But he realized he'd been wrong. These three seemed to be informants of some kind—the Scribes, Iriam had said. Who then did they answer to?

His question was answered in another moment as Iriam placed both hands on the ground, causing deep blue ice to run along the surface of the rock and into the silvery pool. Ripples spread across the water, tugging at the trailing roots.

As the ripples crossed the pool, figures appeared. Mel had seen how the Stars could travel and appear, transported in streaks of golden flame. The Aces could do something similar, shifting across the sky in a dark ribbon of shadow. Yet these newcomers did not do either. They arrived in the cavern with the whispering rush of wind and the gleaming silver of a tumbling waterfall.

Nine tall figures came into focus, robed in deep blues and greens. Six men, three women. Silver markings traced over their skulls like a map of the night sky. In the glimmer of their purple-red eyes, the charcoal gray of their skin, Mel saw another face, one familiar to him.

But they were not Aces. He sensed that immediately. There was no freezing cold, no chill of foreboding in their presence. Only an aura of ancient power as the nine Netrocrians arrived in the cavern.

Iriam, Munben, and Larkin all bowed low, and Mel hastened to do the same. "My brethren," Iriam greeted them, straightening. "I thank you for coming."

The tallest of the nine spoke. His voice, though not especially loud, seemed to fill the cavern. "We have come as we are summoned, Iriam son of Alluvis."

Iriam turned to Mel. "May I present the Druid Council. The last of the Neutrals who remained loyal to the Light during the Dividing War, who have cast off the darkness of Kahlifis and transformed their magic to serve the land and the Light."

Mel managed what he hoped was a friendly smile—inwardly, his thoughts were racing in awe. He'd wondered, occasionally, what had become of the other Neutrals, those who had fought against the Ace-Lord in the Dividing War and vanished shortly after. Iriam alone was known to the mortals—many believed the others had died long ago, or joined the Ace-Lord. But here they were. Standing before him in a chamber where the water reflected the moon.

One of the Neutrals turned her face to Mel, her eyes narrowed slightly. "Why has this mortal been brought before us, Iriam?" she inquired. Her tone, though level, was edged in unease. "Does not the gateway bar all but the Scribes and the Sirens?"

"So it did, Aluna," Iriam answered. "But the gateway will no longer protect this place. Once more it has been opened, and only at my request."

"Then we must find a new place of hiding," the first Druid said. "We know of the unrest in the mortal kingdoms. Should the war continue, our people will cease to exist."

"Perhaps," Iriam said. "But you know, Iraveri, that the time has long passed for exile. The same shadows who once guarded our presence now answer to their master."

One of the other Druids spoke, his voice bitter. "Kahlifis knows not of our existence, Iriam, as we have long fought to keep hidden. If you choose to risk your own life, do not mourn when it is lost. You might still be counted among our number, if you had not chosen to ally with the mortals."

"All I have done has been in accordance to the Prophecy's words," Iriam answered calmly. "I do not regret my actions. The return of Kahlifis is what brought me to ally with the Liznees and their king, and it is what brings us to ask your aid now."

"The trees are stirring," Munben put in, stepping forward. "The dryads of every forest in Orlell know and fear that, should the Ace-Lord's conquest succeed, mortal and immortal alike shall be broken beneath him, and the dead shall reign."

"I would not have come had the times not required it," Iriam said quietly, his voice serious. "But it is for this time that the Druids were placed upon Orlell. Thus, your Scribes ask your help. With us is the New Blood." He placed a hand on Mel's shoulder. "He has seen the horrors Kahlifis is capable of. But so too has he sworn to protect the Star-Stone, despite the darkness to come."

Iraveri's eyes turned to Mel. "Is this true, New Blood?"

Mel met the scrutinizing gaze and nodded, holding the Stone against his chest. When he spoke, his voice was calm. "The mortals need help. We're prepared to fight, but the Ace-Lord's growing stronger with every day. I don't know… what kind of help you're able to offer," he added uncertainly, glancing up at Iriam, "but I do know that many of us have already died in this fight. The Ace-Lord's our enemy as well as yours, so I think our best choice is to fight him together."

"Kahlifis seeks to twist the Prophecy's words," Iriam said. "Only then shall his victory be secured. Such deception, such corruption, can be countered only by the truth. And so the truth must be spread by the dryads, as it was in the days of the Dividing War." He paused. "To reach the dryads is a power few know, and fewer still are trusted by them. But that power was gifted to the Druids for such a time as this."

There was a long pause. Mel glanced at the nine Druids, their faces so similar to the Ace-Lord's. He wondered, briefly, how many of them had known Kahlifis before the darkness had consumed him, before the allure of power had corrupted his spirit and turned the ice of his Essence deadly white. These Netrocrians had fought him, and many had paid for it with their lives. Now, they were being asked to fight again, to rejoin the mortal struggles they had dwelt apart from for centuries.

The time has come. The words of the Prophecy of Three whispered in Mel's mind, as though they had risen from the moonlit pool.

At last Iraveri raised his head, looking up into the trailing roots of the great tree, and nodded. "We shall aid," he said. "By the sacred name of the Light, we shall aid the mortals. The songs shall be sung."

At his voice, the soft rush of wind vanished, as though the very cavern were holding its breath. Hope and excitement stirred Mel's heart, and he felt himself smile. He drew back toward the cavern wall with Iriam, watching with an expectancy he couldn't understand.

The nine Druids knelt at the edge of the pool, placing their hands in the silver water. As one voice, they raised the words of an ancient tongue in a chant, quietly at first, then steadily growing louder. Mel didn't understand the words, yet as the low melody echoed in the moonlit cavern, chills spread down his spine, and it seemed his very Essence was answering the call.

Deep blue water rippled from the Druids' fingertips, streaming toward the center of the pool and the trailing roots. Their chant filled the cavern, and the Blue Stone shimmered brightly in Mel's hand, as though it too were affected by the pure magic crackling in the air.

"Let the trees awake," Iraveri intoned, his deep voice harmonizing with the song of the Druids. "Let the sea stir and the wind gird itself for war. Let all Orlell cast off the darkness of Kahlifis, and let the Light shine through."

As the deep blue reached the center, the roots twisted and stretched deeper into the water. Silvery light rose from the pool, up inside the tree and towards the distant surface. Gradually, the silver spread from the central tree into the neighboring roots, until the entire roof of the cavern glowed silver-blue and the roots twisted and stirred as though waking from sleep.

Wind rippled from far above, blowing into the cavern, carrying the leaves of the trees. In another instant, three dryads flickered into view, pale gray with birch leaves swirling around them. Their whispered voices filled the wind-strewn cavern as they hovered above the pool, suspended by moonlight.

"We have awakened. We shall aid."

In a flicker of falling leaves, they vanished again, riding on the wind as they returned to the surface and spread in a summer breeze through the waking forest.

With one last bow, the Druids faded away before Mel's eyes, their silver markings sparkling like sunlight in a stream before they vanished. In another instant, the great cavern was still, and the pool reflected the pale light of dawn.

2

The Vessel

Dawn had barely lit the camp when Allie sensed something had changed.

Wind stirred the tall trees surrounding the glade, blowing westward. It billowed the tents and tugged on the manes of the sleepy horses, stirring the embers she knelt beside.

Absently, she let red fire crackle from her fingers and set the coals ablaze. The flames glowed scarlet, sparking with energy, but cast the same warmth as though she'd lit it from the tinderbox.

How her fire had changed since the curse had been cast upon her. Channeling the flames of her Essence, which used to take a concentrated effort, now came as easily as her every breath. Allie felt it in her veins constantly, crackling and consuming.

The last time she'd used it in battle had been in Castle Droco some three weeks ago. Since then, her inactivity and the unease of war made the blaze restless, burning hotter and hotter in her chest as though it would sear her heart. But she knew the time would soon come for the fire to burn forth, and the Vessel would join the fight.

The Vessel. Three weeks felt like a lifetime with such a title binding her, yet she could still recall every second of the Ace-Lord's curse. The black-clawed hands gripping her skull in ice. The ominous words of the Life-Blood Spell. The brief burning pain as her Essence was bound to the Ace-Lord's, like freezing chains drawn taut around her heart.

Yes… the fire had changed now.

Allie stood, looking around the camp. Wind rippled the leaves of the tall oaks above the tents. The breeze carried a wild chill that felt strangely familiar, and it took her a moment to place it. "Dryads," she murmured at last, keeping her voice low. Most of the soldiers were still asleep.

Darion, keeping watch a few paces away, glanced over at the sound of her voice, his red hair still tousled from sleep. "I can hear them," he whispered back, hazel eyes scanning the trees. "Or… sense them, rather."

He studied the woods in silence, a hand on his bow. Since the disastrous mission to Wiverrun, he and Rygal had practically become her second shadows, protecting her, keeping her safe. Allie couldn't exactly blame them for their concern; they'd both seen the darker side of her new powers. The three of them had spent the last several weeks searching for any information about the Life-Blood Spell. But, as the days had passed, and Allie's helpless fury stoked the fire's wrath, her determination had begun to wane.

It was part of the reason she'd joined the relief force to Appledale. Get away from the restlessness and unease filling Caer Sia, leave her search for the Life-Blood Spell behind for now, clear her head. Rygal had promised to keep looking through the scrolls while they were gone; his duty to the Guardians of Gayrile meant he would stay in Caer Sia a little while longer. She appreciated his efforts, no matter the outcome.

She turned her eyes back to the trees. They had encountered a dryad on the mission to Wiverrun, who had warned them of Aces in the area—though they hadn't learned about Castle Droco until it was almost too late. But their mission hadn't been a total loss. They'd learned about the Patches—voids of darkness, allowing the Ace-Lord's forces to travel through Orlell undetected. They had yet to learn a way to close the Patches, but for now, as long as they knew where they were, they could better anticipate where the Aces might attack.

Yet the real problem wasn't the Patches, dangerous as they were. The true danger lay in the high tower of Castle Salem, the gateway between worlds the Ace-Lord had crafted with the remnant of the Jewel's magic. Through the gateway, he'd brought the Messenger, Redeyes, whose claws laid terrible curses on the mortals. He had also brought the massive wraith known as the Bruin, which had thankfully been destroyed by the Stars.

Allie had ventured into the Ace-Lord's gateway herself, after entering Ar-Salem through the Patch. The wind and clutching darkness still haunted her nightmares. She had barely made it back out with Jan and Mel, and only because the Ace-Lord had allowed her to.

The fire spat sparks beside her, trailing smoke into the dawn. Allie placed another piece of wood in the flames as the curse overtook her thoughts again.

Despite help from both Rygal and Darion, their search had yielded nothing. They'd scoured Castle Sia's library, looked in hundreds of ancient tomes and scrolls—they'd even begun working their way through the books of Garilian magic that Rygal had been studying. And yet they had found nothing.

Allie was not sure yet what she was hoping to find. A historical record of the Life-Blood Spell would not exactly help her situation. There was no cure, no counter-spell that would release her. The only way to be rid of it was for the Ace-Lord to remove the spell himself…

unless she chose to escape the curse's hold with her own death.

Strangely enough, that very real possibility had yet to set in. When she'd first learned of the Life-Blood Spell, she had felt detached, unable to fully process the truth. Then Dusty had returned, bringing the devastating news of Aryion's death and the attack on Appledale. After that, it had been easy to distract herself with the war—meetings and councils, reports, searching for knowledge of the curse with Rygal and Darion.

So she'd had little time to think or worry over the truth of her future. She could ignore the concern and grief in the eyes of her friends and the growing darkness in her own heart. But anger was better than the fear, and she utterly refused to give up. The alternative would have her fire feed the Ace-Lord's power until it glowed white with corruption, and she was reduced to a pawn in his game.

Sunlight filtered through the trees, and the soldiers of the relief force began to stir awake. Darion stood, looking around the camp as the wind faded away. "I never knew there were dryads here," he mused. "Maybe that's who Iriam went to speak with."

Allie looked at him sharply. "Iriam left? When?"

"A few hours before dawn," Darion answered, sounding unconcerned. "He and Mel headed north—said something about a meeting."

"And you were going to tell me this when?" Allie asked, exasperated.

The young ranger shrugged. "I didn't think to. I'm sorry. It didn't seem dangerous, at least. Iriam told me to let Captain Rosen know when the others were awake. Don't worry about them," he added, seeing her troubled expression. "You know Iriam would never put Mel in danger."

This didn't ease Allie's unease, though she knew Darion was right.

Mel's Blood Oath kept him from charging into danger, not to mention his own duty to protecting the last uncorrupted Star-Stone.

The Stone Isilas had been removed from the hilt of Jan's sword and remained safe in Caer Sia, but Allie knew it would not be remedied easily. Twisting that magic meant to heal and protect into a weapon of war carried a heavy cost—Jan himself had borne the scars of Redeyes for years.

Cahadras had told them Isilas' fate would become clear in time, though Allie couldn't see what could be done. She still remembered the weight of Jan's sword in her hand, seeing Isilas spread white flames up its blackened blade as she'd killed Dal-kerri and enchanted soldiers alike.

She shook the heavy thoughts away for now as morning arrived and the camp stirred to life. They would reach Appledale today, delivering supplies the helpless village would desperately need. Captain Rosen, the leader of the company, issued brisk orders to the men. He shook his head wryly as Darion explained what Iriam had said.

"Leave it to the Neutral to hurry off on a secret task," he remarked. "We may as well be prepared for departure by the time he has returned."

"Mel went with him?" That was Mel's father, Joseph Smallbutton, who had insisted on joining the relief force to Appledale to help his friends and neighbors. Mrs. Smallbutton and Mel's little sister Misty had remained in Caer Sia.

"He did," Darion said, and quickly added, "but don't worry, they'll probably be back soon."

Joseph's rosy face was troubled, but he shook his head, as though banishing his fears for his son. "Oh, I'm sure he'll be safe enough with Iriam. And he's a ranger apprentice."

Allie managed a smile, but she could not understand his optimism. It wasn't just his view of Iriam's strange disappearance; Mr. Smallbutton also held an unshakable confidence that Aryion was still alive and a captive of the Aces. By now, he was almost alone in that belief. Even Mel, Allie could tell, had started to abandon that hope in favor that Aryion had simply been killed. That was almost preferable to the agonizing unknowing of whether or not he yet lived.

"A secret task," Darion repeated wryly, shaking his head as he shouldered his pack. "Well, I don't suppose Iriam meant to give us the morning to sleep in."

The Neutral's deep voice came from behind as he said it, making him jump. "Unfortunately, Master Blackbird, that is not an opportunity this morning allows."

Iriam strode into the camp, black robes billowing about his tall frame. Behind him, looking tired but surprisingly cheerful, was Mel.

"Where have you been?" Allie demanded, unable to keep the edge from her voice. "You wandered off in the middle of the night—you might have been captured or worse!"

"You will have to forgive our haste," Iriam replied calmly. "But you need not fear for us. These woods are protected by a force far stronger than the Ace-Lord and his minions. Know that I would not have left you all alone if I thought otherwise."

His steady answers did not satisfy Allie, especially when Iriam had made such a point to remind them all of the danger of the times. Besides that, Appledale had been attacked by the Ace-Lord's Dal-kerri hounds, and there was a chance the beasts were still in the area. She shook her head, still frustrated. "Even if there wasn't danger, it still seems a risk. Why couldn't Darion and I have come too?"

"That would have been insupportable," Iriam told her. "Our meetings involved the New Blood alone. In addition to that, I preferred to have you here to guard the others."

"We are nearly prepared to depart," Captain Rosen said. "I assume we should head out as soon as possible?"

"Indeed," Iriam told him. "I do not wish to keep the inhabitants of Appledale waiting any longer than needed for our aid. If you will eat, do so quickly."

Allie turned back to the fire, pushing her frustration away as she finished packing up. She glanced at Mel as she rolled up her bedmat, startled to see the hope in the boy's eyes. For weeks, his expression had been filled with grief and fear, the cares for both his mentor and his village weighing heavily upon him. But now, he seemed almost relieved.

"Where were you?" she asked.

Mel looked up and gave her a genuine smile. "I'll have to explain it on the road—if I can explain it."

"We saw the dryads," Darion told him. "At least, we heard them, and felt the wind."

"Well, I guess that's partly because of us," Mel answered. "Like I said—I'll tell you on the way."

They struck camp, loading the horses and continuing the ride east in a clatter of hooves. Allie's frustration at Mel and Iriam for leaving unannounced was replaced now with curiosity. Thankfully, her questions did not have to wait long.

Mel guided his horse to Allie and Darion, speaking quietly. "Have you ever heard of the Druids?"

Allie looked at him, surprised. "A little… I think I've heard the name once or twice in my studies, but that's about all."

"Well, we met them," Mel said, eyes filled with excitement. "They're the last of the Neutrals, servants of the High Light, a council of nine, hiding beneath Grayline Swamp for—I don't even know how long."

"Grayline Swamp?" Darion raised his eyebrows. "Does that mean they're allied with the Sirens?"

"Yeah—well, sort of. The Sirens were guarding the entrance to the Druids' meeting place. But they aren't planning to fight this war," Mel said. "They were leaving just as we got there."

"And Iriam let them go?" Allie asked in disbelief.

"I don't think he was happy about it," Mel answered, "but King Sashan pointed out that we won't win unless we fulfill the Prophecy. Anyway, we met with some of the Druid informants, they're called the Scribes. Chief Munben-Lia of the hama-dryads, a Dwarve from Gayrile named Larkin—I think there's more, too. But Iriam said they're going to… going to help find Aryion."

Allie studied him, finally understanding the relief and elation on his face. As interesting and hopeful as this news was, she couldn't help feeling doubt. "Do they know if he's…alive?" she asked, trying to phrase the question gently.

Mel flushed. "No, they don't—but they're going to find out. And once they do, they're going to free him—they said Lammar can find Bryn, or maybe they'll go help him themselves."

"That's wonderful," Allie said, feeling bad for questioning the plan. Mel was already afraid. Fears for his mentor had threatened to crush him over the last few weeks. But the Scribes' involvement had clearly eased his mind for now, and she was grateful for that.

"So, what are the Druids going to do?" Mr. Smallbutton asked, jostling his fat pony closer to the conversation.

Mel looked up into the summer leaves of the surrounding trees before turning back to his companions. "The Druids are allied with the dryads. They woke up the forest with a song. I don't really know how it works, but the dryads have promised to help."

Allie scanned the forest, both awed and puzzled by this piece of news. "The trees," she echoed thoughtfully. "I think—I think the dryad said something like that on the way to Wiverrun," she said, looking at Darion. "About how the Ace-Lord fears them—the trees see all but speak of none. But if we're able to speak to them…"

"We'll be able to reach anyone," Mr. Smallbutton said, nodding eagerly. "It can take weeks to get messages from kingdom to kingdom, longer in wartime. If the very trees are our allies, they can carry news faster and surer than the swiftest courier."

"They might even be able to gather news, too," Darion pointed out. "Think of all the questions we still need answered—the enchantment, the extent of the Ace-Lord's army, the illusions—and Aryion," he added, turning to Mel.

"If the Aces have Aryion as a prisoner, the dryads will find out," Mr. Smallbutton said, patting his son's shoulder. "It's great news, son."

Mel nodded, but his face had clouded with worry again. *If.* Strange how such a small word could carry such a burden of fear.

Their conversation turned to other subjects as they rode steadily on. Mr. Smallbutton and Darion speculated about the Wildkids' mission back to Kasabren, a journey that would likely take several weeks. Admiral Dessian, leader of the Red Dawn Navy, was personally escorting Dusty's group on his fastest ship. Once they reached Kasabren, they must somehow persuade the Wildkid Clans to join the fight against the Aces. Allie knew this would be no easy task. The Wildkids had distanced themselves from Mainland matters for decades, and they would likely be hesitant to join the war, as Darion pointed out.

But Allie knew the time had passed for such a privilege. The Ace-war, once a thing of speculation, had begun, and every kingdom of Coonsia was aware of it. The bulk of the Ace-army remained in Ar-Salem, shrouded in a darkness so impenetrable no courier team had yet learned more. Other reports warned of outlaws or tribes marching to join the Ace-Lord. The number of enchanted soldiers, Allie feared, was growing daily.

"We're nearly there," Mr. Smallbutton said, drawing her out of her thoughts.

The woods thinned out before a wide stretch of meadow. The road arched down a small hill that overlooked the township before them. Allie was reminded of her first look at Wiverrun as she glimpsed the occasional rooftop ahead.

But Wiverrun had appeared peaceful upon first glance. The same could not be said of what was left of the Appledale township.

Even from this distance, she could smell the smoke.

3

The Return

Morning spread golden light over Castle Sia, pouring through the windows of Jan's study.

The High King stood beside his desk, reading over the latest report from Tinkeeyo. There had been an attack on a small village in the Magno Forest, a township not much larger than the hapless Wiverrun. Its fate had been the same—people taken, buildings leveled, streets left glittering with white ice.

It was the third report of this nature they had received in the past two weeks. Attacking small, defenseless villages did not gain the Ace-Lord much in the way of soldiers, but it had the desired effect. Like a disease, the fear of the common folk spread with every report of destroyed villages and enchanted civilians. Gradually, that fear would erode into a desperate need for action, however inadvisable, in the name of protecting their families. Deceived by the Ace-Lord, they would join his side.

Still, the attacks would eventually escalate. Soon, the Ace-Lord's plan would shift from tormenting the helpless townships of Coonsia. Once the time was right, Jan knew he would strike a larger kingdom, furthering his conquest. Even now, the courier teams had gathered rumors of an impending attack on Mata City.

It was only a rumor, but it was dangerously likely. If the Ace-Lord defeated the Cooper kingdom, he would gain a valuable position on the northern coast.

Ĵan placed the paper on his desk, dismissing the grim thoughts for now. At least this report did not warn of any immediate danger to Mata City, as he'd feared. But he knew better than to ignore the possibility. Ajaha, his sister-in-law and leader of Caer Sia's espionage teams, was working with her couriers to find the truth, and he hoped to receive a more detailed report from her soon.

The door of his study opened, and Dandio entered. "Is that the Tinkeeyo report?" he asked, nodding at the page.

"Did Mother never teach you to knock?" Ĵan asked with a slight smile.

A wry grin crossed his brother's scarred face as he held out an envelope. "This just arrived from Ajaha. She intends to return from Badwater in two days, assuming no other news is gathered in the meantime."

Ĵan took it from him gratefully, passing him the report from Tinkeeyo as he did. "Ah, good. I had hoped to hear her opinion on the Gayrile situation."

"Did Lammar get word to her?" Dandio asked, his eyes scanning the report.

"Yes, but he is still in Bridgeport. Once he returns to Sia, we must decide what is to be done about the rebel factions," Ĵan answered. He shook his head wearily. "I suppose it is no good to wish for a more efficient way to spread news than letters."

Dandio glanced up at him. "Actually, that's what I was going to tell you." He paused, as if deciding whether or not to continue, but then went on. "I don't suppose you remember the stories Father would tell us about the Dividing War… about the actions of the Druids?"

Jan frowned, surprised by the question. The Druids, as told in the stories passed down by their parents, were said to be powerful wizards, messengers of the High Light, serving and guiding the mortals. According to the stories, they were allied with the elements of the mortal world— the dryads of the forest and the Nøkken of the sea.

"We encountered a dryad on our way to Wiverrun," he said after a pause. "I reminded her of the old alliance with the mortals, and advised that she seek the aid of the Druids."

"I think she may have succeeded," Dandio said.

Jan straightened, interested. "What do you mean?"

Dandio folded the Tinkeeyo report. "The courier who brought Ajaha's message arrived early this morning. He admitted he was unsure—a trick of the light, perhaps—but he claimed to see three dryads slipping through the trees last night, carrying a strange melody and waking the trees with the wind."

Jan sat down at his desk, stunned for a moment. Perhaps the rider was wrong, but then… "I spoke with Iriam a few days ago," he said at last. "I admit I had forgotten about it, but I had mentioned the dryads, and he had said he wishes to try to make contact with the Druids again."

"Again?" Dandio echoed.

"My reply exactly," Jan replied dryly. "However Iriam intends to contact the Druids—whenever he plans to do so—I am unsure. But I suspect we may learn more soon." He looked up at Dandio. "Send out the border patrol, just a few riders on the city borders. We do not want to frighten them. But if the dryads have awakened, we may have gained a valuable ally."

Dandio nodded and left the study.

Jan sat at his desk, deep in thought. He knew so little of the Druids, though he had always suspected Iriam knew more than he told about them. Apart from that, they were mostly spoken of in Caer Sian legend. Jan could almost hear his father's voice from long ago, speaking in hushed tones of the Druids and their allies.

"No king can carry the weight of the world. That is why the Druids were sent to bring comfort and encouragement from the High Light Himself."

Jan and Dandio had listened with as much attention as eight and seven year olds can give. "But who are the Druids?" Dandio had asked, hanging upside down off his chair.

"They are the loyal few," their father had replied, a smile crinkling at the corners of his green eyes. "The ones who chose to fight for justice, not join the forces of darkness."

Jan smiled slightly at the memory. Yes, his father had taught them of the Druids and the dryads. But he'd heard about them since then, in his early years as king, from a trusted councilor and friend. He recalled her words, too, spoken during the dark days of the tyrannical human queen.

"Find the Druids, Jan. Seek the Light—He will guide you."

Her face swam vaguely in his memory, shining with bright light. One of the few Stars who had not thought herself above the mortals, but had striven to guide them through those years of fear and shadow.

Luet.

The Aces had drawn her face from his memory, twisted it before his tormented mind while he'd hung suspended in the pit of black water in Ar-Salem. He had watched her death again and again in the illusions, as he had watched it all those years ago. Unable to help.

Jan took a breath, placing a hand on his sword hilt to steady himself. Drisilas felt so much colder without the Star-Stone. Cold as the waters of the pit. Cold as the saltwater that had dragged him down when he'd watched Luet die. Isilas sat in Iriam's study, shining hollow white light, corrupted. A frequent reminder of the darkness he had brought about, harsher even than the scars that Marked his skin.

Fire. He had not realized how much he'd come to rely upon it, and the way it shed comforting light on the darkest hours. Without it, the sword was black, barren.

He tried to remind himself of the hope that still remained. The Stone would be made whole, by some power or other. Cahadras had told him so after the battle in Castle Droco. One day, blue light would again shine from Isilas' core, and the fire would burn away the darkness.

But the uncertainty and fear remained, cold and heavy in his heart, hard as he tried to fight it. Greater than the unease or the old grief was the fear of the simple truth.

With the scars of his failure etched into his chest, not even the hottest fire would undo the corruption of the Star-Stone.

. . . . . .

Smoke trailed in the air as the riders entered Appledale, rising from heaps of rubble and stinging Mel's nose and throat.

The attack had occurred weeks ago, but dark Dal-kerri blood still streaked the cobblestones. Several buildings had been torn down completely, and the broken fences and shattered windows showed the handiwork of the Aces' forces.

A crowd of townsfolk had gathered along the roadside, watching the soldiers fearfully. Women drew their children closer, as though expecting them to be torn away. Many of the men carried farm tools, at work repairing their homes and hauling away the rubble. As the riders approached, they drew close to their families, a few raising pitchforks and spades in futile defense.

Captain Rosen swung down from the saddle and raised a hand. "Be at ease, friends. We have come from Caer Sia with fresh supplies and medical aid for any who need it."

One of the farmers slammed his pitchfork into the ground, folding his arms over his chest. "What does Caer Sia care for a town like this?" he asked bluntly. "We don't answer to your king."

"Be that as it may, the High King has made it his priority to care for all those affected by the Ace-war," the captain answered.

"The Ace-war?" a woman repeated bitterly. "Is that what they call it? Our town paid the price for a war we've never even heard of."

The pain in her voice tore at Mel's heart. He drew breath to speak, though he had nothing to say that could explain away the hurt. But his father had already dismounted, walking toward the fearful crowd.

"Mrs. Wentwood!" he called to the woman. "If you won't trust these fine men, you can trust me. Do you think I'd tell tales about a war if it wasn't a real threat? These soldiers are here to help you."

A puzzled murmur ran through the townsfolk—most of them recognized Joseph Smallbutton, but only as the friendly bookbinder. The first farmer narrowed his eyes in suspicion. "Smallbutton? Thought you'd been killed in the attack—no one's seen you for weeks. What, by the good green river, are you doing with them?"

"Sorry it's been awhile, Mr. Denplough," Mr. Smallbutton answered. His voice was still reassuring and steady despite the farmer's harsh suspicion. "We're back now, and we're here to help."

"Your son with you?" Denplough interrupted shortly.

Mel slipped down to the street and moved through the riders to stand by his father. "Yes, I'm here. And like my dad says, I want to help."

Another murmur rippled through the crowd, but this time, it was filled with undisguised distrust and hostility. Mr. Denplough's glare fixed on Mel. "You, boy—you're the reason for this whole mess, you know that? That's what those shadow men told us—that if we ever offered shelter to you or your family again, they'd be back to finish the job."

"Where have you *been*, Mel?" another man asked. Mel recognized him as Patrick, one of his father's friends. But the postman's usually friendly face showed the same unease as his neighbors.

"I'm sorry I wasn't here to help you," Mel said, fighting to keep his voice level. The suspicion in the townsfolk's voices cut to his heart like a whip. "If there's anything I can do now to fix it, I'll do it—I promise. If any of you are hurt, I can heal you." He slipped a hand inside his pocket and allowed the Blue Stone's comforting light to shine on the fearful faces before him.

"Look, lad," the postman said slowly, "we appreciate the gesture, but don't you see that's what those creatures warned us of? You left a respectable Daffonic future here to run off and get involved in some Caer Sian war, and we've paid the price for it."

He spoke gently, but his words stabbed Mel's heart one after another, as if the postman had seen and called forth every one of his regrets. The guilt of what had happened to his village filled him afresh. Appledale's townsfolk blamed him for this attack… and rightly so.

"We ought to turn him over to the shadow men," another woman stammered from the back of the crowd. "That's what they ordered— said to hand him over if he ever came back, or they'd kill us all for harboring him."

"Can't allow him to stay, at least," Denplough said, snatching up his pitchfork.

Captain Rosen laid a hand on his sword. At his movement, the knights reached for their weapons. Mel felt warmth on his back and knew Allie held the fire in her hands, prepared to fight.

But he took a deep breath and put the Stone away, hiding his guilt, his fear, his pain as he looked up at the farmer. "All right. We don't want to fight you. If you don't want my help, then I'll leave—but at least accept what the Red Dawn brought for you."

"Put the pitchfork down, Denplough," another farmer ordered, placing a firm hand on his neighbor's shoulder. He turned his eyes to Mel, his face worn and weary. "We accept your help—Light knows we need it."

Mel moved to the side of the road at the edge of the township, watching as Captain Rosen's men unloaded the pack ponies. The saddlebags were laden with fresh water, crates of food, and medical supplies. A few townsfolk came forward to help unpack, gratefully accepting the proffered items; the rest remained where they were, their faces wary.

So much fear. He couldn't blame them for it, but that did not lessen the pain it caused.

An old woman hobbled toward him, one arm bound in a bloodstained sling. "Forgive us, child," she said quietly. "People become mighty thoughtless when they're afraid. If you're willing… you said you might help?" She held out her arm with a wince.

Mel nodded. "I can—here." He drew out the Stone again. The blue light played over the woman's weathered features as he placed it in her limp hand, gently closing her fingers over it.

The woman grimaced at the pain, but her eyes widened as she stared at the Star-Stone.

"That's it," Mel said softly. "Just look at the Stone—let its power heal you."

He saw her flinch, but then her face cleared in surprise. "By the Light... my arm." Slowly, she stretched free of the sling, eyes wide with wonder. "Thank you, lad. I—I wish I could do something about all of them—make it right."

"It's all right," Mel said, forcing a smile. "If there's anyone else who's hurt and needs help, send them to me."

"I will—thank you, child." She reached out her hand as if to pat his cheek, but drew back again sharply, and, her expression conflicted, hobbled away.

"That was amazing," Allie said quietly behind him—she had approached partway through the interaction. "I've only heard about the Stone's powers. But... do you think it's smart to use it here? The Aces might sense it." Her silver-skinned face was wary, and the fire still glimmered on her fingers.

"I don't know," Mel said slowly. "I mean... if the Aces are after me, then they probably already know I'm here. And I wanted to help her."

He hadn't given that fear much thought. He knew the Ace-Lord had spies everywhere; his forces would be monitoring Mel in particular, as he carried the last uncorrupted Star-Stone. As long as they left quickly, Appledale would be safe. Its people had made it abundantly clear that Mel and his family were no longer welcome here.

A young woman with a baby walked over, glancing anxiously over her shoulder as she came. "I—I had hoped—you said you could heal."

She held out the baby, who gave a rattling cough and whimpered. "We were caught in our home when the—the shadow creatures came," the mother explained. "They overturned the furnace, and set the house on fire. I think the smoke has hurt his lungs."

Mel held the Stone above the tiny child's head. The little face lit up with interest, and his small hands reached for the glowing blue.

"How many of them were here?" Mel asked the woman.

"So many," she answered, rubbing her face wearily. "I have never seen anything like them. There were wolves, or at least, creatures that looked like wolves. And there were orcs. But the worst were the two shadow men. They just ghosted through the township, shooting ice at everything, leading the beasts and killing. My sister was—" She stopped abruptly, tears shining in her eyes.

"I'm sorry," Mel said quietly, though he knew the words meant nothing. He hadn't been here to help. He'd been in Castle Droco, unconscious in the void, when this had happened. "I lost someone in this attack too," he said after a pause. "I wasn't here to… I couldn't help him. But I knew… I knew he'd want me to be here, keep carrying on."

Tears threatened his vision, and he turned his focus back to the Star-Stone. Blue light sparkled from the Stone's core. The baby coughed again, but a little life had come back to his pale face. Mel drew back slowly. "I think he'll be okay," he told the young mother.

The woman swaddled her child and held him close, her grief-stricken face relaxing with relief. "Thank you—thank you," she stammered, and hurried away.

The familiar weight of his father's hand rested on Mel's shoulder. "I'm going back to the house," Joseph said slowly. "See if there's anything we can take back."

They walked down the road, a path Mel had walked countless times before, until the small neighborhood came into view. The cluster of farmhouses bore the same scars and damage as the rest of the township. But the house on their left had been destroyed entirely, torn to pieces as though made from clay.

Mel stopped, the shock freezing him in his tracks for a moment, as he stared at what was left of the home he'd grown up in.

Bricks, shreds of patterned curtains, shards of wood, or bits of cotton that had once been a mattress or cushion were strewn in all directions, scattered over the road and into the field behind the house. The lawn had been ripped up beneath iron-shod boots and icy claws. Even the flower beds in the front of the house had been attacked—wilted flower petals joined the scattered rubble.

At last Mr. Smallbutton moved forward, stepping carefully over the shattered stones. Allie stood next to Mel; he could sense she was trying to find some reassurance to give.

He took a step forward, his eyes scanning the wreckage in numb silence. Memories, broken memories, were all that remained. Shreds of his mother's favorite blanket, there. Glass from a window or dish, there. Paper and leather binding from his father's workshop, there.

The total stillness of the area, the deadness, cut to his heart deeper than the scene. These walls had once echoed with happy sounds, voices of friends and family. They seemed to echo again as he walked forward, until the ghosts of the past surrounded him: himself and Misty, much younger, running barefoot through the front yard; his mother baking bread while her soft humming filled the house; his father and Aryion playing cribbage and talking at the dining table; the front door where a serpentine had once pursued him and Misty into the night, the night it had all begun.

He knelt on the scarred floorboards, brushing aside the rubble to reveal the monster's claw marks, and heard the hissing voice once again.

Prey. Find. Kill.

Had the Ace-Lord known then? Had he already planned to return and enact vengeance upon Appledale if the New Blood did not cooperate?

Mel laid the tattered rug over the scratches. For a moment, he thought about going to his bedroom to see what there was to salvage, but this soon proved impossible. The entire hallway had been crushed, splitting the house down the middle. Wreckage fully blocked that side of the house.

"I found some books," Allie called softly—she stood near the entryway. The shelf had been overturned, but it had protected a few books from the ruin and weather.

"They're Misty's," Mel told her. His voice sounded as though it came from far away. "She'll like these… we can take them back for her."

Carefully, they uncovered the books and placed them in Mel's backpack. On the bottom of the pile was his father's weathered old cribbage board. The pegs were missing, and one of its corners had chipped, but Mel took this too.

Allie was shaking her head slowly in disbelief. "I never expected this," she said. "I—I know they've attacked cities before, but those were places like Caer Sia or Wiverrun—either a threat or a strategic position. Appledale… Appledale, he just hates."

"It's my fault," Mel murmured, his fingers tracing the etched scars on the floor. "I never should have come back here—I should have just stayed in Caer Sia after the mission to Esile."

"No, Mel." Allie took his shoulders, forcing his gaze to her—a familiar fire blazed in her green eyes. "This is the work of the Ace-Lord, and I promise you we'll make him regret it."

"He would have come either way," Mr. Smallbutton said heavily behind them. "The Aces knew we were here. They knew you cared for us."

Mel let out a breath and nodded. They were both right. If, as he suspected, the Ace-Lord had intended to attack Appledale from the start, there was very little Mel could have done.

But he still wished he'd been here. Wished he could have fought alongside Aryion and the Wildkids in the desperate attempt to protect the township. Even if he'd died with them, that was preferable to this aching guilt, wasn't it?

Even as he had the thought, he knew it was wrong. He could almost hear Aryion's voice arguing otherwise, reminding him of the truth the fears had buried. Protecting the Blue Stone was the best way to help Appledale—and all of Orlell.

Mel stood, shouldering his now heavy pack. His father carried a small bag filled with a few valuables he'd managed to save. Slowly, they left the rubble behind and walked back down the road to the relief force.

Iriam met them with a brief nod. He didn't ask where they had been—he could probably tell from their somber expressions. All he said was, "If you are prepared, we must be off again. It would be unwise to linger here for long."

Mel nodded and climbed into the saddle. He tried to keep his eyes on the road ahead of them as they rode out of town and began the journey north again. Tried to keep his focus on the task before him, on the coming battle, on the distant light of hope that somehow, they would live through this war.

But he couldn't help glancing back one last time at Appledale as they crested the hill. The clusters of ravaged homes, the farmsteads and markets, the memories that lingered with them—he felt as though he were at last bidding it farewell, a goodbye to that old life and who he had been here. Stepping forward into war and darkness, following the words of a Prophecy he was still learning his role in.

Mel took a deep breath and breathed a wordless prayer for the safety of his old home. Then he turned away, casting his eyes on the road ahead of him.

Hooves clip-clopped on the packed earth as they descended the hill and entered the quiet forest. Mel had just moved forward to ask Iriam a question when a haunting howl rose from the trees ahead of them, splitting the peaceful silence.

The riders drew up abruptly, horses whinnying in fear.

Mel had never heard the sound before. But he knew it at once, from Allie's recounting of the harrowing flight through the Magno Forest, or from Rygal's stories of the siege of Castle Droco.

That was the hunting call of the Dal-kerri.

4

The Warning

Allie's horse shied sideways as the haunting howls filled the forest, echoing all too familiar in her ears. Dal-kerri wolves. How she had hoped to never hear their voices again.

She drew her sword as Captain Rosen shouted from the front of the group. "Archers, form up—form up, men, we are under attack!"

Slender, shadowy beasts slipped through the trees to the right, racing towards the road. They would care very little for the Red Dawn knights, Allie knew—there was only one thing they would have come for.

She turned to Mel, who sat stock still in his saddle. His pale face showed that he had come to the same terrible conclusion. "The Stone," he breathed, meeting Allie's eyes. "They're here for the Stone."

Iriam's deep voice broke over the frantic party as the Red Dawn knights swung to face the oncoming attackers. "Ride, men. We must not let them drive us back into the township, nor can we face them here. Ride north, quickly."

The wolves prowled into view, their hulking shoulders bristling with dark fur, their long teeth bared as they snarled. Iriam raised his hands, sending a wave of indigo ice that knocked the closest hounds off their feet. "Go!" the Neutral commanded again. "I will guard your backs."

"Mount up!" Captain Rosen ordered, swinging back into the saddle. "Protect the New Blood!"

Mel seemed to draw breath to argue, but Allie saw his eyes slide back to the Star-Stone's glow and the scar on his palm. The Blood Oath claimed his blade here. Without further hesitation, he bent over the horse's neck and galloped down the road with the retreating soldiers.

"Allie, come on!" Darion's voice was edged in fear.

Another pack broke from the tree line. Ice spread from Iriam's palms, but he could not possibly defeat so many—and the Dal-kerri had been birthed from the same cold and darkness that he wielded. Ice was not an element they feared.

Fire roaring in her chest, she swung down from the saddle, ignoring Darion's urgent cries, and spread flames into the faces of the oncoming hounds. Yips and snarls rose through the curtain of heat, and through the smoke she saw the pack turn their hollow eyes on her.

A hand gripped her shoulder, pulling her back—Iriam stepped in front of her, his ice striking down the wolves that sprang towards them.

"Ride, heiress," Iriam ordered sharply.

"They don't fear your ice!" Allie shouted back, her voice rising with her frustration and fear. "I might actually be able to hold them off!"

Icy blades flew from Iriam's hands, killing four more hounds. With a strength that belied his usual calm demeanor, he hauled Allie to her horse by the back of her jerkin, then swung back into his saddle, red eyes blazing. "We have neither the time nor the numbers to *hold them off,* as you put it. They are not here for us, nor for Appledale, but for the Stone. If you will fight, fight to protect it."

Allie straightened in the saddle as howls filled the woods around them. As much as she hated to admit it, Iriam was right, as usual. There were far too many for either of them to take down. The wisest strategy would be to join the soldiers, riding in tight formation until they outpaced the wolves. She clipped her heels against her horse's sides and galloped after Iriam.

The previously quiet forest had come alive with snarling beasts, bounding through the woods after the retreating horses. The haunting howls chilled her to the core. Fire crackled in her hands, sparking from her fingertips in anticipation. "What's our plan?" she yelled to Iriam as they rode.

Iriam pointed ahead of them, tracing the edge of the road. "The wolves mean to trap us. They shall outpace us and cut us off from the road north. Do not let them pass—keep them behind."

The road spread before them, flat and straight through the dense forest. With that angle, it seemed to go on for miles. She could glimpse Dal-kerri here and there in the underbrush, keeping pace with the riders. Captain Rosen's voice drifted back occasionally, shouting orders. Volleys of arrows sprang from the archers' bows—Allie saw Darion's bow come up with them as the young ranger shot down the pursuing hounds.

The wolves raced alongside them, tongues lolling in their fanged mouths. Allie fired a blast at the pack on her right—the jolting of the horse's stride threw her shot awry, spreading red flames among the rocks. The hounds snarled at the heat and light, but continued on unwavering.

Mel, Allie saw, was in the center of the group, flanked on all sides by the Red Dawn knights. He sat bent over the saddle, gripping the Stone in both hands as though to shield it with his body. Darion rode next to him, arrows leaping from his bowstring, striking down the few wolves that made it past the other archers.

Jostling in the saddle, Allie let another blast fly. The fire cut down two hounds, sending their bodies toppling into the underbrush, but the others came on, eyes alight with the cruel excitement of the hunt.

"Stay close, men!" Captain Rosen ordered—his voice was dry with fear. Iriam rode behind Allie; the occasional flash of blue ice and the steady rhythm of his battlehorse's hooves were a comforting reminder of his presence. To Allie's right, the flash of white fangs and the eager snarls warned that the pack had nearly overcome them.

"Do not let them cut us off!" Iriam warned. Ice spread along the edge of the road before the Dal-kerri could reach the riders, raising an indigo wall between the hounds and their prey. A few wolves managed to leap over the wall as it rose, but the archers cut them down.

"Mind your backs," Iriam warned. The Neutral's face was drawn in focus as the wall on the left rose, and he turned his hands to the right to raise a second barrier. "They may come at our flanks."

Allie nodded, twisting in the saddle to send red flames crackling down the road. Crimson sparks spat on the dew-laden leaves, trailing smoke in the wake of the riders. The tension, the rage, the adrenaline had boiled to the surface, drowning out all other sounds. She glimpsed the icy barrier rising along the road's edge, saw the arrows whizzing past her as the archers felled the few hounds who reached the path.

She had just turned back to Iriam again when something else caught her eye.

Mud-red scales reflected on the icy wall, bat-like wings rose from beyond the barrier, and a nightmarish beast sprang forward with a gurgling hiss.

Serpentines. Allie had only heard of the monsters, which populated her father's darkest stories. They were far bigger than she'd imagined—snake-like, plated with reddish scales, creeping and slithering. Venom gleamed on its long fangs.

"On the right!" Iriam shouted, abandoning the barrier as he sent a blast of ice at the first serpentine. It leapt away, rising into the air with a few quick beats of its dark wings. As it did, four others glided out of the trees, wings tucked in as they dove.

The riders were scattered in chaos under the unexpected aerial attack. Several riders were knocked from their saddles. Two horses fell with screams of pain; the serpentines left the bodies behind and sprang into the air again.

Allie clutched her reins as she galloped beside Iriam. Icy darts flew from the Neutral's hands as he struck at the winged attackers. A serpentine leapt from the trees at Allie's left, fangs snapping at her horse's flanks. She sent a blast of fire into its open mouth, hunching low over the horse's neck as they raced on.

Her eyes scanned the relief force, seeking frantically for her companions. Mel rode in the saddle behind Darion—the boy's own horse had been killed by the serpentines. Mr. Smallbutton bumped along awkwardly on his shaggy pony, keeping up with the group. Captain Rosen shouted orders, fighting to reorganize the startled archers.

Three empty saddles. The sight of them stoked the flames in Allie's veins, filling her with rage.

Gritting her teeth, she turned back, firing into the underbrush as the Dal-kerri lunged for them again. Iriam was shouting something, but his words were lost in the roar of battle. The fire flew again and again from her hands, off target and shaky—the lurching gait of her panicked horse only worsened her aim.

The shadows of the four serpentines cast dark patches on the bloodied path. Deep blue ice flashed, felling one of the winged snakes—its body crashed down among the teeming Dal-kerri.

As it fell, the other serpentines dove again. Iriam's ice disappeared beneath the mud-red scales as two snakes dragged him from the saddle—Allie heard the thud as he hit the ground. In the same instant, the third serpentine swept straight for Mel.

Allie had already turned her horse back to help Iriam, but turned again as the serpentine dove, claws reaching for the boy's back. Darion twisted in the saddle, loosing an arrow into its neck—its body fell forward onto the ranger, and they toppled to the forest path as the rest of the riders galloped on.

Knowing nothing else besides sudden icy fear, Allie swung from the saddle, letting her horse gallop on. With the steady ground under her boots again and the fire primed for battle, she faced the approaching wolves. Dal-kerri teeth snapped at her arms, and serpentine wings fanned the flames, but she did not stop, wreathed by her own crimson blaze that crackled hotter with every moment.

Darion's voice reached her, urging her to keep running. "Go!" she shouted as the fires rose around her. "Help Iriam—keep going, I'll catch up!"

His protest was muffled—Allie shoved him back, leaving red sparks on his black jerkin. At last he turned and jogged toward the fallen Neutral. Allie barely saw them, only heard the horse's hooves as it cantered past her, and thought she heard Iriam's voice faintly as he called her name—but then they were gone, and there was only the fire, only the fury.

Flames licked along the bristling backs of the Dal-kerri, consumed the hissing serpentines, blackened the summer growth of the forest.

She let the red fire rise until she was certain the beasts were gone. At last, exhausted, she lowered her trembling hands, vision blurring as she fought to catch her breath.

Something black drew her eyes, deeper than the shadows beneath the trees. It half-hovered over the ground, like a strange mirror spilling shadows from its depths like smoke.

Had it been there all this time, concealed by the underbrush she'd just burned away? It was far smaller than the Patch that had filled Castle Droco's moat, but she knew it was the same type of thing. A placeholder for the Dark Realm's power. A passage for the Dal-kerri to travel Orlell unseen. Dusty had mentioned it in her report—how else had the Aces reached Appledale without the border patrol's notice?

The swirling darkness seemed to beckon her closer, to that whispering middle world where she'd stood on a silver bridge that arched away into nothingness. Involuntarily, she took a step forward.

In the darkness of the Patch, a face appeared. A face withered by time, by power, by the death it had embraced. Purple-red eyes met her stunned gaze as a tall figure cloaked in shadows stepped out of the void and stood before her.

"Impressive, Vessel."

At first, Allie had thought it was only an illusion, nothing more. But the cold, soft voice that echoed in her ears was no illusion.

The Ace-Lord straightened and studied her. Allie wanted to attack, to fire blast after blast at him until he removed the curse and left Orlell for good. But she seemed frozen in place by his gaze.

"It intrigues me that you insist upon aiding the village of the New Blood," the Ace-Lord said after a pause. "It is an insignificant location in the matter of the world, not even within the Liznees' jurisdiction. Why come you here?"

Allie tried to find her voice; the shock froze the words in her throat. She wished she could scream or curse or throw some witty reply back into his skeletal face. All she managed was, "It was the right thing to do."

"Was it?" the Ace-Lord breathed, folding his hands before him. "Right and wrong are far too narrow a judgment, child. What you must ask yourself, how you ought to act, must be within the domain of what is necessary."

"I know what's necessary for victory," Allie answered. Fire crackled at her fingertips, but she held it back. "I know about the curse now—the Life-Blood Spell. That's what you mean, right? That—that I have to die for us to win the war?"

"Death is required," the Ace-Lord replied calmly. "Yours, perhaps, but who can say? Surely you have seen that fate in the Prophecy. Should you fall willingly or not, I shall remain. It matters little to me."

The cold confidence in his voice brought the fire forth, crackling with anger up her forearms. "If you can't be killed," she snapped, "then the Prophecy wouldn't have talked so much about your defeat. I know you cursed me to corrupt me, and to break down the spirits of everyone else. That's why you gave me these powers."

She raised her hands, the red light reflecting on the Ace-Lord's gleaming armor. "You're trying to turn me into your pawn—well, that's only going to work if I do what you want, and I can promise I'll never join you."

She let the blast fly, summoning her frustration and fear into a crackling ball.

The Ace-Lord raised a hand, letting the blast strike his icy palm. As he did, Allie felt searing pain shoot up her arms through her hands. Gasping in surprise and pain, she clutched her hands close, staring in horror at the fresh blisters rising on her skin.

Bound. Bound to share whatever fate befell the Ace-Lord, but with only a mortal's strength to endure it.

Wincing in pain, she raised her eyes again.

"You, Vessel," the Ace-Lord said, "have no choice in the matter. No matter your words, your heart speaks true. Every breath, every beat of your mortal heart, every bit of the fire within your veins—it belongs to me now. Everything you do will be as I will it, as your power grows and furthers my conquest."

He inclined his head in a slight bow as he stepped back into the void. "Until we meet again."

In a swirl of shadows, he was gone, leaving only the Patch.

Allie staggered forward, uncontrolled fire flying from her hands, piercing the Patch over and over. The void absorbed the blasts at first, but gradually, its edges kindled red hot and, like a match to a page, it simply burned away, its shadows spilling out and dispersing into the underbrush. She stood again in a quiet forest glade, leaves charred and blackened, filled with dead Dal-kerri.

The closed Patch might once have filled her with excitement, a symbol that the shadow would be similarly stopped. But the Ace-Lord's words still hissed in her ears, and she knew he had allowed her to close the void, leaving her with a chilling reminder of her own bond.

Clenching her burned hands into fists, she stumbled back to the road.

. . . . . .

A half mile, perhaps, from the Patch, Allie found the rest of the riders.

They had gathered in a circle, horses still huffing and panting from the grueling race, soldiers standing or kneeling exhausted on the road. At first glance, Allie was relieved to see them all. She'd feared most of the knights had been killed, but saw now that it was not so. Though several soldiers had been pulled from their saddles, their armor had protected them from further injury. Any wounds had come primarily from the Dal-kerri claws.

But her relief turned cold as she drew close. The soldiers waited uncertainly, gathered around someone on the ground.

Fear stabbed her heart, and she ran forward, her eyes scanning the crowd for familiar faces. Captain Rosen stood across from her, his weathered face grim. Darion stood beside Mr. Smallbutton, who leaned on his pony's neck, his usually cheerful face grave.

Allie pushed through the knights and stopped in her tracks.

Mel knelt, holding the Blue Stone. Before him, bearing many serpentine bites, black robes ripped and shredded by venomous teeth, his violet blood streaking the ground, was Iriam.

For an instant her brain could not comprehend what she was seeing. The Neutral seemed so small there, so still. A presence she was used to seeing in command, leading the group, always knowing what to do, completely untouchable in battle. She had long believed him invincible… and yet there he lay.

Numb with shock, she sank to her knees. As she did, her eyes were drawn to faint movement of the Neutral's chest. He was still alive.

Mel straightened, his eyes troubled. "I can't—I don't know what to do. The Stone's stopping the bleeding, but I don't know if it's stopping the venom."

Darion put a gentle hand on his shoulder. "He's alive. If we bear northwest, we might be able to get him to Carna and better medical supplies. If… you believe that wise?" he added uncertainly, looking up at Captain Rosen.

The captain nodded; he looked almost as stunned as Allie felt. "Yes… yes, I do not believe we will be pursued there. And the Neutral needs more help than we can give him. You've done well, lad," he added to Mel.

Mel nodded, but his eyes remained fixed on the still face.

"Let us be off," Captain Rosen said, clearing his throat. He turned to Allie. "I am glad to see you, Heiress. Last we heard, you were fighting the Dal-kerri alone. Were you bitten?"

Allie shook her head mutely, unable to form words.

"Mount up," Rosen ordered, and the tired knights moved to their horses. "Load the wounded, and remain in arrowhead formation."

Slowly, they started down the road again. Adrenaline was still coursing through Allie's veins, so she elected to walk. She kept her eyes on the path before her, unable to bear glancing back at the tall black battlehorse, where the Neutral's battered frame was held upright by another injured soldier.

Darion touched her arm lightly. "Are you all right?"

Allie glanced at him, seeing the concern in his expression. "I'm fine. The Dal-kerri are gone. And I was… able to close the void they came through."

Darion's eyebrows shot up in surprise. "You closed the Patch?" he asked in a low voice.

For a moment, she wanted to confide the full story to him, let his reassurance cause the darkness to fade. But something held her back.

"My fire closed it," she said briefly. "The void's power dispersed, but I doubt it will be fully gone until the Ace-Lord's defeated."

Until the Ace-Lord's defeated. How unlikely that sounded. The Ace-Lord's words had confirmed the black truth she was loathe to accept. The actions of the mortals had been orchestrated by him from the beginning. He could not be killed by mortal weapons. He might be locked in the Dark Realm, as Iriam had once suggested, but Allie had no idea how they'd manage that. The only person who would know more about such things was currently clinging to life.

Darion studied her carefully—he could clearly tell there was another piece to her story, but thankfully he didn't press for more. "Good that you closed it," he said at length. "We'd speculated before that fire might be able to close the Patches, but never had the chance to test it in Castle Droco. I wonder if it's another area of your... powers."

"Maybe," Allie agreed hesitantly, folding her arms over her chest so he wouldn't see the blisters. "I... forgot about the Patch. I should have been looking for it—I might have closed it sooner, maybe before the serpentines..." she trailed off, throat tight.

"It wasn't your fault," Darion said. "It was a stealth attack—there's no way we could have expected it. We responded as best we could, as my mentor would say. And I suppose we should be grateful we didn't lose any more lives."

Allie took a deep breath, staring into the shadows beneath the trees. The darkness was nothing compared to the blackness of the Patch, yet it seemed more akin to the growing black in her heart. The blinding energy and fierce fire she'd tapped into as she'd fought the Dal-kerri hardly felt like her own. That power was vested in her by the Ace-Lord, and it would add to his strength each time she used it.

"I thought I could control these powers," she said finally. "To use them to protect you all, and stop anyone from getting hurt, or… or killed." She shook her head bitterly. "I suppose it was a foolish idea. We haven't learned anything about the curse that might break it… I'm starting to think there's only one way to do that."

She could not bring herself to speak the truth aloud. She'd known from the start that her death was the most likely ending. But the thought filled her with so much rage that it scared her. She was afraid— afraid of the fire that had just seared her own skin and the rising darkness in her heart that was slowly turning her into someone else.

Darion was quiet for a moment. "Cahadras said your choices might turn the Life-Blood Spell against the Ace-Lord," he reminded her softly. "I don't know what magic might break the curse. But I do know we're not giving up until we find the truth." He touched her hand lightly, eyes lingering on the burns. "If you'll protect us, you might start letting us help you."

The concern in his gaze, the quiet question in his voice, eased some of the frustration and worry plaguing her mind. She managed a slight smile. "All right. We can keep looking for answers about the curse in Caer Sia. For now, let's just try to make it back in one piece."

5

§ § § § § § § § § §

Sparks and Steel

Caer Sia

No news had reached Caer Sia from the relief force, but Rygal already regretted staying behind.

He knew Appledale was safe enough, but the troubling reports over the last few days added to his unease of being separated from his companions. It seemed every hour Caer Sia received a new concerning rumor, a recent warning of an impending Ace-attack, or another message telling of a battle in some part of Coonsia.

The Red Dawn and their allies protected most of the northwestern cities, and the Magno regions were well-guarded by the Elven kingdoms. The cities of central Coonsia were not so secure. Nearly all of the flatland villages—small towns and hamlets—had been claimed by the Ace-Lord. Even some of the Hyenin towns on the west side of the Strait had surrendered to the Aces. Most recently, there was a report that the Aces might intend to besiege Mata City.

Lammar had left the Guardians in Caer Sia to direct the investigation in Gayrile. Without the Siren to lead them, there was very little the Guardians could do. Battle strategies had paused for now—a diplomatic solution must be decided for the warring Diren clans in Gayrile before the warriors could return. Allie, Mel, and Darion had gone to Appledale with Iriam, aiding the relief force.

Rygal wished he'd gone with them. Though the long journey from Sia to Appledale was not necessarily enjoyable, it was preferable to the stagnant mire that he waited in now. His mind felt restless, leaping between musings over the Prophecy, worrying for his friends, or—most often—a desperation to act, for the sake of doing *something*.

He shook his head, focusing on the present. Sunlight beamed down upon the courtyard, but it was preferable to the stuffiness of Castle Sia's halls. He had spent most of the morning in the library, pausing his fruitless search through history tomes and scrolls to head outside. The courtyard was filled with cadets, and Rygal could hear Glentree's booming voice calling orders to the lines of young warriors. Most of these men, as Dandio had told him, had only been recruited a few months ago, some barely older than Rygal had been when he'd first come to Caer Sia. But with war on the horizon, their training had been accelerated.

The weeks of respite had given Rygal time to further his own training, too. For the last year or so, he'd worked hard to learn Essence channeling, a unique form of Garilian magic that turned his sword and shield into weapons of flame. The battle in Castle Droco had granted him the chance to use his new skills in action, but it had also reminded him of a cruel truth—that he was running out of time.

The yellow sparks crackling from his sword and shield rim had been effective against the Dal-kerri, but the Ace-Lord had extinguished them with a single blow. Sparks were not enough. He must learn to summon the fire.

He set his stance, inhaled deeply, and tried to calm his mind the way he'd learned to do. The old books of magic, Norrin's notes, and Iriam's training had brought him here.

But today, it was the Prophecy that claimed his thoughts, marching in mocking rhythm.

When the Aces have arisen,
The brightest place will darken.
When a New Blood stands unbidden
Mortal guard what was united,
Then the world shall yet survive.

The time is coming soon, coming soon, coming soon;
Your futile battle sealed your doom.

As he'd learned by now, those first two stanzas had been fulfilled when Mel had joined the Shards. The New Blood had stepped into the role, making his own choice to fight and guard the Stone. The mortal world had lived on, and Caer Sia had been freed from the Ace-Lord. Despite these victories, war had been inevitable from the start, orchestrated by the Ace-Lord to corrupt the mortals. Resisting was futile, as it only played into his plan.

Rygal set his shield against the wall, spinning the sword in his hand as he went through the familiar exercises. The meaning of the next two stanzas—the second stage—had only recently been revealed.

The signs have all been scarred,
By the Messenger of lost Stars
While the Mortal be unwilling,
A spell has made the binding
When the Shadow has arrived.

Light shall ever fade, ever fade, ever fade
Beware the Twelfth who stands unnamed.

After years of speculation, the Messenger had been revealed as
Redeyes, the monstrous black tiger whose claws marked the mortals
for judgment. Rygal didn't fully understand the weight of the scars—
that would probably be a question for Jan, as the High King bore such
Marks himself. Though the Star-Stone Isilas had been removed from
Drisilas' hilt, it was still corrupted, and they were unsure how to undo
that curse.

But Rygal's main concern settled on the words regarding the Unwilling
Mortal: *While the Mortal be unwilling; A spell has made the binding;
When the Shadow has arrived.*

The Life-Blood Spell. A curse binding the Ace-Lord to his mortal
Vessel, vesting his powers in Allie.

For an instant, the sparks dancing from his sword grew hotter, blazing
with the familiar helpless anger. It was a terrible curse—not even the
curses he'd read of in the Garilian spell books held such darkness.
Unbreakable and only able to be removed by the Ace-Lord himself.
Worse still, if by some strange magic the Ace-Lord was killed, Allie
would die with him.

But no one had spoken that horrible possibility out loud. Even while
he, Allie, and Darion had scoured the library and combed through
ancient texts, they had never brought up the chance of her death. It
seemed speaking the fear aloud would somehow bring it about.

All the same, despite Allie's stubborn determination, Rygal could tell
the dread and darkness weighed heavily on her. Nothing they could say
would erase that; nothing could remove the icy chains the Life-Blood
Spell had wrapped around her heart.

The pinwheels of sparks glowed so brightly he had to squint to see
his blade, but not even his frustrated fury could draw forth flames. He

calmed his emotions with an effort.

They'd already searched most of Castle Sia's library for any records of the Life-Blood Spell. While Allie had admitted it was unlikely they'd find a cure or counter curse, it might help to know the curse's history. If there was a way to break it, if there was any loophole at all, they would find it.

But as the weeks had worn on and their search had come up fruitless, Rygal could tell Allie's resolve was beginning to falter. She'd become grimmer, quieter. The futile quest had been one reason she'd decided to go with the relief force to Appledale, and Rygal hoped she'd find peace in helping there. But it would help all the more if he had answers for her once she returned—answers he might still find in the stuffy library.

He shook his head shortly. One thing at a time. He sent another wave of sparks flashing from his blade, dancing over the stone.

He figured he should appreciate his progress. What had once been brief flashes of gold were now sustained pinwheels of swirling sparks, crackling from the blade of his sword and shield rim. While they might not be effective against the Ace-Lord, it was progress all the same, and the glowing sparks reminded him of Norrin.

Norrin would have known more about the Prophecy, Rygal was sure. His mentor had studied all manner of lore and history during his exile by Safacon, and the Prophecy might have been part of that. But Norrin was gone—and so Rygal was left to wonder about it himself, avoiding the painful memories as much as he could as he struggled to both master the flames and decipher the final stage of the Prophecy of Three.

When sun and stars are darkened,
To the call you must still hearken,

When willing warrior be gone at dawn,
Ace-Lord, Mortal, together one
Lest the Shadow ever thrive.

The time has come, time has come, time has come
The heart betrays what must be done.

These lines seemed no less cryptic and foreboding than the rest of the Prophecy. The most he'd managed to gather from it so far was that the forces of darkness would rise all the more before the end of the war. Evil would darken the hearts of the mortals, as it would blacken the night sky. But they must keep fighting, following the words of the Prophecy and striving to fulfill their call.

The fifth stanza also lent further information about the Life-Blood Spell: *When Willing Warrior be gone at dawn; Ace-Lord, Mortal, together one.*

The wording confused Rygal. He supposed that Allie must become the Willing Warrior, transformed from the Unwilling Mortal in stanza three. The choice to fight, to use her new abilities for good, must be hers. But the line didn't say *"willing Mortal,"* it implied a *"willing Warrior,"* which seemed like a different person altogether.

Allie didn't seem bothered by the wording, though. In fact, since learning about the curse, she'd become more of a warrior than ever, throwing herself into the fight with fiery determination and a fury that concerned him.

He sighed. He was worried for the entire relief force in Appledale, worried for what they might find.

And, of course, worried for Allie in particular. By now, he could admit that to himself.

When nameless New Blood knows their call,
If Mortal's heart remains unmarred,
When Lord of Death brings life to all,
The spell that bound leaves deeper scars
Than the Shadow that awakened.

Spells and Stones, mortal roles, hold your hope
Lest the Ace-Lord take your bones.

The last two stanzas seemed a sort of recap, reminding the reader that every stage of the Prophecy was connected. It also introduced the truth of the Ace-Lord's plan, which they had learned about a few months ago. Just as the Marks of Redeyes scarred a mortal's heart, making them do anything to be rid of the curse, so the Ace-Lord would corrupt the mortals through fear, shame, and grief as the war dragged on. As Rygal had seen during the quest for the Shards, the Ace-Lord knew exactly how to break them down, and he would not stop until they had all been broken to the point of surrender.

Hold your hope, the Prophecy commanded. That was, in truth, the only chance they had to counter the Ace-Lord's power.

Rygal spun the sword in his hand, letting the sparks die down, and sighed. With the Prophecy and worries for his friends in his mind, it was impossible to focus on Essence channeling. He sheathed his blade and walked over to the line of cadets.

Glentree was leading the young soldiers in a series of exercises. Each recruit carried a training sword at the ready. At Glentree's order, the pairs of soldiers began their duels, and the repetitive clack of the wooden swords filled the courtyard.

"Keep your feet set, boy!" Glentree bellowed at the nearest recruit as Rygal approached. "All that shufflin', and you'll lose ground. Stand steady, that's the ticket." His eyes landed on Rygal, and a wide grin spread over his face. "Come to watch?"

"Maybe for a minute," Rygal answered, returning the smile. It was good to see Glentree back in action. The giant warrior had been badly injured after an encounter with Redeyes, but had since recovered. "Where's Dandio?" he asked, as the recruits continued.

"That's the question," Glentree replied wryly. "A Commanding General's wanted just about everywhere in times like these, but there's only one of 'im, after all. Last I heard he'd gone to meet with General Leopold about the report from Fort Tinkeeyo."

Rygal frowned. Tinkeeyo, a large city in southwestern Coonsia, protected most of the Magno regions. "What sort of report?" he asked, lowering his voice.

Glentree called another correction to an overeager recruit, then turned back to him. With the constant clamor of dueling cadets, it was unlikely they'd be overheard. But that was never something to risk, and Glentree spoke quietly. "Don't know for sure. My guess is it's about the blockade protecting the Mata Strait—if that rumor Lady Ajaha got wind of turns out to be true, we could have trouble. Still, suppose we won't know till she returns from Badwater."

Rygal nodded slowly. "Lammar should be back in the next few days too," he said. "Maybe he's heard more about it."

"Aye," Glentree murmured, shaking his head as though to clear away the worrisome thoughts. "Well, let's hope there'll be better news from Appledale. When's Asescia's group back?"

"Five days, maybe four if they're fast," Rygal answered without a second's hesitation.

Glentree raised an eyebrow. "*You're* eager to see them back."

Rygal turned his eyes back to the dueling recruits, hoping Glentree didn't see how his face had flushed. "I am," he replied, keeping his voice level. "It's best to have the Star-Stone somewhere safe, after all."

"Mmm," Glentree grunted, but said nothing more.

They stood in silence for a while. Rygal racked his thoughts for something, anything, to steer the conversation away from his worries for Allie, which threatened to bring up a different topic entirely. A topic he wasn't yet sure he could express.

The heart betrays, the Prophecy said. He hadn't realized how true that really was.

6

Fyrocrian Essence

Rygal had intended to practice more that afternoon, but his day soon turned away from such activities. He helped Glentree finish the recruits' exercises, then attended a short and unproductive meeting with the Guardians, which only served to heighten his growing frustration and sense of uselessness.

The Guardians wanted to return to Gayrile and stop the rebel Direns. The warriors had come to Coonsia to aid the attack on Castle Droco, but had overstayed that trip much longer than planned. Without a strategy for Gayrile, though, they would be charging blindly into a potential battlefield. Besides, the hope was to defuse the infighting among the Diren clans before it got any more out of hand, as Lammar had reminded Rygal more than once.

And so the Guardians were left to wait in Caer Sia, listening to the reports of attacks and battle and bloodshed across the kingdoms.

"We'll wait for a few more days," Rygal had finally decided, hearing the discontented murmurs around the small meeting room in Castle Sia. "If we haven't heard from Lammar by then, I'll talk to Dandio, see what he thinks about us going back to Gayrile."

"What if Lammar wishes us to act differently?" one of the older warriors asked doubtfully. The Siren had advised the Guardians over the last few months.

"Then we'll deal with that then," Rygal said. "Gayrile's running out of time—we need the clans allied so they can help protect the north from the Aces. I won't go against Lammar, but I think he'd agree with Dandio."

He could tell the warriors liked this plan about as little as he did. But the meeting was dismissed, and they filed out of the room into the bustling castle. Voices of servants and soldiers filled the corridors. Castle Sia never slept, not in times of war.

Rygal paced the halls restlessly while his thoughts tumbled over each other. Despite the uncertainty of their strategy, despite the debates over the future, the warriors followed him. Even the older Guardians, who had far more experience than he did, who had fought beside Norrin for years, obeyed Rygal's word without question. They offered advice, certainly, and they'd given input during the attack on Castle Droco. But they never questioned his leadership.

Rygal didn't understand why, and it added yet another growing worry. Since Norrin's death, the Guardians had functioned as an extension of the Red Dawn. But soon, the Guardians would choose their new leader. Rygal had acted as Lammar's second-in-command for the last few months, and if Lammar refused the position... would it then fall to him?

He didn't want to think about that now. He wasn't sure if it was his own self-doubt, or the nagging truth that he would never measure up to Norrin's wisdom, that caused him to hesitate. Again, he wished he could talk to Norrin, this time to point out the obvious reasons against his taking such a responsibility.

But he knew what Norrin would say to that. He could almost hear the old man's voice speaking directly into his ear:

"You have a Guardian's blood in your veins. Act wisely."

Act wisely, Rygal's mind echoed bitterly. There hadn't been much of that. He'd made his fair share of mistakes over the years.

"Mistakes make you human, Rygal. Do you believe yourself above it?" There was Norrin's voice again, a gentle reprimand and a firm assurance. Rygal didn't remember when he had said that—it must have been after one of the many failed plans during the resistance years against Safacon. And yet Norrin's to-the-point words had stopped him from wallowing and gotten him back into the fight.

"I'm not enough, Norrin," Rygal muttered into the shadowed halls of the castle. "I'm never going to be you."

Yet again he could hear the old man's rebuke. Words Norrin had whispered over him on dark nights when he was still a child, telling him stories about his father, reminding him of the truth.

"Your purpose is your own. Your father knew his purpose, and he never feared for himself. You are no different, Rygal."

Rygal raised his head, looking out the window at the sparkling sea. Far across the water lay the isle of Gayrile.

If leading the Guardians was what it took to help their broken kingdom… would he do it? The question burned unanswered in his thoughts with the echoes of Norrin's voice.

"You have a Guardian's blood in your veins. Act wisely."

Excited voices of a few young recruits interrupted his troubled thoughts. Wishing for a quieter place to think, he headed up the stairs to Iriam's study. The Neutral had given him permission to look through his scrolls for any history of the Life-Blood Spell, though Rygal doubted he could focus on that topic now. All the same, he needed the solitude.

He slipped past two couriers with a nod as he reached the door, then slipped inside the study.

Jan stood inside, staring out the window, and looked over as the door closed.

"Oh—sorry, sire," Rygal stammered, shaking his head to clear it as he started backward. "I thought this room was—"

"No matter, Rygal," Jan answered, a slight smile crossing his tired face. His dark shirt and jerkin, simple garb for the High King, blended into the shadows beside the bookshelves. He wore Drisilas at his belt, though without the ever-present light of the Star-Stone, the sword seemed colder somehow. "How fare the recruits?" he asked.

"Probably pretty tired after Glentree's finished with them," Rygal said with a grin. His eyes were drawn to the Star-Stone, placed in a golden case on a small silver table in the corner of the room. Pale light radiated from within the small gold case, an ever-present reminder of the corruption that filled it.

Jan followed his gaze, glancing down at the Stone. "Yes, I suppose you have not seen it in this state yet," he murmured. The smile had vanished from his face. His features were grim and somber again.

"No… Allie told me about it a little," Rygal said, glancing hesitantly at the king. He knew the Star-Stone's corruption had come through its purpose being twisted—a power meant for peace turned instead into a weapon of war. It rested here, encased in a protective shield of gold made by the Stars, kept safe until its future was more certain.

"Do we know… if it can be turned back?" he asked at last.

Jan touched the smooth case lightly for a moment, his face illuminated by the white light. "I do not know," he replied slowly. "Even if the matter of the Marks has been reconciled, the corruption is yet to be atoned for. But Cahadras told us that the role of Wielder must be filled again, or the Ace-Lord shall raise up his own."

"Another Wielder?" Rygal asked, studying the Stone. "Who do you think that will be?"

"That I do not know," Jan replied. "I have long lost any claim as Wielder. Yet its light still seems to call to me, all the same." His hand lingered on the Stone before he pulled away, as though the pale light might burn him. "Well—I understand you planned to speak with Dandio?"

"Yes, about Gayrile," Rygal replied. "The Guardians are hoping to return home soon, but we aren't sure when. If we just show up in Bridgeport, the rebel Direns might think we're there to attack, and the fighting would just start again."

Jan nodded thoughtfully. "That is a risk. We cannot allow battle to carry on any longer than it already has—a diplomatic solution must be agreed upon."

"That's what Lammar said," Rygal said with a sigh. "I can understand that, but we're getting tired of waiting with no way to help."

"I do not blame you for that," Jan agreed with a smile, staring out at the sea. After a moment, he turned to face him again. "Well, there's something I wished to ask of you, if you are unoccupied for the moment."

Rygal looked at him curiously, and the High King continued, almost hesitantly. "Iriam has told me of your studies in Essence channeling—I know it is a magic unique to the Guardians of Gayrile, one that must be learned over many years."

Rygal nodded slowly, confused by the change in subject. "Yes… at least, it's unique for the Cantrians—humans and Elves and Dwarves. We can't channel our Essence into an element naturally, like the Liznees or Stars—or the Aces, for that matter." He shrugged. "But we can learn to do it with time and study, and with the right power."

"Iriam has said you have been studying for some time," Jan said.

"Only since the quest for the Shards," Rygal said. "Norrin meant to—" He turned away from that topic abruptly. "I'm getting there. I still can't make fire."

"But you have learned much," Jan persisted. "You can call the Essence forth, and channel it through your blade?"

"Partly," Rygal replied, then looked at him carefully as suspicion entered his mind. "Wait—you don't want me to teach *you* this, do you?"

Jan let out a breath, resting a hand on his sword hilt. "I wish to learn. Fire has been my ally all my life, even before Drisilas was forged. Its blade is not the same now, so I must learn to channel my own fire through it. I had meant to ask Iriam, but as he has not yet returned from Appledale, and you are the only one I know who has mastered it..." He trailed off, looking at Rygal inquiringly.

Rygal stared at him in disbelief. To teach Essence channeling— something he was still fairly new at—was one thing. To teach the *High King* was something else entirely. "Jan—I don't know if I can teach you," he stammered. "I mean—I'm pretty sure you'd know more about channeling fire than I will—like I said, all I can make are sparks—"

Jan shook his head, waving his protests aside. "In this, you are the more knowledgeable. And I am willing—in fact, I am quite hopeful—to learn. If we are to face the Aces, Drisilas must again blaze."

Rygal hesitated a moment longer, seeking for an argument. Finding none, he shrugged slightly. "All right, if you're sure. Umm… the courtyard, then?"

They headed out into the courtyard. The evening sun lit the stone walls, red as the fire of a Liznee's Essence. Black burns still showed on the stones, left by the sparks from Rygal's practice that afternoon. The charred marks bolstered his confidence. It hardly mattered that he couldn't yet summon fire—he'd learned Essence channeling, a complicated power that very few Cantrians could master. And he'd learned it in a relatively short time.

Feeling more sure of himself, he squared his shoulders and fingered his sword hilt, gathering his thoughts. "Right, well—from what Allie's told me, Liznees don't really have to think about channeling their Essence into fire. It comes naturally." He looked at Jan for confirmation, and the High King nodded.

"Yes. I admit we are a bit, ah, spoiled, in that regard. But how does one channel that fire through a blade?"

"I've learned most of this from Norrin's notes, so I'm paraphrasing here," Rygal said slowly, "and I'm not sure if it works the same for Fyrocrians. But I'd imagine it's similar. The most important thing is your focus, where your mind's oriented." He drew his sword. "You already channel your fire through your hands. Focus, and you can bring it out through the sword instead—" He took a breath, set his stance, and sent a brief flash of sparks down the blade of his sword. "Like that," he finished.

Jan arched an eyebrow, clearly impressed. "Like that," he echoed with a wry smile. "Well, I will try."

He took a deep breath as Rygal had done, his hands gripping Drisilas' cold hilt as he closed his eyes. "What do you yourself think of, when you channel the sparks?"

Rygal paused, contemplating his answer. As Iriam had once pointed out, if your mind was not in the right place, you might call on a darker, deadlier power. Norrin's notes had taught him to center his mind upon the High Light, though Rygal could not express what specifically that meant.

"You're meant to focus on the good," he said finally. "The reasons for why you're calling on that power. For me, I—I tend to think about my companions. Thinking that I'm helping them."

He shrugged awkwardly—he'd never talked about that before. But Jan only nodded, eyes still closed, his brow furrowed slightly. "That is wise. The Light's power is a truer strength. I have heard that channeling the darkness is what led Safacon to his downfall."

"That's what the books said, too," Rygal replied.

Jan exhaled slowly, then opened his eyes. Red fire shot up the blade of Drisilas in a crackling bolt, splitting the quiet evening air. It lasted only a few seconds, then vanished, leaving the steel radiating with heat.

Jan's shoulders slumped forward slightly as he caught his breath, his face strained. "I suppose—it becomes easier—with practice."

"Easier," Rygal repeated incredulously. "You've already managed fire—I've been at this for almost a year now and all I can do are sparks!"

A faint smile touched the Liznee king's face. "Well, as you pointed out, I do have one advantage—I have been channeling the fire all my life. To channel it through a blade—that is something else entirely." He spun the blackened sword in his hands experimentally. "All the same, it is familiar, too. Thank you for the lesson."

Rygal shrugged, but pride filled him at Jan's words. "Practice makes it easier. Iriam knows more about this than I do—you might talk with him once he gets back. Although," he added with a grin, "Iriam's methods of practice usually involve throwing a bolt of ice at you."

Jan's eyes twinkled with amusement. "Then perhaps I had better practice more. If Iriam will teach you to fight against ice, then I will teach you to fight fire with fire." He set his stance, Drisilas half-raised in one hand, red fire glittering from the fingers of the other. "Have you your shield?"

Rygal's grin widened. In the weeks since returning from Castle Droco, his restlessness had nearly driven him mad. Clearly, Jan shared the same sensation of pent-up energy—though, of course, he was better at concealing it.

"You're sure the guards will let me attack the High King?" he couldn't resist asking as he lifted his shield.

"Oh, I doubt there will be a need for them to interfere," Jan answered. "From what Allie has told me, there has never been any serious damage done during sparring."

"Allie and I don't spar with fire," Rygal pointed out.

Jan gave a slight shrug. "Fair enough," he said, then stepped forward.

The sparring match continued as evening fell, red flames and yellow sparks lighting the courtyard. For a moment, it was like being back home in Gayrile, like any other evening where Rygal could spar and practice with the Guardians as night fell. He could almost forget about the war, about his conflicted thoughts, about the Prophecy.

But he no longer wished to forget. Not the war or the fear. Not the memory of that old, simple life. Not even the grief that he could not yet manage to speak of. He could look back on it in remembrance, and look ahead to wherever the new path might lead him. To the responsibilities lingering on the horizon. To the hope of a brighter future.

And so he centered his mind on the match, while the two blades danced sparks off the stones and the blood of a Guardian roared with life in his veins.

7

Of the Magics

The five day journey back to Caer Sia blurred with exhaustion and fear in Allie's mind.

Following the Dal-kerri attack, the relief force had reached the city of Carna by evening. The townsfolk evidently knew of Appledale's plight, and they seemed wary to help the Red Dawn knights. Clearly, they feared being branded as enemies of the Aces and suffering a similar fate as the neighboring village. But thankfully, they allowed the group to rest, and offered aid to the wounded. After a night's rest in Carna they began the long ride back north, moving as quickly as they could toward the valley of Sia.

The hours passed in agonizing slowness as Allie rode, rocking back and forth in the saddle. The hurried ride consisted mainly of talking with Darion or Mel, hearing the worry in their voices, as the reins rubbed her blistered hands.

Iriam remained unconscious. In contrast to the usual fevered delirium brought on by serpentine venom, he was completely silent, colder than his own ice. The numerous serpentine bites, as the doctor in Carna had told them, carried enough venom to have killed a mortal long ago. The doctor had been unsure how to even treat the Neutral's wounds, less certain if the antivenom usually administered for humans and Liznees would work at all. But he'd done his best, and Iriam yet lived.

Allie forced herself to focus on that, not the uncertainty of if he would ever wake, not the guilt of how she'd handled the fight with the serpentines. That had been her last conversation with Iriam—arguing against his orders. Her stubbornness had cost them crucial seconds, allowing the serpentines to stalk them from the trees. Had it cost them Iriam, too?

He was too valuable a counselor to lose. He must not die, Allie thought furiously, as tears burned behind her eyes. He would live. He must live, because if he did not, she could never stand beneath the weight of the guilt and grief.

When the farmlands on the outskirts of Caer Sia gave way to the sprawl of elegant buildings and towers in the valley below them, she allowed herself a sigh of relief. Caer Sia was safe. She was home again.

Yet she could sense as they rode through the city that trouble plagued the capital. Groups of soldiers walked the normally quiet roads in the villages, and guards were posted on practically every block in the inner city. Uncertain and fearful voices lingered in the air. Every citizen of Caer Sia was clearly aware of the danger lurking on the horizon.

A squadron of soldiers stood posted at the road to the city center, and stepped forward as the riders approached. A Hyenin general raised a hand, his fox-like face regarding them carefully. "Halt. State your business and purpose."

Captain Rosen saluted, his face puzzled. "Relief force of Appledale returned to report, General Arrex."

Arrex' golden eyes flicked to Allie and Darion, and he seemed to relax. "Ah—it is very good to see you back. This will only take a moment." He nodded to the guards, who stepped forward and began inspecting the supplies and gear.

"Is an inspection necessary, sir?" Allie asked with a frown. She could understand the need for security, but Arrex knew them, and could hardly suspect them of being spies.

"I'm afraid we're under orders to inspect every incoming company, heiress," Arrex replied. "The Aces have many ways of deception. The Star-Stone's presence assures me you are not an illusion," he added with a smile to Mel, "but we cannot be too careful."

The soldiers completed their inspection, and General Arrex waved them on.

Unlike the rest of Caer Sia, where fear stemmed from rumor, here, the preparations of war were visible. Couriers strode past carrying messages. Recruits marched after their commanding officer. The market district of the city center was vacant of the usual bustle of thousands of shoppers and vendors. Instead, a new barracks had been set up.

Allie focused on the castle gates ahead of them. There were twice the usual number of guards along the walls, and she saw a few of them tense at the watchman's bugle.

Dandio met them in the castle courtyard. The armor he wore was leather, a simpler variation of the full plate-and-mail of his battle armor. With him was Rygal, who looked so relieved to see them that Allie almost smiled. But their urgent message erased such joy.

Captain Rosen saluted to Dandio. "Commander—forgive my haste, but several of our men were injured. Allow me to take them to the barracks."

Dandio nodded, but his face paled as his eyes reached the still figure on the black horse. "Light above—Iriam…"

"He's hurt," Allie stammered as she swung out of the saddle. "We were attacked—he needs a doctor, quickly—"

"Call the medics immediately," Dandio ordered one of the guards. "And get him inside." The soldiers carefully loaded Iriam's still frame onto a stretcher and bore him inside the castle.

"What—what happened to him?" Rygal asked, his expression stunned.

"Serpentines," Mel said heavily. "I didn't even know the Ace-Lord still had them on his side—but I guess it makes sense."

"Serpentines," Dandio repeated grimly. "We should have expected they would come for the Stone." He embraced Allie. "Are you all right?"

"Yes, I'm fine," Allie answered. Any injuries she had received paled in comparison to those of her companions. She shook the lingering fear and guilt away as the castle doors closed behind them. "We need to report to Jan."

"Not now," Dandio told her. "You should take the time to rest. Captain Rosen will handle the official report."

"There are more important things to do than rest," Allie protested. "Surely there's something I can help with—a scouting party, or a reconnaissance mission, or—"

Dandio put a hand on her shoulder, stopping her. "Asescia. Your mission is completed. Nothing major will be decided until your mother returns this evening, and there will be war enough to fight after you rest." He smiled slightly, but there was concern in his eyes as he studied her.

"Fine," she said, glancing away. "Call me when the meeting starts."

She moved toward the stairs that led up to her room. But she didn't take the stairs. Instead, she turned left, down a long corridor toward the library.

Even if the next meeting would not be for several hours, she refused to waste time sitting in her room. The sensation of helplessness seemed heightened by the knowledge of the curse. Knowing what the Ace-Lord had done to her—what he still intended to accomplish through her—drove her to action, so she would continue her search for any record of the Life-Blood Spell.

The library was quiet compared to the activity in the rest of the castle, warm and rather stuffy. She cracked open a window, then turned to face the tall shelf before her. It had been weeks since she'd stood here, but the mission to Appledale and the Ace-Lord's words had filled her with a new desperation to seek some knowledge of the curse.

Why had he come? Was it only to speak to her? Was that why he'd sent the serpentines after the others, because he'd expected her to stay behind to fight?

"Everything you do will be as I will it."

No, she shouted back in her heart, *no, you don't know everything. I'll never serve you.*

Yet again, she saw his mocking smile and heard his low voice, which seemed to thunder in her ears.

"You, Vessel, have no choice in the matter."

The Vessel of his strength. A mortal bound. It didn't matter what she decided in her heart; whether or not she wanted to serve him, her very Essence now existed to strengthen him further.

Though the Mortal be unwilling; A spell has made the binding; When the Shadow has arrived.

"I've already looked through the books on that shelf," came Rygal's voice.

Allie glanced at the door, startled. He and Darion walked into the library, each carrying a large book.

"We thought we'd bring the books about Garilian magic," the young ranger said as he sat down. "Rygal's been looking through Caer Sia's records while we've been gone."

"Any luck?" Allie asked him.

"No sign of the Life-Blood Spell," Rygal admitted. "But I did find something in these Garilian books this morning, in the stack Norrin gave me."

"Garilian magic?" Allie asked, puzzled.

Rygal picked up another book, which was marked toward the center. "Dark magic, actually. Unpleasant stuff, I can tell you." He glanced between the two of them. "You're sure you aren't tired? It's a long road from Appledale—trust me, I know."

Allie managed a slight smile—he'd told her about the journey during the quest for Drisilas more than once. "No, I'm fine. These are your spell books, you said?" she added, touching the yellowed pages.

"Yes, the ones I learned Essence channeling from." Rygal held it out to her, and she took it carefully. Its spine was cracked and weathered. "They aren't historical records, though. They talk about the spells themselves, and the power behind them."

Jewel-lore... Cantrian Essence... Of the Trees," Allie read from the table of contents, then looked up at Rygal again. "Wasn't Jewel-lore about the Jewel of Power? Why's it in here?"

"Because Jewel-lore was technically Essence channeling," Rygal answered, as though it were obvious. "That's what made Safacon so powerful, you know—he was using both the Jewel's magic and Garilian spells."

"Cheat," Darion commented, but became serious again as he looked at the book. "That one's about curses?"

"Yes, partly," Rygal said. He turned the pages of the book to a marked section before handing it to Allie. "Read that part, and see what you think."

He and Darion grouped around Allie as she read.

"Of all power there lies a counter-part, just as with all light there is darkness. So too is it possible for dark spells to be learned by an ambitious, yet unknowing, mortal. To invite evil into one's heart holds great power, but also great danger. If a mortal's heart is marred by evil, only the greatest Light may set them free, and even such freedom can come only with cost. Thus, one must shun the darkness, and hold to the light."

Allie looked up at Rygal curiously. "The wording here… it reminds me…"

"Of the Prophecy?" Rygal asked, as she trailed off. When she nodded, he smiled grimly. "The part about a mortal's heart being marred is probably more literal than the Prophecy's—the Ace-Lord doesn't necessarily need a spell to mar the mortals. The longer this war drags out, our resolve will break on its own."

"It's still an interesting comparison," Darion said, studying the page. "Using dark magic mars someone's heart, just as much as fear or grief. Look at the Aces themselves…" He trailed off with a frown, rubbing the scar on his cheek.

Allie glanced at him. "What are you thinking?"

Darion hesitated. "I… well, I don't know if this helps at all… but what if someone were to bind the Ace-Lord with the Life-Blood Spell? If a mortal cast it and then died, wouldn't that mean the Ace-Lord would die too? He'd be trapped by his own curse."

Allie frowned. She had never considered that idea before, not in the slightest. "I suppose it *might* work, theoretically," she said slowly. "But we don't even know if someone could learn the Life-Blood Spell, let alone cast it," she added in irritation, shaking her head. The warm room made her thoughts sluggish.

"Not that we know of," Rygal echoed. His blue eyes were thoughtful. "I wonder if someone could learn the spell—and learn to turn it against the Ace-Lord." He studied Allie carefully.

Allie looked between him and Darion, catching his implication. "I—suppose I'd be willing to try it," she said, "but I've always heard it's dangerous to study any form of dark magic, no matter the reason. Besides, I don't think my spell would override the Ace-Lord's bond over me, would it?"

Darion's face fell. "No. Hang it all, I hadn't thought of that."

"We can keep looking," Rygal said, nodding back to the page.

Allie turned her attention to the book again.

"Just as one must shun the darkness, it is equally vital to understand its danger and workings. All dark spells are flawed in one manner or another. There is always a cost for using such power, a part of a person that is lost, or a strength surrendered."

Cost, Allie's mind echoed with a sudden surge of hope. "All dark spells are flawed—that means there is a flaw in the Life-Blood Spell, something we haven't discovered—what sort of flaw?" Her eyes scanned the rest of the page, desperately seeking more. But the paragraph ended there, and the rest of the page returned to the dangers of dark magic.

"That's what I'm still trying to find out," Rygal replied. He opened another book, flipping through the pages until he reached a portion underlined with blue ink. "This one talks a little more about the magics—Jewel-lore, mostly. But it's this part that got me thinking about something else."

"In the corruption of a Star-Stone, so also comes a corruption of the land," Allie read, feeling a shiver of foreboding. *"Thus, when the Vana Jydra was warped in corruption by the lord of darkness, the evil that entered it polluted the kingdoms of Gayrile, placing an imprint of magic both fell and fair upon the Isle."*

"Gayrile?" Darion repeated, interested. "Wait—the Ace-Lord corrupted the Jewel—in *Gayrile?*"

"It's new to me too." Rygal traced the words thoughtfully. "I always wondered about it. Why the Jewel was given to Safacon, why it remained on Gayrile for as long as it did, how Safacon was able to access the Dark Realm to get it—or if the Ace-Lord accessed Gayrile through him. But it wasn't until I found this that I was sure."

"We haven't found much in Caer Sia's library," Allie said slowly. "I wonder… I wonder if there might be records in Gayrile." She looked at Rygal again. "Your friend there, the Brownae that went on the quest for the Jewel—you said she learned Jewel-lore, right?"

"Morel," Rygal said, nodding. "Yes, she learned the Jewel spells, but Brownaes don't tend to keep written records. Still, I wonder if Morel would know something about the curse. She and her tribe know more about the Jewel than most Garilians."

"Did you make these notes?" Darion asked, tapping the handwritten words etched in the margins of the book Allie held.

"No. These were Norrin's spell books—he learned most of the old lore."

Rygal's tone was subdued and solemn, the light having faded from his eyes at the name. Allie looked at him carefully. She'd heard him mention Norrin before, but knew nothing more than the name. "He was your teacher, right?" she ventured curiously. "Did he ever tell—"

"No. Well, yes—but he didn't—I didn't learn about magic then. And he—I was never taught about the spells, either. Not till later." Rygal shook his head briskly, as if to clear away the pain and grief that had filled his expression. "All right, well—it's interesting that Gayrile is linked to the Jewel's corruption. Might explain some of the trouble brewing there—and why we need to secure the island in the war."

In a moment, the conversation shifted back to the tumultuous present. "Was there any change while we were gone?" Darion asked. "How's the situation in Gayrile?"

"Not great, from the reports," Rygal said. "But last we heard from Lammar, the city of Bridgeport is still secure. It doesn't sound like negotiations are starting any time soon, but at least the fighting has paused, and there's no sign of Aces yet."

"That's good," Allie agreed. "Lammar's there now?"

Rygal nodded. "He went to meet with Morel and the other Brownae leaders. He should return to Sia soon with more information. The Guardians all want to go back to Gayrile, but if we go marching into a war zone, the rebels might see it as a threat and start fighting again." He heaved a sigh. "See, it's times like this that I wish war wasn't so political."

"So you can do your thinking with your sword, you mean?" Allie commented. His face softened in a rueful grin as he shook his head. She liked making him smile; it filled her heart with fireflies despite the dark topics they discussed.

"What about the Diren lords?" Darion asked. "I've heard they're hesitant to hear anything at all from the rebels."

"Yes, well, they're stubborn," Rygal replied wearily, "and I can't say I blame them. King Casper is a decent fellow, and I think he understands the need to join forces. But the only terms his councilors have come up with are just as extreme as the rebels.'"

"They'll have to compromise one way or another," Darion said. "My mentor always said that's the only way anyone agrees to a treaty."

"Sounds like Lammar," Rygal told him with a grin. "And they're not wrong. We should avoid a battle if we can."

The blast of the trumpet made Allie snap the book closed. Through the open window she could just see a procession of riders as they entered the castle courtyard. Several warriors wore the black and gold colors of Badwater.

"Looks as though we're in for more politics," Darion commented.

"As long as they have news," Allie answered as the three of them moved toward the door, "I can live with that."

8

The Council of Caer Sia

Allie could tell from one look at the weary group that her questions would have to wait a little longer.

Her mother and two couriers stood in the entry hall, speaking with Jan and Dandio. Ajaha stood calm and poised as ever, but her voice was heavy and her skirt and vest were dusty from the long ride. Sia's courier teams had been hard at work for months, and now, following the many attacks across Coonsia, they were overloaded passing news among kingdoms.

"I had hoped Lammar would have returned by now," Ajaha was saying as Allie, Rygal, and Darion paused by the stairs, "but I suppose there is not much we can do about that. I take it the situation in Gayrile has not improved."

"Unfortunately not," Jan answered grimly. "But he should be here tomorrow. If you believe it is better we postpone our council until then, we shall do so."

"At least until we have the rest of the information from the north," Ajaha replied. She noticed Allie and gave her a slight smile, but her eyes were tired.

"Then let us prepare for a meeting tomorrow," Jan agreed. "We shall inform the councilors…" He trailed off, seeming to remember something, and looked at Ajaha. "I—don't suppose you might spare one of your couriers to inform them?"

Ajaha frowned in confusion. "Iriam normally reaches the councilors…" As if for the first time, she registered the Neutral's absence, and Allie saw her face pale.

"There was an attack by serpentines," Ĵan told her quietly. "Iriam is in the hospital."

Ajaha's fear turned to shock. "Iriam… when did… will he be all right?"

"We are not yet sure," Ĵan told her. Allie had to strain her ears to catch his muted words. "As far as I know, no one has ever taken that much venom and lived."

Guilt twinged in the pit of Allie's stomach, and she felt sick with fear.

"All the same, we know Iriam," Dandio said, his voice firm and steady. "He's strong. I watched him challenge the Ace-Lord himself in Castle Droco and survive with hardly a scratch to show for it."

"Yes," Ajaha agreed softly, but the worry remained etched on her face. "Well then—I should prepare my report for tomorrow's council. Iriam…would not want us to waste time."

"I'll contact the councilors," Dandio said quietly, and headed down the hall.

Allie stood uncertain for a moment. Part of her wanted to return to the library and pursue their search through the Garilian spell books. But the unease and fear permeating the corridor gave her a need to act elsewhere. She looked back at Rygal and Darion. "I'm going to talk to Ĵan."

They both nodded mutely—it seemed they too sensed the heaviness that had settled upon Castle Sia. Rygal left to the barracks, and Darion said something about going back to the library.

Allie lingered in the entry hall a moment, listening to the faint sounds as her mother's team set to work, then followed the echoes of her uncle's footsteps to the upper levels of the castle. Jan stood at the door to his study; hearing her approach, he turned back to her with a small smile. "I thought you were resting. You've had a long ride today too."

"I'm not tired," Allie replied. "Can I help with anything?"

She saw the concern on Jan's face, but thankfully he didn't press, only held the door open for her as they entered the study. The quiet peace of the sunlit room contrasted with the busyness swarming the rest of the castle. Allie had often come here, sitting in the chair across from Jan's desk, working on her studies, telling Jan about her day, or just to read and rest, listening to the scratching of the king's quill on the page.

Jan sat at his desk, pulled out a small notebook, and looked up at her. "Without Iriam, there is much to attend to. You might help make copies of the summons for the council."

Allie nodded, taking the paper and quill he offered. "Who are these for?"

"The usual crowd of overworked councilors," Jan answered with a faint smile. "Your father's generals—any who can be spared, that is— and my advisors. You will come, of course. Your and Darion's report of Appledale is an important one."

Allie nodded again. It used to be exciting to be included in such councils. Now, though, she had grown weary of the constant talk and planning with so little action to accompany it.

"I take it the mission was successful?" Jan asked after a pause, his eyes trailing down a long list of records.

"We delivered the supplies," Allie answered. "I think Appledale will be safe for now, as long as Mel and his family stay here."

Jan shook his head. "Harsh, but understandable. The Dal-kerri did not attack the town, then?"

"No, they came after," Allie replied, continuing to write. "In the woods… we found the void they came through." Ink welled from the tip of the quill, threatening to blotch the letters. She hadn't meant to mention that last part. He'd worry all the more if he knew the truth, and she was sick of the pity of others, which kindled the wrath all the hotter.

But this was *Jan*. Her uncle, her advisor, the one she'd always confided in about everything. The small corner of her mind that wasn't crystallized by the curse wanted to tell him the whole story, if only to hear his steady reassurance that might help her pretend she'd be all right.

"The void?" Jan repeated, sounding interested. His keen green eyes studied her carefully in that way that always made her suspect he could read the truth in her features. "Were you able to block it at all? That might prevent the Dal-kerri from coming through that way again."

"No, I… my fire closed it." Allie returned her eyes to the page, but pressed so hard that the ink spilled again, streaking the paper in ugly black. She spread a fresh sheet before her, glancing up hesitantly at her uncle, who looked thoughtful.

"We had speculated before that fire might close the voids," he mused at last. "If you share the Ace-Lord's power, perhaps you can destroy the voids as well as travel through them."

"That's what Darion thought," Allie replied. For a moment, she felt her thoughts in turmoil, and wished to lay the whole of the Ace-Lord's chilling words before him. But she closed her mouth and kept writing.

Jan studied her a moment longer, clearly sensing there was something she wasn't telling him. "Sharing power does not make you the same," he said at last, his voice quiet. "No more than night can diminish the sun's light on the moon."

Allie managed a short smile, unable to voice her thoughts. His words held more truth than he knew. She was not one with the Aces. But she was no longer filled with light, either. What was left was a pawn painted gray, dancing the line between sides. What was left was the Vessel.

. . . . . .

Morning dawned bright and sunny, despite the dark discussions the day promised. Allie woke stiff and sore, but the hope of soon having a plan of action drowned it out. She dressed quickly, ignoring the lingering sting of the burns on her hands, and headed for the council room.

Darion met her at the base of the stairs. In contrast to his usual black vest and cloak, he wore the same red leather jerkin as a soldier of the Red Dawn. His quiver and arm guards were new, too, well-made and matching the ensemble of an archer in Sia's forces. "Morning. Ready for more politics?"

"Oh, ready enough," Allie answered, studying him. "A Red Dawn soldier? I thought rangers only served under their fiefs."

He looked down at his new uniform, a flush of pride spreading over his scarred face. "Yes—well—without the duke to order me to serve the Ace-Lord, I've defected to the Red Dawn."

"I'm only teasing," Allie said, smiling. "It suits you. And I'm glad you'll be staying here."

Darion returned the grin as they walked together to the council hall. Voices drifted into the corridor outside; a small crowd had already begun to gather. "Rygal and I read through the rest of that book last night," Darion said. "We didn't find anything about the Life-Blood Spell specifically, but lots about dark magic. But we figured we'd keep looking through the Garilian spell books—the curse probably follows similar rules as other dark spells."

"Probably," Allie agreed. "Thanks for your help, all the same," she added. Despite her own doubts of finding anything about the curse, she appreciated their efforts.

Jan, Ajaha, and two couriers were speaking in one corner of the meeting hall, and Dandio and Glentree had just arrived with some of the generals. Rygal and Mel stood by the door, talking to a Siren with mottled green skin who Allie recognized as Lammar. She waved a good morning to them as she entered with Darion.

Though the stone room was well-lit by cheery torchlight, a shadow still lingered in these walls. The last time Allie had stood in this room had been right after she'd learned about the curse. She could still see Cahadras' penetrating gaze as the Star Queen had spoken of the Life-Blood Spell, and she remembered the concern in Iriam's eyes as he spoke to her.

She shook the dismal thoughts away for now and took a seat. "Do you think they'll have a strategy for battle yet?"

Darion thought a moment. "I'm not sure. Rygal thinks we'll discuss a plan for Gayrile today. And hopefully a strategy to protect Mata City, just in case that rumor turns out to be true." He lowered his voice. "I've wondered if we might attack Ar-Salem eventually, too."

Allie nodded slowly. Her brief journey through the Patch had allowed her to see a portion of it—black marble walls veined in silver, pits of shadow, stairways into darkness—yet she still had no idea what might await them in the towers and corridors of Castle Salem.

"I'd assume we will," she answered. "But I doubt it'll be very soon. From what my father's said, it's a difficult location to strike."

"True. Who knows what the Ace-Lord has brewing there," Darion mused. "Illusions, tricks… and however many more enchanted soldiers have joined him now."

His expression became grim, as it always did when he spoke of the enchanted soldiers. Despite swearing a Blood Oath and betraying several small villages in service to the Ace-Lord, Darion had turned to the Liznees' side after the Aces had claimed his home village of Wiverrun. But that did not change what had happened. His own brother, Allie knew, had been enchanted, and the rest of his family were either lost, or left with shattered minds in the wake of the Aces.

That hadn't stopped Darion from seeking out a cure for the enchantment, if there was one. It was that mission that had originally led to Allie's involvement in the war at all, but with everything that had happened lately, she had nearly forgotten about it.

"Have you looked for any records of the enchantment?" she asked at length. "We know there were warriors that fought with the Ace-Lord in the first Ace-rise."

"Maybe," Darion said, though he sounded doubtful. "I've checked Caer Sia's library. There aren't many details about the Ace-Lord's servants at all, except for the Eleven. It doesn't tell what happened to the soldiers after the battle last time."

He paused, brow furrowed as a thought occurred to him. "If we had time… I thought there might be better records in Tinkeeyo. The scribe houses there are some of the oldest in Coonsia—my mentor and I went there during my training."

"That's not a bad idea," Allie agreed. "There's a Red Dawn fort there, too. We could accompany the next regiment of troops south and check Tinkeeyo's records."

"We?" Darion repeated. "What about looking for the Life-Blood Spell?"

"Maybe they're connected," Allie pointed out. "And yes, *we*. I promised to help you figure this out, and I've been very little help so far."

Darion shook his head, but he was smiling. "Well, I appreciate that. In that case..."

Jan called them to attention before he could finish, and the others took their seats. The High King stood at the head of the table, his voice calm and level. "Thank you all for attending. I will spare little time on formalities. Firstly, allow me to assure you that Iriam is showing improvement. Though still unconscious, the doctors believe the serpentine venom has been cleansed from his blood."

Allie felt herself exhale a sigh of relief along with the rest of the room. All of them respected and worried for the Neutral. Any update on his recovery was good news.

"Now," Jan said, his face becoming serious, "the relief mission to Appledale was successful. Regarding their return trip, however, I ask Darion Blackbird to speak."

Darion gave him a short nod as he stood, taking a breath before speaking. "The people of Appledale were grateful for the supplies we brought, though very fearful of another attack. But they live, and the village itself is not currently threatened by the Ace-Lord, as long as the New Blood remains here." He glanced briefly at Mel. "On our way back, we were attacked by a pack of Dal-kerri hounds and serpentines. Iriam was struck down by the snakes, but Asescia was able to defeat the rest of them." He looked at her expectantly.

Allie felt all eyes turn to her. Everyone in this room knew about her dark new abilities, but that didn't make her feel any better.

"Asescia," Ĵan said, as Darion paused. "You mentioned you found the void in the woods?"

"Yes," Allie replied. She hesitated only a moment longer, realizing the full story would have to be told. "I… I fought off the wolves, and I found the void they came through. I think it led to Ar-Salem."

"Why assume that?" Lammar inquired, his lilting voice both interested and concerned.

"Because…" *Blast*, she hated what she was about to tell them. "Because the Ace-Lord came out of the void and spoke to me."

There was no uproar as she'd expected. The shock, disbelief, and fear were silent things, filling the council room like black smoke.

"The Ace-Lord?" one of the generals repeated blankly.

"The Ace-Lord himself?" Ĵan asked. His face remained calm, but she could hear the dread in his voice.

Allie nodded, glancing apprehensively at the others. Rygal looked at her in disbelief. Darion shook his head slowly. "You left *that* out of the story before," he said.

"I wasn't sure… I didn't know how to bring it up," Allie said haltingly, looking down at her hands. The blisters still creased her hands in pale streaks. "I don't even know what it means."

"What did he say to you?" Ajaha asked, her eyes fixed on her daughter.

Allie did not want to repeat those words. The finality and futility within them—wouldn't that only serve the Ace-Lord, breaking down the determination of her companions? But she could not avoid the answer. "He wanted to make sure I understood the meaning of the curse. He said there were things he wants me to do for him. And… when I said I wouldn't serve him… he said I didn't have a choice."

The generals murmured something uneasily. Mel and Darion both looked stunned. Rygal's jaw was set in an angry line, but he didn't say anything.

"There is always a choice," Dandio said at last, his voice firm. "We have learned that more than anything by now. No matter what the Ace-Lord has told you, Allie, your actions are still your own."

Allie nodded, trying to find some comfort in her father's words. But such hope seemed to have been snuffed out by the inevitable truth. Who she had been, the fire in her veins… that was claimed by the Ace-Lord now. Transforming her into a tool to destroy the resolve of those she loved.

"There are other actions he won't expect, too," Mel said, determination in his young voice. "Iriam made sure I understood that even before we got to Appledale. The dryads are wakened again."

This time a ripple of hopeful interest filled the room. "I had thought the dryads were nothing but legend," one of the couriers said in wonder.

"We thought the same of the Aces," Jan pointed out. "My father used to tell Dandio and me tales of the prophetic messages the Druids brought from the High Light. In the Dividing War, it was said that the dryads carried those messages among the mortal kingdoms."

"Our outriders have already reported seeing dryads," Dandio added. A fierce light had re-entered his eyes. "The Magno Forest is waking." He turned to Mel. "Did Iriam say when to expect their messages?"

"No," Mel said, uncertain now. "I know the dryads aren't eager to work with the mortals, but they promised to help anyway. Munben-Lia said his tribe will help us maintain contact with them."

"That is good to hear," Jan said. "Ever since the creation of Drisilas, we have maintained the alliance with the tribe of Lia. If they can contact their dryad brethren, we would do well to send word to them."

"We must be cautious, sire," General Leopold said hesitantly. The Cagari's panther-like face showed his unease. "To know the dryads have allied with us is good news, but I fear we must keep it secret as long as we can. If the Ace-Lord were to learn of the alliance, I have no doubt he will do all he can to stop them."

"His forces are growing," Ajaha added heavily. "Three of my informants reported villages that have surrendered to the Aces out of fear."

"Those are not the only reports of mortals swearing their allegiance to the Ace-Lord," Jan said, sounding frustrated. "Still, whether those soldiers were deceived, or chose willingly, I fear we will not know until we understand the enchantment itself." His gaze turned to Darion. "You have sought the truth of the enchantment for some time, have you not?"

"Yes," Darion said slowly, "but I admit I've learned very little. Even when I was closer to the Ace-Lord's plans, I never saw the actual enchanting, much less knew the motives of the warriors themselves."

"You think some of them were bribed?" Rygal asked.

"Bribed, tricked—some probably thought they could protect their homes or families by choosing it," Darion replied. "I know some are mercenaries. But I also know a lot of them were... in a similar situation as I was." His hand rubbed the scars as though he could wipe them away.

"What sort of enchantment binds them?" Rygal wondered, folding his arms over his chest. "If we knew that, we might find out how to break it."

Allie raised her hand slowly, catching her uncle's eye. Technically, as she'd been invited to this council, she was allowed to speak whenever, but it was still new to her. "Jan... Darion and I were talking about that earlier. There are hardly any records about the enchantment or the Ace-army during the first Ace-rise, at least, not in Sia's library. We were wondering if we might find more in the archives of Tinkeeyo."

Jan's face became thoughtful. "Tinkeeyo," he murmured, his voice suddenly distant. "Now *that* is an idea."

"Their records may cover the first Ace-rise," Dandio said, glancing at his brother. "Luet's writings… aren't they?"

"Yes…" Jan's brow was furrowed. Allie sensed her suggestion had brought up a different idea entirely, but she wasn't sure what it could be. She'd never gone to the scribe houses of Tinkeeyo—her only visits to the Elven city were to the fort itself, when her father had gone to inspect the garrison.

"Do you think they'd leave the Aces?" Mel asked, looking at Darion. "If we figured out how to break the enchantment, do you think they'd join us?"

"I can't speak for all of them," Darion replied, "but I owe it to the people of Wiverrun to find out. If there are records of an enchantment during the first Ace-rise, I'd be interested to find out more about it."

Dandio looked at him thoughtfully. "I intend to travel to Tinkeeyo soon to meet with Lord Andros. Perhaps you might accompany us."

"It may be worth checking those records regardless," Jan said. "Unfortunately, there are more pressing matters to attend to before we seek a cure for the Ace-Lord's forces." He turned to Ajaha, seeming to pocket his unspoken idea for now as the conversation shifted back to the war. "On the situation in the north, I ask Lady Ki and Lammar Skytooth to speak."

Ajaha stood and exchanged a glance with Lammar before speaking. "Gayrile has always been split into factions—the rebel Diren clans both despise the alliance that placed Caer Sia in authority, and desire to overthrow their ruling lord in Flameton. Now, it seems they have used the unrest of the Ace-war to ignite a civil war in Gayrile. My couriers in Badwater have worked with our comrades in Bridgeport for the last few weeks, struggling to better understand the conflict. Now, I believe, we have a course of action." She nodded to Lammar.

The Siren's vivid green eyes glittered as he looked at the assembly. "In a few days, the Guardians will return to Gayrile. We're not there to fight," here he cast a wry smile in Rygal's direction, "not unless necessary. We'll be escorting a representative from Caer Sia and spearheading negotiations with the rebel Direns, and hopefully end this pointless battle so we can fight the Aces together."

"That would be ideal," Jan agreed, looking at Ajaha. "Do you intend to lead this negotiation?"

"I would," Ajaha said with a sigh, "but I will be in Mata City, meeting with Lord Roan. I intended to appoint one of my couriers over the task, but I admit there are few I can spare."

"Any of my generals would volunteer for the mission," Dandio said. "But we're in a similar predicament. Until Mata City is secured, I would be hesitant to lose any one of my officers."

Allie raised her hand again. "Couldn't—couldn't I represent you?" she asked, looking at her mother. "I know I'm not a courier, but I've studied negotiations and I could represent Caer Sia."

"It is not a bad idea," Ajaha said after a pause, "but there is a problem. Though you are the Heiress, you are not yet qualified to sign any treaty."

"Rangers are," Mel jumped in, his eyes lighting up. "Aryion taught me all about treaties—he said a lot of the agreements were led by rangers."

"They were," Ajaha agreed with a slight smile, "but you could not accompany her either, Mel—you have not yet been appointed a fully-fledged ranger."

"He hasn't," Darion said, "but I have. If all she needs is a ranger to sign the documents, then I can go too."

Allie looked at him, grateful but surprised. "But what about your mission to Tinkeeyo?"

"The records will still be there after we get back from Gayrile," Darion replied with a shrug. "I doubt the war will be over by then, either."

"The Guardians can escort you both," Rygal said. His face was hopeful. "This treaty negotiation should stop the fighting, and it'll hopefully get the Direns on our side too. You've both fought the Aces, and your report will carry more weight than anything."

Ajaha looked between Allie and Darion, as though trying to decide whether or not they could handle such a mission. But finally, she nodded and looked at Jan for his decision.

The High King rested his hands on the table. "The tensions in Gayrile must be ended. Master Blackbird, you will escort the Heiress with the Guardians. You will both represent Caer Sia in the negotiations for peace."

Allie shared a quick, excited smile with Rygal and Darion. She could see the same energy and hope in both their faces. At last, the Guardians would return to Gayrile. There was a plan to be acted on, a mission to be accomplished.

All the same, the Ace-Lord's quiet words and the lingering burns on her hands chilled her determination with a breath of fear.

9

The New Blood's Mission

Mel lingered in the council hall after the meeting ended. The voices of his companions faded away into Castle Sia, filled with fresh determination and hope following the decisions and plans made in this short meeting. He was glad his own report of the Druids had helped encourage his friends.

Nevertheless, he could not help but feel utterly useless.

Duty to the Stone, important as it was, forbade him from joining the battlefield. He'd debated asking Rygal and Lammar if he could go to Gayrile with them, but there wasn't much he could offer to help with. The Guardians would handle the unrest, and the treaties that Darion and Allie would help forge would hopefully bring peace to the warring clans. The Red Dawn protected the northern coast, and Ajaha's couriers would uncover any plot against the threatened Mata City.

And so the New Blood would stay safe and protected in Caer Sia while war raged around him. It felt so wrong.

Hearing about the many attacks across Coonsia troubled him. Many small towns in the Magno Forest had been laid waste by the Aces, Dandio had told him—those that hadn't been attacked had joined the Ace-Lord. In fact, they had only recently received a report from Elimar about a battle near the southern fiefs.

The sheer number of conflicts and battles muddled his mind. War,

Mel had come to realize, was far more complicated than he'd first thought. He had pictured a straightforward battle, where the Red Dawn would clash with the Ace-army and the war would end one way or another. The truth was a convoluted tangle of kingdoms, politics, and conflicts to keep track of.

Soft footsteps in the corridor drew his attention. "Mel?"

Mel smiled as he recognized the hesitant yet curious voice of his younger sister. "Hey, Misty. You can come in—the meeting's done."

Misty walked inside, looking around the council room with interest. Since the attack on Appledale, Mel's family had been staying in a small suite of rooms in one of the wings of the castle. Here, they could be both protected and near enough to the reports and meetings for Mel to be involved.

"Mom was wondering if the meeting was over," Misty said, stepping close to the table to look at one of Dandio's maps.

"For now. Jan said he wanted to talk to me later," Mel said. He wasn't sure what about, but there had been a curious glimmer in the High King's eyes when Allie had brought up Tinkeeyo and the records there. "Did you see the books we brought back?"

She nodded, though a shadow had come over her face at the thought of their home. "Yep—thanks. Those are good books," she said, seeming to avoid the painful topic. "That way I can get some studying done while we're here."

Mel couldn't help grinning. "It's practically summer. Do you ever take breaks from schoolwork?"

"I did, when we first got here," Misty informed him, pushing her braids off her slim shoulders. "Now I need to get working again. It's more fun reading in a castle, anyway."

Mel shook his head. "Okay, that's fair. I still don't get why you like studies so much, though."

"They're interesting. History and languages and lores no one knows anymore. And the High King even said I could borrow some books from the castle library if I wanted," Misty said, beaming. She sat beside him, fidgeting with the sleeve of her dress. The dress was too big—it was probably one of Allie's. "Have we heard anything from the dryads yet?"

Mel felt his smile disappear in an instant. "No… not yet," he replied, trying to sound unworried. It was unsurprising that the dryads were taking their time to make contact. Any news they brought would likely be regarding the various conflicts, anyway. But he couldn't help hoping that their report would be for him—and that it would finally answer the consuming fear about his mentor.

It would be easier to assume Aryion was simply dead… but Mel refused to accept that. Whatever the Scribes' plan was, he'd have to trust them. He had resisted asking Lammar about it today, though he was certain he'd glimpsed the red Dricaster pin vanish in the Siren's hand before the meeting.

"We don't know when the dryads will come," he said after a pause. "Hopefully they'll bring news about Mata City, though. There's a chance the Aces are planning to attack there."

"Do you think they'll come to Caer Sia?" Misty asked, clearly trying to hide her worry.

"I don't think so," Mel said quickly. "The Stones protect Caer Sia, and we'll protect the Stones."

He knew it wasn't that simple. The Ace-Lord wanted the Stones too, and even with their protection, Caer Sia was still far from safe. But he didn't want to remind Misty of that. She'd already experienced too much fear in her nine years.

Footsteps sounded in the corridor again, and in another moment, Dandio reappeared. "There you are—ah, hello, Misty. If you're ready, Mel, Jan and I need to speak with you."

Mel got to his feet, looking curiously at the tall Liznee. "I'm coming. What is it?"

"Nothing serious," Dandio reassured him. "There's a mission we think you may be able to help with."

The frustrated helplessness vanished in a flash. A mission. Finally, something he could do to help. "A mission? Where? When?" he asked eagerly.

"We'll discuss that in a moment," Dandio said with a patient smile. "You may come as well, Misty."

The two siblings followed him up the corridors to the High King's study. Mel still remembered the first time he'd been in this room, right after the fight with the Darkness—it was here that he had first learned of the Ace-Lord by the name Kahlifis.

The study looked much the same, well-lit by a large window overlooking the sea. Misty stepped immediately to the book shelves, looking with interest at their weathered spines. Jan stood beside his desk, reading a report, and looked up as they entered.

"Thank you for coming, Mel. Good afternoon Misty—you might find those tomes difficult to read," he added with a slight smile, as Misty reached for a large book, "as they are written in Liznaeic."

Misty nodded, undaunted. "I've been learning to read it—I still can't speak it though."

Jan raised his eyebrows. "That is impressive." He turned to Mel. "I am grateful for your report about the dryads—besides Iriam, you were the only one to witness their return. That knowledge alone is cause for hope."

"I think Lammar knows about the Druids, too," Mel said slowly.

"He does," Jan said with a mysterious smile, "as he has mentioned to me this morning. But he was not there to speak to them. He did tell me, in part, about your decision to allow the Scribes to seek for Aryion."

Mel nodded, suddenly breathless. "Have… have they learned anything yet?"

Jan shook his head, which steadied Mel's racing heart. "No, not yet. But trust that you will be first to hear if we do. There is a different mission we thought to ask of you." He looked at Dandio.

"We did not have a plan yet until Allie brought up Tinkeeyo today," Dandio said. "I had already intended to go there to make sure the southern regions are well-secured, but I was rather hoping you could join me."

"Me?" Mel repeated, puzzled. "What do you want me to do?"

Jan spoke slowly, as if drawing the words from memory. "Mel… what do you know of the Star called Luet?"

Mel frowned, trying to recall the knowledge. The name was vaguely familiar—he'd heard it mentioned long ago on the quest for the Shards. "She was a messenger like Cahadras, right?" he said slowly. "I think I remember hearing that she brought the High Light's wisdom to the mortals."

"She did." Jan paused. "Unlike the other Stars, Luet allied herself with the mortals. She advised us, helped us, even fought with us at one point against a tyrannical queen. I have her to thank for Caer Sia's survival during the reign of Kircadash, in fact." A bittersweet smile crossed his face.

Mel hesitated, sensing the end of Luet's story had not been a good one. "She… died?" He knew it was possible—despite the great power and long years granted to the Stars, not even they were immune to the consequences of war.

"Fighting Kircadash's forces," Dandio said gravely. "She saved many lives with her sacrifice."

"She saved my life," Jan said quietly. For a moment he was silent, then shook his head as though to banish the old pain. "Luet dwelt among the mortals for centuries, exploring, charting maps, and establishing peace among kingdoms. Her writing, her messages, were all kept safe in the scribe house in Tinkeeyo, a city she helped to establish. Centuries of records are kept there, many of them in Luet's own hand. The last message she brought from the High Light was some thirty years ago, during the first Ace-rise."

Something seemed to connect in Mel's mind at Jan's words. "Wait… are you saying Luet was the one who brought the Prophecy?"

"It was the last message she brought from the Land Immortal," Jan said. "The Prophecy caused the Ace-Lord to retreat then—we believed him defeated, but as we have learned now, with the Prophecy in play, he had to craft a new strategy for his conquest that aligned with its words."

Misty listened in wordless wonder. Mel shook his head slowly, stunned. "I—I remember hearing that the Aces attacked a scribehouse in Tinkeeyo while we were on the quest for the Shards," he said. "Norrin brought word of it—he said an Ace destroyed a bunch of records and stole the copy of the Prophecy."

"Was that the original copy of the Prophecy?" Misty asked curiously. "The one Luet first wrote?"

Jan shook his head. "I doubt it—there were many copies of the

Prophecy made during the first Ace-rise, and none of them held more power than another. Unfortunately, when the Aces left, many disregarded the Prophecy entirely, believing its words irrelevant. We chose to focus on the fight with the Darkness, along with the unrest among the human and Elven kingdoms." He shook his head grimly. "In that, we were fools."

"The good news is, Luet's writings survived the Ace attack on the scribehouse," Dandio put in. "And this is where your task comes in, Mel."

"How?" Mel asked, still confused how this involved him.

Jan folded his hands on his desk. "I knew Luet very well—after I was Marked by Redeyes, she helped guide me back to the Light. She knew a great deal about the Star-Stones, and the deeper power within each one."

"Deeper power?" Misty repeated. "Like how the Jewel was a doorway?"

Jan nodded. "Each of the Stones have a distinct power, as you have both seen. The Jewel, a gateway from one world to another, whose magic might open a void to another place; Isilas, a source of fiery magic that protected the people. The Blue Stone's powers, however, are two fold. You know one," he said to Mel. "The power to heal. But the other power is one I have only heard of from Luet."

Mel's fingers closed over the Blue Stone in his pocket, his interest piqued. "What power?"

"A way to draw power from the Land Immortal, as the High Light intended for the mortals," Jan replied. "The Druids actually taught this power to the first wielders of the Stones, but few know of it now. I admit I do not know how it works. From what Luet said, once accessed, the Stone forms a shield that can protect the mortals. It is said that King

Grisham of Arkran, the first Wielder of the Blue Stone, used this magic against Kahlifis in the Dividing War and protected his kingdom."

"And you think Luet wrote about that magic?" Mel asked, finally guessing where this conversation was going.

"I would imagine she did," Jan said. "She wrote a great deal about the Star-Stones in particular, and she told me to seek the Druids when the kingdoms were at war. Our searches were unsuccessful, and I believe we were meant to understand the power without the guidance of the Druids."

"Do you think Iriam knows how to access that power?" Mel wondered.

"I expect he knows something of it," Dandio said grimly, "but until he wakes, we won't know. That is why I want to travel to Tinkeeyo. While I meet with Lord Andros and deal with military matters, you can go to the scribehouse and seek Luet's guidance about the Blue Stone."

Mel was nodding even before he finished. "I can do that—I can try to find the writings. Maybe there will be something about the enchantment, too, like Darion thought."

"Maybe," Dandio agreed. "Until Darion returns from Gayrile, we might as well seek the writings in Tinkeeyo."

"You'll need my help too," Misty put in unexpectedly.

Mel turned to her with a frown, a protest on the tip of his tongue, but she spoke over him. "Mel—I spent all of last summer studying Liznaeic. I'll know which books might have the information we need, which eras of history we can look through—and I can read the language," she added, with a glance between Jan and Dandio.

Mel hesitated. It wasn't that he didn't want Misty with him—he loved being with his little sister, and he didn't doubt she could help. But there was one matter. "You know Mom won't let you go."

"She won't want you to go either," Misty pointed out. "But she knows you can't go into battle with the Blood Oath, and if you're protecting me, that keeps me out of the fight too."

"I will protect you both," Dandio said. "Your mother has the final say, of course. But I think I can promise that this mission will be considerably safer than the quest for Drisilas."

"Don't promise that," Jan said wearily. "You manage to find a battle almost everywhere you go."

Dandio spread his hands. "And I will avoid said battle for Mel's sake. I know it is not ideal, but this is war—very little is truly safe now, nor will it be until the Ace-Lord is defeated."

Jan shook his head, looking at Misty. "I do not wish to put you in danger, no matter how slim the chance is," he said. "But I agree with Dandio—and I know he will keep you safe. If your mother allows it, then so will I."

Misty threw Mel an excited smile, and he grinned back. It was almost like old times, he thought—he and Misty going on a quest with Dandio. But this time, it would be a mission he could truly help with. "When do we leave?" he asked. "Isn't it almost a week's ride to Tinkeeyo?"

A little of his excitement faded as he said it. He could already picture the long, muggy trek through the Magno Forest, up and over the rolling hills as they slogged southward.

But Dandio gave a familiar half-smile, his green eyes twinkling. "Indeed it is. But we'll spare the horses the ride. It is high time we took Nella on an outing again."

10

Blood Right

Murky shadows filled Castle Salem as the night faded before the dawn, yet not even the rising sun could penetrate the black cloud shrouding the Ace-Lord's fortress.

The Ace-Deputy stood with his back to the wall that had once held the second gateway. Gray light filtered through the stained glass window, far dimmer than the glaring sunlight that had once pierced his eyes within his master's palace. Now, Castle Salem wore a cloak of darkness so impenetrable not even the brightest blaze of dawn could pierce it. To the mortal eye, only a wall of fog was visible, a cloud of shadow and illusions, dyed black by death. It must remain thus, to further foil the futile attempts of the mortals' reconnaissance teams.

The Deputy had seen enough of the Red Dawn's forces to admit, albeit unwillingly, that they were a strength to be reckoned with. He well-remembered the hated red fires that had blazed in Castle Droco, before the Bruin had come and crushed them all. Yet even the massive wraith had been destroyed by the Stars—darkness claim them all!

Fury filled him at the memories, along with the biting shame of his defeat. He straightened, silver armor clinking slightly. No matter. His master had allowed him a second chance, a new task, as he had promised all those years ago. The Ace-Lord no longer looked to the depths of the Magno Forest, nor the skeletal ruin he had once ruled from. Now, the plan had shifted elsewhere, and his master would require an update. That was likely the purpose of the meeting today, the Deputy guessed.

A shadow appeared from the entry hall, drawing him out of his thoughts. But it was not the Ace-Lord. The beast prowling towards him, eyes glowing like blood-red fires, brought a twinge of loathing into the Deputy's heart. But he kept his tone calm and smooth as ever.

"I take it our master has a new task for you as well, Redeyes?"

The massive cat looked up with a short growl. "Where have you been these last few weeks?"

Ah, Redeyes was nervous too. Good. They both were acutely aware of the frailty of their own power in the Ace-Lord's service.

"That is none of your concern," the Deputy replied coolly, clasping his hands behind his back. How he would have liked to spill the full story of his delightful success to Redeyes, if only to see the hatred and jealousy on the prideful cat's face. But he restrained himself, keeping his words vague. "I have been occupied with my task in our lord's strategy. I understand you have been given a similar assignment, else you would not be here to meet with him."

"No assignment," Redeyes replied, flicking his tail. "Only the purpose I was brought here for, and none other."

Short-sighted brute. He'd never appreciated the intricacies of the Ace-Lord's plan. He had been returned to the mortal world to kill, a purpose he carried out with morbid enjoyment. *The Ace-Lord's Messenger,* the Deputy thought in disgust, *the title Butcher would suit you better.*

A rustle of movement on the stairs above caused them both to turn and watch as their master strode down to meet them. Shadows swirled about the Ace-Lord's tall frame, mingling with his robes, as though the black fog were as much his cloak as the fortress'.

"Purpose, Redeyes?" he echoed quietly, his rich voice chilling the air. "Purpose is never made up of one singular action, one life to be taken. I trust you have come to understand this now."

"Yes, my master," Redeyes answered, his voice a low growl. "The fate of the Marked must be mine to claim. My mission calls me north."

The Deputy glanced at him swiftly. He would never dare to speak so presumptuously to the Ace-Lord.

But the Ace-Lord showed no anger, no disdain, only nodded slightly. "Indeed it does. You shall claim the Marked Ones, lest it be said I do not deliver on my promises." His purple-red eyes flicked to the Deputy. "How many now number among the vanguard?"

"A dozen have claimed the darkness, my lord," the Deputy answered, hearing the pride in his own voice. "I expect another seven to surrender before tomorrow's dusk. The mortals' fear sustains them, as it strengthens us. They await your orders." He hesitated a moment before voicing his concern. "That said…without the presence of the Messenger on the Mainland, I doubt the fear of the mortals shall continue to grow."

He glanced at Redeyes, unable to hide the dislike twisting his ruined face. A soft snarl rose in Redeyes' throat as he glared back. "If I am needed in every aspect of the conquest, then perhaps you should not have caused the Bruin's destruction."

Ice crusted the Deputy's knuckles in a surge of rage. Curse the wretched beast, he knew exactly how to rub salt in the wound.

"Silence," the Ace-Lord ordered, as the Deputy drew breath to retaliate. "Your purpose is decided, Redeyes, as you wished it. You shall go to Gayrile."

The Deputy looked to his master, startled. Redeyes' ears flicked back, confusion in his soulless eyes. "Gayrile?" he growled at last. "Why not Caer Sia?"

"In this *aspect* of my conquest," the Ace-Lord replied, drawing the words out icily, "the fate of Gayrile is of greater importance. There you shall go, and fulfill the purpose you were brought for. Fracture the mortal alliance, kill the Marked One, and return when you have done so."

"As you wish, my lord," Redeyes replied, seeming to know better than to question further.

The Ace-Lord turned to the Deputy. "Do not fret over strength, Deputy. Fear cannot be snuffed out so easily. Already it spreads like a plague, filling every mortal heart. Time itself serves my conquest now. All I require is patience."

"Yes, my lord," the Deputy answered, bowing his head. The Ace-Lord's voice raised his eyes again.

"How fares your prisoner?"

The Deputy's irritation vanished in an instant at the word.

The prisoner. Oh, how long he had waited to give this report, waiting for his master to return. How pleased he'd become with the twisted combination of magic and persuasion he had learned to perfect. How eager he was to share the satisfying results. His failure at Castle Droco would be forgotten once he had finished with the prisoner—his greatest triumph was yet to come. Only one question remained to ask of his master.

"The darkness has been planted within him, my lord. However, I wish to try a...different tactic to ensure the changing proves successful."

. . . . . .

Evening spread a fiery sunset in the western sky as Rygal returned to the harbor with Lammar.

The last few weeks of frustrated expectancy and waiting impatiently for news had fallen away, replaced by a determined hope. At last, the Guardians would return to Gayrile.

"We'll set sail in a few days," Lammar said. The Siren padded ahead of him, eyes glittering as he thought. "Get the Guardians prepared and head out with the delegation from Sia. That was a smart move of her," he commented, with a glance up at Rygal. "The Heiress. While she can't officially sign the treaty, her presence at the negotiations will assure the Garilians that Caer Sia is on their side."

Rygal nodded, shifting the spellbooks under his arm. With Allie representing Caer Sia, and Darion backing her up with the technical requirements, they could hopefully bring the conflict in Gayrile to an end. He was grateful they would both be there to help.

"I still wish we could have returned sooner," he admitted as they walked down the pier. While he was glad they had a plan, he knew the last few weeks had been difficult ones in Gayrile. Clans fought and people died, and the Guardians had not been there to prevent it. The flagship of the Guardians' fleet—*Ignis Veritos*—had waited in Caer Sia's harbor for so long that Rygal had begun to wonder if it had grown barnacles.

"Couldn't be helped," Lammar pointed out in his usual matter-of-fact way. "It was all in the timing, and now the right time has finally come." He shook his head as they walked up the gangplank. "It's another reason why I've always enjoyed the freedom of espionage."

"You've had plenty of that lately," Rygal said with a slight grin. "Barely even took time to rest in Caer Sia at all, and now you're off again. You're going to wear yourself out."

Lammar threw him a withering look. "Oh, please, now you really sound like Norrin. I'll be in Caer Sia a few days longer, or at least for supper—have you tried the clams at Madrona Lane? They're positively delicious. I've always been skeptical of the Sian cuisine, you know, but these..."

Rygal felt his smile widen as Lammar continued his spiel about the Liznees' cooking traditions. The Siren, he'd always thought, would have been better suited as a food critic than a warrior and spy. Then again, Lammar did both very well.

"Are the others on their way?" he asked as they boarded the ship.

"Oh, they'll be here soon enough. Thought we might get the *Veritos'* berth tidied up a bit more for them," Lammar answered.

Rygal followed him down into the officer's quarters. A table dominated most of the room, and a large map of the Northern Isles hung on the wall to his left. The Guardians who'd waited in Caer Sia—some fifty warriors in all—would meet here for the briefing now that a plan had at last been decided for Gayrile. They wouldn't leave just yet—more details had to be finalized first. All the same, Rygal was glad Lammar had decided to have them meet onboard the ship. He'd seen enough of the council hall over the last few weeks to appreciate the familiar half-darkness below decks.

"So," Lammar said, drawing Rygal's attention back. "I trust you know how to behave in a treaty negotiation."

"Sit quiet and let the delegates argue it out, right?" Rygal asked with a grin, setting the spell books on the table.

"Precisely. And pay attention—get everything put down in writing," Lammar said firmly. "I imagine the scribes will handle that, but it can't hurt to have it written down for our own records. You'll be representing the Guardians, after all."

Rygal blinked. "Representing the Guardians?" he repeated, his voice cracking in disbelief. He cleared his throat and tried to speak calmer. "I mean—why? Won't you be there?"

Lammar shook his head. "As much as I'd enjoy signing off matters with those bickering Direns, no, I won't. I've been assigned a different mission, but it is one that is, I dare say, equally important."

His scaled fingers played over a small red pin that bore the insignia of a snarling bear before it was concealed again.

"What mission?" Rygal asked, interested.

"I can't say too much—hardly anything at all, in fact. The most you can know is that it was assigned by the Druids' Scribes—and that it was a request from Mel."

Rygal paused. A guess had entered his head with those words, and he could understand why Lammar needed to keep it secret. "You think… he's alive?"

He admitted he had half resolved himself to the terrible truth of Aryion's death for these last few weeks. He'd felt the horrible grief when Dusty had first brought the news, hard as he tried to convince himself Aryion yet lived. But with all that had happened since, he'd had little time to wonder over the ranger's fate.

"Let's hope, for Mel's sake, that he is," Lammar said quietly. He seated himself beside the table, green-scaled hands moving over the charts, before looking at Rygal again. "So, with that said, I won't be able to accompany you all to Gayrile, which is why I need you there."

"To represent the Guardians," Rygal guessed.

"Not just represent, Rygal. I need you to lead them."

Rygal stared at him, speechless, for several moments, wondering if he'd heard wrong. That thought had been in the back of his mind for weeks, but hearing it spoken aloud stunned him to silence. *Lead.* Lead the Guardians, as Norrin had.

In an instant, all his old hesitations and fears came flying back. "Me…no, Lammar, I can't lead them," he said, shaking his head firmly. "Choose someone else—someone with more experience, maybe one of the captains, or—"

"I've spoken with our captains, with the warriors, and with many of our advisors," Lammar answered calmly. "They don't want someone else, Rygal. They want you."

Rygal stood wordlessly for a moment, unable to put his unease into words. "Why?" he said at last.

"Because it's what you've been trained for." Lammar looked him in the eye as Rygal stared in disbelief. "Norrin never told you that was his intent, though I wonder if you would have picked up on it eventually. All those years of studying, training you, teaching you the old lore, guiding you to lead the resistance against Safacon—you think that was all for nothing?"

Rygal remained silent. Memories of his mentor, of everything he had taught him, filled his thoughts. His gaze fell on the spellbooks. Even what Norrin had been unable to pass on were still available to Rygal to learn. Preserved by his hand in the ancient tomes.

"Iriam and I were the only ones he told," Lammar went on. "Norrin didn't want some sense of authority to go to your head, nor did he want you to be weighed down with it should anything happen to him." He took a breath. "For his sake we told you that Norrin chose no successor, just as he'd asked of us. But we also made sure you kept training, kept fighting—made sure you steeped yourself in the magic Norrin wished for you to learn."

Rygal's hand traced the hilt of his sword, his throat tight. Everything Lammar said aligned with his assumptions, but he'd never known that this had been Norrin's intent. Now, though, he could not deny the truth. He could almost see the old man's face again, the smile twinkling in his dark eyes.

"I… I knew he was training me for something," he said at last, his voice hoarse. "I didn't think… I didn't think it was to take over for him."

"It wasn't just that. It was to equip you for this fight. Norrin suspected something dark was coming as soon as the Jewel turned up again. He wanted to make sure you were prepared—prepared, if it was your choice, to take on the responsibility for him." The Siren gave a slight, sad smile. "You know he always wanted what was best for you, lad."

Rygal looked down, hiding the tears burning behind his eyes. The responsibility spread before him was one that Norrin had always borne so well. He did not know whether he could bear it too.

"I don't know… I don't know if I'm ready for this," he admitted at last. "I don't have as much experience as the rest of the Guardians. I've only been learning magic for a few months—I still can't even channel fire."

Lammar gave a short laugh. "Your hesitation is reassurance enough. A leader's strength is never defined by his own abilities, you know—it's in the people that trust him."

"That sounds like something Iriam would say," Rygal said, forcing a wry smile.

"It's a Norrin quote, actually. One he lived by." Lammar studied him for a long moment. "It's your choice, just as it's always been. But this is what you've been trained for."

Rygal closed his eyes for a moment as Norrin's face swam in his mind. The wizard's guidance, his teaching, his power—that was something

Rygal knew he would never measure up to. But at the same time, he understood that he wasn't expected to. This was the purpose he'd been prepared for—to lead in his own turn. This was his blood right. The Guardians must be led by a son of Gayrile. Norrin's teaching filled his heart and his father's blood flowed in his veins.

The rhythm of footsteps sounded on the decks above as the Guardians reached the *Veritos*. They would be waiting.

He took a deep breath and looked at Lammar. "Very well. I'll lead them."

A smile crossed the Siren's face, and he nodded to the stairs. "Then let's introduce the Guardians to their new commander."

11

The Garilian Strategy

"Have you ever been to Gayrile before?" Darion asked.

Midmorning sun warmed the streets of Caer Sia as Allie followed the young ranger to the harbor. The flurry of motion filling the city still warned of wartime, yet not even the curse could daunt the energy filling her heart. The two days since the council had seemed to drag by, grating on her patience. But now, the Guardians had cleared out their barracks and the ship had been loaded.

Today, they would finally travel to Gayrile.

"A few times," she answered Darion, shifting her pack to her other shoulder. "I've gone to the Diren's city, Flameton, once or twice—it's a beautiful place to visit in the winter when it's so cold here in Sia. My father likes to sail through the Kilean Strait between the Northern Isles to see the reef. What about you?"

Darion had traveled most of Coonsia with his mentor, the Meadowlark, during his training. He'd told her about those travels during their journey to Wiverrun. But he shook his head ruefully. "No, actually. I went to Kilee to meet with the Hymian emperor when I was still an apprentice. But I've never gone to Gayrile."

"Well, this will be my first time actually exploring Gayrile itself," Allie said. "I've never seen much scenery —the only times I've gone have been short visits, and mostly from the inside of a meeting hall."

"We'll probably see plenty of both," Darion replied wryly.

Crowds of Red Dawn soldiers walked the waterfront of Caer Sia's harbor, and Allie recognized a few captains calling orders from their ships. The Guardians were not the only ones preparing to disembark this morning. Many others would be off to other regions of Orlell on one mission or another.

A security check point, like the one they'd met upon returning to Caer Sia, waited at the entrance to the docks. The guard on duty allowed a few townsfolk through and paused as Allie and Darion approached. "Halt—we'll be needing to know your names and business. King's orders."

"Let them pass, private," a voice ordered as Allie drew breath to reply. General Leopold moved toward them. With Admiral Dessian escorting Dusty's squadron back to Kasabren to rally the Wildkids, command of the navy had fallen to the tough old Cagari warrior. "You are with the Guardians? The *Veritos* is anchored at pier seven."

"Thank you, General," Allie said. "Have you seen Rygal this morning? He was going to meet us here."

Leopold nodded toward the pier. "I believe he is already on board, Heiress. At any rate, he did not leave with the Siren."

Allie frowned slightly, wondering where Lammar had gone. If he was not going to Gayrile, who would lead the Guardians? "Ah... all right. Thanks," she said, and she and Darion continued on.

"Wonder where Lammar's headed," Darion murmured.

"I don't know... but Mel mentioned he's part of the mission from the Scribes," Allie replied in a low voice. She didn't know the exact details of that mission, no more than anyone else did, but that was probably for the best. From the little Mel had told her, it seemed the Scribes intended to seek news about Aryion, which meant if the ranger still lived, whoever tried to rescue him would have to go deep behind enemy lines.

They reached the pier, where the *Ignis Veritos*, flagship of the Guardians' fleet, waited. She was slightly smaller than the Red Dawn warships, but her sturdy build and steady masts were well-made to weather the rough waters of the North Sea. Guardians brushed past them as they walked up on deck, and Allie could tell everyone was as eager to be off as she was.

Rygal stood near the helm. The armor he wore was a mix between the simple leather of the Garilian warriors and the steel pauldrons of the Red Dawn, and his shield was slung over his back. He noticed Allie and Darion and walked over with a tired grin. "Good to see you two. Ready to head out?"

"Can we help with anything?" Darion asked.

Rygal gave a slight shrug. "We're nearly prepared. You might ask Captain Pike, if you want something to do—he's had the men at work all morning."

"He's leading the mission, then? We heard Lammar was gone," Darion said.

Rygal opened his mouth to speak, shut it again, and hesitated. Allie frowned at him, confused, but then the captain called out behind them before Rygal could say anything. "Commander, we're prepared to leave at your word."

Allie looked back at Rygal in disbelief. "*You're* leading us?"

Rygal flushed. "Yes—it didn't happen until a few days ago. Lammar said that was what Norrin—that it was what the rest of the warriors had chosen."

"That's great!" Darion congratulated him, clapping him on the shoulder. "I suppose I should have guessed, especially after you led the Guardians in the attack of Castle Droco."

Allie finally found her voice. "Yes, Rygal, it's wonderful—I didn't mean to doubt you, I'm just… surprised."

"So was I," Rygal admitted with a grin. "I never thought—that is, I led the attack, but I didn't think I'd end up in charge of this mission, let alone the Guardians."

"You'll do great," Darion told him with a confident nod. "Though don't expect us to salute you whenever you walk into a room now."

"Please don't," Rygal agreed fervently, then turned back to the tiller. "Thank you, Captain—all right, let's, ah, meet down in the captain's quarters, please, everyone."

The warriors headed down the stairs. Allie and Darion followed Rygal into the stuffy half-darkness below decks. The *Veritos* carried no cannons, but Allie had noticed several small catapults stored in the berth. In case of battle at sea, they could still return fire. The Red Dawn had also sent them with a few crates of firearms—rifles and pistols to better equip the allies of Gayrile.

They gathered in the captain's quarters. A lantern sat on the table beside the sea charts, and a round window allowed the sun to further light the interior.

"Better introduce you both before we carry on," Rygal muttered, weaving through the crowd. "Allie, Darion, this is Captain Robert Pike, helmsman of the *Veritos*. Captain, this is Darion Blackbird, ranger of Wiverrun, and Asescia Ki, the Heiress and delegate of Caer Sia."

Captain Pike's iron-gray hair and beard were cut short, and there was a strict set to his weathered face. But his eyes were kind as he shook their hands. "Glad to have you both aboard. I trust you know our plan?"

"Parts of it, sir," Allie answered.

"Well, I'll let the commander fill you in," Captain Pike replied with a nod to Rygal.

Rygal threw him a smile that seemed forced before clearing his throat and turning to the assembled warriors. "All right, everyone—we'll be off in a few minutes, and the details of the negotiations will probably be discussed further once we've met with the other delegates in Gayrile. But I wanted to share more about our mission before it begins."

He took a breath, seeming to gather his thoughts. "The most important part of this—something Lammar's impressed on me more than anything"—a ripple of amusement ran through the warriors; they had all heard the Siren's repeated warnings before—"is that we can't go into this with the intention of battle. We're prepared, of course—better safe than sorry in my book. But if fighting starts again, the Aces will capitalize off it. They might attempt to seize Gayrile then and there."

"What's stopping them from doing it now, sir?" one of the Guardians inquired.

"Technically, nothing," Rygal said grimly. "Our latest intel shows their focus is on Mata City, not Gayrile. Still, we need to settle the unrest in the north before it costs any more lives."

He stepped to the side, nodding to a large map of the Northern Isles hanging on the wall. "If we sail directly into Bridgeport, there's a good chance the rebel clans will see it as an attack before we've even disembarked. That's why we're making port here," he tapped an edge on the east side of the uneven coast. "There's a small cove in the Wandering Wood. The Chanterelle Brownaes will send warriors to meet us there."

"Then what of Bridgeport?" another warrior wondered. "We've heard reports that the people there are in a bad way."

"We'll go there soon enough," Rygal replied. "The main concern is that we don't actually know what's going on, only that there's news of attacks on the city outskirts. We've speculated rebels, but our informants haven't seen anything. Whatever's causing trouble there, it's very good at staying out of sight."

A prickle of fear ran down Allie's spine, and she reached involuntarily for her sword hilt.

"We'll start in the Wood," Rygal went on. "Assess what's happening and meet with the Chanterelle forces. The treaty discussions should be held soon—once that's decided on, we can actually help the people of Gayrile again."

He looked back at the group. "Ah… any questions?"

Darion raised his hand slowly. "Are the Brownae tribes allied under the Chanterelle?" he asked. "From what I've heard, the tribes have been fighting each other more than anyone else in the last decade."

"They have," Rygal said. "Morel has more information than I do. Her last report stated that a few of the tribes have joined with the rebel Direns—radicals, trying to use the Ace-war to claim Gayrile for themselves. Thankfully, the Chanterelle tribe still has control over the Wandering Wood."

"Do we know if there's any Ace activity in Gayrile yet… Commander?" Allie asked, adding the last word with a slight grin.

Rygal folded his arms over his chest, but the hint of a smile threatened his face before he was serious again. "No, we don't. I think there's a good chance the Aces are behind the trouble in Bridgeport somehow, though we don't know what they'd be after."

Captain Pike spoke slowly. "I have a guess about that, Commander… it's one of Norrin's theories, in fact." He paused as all eyes turned curiously to him. "As we've learned, Safacon gained the Jewel of Power from the Ace-Lord through some way or another. He didn't create it himself, though we thought so for years."

Rygal nodded. "Right—even Norrin thought Safacon made the Jewel. We only learned that it was a Star-Stone when the Aces showed up again."

"Yes," Captain Pike said. "The true origins of the Jewel faded into folklore. But there's one legend among the northern provinces of Gayrile that no one forgot—the tale of the Mad King."

"The Mad King?" another Guardian, a Liznee archer, repeated. "We have that story in Caer Sia too, but it's considered a folk tale."

"A lot of folk tales have been proved true lately," Darion said grimly. "Trust me—I got these scars from a twice-dead beast."

No one could argue with that. Captain Pike went on. "The Mad King was said to have come from a Mainland kingdom, traveling in secret to the wilds of Gayrile. He had great power, and was said to carry an artifact that allowed him to enter another world. As the legend goes, the Mad King went deep into the mountains of Gayrile and opened a doorway into this other world, where he would vanish for years at a time. But it's said that the tribes of the north would occasionally see a black gateway of swirling shadows open in the valley, and know that the Mad King had returned from wherever he had been."

Allie listened in stunned silence. She'd wondered about the Ace-Lord's interest in Gayrile, and her conversation with Rygal and Darion in the library a few days ago had piqued her curiosity. If the legend of the Mad King was true, Gayrile was not only the place of the Jewel's corruption— it was also the original home of the gateway voids. "Do you think it was the Ace-Lord?" she said at last.

"I've heard other tales that might prove it true," Darion said, looking like he was thinking hard. "The Mad King story fits with the Ace-Lord's mortal history—back when Wiverrun was part of his domain, there were reports of our ruling king vanishing for long portions of time."

"And if Gayrile was the place where the Ace-Lord first accessed the Dark Realm, that explains how Safacon was able to get the Jewel at all," Rygal mused. "He was trained as a Guardian before he went bad. I bet he somehow stumbled upon whatever void the Ace-Lord had been using to travel between worlds."

"I agree," Captain Pike said. "There's no way to confirm it's true, of course. But if that was the birthplace of the Ace-Lord's dark magic, perhaps the darkness is stronger there."

There was a solemn pause. Allie thought of all she'd learned of the tyrannical sorcerer Safacon and his cruel reign of Gayrile. She'd never thought about why Gayrile had been the birthplace of so much darkness.

Another thought came to her, chilling her heart like a breath of ice. The Ace-Lord intended the Vessel's corruption to further his power. With Castle Droco gone... what better place to guide the Vessel than to the origins of his power?

"Everything you do will be as I will it."

She gritted her teeth, fighting down the angry flames that blazed to life at the thought. No, even if he meant to guide her to Gayrile, her fire would not blaze for him. But the thought did not ease this new fear of the curse, which wrapped icy chains around her heart.

She forced herself to focus on Rygal's voice as he spoke. "It's something to be aware of. But remember, the Guardians defeated Safacon, and Light willing, we can defeat the darkness that he drew from, too. Let's get to Gayrile and learn what's happening there, and decide our strategy then."

"Well said, sir," Captain Pike agreed. "All hands on deck—back to work, men."

The warriors jogged back up the stairs. The billowing sails were unfurled, the rowers sent the *Veritos* riding over the water, and Allie felt the familiar tug and lurch of the waves lapping at the prow. Wind whipped over the decks, pulling at her hair as she moved to the rail. Rygal's voice ordered them north, and she turned her eyes across the sparkling water.

Toward Gayrile, and whatever awaited them there.

12

Aboard the Veritos

It was a two day voyage from Caer Sia to the wooded port Rygal had mentioned on Gayrile's western coast. The *Ignis Veritos* made excellent time, heading northwest through the sulfur-scented winds of Badwater. By evening, the rocky outcrops of Mata City came into view, marking their last stop on the Mainland.

Under normal circumstances, Rygal said, they'd stop in Mata City and enjoy the rest and companionship of the Coopers. But the urgency of their mission forbade that. Jarus Puddlepaw and the rest of the Cooper delegates would meet them in Bridgeport after the negotiations were complete.

Allie passed the time aboard skimming through the protocol notes her mother had sent with her, which detailed the process of forming a peace treaty, as well as regional customs to expect in Gayrile. There were years of disagreements, alliances, and battles to learn. While the clans of Gayrile had joined together in the battle against Safacon some four years ago, those alliances had always been strained.

Beads of sweat pearled on her brow as she sat in the shade of the mizzenmast, thankful for the steady breeze stirring the warm air. She tried to focus on the words and prepare herself for the treaty discussion. Darion carried the authority needed to make any significant decisions. Rygal and the Guardians would be there to protect the delegates in case battle erupted again. Her only role was to represent Caer Sia.

Despite this, she could not shake the cold foreboding. Dark magic and corruption still lingered over Gayrile, no matter the years of peace and light that had filled it since. She could almost sense it, as if the curse was answering to a distant call: *Come, Vessel, come and see what our master will make of you...*

"Sorry to interrupt you," came Darion's voice, drawing her out of her thoughts. He stood above her, holding one of the Garilian spell books.

Allie looked up, shaking her head to clear it. "No, it's fine. What is it?"

To her surprise and concern, his face was grim. "I was reading that chapter about dark magic, and... I found something you should see. It's a section on enchantments and curses."

He crouched in front of her, holding out the book. Allie took it, her eyes scanning the page. This was the same book that had detailed the Jewel's corruption.

"To enchant and to curse are two entirely different spells, and must not be misconstrued. An enchantment is not always linked to dark magic. For an enchantment to be properly cast, both parties must be willing, fully choosing the magic they take part in.

"A curse, rather, relies upon dark magic. Often more complex and difficult than a spell, a curse is wrought of darkness. Except in rare cases, the one bound by the curse is unwilling, trapped in an arrangement the caster has placed. It is of far greater importance for a student of magic to learn the counter-spells than the curses themselves, that they may protect themselves from a worse fate."

Wrought in darkness, Allie's mind echoed. Bound by the same evil that the Ace-Lord steeped himself in, and slowly becoming corrupted by it.

With a deep breath, she pushed the thought away for now and looked up at Darion again. "I'd heard you had to be willing to be enchanted, but... I didn't know it worked like this."

"Neither did I," Darion replied. His face was troubled. "That line there—*fully choosing what they take part in*—I'd thought that even if some of the enchanted soldiers were tricked or bribed, they—I wouldn't have expected them to have chosen that fate willingly."

Allie studied him, seeing the conflict and pain on his face. She could understand that—he'd been looking for some cure to the enchantment for months. Now, the little hope he'd gathered seemed dashed by the book's words. "I'd wondered if I might be able to help them," she said slowly. "Not in battle, but maybe if we managed to talk to one of them outside of that. My fire breaks the immortality part of the enchantment, at least."

How gentle it sounded out loud. It didn't encapsulate the violent way she'd learned that. She still remembered the flight through the fog with the Wildkids, the red sparks sprinkled over the rocks, the way her fire had cut down the very soldiers she'd sought to free.

Darion thought a moment. "It's an idea, though I don't know when we'd get a chance to talk things through peacefully. You've seen how the Ace-Lord controls them—we'd be cut down before we got a word out."

"That's true," Allie agreed, "but what if... I don't know, what if... your brother's enchanted, right?"

He nodded slightly. He didn't like discussing this, not that she could blame him, but she pressed on carefully. "If he chose the enchantment, he might still be able to choose a way out. If we were able to find him, maybe you could talk to him, try to help him remember."

Darion let out a breath. "Allie... I've tried that. When I was still working for the Aces, I—I tried to get him to come back to himself, help him remember, so that we could both get away. Nothing happened—I doubt any of my words got through. The last time I saw him was when we were running to Mata City with the Wildkids."

Allie felt her heart drop. "Did I…"

"You didn't kill him," Darion reassured her quickly. "He was in the back of the group. I could hear him calling orders."

A voice and a face swam into Allie's memory, the face of the captain who had met them in the cabin when Darion had betrayed them. A young man in a blue-plumed hat whose expressionless face had been somehow familiar. If she focused on that face, she could almost imagine those hollow blue eyes had once been hazel.

The realization dawned on her, and she stared at him in disbelief. "Your brother?" she breathed. "The captain of the group that captured us—the one you'd planned to meet—"

"Fargrin." He gave a tight smile. "Not much resemblance, I'm guessing. I didn't expect him to be made a captain—but he's always been the one in charge."

A captain. Strange how this simple truth completely shook her previous views of the enchanted soldiers, who they were, who they'd been. She knew that many of the warriors had chosen the binding spell in a desperate attempt to protect their homes and families. But she'd assumed this applied only to the footsoldiers, to the servants that had filled the halls, to the slaves working in the bowels of the black palace of Ar-Salem.

But some had been made captains, generals maybe, leaders of the Ace-army. Commanding warriors into battle, decimating helpless villages, killing and destroying as their dark lord ordered.

Was there freedom for them too? Or were they too far engulfed by the power that had claimed them?

"I didn't know," she said at last, stunned.

"Of course you didn't," Darion said quietly, shaking his head. "I didn't tell you—I wasn't sure if I should, and I'm sorry for that. I was… I know you hate them for what they did to Caer Sia."

"That was the Ace-Lord, not the enchanted soldiers," Allie said quickly, though it hardly mattered. Nor could she forget the vengeful thoughts and the twisted satisfaction that filled her mind so easily. The Ace-Lord's curse fed upon the helpless rage and fear that arose when she fought. Worse, it gave her a way to gain the vengeance that fear demanded.

"I won't give up the hope of freeing them yet," Darion said after a pause. "I owe that to them—and it might be the only way to atone for this." He rubbed one of the scars creasing his face as though it had suddenly burned him.

"You're past the curse now," Allie said, trying to reassure him.

"Not fully. It was my doing that brought Wiverrun into the Ace-Lord's hand." Darion straightened, glancing across the water. "The curse might hold no weight without judgment, but the enchantment does—and until that's broken, the Marks must be atoned." He turned back to the book. "This part is more important, though—the line about curses. Did you catch it?"

"*Except in rare cases, the one bound by the curse is unwilling, trapped in an arrangement the caster has placed*," Allie read from the page, feeling a familiar frustration at the words. "Cahadras said something like that when she first told me about the spell. It doesn't sound like the Mortal's usually willing."

"Right—which is strange that the Prophecy implies a *Willing Warrior*," Darion said slowly. "What if that's about someone else entirely?"

Allie met his gaze, seeing the hesitant hope in his eyes. When she'd first learned of the Life-Blood Spell, her death had been presented as a very real possibility. But she'd pushed it away, fighting it with the fury, and allowing the fire to rise. Yet perhaps Darion was right. With the Life-Blood Spell cast upon her, she'd never been truly willing. Maybe there was still hope, a chance to escape the chains of the curse, to forget the darkness the Ace-Lord had imbued in her.

"I'm not sure," she said at last. "From what Cahadras said… I'm the Willing Warrior now. But maybe…"

She trailed off, unable to fully voice that hope of life for fear it might be crushed, and left the unanswered question hovering over the waters.

······

The wind picked up as they as they sailed farther on. By the second morning at sea, the dawn light outlined the Northern Isles, and Gayrile lay before them.

The mountains came into focus first, rising like craggy teeth along the east side of the island. Allie could make out the tallest peak, the Topstorm, wreathed in clouds.

Rygal pointed towards the mountains. "That's Sorcerer's Valley—Safacon's old domain. His fortress is gone now, thankfully—it was dismantled by Lord Casper after the Jewel was destroyed."

"Good," Darion said, folding his arms over his chest. "That's one less old ruin for the Aces to inhabit. But why not make port on that side instead? Isn't it closer to Bridgeport?"

"It is," Rygal told him, "but it's also much closer to the lands of the rebel Diren clans. Until we know what's going on, the Wood is the best place to hide out."

A dark haze hung in the air overhead as they sailed west along the coast, and the stench of burning oil stung Allie's throat. Gradually, the outlines of buildings came into view, perched along the rocky coast. Smoke coiled in the wind, blurring the details of the city, but Allie could make out a few small fishing vessels filling the harbor.

"Good old Bridgeport," Rygal murmured, looking relieved. "Never thought I'd be happy to see all that smoke."

"Better than ice," Allie pointed out, her eyes scanning the distant city.

"From what we've heard, the reports of trouble came from the west side of the city, near the swamps," Rygal said. "Whether it's the rebels, or something else, I would assume they're hidden there."

"They'll have plenty of places to hide, sir," Captain Pike remarked grimly. "Bridgeport itself seems safe, at least from a distance."

The wind picked up as they passed the city, as though propelling them onward. The Guardians stood on deck, studying their homeland with both longing and concern. All appeared well, Allie thought, but she decided to reserve judgment until they were on land.

Bridgeport fell away behind them as they rounded the western coast, and the hills rose in a dark green expanse of forest. It reminded Allie somewhat of the vastness of the Magno Forest, which they'd traveled through on the mission to Wiverrun, with its towering trees and arching hills filling mainland Coonsia.

The Wandering Wood was much smaller, but it daunted her nonetheless. It seemed a darker shade of green, murky as a bottomless pool, enticing unsuspecting travelers down endless roads.

"We're walking through there?" she asked slowly, trying to hide her unease.

"Well, not the entire thing," Rygal reassured her. "Trust me—the Wood's not an enjoyable place. We got turned around in there during the quest for the Jewel and spent almost a week trying to find the right road. This time, the Brownaes should meet us near the river mouth to guide us to their camp."

He turned back to the forest before pointing ahead. Half hidden by the dense trees was a river, spilling reddish silt into the sea. Tall cliffs rose on each side, further concealing the harbor from view before melding into the hills beyond.

"There, Captain," Rygal said. "We'll anchor just inside the mouth of the river and conceal the ship."

"Aye, sir," Captain Pike replied, guiding the *Veritos* forward. The river's current pushed against them, but the rowers hauled the ship upstream until they were within the shadows of the cliffs. To Allie, the Wandering Wood seemed to embrace them, pulling them within itself. She could not decide if the thought was comforting or not.

Here they anchored and lowered the rowboats. A small landing of stone formed a slight shoreline on the right side of the river, carved from the cliffs by the rushing water. Steps led up the cliff side to the Wood above.

They disembarked, paddling through the shallow water to the bank. Most of the Guardians moved to shore with an ease that showed they'd done it before. Captain Pike and a few others remained on board, guarding both the ship and the supplies until the others had made contact with the Brownaes.

Wind whispered through the Wandering Wood, tousling the ferns and branches as they headed up the slippery steps. Allie shivered as the breeze cut through her thin sleeves and looked at Rygal. "Where to?"

Rygal paused, his eyes scanning the forest. His initial hesitation to lead the Guardians seemed to have left now that they were finally back in Gayrile, and she could see that his confidence had grown, too. "All right," he said, as the last of the warriors reached the top of the steps. "These are the lands of the Chanterelle, but we weren't given an exact meeting place. We'll follow this road north for now. The Brownaes will meet us soon."

"How will they know we've arrived, sir?" one of the Guardians asked, puzzled.

"That's something I've never fully understood," Rygal told him. "But they will. Keep an eye out for them."

At his order, the group turned and began a brisk march down the overgrown path. Allie jogged to catch up to Darion, trying to warm up, scanning the woods for any sign of the Brownae warriors.

"I finished reading that protocol book my mother sent," she commented as they walked, "but I don't know how much of it really applies to the Brownaes."

"It doesn't sound like you'll need to know those kind of rules until the negotiations begin, anyway," Darion reassured her. "Even then, don't overthink it. You're mainly there as the voice of reason." The faintest hint of a smirk crossed his face. "Now *that's* a terrifying thought."

"You're one to talk," Allie fired back, but she was smiling. "You've had some experience with these sort of things, then?"

"Two missions was all," he answered, ducking under a low-hanging branch. Moss hung from the limbs of the ivy-choked trees, further darkening the forest as they walked onward. "We went to Kilee in my second year as an apprentice, to deliver a message to the Hymian emperor. And there was a mission a couple months after that to West

Coonsia, overseeing a trade route agreement."

"I didn't know the Meadowlark was so involved," Allie said, impressed. She'd only met Darion's mentor in passing, several years ago. The white-bearded ranger had been more of a diplomat than she had realized.

"Yes, Kenneth likes diplomacy. He used to joke that he would have apprenticed to be a senator, if he had better handwriting." Darion smiled, but his eyes were sad.

Allie pushed a moss-heavy branch out of her path, glancing over at him. "You said he was captured when the Aces first came to Wiverrun? Was he enchanted too?"

"I don't know," Darion answered slowly. "He was captured. I doubt they could have convinced him to choose the enchantment, even with their lies. I never saw him when I was working for them."

"He might have escaped them," Allie ventured slowly, though she knew it was unlikely. Even a ranger would be hard-pressed to escape the Aces. And the Meadowlark would be a key prisoner, with his knowledge of Wiverrun and the surrounding areas.

But he hadn't been enchanted—at least, not that Darion knew. Maybe the Aces were keeping him hostage.

Or maybe there was another purpose they intended for him.

Cold fear chilled the pit of her stomach. Darion, seeming to need the change in subject as much as she did, moved forward slightly to Rygal. "Do we know if the rebel Direns are in the Wood at all?"

"Not to my knowledge," Rygal told him. "The Chanterelle tribe guards this land fiercely, and I doubt anyone's slipped past their watch."

"That's good," Allie said, relieved. "But what about the Brownaes who aren't on our side—the ones who've joined the rebels?"

"We don't know much about them, either," Rygal said. "Thankfully, we know that most of them are hesitant to challenge the Guardians. They hate us, but it'd take a lot for them to attack us outright." He grinned. "Just be glad you weren't here during Deathcap's reign."

Even as he said it, the underbrush around the trail rustled as several furry figures seemed to materialize from the shadows before them, so quickly it took Allie a moment to realize they had come. The Guardians stopped abruptly. Allie's hand flew involuntarily to her sword hilt, but a voice spoke from behind them—female, and holding a wry note of amusement.

"Oh yes, Deathcap is gone. But it seems you've found a new war to fight, Rygal."

"Lower your blades," Rygal ordered. Several warriors had drawn their weapons, startled by the Brownaes' sudden appearance. But at Rygal's command, Allie and the others relaxed, turning to see the allies they had come to meet.

Five Brownaes had emerged from the woods in front of them, their dappled brown fur concealing them so well that she hadn't even seen them until they'd moved. Four others remained in the underbrush beside the path; the one who had spoken stepped onto the trail and walked briskly toward the group.

She stood around four feet tall, well-built and stocky, with a strength built from years of fighting. The armor she wore was made of a tough, leather-like hide. Turquoise stones glittered in her cat-like ears. The slight smirk on her face further displayed her cool confidence, and she carried herself with an air of unrivaled authority, shoulders back, head held high as she regarded the warriors.

"Thought you'd be back sooner," she commented.

Rygal stepped forward, stooping slightly to clasp the warrior's hand.

"Morel—it's good to see you."

"You as well," Morel replied, a genuine smile of greeting crossing her face. "How fares the Mainland?"

"As well as can be expected in times of war," Rygal said, shaking his head, "but it'll be better as soon as we can establish peace here."

"Hmm, well, that's easier said than done," Morel answered, her eyes scanning the rest of the group. She seemed to recognize a few of the Guardians; Allie knew the Chanterelle Brownaes had fought alongside them against Safacon.

"Morel, meet Darion Blackbird and the princess Asescia Ki," Rygal said, ushering them forward. "They're representing Caer Sia in the treaty discussions."

"Good to meet you both," Morel said with a short nod. She regarded Allie carefully. "I had not known our little war here was enough to catch Sia's notice, enough to send their heiress here to calm things down?"

Allie managed a weak grin. "I'll help how I can, though I can't say I'm very good at calming things down."

"Good," Morel said, satisfied. "That's exactly what I hoped to hear. Frankly, all these discussions for peace concern me, considering what's going on."

Unease prickled in Allie's chest at her words. Rygal frowned. "How do you mean?"

Morel nodded down the road. "Not now. Too many ears in this part of the Wood. We've made camp a few miles from here, and I'd prefer to discuss this matter in secret."

13

∽ ∽ ∽ ∽ ∽ ∽ ∽ ∽ ∽

Into the Wood

The cool coastal breeze faded away as the Brownaes led the Guardians deeper into the Wandering Wood. Sounds filled every part of the forest—rustling underbrush, cries of strange birds, yips and howls from other beasts that made their homes here.

Allie kept her hand on her sword hilt, but she did not feel afraid with the Brownae warriors. Morel led them confidently ahead, even as the path dwindled away and the mossy trees wrapped a seemingly impenetrable barrier around them. Without a guide, Allie had no doubt they'd be completely lost within minutes. But the Chanterelle had dwelt here since the beginning of time, guarding their lands fiercely for centuries past.

At last, they descended into a hollow earthen draw overshadowed by evergreens. Once, Allie guessed, this had been a creek bed, but now it was nothing more than a narrow valley carved into the ground. Tents and wooden crates of equipment and weapons were set amid the ferns. Brownae warriors filled the camp, tending their fires, sharpening their weapons, speaking quietly in their own tongue. Allie glimpsed a sentry perched in a tree at the top of the ridge, and knew others likely filled the forest, keeping watch.

"I expect to hold camp here for a few weeks," Morel said to Rygal as they headed down. "The treaty discussions have been postponed twice now."

153

Rygal frowned. "What? I thought we were set for next week."

"So did I," Morel said, shaking her head. "But the rebel clans refused to show. Last I heard, they're insisting that a delegation from Mata City join the discussions, too."

Rygal sighed. "Jarus' last letter mentioned something along those lines, but I'd hoped the meeting could still happen on schedule."

"Why involve Mata City?" Allie asked slowly. She knew Jarus was the main diplomat who maintained the Coopers' relations with Gayrile, but for them to be included in a treaty between Diren clans was odd. The rebel Direns needed to ally themselves with the king of Flameton and the other Garilian nations. Bringing the Coopers into the discussion wouldn't change that.

"That's what I've been wondering," Morel said. "With luck, the meeting will be rescheduled soon. Either way, you might as well settle in and unpack your gear. I'll be back in a moment." She disappeared down the draw.

The Guardians set up their tents. Allie set her pack inside her tent, which, along with her supplies, carried the books and a few changes of clothes. Once they had set up, she moved to sit by a fire with Rygal and Darion.

Morel joined them shortly with a second Brownae, a young male with dark brown fur. He couldn't be much younger than Allie, though it was hard to tell with the Brownaes. In contrast to Morel's brisk, soldier-like nature, he held a friendly kindness about him. He greeted Rygal joyfully, then smiled widely to Allie and Darion. "Hello—good to meet you. I'm Porcini."

"The Chanterelle's delegate, and my youngest brother," Morel added with a smirk, but her eyes sparkled with pride.

Allie and Darion introduced themselves. Porcini, Allie knew, had gone on the quest for the Jewel—according to Rygal, he'd even led Safacon's prisoners into battle against the cruel sorcerer. She could hardly believe this cheery-faced youth had been a critical leader in that war.

Rygal shook his head in mock dismay. "You and Jarus both becoming politicians—I don't know whether to be proud or not."

"I'm not exactly a politician," Porcini returned. "But Lammar said I should represent the Brownaes—he said I'd do a better job at—"

"Establishing peace," Morel broke in.

"Negotiating," Porcini said. "He really just meant that I wouldn't start yelling at the rebels for causing all this trouble—"

"Which I'd say you should, as they deserve it," Morel added.

Porcini turned to his sister. "And that's why Lammar said *I* should do it."

"And that's why I agree with him," Morel replied with a slight shrug. "Either way, Father believed you could too." Her smile faded.

Rygal's face became somber. "Your father...Chief Cedar?"

"We lost him about a month and a half ago," Morel told him, shaking her head. Her voice was calm, but Allie saw the grief on her face. "We were ambushed by the rebel clans, a few miles from Safacon's old haunts."

"What were you doing there?" Rygal asked.

"Investigating. There were far too many strange reports coming from that side of the mountains—our father wanted to know what was going on, and he thought if he went with the intention of a peaceful meeting, the clans might let us pass. They might have, if they'd stopped to ask questions." Morel folded her arms over her chest and let out a breath. "Either way...those of us who survived made it back to the Wood, and we've stayed out of the Direns' petty fight since then. We never did find out what was going on in the mountains—not, at least, until a few days ago, which brings me to my concern over whether or not the negotiations should happen at all."

Allie listened silently, both interested and concerned. Morel paused before continuing. "Three days ago, we came across an old rebel camp on the Bridgeport side of the Wandering Wood. The Direns had abandoned it, it seemed, but they'd left some supplies, and we ended up sheltering there for the night. But the sun was barely down when these…things…came out of the forest." Her face was grim. "They looked like wolves, if wolves can die and crawl back out of the Dark Realm. I think you called them Dal-kerri."

Allie straightened, feeling herself tense.

"Dal-kerri?" Rygal repeated, stunned. "In the Wood?"

"Fifteen of them that we saw. There might be others," Morel answered. "We climbed into the trees and watched them. They strolled into the camp as if they belonged there—and what's worse, I'm starting to wonder if they *did*."

"How so?" Darion asked.

"The same reason the rebels keep postponing the treaty hearings," Morel replied. "We need the clans allied before we can fight the Aces, and I imagine the Aces know that. The Dal-kerri got here somehow. I don't know how, but I'm worried the Aces have convinced the rebels to side with them—and now, they've joined forces to drive us out of Gayrile."

A heavy silence followed these words. "I doubt the rebels would fully join the Ace-Lord," Porcini at last. "They'll wait until we're weakened, and then they'll try to betray the Aces too."

"The Aces might betray them before they have a chance," Darion said darkly. "They can be very persuasive if they need someone on their side, but they don't exactly care about loyalty."

"Now, here's our predicament," Porcini continued. "The negotiations have already been postponed several times. If we back out now, we would avoid playing into the rebels' trap. But if Morel's wrong, then we'll be the reason the treaty never happens. We'll have ruined any chance of making peace with the rebel clans—maybe forever."

Allie looked at Rygal. The firelight played over his face, showing the conflict of thoughts within him. At last he turned to Morel. "How confident are you that the Dal-kerri were actually there to meet the rebels?"

Morel frowned. "I'm certain I'm right, and the rebels plan to betray us. That said," she added, with a glance at Porcini, "there's no way to prove it. And like my brother's pointed out, if we call off the treaty discussions altogether, we may not get this chance again."

Silence fell a moment. Allie could sense the helpless frustration of the decision looming before them, like smoke filling the valley. Her fire crackled to life in her heart, hot with the energy to act. "Maybe we don't have to call it off," she said finally. "We're here to protect everyone who wants peace. If the rebels plan to spring an attack on us, they'll soon regret it."

Rygal grinned faintly and looked at Morel. "See what I said about not calming things down?"

"It's good," Morel said, nodding. "It's the same way I feel about it."

"Then what about the Guardians?" Porcini asked uneasily, looking at Rygal. "You came here to help negotiate peace. What if this *does* turn into a fight?"

Rygal let out a breath. "The Guardians are here to protect the kingdom. If we have to fight this war, then so be it."

"We can hope it doesn't escalate to bloodshed again," Morel said. "And let's hope the negotiations will take place as planned. But you can trust we'll be prepared for the worst."

A soft breeze played through the Wandering Wood as night fell. To Allie, the wind seemed to fill the forest with heat, as though tempting a blazing fire to spring to life.

. . . . . .

Torches lit Castle Sia's stables as Mel followed Dandio inside.

It had been four days since their conversation in Jan's study. Despite Mel's excitement to begin the mission as soon as possible, many things had to be attended to before they could leave to Tinkeeyo. Dandio, as the commander of the Red Dawn, needed to make certain the armies were at the ready in his absence. Many tasks had already been turned over to Glentree.

That time had also been enough to persuade Mrs. Smallbutton that the mission would be safe. She didn't argue against Mel's going—by now, she understood her son's role, and as much as she would worry for him, Mel knew she trusted in his ranger training. But she was less convinced that Misty should go too. At first, she'd refused outright, leaving Mel and Misty to persuade her as best they could. In the end, though, it had been Jan's reassurance that convinced her. Tinkeeyo was not an active battlefield. Should an attack occur, Dandio had assured them the fort was well-protected and difficult to infiltrate.

Now, finally, their last evening in Caer Sia had arrived, and Mel had come along to help Dandio with preparations before they left in the morning.

The stables were connected to the east side of the courtyard. Rows and rows of stalls filled the building where the war horses of the Red Dawn snorted and nickered in the early dusk. A pasture opened behind it, facing the darkening foothills.

Mel remembered running in here right before the fight with the Darkness—he and Rygal had raced into the stables to recover Drisilas. They'd ended up with a front-row seat to witness the Darkness as it engulfed Terrax's outlaws.

"Come along, Mel," Dandio called from up ahead, pulling Mel out of his memories.

Mel jogged after the tall Liznee. "Are we loading Nella tonight?"

"No, we'll do that in the morning. But I need to oil down the saddle and tack. It's been several months since I last took her on a journey." Dandio smiled. "I rather think she'll enjoy this mission more than we will."

He stopped at the end of the corridor. A soft purr of greeting came from within the stall, then came a rustle as the creature rose and stretched from its bed of straw.

Mel reached Dandio and grinned at the beast inside. "Hey, Nella. Remember me?"

The gryphon padded forward on lion-like paws, nudging Mel's hand with her muzzle. Her powerful wings were folded on her back, and bits of straw stuck to her feather-like fur.

"Look at you, you lazy beast," Dandio chuckled, scratching Nella behind her ears before opening the stall gate.

"She's bigger," Mel realized, as Nella bounded out to the pasture. The last time he'd seen the gryphon, she'd stood about the same height as a pony. Now, she was nearly as tall as the battle horses, and her lean, cat-like form rippled with muscle.

"Of course she is," Dandio replied. "When you saw her last she wasn't full grown." He opened a cabinet in the back of Nella's stall and hauled out the saddle. "Could you grab that basket of tack?"

Mel picked it up and followed Dandio into the pasture, where they lowered the slightly dusty gear to the ground. Nella rolled in the grass with a soft chirruping purr of pleasure. At last, she got to her feet, ears pricked forward, listening to the many sounds of late evening. The wide clearing ended some fifty yards from where they stood, and the forest stretched up into the foothills.

After a pause, the gryphon spread her wings and launched into the air, soaring as silently as an owl towards the woods. Likely, she would hunt down a meal to sustain her for the long flight tomorrow.

"This is truly shameful," Dandio muttered as he oiled the tack. "I forgot to do this last time I used the gear, told the stable hands not to bother with it, and it was raining—now the leather is beginning to crack."

"Will it be all right?" Mel asked, watching as the gryphon soared over the forest.

"Oh, it will be fine," Dandio said with a wry smile. "I only regret not having done it sooner." He set the bridle and reins aside and set to work on the saddle.

Mel turned back to him, reminded of something else. "When we were in Esile City, we saw the Randuins fight Terrax's men," he said. "Do you think they'll come join us against the Ace-Lord?"

The Randuins, as he'd learned on the mission to Esile, were an elite sect of knights who protected eastern Daffodalion from Jenna attacks. They were well-known for both their skill with the sword and their cavalry of dragon riders. They'd be a valuable ally against the Aces.

But Dandio shook his head. "Unfortunately not—at least, they will not fight the Aces here with us. From what Jan has told me, the Randuins are working to secure the far eastern front, in case the Jenna tribes seek to join the Ace-Lord again."

Mel nodded, a little disappointed, but understood this reasoning.

He saw Nella wheel mid-flight and dive back toward the pasture, and moved to her as she alighted in the field. As the gryphon touched down, he felt a sudden stir of unease. Nella's ears were flattened to her skull, and she swung to face the forest as she landed, a low growl building in her throat.

"Whoa, Nella," Mel said, startled. He patted her neck, staring at the tree line. He saw nothing. But Nella growled again, and took a half step back.

Dandio had moved to them as soon as he'd heard Nella's growl, red flames glowing at the ready in his hand. "Easy, girl," he murmured to the gryphon. At his voice, Nella ceased growling, but her tail continued to lash the grass behind her, and her ears twitched uncertainly.

"Do you think something startled her?" Mel asked.

"It is not easy to startle a gryphon," Dandio replied. His eyes were fixed on the trees.

The figure seemed to rise out of the ground directly in front of them in a swirl of leaves and wind. Mel stepped backwards with a short cry of alarm, and Dandio raised both hands, flames licking down his arms. Wind rolled over the pasture, gathering around the figure before them.

Willow leaves framed a woman's face with translucent green skin and blue eyes as deep as the midnight sky. She raised a hand, her voice reminding Mel of a breeze whispering through a forest. "Be not afraid. I come bearing a two-fold message."

Dandio lowered his hands, the fire fading away as he bowed. "Thank you for coming to us, lady of the dryads. What is this message?"

The dryad looked down at him. "The first message of our people comes from the far south. The Aces remain in Ar-Salem, but their forces will soon march on the north. You must prepare. Do not seek to enter the cursed palace—the black road leads only to death, and not even the dryads can reach within the shadows that shroud the Flats. Be prepared."

Mel looked at Dandio. The Liznee's scarred face filled with concern. "The north? Then the Aces intend to besiege Mata City?"

"We do not yet know. When their intent becomes clear, another message shall be brought," the dryad answered. "My second message comes from the Druids and their Scribes, news for the New Blood." Her eyes fixed on Mel.

Mel felt as though he were suddenly suspended in the void again, where time had stopped and he could feel every beat of his pounding heart. News. Weeks of fear and uncertainty were about to end. He would know the answer to his deepest fear, and yet now, he was terrified to hear it. His throat was dry, and he could hardly speak. "I—I'm here," he managed to choke out.

"The Druids and their Scribes sought the ranger," the dryad told him. "They asked the knowledge from us, to know if our roots had felt his body fallen. We did not find him among the slain."

The world spun beneath his feet, and he put a hand on Nella to steady himself.

"We cannot enter Ar-Salem," the dryad continued. "It is a dead land, where even the roots of our trees are cut off. But the wind knows no restraints, and has entered the black palace of the Ace-Lord's domain.

There it has heard the echoes of the Hummingbird's voice in the depths of the fortress. How one is to reach the Ace-Deputy's prisoner, only time shall tell, but I bring this news for your benefit, not your trouble."

"Thank you for your report," Dandio said. The dryad bowed, then vanished with a final gust of wind.

Mel sensed Dandio's eyes on him, but he could not speak, emotions drowning out his voice. All he could hear was the dryad's message, over and over again in his mind.

Echoes of the Hummingbird's voice.

We did not find him among the slain.

If one is to reach him…

"Mel?" Dandio asked gently.

Mel felt himself take a shaking breath. His whole body trembled with the onslaught of emotions. The shock, the fear, the uncertainty had evaporated in a moment. Weeks of accepting grief as the agonizing truth now paled before the soaring hope, a hope as wild as the wind that whistled through the darkening field.

"He's alive," he whispered at last, his heart pounding as he looked at Dandio. "Aryion's alive."

14

In Blackness Bound

Ar-Salem

Darkness. It was all he knew. An empty world silent as the grave.

Had he died? As if there were a way to answer that question.

It was the cold that roused him, forcing air into his lungs and his eyelids to open as he lay flat on a freezing surface. Frost dusted his skin and shimmered faintly on a black floor as smooth as marble.

Marble.

The bridge.

"I'm sorry."

The voice floated through his mind, and his heart ached with grief, but he did not know why. He tried to move, but his limbs did not respond, and fear shot through his heart. Perhaps that final blow had broken his back, rendering him incapacitated and helpless for whatever remained of his life.

There had been a blow, he remembered. A black shadow looming up behind him, striking him so hard in the back that his sword had gone flying from his hand. He remembered screaming in pain as he'd fallen to the blood-streaked cobblestones, certain his Essence had been stripped from his body, and he would join the rest of the dead in Appledale's street.

But he hadn't died.

Frozen hands had lifted him, dragging him into the forest, while ice crusted his spine and stabbed his muscles every time he tried to struggle. There had been a black void waiting in the woods. The swirling shadows of the Patch had engulfed him, and after that, there had been nothing.

Who he was, who he had been… all had died in a wave of pain and darkness.

Again, he tried to move, and managed to slide his right leg across the floor. Icy chains were wrapped loosely around his chest and clasped at his neck, seemingly secured to the invisible ceiling. His leather chest plate and arm guards, his cloak, and his sword belt were all gone—not as though they would offer much protection or warmth now. What remained of his shirt and pants were ripped and stained with blood. Dal-kerri blood—the color of charred bones.

Shivering, he rolled onto his chest with a clink of chains, gasping as searing pain shot down his back. In addition to the freezing ache, he could feel another wound, too, a cut across his shoulder blades. That wound… it hadn't come in the battle where he'd been taken. No, it had come before that, when he had lain flat on the marble bridge trying to pull someone back to safety. But Mel had fallen despite his efforts.

Mel.

Appledale.

The words were familiar, but he could associate no meaning to them. The few memories he could grasp were raw and scattered, and his head ached as he sought to recall them. Why had he been fighting? How much time had passed?

More pressing—at least, as far as he could tell—where was he now?

Raising his head with an effort, he looked around. The black room was surprisingly large, perfectly square, its dark walls glossy with white ice. There was no door, no windows, only shadows. The black room was a box with no way out.

He dragged himself to his knees and elbows, teeth chattering against the chill. Urgency lingered in his mind, but could not understand why. Why did he feel no fear? His mind seemed numb to all besides the pain.

Movement to his right drew his eyes as a tall figure ghosted into the room, his silver armor giving off a pale white light. The face was ruined—half skull, half skin, with purple-red eyes that glinted with satisfaction.

"I imagine you are still feeling the effects of the ice." The smooth voice seemed to echo in the black room, filling his mind as well as his ears. "Fear not, your body and mind will return to you soon. Tell me your name."

He tried to speak, but his voice was gone. His name. Why could he not remember?

"*Tell me your name,*" the hissing voice ordered in his head.

"What…" He forced the word out in a weak rasp. "What… did you do to me?"

"Only shown you a portion of our power, so that you learn to fear it," the armored shadow replied calmly. "Power is nothing without fear, Hummingbird. If so little power affects you, perhaps you are not fit for the future I intended for you."

Hummingbird. Yes, he knew that name too.

"*Speak,*" the voice ordered in his thoughts. "*What is your name?*"

"My name…" Pain seared his mind as he strove to remember. He tried to sit up, but agony shot down his spine again, and he slumped against the wall. Yet he felt the return of memory like a slap of cold water. "My name is Aryion Paya."

And with the words, he remembered everything. Remembered the mission to Appledale to rescue the Smallbutton family. Remembered the Dal-kerri in the woods. Remembered the journey to Wiverrun. Remembered Mel, falling into the eternal darkness of the Patch.

The Ace-Deputy looked down at him with a slight, mocking smile. "Wrong," he chided softly. "You have no name. None but the name my master will give you. Your purpose is one you must accept yourself."

Aryion forced another breath into his aching lungs and raised his head. "I'll never choose your power," he said through gritted teeth. "It's an illusion… just like this prison, I imagine." He glanced around the black room, trying to get his bearings. "None of this is real."

"Real?" the Deputy repeated. "Nothing is real, Hummingbird. There is no reality beyond the darkness, no constant besides death." He stepped forward. "My master intends a new purpose for you, and it is my task to ensure you understand it. I recommend you accept your fate. Do you not know that your apprentice is yet our prisoner?"

For the first time, something cut through the fog in Aryion's mind— fear. A fear so strong it took his breath away. Mel. They still had Mel as their prisoner. But… no, that couldn't be right. If that was true, it meant Asescia had been wrong about the Patch, and she'd been unable to free Jan and Mel. That had been her plan, right? He thought he recalled it, but it may have been another dream.

"You lie," he whispered, though he could not shake the sudden dread.

"Do I?" The Deputy laughed softly. "The Heiress' gifts were never her own. She is my master's Vessel now, and to traverse the voids is a skill only he may grant. The New Blood is yet ours, and he will die if you will not serve."

Aryion's exhausted, agonized mind fought through the fear. The Deputy's words had rung false. The Ace-Lord needed Mel alive to use the Blue Stone—the Aces wouldn't have killed Mel. It was all a lie, an illusion… but why could he not make his mind believe it?

"Why am I here?" he asked at last, defeated.

The Deputy nodded, satisfied. "You are here because my master considers you to be useful to us. Yet, while he wished to make you only another voiceless pawn, I desire to make you something far greater. Thus, he has granted that I may test this new power, for however long it takes to yield results." His smile sent a fresh wave of fear into Aryion's heart. "My master is generous. But unfortunately, we have only so much time."

He flicked his fingers. The icy chains tightened around Aryion's chest, dragging him upright. The sudden jerking movement wrenched his spine—he choked down a cry of pain, his entire body trembling as the Deputy stepped close.

"Kill me, then," he rasped, hands shaking as he clutched the chains. "You're… wasting your time… with me. I'll never serve you or your master."

"I do not doubt that," the Deputy agreed calmly. "But I intend to craft a prisoner who will serve, and until such a prisoner can be brought before my master, here you will remain." He gripped Aryion's head in his withered hands. "No, I will not kill you. I have had decades to perfect this persuasion, so trust that I know the limits a mortal can take."

Icy blades pierced his mind, tearing and shredding all thoughts. Memories, truths, any recollection of a time before, were swept aside as though by a powerful wave, hard as he fought to hold onto them. Excruciating pain split his skull as he was plunged into the Deputy's illusions.

There were no questions during the torture. The Deputy did not speak at all. The only voice was his own, until even that gave out from the screams and the little he had recalled of himself fell apart again.

When the Deputy at last lowered his hands, the chains loosened, allowing the prisoner to crash to the floor. Any memories he had regained seemed rimmed in white ice, stabbing his thoughts if he ventured too close. Cries echoed in the black box—Mel's voice, raw with terror and pain, thundering in the stillness. He covered his ears, but the scream filled his mind so that he could not escape.

The Deputy's voice cut through the horrible cry. "I will leave you with one last lesson. Our illusions work through sight—we cannot create sound. Thus, all sounds have existed at one point in time or another. If you will not trust my words regarding the New Blood, then trust his cries."

Aryion clutched his head, nails digging into his scalp as he curled against the wall. Vaguely, he sensed the Deputy had gone. His body trembled in agony, but worse—far worse—were Mel's screams, which grew louder and louder with each passing moment.

It was an illusion. It was only an illusion. But that did not stop the tears from streaming down his face as the darkness and pain engulfed him again.

PART 2

The Blood of Mortals

15

A Place to Rest

Mel slid off Nella's back, his legs aching from the long ride. The summer breeze blew in his face as he took a deep breath, and after the sun glaring in his eyes all day, it was a welcome change. Now that they'd descended to a hilltop deep in the Magno Forest, the air was cool with coming evening.

Dandio helped Misty dismount behind him. The Liznee's green eyes surveyed the hilltop, and he nodded in satisfaction. "Yes. We'll make camp here for the night."

They had left Caer Sia that morning. Nella's powerful wings had carried them over mountain passes, over the foothills east toward Elimar, and steadily southwest. The Magno Forest spread in a forested carpet of never-ending hills beneath them. From the air, the forest's sheer vastness could be fully appreciated. Mel had last experienced the view when he'd ridden to Sia on the back of Lord Fireclaw, near the end of the quest for the Shards.

That flight had been around six hours. They'd go slower on Nella—the young gryphon was burdened with three riders and travel supplies, and would need to stop more often. But Dandio was confident they'd reach Tinkeeyo tomorrow afternoon.

Now, the sun had set, and the cries of birds and the chorus of insects filled the Magno Forest. The grassy hilltop allowed a clear view in all directions, though all Mel could see were more arching hills.

Dandio unloaded the saddlebags, allowing Nella to stretch. "Mel, get a fire started—I suppose you have your own flints?"

Mel nodded, sliding his pack to the ground. It was good to be back in the wilderness, on the way to the next mission. He'd gotten so used to hiking and camping during ranger training that the sudden break from it all had felt unnatural. Then again, everything normal had been uprooted since the mission to Wiverrun.

Echoes of the Hummingbird's voice… if one is to reach him…

He searched for kindling in silence, listening to Misty chatting happily to Dandio. The dryad's news the evening before had filled him with an entirely new set of emotions. The uncertainty and grief were replaced with relief so sharp it seemed to punch the air from his lungs. Aryion was alive. Alive.

Mel wished he could just rest in that truth for a moment, but it wasn't that simple. Along with relief had come fear, new and icy cold. Aryion was alive—for now. But he was also a captive of the Aces, a fate little better than death. He would be held in Ar-Salem, which not even the dryads could enter.

Along with the impossibility of a rescue was the fear of why the Aces had kept Aryion a captive at all. The Ace-Lord was smart, dangerously so. Mel knew every one of his actions had a purpose in his conquest. Ransom was not the way of the Aces. Aryion wouldn't know any crucial secrets the Ace-Lord might want, so Mel doubted he'd been captured for questioning.

No… whatever the purpose, his mentor was a pawn in the Ace-Lord's game, and try as he might, Mel could not shake the dread that the Ace-Lord's plot had something to do with him, too.

He carried the dry branches back to the hilltop. Dandio unpacked the cooking supplies, and Misty had already set up Mel's bed roll beside her own. She seemed in high spirits—likely, she was as glad to be out of the castle and doing something helpful as Mel was.

"I'm supposed to write an essay about Fort Tinkeeyo next school term," she was saying as Mel got to work on the fire. "But I can get a head start on it now."

"You certainly can," Dandio answered with a slight smile. "You will be searching the libraries with Mel."

"I'm not sure what I'm looking for," Mel admitted, sparking the fire to life. "Jan said Luet's writings will be in the scribe house, so I guess we can start there."

"There will certainly be many records to search," Dandio agreed. "Luet was an explorer as well as a scribe—her writings will likely span several centuries. I expect you could ask the librarians to help."

Mel's heart sank a little. Searching shelves of old scrolls might take weeks, considering no one knew exactly what he should look for. But he knew this mission was important—and thankfully, he'd brought along the one person he knew would enjoy such a task. He glanced at Misty with a grin. "Don't get too busy with school work. I'm going to need your help reading through all those scrolls."

Misty shrugged nonchalantly. "Don't worry, I can do both."

With such a short journey, they had the luxury of packing fresh meat. There was cold ham and roast potatoes for supper, and Mel ate gratefully. It had been so long since he'd been on a mission with Dandio and Misty, he thought with a smile, almost two years since the quest for Drisilas. His childhood hero, who had since become a councilor and friend, and his little sister, whose clever mind was perfect for this mission. He was very glad they were both here.

"What are you going to do while we're in the scribehouse, Dandio?" Misty asked, looking inquiringly at the Liznee.

Dandio leaned forward to add another branch to the fire. "Tinkeeyo is a critical location in the Magno Forest; frankly, its forces are the only thing keeping the Aces from invading further southeast. I intend to keep it that way, but according to Quinn's last report, there are some in Tinkeeyo who would prefer to flee."

Mel frowned. "Flee? Where?"

"Further south, I assume. Remember, there are some who believe the Ace-war is nothing more than another Caer Sian battle." Dandio shook his head. "I can understand their fear—many small villages have been attacked in the Magno already. But we cannot lose Fort Tinkeeyo. If it were overthrown, the Aces could advance further and further east."

"Do you think the Aces will attack the fort?" Misty asked uneasily.

"Possibly," Dandio admitted. "That's mainly why we are choosing to further fortify Tinkeeyo. If we get wind of battle, you can both return to Caer Sia safely on Nella. I know that is not an ideal plan," he added, as Mel frowned, "but we cannot risk the Star-Stone, and I do not wish to risk you two, either."

Mel nodded. He knew better than to argue. While fleeing an impending battle was the last thing he'd like to do, he knew that would be the wisest move if such a situation arose. His mother had made him promise to keep Misty safe, and he had the Blood Oath to keep to as well. He'd stay off the front lines to keep the Star-Stone safe. Hopefully whatever he learned from Luet's writings would ensure he could still help.

Night fell. The Magno Forest came alive with the sounds of small animals, the hoots of owls, and, occasionally, the distant rumble of some beast Mel could not identify. Misty lay by the fire, hunched over a large book. Eventually she dozed off, the book resting face down on her chest. Mel gently slid her bookmark back in and closed it next to her.

Dandio returned from the woods, carrying more firewood. "I will take first watch tonight. Get some rest—it has been a long flight."

"I'm all right," Mel answered with a shrug. "I haven't really… slept normally since Castle Droco," he added slowly. Since Cahadras' healing had drawn him out of the dark coma, he barely felt the need for sleep. He could doze off for a few hours here and there, but he barely felt tired—or at least, it was not the type of weariness that would go away with sleep.

"I can understand that," Dandio answered. He sat across the fire, the golden light illuminating his scarred face. For the first time, Mel noticed how worn his features were, how weary. The larger-than-life hero he'd idolized as a child was far from reality. Dandio had been in this fight much longer than Mel had, and Mel could tell he had long grown weary of it. Somehow, he admired that more than the legendary warrior he'd once pictured.

He took a breath before voicing his question, but the thought had been nagging in his head for months. "Dandio… I never really asked about when the Aces had you as a prisoner. I didn't want to press." The Liznee glanced up at him, and he continued. "I just want to understand—I want to know what the Aces will do. I want to know what… what they'd do to Aryion."

Dandio shook his head slightly. "I don't think answers would help, Mel," he replied, his voice low.

"I know, but I don't know why they'd want to capture Aryion at all," Mel said, looking down. "It can't be for questioning, and he's not a Wielder or anything that would be important to the Ace-Lord."

Dandio stared at the fire for several moments. "Can you remember what they did to you?" he asked at last.

Mel shook his head wordlessly. He had never admitted it, feeling almost guilty that in the week of horror, he remembered absolutely nothing. Jan had memories of the prison and torture, though they were fragmented and confused. But to Mel, there was nothing, only a black hole where the memories should have been. The Aces might have questioned him, tortured him—he was certain they had, there must have been something to plunge him into that comatose state—but it had been removed from his mind.

Dandio nodded slowly. "The Aces have ways of altering the mind," he said at last. "They can read your thoughts if one is not prepared to resist them—draw out memories and create illusions from them. But we also know they can erase thoughts to a point, like they've done with the enchanted soldiers."

"So you think the Aces erased those memories?" Mel asked uneasily, touching his head involuntarily. "Why?"

"They may have. Perhaps they used some new power they did not wish you to know about. Perhaps they simply wished to instill you with doubt." Dandio gave him a half-smile that did not quite reach his eyes. "Whatever the purpose, be grateful all the same that it was taken away."

Mel nodded again, staring into the fire. He was glad the memories had been removed, but at the same time, he disliked knowing it had happened. As if a part of him, however painful, was missing. What if those memories could somehow help Aryion?

Another thought struck him, too terrible to voice aloud. If the Aces could alter minds, what if they erased Mel himself from Aryion's mind? What if, if by some miracle Aryion was freed, he didn't even know his apprentice when they met again?

He placed his head in his hands, trying to shake off that horrible idea, though it chilled his heart with fear. The dread seemed to transform into illusions before his eyes—a vision of Aryion, broken and bleeding in a dark prison, dying where Mel was unable to save him. He saw, too, other memories, springing to life in the shadowed forest—dark, sad memories from other times.

He took a shaking breath, closing his eyes tightly for a moment. "Does it… go away?" he asked finally.

He could not put into words what he meant. The horror, the grief, the fears of the past, the sounds that still echoed in his ears, the dreadful darkness that seemed to cling to his skin like grime—no matter how many times he thought they were behind him, they returned so easily, a part of him now. The guilt of Llyrion's death. The terror he'd experienced in the void. The Ace-Lord's voice hissing from the darkness, searing his thoughts. He did not know if he could live the rest of his life if it meant he would be forever choked by the shadows of the past.

Dandio did not ask what he meant, only thought for a long moment. "It never goes away," he said finally, his voice soft. "None of it will simply go away. But it does get easier to bear when you allow yourself to move on. The raw memories will heal like a wound. The burdens of guilt and grief gradually become lighter."

His green eyes flicked up to meet Mel's gaze. "Your past is a part of you, but it does not rule you. Live in each day. Keep moving forward, away from the darkness, away from the shadows. Follow where the Light calls you."

Mel let out a breath and nodded, pushing the dark memories away as he centered on the here and now. The warmth of the fire on his face.

The peaceful breathing of his loyal little sister. The chirping of the crickets. The stars shimmering above him in the constellation of the North Sword.

When his mind spiraled into the past, or became crushed by the fears of the future, he could ground himself here. Locking this moment away and holding it close in his heart, until not even the Aces could take his peace.

Eventually, he let that peace carry him into sleep.

16

Weapons of War

Rygal nodded to the sentries and shifted the crate to his other shoulder as he entered the Chanterelle encampment.

Activity filled the narrow valley. Brownae scouts slipped in and out, their dark fur blending with the shadows of the Wandering Wood. Distant voices came from the ridge above him to the right, where the Guardians had staked their tents, and Rygal could hear Captain Pike among them.

Five days had passed since arriving in Gayrile. Today, Rygal had decided to unload the weapon cargo from the *Veritos* and haul it back to camp. While they would only need the supplies if matters escalated to a battle, it was better safe than sorry, especially if Morel's guess about the rebels betraying them was correct. Porcini was still doubtful of the rebels' treachery at all—but then, he'd always been inclined to think well of everyone. That was a positive trait under normal circumstances, but could become a naïve sentiment in times like this.

"Not everyone will be acting in the best interest of their tribe," Morel had said bluntly last night. "Some of the rebels just want bloodshed."

They were both wrong and right in their own ways, Rygal knew. Some of the rebel clans aligned with Porcini's statements; much like the Ace-Lord's enchanted soldiers, they may have joined the battle out of fear, fighting a cause they did not truly believe in. But other clans were as Morel had warned—radicals who would see Gayrile purged of all

181

non-Diren blood. Those clans had joined with Deathcap during the time of Safacon, and after the maniacal Brownae prince had been defeated, they'd retreated back into their own lands, biding their time to strike. The unrest of the Ace-war had given them the opportunity to rebel.

This morning, though, the news that reached the Chanterelle was good—a letter from Jarus, brought by an informant in Bridgeport. The Coopers had agreed to join the negotiations, which meant they could soon select the date for the meeting. King Casper of the Direns would also be there, with his councilors and the other representatives.

Rygal lowered the crate to the ground inside the supply tent and turned to the men behind him. "Stack them here—these need to stay sheltered from the rain."

There were a few grunts from the others as they set the crates inside the tent. The pleasant breeze from the first day had faded away, and with the overcast sky and slight drizzle, the Wandering Wood was exceptionally muggy. Sweat drenched his shirt as he tossed a canvas tarp over the crates.

"That the last of them?" Morel asked, stepping into the tent.

Rygal straightened stiffly, stretching his arms. "That's all of it. Captain Pike's leaving the *Veritos* anchored upstream until the negotiations."

"Sounds smart," Morel said. "No good compromising the plan now that they've nearly settled on a date." Her eyes shone with interest as she noticed the Liznee crest on the crates. "Supplies from Sia? Are those the new designs I've been hearing about?"

Rygal threw her a grin—he'd expected she might be interested in these particular supplies. "Yes, they're from Sia. I don't know what designs you've heard about, though."

Morel gave him an exasperated look. "The new rifles? I asked if you could bring me at least one."

"Oh, those. I think Dandio threw one or two in for you," Rygal said. He drew a short knife from his belt and pried open the lid of a crate. Packed beneath the straw was the gleam of metal and polished wood. The Red Dawn were famous for their skills, yes, but it was their technological advances that made them feared throughout the north.

Morel brushed aside the straw and lifted a rifle from the pile, looking as though she were beholding the Star-Stones themselves. "Ah, these are the new ones. You remember the rifles we had during the battle against Safacon?"

"Vaguely. I never learned to use one," Rygal replied. "I probably would have been killed by a Serventiri by the time I finished loading the thing."

"Well, those were rough designs, and the Serventiri could barely shoot straight with them. Loose powder only—it meant every shot took minutes to prepare, twice that if you had double barrels..." Morel shook her head and ran a hand down the barrel of the rifle she held. "These are the new ones, Rygal. Now, we have paper cartridges. A pre-loaded shot, without the need to measure powder." She opened one of the small wooden boxes stacked beside the rifles in the crate.

"Not bad," Rygal said, "but how'll that help you? You'll still have to load every shot."

Morel flashed a grin. "Because now I can load more than one round." She set the box of paper cartridges down and turned the rifle on its side in her hands. "Here. You see this rotating part above the trigger? That's a revolving cylinder—six shots, one after another. *That's* why I'd been hoping to have this new design."

Rygal nodded, impressed. "Well, that's definitely more practical.

Assuming you can reload the next six shots before you're hacked to pieces, of course."

"That's why we have practice," Morel replied with a shrug, and set the rifle back in the crate with some reluctance. "As soon as the rain lets up, we can start running drills."

Rygal nodded, securing the lid of the crate. Most of the Brownae warriors, Morel had said, had also stolen Serventiri firearms during the time of Safacon, which meant they'd already learned the basics. He was glad the weapons would be helpful, but it still felt strange bringing these firearms into the Wandering Wood. The Brownaes, while skilled in the traditional weapons of slings or spears, had long since set those aside in favor of the firearms. The changing times demanded they adapt, or be crushed by their enemies.

All the same, they weren't the only ones who had learned new ways of defense, he thought. He'd brought the spell books from the *Veritos* along with the crates. Since the negotiations were not to be for several more days, he might as well keep working on channeling the fire.

Morel glanced at the books as he set them inside the tent. "The heiress mentioned something about you learning fire-forms?"

Rygal looked at her. "Well, I'm still learning it. Allie told you that?" he added slowly.

"She and Darion told us about the siege on Castle Droco this morning, while you went to get the crates," Morel answered.

"Oh. What did she… say?" Rygal asked, trying to sound casual.

"Not much, only that you'd been learning from the books. And she said you'd gotten pretty good."

An absurdly giddy smile threatened his face at those words. *Pretty good*, Allie thought it, *pretty good*—with great effort, he managed to keep his expression neutral. "Ah. Well, yes, I've been working on it. I've learned the magic, at least—channeling the fire has been more work."

"Fire is difficult," Morel agreed. "But that's impressive, all the same."

"Thanks," Rygal said. Her words brought a new thought to light, and he looked at her curiously. "You studied fire-forms, didn't you? At least—the Jewel-lore? Where did you learn it?"

Morel glanced up at him. "My mother studied the old lore," she replied after a pause. "The language of the trees, the songs of old—the Brownaes used to learn and teach the old magic, the same power as the dryads. Pure, natural magic gifted to us by the High Light, before the dryads left."

"Dryads?" Rygal repeated, startled. "There were dryads in Gayrile?"

"Of course." Morel arched an eyebrow. "All the confusing paths in the Wandering Wood, the way the forest seems to swallow you up—that would have had a source, wouldn't it?"

"I suppose so," Rygal said, shaking his head in awe. "I never knew the dryads lived here."

"They didn't last long after Safacon rose to power," Morel said grimly. "His forces fought them, intending to wipe them off Gayrile for good. Many of them were killed—those that survived retreated so far into their trees that not even the end of the world would bring them back." She paused. "At any rate, I believe that's where my people first learned the old magic, and the rest was passed down through our families. I couldn't tell you where my mother learned the Jewel-lore—part of me thinks she stole some of it from Deathcap, actually."

"And you learned it from her," Rygal guessed. He remembered the spells Morel had called forth from the Jewel, the way the light had flashed from her hand. "Were there any other spells you learned about, though? Any curses?"

Morel folded her arms over her chest. "If the reason for all these questions is to help you channel fire," she said, "you can forget it. Studying dark magic, for any reason, was something we were always cautioned against."

"I'm not trying to study it," Rygal replied slowly. "Not for Essence channeling, I mean. But there's one curse that I've been trying to learn about—maybe the most important one in this war."

Morel frowned slightly. "Really? Do you know its name?"

Rygal hesitated. Allie hadn't told Morel about the Life-Blood Spell yet, only alluded to the curse. She clearly wanted to keep the truth quiet for now—and he couldn't blame her. Nor did he know if it was his place to share it. But Morel might know more about this sort of curse—and more importantly, know some way to break it.

He lowered his voice as he answered. "It's called the Life-Blood Spell, a binding curse cast by the Ace-Lord—and it can only be affected by the Ace-Lord's hand. We've been trying to find any other knowledge of it over the last few months, but so far we've had very little luck."

"We?"

"Me, and Darion... and Allie."

He paused, not sure how to put the rest into words, but the heaviness of his tone must have revealed the truth. Morel's face cleared as she understood. "So *that's* what the Heiress meant," she mused quietly. "I'd thought there was something...off... about her, but I couldn't place it. We can usually tell when someone's cursed—something wrong about their scent."

"Do the others...?" Rygal started, glancing worriedly toward the Brownae scouts.

"I don't think anyone else suspects anything," Morel reassured him. "This entire forest reeks of all manners of strange creatures, and the curse's trace is faint. Only reason I recognized it was after spending all that time with the Jewel." She shook her head thoughtfully. "The Life-Blood Spell… a binding curse, you called it?"

Rygal nodded, feeling a familiar helpless anger and grief clutch his heart. "The Ace-Lord cursed her in Castle Droco. Allie's Essence is bound to his—she shares his power, he grows stronger off her fire. But she still has mortal weakness, so if we were to attack the Ace-Lord, she would…" He trailed off, unable to finish the sentence.

"Yes, that's typically how a binding curse works," Morel murmured. Rain had begun to fall, shimmering down upon the Wandering Wood. Fog rolled over the surrounding hills, spreading a veil of gray over the encampment. The dismal light seemed to reflect the unease and fear in Rygal's heart.

"It's strange," Morel said at last. Her cat-like eyes were intensely thoughtful. "I *have* heard of the Life-Blood Spell. But not in the realm of the binding curses—we knew it as a covenant."

Rygal frowned. "A covenant? What do you mean?"

Morel turned to him. "The Brownae tribes know the stories of the world before the Dividing War, back when the Stars were said to walk the mortal world and prophecies weren't such a rare thing. As we've heard it, the High Light created the Life-Blood Spell—not as a binding curse, but as a covenant between Himself and the mortals."

"The Life-Blood Spell?" Rygal repeated incredulously, as Morel paused. "The Life-Blood Spell was created by the High Light?"

"Not in the way you know of it," Morel said, "but think of all the other magic the Ace-Lord's corrupted. This spell didn't originate in the darkness, according to the stories—through it, the mortal's very Essence reflects the Light, while the Light's power flows through them." She shook her head bitterly. "Of course, the Ace-Lord twisted that spell too—turned it into a one-sided curse, like you've described."

Rygal stared into the shadows of the trees, his mind a blur of thoughts. He'd never considered this possibility. Iriam and Cahadras had both described the Life-Blood Spell as something so utterly evil that it seemed impossible for it to have ever originated from the Light— but then again, wasn't it the same with the Jewel of Power? A Star-Stone, corrupted and twisted to draw on dark magic; a spell, warped into a curse by the Lord of Death…

No, it did not seem so impossible when he thought of that.

"Mel talked about the Star-Stone's power," he murmured, trying to put his thoughts into words. "The way he describes it, it's not anything he can do, any strength he can give. He channels its power… I wonder if that's how the Life-Blood Spell was originally intended."

"It might make sense," Morel agreed. She paused. "I can understand wanting to find a way to break the spell—I won't tell you to stop. But I will warn you, you won't find any answers studying dark magic. Believe me—I spent far too long in that area."

Rygal nodded. "I know, and thank you. This is the most I've learned about it so far." He sighed. "I just wish there was some way I could find something that might counter the curse."

The Life-Blood Spell's true origins, though interesting, did very little to help their current predicament. Even if the spell had once been a thing of light, the curse binding Allie promised nothing but darkness. Nor did anyone—not even the ancient tomes in the library—know of any counter-spell that might loose the chains. Hard as he fought it, he could not ignore the horrible image of Allie, alone in the darkness, swallowed by the void and blackness of the curse. Even if the war was won, she would still be lost, and there was nothing he could do to change that.

When Willing Warrior be gone at dawn; Ace-Lord, Mortal, together one; lest the Shadow ever thrive.

The Prophecy of Three's words floated through his mind, mocking his struggling hope.

Morel spoke slowly. "There may be nothing to destroy the spell itself—I doubt anyone but the Ace-Lord can remove it. Most binding spells call for drastic measures in order to escape them—I'm guessing there's something Asescia could do to be rid of it, if not by the Ace-Lord's hand?"

"Death," Rygal replied hoarsely. He cleared his throat, fighting down the pain and despair that gripped him. "That's the only alternative the curse allows. Either the Ace-Lord removes it himself, or Allie could— she escapes it in death."

"That said," Morel pressed, looking at him carefully, "all dark spells have a flaw. While that doesn't make the curses any less effective, it's still something you can look for. I don't know what it might be, what scenario would bring it about—but now that you know the truth of the spell's origins, you'll be able to see what magic is the Light's, and which is the Ace-Lord's. Corrupted magic is unstable magic—there's some flaw the Ace-Lord had to reckon with, something he's concealed." She stood. "I'll ask the elders what they know. It might not be much, but there's a few of us who still know the old magic."

"I appreciate that," Rygal said. "Just—don't tell them about Allie herself just yet. I don't think she wants everyone to know about it."

"Fair enough," Morel replied, standing and stretching. "Look in your spellbooks too—you never know what else Norrin might have written about."

"Well, add it to the list of things I wish I'd asked him about," Rygal murmured.

Morel was quiet a moment. "We all have a list like that," she said at last. "But there's nothing we can do about it. The best we can do is work with the little we have, keep moving forward."

Rygal managed a slight smile and nodded. "Thank you, all the same. I'll keep looking."

He headed toward the tent as the rain continued its steady shower. His search would continue, but not in the black web of dark magic, which had offered only confusion and fear. No, if the spell had once come from the Light, then he would seek there for guidance.

Strangely, it was not the Prophecy's words, but those of the spell itself, that filled his mind as the day wore on. *Aranac, co vey devarris, dovannon.*

Cursed words in an ancient tongue—yet they had once been words of life, of light. Mel had once explained that words themselves had little power. The true magic lay in their intent—where your mind and heart were centered. How similar that was to the magic of the fire-forms, to the power of the Star-Stones, to the oaths and spells that filled the mortal world.

Perhaps it was all interconnected by a deeper light.

Perhaps, somehow, that light would be the way to free the one he loved.

17

Fort Tinkeeyo

Late afternoon sun beat down on the Magno Forest as Nella flew over the city.

Dandio had awakened them a little after dawn. Mel had slept well for the first time in weeks, without any images of dark voids or dying companions plaguing his dreams. They'd packed up their little camp on the hilltop and flown out on Nella again, flying steadily south. With the sun warming him and the slight rocking motion of Nella's flight, Mel nearly dozed off, but his mind had left the fears he'd worked through last night and focused again on his upcoming mission.

Now, the first buildings of Tinkeeyo came into view, lit by the brilliant sunlight.

The city was nestled in the hills of the Magno Forest, its buildings as tall as the massive redwood trees. Roads wound in from all different parts of Coonsia, and even from this height Mel could see the flurry of movement from thousands of carriages, riders, and townsfolk. Tinkeeyo looked like a slightly smaller, more wooded version of Caer Sia, a crossroads for travelers headed to and from the kingdom.

"The principle scribe house is on the north side of town," Dandio called to him, raising his voice over the whistling wind. "I'll show you two there as soon as we've settled at the fort." He clicked to Nella, and the gryphon tucked in her wings and swept downward.

"I can see the fort!" Misty cried, pointing ahead.

Mel pulled his eyes away from the bustling city below and followed Misty's eager gaze.

Fort Tinkeeyo stood on a slight hill overlooking the city, a large square fortress as wide as Castle Sia, though not as tall. The fortified walls were slate gray, standing firm and strong despite the years laid upon them. Two banners—Tinkeeyo's green, and the red and black of the Red Dawn—flew from the watch tower. The walls of the fort were wide enough for five men to stand side-by-side, and Mel could see many soldiers standing guard as they flew over.

Nella descended into a wide courtyard. Three elven soldiers moved to meet them, reaching uneasily for their weapons. Dandio swung out of the saddle, raising his hands. "Easy, men. I am Commander Ki, and my companions and I are here to meet with Lord Andros."

The guards snapped into salute as they recognized the commander, and their captain stepped forward. "Welcome, Commander. Please come—Master Goldfinch let us know you would be coming."

Mel and Misty dismounted. Misty's eyes were wide as she looked around, and Mel found himself staring in awe at the rugged walls of Fort Tinkeeyo. He'd never been as interested in history as Misty was, but here, every scar and chip of the gray stones told a story, each scratch and burn a sign of the many battles that the fort had withstood.

Thousands of years ago, he thought, elves would have stood in the same place he did, greeting visiting dignitaries. Perhaps Luet herself had once stood here, casting her gaze up to the sky while she wrote the High Light's messages.

Dandio, after arranging for the stable hands to take care of Nella, followed the captain inside with Mel and Misty at his heels. The heavy double doors fell closed behind them as they entered the cool stone hall. There were no windows, and the golden light of the lanterns gave a warm, rustic feel.

A tall, blond elf stood in the entry hall, wearing the garb and weapons of a ranger. He was speaking to a younger elf with reddish hair, but turned as they entered, a wide smile of greeting crossing his face.

"Commander—you made it. I thought I saw the gryphon fly over."

"Good to see you," Dandio said, clasping his hand and returning the smile. "I've brought help, as you can see." He motioned to the Smallbutton siblings with a wink. "Mel and Misty Smallbutton of Appledale—though of course, you've met Mel before."

"Fought beside him, in fact," Quinn replied with a grin, and Mel saw the relief in his eyes as he clasped his hand. "It's very good to see you. The last time I met with the Commander, we were unsure if you yet lived." His lively eyes turned to Misty. "And I expect this lovely young lady is your sister?"

"Misty, this is Quinn Fireleaf," Mel introduced them. "He went on the quest for the Shards with me—and I heard something about you helping with the elven alliance," he added, a little unsure of that fact. He'd heard about the council of Mata City after he'd woke up in Caer Sia. He knew the elven kingdoms of Tinkeeyo and Elimar had at last put aside their past arguments and joined the war against the Aces, fighting side by side.

"Partially," Quinn said, straightening and beckoning the other elf over. "Since then, the Elimarian delegation has come to Tinkeeyo, along with a company of their finest warriors."

"I'm not exactly part of the delegation or the soldiers," the younger elf admitted as he approached. He looked to be around seventeen or eighteen, and there was something strangely familiar about his red hair and twinkling blue eyes.

Dandio studied him for a moment. "You've grown since we last met," he said at last, a smile crossing his face as he shook the lad's hand. "What brings you to Tinkeeyo?"

"The war, unfortunately," the young elf answered ruefully. "I'm studying as a scribe, so for now, I'm here with Quinn to keep a report for the Elimar Council." He turned to Mel with a slight grin, offering his hand. "You're the New Blood?"

"I'm Mel," Mel replied, shaking his hand.

"It's good to meet you. I've only heard about you—but I think you knew my father. I'm Alder Tarash."

Mel stared at him, finally realizing why he seemed so familiar. "Tarash? You're… Llyrion's son?"

A flicker of pain crossed Alder's face at the name as he nodded. "Yes. I heard you met him… on the mission to return the High King's sword?"

"Yeah," Mel said, already feeling terrible for mentioning the name. Alder had never met Mel. But he would have heard about what happened on the quest for Drisilas, where his father had been killed. Did he know that Llyrion had died saving Mel's life?

But Alder gave him a small smile. "My father always said… he said we were made to help others. He made his choice."

"He saved my life," Mel said, looking down. "I'm still… trying to understand why. But I know I can try to live like he did."

Alder glanced away, and Mel saw tears in the eyes of both Quinn and Dandio for a moment. He'd only known Llyrion a short time, yet the effect he'd had still fueled Mel's own mission as the New Blood. But to these men, Llyrion had been a close friend, a father, and the pain of the loss would always be there along with the memories.

"Well," Quinn said briskly, turning to walk down the hall, "let us speak of other matters. My father is waiting for us in the council hall. Mel, Misty, you are both welcome to join us."

He led the way to a large room that reminded Mel more of a hunting lodge than a council hall. Warm torchlight lit the stone room, and on the far wall hung a rack of antlers that must have once belonged to the largest elk in the Magno Forest.

Five other elves waited in the room. Three wore the armored uniforms of generals, while the other two appeared to be a government official and his aid.

"Mel and Misty Smallbutton, meet my father, Lord Andros of Tinkeeyo," Quinn introduced them.

Mel looked at Quinn in surprise—he hadn't known Quinn's father held such influence in Tinkeeyo. Then again, the topic had never really come up on the quest for the Shards.

He and Misty both bowed. The lord saluted Dandio respectfully, then shook Mel and Misty's hands in turn. His hair was the same pale blond as his son's, and while his brown eyes were kind, there was a weariness in them that showed his concern of the times. His face reminded Mel of Jan's: strong and calm, yet worn with care and weary of a war that had already cost them so many lives.

Andros smiled slightly to Mel. "Quinn has told me of the New Blood's actions," he said. "I believe we have much to thank you for."

Mel gave a small shrug, not sure how to respond. "Well… I had a lot of help," he said, glancing at Quinn.

"Indeed," Andros conceded. "And I hope we may offer some aid while you are here as well. Let us sit, and we shall speak."

Mel felt a little out of place among the Elves, but at Dandio's encouraging nod, he and Misty sat down at the round table. Misty, for her part, looked fascinated, her eyes both excited and serious as she perched on the edge of her seat.

"The alliance between Tinkeeyo and Elimar has aided us in many ways," Andros said once everyone was seated. "While our ancestors were enemies, we have now put aside the past, and joined this war as one. Nonetheless, I trust you are aware of our people's fears," he said to Dandio. "Tinkeeyo stands on the front lines against the Aces. Should their forces march from Ar-Salem, I have no doubt they will strike here."

"You are not alone in that concern," Dandio said slowly. "Fort Tinkeeyo has stood against the Aces twice in the past, in both the Dividing War and the first Ace-rise. That is something the Ace-Lord will remember. We've also received a report that the Aces intend to strike north and attack Mata City."

A worried murmur ran around the table. Quinn looked at Dandio with a frown. "Mata City? I thought the Strait was protected."

"It is," Dandio replied. "But you know as well as I that if the Aces want Mata City, they'll strike through the blockade and fight their way to the city. It may cost them many lives, but when has that ever stopped the Ace-Lord?" He paused. "It's yet to be confirmed. But it's a possibility we should be prepared for."

"What would you advise us to do?" Andros inquired.

"For Mata City, there's very little Tinkeeyo can do," Dandio said. "Nor would it be wise to strike against Ar-Salem at this time. None of our spies have managed to infiltrate that fortress yet—we have no knowledge of what the Ace-Lord may be concealing there."

Mel stared at the table top, trying to fight the fear that filled his chest at those words. But his mind had returned to thoughts of Aryion, a captive in the depths of Ar-Salem.

His fear must have showed on his face—Dandio glanced at him and paused for a moment before continuing. "I would recommend preparing for a siege. This fort is well-protected. Your danger would come from being trapped in here without supplies."

"Do you believe a siege is impending?" one of the generals asked.

"Maybe not. You'd do well to prepare all the same. I would prefer to be wrong," Dandio said with a wry smile, "but I rarely am."

"I will double the border guard," Andros said. "We will reinforce the southern outposts. If the Aces plan to besiege Tinkeeyo, they shall soon find it is a difficult tree to fell."

"It will not have to face the Aces alone, either," Dandio told him. "I've ordered three companies from Caer Sia to join us in five day's time. We also have other allies, ones we've only been made aware of in the last few months." He paused. "I understand it's been some time since Tinkeeyo has had dealings with the Alfona people."

Andros frowned. "The Alfona… yes, it has been many years. Our last meetings were not pleasant, I fear. Tinkeeyo relies on lumber, exporting through the Magno Forest. The Alfona have always resented it, though we never cut from their lands."

"The Alfona believe the forest is one living being," Quinn put in. "Ever since the dryads vanished, the Alfona jealously protect the ancient trees. They used to attack our trade caravans."

"I remember those days," Dandio said. "The Red Dawn offered protection for your caravans against the Alfona. But you must put those times aside now. The Alfona are against the Aces just as we are, and you must ask their aid."

Mel looked at the elves. He could tell none of them liked this suggestion. Quinn looked unsure, Lord Andros was frowning deeply, and the generals looked as though Dandio had suggested they ally with the Aces themselves.

"The Alfona are on the Wildkids' side too," Mel ventured hesitantly. "I—I wasn't there to meet the Alfona, but my friend Dusty always spoke highly of them. The dryads are awakened again, and they've promised to help us."

That statement got everyone's attention. Andros looked at him in disbelief. "The dryads?" he repeated. "They have joined the war?"

"They've already brought news to us," Mel said. "They warned us about an attack to the north before we left to Tinkeeyo." *And that Aryion is trapped in Castle Salem,* he added in his mind. But he forced himself not to think of that.

Alder's face was thoughtful. "My father once told me of the tree spirits. He said they passed their words on to their cousins the hama-dryads, and the Alfona."

"Yes," Dandio said, studying Lord Andros. "My daughter has assured me they are on our side. In addition to their alliance with the dryads, their loyalty and devotion to this region is an asset we cannot overlook. Together, Tinkeeyo and the Alfona can protect the Magno Forest far better than the Red Dawn. If there is any way to reach them, I suggest you do so."

There was a moment's pause in which Mel saw the Elven lord considering his options. But at last Lord Andros nodded. "You have spoken well, Commander. Now is not the time to hold onto past wrongs." He turned to his son. "The rangers know of the trading posts of the Alfona, do they not?"

Quinn nodded. "There's a post only a few day's ride from here, where the rangers used to meet with the Alfona. It's been years since I've gone there, and I expect it was abandoned when the Aces claimed Wiverrun. But I may be able to track them from there."

"I trust your abilities," Andros replied with a nod, turning back to Dandio. "Very well, the Alfona shall be sought out, and we will seek to remedy the old harms." He stood. "If we are to prepare for a siege, I will send for the rest of my officers. I hope you will offer your insight into our strategy?"

"I will," Dandio replied. "In the meantime, might someone show Mel and Misty to the scribehouse? They hoped to research the records there."

"I'll take them," Alder offered.

Dandio nodded to Mel with a smile. "Go with Alder. I'll meet you two back here this evening."

Mel and Misty followed the young elf to the door. Alder looked at them with a grin as they headed down the halls. "I wondered if you'd want to see the scribehouse—there are probably plenty of records that might help us against the Aces. Are you looking for anything particular?"

"I'm still figuring that out," Mel answered ruefully. "But Jan told us to start with the writings of Luet."

Alder raised his eyebrows. "Well, in that case, you'll be reading for a while."

18

∽ ∽ ∽ ∽ ∽ ∽ ∽ ∽ ∽

The Scrolls

Townsfolk crowded the roads of Tinkeeyo as Alder led Mel and Misty to the carriage station. At the young elf's request, the carriage left the fort behind, headed toward the scribehouse. Voices of travelers and market-goers alike filled the air, drifting through the carriage windows.

"Everything's become busier here in the last month, with the war and all," Alder explained as they bumped along the noisy streets. "When I was your age we used to come from Elimar on holiday visits to enjoy the peace and quiet."

A series of loud shouts as they passed the market punctuated his words. Mel grinned. "Can't see it being very quiet now."

"How do you know Quinn?" Misty inquired curiously. "I always heard that elves from Elimar don't like elves from Tinkeeyo."

Mel nudged her, exasperated, but Alder shook his head with a slight smile. "Well, that's still true for a lot of people. But my father always believed we were stronger as allies. He and Quinn grew up together— the son of an Elimar councilor and the son of the lord of Tinkeeyo. You can see how they wanted there to be peace between the two kingdoms."

"And now there is?" Misty asked.

"Partly—things have gotten better," Alder said slowly. "At least, the war's made everyone need to get along."

"Let's hope that's true for Gayrile, too," Mel murmured. He'd heard

200

enough about the rebel clans and uprisings to worry for the turmoil there. His thoughts strayed to Rygal, Allie, and Darion, and he wondered what they might be doing now.

The carriage headed away from the center of town, towards the forested hills to the west. At last, they stopped before a wooden building that looked like a large log cabin. A group of guards stood posted at its doors. This, Mel thought, was not too surprising. Security would be tighter in times of war.

One of the guards moved forward as the carriage rolled to a stop and the passengers stepped out, his eyes wary. "Halt. What is your business here?"

Alder gestured to the two siblings. "We're here with Lord Andros' permission, Captain. I'm escorting the New Blood to view the scrolls of Luet."

The captain's face softened as he saw the three youths, and his gaze centered with interest on Mel. "Well then, carry on. I hope you mean to find something that will help win the war?"

"Maybe," Mel answered uncertainly. He realized he had no idea what he was looking for. The "deeper power" that Jan had said Luet wrote about might be anything—a weapon, a spell, some other special artifact that must be sought out—he didn't know. "It should help," he said at last.

The guards permitted them inside without further questions. In contrast to the warm summer light filling the city, it was cool and dark inside the scribehouse, filled with the smell of wood and parchment. The cooler air was pleasant after the heat outside.

Mel blinked, letting his eyes adjust to the dimmer light. They stood in a short hall that opened into a wider room. Rows upon rows of shelves were visible beyond.

Alder led them forward, looking around with interest. "The last time I was here was with my grandfather, Llio," he said. "He wanted to study the old texts, but I was so small I don't remember it much."

"I thought the Aces destroyed most of the scrolls here," Mel said. "We heard about that on the quest for the Shards—an Ace came and attacked a scribehouse in Tinkeeyo, looking for the Prophecy."

"Not this scribehouse, thankfully," Alder answered. "The one you're thinking of is a few miles from here, on the other side of the city. It held prophecies specifically, as well as poems and songs."

"Are you sure we don't need to go there?" Mel asked.

"We might," Alder admitted, "but I figured we'd start here. This is where you'll find the records of Luet's writings."

"That narrows it down for us," Misty pointed out optimistically, then turned curiously to Mel. "But why did the Aces try to get the Prophecy?"

"They wanted to keep us from reading it," Mel replied. "And the Ace-Lord wanted to study the words, too—figure out a way around them."

He knew the Ace-Lord's plan didn't involve simply destroying the Prophecy. The words offered hope to the mortals, and could not be overcome. But those words could be twisted, corrupted by lies. The Ace-Deputy had told him that while he'd been captured in Castle Droco. Lies and illusions, like everything else the Ace-Lord dealt with… but they were very convincing.

The hall ended. Daylight shone through large paneled windows, lighting the rows of shelves arranged like the spokes of a giant wheel. The shelves reached all the way to the ceiling; rolling ladders allowed readers to access the books at the top. Each shelf was packed with books and scrolls of all sizes, some written in Coonsian, others in flowing

Liznaiec runes, and others in languages Mel could not even guess. They seemed to span every century of Orlell's history, books with crisp new leather covers or scrolls cracked and yellowed with age.

Misty's eyes were wide as she looked at the shelves. "Wow," she breathed at last. "We should have brought Dad—he could have restored some of those books."

"Yeah," Mel said vaguely. He rubbed his forehead, already overwhelmed. Thousands—perhaps tens of thousands—of scrolls lay before him to search through, some in languages they wouldn't be able to understand, and he had no idea what exactly he was looking for. The words and letters muddled before his eyes as he tried to read the labels on the shelves, and he felt an unwelcome sensation of defeat.

It may not be a battlefield, but he felt twice as daunted by it.

"Where would you like to start?" Alder asked.

Mel let out a breath, forcing his anxious thoughts to calm. This was important, for his friends, his family, for Aryion. "Okay. Umm… Jan said Luet died during the reign of Queen Kircadash, so we can rule out anything in the last twenty-five years or so, right?"

"That would be logical," Alder said, his gaze scanning the shelves. "We can also rule out this side of the room." He gestured to the left. "They're labeled as Elven history only—I don't think Luet's writings fit that category."

"Then we should start with those," Misty said, pointing to three shelves on the right.

Alder squinted at the sign. "*Exploration and Navigation…* are you sure?"

"Jan said Luet was an explorer," Mel said, catching onto Misty's line of thought. "Most of her writings were about her travels, hundreds of years ago—maybe her notes about the Stones would be there, too."

Alder led the way forward. These shelves, Mel noticed, were primarily scrolls, and very old scrolls at that. He stepped close to read the delicate writing on the edge of one: *"The Culture & Chronicles of the Matrizel Elves."*

"I've never heard of the Matrizel," Misty commented, touching the scroll lightly as if her fingers itched to read it. "Were they a tribe, or just a family?"

"They were a nation," Alder replied. "Thousands of them once dwelt in the Magno Forest. No one is really sure what happened to them— they didn't fight in the Dividing War, simply vanished. Some say the Darkness killed them, but my grandfather thinks they left the Mainland entirely."

"And went where?" Mel wondered.

"Past the edges of the maps, maybe. My grandfather thinks you can keep sailing north, up and around the known lands and beyond, maybe to another land altogether."

This idea intrigued Mel, but he turned his attention to another scroll. He couldn't read the words, but knew the runes were Elven. Aryion had been teaching him Elven—his upbringing in Elimar had taught him some of the language. But Mel was still learning the alphabet.

"Alder… could you write down a chart for these letters?" he asked, as an idea came to him. "I can sort of speak Elven—not very well, but if you could write down the letters next to the Coonsian alphabet, then I could read the scroll titles too, and we'd get through it twice as fast."

"That's not a bad idea," Alder agreed. "I'll write down a key."

"And I can make one with Liznaiec runes," Misty added. "I've been learning them in school, and I brought two of my textbooks that should help us translate."

"Good. That'll help a lot," Mel said, his confidence gradually returning. "We can probably skip over the scrolls written in Coonsian—I think Luet wrote primarily in Liznaiec and Elven."

"That rules out these ones," Misty said, motioning to the lower two shelves.

Alder rolled over one of the ladders and climbed up, scanning the scrolls above while Mel and Misty read over the lower ones. Several minutes passed before Alder's triumphant voice filled the quiet hall. "Found one—there's a few of them up here. I can't read Liznaiec runes, but they have Luet's crest."

He carried three scrolls back down the ladder, holding one out to Misty. Mel noticed the crest—a simple compass rose, emblazoned like a shining star upon the corner of the parchment.

Misty opened the scroll carefully, reading slowly and meticulously.

"Well?" Mel asked eagerly, after a few moments.

"I think... it's a travel record," Misty said finally.

"Travel where?" Mel asked, an edge of impatience in his voice.

Misty's eyes narrowed at the parchment. "Mata City... it sounds like Luet met with the Cooper lord. Yes, that's this word—*Huvá*. This journey was about a hundred years after the Dividing War."

Mel sighed. "Is there anything about Star-Stones?"

"Maybe. I can't read that fast," Misty said reproachfully.

Mel nodded, feeling bad for his impatience. Misty was doing all she could, which was excellent. That said, it would be better if they had another person here who could read Liznaiec.

"Dandio," he said slowly, as the thought came to him. "We could bring some of these scrolls back to the fort for Dandio to look at—he'll be able to read them faster than we can." He looked uncertainly at Alder. "We're allowed to do that, right?"

"If it's permitted by Lord Andros, then yes," Alder said. "We can send a request to take some of these scrolls on loan."

"This was a really interesting journey," Misty commented, eyes still glued to the scroll. "Luet says they traveled from Mata City and encountered the kragons in the Magno Forest. And she said the kragons taught them…" she frowned, studying a word uncertainly for several moments, "to… sing."

"That can't be right," Mel said.

"It's the right verb," Misty said. "It's just the placement of the words together—*Allá Alené*. Normally it'd be written *Allá Ultave* when you're talking about singing, or teaching someone something. The word for 'sing' is different here—*Alené*."

Mel looked at the scroll skeptically. "You're saying the kragons taught them to sing?"

"That's what it says. But it's not… oh, I don't know," Misty said, frustrated. "That word's confusing me—*Alené* usually refers to power, or fire. So it's basically saying '*The kragons taught us to sing power.*' It doesn't make sense."

"Might just be the old dialect," Alder pointed out. "Don't worry. The important thing is, we've found the scrolls of Luet."

"And you can read them, Misty," Mel added encouragingly, trying not to worry. They'd already have their work cut out for them trying to translate the scrolls—if the old dialect was this confusing, their search would take even longer. "This scroll doesn't talk about Star-Stones, right?" he asked.

"No. Unless that's what she means by *Alené*," Misty replied, but she sounded doubtful.

"We can read over the next few," Alder said. "I'll put that one back while you look at the next."

Misty reluctantly closed the first scroll, her brow still furrowed over *Allá Alené*. But she opened the second scroll and peered at it carefully for several minutes. Mel forced himself to wait patiently, knowing he'd only frustrate her if he pressured her to read faster.

At last Misty looked up. "This one isn't about Star-Stones either. It's about a journey to Caer Sia during the reign of…" she looked at the parchment, then up again. "King Azdiel."

"I believe he was crowned after the Dividing War," Alder said. "That means this scroll happened before the last one we read."

"Probably," Misty agreed. She scanned the words for a few more minutes, then shook her head, disappointed. "Nothing here. The first part talks about the king and who his advisors were, and the next part is a lot of details over the different councils they had."

Mel looked up at the shelf, starting to feel overwhelmed again. Whether they were looking for one specific scroll, or several, there was no telling. Nor, he realized, was there a way to know if that scroll actually existed. What if Luet had only talked about the Star-Stones, and never written her theories down? Or what if those writings had been lost long ago?

"I'll grab a few more to look over," Alder said. "We might want to check the Records side of the scribehouse later, just in case."

They spent the rest of the afternoon at the same bookshelf, looking over scrolls. Mel and Alder read a few written in Elven, as some bore Luet's compass crest as well. Misty toiled dutifully over the Liznaeic scrolls, occasionally calling out interesting things she read. Luet seemed to have traveled all over Orlell. Her travels ranged from exploration to diplomacy. A few times Misty mentioned something Mel recognized—a war, or the name of a long-dead ruler. But most of them were totally unknown.

Sunset painted the sky by the time they stopped for the day. Mel's stomach was rumbling, his eyes were tired, and they were no closer to learning anything of importance. On the plus side, he was gradually learning to decipher the Elven runes, which filled the majority of the scrolls.

"We can take a few back for Dandio," he said, rubbing his eyes.

"Tomorrow," Alder said firmly. "We'll need Lord Andros' permission, and we're all tired."

They headed back outside, waiting for the carriage to return. The sun had set, leaving only the muggy heat. Mel took a deep breath of the warm air, trying to rid his thoughts of tangled runes and ancient records.

Misty was frowning deeply. "*Allá Alené,*" she muttered to herself. "I didn't read it wrong… why was it written like that?"

"Must have been a mistake," Mel suggested. "Don't worry about it, Misty. That's not the scroll we need to worry about understanding."

19

Hounds in the Hills

Time passed in agonizing slowness in Gayrile.

A heatwave gripped the Wandering Wood, dousing the Chanterelle encampment in a muggy haze. It was so hot that Allie barely wanted to think about fighting, and hoped that the negotiations would be resolved quickly just so they could return to the cool and comfort of Sia. She had intended to study more from the protocol notes her mother had sent with her, but there were far too many things on her mind this morning.

Strange tracks had been found, ones the Brownae scouts had not recognized, intermingling with the charred paths left by the Dal-kerri. They belonged, the Brownae captain had said, to large beasts that crept and slithered, leaving long trails in their wake as they had dragged themselves through the underbrush.

Serpentines. Allie had no doubt about it, since they'd already learned the snakes filled the Ace-army, and she understood the fear in the eyes of the scouts. Even with the anti-venom they'd brought, the serpentines posed a significant threat.

Yet the week had passed with no further sign of potential invaders, leaving them to worry and wait in the humid forest.

So far, she'd felt about as useless here as she had in Caer Sia. With the negotiations finally decided upon, there was not much the Brownae warriors could do until the meeting. Morel kept them training with the new rifles; the distant crackle of gunfire was a frequent occurrence. Allie wondered if she should learn how to shoot too, just in case. Then again, her fire was easier to master.

Her eyes trailed to the spellbook beside her pillow, open to the place she'd read over last night.

Of the Old Magic.

In contrast to the stagnant, blurred futility that had filled everything they'd read before, the words last night had seemed sharp and piercing, tiny blades that stung her heart and whispered an ending she refused to accept. The Life-Blood Spell had not always been a thing of darkness. But darkness claimed it all the same, just as it claimed her.

Rygal had explained what he'd learned from Morel a few days ago, his blue eyes alight with hesitant hope. Did he truly believe that someone could overrule the curse the Ace-Lord had on her? Speak the same words that had bound her, and free her? No matter the interesting story of the spell's origins, no matter the light that had once filled its words— she was bound by darkness, and nothing but death would break that curse.

The grim truth chilled her thoughts again, and she had to fight to take a breath, shaking her head fiercely. No. Now was not the time to think about that.

She headed outside. The sun had barely risen, and the cool in the air helped ease her frustration. Rygal, Darion, and Morel stood talking around one of the cookfires. Allie could tell in a moment from the tone of Morel's voice that something was wrong.

"They should have joined us days ago," the Brownae princess was saying quietly as Allie approached. "I don't know if they just intend to sit this whole thing out, but I don't like it."

"There's a chance they reported to one of the other chieftains, and we weren't told," Rygal pointed out slowly, "but I agree with you."

"That's the same ridge as the tracks, right?" Darion asked, and Morel nodded.

Allie looked between the three of them uneasily. "Tracks? Have we seen more Dal-kerri?"

"No," Rygal replied slowly. "But the Rufa tribe was supposed to meet us here a few days ago—their warriors promised to guard Bridgeport while the negotiations take place, and we needed to arrange their defenses. They should be camped a few miles from here."

"They might still be debating over joining the negotiations at all," Morel reminded him grimly. "Many tribes think they can just sit this war out."

"But they promised to, all the same," Porcini pointed out, sitting across from her by the fire. "I know they didn't bring as many warriors as you'd hoped, but they're allied with us."

"Only so we can protect them," Morel said flatly. "They haven't attended our war meetings or offered any resources to help whatsoever." She shook her head. "Either way, we need to check in. The ridge they've encamped on is near the place where Captain Boli saw the Dal-kerri tracks. Old tracks, but we can't ignore them."

"We'll head up and check in on them," Darion said, standing and shouldering his bow and quiver.

"Take a troop of Chanterelle and a few Guardians with you just in case," Morel told him. "Better safe than sorry."

There was likely no danger, Allie told herself. The Rufa had neglected to communicate before, as Morel said. But her chest was suddenly tight with worry.

She forced a casual smile as Rygal and Darion rose to go. "Try not to hurt yourselves."

"We'll be fine," Rygal answered. "You and Morel can handle packing the gear, right?"

Morel snorted. "Oh, I'm sure we can manage. You boys have fun."

They'll be all right, Allie told herself firmly. Rygal's eyes studied her face in a way that told her he could tell she was worried. He seemed about to say something, but instead turned away and joined Darion and the Brownae troops.

Allie let out a breath, trying to force away the nervousness. But her gaze lingered on the warriors until the trees hid them from sight.

"Well, we'd best get to it," Morel said briskly.

Allie shook her head and stood. "Right. What do we need to do?"

Morel led her to the supply tents where a group of Brownaes were already at work loading the crates onto a small wagon. "Now that the rain's stopped, we need to start packing up the gear. Assuming everything goes according to plan with the negotiations, we'll be heading out soon."

"Do you think there might be trouble?" Allie asked, catching the doubt in her tone.

Morel called an order to one of the Brownaes, directing them to start moving the crates, then turned back to face her. "To be honest, I don't know. The last message we got was promising—all the delegates have agreed to attend. But since these reports of wolves, I'm worried there's something else going on here."

"I've heard that Gayrile is… well, that it sort of attracts dark magic," Allie said slowly. "Because the Jewel was corrupted here. You've studied some spells, didn't you?" she added curiously. "Where did you learn of the Jewel-lore? I've only heard of it in the last month or so."

A wry smile crossed Morel's face. "Grab that side," she said, nodding to the end of a crate before answering the question. "Brownae history is passed down through our families. My mother learned of the old magic from her mother, as well as the danger of dark magic. We even learned some things from the Guardians."

The clink of metal came from within the crate as they lifted it, and Allie's fingers nearly slipped on the wood. "The Guardians?" she repeated with an effort. "Thought they were—exiled by Safacon."

"They were, but that didn't mean the knowledge just went away," Morel replied. "Safacon ordered all records of their magic destroyed, but it was Norrin who kept most of it safe. And that's how you have his spellbooks."

Allie slid her end of the crate onto the wagon bed, pushing it flush with the others, and wiped a strand of damp hair from her brow. The air was unbearably warm and sticky. "Norrin was the leader of the Guardians before Rygal, right?" she asked slowly. She knew very little of the man Rygal so respected, besides his name and that he had died during the quest for the Shards.

Morel glanced at her. "Yes, he was. What has Rygal told you?"

"Hardly anything," Allie said. "He doesn't seem especially talkative about him."

"I don't blame him," Morel murmured. "We all have pain we'd rather forget."

Allie frowned, but before she could inquire into this cryptic statement, a gunshot split the air behind them.

Morel's head snapped up, cat-like ears flicked forward. Fire sparked in Allie's heart, crackling in her veins—she fought it down, but her pulse was racing. "Was that from the ridge?"

The Brownae soldiers had all paused, listening tensely. Morel was silent for several seconds. "Sounded like that direction," she said at last, sounding unsure. "But I don't hear anything more."

Even as she said it, three more gunshots sounded in rapid succession from the same direction, and with them, a sound Allie knew too well—the haunting, shrieking cry of the Dal-kerri.

Morel swore in the Brownae tongue, running back towards the command tents while shouting a rapid stream of orders. Allie ran after her. Gripping fear fanned her fire into an uncontrollable blaze, barring any attempt to calm herself. All she could think of was Rygal and Darion, fighting the Dal-kerri on the ridge.

Why didn't I go with them? The thought screamed in her mind. If there were enchanted soldiers among the ambush on the ridge, they'd be outmatched and defeated—both would die.

Rygal and Darion would die.

The image of them lying in the ferns, cold and lifeless and covered in blood, flashed before her eyes, and helpless fire sparked from her fingertips.

Four guards met them at the command tents—Porcini was with them, his face drawn with fear. "None of our scouts have seen any signs of enemies," he stammered. "We think the wolves are on the neighboring hill, near the Rufa encampment."

"Double the guard," Morel ordered immediately. "If you hear my battle horn, evacuate the warriors to the coast as fast as you can." Porcini nodded mutely as Morel turned to the captains. "Squadrons one and two, with me. We're heading up the hill to hold this side of the valley."

"I'm coming with you," Allie said. Her voice was hoarse with fear.

Morel didn't argue, only slung a rifle onto her back and led the way uphill. Allie ran after the Brownaes, stumbling as the ferns tangled at her knees. The gunshots had faded, but she could still hear distant howls. Horrible images filled her imagination. She'd seen what the Dal-kerri could do.

They reached the top of the ridge. The hill opposite them was just visible—there was no sign of battle on this side, but she could hear the sounds of fighting filling the neighboring valley.

Gripping her sword, she started down into the next draw.

"Wait, Heiress," Morel ordered behind her. "We'll hold here."

Allie swung back in disbelief. "What are you talking about? We have to help them!"

"If we go too far, we'll leave the camp completely unprotected," Morel told her. "We'll wait here, stop any Dal-kerri that slip through the battle."

Allie walked back up the ridge, her mind reeling. Beyond, the howls of the wolves heightened her growing desperation. "They'll die, Morel," she said, voice raw with panic.

"They're prepared," Morel said levelly.

"I don't care," Allie snapped. Fire sparked at her fingertips as she turned away. "I'm not going to let that happen."

She started forward again—Morel grabbed her arm and hauled her back. For her short stature, the Brownae was incredibly strong. Her voice was low and firm. "Listen to me, Heiress. You might have more power in your new state, but the Ace-Lord knows that. The curse binding you—you think that's there for your benefit? If you go charging into that fight, you'll only give the Ace-Lord more power."

Allie yanked her arm away. "Who told you about the curse?"

"Rygal mentioned it," Morel said quietly.

"Then did he mention that I can't do anything to help it?" Allie snapped, her body trembling with rage. "Did he make it sound like I'm glad I have this power—that I'm *glad* the Ace-Lord did this?" She kept her voice low, but the words tore her throat like barbs. "Did he tell you how to break it, Morel? I have to die. That's the only way. I'm the willing warrior in the Prophecy. I have to *die*."

There. She had said it aloud. She'd wondered, worried, resisted the truth. But she'd never stated it out loud. Fire heaved in her chest, but it did not blaze forth, as though utterly crushed by the horrible finality of the words. She was going to die.

Through a haze of furious tears she saw Morel shake her head. "Rygal told me that too. Because he's worried for you, and he's seeking a way to break the curse that doesn't involve your death. I don't know if what he plans is possible…"

"It's not," Allie whispered. "Even if the curse wasn't always a curse, only the Ace-Lord can remove the Life-Blood Spell. Only the one who cast it can get rid of it."

"And he cast it to use your strength," Morel stated, nodding at the opposite ridge. "That's what he's trying to do now—draw you out, corrupt your heart. We know he means to mar the mortals."

A Dal-kerri shriek split the air, followed by four more gunshots. Allie closed her eyes. "Maybe I'm already marred," she said quietly. "Maybe that's what the curse does."

"I doubt it. If that were true, there'd be no reason to force you to fight now," Morel told her. "Don't fall for it. This fight isn't yours. You have to trust Rygal and Darion to handle it on their own."

Allie gritted her teeth, forcing the blaze away with an effort. Morel was right. She could say nothing to argue about it.

She set her stance and waited, listening to the howls of the wolves and the clash of steel. Occasionally, a brilliant flare of fire came from the opposite ridge, and she knew one of the Guardians was fighting there. But she didn't see Rygal's sparks among them.

They stood there, weapons ready, as the minutes dragged on. The sounds of battle began to fade away. Allie couldn't see anyone on the far ridge—the fighting must be contained on the other side.

What if they were already dead? Worse, what if they were still clinging to life, and needed her help?

The fire roiled to life again, an inferno of fear and uncertainty.

Something rustled in the ferns beneath them, snapping her focus back to the present. Three Dal-kerri bounded through the underbrush, straight up the hill. The fire building in Allie's chest burst from her hand, smiting the first wolf in a single blast. Morel's quick shots took the other two down.

"Look at that," Morel murmured, nodding to one of the wolves she'd hit. A black-feathered arrow stuck in its flanks. "Looks like that ranger of yours is still kicking."

The ferns below them rustled again. A creature with dark fur ran towards them—but not a Dal-kerri. A Brownae warrior jogged uphill, stumbling in weariness. Umber blood streaked his leather armor, but he seemed uninjured.

"General," he said, saluting to Morel.

Morel lowered her rifle. "Captain Boli—talk to me. What's happening over there? Do they need reinforcements?"

"No," the captain panted. "Don't send anyone this way—you'll be trapped. There are more wolves on this side of the ridge, waiting for you—don't come that way. We've nearly beat them, but they're waiting for the chance to flank us and infiltrate the camp."

Allie looked at Morel, but the Brownae princess had the grace not to say *I told you so.* She only nodded to the captain. "Go tell Porcini to form a perimeter. If there are Dal-kerri on this side of the ridge, we're not taking any chances."

"Aye, General," Boli replied with another salute. "Our warriors have the hounds backed up, but we've taken casualties."

"What of the Guardians?" Allie asked, almost afraid to know the answer. "Commander Rygal and Darion Blackbird?"

"The ranger was still fighting last I saw," Boli said. "The Guardians are holding their ground, but two of their leaders were killed when the Dal-kerri ambushed us."

Freezing fear seized Allie's heart, and she had to fight to take a breath. "Who?" she choked.

"I don't know their names," the captain answered. "Even if I did, you've seen how the wolves kill—they leave hardly anything left." He shook his head grimly.

"And the Rufa?" Morel asked.

"Fighting with us—the ones who can, anyway. A lot were hurt or killed. Seems they were caught off guard too."

"For three days?" Allie demanded in disbelief.

"We'll figure that out later," Morel said. She dismissed Captain Boli, who jogged back toward camp.

Two dead Guardians. *Not Rygal,* her mind pleaded, *please, please not Rygal.*

"We have to help them," she said, unable to stand the uncertainty. "They're outnumbered, and they're taking casualties."

"Not as we've heard," Morel countered. "They're driving the Dal-kerri out, which means the hounds might be headed this way. Form up," she called to the soldiers. "Crescent formation. Hold this ridge at all cost—we must protect the camp."

Allie stood next to her, gripping her sword. *Two dead Guardians.* The words echoed tauntingly in her mind, and she felt sick.

The minutes stretched into silence. No more howls, no more gunshots, no more fire lighting up the distant trees. The sun began to dip for the west.

"There's someone coming this way," Morel said, breaking the tense quiet. "Quite a few of them."

"Dal-kerri?" Allie asked.

"No—Brownaes, it sounds like. With the noise they're making, there are Guardians with them too."

Allie waited tensely, peering through the shadowed trees. At last she saw them. The colors on their leather armor marked both Chanterelle and Rufa Brownaes. Guardians walked among them, some limping or supporting injured comrades.

She didn't see Rygal or Darion.

The warriors reached the ridge. Morel sent four of her men down into camp to make sure the injured received critical supplies. "There were no serpentines," one of the Brownaes reported. "Only wolves."

Allie kept her eyes on the draw as more warriors slowly returned, her fear growing as the minutes ticked by. A Guardian reached the ridge—Allie stepped toward him. "Sir—your commander, and the ranger, are they—"

"Asescia," Morel said quietly, nudging her.

Allie swung her eyes back to the valley below.

Rygal and Darion were walking at the back of the group.

Relief swept through her so fast it took her breath away. She ran downhill to meet them. They both saw her coming, and smiles spread over their weary faces. Darion was supporting Rygal, whose pantleg was streaked with blood, but his eyes fixed immediately on her.

"Are you all right?" he demanded as soon as she reached them.

"I'm fine—are you—what did you—" Allie could barely form words, the relief choking out her voice. Emotions clutched her throat, and she blinked away the burning tears. She hugged him before she could stop herself, then pulled away awkwardly. "What—what happened?"

"Dal-kerri," Darion told her. His scarred face was drawn with weariness, but aside from a score of cuts and bruises, he was unhurt. "A whole pack of them, surrounding the Rufa encampment."

"That explains why we didn't hear from them," Allie murmured.

"Well, the real question is why the wolves didn't attack sooner," Rygal replied grimly. "I don't like it. Why'd the Dal-kerri just wait there? They had numbers enough to destroy the Rufa camp."

Allie looked at him uneasily. Darion shook his head. "Let's worry about that later. Right now, the Rufa are here with us, and they've sworn to fight for Gayrile."

"And I think we've gotten rid of the Dal-kerri," Rygal added. "Boli only reported seeing one pack, and we've just defeated them."

"Did you find out who was leading them?" Allie asked.

"Not a sign," Darion said. "We can hope it was a rogue group of wolves, but I don't know."

"We'll scout the area further," Rygal said. "Check the neighboring hills for tracks—make sure there aren't any more. I'll ask Morel about sending some scouts west, too."

"Not till you're patched up, *Commander*," Darion informed him dryly. "You've bled enough to attract a whole new pack of unpleasant creatures."

"It's barely a scratch," Rygal said, but winced as they started downhill towards camp. "Blazes—why is it always my leg?"

"Because you're tall, and it's a difficult target to guard," Allie told him, echoing his words during one of their many sparring matches. He returned the smile weakly, but the pain and weariness on his face cut to her heart. "I thought I told you to be careful," she added reproachfully.

"I'm always careful," Rygal replied.

"The gaping cut above your knee argues otherwise," Darion told him. "Now shut up and let's get to the medical tent."

. . . . . .

Morel called a meeting that evening, after the injured had been tended to. In addition to the many bites and scratches, five warriors had been killed. Rygal's wound, thankfully, was not serious, and he seemed more worried for the fate of the rest of the camp.

"No one else was hurt," Allie reassured him again, as they settled by the campfire. "The battle didn't even reach the valley."

"Good," Rygal breathed. His gaze lingered on her. "And you're— you're sure you—"

"Better now that you're back," Allie said, managing a smile, and sat down between him and Darion. The gripping fear of before had faded now that the battle was over. She thought she noticed a suspicious smile on Darion's face as he glanced between the two of them, and frowned slightly. "What?"

Darion raised his eyebrows innocently. "What?"

Allie turned away, fighting to keep herself from blushing. Whatever Darion was alluding to... no, now wasn't the time to think about that. She fixed her gaze on the fire, forced her thoughts away from Rygal, his smile, the relief in his eyes when he'd seen her...

She shook her head sharply as Morel and two of the Rufa leaders joined them. The Rufa Brownaes were taller and wirier than the stocky Chanterelles, with a wily, wild light in their eyes, and they thanked the Guardians profusely for their aid.

"Glad we could help," Rygal told them. "You're lucky the Dal-kerri decided to wait in the woods, instead of attacking your camp."

His direct tone implied his suspicion, but the Rufa leader only nodded. "Yes, very fortunate. Now, what is our plan, General Morel?"

Morel stood beside the fire, thinking. "I'm glad to hear the Dal-kerri are gone," she said after a pause. "But we can't afford to lower our defenses. We'll discuss continued perimeter protection when we reach Bridgeport. I trust your warriors are prepared?" she added to the Rufa chieftains.

The Brownae nodded. "We are unaccustomed to allying with humans," he admitted. "But for this cause, we will make certain the city is secure."

"Good," Morel said. "We march at first light. I would recommend you rest up—it's a long journey."

The two chieftains nodded again, moving away from the fire to join their warriors.

Porcini looked at his sister. "You still don't trust them?"

"I tend to distrust everyone until proven otherwise," Morel told him, shaking her head slowly. "There's one thing that still bothers me—not about the Rufa. Even if the wolves are gone, I've never heard a report of the Ace-Lord sending them to act alone. My question now is, if all the hounds have been killed, who was leading them, and where have they got to now?"

Allie glanced between Darion and Rygal, seeing their troubled expressions. But Morel's question remained unanswered as night fell.

20

Twilight in Tinkeeyo

A long, busy week passed in Tinkeeyo. Soldiers marched the streets, the rhythm of their ranks filling Mel's ears no matter where he was. Couriers came in and out of the fort daily with news from across the country. Every day seemed to bring a new report of a different battle.

The couriers were not the only ones bringing news, though. Each morning, in the blue hours of dawn, Mel could glimpse the dryads slipping like shadows through the city. They did not enter the fort itself—they were still slow to trust the Elves. Dandio often rode out on Nella in the morning, waiting for the dryads on the city outskirts. Sometimes they simply ghosted past, observing silently, but other times they delivered a message from another part of Orlell.

The most recent message had come from Jan, who, it seemed, had gained the dryads' trust. A battalion of Red Dawn knights, led by Glentree, had marched to Elimar to strengthen the border defense. Jan had also sent word to Lord Roan of the Coopers, warning his people to be on high alert. No new report had come regarding Mata City, but the city was still under threat.

Despite the activity filling every waking moment, Mel was no closer to learning anything about the Star-Stone. The reports of war only heightened his growing desperation to find Luet's writings about the Stone.

He had help, thankfully. Misty was by his side constantly, becoming faster and faster at reading the runes. Alder joined them in the scribehouse when he was not busy with his own duties. Even Dandio, when he was not needed elsewhere, offered help where he could, and occasionally had to convince Mel to take a rest.

"You'll do more harm than good at this point," the Liznee had said firmly last night, after Mel had nodded off over a scroll. "Imagine telling Lord Andros you fell asleep and drooled on a four hundred-year-old record of his ancestors. Take a break and start again in the morning."

Mel had relented, though reluctantly. He loathed stopping, even for a short rest. His worry for his mentor crept into his dreams, filling him with gnawing urgency. The dryads had not brought any other news regarding Aryion since their first message. The wind, they said, could reach the borders of Ar-Salem, but the Aces had concealed Aryion in a place not even the wind could find him. Hard as Mel fought to hope, the fears were a part of him, an ever-present concern.

The scrolls took his mind off it for a bit, at least. Alder had written up a chart depicting Elven runes beside their corresponding Coonsian letters, so Mel could translate the alphabet. From there, he had to carefully and meticulously make out the Elvish word. Certain words appeared often enough he didn't need to translate them now—he could recognize "*war*" or "*census*" or "*genealogy*," which usually meant he could skip those scrolls. He'd also written down the words "*Star-Stone*" and "*power*" in Elven so that he could immediately recognize them if they ever appeared in the title.

All the same, it was slow work, with very little results.

He and Misty returned to the scribehouse after breakfast. Dandio had allowed them to ride Nella there, instead of taking a carriage every time. The guards had come to expect them, letting them in without question. The summer sun warmed the morning, promising another hot day.

"We've pretty much finished this side," Misty said as they walked inside, pointing to the Exploration shelves.

"I know," Mel said, scanning the room. By now, he knew what the labels said. He pointed to one. "We can keep working through '*Records*.' And I thought we might try skimming through the history side—most of them are in Coonsian, but there are a few of Luet's scrolls over there too."

"Okay," Misty agreed, starting forward. She would never grow tired of this, Mel thought. She was getting faster at reading Liznaeic, too, as she reminded him constantly.

Mel was glad she enjoyed the task. To him, this was his hardest mission yet—and that included the exhausting trek to Kamon during the quest for the Shards. He would take a difficult trail, a long hike in the rain, even a troop of immortal orcs over this tedious work.

Together, they rolled one of the ladders over to the shelf, and Mel climbed up to the top while Misty started on the lower row. Misty found a Luet scroll first, pulling it out. "Here's one—*The Rise & Fall of Lord Danioshi*. He was a Cagari lord—probably not about Star-Stones…"

"Probably not," Mel murmured, his eyes searching the titles. At last he spotted Luet's compass crest, emblazoned on a scroll written in Liznaeic. "What's this say, Misty?" he asked.

Misty peered up at the title. "*A Genealogy of Elven Drakes*—no, *Dukes*. It's a list of names."

Mel slid the scroll back into place. Most of the records were genealogies—seemingly endless lists of names. Why anyone would ever need that knowledge, he had no idea, but they made up at least half this shelf.

He pulled out another scroll, which was written in Elven, and unfolded his chart of runes. Painstakingly, he set to deciphering each letter. Once the word was clear, he could translate it into Coonsian. If he didn't recognize the word then, which happened often enough, he could set the scroll aside for Alder to read once he joined them here.

"Mel," Misty said slowly, a question in her tone.

Mel glanced down at her. "Yeah?"

"I'm just wondering. You don't think we should be looking in the other scribehouse Alder told us about—the one holding prophecies?"

Mel frowned slightly. "I don't know. Alder said Luet's writings were kept here, and we're not looking for a prophecy."

"No, but we're looking for writings about Star-Stones," Misty countered, her brow furrowed. "What if some of Luet's writings are kept with the prophecies?"

Mel looked at the packed shelves around them, considering this. Perhaps they were looking in the wrong place. Perhaps Luet's writings were also kept with the prophecies, since Luet had first brought the Prophecy of Three.

"We can ask Dandio later," he said finally. "Jan didn't tell us Luet had written any other prophecy."

"I know," Misty said, sounding slightly disappointed. "It's just… I think we're looking for something besides just records. Something… magical, like the prophecies."

"There's nothing magical about the prophecies, Misty," Mel said, but he had to smile. "At least—the High Light gives us a type of magic, and the Stars have magic—but the scrolls are just scrolls."

"I don't know," Misty said thoughtfully. "Whatever other power you're hoping to find, I think it's another type of good magic, one we don't know about."

Mel nodded, turning his attention back to the scrolls before him. Misty wasn't wrong—once they found whatever scroll they were looking for, it would hopefully detail some new sort of power, a true, pure magic that could help in this fight. But first, they must find that scroll, which seemed hidden as a needle in a haystack among Luet's many writings.

He worked his way along the top shelf, skipping the genealogies. He found a recounting of another of Luet's adventures, which had been translated into Coonsian by one of the scribes. The story detailed a battle between the dragons of West Coonsia and the kragon lords. The tale drew him in, painting desert plains on the scroll before his eyes as contrasting flames clashed in the sky.

"Mel?"

Misty's voice drew him out of the story. Noise reached his ears— muted voices outside, and the shuffling of hurried feet.

He climbed back down the ladder as the door opened, and the captain of guard entered. "Excuse me, but you have both been summoned back to the fort by Lord Andros."

"Is something wrong?" Mel asked, a prickle of unease running down his back.

"No, child—in fact, it seems quite good." The captain's eyes shone with hope. "The ranger Goldfinch has returned. It seems the Alfona have joined our cause."

Mel's heart leapt. He'd been so busy reading scrolls over the last week that he'd completely forgotten about Quinn's mission to meet and ally with the Alfona. Now, at last, there was good news.

He and Misty hurried outside. Nella, who had been napping in the shade of the redwood trees, now stood, ears pricked forward as though sensing the excited energy in the air. Mel and Misty both climbed into her saddle, and the gryphon swept into the sky.

From the aerial vantage point, Mel noticed the newcomers—but only because the usual crowds were giving them so much space. The Alfona warriors blended perfectly into the tree-shadowed roads of Tinkeeyo, gathering in the courtyard of the fort. Their muffled voices grew louder as Nella swept downward.

Quinn's voice, heavy with urgency, brought all of Mel's fears rushing back. "We cannot know how long we have, we must act quickly—"

"Our defenses will not hold them for long," another voice said, deep and somber like the wind through the fir trees. "If your lord intends to act, it must be now."

Nella landed at the courtyard entrance. The Alfona glanced at them carefully, clearly startled by the sight of the gryphon with two children clinging to her saddle. Their faces were human-like, chiseled and tan, and black, bark-like markings streaked their faces in unique patterns. Dark, plate-like skin covered their forearms and shins, too.

Mel hesitated beneath the fierce gaze, but as Dandio's voice reached him, he felt a rush of relief.

"Come, good chief. Lord Andros desires to speak with you. Your warriors may rest in the barracks."

The Liznee's tall form appeared through the crowd, ushering the Alfona inside. His eyes landed on Mel and Misty. "Glad to see you both. Come inside."

"What's going on?" Mel asked, looking at the warriors uncertainly. "Is...something wrong?"

Dandio let out a breath, as if seeking a different answer, any answer, to ease Mel's mind. But the time for comforting lies was long past. "The Alfona sighted a large force marching from Ar-Salem, headed for Fort Tinkeeyo," he said at last. "The Aces plan to besiege us."

Siege. Of all the bad news Mel had feared, that had been low on the list, as it seemed so unlikely. He followed Dandio inside, too startled to form words.

"Does that mean we have to go back?" Misty asked softly.

Dandio paused beside the door, looking at the two of them. "That was the plan at first. But we had also hoped that you would have found Luet's writing by now."

"We're trying," Mel said, his frustration rising to the surface.

Dandio spread his hands. "That is not what I meant. In fact, your mission may have become all the more crucial with this new development. If there is a way to protect, to harness the Stone's power for the good it was meant for, it is imperative we find it. However, we cannot risk the Stone, or either of you."

"We'll find it," Mel said firmly. "Dandio—I can't go back now. This is what I came here for—what the New Blood is meant to do."

A faint smile crossed the Liznee's scarred face. "There's that fire. I trust you both." He turned, leading them to the council hall. "We can discuss this later. Come."

Lord Andros stood with his generals in the council hall, his face grim. Quinn stood beside a tall, wizened Alfona who wore a feathered headdress and whose calm eyes seemed able to see deep inside the people around him.

"My father," Quinn said, with a slight bow, "this is Chief Kadryion of the Alfona."

Andros bowed before him. "It is an honor to meet you, chieftain. I hope we may repair the wrongs done by our ancestors."

"As do I, my lord," Kadryion answered warmly. "It is a shame this war is what drives us to alliance."

"Yet it is a battle we must fight together," one of the warriors said. His flashing eyes and grim expression reminded Mel of a wolf on the trail.

"Indeed," Kadryion agreed, beckoning to the other warrior. "Meet you Wolfsbane, my captain. If not for him, I fear we may not have reached you undetected."

"Do the Aces know of your coming here?" Lord Andros inquired.

"We're not sure," Quinn said, exchanging a glance with Wolfsbane. "We left the outpost two days ago to travel back to Tinkeeyo. Wolfsbane saw the outriders—thank the Light he did. We managed to reach higher ground off the main road, so that we could see their army marching onward."

"Army?" Dandio repeated.

"A siege force," Quinn said, shaking his head grimly. "Thousands of them—Dal-kerri, enchanted soldiers, serpentines, and other beasts I couldn't recognize. We traveled lighter than they, but they are not far behind us."

"We have delayed them," Kadryion put in. "A barrier of trees stand between them and the fort. But I admit I do not know how long it will hold them."

"We are prepared for a siege," Andros said with a sigh, "though we hoped it would not be this soon. We must act now." He turned to his generals. "Secure the city boundaries. Issue an order for all to barricade themselves in the inner city."

"I will alert the Red Dawn," Dandio said, and left the room with the generals.

Andros turned to Mel and Misty. "It would ease my heart if you were both safely away before the Aces arrive. Should you wait too long to flee, your chance will be lost."

Mel took a breath and glanced at Misty. "We're staying. I came here to understand Luet's scrolls, and I can't give up on that now. There might be a power that could save this whole city."

He half wondered if the lord would order him to go, but Andros only nodded. "So be it. We will protect the New Blood."

Mel nodded gratefully, trying to calm his fear. He'd promised to keep Misty safe, to return if the mission got too dangerous—but what they were working to learn was too crucial to abandon now. They would stay together, seeking the elusive secrets Luet had left for them.

The council hall became a blur of movement as the respective generals and captains carried out their orders. Mel and Misty made for the door, weaving through the many people. Chief Kadryion's dark eyes met Mel's as they entered the corridor beyond.

"You are the New Blood?" the chieftain inquired.

"Yes, sir," Mel said.

Kadryion smiled slightly. "Your mentor told us much about you. I am very glad to see you released from the Aces' clutches. It is good that you are staying," he added softly. "Your task is not yet complete."

He turned down the corridor, leaving Mel staring after him in confusion and curiosity. *Your task is not yet complete.* He'd heard those words before, from Cahadras, when he'd first sworn the Blood Oath.

Perhaps he was exactly where he was meant to be for this moment. Perhaps the knowledge awaiting him was worth the risk of staying.

Voices echoed through the halls and up the stairs as they headed to the suite above the fort. The setting sun filled the quiet space with red light. Mel moved to the window, his mind still reeling from the turn the afternoon had taken.

So the battle had come to Tinkeeyo. The siege Dandio had feared was coming, and soon, he and Misty would be caught in the middle of it, entangled in a mission they were yet to understand.

"I'm going to write a letter to Mom," Misty said finally. "In case… in case the roads get blocked, and we can't get word to her later."

Mel nodded wordlessly.

Outside, red sunlight illuminated the forested hills and the crowded streets of Tinkeeyo, where the rumor of fear began to spread. It whispered on the wind like a dryad's voice, returning Mel's thoughts to Aryion.

By the time the sun vanished over the hills, Mel heard the distant thud as the gates were closed. Already, a dark shadow had appeared in the west, spreading its merciless reach toward the waiting city. From this distance, Mel could not make out details, but the darkness and icy cold were all too familiar.

There was no time for second guessing, no chance to flee now. The Aces were coming, and the siege had begun.

21

A Meeting of Peace

Heavy smoke filled Allie's nose and stung her eyes as she and the warriors entered Bridgeport.

Aside from the soft voices from a few wondering townsfolk as they watched the group of Brownaes and Guardians, and the distant clinks of machinery from the whale oil refineries, the city was nearly silent. Allie figured this was a good sign—it reiterated the hope that the Dal-kerri had been driven from Gayrile. In fact, since the attack on the ridge four days ago, they had seen no sign of wolves nor serpentines. Still, the dull silence of Bridgeport grated on her nerves, and she tightened her grip on her sword hilt.

"It's all right," Darion said beside her, seeing her tension. "I don't see any signs of Dal-kerri here—nor rebel Direns, for that matter."

"The delegates should arrive at the meeting hall around noon," Porcini said, glancing around. "That's what we arranged." He sounded calmer than anyone else, but there was nervousness in his eyes too.

Still, maybe they were worrying for nothing. The rebel groups had already agreed to come peacefully, granted the same rule applied to the Chanterelle and their allies. Those who attended the meeting must come unarmed.

Allie didn't like this part of the agreement, but she knew it was necessary. Assuming all went well today, the conflict would be resolved, the Direns would be united, and they could turn their attention to fighting the Aces together.

No—her concern was less in the outcome of the meeting, and more in the day itself.

Bridgeport sat perched on craggy cliffs overlooking the sea, tilted slightly toward the sea by the gradual rise of the slope. The waterfront, typically filled with fishermen or boatmen tending to their crafts, was as silent as the rest of town. Allie noticed two Cooper ships among the vessels in the harbor. Jarus and the delegation from Mata City would be waiting for them at the council.

"It's very quiet," Rygal murmured, brow furrowed with concern. The cut on his leg had begun to heal, but he still walked with a slight limp.

"It's been like this for weeks," Morel replied. "People are afraid to be outside for long periods of time since the rebels attacked the oil refineries."

"Why the refineries?" Darion wondered.

"Whale oil is Bridgeport's main export," Rygal told him. "Attacking the refineries is a sure way to cripple the economy here. Plus," he added with a crooked grin, "they're quite impressive when they blow up. If the rebels want to send a message, that's a clear way to do it."

Morel rolled her eyes in his direction. "Oh, you *would* know that. Point is—Bridgeport's quieted down. Now that the Guardians are back, things should start to improve."

Allie glimpsed a few faces peering at them through the dirty windows of the houses, their eyes following the armored Guardians in the midst of the group. Two small children played in a muddy side street, and looked up with interest as they walked by. Hope lit their faces, and Allie smiled at their excited whispers.

Word traveled fast. Through every soot-streaked hovel and worn down neighborhood, shutters opened and people peered out, eager to glimpse the return of the Guardians. Others opened their front doors, some calling out a greeting or raising a hand in exuberant welcome.

Rygal gave a brief salute to one of them, looking as though he was trying to conceal a smile.

"You're enjoying this, aren't you," Morel said.

"If there's ever a reason for a little publicity," Rygal told her, "it's this. The Guardians are back, Bridgeport is protected, and we're finally making peace with the rebels."

"Fair point," Morel conceded, as she gave a rare smile to a small child waving excitedly to them.

Voices filled the streets as the group walked on, joyful and eager. The Guardians represented more than skilled soldiers to the people here. To the people of Gayrile, these were the warriors who had always defended them, protected them, battled foes against insurmountable odds and risked everything to save them. These were the warriors who had faced the tyrannical queen Kircadash, the cruel sorcerer Safacon, and now, the Guardians would protect Gayrile from the Aces.

Allie turned her attention back to the coming meeting as they reached the town hall, a squat brick building with the flag of Gayrile fluttering in front of it. A group of government officials awaited them outside, along with a delegation of Coopers. One of them padded forward as they approached, his dark fur tousled by the sea wind and a smile shining in his blue eyes.

"Glad you could make it. How's the Wandering Wood?"

"Good morning, Jarus," Rygal said with a grin. "The Wood's exactly as you'd remember it."

"Oh, not too fondly," Jarus replied wryly, turning his smile to the others. "Hello, Allie, Darion. It's very good to see you again. Morel, Porcini—it's been too long."

"Good to see you, Jarus," Morel said, no longer bothering to conceal her smile. "How's Maya?"

"Very well—one of her ship designs has been adapted by the Mata City navy," Jarus said proudly, moving back toward the delegates. "But I suppose I'll have to tell you more later. Let's get this meeting underway. You've met Governor Geoffrey, I assume?"

A portly man with rosy cheeks stepped forward, greeting them enthusiastically. "Welcome back, Guardians, welcome back."

"Thank you, Governor," Rygal said, shaking his hand. "We're ready to put this business behind us." He introduced the rest of the group. The governor bowed low to Allie.

"Thank you for coming, Heiress," he said. "You cannot imagine the comfort it is to know Caer Sia wishes to aid our cause."

Allie curtsied to him with a smile. She'd worn her leather armor over a knee-length tunic. Not particularly fancy, but more formal than her usual trail clothes, and it gave her security knowing she was somewhat prepared for battle.

"The forest clans should arrive momentarily, but Lord Casper and his councilors are here already," the governor said, ushering forward a tall Diren with glittering red scales. His face was young—mid-twenties, Allie guessed, though it was hard to tell with a Diren. His golden eyes were serious as he clasped Rygal's hand. "I am glad to see you again, son of Maran. It has been some time since your companions met us in Flameton."

"It's good to see you, your highness," Rygal replied, smiling. "Will Neely join us today? Lammar mentioned she's been studying diplomacy."

The Diren lord's eyes sparkled at the name, and he glanced down with almost boyish pride. "No, I am afraid not. She sends her regards. We are to be wed this spring," he added, as though he could not contain himself.

"That's wonderful, sire," Morel said with a warm smile. "You are a very lucky man."

Casper nodded. "Yes—indeed. However, I fear we have more pressing matters." He was serious again in an instant. "Let us go inside."

They left their weapons in a chest just outside the door. Morel gave a few short orders to the Brownae warriors behind her. The Rufa would form a barrier around the city, as Allie recalled the plan, guarding the streets near the council hall. Meanwhile, a group of Guardians led by Captain Pike would protect the seaward side.

Bridgeport's council hall reminded Allie of Mata City's—blocky and square, with a similar layout to a courthouse. The foyer they gathered in was a rectangular corridor, with a side door to the left and a set of doors directly in front of them leading into the meeting room.

The rest of the Coopers waited inside. Jarus moved to speak to them—it seemed they already had a plan for the meeting.

"Governor, I trust you have the agenda?" Rygal asked once they were gathered.

"Ah, yes, yes," the governor replied, pulling a folded piece of paper from his breast pocket. "Well then—let's look it over before the negotiations begin. Five chieftains and three captains will represent the Forest Clans today. For the Coonsian alliance, the representatives shall be from the Brownaes, the Guardians of Gayrile, the Crown of Flameton, and the High Crown of Caer Sia."

He pulled out a different page. "The Clans have three requests, which they will present today. They are," he cleared his throat briskly, "as follows. One: the Crown of Flameton will restore all areas of the western mountains to them. Two: the Clans shall remain independent of Caer Sia's rule and submit only to their respective chieftains. Three: the Clans shall remain independent of all Mainland conflicts they are not directly involved in."

Mainland conflicts, Allie thought dryly. Was that their view of the Ace-war?

"And… if we aren't able to grant them these terms?" Porcini asked slowly.

"We *can't* grant them those terms," Morel said bluntly. "Remaining independent of Caer Sia is just a request to keep starting petty fights whenever they feel like it." She looked at Allie. "Be prepared to argue that point, Heiress. They need to submit to Caer Sia if we're going to get anywhere."

"I'm prepared," Allie said, though she felt anything but. "But what are we going to do if we deny all their terms? Unless you give them their land," she added, looking at Lord Casper and his councilors.

The Diren lord shook his head firmly. "Those lands were hard fought and hard won. Many of them now house farms and villages. I cannot just hand my people over to these insurgents."

"Right, then," Rygal said tiredly, running a hand through his hair. "Do we have any counter-terms?"

The governor nodded. "Of course. We have two terms we request the clans comply with: firstly, that the Forest Clans swear allegiance to Caer Sia, and secondly for them to present a set tax to the Sian Crown as surety."

"They'll never agree to that," Darion said, frowning deeply. "Besides, we can hardly enforce those terms, governor. None of the other Garilian nations have to pay tax to Caer Sia—that's the whole reason the Garilian

Agreement was ever formed. It meant the people of Gayrile could remain independent of Caer Sia and elect their own leaders, but appeal to the crown if they ever needed protection."

"That's true," Rygal agreed uneasily, "but what would you suggest to the rebels, then? They've never followed the Agreement."

"They need to understand we're on their side," Darion said. He seemed to be thinking hard. "They need to be assured that we're here to help them, and that we actually want to stop the fighting. They can't just be told the only way to peace requires them surrendering and submitting to a lord they don't want—that's just tyranny."

"As much as I'd like to argue," Morel said, "he's right. Ordering the rebels to do something they're already opposed to will just escalate the fighting again."

"So what should our terms be?" Allie asked.

The governor folded the page and mopped his brow. "Well, we might try discussing it with the rebels themselves. That's what this negotiation is for—examining both sides of the issue. Perhaps they will be more inclined to hearing us out after we've talked the matter through."

"Assuming the rebels haven't made any new friends lately," Morel said darkly.

"The perimeter's secured," Rygal reminded her. "The Rufa will keep any lingering Dal-kerri out of Bridgeport."

"We may as well go take our seats," the governor said. "Lord Casper, shall we?"

He headed into the room with the Direns and Coopers, speaking quietly. Rygal and Porcini went to talk to Jarus.

Allie lingered in the foyer, her eyes scanning the streets outside from the open door. Rygal was right, she told herself. The city was protected.

Any attackers would have to get past the Rufa warriors to reach Bridgeport.

Her gaze rested on a side door to her right. Three barrels were stacked in front of it, seemingly blocking it from use—at least from this side.

"You all right?" Darion asked. He faced the front entrance, leaning against the wall.

"Where do you suppose that door leads?" Allie asked, nodding to it.

Darion studied the door. "I'm not sure. Storage, maybe?"

"Storage in a foyer?" Allie repeated, raising her eyebrows.

"I think it goes outside," Morel told her. "And now that you've brought it up, we should secure that door, wherever it goes. I'd rather be certain of our entrances and exits."

She moved toward the main entrance, but stopped at the sound of rhythm of marching feet. In another moment, the Direns entered the meeting hall.

Allie stepped aside to allow the rebel Direns to pass, watching them intently. In contrast to the Direns from Flameton, with polished scales and elegant manner, these warriors were filthy, scales streaked in mud and stained by travel. Several of them had tattered wings or large scars. Their eyes were different, too—shifting about the room, taking in each person present, scanning for potential threats or escape routes.

"Smile at them, Allie," Darion said through a tight grin, nodding respectfully to the rebels.

Allie realized she had been staring with undisguised hostility—she adjusted her expression, putting on what she hoped was a welcoming, understanding smile. The chieftains ignored her entirely, but the three captains, to her surprise, returned her smile with simple nods. That was encouraging. Perhaps Darion's hope was right, and the rebels were just as tired of fighting as their opponents.

"Something's off," Morel hissed as the rebels headed into the meeting hall. "Didn't you notice? There were supposed to be eight. There's only six—three captains, and three chieftains. Where's the other two?"

"Maybe they backed out?" Allie suggested.

"They can't back out," Darion murmured, voice heavy with concern. "We need all five clans represented for the negotiations to be signed. Is there a way we can get word to them?"

"Nothing that would return in time," Morel replied. "Their clans are in the north—near the place we've seen Dal-kerri activity. Either they're long gone… or they're coming with company."

Chills ran down Allie's spine, and she was suddenly acutely aware of their unarmed state.

"What should we do?" Darion asked quietly. "Postponing the meeting will cause problems."

"Without the other chieftains, we can't negotiate anything," Morel said shortly. She thought for a moment, her jaw set in a rigid line, before starting for the door. "Go inside and stall them. I'm going to check on the guard posts, see if they've seen or heard anything. And I'm going to block up that door," she added, nodding to the side door.

This was hardly much of a plan, Allie thought, but she could do nothing besides follow Darion into the meeting hall.

Daylight streamed through the soot-stained windows. The delegates were seated around a circular table that took up most of the room. The representatives sat in distinctive groups—rebels and allies. Muttered and suspicious conversations filled the room like the black smoke outside.

She and Darion moved to sit near the Guardians. Rygal leaned over, his face worried. "What's going on? Where are the other rebel chieftains? And where's Morel?"

"We don't know, she went to find out, and she told us to stall," Darion answered.

Rygal shook his head. "That's very like her."

"Stall?" Jarus whispered, his furry face wrinkled in concern. "Stall for how long?"

"Figure something out," Allie said with an uncertain shrug. "Morel should be here soon."

One of the rebel chieftains spoke up crisply. "I assume this meeting will now commence?"

Jarus straightened, forcing a friendly smile. "Soon, sir. We're waiting for your brethren from the north to arrive."

"Perhaps we could start with roll," the governor suggested pleasantly.

Roll. Good. Anything to stall for time. Allie listened as the governor listed off the names of the representatives, the councilors, and the rebel chieftains and captains, skipping over those who had not yet arrived. That was over quicker than she'd hoped.

"Well, then," Governor Geoffrey said awkwardly, as tense silence stretched on again. "I, ah, trust you've all had time to look over one another's terms?"

"We have," Lord Casper said, his voice edged in distaste as he looked across the table at the rebels.

"Likewise," one of the rebel chieftains replied shortly.

Rygal cleared his throat. "Terms aside," he began slowly, "I believe I can speak for everyone here in saying we wish to end this conflict before any more of our warriors are lost. Lord Casper, your soldiers have given their lives defending their homes," he said, gesturing to Casper, who nodded briefly. "And you've lost warriors too," Rygal added, looking at the rebel leaders. Allie noticed none of the chieftains deigned reply, but two of their captains nodded.

"This argument is not worth losing any more lives," Porcini said. "Regardless of what you fight for, you raise your blades against brothers."

"Hasn't there been enough Diren blood spilled in Gayrile?" Jarus asked gently. "You fought against Kircadash, against Safacon, against Deathcap, and now, against one another. We brought our own terms," his paw touched the page before him lightly, "but we lay them down now, in favor of discussion."

Casper glanced at him uneasily, and the governor looked surprised, but Allie understood what he was trying to do. The rebels were wary to cooperate, believing they would be forced into a decision. They needed to be assured this meeting, and its terms, would benefit them too.

"We have little to say," one of the captains said at last, his emerald green scales bearing the scars from many battles. "We were told..."

"There is nothing to say," his chieftain interrupted, turning to face Casper. "Our terms are before you, *my lord*. Accept and we will have peace. Deny and there will be blood. There is nothing to discuss."

"I could say the very same to you," Casper snapped. "What lies were you told? That we intended to ensnare you in false promises and force you to bow your knees to another tyrant?"

"Flameton abandoned our people to Safacon," one of the other chieftains argued. "Are we to believe this will not happen again?"

"Safacon betrayed us all," Rygal cut in. "He betrayed everything we stand for—Diren, Brownae, human alike, we were all wronged by Safacon."

"Safacon is dead," Darion said, speaking slowly and clearly. "That past is behind us. This is the war you need to concern yourselves with now. Now is the time to forge an alliance, for the good of all your people."

"We have heard of your war, Mainlander," the first chieftain said shortly. "We have been assured our clans will not be involved, as long as we remain as we are. If *you* choose to fight against the shadow," he added, looking at Casper, "that is not our concern. But do not weep to us when your sons and daughters lie slain in the streets, when the white ice consumes their Essence, when darkness claims your land."

Allie exchanged a quick glance of unease with Darion. Rygal looked between the waiting rebels, his face drawn with sudden fear. "You were assured?"

The leader raised his chin defiantly. "We trust the source. The Messenger of old has told us of the great power of his master and the futility of your fight. There will be no further negotiation."

Cold, icy cold, seemed to grip Allie's heart in dread. She realized, far too late, that they had been tricked. Trapped. The rebels had nothing to say, because someone else had come to speak for them.

In another moment, as though on cue, a massive shadow prowled into the room. Claws raked the polished wood floor and a snarling voice as cold and dark as night filled the room.

"There will be no negotiations," Redeyes echoed, his pitiless eyes flashing in satisfaction. "The Ace-Lord may take your bones. I," he hissed, teeth glinting, "will have the blood promised me."

22

Inferno

Allie's hand reached to her side where her sword usually hung, already knowing it wasn't there. It was outside—outside where the defenses Morel had so carefully planned still waited, unaware of the deception that had occurred within.

At Redeyes' appearance, everyone reacted at once. Rygal and the Guardians leapt to their feet, along with Lord Casper and his councilors.

"What treachery is this?" Casper shouted at the rebels. "We agreed to negotiate this conflict. Now you claim that was never your intent."

"Do not claim treason, Casper," the leader snapped back, but he was the only one of his party who seemed able to speak. The rebel captains were staring at Redeyes in shock, and the other chieftains looked nervous. "We brought our terms. You refused them. This battle will be by your own making."

"There will be no battle," Rygal barked, raising his hands for silence and staring at the rebels. "Listen to me. This won't help anything. You can still walk away from this—leave the Aces and join us, before the Ace-Lord claims Gayrile."

Redeyes' low growl held a cruel note of amusement. "No battle? There can be nothing besides it. These loyal clans led us into Gayrile, to their lands," he said, his flashing eyes fixed on the six rebels. "Their choice is already made."

Approaching feet and panting snarls came from the door. Allie swung around, fire sparking in her fists, but what she saw seemed to snuff the flames away. Framed in the doorway, prowling into the room, were more Dal-kerri than she had ever seen before. They filled the entry hall like a foul fog, a sea of teeth and hackles, huffing and scenting the air for blood.

Darion's voice spoke over the wolves' growls. "Whatever deal you've made with the Ace-Lord isn't worth it—please believe me. Turn away from them and help us fight."

"Listen not to the ranger," Redeyes purred, eying Darion with so much hatred that Allie gripped his arm as if to shield him. "His curse will only continue to harm those near him."

"You know nothing of our deal, ranger," the rebel chieftain snapped back. He and his comrades stood, moving out of the way as the Dal-kerri entered the room. "You do not know our purpose here. Centuries of oppression and wrongs—now, we will have revenge. The Aces will rid Gayrile of your filth," he spat, jabbing a finger in Casper's direction, "and we shall rule when you are gone."

Darion's face was pale, but his eyes remained fixed on the chieftain. "I might not know the details of your deal," he said, "but I understand your fear. You've allied with the Aces out of desperation, trying to protect your clans, your warriors, your families. This isn't the way to help them."

For the first time, a glimmer of uncertainty showed in the eyes of the chieftain, but then he shook his head. "No. No more words. There will be death, as was promised."

"Indeed," Redeyes growled softly. He prowled closer to the rebels, his gaze sweeping over them. "And the Ace-Lord knows how to reward those faithful to him."

Allie knew what was coming moments before the Dal-kerri lunged forward. Redeyes sprang, leaping upon the rebel leaders—a swipe of his massive claws, and the chieftain fell, headless, to the floor. In a blur of startled cries and flashing fire, the other rebels fought back—Allie could hear their frantic struggles as the wolves sprang over the table to attack.

A hound slammed into her, knocking her backward. The room filled with screams and shouts. The councilors were helpless—even those who could fight were unarmed. She'd lost sight of Rygal in the fray—he seemed to have moved to help Lord Casper. Fire flared from the hands of the outnumbered Direns, fending off the snapping fangs.

She kicked a wolf that lunged at her—its teeth closed on her trouser leg, ripping the fabric. Staggering upright, she let the red flames fly. The room was in chaos, chairs toppled, table broken in half under the Dal-kerri. Blood streaked the floor, making it sticky. Two Diren councilors had fallen defending their king. She saw the furry forms of four dead Coopers, and felt a flare of panic, looking around for Jarus.

"Allie!"

Darion's shout drew her attention. He knelt, reaching for something in his boot. "We need to get the delegates out of here—see if there's a way outside!"

Allie jumped onto a chair, peering back toward the entrance. All she could see was a sea of bristling black fur and snarling teeth. "I can't!" she cried with a surge of panic. "The main door is blocked!"

"We'll try the side door, then," Darion called back, drawing a short knife from its concealment in his boot. He gave a slight shrug at her surprised expression. "What? I'm understanding, but I'm not dumb."

Allie shook her head, unable to come up with a retort. "Find Jarus and the other Coopers and try to get them out the side door. I'm going to help Rygal."

"What about Redeyes?" Darion asked.

"Don't attack Redeyes!" Allie ordered. "Stay away from him—don't you dare take him on alone!"

She plunged back into the fray before she heard Darion's reply. Red fire crackled in her hands, searing Dal-kerri fur. Wolves howled in fury and pain, snapping at the hated flames. Allie kept her gaze focused on the barrier of Direns, who were desperately fending off the hounds.

The fear, the fury, the emotions she'd pressed down since the fight in Appledale, blazed to the surface. Fire roared in her veins, licking up her arms, dancing in her hair. Teeth snapped at her hands, but she blazed on, striking again and again until she lost track of time. Only when a sickening headache replaced the fury did she stop, bracing herself against the blood streaked table, gasping for breath.

Her vision blurred. Someone was shouting, the voice echoing past the ringing in her ears—Rygal, maybe, but she couldn't tell. "Go! Go now!"

Vaguely, she saw the Diren delegates hurrying past her, fleeing through the breach she'd opened. She stumbled after them, trying to summon the flames again, but they did not come, exhausted by the inferno of red. Her heart ached with each beat as if her very Essence had been torn from her. Her breath rasped in her lungs.

The bodies of the rebel Direns lay broken and torn where they'd fallen. Five, all killed by Redeyes. The sixth must have fled in the chaos of the attack. There was no telling if he'd made it out, or if it mattered anymore—the negotiations had gone up in flames.

She tripped over a body—someone caught her arm before she fell.

"Allie? Allie?" Rygal's voice was filled with fear.

"I'm all right," Allie mumbled, blinking to clear the dizziness. "Just… fired… too much." She'd been warned of this before, at some point in her life. A Fyrocrian only had so much Essence to be spent at a given time. She'd never come this close to expending it all, leaving her as faint as if she were bleeding out.

"Come on—we're getting out of here." Rygal slung her arm over his shoulders, half dragging her to the door.

"Where's Redeyes?" Allie managed to pant.

"I don't know—I think he went back out this way after he killed the rebels." Rygal's face was pale. "Darion was right—the Aces just needed the rebels to get them into Gayrile undetected, and then Redeyes was here to take care of them once they'd served their purpose."

"Then… why arrange the negotiation at all?" Allie stammered weakly.

"It got everyone in one place. Made it that much easier for the Dal-kerri to take us out, just like Morel thought—have you seen her?"

"No," Allie replied, a fresh wave of fear chilling her throbbing heart.

They entered the front hall. Dal-kerri pressed against the main door, held back by a faltering line of Brownaes. Porcini was with them, wielding a short spear. "Head that way!" he called, gesturing to the side door. "Watch out for the Rufa—they're guarding the exit, I don't know if Morel's cleared them out yet."

"The Rufa?" Allie repeated, shocked.

"They're on the Aces' side too," Porcini stammered. "They let the Dal-kerri through the perimeter."

Rygal swore under his breath. "We should have expected that—who lets Dal-kerri camp beside your base for three days straight?"

"Get your group out of here, Porcini," Allie said, stepping forward unsteadily. "We can hold this door—get your warriors out."

Porcini hesitated, but nodded. "Here are your weapons," he said, holding them out. "You'll probably need them."

Allie took her blade, but slid it back into its scabbard. Fire would be a stronger defense against the wolves. She turned back to Rygal. "You need to go with the Brownaes—help them get out."

"Sorry, princess," Rygal replied with a wink, "but you don't outrank me anymore." He clashed his sword against his shield, sending golden sparks flashing along the rim and blade.

Allie managed to grin. "All right, then."

"Whenever you're ready," Porcini called. "Three… two… one… go!"

At his order, the Brownaes broke away, sprinting for the side door. The Dal-kerri howled in triumph as their opponents retreated, leaping through the door into the council hall—directly into the fire waiting for them.

As before, Allie sensed the inferno coming, but this time she fought it down. Another attack like that might render her unconscious from the loss of Essence. Instead, she remained on the defensive, back to back with Rygal, sending blasts of red at the wolves lunging at them. Over and over she let the fire fly, and yet the hounds kept coming. Her heart throbbed in her chest, her arms ached, but she fought on. Any pause, any faltering, and the wolves would kill them both.

Rygal's sword was a blur as he cut down the Dal-kerri before him, but fresh blood streaked his pantleg, and Allie could sense he was tiring. "Go," she panted. "Get to the door—get out of here."

"Not today," Rygal grunted back.

Allie sent another wave of flames at four wolves—they were flung back, red sparks glistening on their fur, but she felt her legs give out.

She fell to her knees, head pounding, hands stained by umber blood. "Rygal… go…" she rasped, trying desperately to stand.

A new pack of Dal-kerri sprang through the door, leaping towards her. Allie raised herself to her knees, fire flickering uncertainly in her hands, bracing herself for the blast that would undoubtedly end it all.

Until a golden plume of fire caught the nearest hound, flinging it back before it could bite her.

Fire filled the room, blasting the Dal-kerri back through the door, joining her weary red flames. Allie turned, gathering her breath painfully.

Rygal stood behind her, pressing the Dal-kerri back. The sparks had transformed into golden fire, spreading up his sword and shield, wreathing him where he stood. The wolves fled before it—those that didn't were cut down.

A hand grabbed Allie's arm, pulling her to her feet—Darion. Through the ringing she heard him calling for Rygal to follow. Rygal retreated slowly, sending blasts of gold flame at any hounds that pursued.

They stumbled through the side door, descending a short flight of damp stairs leading to a narrow hall. Allie placed her hand against the cold wall, steadying herself as she caught her breath.

"Looks like you've figured out fire," Darion commented, impressed, as Rygal slammed the door behind them.

"I suppose so," he answered, sounding as surprised as they were. Allie felt his hand rest on her arm, still warm from the golden flames. "You're all right? You're not hurt?"

"No, I'm—I'm fine now," Allie answered. Her head still ached, but she felt her strength returning.

"The delegates made it out safely," Darion said as they hurried down the hall. "This passage opens out on the far side of town, facing the mountains."

"That means we'll be cut off from the Wandering Wood," Allie said worriedly.

"I don't think we can go back to the Wood anyway," Rygal said. "We'd only lead the Dal-kerri back to the Chanterelle tribe. Our best bet is to get out of Bridgeport and regroup somewhere secure."

Distant cries and howls came from outside. Allie forced herself to keep moving, pushing away the chilling fears of what was likely happening in the streets. As soon as they got out of the council hall, they could join the battle and save the people of Bridgeport.

A massive black shadow moved in front of her in the hallway, crimson eyes flashing in the dark.

"Darion!" Allie shouted, shoving him back. Claws raked the air before her face. Light blazed as Rygal sprang in front of them, lowering his sword at Redeyes.

The great cat snarled in hatred, teeth glinting. "Fools," he hissed. "Protect the Vessel if you will—there is nothing you can do to save her."

He lunged. Rygal raised his shield—Redeyes shoved him down, claws shrieking over the steel. Yellow fire licked the cat's face, but he did not relent, clawing at Rygal's shoulders and neck. Darion loosed an arrow into Redeyes' back, and the beast rounded on him with a growl.

"No!" Allie yelled, leaping between Redeyes and her two companions. "Get out of here, both of you—he's not going to hurt me."

Rygal staggered to his feet, hesitated, but finally obeyed, and he and Darion rushed for the door.

"Vessel," Redeyes snarled again. His bloodied claws glinted in the red fire, but he did not attack her. "You are very lucky my master has ordered you to be kept alive. Trust that your purpose has a limit—as soon as it has expired, I shall tear your head from your body."

"Too bad that time hasn't come yet," Allie retorted, backing slowly down the hall.

"No," Redeyes hissed. "I cannot kill you—but that does not protect your friends. Nor does it prevent me from bringing you near to death, either."

He sprang, claws slashing at her face. Allie ducked, letting the fire fly, but it was still weak, and flickered out as it left her hands. She stumbled back against the door, collapsing into the smoke-filled alley behind the council hall.

Redeyes' breath wafted in her face as his teeth snapped above her, and she crawled back, unable to defend herself. Three gunshots split the air behind her before the claws could make contact. Redeyes reeled back into the hallway with a roar of pain, vanishing into the shadows.

"You talk too much," Morel said, smoke trailing from the tip of her rifle.

Rygal's hand pulled Allie to her feet, and she caught her breath shakily. The side passage opened onto a cobblestone alleyway between the council hall and the neighboring building. Black smoke hung thick in the air along with the distant echoes of Dal-kerri howls.

The weary group around her consisted of Brownaes, Coopers, Direns, and Guardians. Nearly everyone who'd attended the deadly council was injured in one way or another. Jarus' fur was streaked in Dal-kerri blood.

"Was that the end of Redeyes?" the Cooper panted, looking uncertainly toward the hallway.

"I doubt it," Morel said, shouldering her rifle.

"It was satisfying to watch, all the same," Darion commented. "But what are we going to do about the Dal-kerri?"

Morel let out a breath as she turned to Rygal. "Negotiations are scrapped—our priority now is to get out of here. I'd expect the Dal-kerri to follow us."

"Yes," Rygal said uncertainly, "but we're in the center of the city. We can't lead them back to the Wandering Wood."

"I figured," Morel said heavily, shaking her head. "Well, we can head into the hills. We should be able to throw the wolves off our trail, and we can make camp up there." She pointed northeast, toward the slow rise of craggy mountains.

"That is rebel land," Lord Casper informed her. "The Clans will undoubtedly kill us if we go there."

"Would you rather fight them, or the Dal-kerri?" Morel asked dryly. "It's probably our only chance."

"There's a port to the east," Rygal added. "Near Safacon's old haunts. If we could send for help, a relief force could meet us there."

"*If*," Allie repeated worriedly. "No one knows what's happened here."

"I can make it to the harbor," Jarus put in. "The Cooper frigates are still there. I can get to Mata City, let Lord Roan know what's going on, and request help. Then we can meet you at the port in the valley."

"That's too risky," Rygal said, shaking his head.

"If we don't try, we can say good bye to Gayrile," Jarus said firmly. "You'd take the same risk for me. I'm smaller and less noticeable than any of you—I can slip back through town and reach one of our ships."

Rygal still looked worried, but Morel nodded. "I trust you can make it. Go quick and be careful—I don't know how we'd face Maya if you got hurt."

"Me neither," Jarus said with a weak grin. "Just try to stay alive until I'm back." With that, he turned and bounded down the road.

Allie had little time to fear for him—a new round of howls sounded nearby. Morel turned to the weary group. "Porcini, lead them north. We'll cover your backs. Move fast, and don't stop, not for anything."

Her brother nodded and led the councilors at a brisk but maintainable pace up the road. The warriors—around thirty Guardians, and the same number of Chanterelle Brownaes—formed up at Morel's command. Allie walked beside Rygal and Darion, letting the fire flicker from her fingertips.

The council hall had only just vanished from view behind them when a Brownae gave a cry of warning. Teeth snapping, a pack of Dal-kerri sprang from the shadows, bounding uphill after them.

Morel shouted a command, her voice quickly drowned out by the crackle of Brownae gunfire. Allie blasted down a wolf that sprang for Darion's turned back, and saw his arrow strike down a hound before it attacked Rygal. Golden fire leapt from Rygal's sword and shield, mingling with the red flames sparking from Allie's fists.

At last the hounds pulled back, and the warriors pressed on, running north. Bat-like wings flapped overhead—Allie ducked just in time. "Get down!" she managed to scream. Four serpentines alighted on the road, bearing viperous fangs dripping venom.

"Don't let them bite!" Rygal warned, his sword cleaving the neck of a snake that pounced for Morel. Morel shot down another. More serpentines dove from above or crept from the alleyways like rats.

"Bear left!" Morel shouted, sliding six new shots into the revolving chamber of her rifle. "Get off this street!"

Allie fired another blast, edging back towards the alleyway Morel indicated. The rooftops nearly touched above them, protecting them from the serpentines' aerial assault. Porcini and the councilors vanished within, followed by the slowly retreating warriors. Darion brushed past her, supporting an injured Guardian.

Allie had just turned to follow when an icy cold gripped the air, and dread chilled her heart.

Darkness spread up the street behind them. Ice crystallized the puddles on the cobblestone ground. Through the refinery smoke strode an Ace—not the Ace-Lord or the Deputy. This one was bulkier, clad in iron armor, likely one of the guards Allie had noticed in Castle Droco. White ice glittered on its gauntleted hands.

"Go!" she screamed, gesturing wildly to the remaining Brownae warriors, her voice raw with fear. "Go now—before the—"

The Ace raised its hands, sending ice flying down the street— Allie fired a return blast, knowing the shot had gone awry as it left her hands. The pale ice struck a Guardian in the back of the group, and he fell lifeless to the street, Essence destroyed from within.

"In the alley, now!" Morel ordered, and the warriors retreated frantically.

Allie let the fire crackle towards the Ace, willing it to burn and destroy, but the wraith only brushed the flames aside with ice. Even if it could be destroyed by fire, it would take more than what she could summon. She stumbled into the alleyway after the others.

"Do they have a weakness?" Morel asked as they ran. "Anything we can use against it?"

"Fire," Allie said doubtfully, "but aside from that, I don't know."

"We'll need more than that," Rygal panted, his face drawn. "I've seen what they can do. Iriam's the only one who ever stood a chance against them—or Jan, maybe—but we don't have that kind of strength."

"I can," Allie said slowly. "I've done it before." This was a slight exaggeration—she'd barely managed to survive an encounter with the Ace-Deputy. But she *had* survived it. "I can hold it off while you retreat."

"Not in your condition," Morel replied shortly. "You're nearly spent. No—best thing we can do is keep going together."

They left the alley behind, turning up another street. A dead serpentine lay sprawled across the road, alongside the bodies of three Brownaes and a fallen Guardian. The clatter and cries of battle came from up ahead, and Allie could see warriors battling another pack of Dal-kerri. More hounds bounded into the fray as they watched.

Rygal and Morel ran to aid the weary warriors, and Allie jogged after them, the fire already flaring in her hands. She sensed exhaustion on the fringe of her efforts, warning her against channeling the inferno again, and she fought away the temptation to set the street ablaze. Not here. The fire must be precise, calculated, opening their way to freedom.

But there were so many hounds. She sensed her companions falling back, sensed the defense crumbling before the wolves. White ice flashed behind her, and a Brownae captain collapsed lifeless. Rygal's golden fire flickered away as he tired.

Now or never.

"Keep going!" she yelled. Gritting her teeth, she summoned every bit of fire she could manage, spreading her hands and trying to create a wall as she'd seen Iriam do with his ice. Red fire flashed around her in a perfect circle, searing Dal-kerri fur, intercepting a blast of ice before it struck a Guardian. Her arms trembled as the fire rose, the blood pounding in her head, her ears ringing. Through the haze she saw her companions retreating, fleeing up the road leading to the hills. The barrier rose to her height, trembled in place for a moment—and then flickered away as her strength vanished, and she collapsed to the bloodstained road.

Shouts pierced the fog in her head. Morel's voice—then Rygal's, filled with fear.

"Get her out of here, hurry—"

"Morel, watch your back!"

Wings swept the air above her—Allie drew herself up on her elbows, blinking rapidly, trying to clear her vision. Through the haze of pain she saw three serpentines close around Rygal and Morel. Morel shot the first down even as the teeth of the second snapped closed on the back of her neck. Rygal's sword hewed off its head—the third sprang at his back.

The fire came without being summoned, the last blast she could manage, finishing off the third serpentine.

Her vision blurred again, her hearing drowned out by her throbbing heart. She sensed Rygal raising her to a sitting position, heard his voice, edged in fear. "We can't just leave you…"

Morel had fallen to her hands and knees, gasping, bloodied froth leaking from the corner of her mouth. Blood trailed down her neck from the serpentine's venomous bite. She leaned on her rifle, raising her head with an effort. "Light above… just do as I say…"

"Morel…" Allie breathed, trying to stand—her knees gave out, and she sagged into Rygal's arms. She felt him lift her, sensed him retreating, and fought his hold weakly. "No—Morel—we can't leave her—"

At the end of the street, sweeping through the smoke from the city's largest refinery, came the Ace, moving relentlessly forward.

Morel dragged herself to her knees and coughed, blood running down her chin. Arms shaking, she raised the rifle at the Ace.

Rygal stopped at the edge of the next building. Allie leaned against the wall, knowing she could not help, knowing she had to be ready for the Ace after it finished Morel. But the sight of the Brownae warrior, alone before the oncoming wraith, broke the little calm she had left.

Dal-kerri swarmed behind the Ace, prowling up the road. Slowly, mercilessly, the Ace stepped forward, ice crusting the stones at its feet as its eyes fixed on the dying Brownae.

"Morel…" Allie choked, her voice nothing more than a weak croak.

Morel's hands steadied on her rifle. Allie saw her take a deep breath, her eyes fixed on the Ace as it stepped into the shadow of the refinery.

And Morel smiled just before the gunshot split the expectant silence, shattering the window of the oil refinery and flinging a single lantern into a vat of oil.

The Ace swung around, far too late—in a deafening whoosh, the building exploded, spreading fire up the street. It engulfed the oncoming Dal-kerri, swallowed up the Ace and the lifeless bodies before it.

A wave of heat and rancid black smoke whipped Allie's face—Rygal pulled her into the alleyway, half-dragging her uphill as fire consumed the street behind them. Allie glimpsed the path before them leading toward the mountains, and could make out the distant forms of their worried companions far ahead.

Then her vision finally blurred away, and she was left in semi-conscious darkness, stumbling blindly to freedom, her back warmed by the fire's heat and her ears ringing from Morel's final shot.

23

∽ ∽ ∽ ∽ ∽ ∽ ∽ ∽ ∽

A Call to War

Cold. Gripping cold. It was the first time in her life that the fire had truly left her, and it returned slowly, bringing painful waking with it.

The darkness faded as the world came gradually into focus, along with a pounding headache. Allie put her hand to her forehead, grimacing as the light pierced her eyes. Dusk filled the woods around her. The trees above her were shorter and shabbier than those of the Wandering Wood, choked by sagebrush and scotch broom.

A fire burned a few paces away, and she could make out the outlines of a few Brownaes and Direns. Muted conversations murmured around her. Two people sat in the shrubs to her right, talking quietly—Darion and Rygal.

"We saw the fire… I thought she might have…"

"She's spent. I've heard about that—Fyrocrians using too much of their Essence—I don't know if she'll…"

"She's alive," Darion told him quietly. "Thanks to you." Allie saw him turn to look back down the hill, toward the smoky haze of Bridgeport. "I… assume there's no chance that…"

"You saw the explosion." Rygal shook his head, his voice heavy. "I suppose everyone saw it. Quite a show of strength, like we said earlier." He gave a short, humorless chuckle. "Everyone in Bridgeport would have seen the Ace go up in flames."

261

Morel.

Allie closed her eyes as the Brownae's last stand played in her memory. She'd only known Morel a few weeks. Yet that had been long enough to demonstrate her strength, her bravery, her loyalty. She'd stayed calm even when Allie had panicked during the Dal-kerri attack in the Wood. And she had remained steady and focused right to the end. Allie had seen the last triumphant smirk on her face before she'd blown up the refinery, taking the Ace and a whole pack of Dal-kerri with her.

A lump rose in her throat, but she swallowed it down as she sat up. Rygal and Darion looked over as she moved, relief spreading over both their faces. "How do you feel?" Rygal asked immediately.

"Sore," Allie replied. Her voice still rasped. Every muscle in her body ached, but that breathtaking exhaustion had gone. "Where are we?"

"Somewhere safe, for now," Darion said. "We're about five miles outside of Bridgeport."

Allie looked around, her eyes adjusting to the glaring evening sunlight. Rolling hills speckled with hedge-like trees stretched behind her as far as she could see, but the faint lights and smoky haze of Bridgeport still showed to the south. To her left, Topstorm Mountain lifted its craggy peak over Gayrile. Campfires burned around the hilltop, and she could see Brownaes, Guardians, and the surviving Direns of Lord Casper's retinue.

"The Coopers," she said slowly, as the thought occurred to her. "Did Jarus…"

"No word yet," Rygal said. "All we've heard was from one of our informants, who was in Bridgeport when the fight started—he confirmed Jarus reached the ship and headed back to Mata City."

"He made it out safe," Darion said, clearly searching for some encouragement. "With luck, he'll be back soon with help."

"Help," Rygal echoed wearily. "I'm not exactly sure what they can help with. We didn't come here to fight a war—now that war's come here, we're not equipped to end it."

"Could we get word to Sia?" Allie asked hesitantly.

"It'd take days—maybe weeks. The Aces have already locked down Bridgeport's harbor—Jarus barely made it out," Rygal replied. "No… any help for Gayrile will have to come from within." He let out a tired sigh. "We can rest here for now. I'll talk with the others and… try to come up with a plan," he finished uncertainly.

He looked so tired and defeated, grief etched on his face, so Allie didn't press for more. The three of them sat beside the campfire with the remaining leaders. Captain Pike sat with two other senior Guardians. Porcini was there too, his young face a mask of sorrow and exhaustion.

"I'm… sorry about your sister, Porcini," she ventured slowly, knowing no words could ease the hurt.

Porcini gave a small shrug, smiling sadly. "It's… it's how she always said she wanted to go down. Fighting for Gayrile." He turned away, his eyes bright with tears.

"It is how we all may go down now," Lord Casper said grimly. "If we could get word to Flameton, our forces might join us… but it is several day's journey through enemy land."

"Might be a better chance than Caer Sia, though," one of the Brownaes pointed out. "Assuming the Aces haven't blocked the northern roads as well as the sea."

"They will have them blocked soon," an older Diren councilor said, shaking his head.

"What about Kilee?" Darion asked. "Could we get help from any of the other Northern Isles?"

"The Hymian Empire collapsed years ago," Casper told him. "Any warriors still living there are little more than mercenaries, and we have nothing to offer them to buy their services."

"I think the only warriors we'll get are already here," Rygal said.

"And we're all prepared to follow you," Captain Pike said quietly. "With Morel gone, you are in command now. If you have a plan to reclaim Bridgeport, we will follow you."

Allie looked at Rygal. He stared into the fire, the light playing over his features. Finally he looked up, studying the warriors before him. "None of you came here to fight a war, and I won't ask it of you. But… if you're willing… I do have an idea."

No one spoke, but the expectant silence answered Rygal's question. He hesitated a moment longer, then spoke. "Norrin always said, in situations like these, the best thing to do is strike back soon. We lost, but we also took out a lot of Dal-kerri, and Morel killed the Ace that was leading the invasion. The only leadership they'll have left is Redeyes."

"Which isn't exactly a comforting thought," Darion said, frowning.

"No… but we know Redeyes isn't a strategist," Rygal said. "He's here to kill us all, and I think he'll take any bait we offer. Our scouts indicate that the Dal-kerri are all in Bridgeport. What I'd like to do is lure them this way, out of the city and to the port on the other side of the hills. Once we get them there, we can trap them by the sea, and the Cooper ships can help us defeat them."

"You believe the Coopers will come in time?" Casper asked uncertainly.

"Jarus will come through. He's never disappointed me yet," Rygal said firmly. "Either way, these hills are difficult to defend. A wide, clear space, like the beach where Safacon's fortress used to be, will ensure the Dal-kerri can't sneak up on us. We'll lure them into the open."

There was a pause. Casper finally shook his head. "I do not know if it will work. But it may be our best option."

"The Chanterelle will fight," Porcini said softly.

Rygal glanced at Allie. She managed a wry grin. "We don't really have anywhere else to go. I'm with you."

A faint smile crossed Rygal's face, and he nodded. "Good. Well… we'll work out a more detailed plan tonight."

Sagebrush rustled behind them as a Brownae scout moved to the fire. Allie gripped her sword hilt as she saw the worry on his face.

"Sir… the rebels are here," he stammered.

Everyone leapt to their feet. "How many?" Rygal asked immediately.

"Only three," the scout answered. He seemed more uncertain than afraid. "I recognize one of the captains—he attended the council. He said he wants to talk."

"Talk?" one of the Diren councilors repeated warily. "With their swords, I expect."

"I thought all the rebel captains were killed by Redeyes," Porcini said slowly.

"Not all of them," Allie said as she remembered the grisly scene. "I only saw five bodies—one must have escaped."

She looked at Rygal again, seeing his brow furrowed in thought. At last he nodded to the scout. "We may as well hear them out. But make sure they come unarmed."

Since the Direns could channel fire, that wouldn't help much, Allie thought worriedly. She kept a hand on her sword hilt, waiting tensely.

After a long pause, the scout returned with three Direns, surrounded by Chanterelle guards. The captain leading them had emerald-green scales, and his golden eyes regarded the wary faces carefully.

"We did not expect to see you still alive," he said at last.

"We might say the same about you," Rygal replied. His tone was level, but Allie could sense the distrust in every fiber of his body. "From what we've seen, you're the reason the Dal-kerri are here in Gayrile in the first place."

"That was not my decision," the captain informed him. "But as they are here now, it matters little." He glanced around the camp, then back to Rygal. "May we speak?"

"What is there to speak on?" Casper asked coldly. "You cannot expect us to agree to your terms now."

"Let us speak of Gayrile, then," the rebel replied.

Rygal seemed to consider this for a moment, then nodded slightly. "Very well. Come and sit."

He returned to the fire, motioning for the others to follow. The rebel captain sat across from him, his warriors standing close behind their leader. Allie remained standing behind Rygal. This captain may not have chosen to bring the Dal-kerri here, but that didn't mean they could trust him.

"I understand you are the Commander of the Guardians," the captain said after a pause.

"I am." Rygal's tone gave nothing away. He was getting good at this, Allie noted. A few years ago, he would have blustered and stammered his way through this sort of conversation, far more confident in his sword than in his words. The young man staring down the Diren before him was a completely different person, steady and sure.

"I am Captain Terivis," the Diren said. "Previously, I served under Chief Rellak, the leader of the Forest Clans. It was his plan to join with the forces of the Aces, to lead them into Gayrile undetected. In exchange, we were promised that they would defeat our enemies and leave us the kingdom."

"You betrayed Gayrile," Casper said, shaking his head in disgust. "You are here now only because you are desperate—had your chieftain's plan succeeded, we would be dead, your Clans would have their kingdom, and we would not be having this conversation."

"I did not agree with my chieftain's choice, Lord Casper," Terivis said crisply. "Nor did many of our clans. We are not the barbarians you believe us to be—few still adhere to the radical beliefs that Gayrile must be purged of all Cantrian blood."

"Then why fight for their cause?" Rygal asked.

Terivis looked down. "We… had families, homes. Many of us suffered under Safacon. Our own countrymen in Flameton offered no aid."

"We had no way to send aid to you at that time," Casper said with a frown. "King Makana would have helped if he could, but Safacon had us by the throat."

"Whatever the reason," Terivis said pointedly, "the Forest Clans suffered, so we rebelled, even if we did not fully agree with the extremist ideals of our leaders. After Safacon fell, we never thought to leave the rebellion. Our chieftains drew us into battle after battle, until we barely remembered why we fought. I lost countless men to a cause I could no longer explain."

He glanced around the evening camp, his green-scaled face grim. "When the Ace-war began, we were told that this fight would bring about our victory—the return of our lands and the end of Flameton. So our chieftains allied themselves with the Aces, with the intent to break from them as soon as our part in the war was over. But the Aces learned of this intended treachery. Instead of severing our arrangement, they offered something else. An enchantment, binding us forever to their dark lord."

Darion leaned forward, his face suddenly tense. "An enchantment?" he repeated slowly. "What did they tell you about the enchantment?"

Terivis looked at him, slightly confused by the unexpected question. "We… were told it is a powerful spell. But one must choose to take it. I watched many of my comrades do so. It is a spell that gives great strength, keeping one even from death."

"Yes," Darion said breathlessly, nodding. "Yes, we know what it is—but tell me how the Aces cast it. Tell me what happens when someone chooses it."

Allie looked at him, suddenly understanding. Up until now, everything they'd learned about the enchantment had come from their own investigations. Darion had known the Aces had claimed Wiverrun, but he hadn't been there to witness the actual enchanting of his friends and family. The only witness they'd talked to had been after the Kamon battle—Jan had told her that they'd interrogated a captive goblin who'd told them of the enchantment. But even the goblin servant hadn't seen the actual enchanting. This rebel sitting before them had.

Terivis thought for a long moment. "There is an oath, sworn in blood. A promise that binds the life of a mortal to the will of his master. Once sworn, the choice is irreversible—if blood will forge it, only blood can break it."

"But could the enchanted choose to leave the servitude?" Darion asked.

"That I do not know," Terivis said, looking uncertain. "Surely you have seen the enchanted—their minds are not their own. The curse itself would have to be broken before such a choice could be made."

"And… how would the curse be broken?" Allie asked, though she already knew. She'd known from the moment the words had hissed in her mind back in the middleworld between realms.

"I have told you," Terivis replied heavily. "Blood alone may break the curse—the Ace-Lord's. His Essence sustains the enchanted ones, and only in his death can they be freed."

When Lord of Death brings life to all.

So that was it. Allie had known it, had wrestled with it, and yet now, the fact seemed to snuff out any dread, any grief, that surrounded it, leaving her only with the fire. Death. The Ace-Lord must die if the soldiers were to be freed—and when that happened, she would die with him. The Vessel dragged into darkness by the icy chains that claimed her.

She sensed Rygal and Darion looking at her, felt the concern in their glance. She fought down the despair and managed a tight smile. "Suppose we should be glad to hear that as fact. There is a way to break the enchantment."

"Not like this," Darion said quietly. His scarred face was filled with emotions—disbelief, denial, fear.

"We already knew it was likely," Allie murmured back, looking down at her hands. The burns had faded, leaving the faint outlines of pale scars. "The Ace-Lord's death will end the war, and break the curse." Why did the thought not fill her with terror? Shouldn't she be angry at the very least? Her mind simply denied it, unable to accept the truth.

Terivis looked at his silent audience, pausing before continuing. "My clan, and the warriors with me, have no desire to choose the enchantment. That is why we left. We wish to strike against the Aces."

"Then why come to us here?" Casper asked slowly.

Terivis hesitated. "We do not have the numbers to defeat them alone. The Dal-kerri, the enchanted soldiers, the red-eyed demon—I do not know how many more are now here. Regardless, we are both outnumbered." He glanced between Casper and Rygal. "That said, together, our warriors may succeed."

Allie looked up, thoughts of the curse vanishing with surprise. The Diren councilors were frowning uncertainly. Porcini and the Brownaes looked startled. But Rygal looked like he was thinking hard. "An alliance?" he asked at last, studying the captain.

"Against the Aces," Terivis answered. "Our chieftains brought them here; it is only fitting we fight to drive them out. But we cannot do it alone. With your armies," he said, gesturing at the camp, "we may have a chance."

Rygal turned to Casper. The Diren lord thought for a moment. "I agree we cannot fight alone," he said at last. "My men are already weary, and we do not know these lands like the Forest Clans. But I cannot accept the terms your chieftains wished to put forth," he said firmly. "Not in good favor of my people."

"I have no other terms to offer," Terivis said uneasily. "But we must have assurance that you are on our side. My warriors will not fight without such terms."

There was a tense pause. Darion finally spoke. "What if… we suggest new terms, then. And make them the same for both sides."

Both Diren leaders looked at him uncertainly, and the young ranger went on. "You'll both have the freedom to choose and follow your own leaders. But you'll swear loyalty to Sia, just as the Garilian Agreement demands. You'll remain in your current kingdoms, and stop fighting for more land."

"Much of their kingdom was stolen from us," Casper argued. "That land must be returned."

"I could say the same," Terivis said briskly. "And I refuse to join the Liznee King. I will fight for Gayrile, but I cannot continue sending my men to die for meaningless wars."

"Meaningless?" Allie repeated. The fire flared hot in her veins, but her voice was calm. "After everything you've seen, you can't truly think this to be a meaningless war. You've seen what the Aces are capable of, you've seen the enchantment, you watched your chieftains die. This isn't some petty struggle on the Mainland that you can sit back and watch. Whether or not you want to fight, you're drawn into it now just like we are."

Terivis hesitated. Rygal spoke, his voice low. "This war involves Gayrile now. If we don't fight for it, the Ace-Lord will."

"And trust me when I say he'll win," Darion said. "By the time you've stopped arguing over whose land is whose, it will all belong to the Ace-Lord."

The Direns were silent. Allie sensed the rest of the camp listening intently. The warriors beside the fire watched with nervous expectancy.

At last Casper sighed. "Very well. I agree to these terms, if you will."

Terivis nodded. "As will I. For the good of our people."

The two stood and shook hands. Allie figured they should have written everything down. This alliance was far less formal than the one they'd planned to negotiate, without the politics or protocol that should have surrounded such a treaty. This was one forged by two leaders, both bearing recent scars and injuries from a battle that had lost them many friends and brothers, both exhausted of war. Despite the lack of formalities, she felt that this kind of agreement would last.

"Well, then," Terivis said, glancing at his warriors before fixing his gaze on Rygal. "You intend to fight against the Aces, despite the risk?"

Rygal turned to the waiting warriors. Direns, Brownaes, and Guardians stood silent on the edge of the fire. Allie could sense their fear, their grief, just as she felt her own.

"There's always a risk," Rygal said at last. "Anything worth doing comes with a risk. We will fight—not for our gain, not out of a foolish hope." He straightened, eyes scanning the warriors. "The Ace-Lord seeks to destroy us, and the enchantment may yet bind his warriors. But in that, he will fall. Thus fell Kado, and thus fell Safacon, and thus always to tyrants."

He drew his sword. A rising murmur of energy seemed to ripple through the waiting army.

"We will fight," Rygal said again. Fire played along the edge of his sword. His voice was firm with an authority Allie had only caught glimpses of before. "Fight for our families, fight for our homes, fight for those we've lost. We will fight for Gayrile."

"For Gayrile!" The words rose in a roar as the warriors shouted with one voice. The Guardians raised their staffs in answer, lighting the camp with multi-colored flames. Answering orange fire flashed in the hands of the Direns. The Brownaes shouted in response, clasping furred paws to their chests and raising their rifles above their heads.

Allie looked at Darion. His jaw was set in determination as he nodded. She turned back to Rygal, letting the crimson flames play on her fingertips, and felt herself smile at the anticipation of coming battle.

"For Gayrile."

24

Siege

Echoes of the surrounding enemy filled every waking moment as the siege of Tinkeeyo stretched on.

Mel had never observed a fight like this. The only battle he'd been a part of before had been in Kamon. That conflict had been relatively short—a full day spent fighting, until at last the battle had been won.

A siege was a slower, more brutal conflict.

The Ace-army arrived the same night as Quinn's report. Mel had lingered by the window in the upper room, unable to sleep, as the light of the city's lanterns illuminated the swarming army along Tinkeeyo's outskirts. He had never seen so many warriors in one place. The distant figures of enchanted soldiers—orcs, humans, goblins, Dwarves, and others—gathered at the edge of the city.

But it seemed the larger part of the force was comprised of Dal-kerri wolves. Serpentines had come too, along with four hulking creatures that seemed like smaller versions of the Bruin that Dandio had told him about. "Smaller" hardly meant much—while the beasts were nothing compared to the behemoth that had destroyed Castle Droco, these bear-like brutes were the size of carriages.

The creatures had yet to infiltrate the city, confined to skirmishes along various parts of the wall. But the noise still reached the fort periodically—clashing steel, cries and screams, shrieks and howls of the Dal-kerri.

And then the silence would settle again as the fight ended and the Dal-kerri withdrew into the tangled forest. The jarring quiet, where the fallen were counted, was somehow more terrifying to Mel than the previous sounds.

Mel supposed he should be grateful he didn't have to fight this battle. All the same, the unknowing of what was going on out there was nearly unbearable. Hearing the constant sounds, knowing he couldn't help, knowing that good soldiers were laying down their lives right now filled him with restless anxiety.

Dandio worked tirelessly, organizing the defense, joining the skirmishes, riding Nella to and from the walls. Occasionally he'd enter their rooms late at night—never for long, never more than a few hour's rest. He seemed as steady and determined as ever, but Mel could not ignore the gnawing fear that every time he left might be the last time he saw him.

Time passed slowly, the days blurring together. They had been in Tinkeeyo nearly three weeks—thirteen days of that were claimed by the siege, which showed no sign of lifting.

"The tide may turn in our favor soon," Dandio had told them last night, clearly hoping to reassure them. "Lord Andros has attempted to contact the kragons."

"The kragons?" Misty had asked hopefully, and Mel looked at Dandio in surprise. The massive hawk-like creatures inhabited the depths of the Magno Forest, and he knew Lord Fireclaw was loyal to Sia.

"Do you think they'll come?" he asked, studying the Liznee's scarred face carefully.

"We hope so," Dandio answered with a tired smile. "The kragons are historic enemies of the Aces. Our only concern is that our message may not be able to reach them—the Aces are watching the roads."

That was a problem. The Aces had Tinkeeyo gripped in a vice, barring all possibilities of travel. The kragons may fight willingly, but they may not even receive the call for help in time.

The door closed behind him, and Misty's voice drew him out of his thoughts. "Alder brought us some more scrolls."

Mel turned away from the window. A look at Misty's face told him not to bring up any of his worries. Misty was clearly stressed enough. She might not feel the same urge to join the battle as her brother, but her fear seemed to grow with every day that passed in fruitless search for the knowledge of the Stone.

He shook away dark thoughts for now. Finding the secret Luet had written would ease both their minds. "Well, we can work on those this afternoon," he said, fetching the pile of notes and sitting on the floor. It was already quite hot. The stuffy heat of early afternoon did nothing to encourage him as he faced the next stack of scrolls.

Misty sat beside him. "Okay… this one's in Elven. Can you translate the runes?"

Mel nodded, taking it from her and setting to work. Weeks of practice hadn't made him much faster at reading, but he'd begun to memorize the runes and translate them into letters mentally. He barely needed the chart Alder had made for him anymore.

A word jumped out at him as he translated it, and his heart skipped a beat. "*Stone*," he breathed, looking up. "This word means stone—Misty, I think this might be important. Hand me the dictionary."

Misty slid the massive tome to him, which translated Elven into Coonsian. Slowly, painstakingly, the two of them set to work on the scroll. Though not especially long, it took them the better part of the hour before they had a translated copy.

"It's a history," Misty said, as Mel studied the words. "The Gifting of the Star-Stones. It's about how the Star-Stones were given."

"Is there anything about the Blue Stone itself?" Mel asked.

Misty's eyes scanned the page, and she shook her head slowly. "No. It's just a record of when the Stones came to Orlell: *Three were given to the great rulers, to be a shield and blessing to their people. To the Cantrians, the Blue Stone, the purest of the three, to heal and protect mortal life. To the Fyrocrians, the Stone Isilas, to guard a people of many enemies. To the Netrocrians, a people apart from the rest, the Vana Jydra, that it might be a bridge between their kingdoms and that of their mortal counterparts.*" She frowned. "But I guess the Netrocrians ended up using the Jewel of Power for wrong."

Mel sighed and shook his head. The story was interesting, but there was nothing in this scroll that they hadn't yet learned. "Well… let's look at the next one."

Misty kept the scroll open as she fetched one of her textbooks, glancing between the two pages as she wrote on a fresh sheet of parchment.

"What are you doing?" Mel asked, confused.

"I'm going to translate it into Liznaeic, in case we missed something," Misty answered without looking up.

"Liznaeic?" Mel repeated, even more lost. "Why?"

"I just told you. Alder said Coonsian is a technical language, so you might not get the deeper meanings if you just translate word for word. But Liznaeic is more…" she paused, searching for the word, "poetic."

Mel shrugged, confused but not enough to inquire further. "Fine, if you want to. I'm going to work through the rest."

He made it through two more scrolls—one, a record of Tinkeeyo's lords in the century before the Dividing War, and the other a correspondence between Luet and a Caer Sian noble—before Misty spoke again.

"That's odd," she murmured. "The Liznee word for Star-Stone is different. I thought it was *Leva-Tiri*, which is just 'star' and 'stone' put together. But it's *Alena*."

"Odd," Mel said, not really understanding why that mattered.

"It's really odd, because that's not even used as a noun," Misty said, frowning. "*Alena* is written as a verb—something that you can do, not something that is."

Mel glanced at her. "*Alena?*" he repeated. The word seemed familiar, but he didn't know why. "Well… if that's the word for Star-Stone, we could ask Alder to look for scrolls with that in the title."

"That's true," Misty said. She shook her head. "I wish we could go look ourselves. I feel useless here."

You and me both, Mel thought, but didn't say it. "We could head downstairs to the fort and ask Dandio," he suggested. "Or if Dandio's not here, we could ask Lord Andros if we can go to the scribehouse. He's willing to help too."

They headed down the corridor, then down the stairs that connected the flight of rooms to the fort itself. Voices grew louder as they approached. The urgency in them made Mel hesitate.

Two guards stood posted at the doors to the hall, and straightened as they approached. "Hi," Mel said, forcing a smile. "Um—can we talk to Commander Ki?"

"He is not here," the guard answered shortly. "I suggest you return to your rooms."

"We just have a question," Mel pressed, refusing to give up so quickly.

"Please—it's about our mission."

The guard hesitated, glancing at his companion. The other soldier sighed. "I will go speak to the attendants. Please wait here."

Mel leaned against the wall, trying to hide his impatience and unease. When the door opened, it was not the guard nor Dandio, but Quinn. The Elven ranger's face was drawn in weariness, and one arm was bound in a sling. "You can come in, you two," he said quietly.

The heaviness in his voice told Mel something drastic had occurred. "Are you all right?" he asked hesitantly as they followed.

"An unlucky slash from an enchanted soldier, nothing more," Quinn replied, smiling bitterly. "I can assure you it is a better fate than that of many of our troops."

"We can hear the fighting," Misty ventured.

"You will soon hear it all the more, I fear," Quinn told them grimly, leading them to the council hall. "The Dal-kerri have breached the outer walls to the south and west, and march into the city."

Icy fear gripped Mel's heart. "Is Dandio…"

"Last I saw him, he had flown back to the battle lines on the gryphon," Quinn answered. "That was several hours ago. A garrison of Red Dawn sought to reach us, but they were forced to fight through the Ace-army to get here, and many of them were injured. I believe Dandio and the Red Dawn regiment intend to reinforce the blockade on the southern walls. The Alfona held the perimeter as long as they could."

"The Alfona?" Mel asked, his heart sinking as he guessed what had happened.

Quinn let out a breath. "Chief Kadryion is dead. He fell with a host of his finest warriors on the southern wall. The rest of the tribesman have retreated to the fort for now."

Mel stared at him wordlessly, shaken by the news. He hadn't known Kadryion well, or any of the Alfona warriors, for that matter. But the fact that the chieftain had joined Tinkeeyo despite years of wrongs spoke volumes about his character. Not only that, he'd helped Aryion after Mel had been captured, which further improved Mel's opinion of him.

And now he was dead.

"What… what's going to happen now?" Misty asked, her face pale.

Quinn was silent a moment. "I don't know," he said at last.

Soldiers marched past them to the meeting room. Two of the warriors they passed were Alfona, their buckskin garments covered in blood. Low, hurried voices filled the halls of Fort Tinkeeyo.

Lord Andros stood inside the meeting hall, speaking with three battered generals. Quinn had them wait by the door until the generals left, and Andros beckoned them within.

"Well met, New Blood," he said, his voice heavy. "How fares your mission?"

"We haven't found anything yet," Mel said slowly, then, in a desperate attempt at optimism, added, "but we did find Luet's writings about Star-Stones, so I think we're getting close."

"Close," Andros echoed, shaking his head. "I fear 'close' may not be enough. The principle scribehouse has been overrun—any access to it is impossible. The Dal-kerri have taken over that portion of the city."

Mel felt as though a heavy burden had settled on his shoulders, crushing him down into the ground. "Overrun?" he repeated numbly.

"But—but we need those scrolls," Misty stammered. "Sir, we're really close—maybe Dandio could take us on Nella, or maybe—maybe we could sneak in—"

"Dandio is currently fighting to save any civilians trapped in that part of the city," Andros said gently. "As for 'sneaking in', while I do not doubt your courage, I cannot allow you to risk that. The Dal-kerri are not easily fooled—by now, we have learned that."

He glanced at Quinn, then turned to them again. "I am sorry, children. I know this mission meant much to you, but now, I fear, the best thing you can do is return to the safety of Caer Sia. Dandio insists that as soon as he returns, you will embark north on the gryphon."

Mel was shaking his head rapidly before he finished. "No—no, we can't just leave. Even if we can't get to the scribehouse, we'll figure something else out—we can learn from the scrolls we have, or maybe— maybe we could get word to the dryads, and they could look for us—"

"To reach the dryads, one would have to leave the city on foot," Andros said. "And that is not possible at this point." He paused, thinking. "I will not order you home. If you believe there is some knowledge here, then I recommend you seek it as quickly as you can manage. See what you can find before Dandio returns. It is he you must convince."

Seek? Mel's mind echoed in despair. *Seek in what? The scrolls we have here?* None of them contained any new information. Nothing they'd found yet had aided their quest. Worst of all, he had no idea what exactly he was searching for.

"We'll do that," Misty said, slipping her little hand into Mel's. "Thanks, sir."

A faint smile touched the Elven lord's weary face, and he nodded slightly. "May the Light guide your search," he said, then turned back to the table.

Mel allowed her to lead him from the room, then pulled away once they were in the halls. Misty looked at him, her eyes wide with worry.

"What are we going to do now?"

Mel took a breath, already knowing she wouldn't like his answer. "Misty... you're going to go back to Caer Sia. I don't think I can convince Dandio to let you stay, now that the fighting's inside the city. But he might allow me—it's better than giving up the mission entirely."

Misty's face crumpled with disappointment. "But... but it's my mission too," she protested. "I've been helping—I can still help."

"I know. But I promised Mom you'd be safe," Mel said. "We're already trapped in the siege—if Dandio wants you to ride Nella out of here, you can make it back to Sia. You can share what we've learned with Iriam, if he's recovered—maybe he'll know more."

Misty's slim shoulders slumped, and she looked down. "All right," she said at last. "But I'm going to keep helping until Dandio's back."

"I'd hoped you would," Mel said, forcing a grin.

They jogged back to the room. Three scrolls still sat on the bed. The last three scrolls, Mel thought grimly. Perhaps, by some magic, these would be the ones they'd been looking for this whole time.

They were all written in Liznaeic. With Misty's textbook between them, they set to work translating the words. Mel strained his eyes, trying to find something, anything that would help them. Letter after letter, word after word, as the time stretched into hours, yet each rune seemed to mock the futility of their search. Hard as he fought it, Mel's thoughts taunted him: *This isn't something you're good at, it never has been. You don't even know what you're looking for. How do you think this is going to help anything?*

He gritted his teeth and closed his eyes for a moment, trying to steady his spiraling thoughts. Aryion's face swam into his tired mind. Perhaps he was already dead, and Mel's mission would change nothing.

No.

Taking a deep breath, he turned his eyes back to the pages.

The red glow of evening filled the room by the time the door opened. Dandio stepped inside slowly and leaned heavily on the door frame, his armor streaked with blood and grime.

"Lord Andros said you requested more time," he said, his voice hoarse. Alder came in behind him, his young face troubled.

Mel had readied a whole argument for staying, but Dandio looked so worn out he didn't bring it up now. "We're just… working through these last ones," he said instead, glancing at Misty. "What's going on out there?"

Dandio sat down in the wicker chair beside the window and leaned back wearily. "Nothing good," he answered. "We have managed to keep the Dal-kerri from advancing further into the city. My men are securing the southern wall. I will return to them shortly, but I needed to speak with you two."

Alder set three more scrolls on the table. "Here. We were able to get a few out before the scribehouse was taken."

"Thanks," Misty said. "Hey—we already read this one," she added, picking one of the scrolls up. "It's the first one we started with."

"Did we?" Alder asked tiredly. "I guess I forgot."

"It's all right. At least you saved it," Mel said, turning back to Dandio. He could already guess what he wanted to talk about. "Dandio—we can't abandon the mission. Misty's agreed to go back, but—she's been helping more than I have. And we both want to find Luet's writing."

"I don't doubt you," Dandio said. "But the fact remains, Mel, Tinkeeyo is now an active battlefield—one that grows more dangerous with each hour. Now that the Dal-kerri have breached the outer walls, there is no telling how long it will be before they reach the fort. Without the scrolls, there is not much you can look for. And you need to protect the Blue Stone."

"The Blue Stone is why I'm here," Mel pressed. He sensed he was grasping at threads, desperate for a convincing argument. "Jan said there's another power Luet wrote about—the last scroll we found was about Star-Stones. We're close, I'm sure."

"How close?" Dandio asked gently. "You know I would protect you here if I could, but I have seen more men die today than I wish to count. I promised your mother that you and Misty would be kept safe. Tinkeeyo is no longer secure."

Mel looked down, knowing he was right. All the same, the idea of giving up, of returning to Caer Sia having failed his mission, was unbearable. "Could... couldn't we have till tomorrow?" he asked at last. "One more day of looking—and if we don't find anything, then we'll go."

Dandio hesitated, but finally nodded. "Very well. One more day. Now, I must return to the south wall." He stood and started for the door.

"Light above!"

Mel jumped at Misty's shrill voice. Dandio and Alder turned back sharply in confusion.

Misty had recoiled from the scroll as if it had burned her, her fingers a blur as she flipped through her notebook. "I read—I knew I didn't—I should have seen it right off—"

"Misty, what are you talking about?" Mel demanded.

She didn't respond, still searching through pages, her face white as the paper. "I *didn't* read it wrong, I *knew* I didn't—Light above, I'm an *idiot*—"

"Misty..." Mel started again.

Misty looked up sharply, turning to Dandio. "How would you say 'Star-Stone' in Liznaeic?"

"*Alena*, I believe," Dandio said slowly, looking confused. "Though it has been awhile since I studied the old tongue."

Misty nodded rapidly. "Right—and how would you say 'the Stone sings?'"

Dandio frowned, but not in doubt. "The verb must reflect the noun—or something along those lines, I could never remember the proper conjugation. *Alena Allá—no, Allá Alena—*"

"*Allá Alené*," Misty said, emphasizing each syllable. "I *knew* I didn't read it wrong."

Mel looked at her, still at a loss. "What does that mean?"

Misty's brow was furrowed as she fought to turn her thoughts into words. "Mel—I thought the scroll was trying to say '*Allá Ultave*,' which means 'taught to sing'—and we said it didn't make any sense."

"And it... doesn't," Mel said haltingly.

"I know it doesn't, because that's not what the scroll said. It wasn't a mistake. It said *Allá Alené*, which I thought meant 'taught the power to sing'—which still doesn't make much sense, because I was reading the word wrong. It's not 'power.' It's the word for the Star-Stones themselves—*Alena*, but in a different form."

Something connected in Mel's mind. "Wait—so that's saying the kragons taught Luet about..."

"About the *Alené*. Mel, this was the scroll we should have looked for all along." Misty's eyes scanned down the ancient words, her frame practically trembling with excitement. "What we're looking for isn't a story, or a record." She looked up. "It's a song."

Mel's heart leapt. "Misty, you found it!" He turned to Dandio and Alder. "We have to get to the scribehouse."

"It won't be with the records," Alder said. "If we're looking for a song, that would be in the house of prophecies."

"The west side of town," Dandio stated. His face was grim. "The Aces and their forces have already breached the west walls. You will need to hurry." He turned to Alder. "Go with them. Take Nella and go as quickly as you can. Stay with them and bring them back safe."

Misty snatched up the books and notes, shoving them into her bag. Mel started for the door but hesitated, looking back at Dandio. "What about the battle?"

Dandio met his eyes. "Jan believed this is worth the risk—and I trust you to see this mission through. We'll fight for you however long you need."

Mel nodded, took a breath, then ran after Alder and Misty, heading for the courtyard.

25

Allá Alené

Fort Tinkeeyo swarmed with the energy of battle. Mel nearly collided with a courier and had to weave his way around a group of soldiers in the hall. But he hurried on, following Alder and Misty out through the main doors. His right hand gripped the Blue Stone in his pocket. After weeks of searching the scrolls, they finally knew what they were looking for. The only question was if they could find it in time to help Tinkeeyo.

Nella waited saddled in the courtyard. Her ears flicked forward as she saw them, clearly sensing their urgency and excitement. Alder helped Misty up onto her back and hesitated. "Should I…"

"Get in front," Mel told him, swinging up behind Misty. "You're going to have to show us the way to the scribehouse—you know where it is, right?" he added worriedly.

"I know where it is," Alder mumbled, climbing unsteadily onto Nella. "I've never *flown* there, though."

"Just hold on tight," Misty told him.

Mel clipped his heels against Nella's sides, and the gryphon bounded forward, launching into the sky. Alder gripped the reins white-knuckled, squinting against the rush of wind, and managed to carefully turn Nella's head to the right.

The sounds of battle echoed behind them, where the south wall still stood, and Mel felt a surge of fear for Dandio and the rest of the warriors there. But he couldn't help them now—the best help he'd offer would lie in finding the mysterious song that detailed the Blue Stone's power.

A song, he thought wryly to himself. A song was their secret weapon against the Ace-Lord? How on Orlell would that help anything? Then again, his father had always told him there was magic in music—deep magic gifted from the High Light. Maybe he was right.

"We're not far!" Alder shouted over the wind. "But the west walls are teeming with Dal-kerri!"

Mel squinted west—the setting sun glared in his face, making his eyes water. "Is the scribehouse still safe?" he called back.

"I believe so," the Elf replied. "I'd point it out to you if I didn't think I'd fall."

"Mel, look!" Misty cried, her voice edged with fear. Directly below them, making their way steadily down the street, was a pack of Dal-kerri. Mel could see enchanted soldiers among them, seemingly headed back toward the walls. Fallen soldiers littered the street behind them like dead leaves, and his heart lurched.

"There!" Alder called. Mel tore his eyes away from the scene below. The roof of a small building appeared before them, sheltered in a grove of trees on the edge of town. Nella seemed to understand—with a toss of her head, she descended gracefully.

The second scribehouse was much smaller than the one Mel had spent the last few weeks in, though its build was similar—square and simple, constructed of reddish wood. Five guards stood posted outside, and they raised their bows as the gryphon landed before them.

Mel held up his hands, sliding from the saddle. "It's all right—it's all right!"

"We're here with Lord Andros' permission," Alder said quickly. "He is the New Blood."

Mel nodded. He didn't usually throw the title around, but here, he realized it offered some reassurance to the Elves. The guards lowered their weapons, and the captain studied him carefully. "The New Blood? Why have you come here? It is not safe—the Dal-kerri are headed this way."

"I'm here to help," Mel said. "We need to look for Luet's scrolls—are they still here?"

"I believe so," the captain answered, looking uncertain. "But I do not know how many of the prophecies remain intact. The Aces attacked this scribehouse last year, you know—left the librarian half mad, poor fellow, and tore up most of the ancient scrolls."

Mel's heart sank. After all their efforts, what if the scroll they needed had been destroyed months ago?

"We'll look all the same," Alder said, starting toward the door.

"Go quickly," the captain warned. "If the Dal-kerri reach us, you will be trapped inside."

Misty lifted her book bag with an effort and ran to the door. With a brief nod of thanks to the guards, Mel hurried inside.

It was darker and dustier in this scribehouse, he noticed. Instead of the spiral array of well-ordered shelves, only ten or twelve shelves stood before them, about six feet tall, stacked with scrolls and books. Shreds of paper lingered in the corners, the last remnants of the Aces' fury when they'd stolen the Prophecy of Three.

"Where do we look?" he asked, trying to dismiss his fears.

Alder pointed to the shelf on the left. "There—those are the old songs. Look for Luet's crest—I'll look on the other side."

Misty had already ran to the shelf, kneeling to peer at the books near the floor. Mel joined her, his eyes racing over the scrolls. Everything on this shelf, he noticed, was written in Liznaeic. That meant Misty would have to translate the scroll before he could read it himself, which would cost them more time.

"There are several empty spaces on this side," Alder called worriedly.

"There's some here, too," Mel replied, dread gripping his heart. He remembered the news Norrin had brought them on the quest for the Shards—that an Ace had come to this scribehouse, shredded its way through the ancient texts, and left with the copy of the Prophecy of Three. Had Luet's writings all been destroyed? If so, their entire mission here had been for nothing.

Sickened by the idea, he turned to the next shelf.

"I found it," Misty said as he did so.

Mel whipped around. Misty had selected a scroll and unrolled it carefully. Her eyes widened in shock. "Someone's translated it," she said in disbelief. "Luet's writing is in Liznaeic, but someone's already written the translation in Coonsian underneath it."

"What?" Mel asked, looking over her shoulder.

Alder joined them, studying the scroll. "I don't recognize the handwriting," he said, frowning. "I doubt any of the scribes or librarians would have done it, they're not allowed to make their notes directly on the scrolls."

"Who would have translated it?" Mel wondered, stunned. "And do you think… they knew…" He trailed off, unable to voice the impossible suggestion, yet it remained in his mind. Someone, however long ago, had translated this scroll into Coonsian. For what reason, no one could know. Yet it had saved them precious hours of time. Someone had devoted their time to see that this scroll—deemed only an old song, nothing more—was translated into the common tongue.

Had that someone known that one day, lives would depend on it? Had they known that eventually, the New Blood would need this very information?

He shook his head in wonder, turning back to the scroll. "What's it say, Misty?"

Misty took a breath. "*Allá Alené*—the Song of the Stars. It seems like a type of spell, a way for the Wielder of the Blue Stone to access the High Light's power, and let that power flow through them."

Mel frowned, confused. "So… what do I have to do?"

Misty held it up. "Luet wrote the lyrics in Liznaeic. She also wrote something else… that's funny," she mused, studying the note on the top of the scroll. "Luet said it's not the words that have power—that they're words, nothing more. She says it's your heart that matters, and the reason you're using the Stone."

"Iriam said something like that once," Mel murmured, remembering it. He took the parchment from her, looking at it uncertainly. "So… I have to sing this?" he asked, with a twinge of discomfort. He liked music, but he'd never been much of a singer, unless they were the lighthearted and often ridiculous tunes he came up with on the trail to make Aryion laugh. Those songs would *certainly* not help here.

"I can't read the Liznaeic words," he said finally, studying the foreign script. "I don't even know what it's supposed to sound like."

Growls and shouts came from outside. The captain's hurried voice reached them. "New Blood, the Dal-kerri are here—you must hurry!"

Alder turned. "I'll block the door—Mel, figure out the song."

"I…" Mel stammered, looking helplessly at the parchment.

Howls sounded outside, growing steadily louder. Alder pushed one of the shelves in front of the door to bar it, his face drawn with fear.

Misty took Mel's arm. Her eyes were scared, but her voice was steady. "Mel, it's not about whether or not you can do it—it's not about what you can do at all. That's why Luet made sure to write that—it doesn't matter what the song is, as long as you're singing for a good reason."

Mel took a breath, calming his panicked mind. He hadn't pictured a song to be the power they had sought—but if a song would somehow help them, then he'd sing. "All right. Start singing, Misty—I'll follow you."

He took the Blue Stone out of his pocket. Comforting light filled the shadowed scribehouse, falling on the letters of the scroll and causing the ink to shimmer.

Misty began to sing quietly next to him, simply making up a tune for the lyrics. She sang the Liznaeic words, while Mel allowed his eyes to follow along on the translated version, reading the meaning to what they sang.

Despite the title, it was not the Song of the Stars as he'd heard it before. It was not a war song, or a cry to battle, as he would have imagined. This was a lament. A prayer to the High Light, words in an ancient tongue, praising the goodness and power while pleading for deliverance and safety from the darkness.

He whispered the words in Coonsian, though they did not feel as powerful or flowing as the ones Misty sang in Liznaeic:

O here, through darkness deep,
Shine light that life yet keeps.
Hear now my mortal tongue,
Fire wrought, atoned by blood.

The Blue Stone glimmered in his clenched fist, light sparkling faintly between his fingers.

Dal-kerri howls and snarls filled the air outside, accompanied by the low thrum of bowstrings and the cries of injured soldiers. The growls drew nearer.

"Mel..." Alder called uneasily.

Mel took a deep breath and picked up the words as Misty sang softly beside him. His voice was shaky and uncertain, but he ignored it. *Remember the Stone*, he ordered his racing thoughts. *Remember why you're here. Remember your call.*

Every event of his life seemed to swirl before his eyes, every step leading him to this moment. He thought he heard the voices of the lost whispering the words beside him, thought he saw Aryion's face, dark eyes shining with pride.

The Stone was glowing so brightly it lit the entire scribehouse. The words on the scroll seemed to glow with it, though perhaps it was just his imagination. Misty's voice grew stronger with excitement.

Then the captain's cry cut through the spell. "They are coming, New Blood—they are coming!"

Something heavy slammed against the door, splintering wood. Alder leapt back, drawing the dagger from his belt as he placed himself between the siblings and the doorway.

Mel's voice faltered with fear. He couldn't fight them—the Blood Oath had forbidden him to put the Stone in danger, and now his own life would be forfeit, the Stone would be lost—and Alder and Misty would die too.

"Keep singing!" Misty cried. "Mel, keep singing—we—"

She was cut off by a howl of triumph. The door broke inward beneath the hounds' assault. The shelf crashed into the room, scattering pages in all directions.

Snarling, the pack sprang inside. Alder slashed at the first wolf as it rose on its hind legs, tackling him to the ground with a sickening thud. Misty's terrified scream split the tense air.

"No!" Mel yelled, lowering the scroll and reaching for his dagger.

Then, out of nowhere, he heard the voice.

For a horrifying moment, he thought it was the Ace-Lord's voice again, echoing in his mind as it had in the void. But this voice was far different. Not the cold, cunning tone that had plagued his nightmares for so long. It was low, quiet, as powerful as a lion's roar yet as soft and gentle as a summer breeze.

"I am with you."

Mel froze. Chills ran down his arms, but not in fear. Time seemed to slow. Misty's screams, the Dal-kerri howls, the shouts of the soldiers outside, seemed to have faded away. He heard nothing besides the voice, which seemed to fill his heart with fire.

"Surrender your fears. Surrender your burdens. Rely on My strength."

Mel took a deep breath and relaxed his grip on the Stone, holding it out in his open palm. He stepped forward, standing over Alder's unconscious form and pressing Misty behind him.

The wolf snarled, but Mel no longer heard them. He felt himself singing again, felt the doubts of the last few weeks falling away—and the Stone was shining, brighter than he had ever seen it.

The Dal-kerri reeled back with cries and growls of hatred. The enchanted soldiers faltered in their attack, weapons falling from their hands, stumbling and clutching their heads.

Yet Mel barely saw any of it. The Blue Stone shone blindingly bright, spreading fiery tendrils of blue light from the scribehouse, over the exhausted guards outside, over the besieged walls and the army of Tinkeeyo.

Through the broken door, Mel saw the city, outlined in brilliant flames of blue. The Dal-kerri were pulling back. Massive shadows swept over the city—for an instant, he thought they were serpentines, but no, these newcomers were much larger, their great wings beating in rhythm as they glided to aid Tinkeeyo's exhausted armies. The fire of the *Alené* illuminated the kragons as they descended on the siege force.

The light grew brighter, spreading down his body like fiery armor, and coiling around the city in a glowing embrace.

Only when the Dal-kerri had fled the scribehouse and he felt Misty's hand take his did his strength finally fail him. He fell to the ground, fingers closed around the Stone, Aryion's voice echoing dimly in his thoughts as his vision faded to nothing.

26

♨ ♨ ♨ ♨ ♨ ♨ ♨ ♨ ♨

The Message

He was in the void again. Sounds swam around him, the past and present seeming to blur. Voices, some he recognized, faded in and out of his thoughts. A brief image of a figure standing in a ruined scribehouse, wreathed in blue light, flickered into his vision, and he heard the Ace-Lord's voice drifting from memory.

"What an interesting mortal."

With an effort, Mel opened his eyes.

The first rays of a brilliant sunrise blinded him. He was no longer in the dusty scribehouse, shrouded by the shadows of evening. An open window let in the early light of day. He recognized the itchy woolen blanket of the bedding of the suite. Was he back at the fort?

"Misty?" he called hoarsely. His throat ached. How long had he stood in the scribehouse, half-screaming the words to a song he'd never heard before?

Well, at least it wasn't his technique that mattered. What mattered was his heart, centered on the source of the Power he called upon. He remembered the voice speaking over him, deep and powerful, and felt a warm sense of awe.

He pushed the blankets off and sat up slowly. Misty's head appeared in the doorway, her tired expression lighting up as she saw him. "Mel!"

She ran to him, nearly knocking him flat with a hug. "Ouch—hey,

Misty," Mel said, giving her a squeeze.

"I figured you'd be okay—but I was so scared—you were so pale, like when you were unconscious in Caer Sia," Misty stammered.

"I'm okay," Mel reassured her. His right hand ached—when he looked down, his fingers were still closed around the Blue Stone. He loosened his grip, wincing, and slid the Stone back into his pocket. "How long have I been out?"

"All night," Misty answered. "I barely saw what happened, it was so bright—Alder got knocked out by the wolves, so I had to help you both."

"Alder," Mel repeated with a surge of fear. "The battle—what happened?"

"Alder's alive," Misty told him. "The doctors said he got a concussion, but he still wanted to return to the fort as soon as he could stand steady."

"And the fighting?" Mel asked.

Misty's eyes showed a wondering awe. "The Stone made a shield— well, not really a shield. It looked like armor, glowing armor for everyone around you. Then the kragons got here and attacked the bear creatures. The Dal-kerri left—I think the light hurt them. The walls are secure again."

Mel let out a sigh of relief. "Where's Dandio?"

"He's meeting with Lord Andros," Misty replied. Some of the relief had faded on her face. "The Dal-kerri broke through the south walls right as we found the song, remember—a lot of people were hurt. The fighting's stopped for now, but the light didn't make them all go away. Dandio thinks the Aces could be preparing for another attack."

She looked exhausted. Worry had etched lines beside her blue eyes, making her look older. Then again, the complexities and horrors of war were something no nine-year-old should ever have to experience.

Mel pulled on his boots and stepped toward the door. "I'm going down to the fort."

"I'll come too," Misty said, but she stumbled slightly as she turned to follow.

"No," Mel told her, guiding her gently to her bed on the opposite side of the room. "You need to get some sleep."

"But… I want to help too," Misty protested, looking up at him blearily.

"You've already helped plenty," Mel assured her. "If it weren't for you, we would have never found the song. I won't be gone long"

Misty finally agreed, and was asleep almost as soon as she'd laid down. Mel closed the door quietly behind him and headed down the halls.

. . . . . .

The lower levels were quieter than they had been last night. The frantic voices, the fearful cries, the shouts of battle had transformed into a low hum of conversations filling the fort. The voices sounded more purposeful than afraid. Though their enemy remained at their threshold, the brilliant display of the High Light's power had been seen by everyone in Tinkeeyo. That reassurance—that they were not fighting in vain, that their lives had a purpose—filled Mel with calm.

The guards let him into the halls without a word. Several people paused to smile or nod to him as he passed them in the corridors. One general even gave him a slight bow. Mel felt his face warm, and he nodded back.

Dandio's voice came from behind him. "I take it you learned the secret of the *Alené?*"

Mel turned. The Liznee moved slowly, evidently sore from the long day and night of battle. His face was bruised, but his eyes shone as he smiled at Mel.

"We did," Mel answered, returning the grin. "Are you all right?" he added.

Dandio nodded. "Yes—yes, I'm quite well. And you? Misty told me about the Dal-kerri in the scribehouse."

"I'm fine," Mel replied. "The Stone protected us—or at least, the High Light used it to protect us. I… I'm not sure I can explain it." The shining power of the Blue Stone, the voice that had spoken such peace over him, the other Being whose power had flowed through him… he had no idea how he could put it into words. "What's happening out there?" he asked instead. "Is the siege over?"

Dandio's smile vanished, and his face became serious. "No, unfortunately. While the song and the Stone saved many lives, the Aces have only been driven back behind the walls, not defeated. With the timely arrival of the kragons, the northern roads have been secured."

Mel glanced up at him. "Does that mean we… have to leave?" Technically, his mission was completed. He'd learned what Luet had wrote about, and had managed to save the warriors of Tinkeeyo. But he didn't want to leave now. The determination and hope, renewed by the High Light's voice, called him forward.

Dandio seemed to sense his thoughts. "I had thought your mission would be over after the song was found," he answered, "but of course, you have proved me wrong. No, I do not believe we will leave yet. The true power of the Alené may yet help Tinkeeyo—this fight is not yet won."

"Won or not, we've dealt them a severe blow," came Quinn's voice. The Elven ranger strode toward them with Lord Andros, and Alder behind him. The young Elf had a bandage around his head, and his face was pale, but his eyes lit up when he saw Mel.

"New Blood—it's very good to see you're all right," he said eagerly, clasping Mel's hand.

"You too," Mel said with a grin. "Thanks for protecting Misty."

"Well, thank you for saving us both," Alder replied.

Mel gave a slight shrug. "I didn't really do anything, you know," he said. It felt wrong to claim that power as his own. The Stone's magic didn't rely on him. "The song, the Stone—that didn't come from my strength."

"Not your strength," Lord Andros said thoughtfully, "but it did come about through your willingness. The High Light has never chosen His servants based on their abilities, as the Old Stories say, but on the nature of their hearts." He smiled at Mel. "For your willingness, child, we are very grateful."

Mel returned the smile, touched by the praise.

"Now," Andros said, "let us speak of other matters." He led them into a room a few doors down from the council hall. It reminded Mel of Jan's study back in Castle Sia, with a neatly organized desk and furniture made of deep mahogany.

Lord Andros sat behind the large desk as the others seated themselves around the room; Mel, glad to be included, sat down too. The Elven lord's worn face was serious as he looked at Dandio. "Your strategies thus far have been highly effective, Commander. We owe you our thanks—the south walls are again secured, and many lives have been saved by the knights of the Red Dawn."

Dandio gave him a short nod, acknowledging both the compliment and the heavy price his men had paid.

"However," Andros said, hesitating slightly, "I am uncertain. The city's gates are again protected, the Aces drawn back, and our allies the kragons guard our walls. Lord Fireclaw has promised his army will remain until the siege force is defeated, and the roads are secured."

"Yes, I spoke with him when they arrived," Dandio said. "The kragons have always hated the Aces—it was Kahlifis who drove them from their lands in the Magno Forest. I do not doubt their loyalty, nor their strength."

"Nor I," Andros replied. "No, my uncertainty does not lie with them." He folded his hands on the desk and turned to Quinn. "Might you share your concerns?"

Quinn spoke slowly, his expression both thoughtful and troubled. "Commander... I am not as learned in strategy as you. But I've trained as a ranger for many years, and one of our core principles is to know your opponent. I've fought the Aces before, and I have to point out, it's very strange for them to simply withdraw their forces from attack."

Dandio folded his arms over his armored chest, frowning slightly. "Well, I agree with you there. I doubt they've simply given up—we know they're still guarding the walls fiercely, preventing anyone to go in or out of the city."

"Exactly," Andros said, shaking his head. "I do not like it. They retreat to our perimeter, but they have not attempted to infiltrate the walls, strike our defenders, or even send out the Dal-kerri against the weaker parts of the barrier."

"Maybe it's the Stone," Mel ventured, trying to come up with a positive reason. "I mean... we saw the Dal-kerri retreat at the Stone's light."

"I will hope that is the case," Andros replied, "but even if that is so, I will point out that the Aces began withdrawing their main forces from battle even before you sang the song."

An uneasy prickle ran down Mel's back. He remembered glimpsing the packs of Dal-kerri when they'd flown over the city to the scribehouse. But now as he looked back on the memories, he realized Andros was right. Those forces hadn't been fighting. They'd been moving steadily out of Tinkeeyo, forming up at the city's edge.

Concern showed in Dandio's green eyes. "In my experience, when an enemy unexpectedly retreats, there is one of two reasons to blame," he said after a pause. "One is as Mel suggests, and they retreated because they suffered losses. They'll pull back, recover, and try a new strategy once they're stronger and more prepared."

"And the alternative?" Andros asked.

Dandio let out a breath. "The alternative is that their plans have shifted, and the Aces no longer need Tinkeeyo—at least, they do not need it destroyed. It seems locking down the city has had the effect they want, and they will not bother wasting further resources in a prolonged battle. They are satisfied to wait out the siege."

"But… why do that now?" Alder ventured uneasily. "Even if they barricade the roads, it would take months—years even—before we run out of supplies."

"I wonder," Dandio said slowly, "if their concern is less in allowing supplies in, as it is in allowing us *out*."

Fresh fear chilled Mel's heart. "Why?" he asked.

"Tinkeeyo protects more kingdoms than the south alone," Andros mused. "Our forces stand ready to aid against any attack to the north as well, particularly the kingdoms along the coast." His face was grim as he looked at Dandio. "Sia's espionage teams warned against an impending attack on Mata City, did they not?"

Mel looked at Dandio anxiously. He had never been to Mata City, but the thought of the Aces attacking it, destroying it the way they had Appledale, sickened him. He thought of Jarus and his family, of the peaceful Coopers who had thus far managed to stay safely out of the main conflict. The Aces threatened to destroy every part of their happy lives and wreak havoc upon the Cooper kingdom.

But Dandio was frowning. "They did, but… that was weeks ago. Surely our spies would have learned by now if the Aces were planning such an attack—we would have seen their forces headed up the Strait."

"Unless the news was blocked from reaching us," Alder pointed out.

"Then we would have heard from the dryads," Dandio countered. "The siege has not stopped their news from reaching us so far. The dryads would have seen the Aces' forces marching to Mata City, and they would have brought that news here…"

He trailed off, his expression changing from doubtful, to concerned, to pale with sudden dread. "Unless… the Aces never intended to attack Mata City at all."

"Then where would they go?" Andros inquired. "Our sources have all stated they meant to attack to the north."

"To the north, yes… but we never knew exactly where," Dandio replied, his face drawn.

As if on cue, the rhythm of hurried footsteps reached Mel's ears, and he could hear the rising sounds of confused and urgent voices.

The door was flung open, causing everyone to jump to their feet. One of the aides and an Elven general entered. "Forgive the interruption, my lord," the aide stammered.

"There's been an attack, sir," the general said at the same time. "The trees—you must hurry."

Dandio and Quinn left in a flash, with Andros and Alder following. Mel jogged behind them, his heart suddenly racing in fear. As he ran down the halls after the men, a new sound reached his ears—a horrible noise that shook the walls of the fort and gripped his chest with icy hands of dread.

At first, he thought it was Dal-kerri, howling as they charged into battle. But this sound was different—wilder, stranger, filled with agony. A soft, keening scream reverberated in the air.

A crowd of generals, courtiers, and soldiers had already gathered in a group, amassing on the walls as Mel ran into the courtyard. Some soldiers had drawn weapons, staring around in confusion for the unseen source of the horrific cry. It was not especially loud, yet it seemed to thunder over Tinkeeyo, inescapable, eerie and tortured.

Mel covered his ears, hands shaking. He'd lost sight of Dandio in the crowds, and pressed his back against the wall by the door, trying to calm the surging terror. He'd felt this gripping panic before—when the Ace-messenger had caused an illusion of Misty's screams to draw him into the forest during the quest for the Shards.

But this was no illusion. This was far worse, a cry that seemed to rise from the very core of the world.

"Mel!"

Misty's voice cut through his rising panic. He felt her grip his arm, her hands trembling. The sound had likely woken her, and she'd come looking for him.

"It's—it's all right," he managed, huddling with her beside the wall.

"It's the trees!" Misty stammered, her eyes brimming with tears. "Mel—look at the forest—"

Mel stared at her, not comprehending, but at her urging they jogged up the stairs to the top of the walls, joining the groups of soldiers. He turned his eyes eastward into the vast expanse of the Magno Forest. The sight turned his stomach with horror.

The trees were twisting, branches cracking before his eyes, warped and torn by white ice. Some were wrenched into the ground, breaking into pieces by the frozen soil as their roots were dragged down. Others had been shattered into pieces by the pale frost.

The screams came from the dryads. He could glimpse them here and there, leafy shadows racing for the fort. Two of them dissolved into nothing before his eyes as their trees were destroyed behind them.

"What—what's attacking them?" he finally cried.

He spotted a group of kragons hovering around something in the forest, raining down fire or diving to slash with their claws. A blast of white ice answered, and a kragon fell from the sky, disappearing into the frozen trees.

"Aces," Dandio hissed. He strode along the walls of the fort to reach Mel and Misty, his jaw set with helpless rage. "Two of them, as far as our watchmen can make out."

"Why are they attacking the trees?" Misty asked in a trembling voice.

"They fear them," Dandio answered, shaking his head. "The Aces hate the dryads for siding with the mortals, as they did in the Dividing War. We'd hoped it would be some time before the Ace-Lord learned of the alliance, but evidently not."

Another kragon dropped lifeless. Four dryads were flying through the woods, speeding desperately for the fort.

Mel's hand flew to his pocket. "The song—I'm going to sing the song again," he said, holding up the Blue Stone. "It can shield the dryads—it can help."

"Archers, with me!" Quinn ordered, jogging down the wall. "We cannot just stand by and watch."

Mel saw him and the Alfona captain, Wolfsbane, rallying their troops in desperate defense of the dryads. He glimpsed the four in the forest drawing closer, climbing the hill to the fort. One of them collapsed in a cloud of birch leaves as its tree shattered behind it.

He took a deep breath, held the Stone in his open palm, and raised his voice in the first lines of the song.

"Hello, New Blood."

Mel's voice faltered. That voice. It was familiar, but it was certainly not the gentle, powerful tone he'd heard yesterday. It did not belong to the Ace-Lord, nor was it the Deputy's smooth, sneering tone.

This voice belonged to another time, another place, before he'd understood the title New Blood.

That's impossible, his mind argued. *I watched him die.*

He continued the song. Blue light had begun to flicker from the Stone's core when the Ace's voice spoke again. And this time, he knew he was not mistaken.

"How long it has been, boy. My master was not mistaken—you have grown quite great. When we last met, you were but a child, drawn into the quest for the Shards and following the voices I made you to hear."

"Keep singing, Mel!" Misty cried—he could hear her singing the words to the song too. But his focus had broken.

The Ace was speaking again. How Mel remembered that hissing tone, the satisfaction in the ruined face when the Ace had killed Norrin. *"You must be surprised to hear it is I. But of course, another of our number was recently slain, and my master must maintain the rule of Twelve. Thus, I have been revived for this purpose, though I no longer exist in my previous role."*

Mel's throat was raw—he was practically screaming the words to the song now. The blue light shone weakly around the fort, not the blazing fire he needed. *Help me*, his mind cried desperately, begging the High Light to aid him again. And for an instant, he felt the peace, felt the calm, felt the assurance in a power greater than the Aces. His voice grew stronger. The Stone bathed blue light over the fort, spreading towards the battle in the forest.

Until the Ace spoke again.

"I have a message for you, New Blood, regarding the one called the Hummingbird."

Mel's heart froze. He tripped over the words of the song. The light, the peace he'd centered on, seemed to evaporate, replaced again by a fear unlike any he'd ever known before.

"Mel, keep singing!" Misty's urging came from far away. There was only the Ace-messenger's voice now.

"Do you know he yet lives? We expect the trees have brought you such a message; allow me to bring you another. Would you like to hear his voice?"

"No," Mel gasped, horror clutching his throat. "No—get out of my head—I know it's not real—"

He took a breath to resume the song, and as he did, a scream pierced his mind like a blade, louder even than the cacophony of battle or the cries of the dying dryads. It thundered in his head, shattered his desperate resolve to channel the Stone's power.

Aryion's voice. Filled with agony. Crying out from some dark place where Mel could not reach him.

A cry half of grief, half of blinding pain tore from Mel's throat, and he fell to his knees, clutching his head as his mentor's voice seared his mind. The Stone's light still blazed, but the scream continued unhindered. The blue light that had previously shielded him now stood as a cage, and the illusion was inside with him. He crumpled, curled into a ball, crippled by the deafening cry throbbing in his mind.

Only when the scream faded away was he aware of the wind tearing over the fort, of the worried voices around him, of Dandio's hand gripping his shoulder. His ears were ringing, his head ached as though it would split in two. Dandio's face swam into his vision. "Mel—Mel— look at me, Mel—"

Painfully, Mel raised his eyes, trembling all over. The Liznee's expression was drawn with concern. "It's over," he said firmly. "It was only an illusion. None of us heard it—it was not real."

"It… it was Aryion, Dandio," Mel rasped—his voice was gone. "It was Aryion." Then the tears came, as much as he wished he could stop them, and appear brave and confident before the warriors. But the sheer horror of what he had just endured tore the strength from him. He fell forward, face pressed against Dandio's shoulder. Dandio held him tightly—he alone could understand the pain.

"It's all right," the Liznee said quietly. "It's over now. Try to breathe."

Mel pulled back, rubbing his face with his sleeve as he got to his feet shakily. The tortured scream still echoed in his ears, and it took him an effort to catch his breath. "I—heard—Aryion—I think he's—they're doing something to him—he—" He choked on the words, unable to go on.

The wind whipped over the frozen trees, over the desolate patch of forest where the kragons tended their dead. The Aces had vanished, their task completed, their message delivered.

Wind rolled over the fort, carrying the leaves with it. Two dryads appeared before them. One had the reddish tint and fir-needle hair of the Magno Forest dwellers, but the other was smaller and gray, like the trees near the Flats.

"Son of Sia and son of Tinkeeyo," the first said, turning flashing eyes to Dandio and Lord Andros. "We bring fell news."

"We are listening," Andros answered.

"The Aces seek to silence our voices," the dryad said, his voice heavy. "They found that we had learned of their plans for the north. They sought to destroy us before we could deliver our message."

"You must make haste," the second dryad whispered, her voice shivering with urgency. "You must make all haste to reach the north. The Aces march to attack."

Mel looked up in disbelief. Misty's face was fearful.

"Mata City?" Lord Andros asked. "The Aces—they intend to attack Mata City?"

"No—they never intended to attack the Cooper kingdom," the silver dryad replied. "They made certain you would believe the lies that led you to believe thus. The Aces march on Caer Sia."

The words struck Mel in the chest, each filling him with dread.

"When?" Dandio demanded, his face tense. "When should we expect this attack?"

"It has already begun," the first dryad answered, bowing his head. "By tomorrow, the Ace-Lord's forces will reach Sia's gates."

27

The Battle of Gayrile

It was too quiet.

Allie shifted her position, the sagebrush crunching softly as she did so, and studied the wide space of rocky beach across the road below her. Further out, the sea stretched on for miles, morning sun glaring off the mellow waves.

If all went to plan, they'd see Cooper ships riding those waves today, speeding to aid the allies of Gayrile. Even with the rebel Direns joining them, they were drastically outnumbered. Rygal's strategy should draw every Dal-kerri, enchanted soldier, and serpentine to the sloping beach where the others waited. Then there would be battle, until the Coopers arrived to help.

If it all went to plan.

She took a deep breath, trying to settle herself, and looked around the hilltop. About a hundred Brownaes crouched with her, their mottled fur blending into the sagebrush. Another hill rose to her left, and she could make out the occasional glint of color from a Diren's scales, or the gleam of a Guardians' blade. But most of the Guardians had gone back to the city with Rygal.

She looked to the right, but from here, all she could see of Bridgeport was the distant smoky haze. Perhaps they were fighting already, clashing with the Aces' forces. Perhaps they were on their way back, pursued by hoards of Dal-kerri and Redeyes.

The thought of Redeyes twisted her stomach. Since the Ace had been killed by Morel, Redeyes would assume command. She didn't doubt he would take the bait the Guardians offered. Rygal was right—as he'd mentioned yesterday, the black tiger was no strategist, here only to bring death and revenge. Besides, there was hardly a need for him to strategize, considering the sheer advantage of numbers.

She wiped the sweat from her brow and looked down at the road directly below, which ran between the beach and the hills they waited on. Rygal's group had headed to Bridgeport just before dawn. There, they would goad the Dal-kerri to attack, drawing them from the shadows, then feign retreat, leading them along the road and into the trap they'd prepared.

"Stay still, men," Lieutenant Porto called softly behind her, settling the restless Brownaes. Every heart on the low-lying hills raced in nervous anticipation of the fight.

Allie took another deep breath, trying to calm herself. She couldn't remember ever being this anxious before a fight—though she'd really only been involved in two battles. The first had been the fight with the Darkness, which had started and ended so quickly she'd never had time to be nervous, and the other had been the battle against the Aces when they'd taken over Caer Sia last summer. Her view of war had been so narrow then, so confident that they would win—which they had, thanks to Mel joining the Shards.

But Mel was not here today. He would be in Tinkeeyo, miles and miles to the south, and hopefully in a safer place than they were.

Darion crouched on a stone above her, an arrow on his bowstring, his eyes scanning the south.

"Any sign?" Allie whispered, more to break the tense silence. If the Dal-kerri appeared, she'd likely see them the same time as Darion.

"Not yet," he answered quietly. "Rygal's group would have reached Bridgeport a few hours ago. If it's all gone according to plan, they'll be fighting now."

Allie nodded, trying to fight down the fresh wave of fear that gripped her at the thought of Rygal, facing off with the Aces' forces, with only a handful of warriors as backup.

Darion studied her fearful expression. "He'll be all right. You know he'll retreat the moment they've got the Dal-kerri headed the right way."

"I know," Allie answered shortly, not quite up to discussing her thoughts for Rygal at the moment. She gripped her sword hilt to steady her trembling hands. It would work. It must work, because if it didn't, Gayrile would be lost.

A young Brownae warrior jogged up the hill to them, slipping silently through the dry brush. "No sign from the hilltop," he reported to the lieutenant. "Captain Terivis has sent a scout to fly closer to the city and see how the battle fares. If he's spotted he knows not to return here."

"Good," Porto replied with a nod. "We can't give away our position."

Allie turned back to Darion, needing the distraction of conversation. "So… after this battle… are we still planning to go to Tinkeeyo?" she asked, managing a faint smile.

Darion smiled back. "After this, I'd almost enjoy searching all those scrolls. And now we've learned how the enchantment is forged." His smile faded at the words, and he hesitated a moment. "You don't suppose… there's any other way to break it?" he murmured softly.

Allie paused. Terivis' report yesterday evening had answered many of their questions about the enchantment. Though the enchanted soldiers might wish to leave the Ace-army, their minds were no longer their own, their whole being was completely controlled by the Ace-Lord. That bond would not break until the Ace-Lord himself was defeated and locked forever in the Dark Realm, as Iriam had once described.

And she would share that fate, as the Life-Blood Spell required.

She shook the thought away. That wasn't a concern she needed to worry about today. There were far more pressing fears. "I don't know," she said. "We might find something in Tinkeeyo. Or if Iriam has recovered, we can ask him when we're back in Caer Sia."

There was a moment of silence. Allie tried to think of that return, looking forward to a time after this fight. Gayrile would be won, they'd return to Caer Sia, and she, Darion, and Rygal would resume their search through the old books. She'd gladly take the stuffy library of Castle Sia over the fear and bloodshed that had filled the last few weeks.

She shifted her position again, easing her aching knees. "Can you… tell me about your brother?" she asked finally, steering the conversation away from the war for now.

Darion looked at her, seeming to understand the reason behind her request, and thought for a moment. "He's smart," he said at last. "Good at talking to people and making friends. He was my best friend growing up." A small, bittersweet smile touched his face as he spoke.

Allie listened in silence, trying to ground herself on his voice, to allow his words to carry her back to the times he spoke of. Simple, peaceful times, when Darion had been a ranger's apprentice, and his brother Fargrin simply an ambitious young man.

A time before the Aces had claimed both their lives.

The lilting call of a hunting horn jarred her mind back to the present. Darion became still immediately, his eyes turning to the right. "That's

Rygal's signal," he whispered. "They're close."

The Brownae warriors straightened with only the softest rustle, gripping their weapons. Allie hunched behind the sagebrush, keeping her sword low so that it did not catch the glint of sun. That might betray their position, and they couldn't afford to lose a moment of the surprise before the proper time. Rygal's horn meant the plan was working. The thought filled her with both excitement and fear.

Gradually, she became aware of more sounds—the rhythm of many running feet, the garble of urgent and frantic voices, and, steadily growing louder, the pants and snarls of pursuing Dal-kerri. Her fire kindled in her chest.

At last, the Guardians appeared on the road, running in a chaotic, confused retreat towards the beach. They were playing the part perfectly, thoroughly beaten, disorganized, and terrified—at least, Allie hoped they were pretending.

At their heels came the pursuers.

Allie had known there were still a large number of Dal-kerri here, but she'd never imagined so many. Hundreds of wolves bounded down the path, snarling and snapping at the weary Guardians. Serpentines reeled in the sky above them, bulging eyes gleaming as they watched their tiring prey. Still they kept coming, blotting out the road behind in a crowd of bristling black fur and mud-red scales. Enchanted soldiers marched on the edges, herding the pack forward.

Allie didn't see Redeyes yet, but she did see Rygal, surrounded by hounds and yellow fire, guarding the back of the retreat. He looked exhausted, his armor streaked in umber blood. Allie couldn't tell how much of his weariness was real.

"Hold," Lieutenant Porto ordered in a low voice. The warriors waited tensely, watching as the force spread on below them. Fire blazed in Allie's veins, spreading restless heat through her body and sparking across her knuckles. She gripped her sword to steady the blaze.

"There's Redeyes," Darion whispered beside her.

Prowling at the back of the pack came the great cat. The gunshot wounds on his huge head still leaked dark blood, but he seemed unhindered by them, snarling orders to the enchanted soldiers. Seeing him replaced Allie's fear with fury. Here was the monster who had killed so many, who had cursed both Jan and Darion.

"Hold," Lieutenant Porto repeated, as several Brownaes shuffled nervously.

Rygal stumbled, still shouting orders to his ragged group. The Guardians angled toward the beach, setting their stance in the packed sand and bracing themselves for battle.

At the same time, Allie saw Redeyes pause directly beneath her, turning his huge head to the wind. His fiery eyes scanned the hill.

Rygal's horn sounded a second time, summoning the allies of Gayrile.

"Now!" Porto shouted.

Allie sprang to her feet, leaping down the hill with the Brownaes, gripping her sword in one hand and letting fire crackle in the other. She launched a blast down at Redeyes. The black tiger dodged beneath the flames; eyes blazing in fury, he roared a command to the Dal-kerri, who spun to face the sudden attack.

The Brownae warriors charged downhill, crashing into the wolves like a battering ram. Redeyes had given the warning too late—most of the nearest pack died before ever seeing the waiting threat, and the rest were caught off guard.

Allie sprang through the sagebrush, her boots landing on the gravel road. Bodies pressed against her in the fray as she slashed and stabbed. Teeth ripped at her left arm, bringing a flare of pain and ripping her sleeve, and she sent the fire blazing forth. Something heavy slammed into her from the other side, nearly knocking her down. Blood splashed across her face as she stumbled, but it wasn't her own. Blindly, she brought her sword up in time to intercept a wolf that lunged at her.

A bright blast of flames came from her left as the Direns launched their assault. The reek of charred flesh, the shrieks and howls of the furious Dal-kerri, the screams of the wounded and dying, seemed to fade away as her senses heightened and her fire blazed hotter. The fury had cleared. The fear seemed to have left. Her mind was centered entirely on the battle, the flames crackling in her veins and spreading from her fingers. Dal-kerri were everywhere, snapping and clawing. Gunshots crackled in the air in a deafening cacophony.

Any battle, any fight she'd ever experienced—they were nothing compared to this mad rush of killing. She barely saw her companions, barely knew where she was, only the heat of the fire in her hands and the chill of adrenaline drowning out all else. On and on it went, until the dust of the path was soaked with blood and the attacks gradually faltered.

Wings swirled the air overhead, and she looked up as a serpentine dove, venom glinting on its fangs. Darion's arrow caught it in the neck, and it hit the ground lifeless. Allie swung to face him, catching her breath. "Where are the Guardians?" she called.

Darion's leather armor was soaked in Dal-kerri blood, and there were several cuts on his face and forearms, but he wasn't badly injured. "Rygal's drawn the battle further down the beach," he panted. "Lieutenant Porto's garrison will stay here—make sure the wolves don't slip away."

Allie turned. The road beside the hills was carpeted with bodies. Beyond, the rocky beach churned with battle. The Dal-kerri seemed almost hesitant; she could sense them pulling back. But the enchanted soldiers showed no sign of weariness. Several Guardians had fallen to the serpentines' fangs.

"They'll be pinned down there!" she cried, feeling a surge of fear. Rygal's plan had been to draw the battle away from the hills, hoping to keep the Ace-army from escaping into the wilds. But now, with the full force of the enraged invaders, the Guardians would be trapped at the ocean's edge.

"The Coopers are coming!" Darion yelled back. "Rygal wants us to hold the line here."

Allie turned toward the sea. A haze of fog mingled with the smoke of Bridgeport, blocking any view of the approaching ships—assuming they were coming at all. But she shook that fear from her mind and set her stance in the bloodied ground, slashing the last few hounds that attempted to flee. Now that she was out of the chaotic fray, she felt incredibly calm, her mind vacant of everything except cold focus.

Darion's voice drew her attention again. "Allie—look." He pointed north, his face drawn. Further down the beach, a squad of enchanted soldiers had broken from the main battle and were engaged in a fight with a group of Guardians. Whether they intended to forge an escape route, or they simply meant to weaken the already exhausted warriors, Allie couldn't tell, but that hardly mattered—what mattered was that they were moments from attacking.

"Let's go," she said, jogging down the road toward the fight.

Darion ran after her, his voice tense. "Allie—you can't just kill them— they don't know what they're doing, or why they're here."

"I don't want to kill them," Allie replied shortly. "But they're here to kill us, so I don't really get a choice." The tone of her voice startled her. Cool, collected, and with a hint of something like excitement. The thought sickened her. Where had that come from? She hated killing, no matter the situation. Even the battle in the woods with the Wildkids, when she'd first learned of her new powers, had filled her with dread. She had hated killing those enchanted soldiers, knowing their actions had not been their own.

But there was no remorse now. Only a rising darkness, drawn forth by the horror around her, that threatened to encase her heart in ice.

"I won't kill them," she said aloud, hoping to banish the strange darkness that had suddenly overshadowed her. "Not unless I have to. We can press them into the sea—the waves will slow them down."

Darion's gaze lingered on her uneasily, but he only nodded wordlessly and followed like a second shadow, an arrow on his bowstring as they reached the struggle.

The rocky coast sloped upward before her, dropping away before the waves in a short but steep cliff to the right. A small squadron of Direns had come to aid the Guardians, fire flashing from their scaled hands, but they too were beginning to tire. She raised her hands as she and Darion reached the group, spreading a wall of red flames into the faces of the enchanted soldiers.

"Don't try to fight them!" Darion called to the exhausted allies. "Press them back to the edge!"

An orc lunged at Allie, breaking her concentration, and the fiery barrier flickered away. She raised her sword—the strength behind the orc's blow shuddered her tired arm, sending her stumbling. She managed to parry, trying to recover her balance. As she'd observed before, the enchanted soldiers had no qualms about killing her—probably unable to recognize their master's Vessel in the heat of battle.

Or, as a darker thought entered her mind, perhaps this was the Ace-Lord's strategy to force the Vessel's hand.

The Ace-Lord's voice whispered in her thoughts as her fire blazed again. *"Every bit of the fire in your veins exists to serve me now."*

She tried to settle herself, turn her thoughts away from the rage and darkness—but the fear and adrenaline of the fight drowned it out. In a flash, the wrath was back. Her fire struck the orc in the chest, leaving red sparks on his jerkin, and he staggered back, his hollow blue eyes holding both surprise and fear as he felt the pain.

Allie loosed another blast, sending him toppling backward over the short cliff and into the frothy spray below.

"I thought you said no killing," Darion said behind her, his teeth gritted as he loosed an arrow.

"I didn't kill him," Allie snapped back, blasting another enchanted soldier. One of the Direns kicked him in the chest and knocked him backward.

A horn blast sounded—it took Allie a moment to remember what the signal meant. "Regroup," she panted at last, wiping the sweat and blood from her face. They headed back down the beach toward the battlefield.

Bodies lay sprawled across the space between road and waves, Brownaes, Guardians, Direns, and Dal-kerri alike. The enemy force had gathered a mere arrow shot away, teeming and snarling like one massive beast. Hours of bloodshed and battle, and yet the allies of Gayrile were still vastly outnumbered—nor did the Ace-army show any signs of tiring. Doubt and unease twinged in Allie's chest.

The allies had formed up in a wide half-circle, keeping the

Dal-kerri before them. Rygal's voice rose amid the crowds, hoarse with exhaustion. "Hold, men. Lord Casper, stay with your warriors on the rocks."

He stood slightly in front of them with a group of Guardians, battered and bruised. Flames still sparkled from his sword, but blood streaked his injured leg, and he moved with evident pain.

"Where to?" Darion called to him.

Rygal glanced over—Allie saw relief cross his face as he saw them both still alive, and he nodded to the left. "We're holding here. Don't let them get any further north."

Allie frowned uncertainly. "Hold? For how long? We can't beat them all."

Rygal pushed a lock of bloodied hair off his forehead, taking a breath. "Not long. We're going to drive them back soon—we just need to wait for reinforcements."

"Reinforcements whose arrival we have no certain knowledge of," Lord Casper pointed out grimly behind him. "Do you believe they will come in time?"

"Do you have a better strategy, sir?" Rygal asked tiredly.

The swarming hoards of Dal-kerri stirred restlessly, eager for the fight to begin again, but a low growl held them back. Through the ranks prowled Redeyes. The great cat's eyes blazed with anticipation as he studied the weary warriors, and his voice rumbled across the battle-stained beach.

"If you plan to surrender, know that the Ace-Lord has ordered no quarter," he snarled, teeth glinting as he smiled wickedly. "Your only choice is to serve him, and swear the enchantment with the rest of your meager brethren."

Captain Terivis spat on the ground before him, his green scales covered in grime. "Even if my people once considered that offer, we will never accept it now. Not after you have murdered our chieftains and brothers."

Redeyes' fiery gaze fixed on him. "Then you choose death," he breathed, and with a roar, the Dal-kerri lunged forward in a renewed assault.

Allie slid her sword back into the scabbard—she could hardly trust her weary arm to wield the blade in the tight, confined fray of battle. Instead, she allowed the flames to blaze at her fingers, placing herself between Rygal and Darion. The oncoming rush of Dal-kerri drowned out Rygal's voice as he called orders to the Guardians. Multi-colored flames lit Gayrile's shore as the battle began again.

Allie felt the eerie calm, acutely aware of her every heartbeat. Through the blur of blood and madness, the red fire seemed to grow hotter and paler with every second. She felt as though she were observing the fight from afar, as if her body were possessed by someone else and she were only a spectator.

Three enchanted soldiers collapsed lifeless. A wolf crumbled beneath the blazing fire. Waves of heat wafted in her face and hair. Her skin blistered at her fingertips.

"Allie!" Darion was shouting nearby, but she barely heard him. The fire had come forth—not that breathless inferno that had claimed her the day before—this was something else entirely, some other power that filled her now.

"Allie!" Rygal's voice, right beside her—with an effort, she drew herself out of the detached darkness.

The dead lay piled in heaps around them; she hardly recognized their charred bodies. Yet her eyes were drawn to the opponents before her.

The Dal-kerri were… falling back, their hollow eyes turned to the sea, uneasy snarls rising in their throats.

Through the haze of smoke and ash, six ships were speeding for Gayrile's coast, their triangle sails rising above the water like the wings of a sea bird, the wind propelling them forward. Mata City's blue and silver banners fluttered triumphantly in the breeze.

The Coopers had finally arrived.

28

Triumph and Death

Allie felt herself exhale a pent-up breath. Her hands ached, and she felt the pain from a score of injuries all over her body, but it was dismissed by a surge of hope as she watched the Coopers draw near.

Jarus had done it. He'd rallied the armies of Mata City, bringing them to the battle, and not a moment too soon.

Allie saw the Coopers spring easily into the waves and climb up the rocks to the battlefield, saxe knives clenched in their teeth. Each warrior wore plated leather armor over their backs and forelegs, and their eyes gleamed beneath their steel helmets as they swarmed to shore.

Redeyes turned sharply to see the approaching opponents, his face filled with hatred as he realized he had been tricked a second time. "Fight them, you fools!" he roared, bounding toward the Cooper warriors. The Dal-kerri followed, but their attack was confused, uncertain. The Ace-army split into two groups, some continuing to clash with their previous opponents, others moving to fight the newcomers.

With the piercing battle cry of Mata City—*"Huvá! Huvá!"*—the Coopers lunged into the fight. Despite their small size, they were deadly warriors. Saxe knives cut down the startled Dal-kerri. Several Coopers wielded atl-atls, flinging darts up at the hovering serpentines. Allie watched in awe as four Coopers overwhelmed an enchanted orc, hauling him to the ground.

"Let's go!" Rygal ordered, raising his sword.

Allie ran after him, fresh energy replacing the doubt and dread. Their gamble had paid off. The Dal-kerri, splintered and startled, had nowhere to flee. Behind them was the line of Brownaes, protecting the hills. Before them, leaping from the sea, were the Cooper warriors, far more in number than Allie had first thought, fearlessly attacking wolves twice their size.

A serpentine dove at her from above, and she fired a blast before it reached them. Jarus, his dark eyes alight with excitement, bounded toward them. He wore the same plated leather armor as the rest of the Cooper forces. "Glad to see you're all here and alive," he commented. "Looks like we made it just in time. What's our plan now?"

"They'll try to flee," Darion warned, nodding back toward the mountains. "Once they realize they're outmatched, they'll try to make for either the hills or back to Bridgeport."

Rygal nodded with a tired smile. "Don't worry, I thought of that this morning." He pointed to the road. "Captain Pike has a squadron of Guardians waiting with the Brownaes to the south. We'll drive the Dal-kerri back toward Bridgeport, catch them in a vise and finish them off."

Four Dal-kerri turned from fighting the Coopers and lunged at them. Allie blasted two, and Rygal and Jarus killed the others.

"Sounds like a good plan," Darion said, lowering his bow. "But I doubt Redeyes will be 'finished off' easily."

Rygal let out a breath. "I know. But he won't continue the invasion without any forces to command. We'll deal with him later—right now," he grunted as he caught another hound against his shield, "I need these blasted dogs out of Gayrile."

Darion released an arrow, dropping the Dal-kerri to the rocks.

"We can't leave both sides undefended," Rygal continued. "Lieutenant Porto is holding his side of the perimeter, but he's taking heavy losses—we saw a pack of Dal-kerri head his way before the Coopers got here."

"We can go help them," Allie said, with a glance to Darion. Her voice barely sounded like her own. She supposed she should prefer this cool detachment to the crippling nerves of before, but even that was preferable—at least she had felt *something.*

Rygal looked back at the hills, then nodded to her and Darion. "Just be careful. We'll regroup back here—shouldn't be long now."

"Don't say that," Jarus berated him as Allie turned away. "You're going to jinx it."

Allie ran back toward the dusty road with Darion following close behind. The dying and wounded were everywhere, some crying out in agony. Others were silent. She tore her gaze away from the carnage, though it chilled her to the core. Her eyes scanned the sagebrush of the rolling hills, watching for mud-red scales or bristling fur. No sign of attackers. The Dal-kerri and serpentines seemed confined to the fray on the beach.

Where was Redeyes? She'd seen him intercept the Coopers, but now he seemed to have vanished.

Clouds shrouded the sun, and a muggy haze embraced the battlefield. Carrion birds soared overhead. Sweat and grime covered Allie's face. The gash on her sword arm, torn by Dal-kerri teeth, ached over the adrenaline that had gripped her through the fight. Her chest felt chillingly cold. She let the fire play on her fingertips, yet her skin stung at the heat.

"You, Vessel, have no choice in the matter."

The Ace-Lord's voice filled her mind again, sending the anger surging back.

They reached the hilltop. A group of Dal-kerri clashed against the Brownae warriors, who were stubbornly protecting the path leading into the hills. Darion's arrows took down three wolves in rapid succession; Allie's fire consumed the rest.

Lieutenant Porto stumbled forward to meet them. The Brownae's black fur was crusted in Dal-kerri blood, and there was a nasty cut on his brow. "We've held the road," he panted. "None of them escaped the battlefield. We saw the Coopers arrive—I take it the Commander's plan worked?"

"Better than we hoped," Allie told him. She studied the Brownae squad. There were eleven of them left, all injured. Three were semi-conscious, supported by their comrades. "Let's get you all out of here. You've done well."

Porto smiled weakly in thanks, following as they started downhill. Darion moved to the rear of the group, making sure none of the injured fell behind, and they began the slow descent toward the road. Allie kept her eyes on the beach. Only hours ago, she realized, she'd crouched on this same hillside, waiting tensely for the fight to begin. The clamor of battle filled the air, and from this vantage point, she could tell the Dal-kerri had begun to fall back.

Brush crackled to her left.

She turned sharply. An enchanted soldier stood before her, crossbow pointed at her chest.

The Brownaes stopped abruptly, looking uneasy. Fire crackled in Allie's hands for an instant, but she forced it down. The enchanted soldier's hollow eyes fixed on Allie's. He was young—probably younger than she was.

"Allie…" Darion started worriedly. He had an arrow on the string, but didn't draw it.

"Keep going," Allie told Porto, keeping her eyes on the young soldier. "Get them to the beach."

The Brownaes started forward again, glancing back worriedly. The enchanted soldier stood silently, face expressionless. He was human, not one of the orcs she'd fought earlier. Perhaps he'd been one of the many taken from Wiverrun.

"It's all right," she said quietly, trying to recall everything Rygal had ever told her about curing the Hazes. "It's all right. Do you remember your name?"

The enchanted soldier did not move, the crossbow still aimed at her.

"You're in Gayrile," Darion said behind Allie. "You're fighting for the Ace-Lord's forces. You took a Blood Oath. Do you remember that?"

At the mention of the Oath, the soldier lowered the crossbow slightly, seeming to hesitate. Allie saw momentary confusion cross his expressionless face. Now was hardly the time for this, but it might be the only chance they had to speak to one of the Ace-Lord's enchanted slaves.

"It's all right," she said again. "Tell us your name."

At the words, a new light entered the young soldier's eyes and he finally spoke, voice dull and lifeless. "I have no name. None but what my lord gives me."

"We can help you," Allie pressed. "But you have to choose it for yourself. Do you want to be free?"

The soldier's gaze slid down to the ground. For an instant, Allie thought the blue light faded away slightly in his eyes. His soft voice held a distant note of longing. "Many of us wish a choice. But it is not ours to choose."

"It could be," Allie insisted. "You could choose it. You just need to remember who you are."

For a moment, she thought her words had reached him. But then the young soldier seemed to shudder. He raised his head again, his unblinking eyes fixed on her. The voice that issued from his mouth was low, deathly cold, and chillingly familiar. *"This is a strange strategy."*

Chills spread down Allie's arms, and she took a step back. The enchanted soldier stared at her, a new light in his lifeless face as his master spoke through him.

"How many have you killed, Vessel?" the Ace-Lord's voice inquired, mocking amusement in his words. *"Do you wish to help them? There is only one language they understand."*

The soldier raised the crossbow, the bolt aimed at Allie—Darion loosed his arrow into the man's chest before he could shoot, sending him toppling back into the brush.

"Heiress!"

A shrill cry split the tense air further downhill. Allie turned sharply. Gunfire sounded below them, and with it, the rising hiss of serpentines.

She stumbled through the underbrush, her calm shattered by the Ace-Lord's words as she and Darion raced downhill. By the time they reached the road, two Brownaes already lay lifeless, white venom rimming their fresh wounds. The others were grouped together, desperately fending off the new attack.

"Go!" Allie yelled, fire sparking from her hands. "Get to the water— the Coopers can help you there—"

The small party turned, stumbling across the rocks. The pale fire was rising again, so much stronger than the usual crackling red, tempting her with every frantic heartbeat. She struck down two serpentines as the others took to the air.

She ran after the remaining Brownaes. Darion jogged among them, occasionally pausing to loose an arrow at the sky. The cold was filling Allie's chest again, a darkness she could not stop, a fear that fanned the flames to an uncontrollable heat.

Twenty enchanted soldiers marched towards them as they reached the beach, barring the injured Brownaes from escape.

Allie sprang forward as the soldiers charged, knowing dimly that there were too many for her to fight alone. Fire blazed in blast after blast as she struck at her targets—lives she had hoped not to take, lives drawn into a fight they didn't understand, lives snuffed out in succession by her fire. A club glanced across her left shoulder, flinging her forward. Another injured Brownae collapsed without even the chance to fight back.

Darion stood just ahead of her, fending off an enchanted soldier with his dagger, gripping his bow in his other hand. Only three arrows remained in his quiver.

"Get them to the beach!" Allie shouted at him. "Just go—I can cover you."

Darion called something back, but his voice was drowned out as the fire blazed again, spreading across the rocks around her. Another enchanted soldier fell. But more came from the beach, splashing through the ankle deep water to join the fight.

They couldn't be coordinating this attack alone. Who…

A snarl rumbled behind her, sending a jolt of fear through her chest as she understood.

She swung around as Redeyes stalked forward, triumph on his face. She sent a blast at him—a sword glanced across her shoulder, and a cry of both pain and anger tore from her throat. Fire launched from her hands as she fought blindly. The seconds blurred, too fast for her mind to process.

Redeyes sprang into the fight, his claws easily dragging down two injured Brownaes. Darion fired two arrows in quick succession, sinking them into the tiger's face and shoulder. Redeyes roared in pain as the arrows struck his recent injuries, and for a moment he seemed to falter.

"Go!" Allie screamed again, turning her fire to the massive cat. Darion, finally, moved onward, leading the remaining injured away. She sensed him retreating down the beach.

Then she was alone, alone with the fire and the dead piling up around her.

The enchanted soldiers closed around her. A crossbow bolt whizzed past her side, inches from her ribs. Her breath came in ragged gasps, exhausted from the toil of the day and the sheer horror of the present.

She edged backward after her companions, tripping over another dead Brownae—Porto. Waves lapped at her boots. Enchanted soldiers closed in again, striking relentlessly. Darion slashed at one with his dagger, then brought his bow up, his last arrow aimed at Redeyes.

As he did, Allie saw his eyes widen in fear as his gaze fixed on something to her left. Out of the corner of her eye, she saw the serpentine dive down at her.

Darion's last arrow pierced its throat in the same instant that Redeyes loomed up behind him, his claws raking down the ranger's unguarded back.

The serpentine's body crashed onto Allie, flinging her into the bloodied surf. Gasping, she fought to her knees, blinded by salt and sand. The hulking figures of the enchanted soldiers advanced upon her, and she raised her hands, pale fire spitting at her fingertips. "Darion—get back—"

There was no tempering the flames this time—she called forth the inferno, letting it engulf the oncoming warriors. Fire crackled over the waves and packed sand. Her red flared to white in the same moment that, abruptly, her vision plunged into darkness, and she felt herself fall face-down to the beach.

All was dark. Her ears were ringing. Cold seawater lapped against her face as she lay in the surf.

As if through a haze, she saw Redeyes move away, saw the remaining enchanted soldiers stumble after him, red sparks still glowing on their armor.

The Brownae warriors lay unmoving, bodies spread from the hilltop they'd protected to the sea they'd fought so hard to reach.

Eleven bodies.

Porto's entire group, the lives she'd been tasked to protect.

Painfully, she crawled to her hands and knees. A hand gripped her shoulder as she did, making her jump. Her vision focused on Darion's pale face.

"Allie—are you—"

"I'm all right," she managed to answer, though her head was pounding as if it would split in two. "Let's just… get to the Coopers… see how we can help."

Leaning on each other, they got to their feet. Darion gripped the rocks, his entire body trembling as they moved forward. Allie put an arm under his shoulder, helping him move down the coastline.

"I'm—sorry," Darion panted. "Didn't—see Redeyes—" He stumbled and fell, pulling Allie down with him.

Alarmed, she knelt beside him. "It's all right—just catch your breath." Her right arm was pressed against his back, and she became aware that it was soaked in blood. His Red Dawn armor had been shredded by

Redeyes' claws. A gaping wound had been torn from his right shoulder across his back to the left side of his ribs. His breath came short and shallow. He looked up at her, confused by the fear on her face.

"Is—everything all—right?"

"It's okay. It's not your fault—just breathe," Allie told him, ignoring the fear that had crept into her heart. "We're going to the medics, just to make sure."

With an effort, she hauled him to his feet again. He leaned heavily against her, too heavy for her to manage, not after the exhaustion of the day. She stumbled over a fallen Guardian and they fell again to the coarse sand of the beach. Darion lay on his back, his face more confused than in pain as he gasped for breath.

"Stay with me," Allie ordered, tearing a strip of fabric from her tunic and pressing the cloth against the gaping wound under his arm.

"I—shouldn't have argued—didn't want you—in danger," Darion said haltingly. He coughed, blood rimming his lips.

"I know. It's fine. We're going to be fine," Allie said firmly, ignoring the rising cold in her heart. "Just stay with me, all right?"

Darion let out a shallow breath and nodded. "All right. All right." His eyes remained fixed on her face, his expression relaxing, as blood steadily stained the sand around them.

"Hold on," Allie murmured, hearing the futility in her own voice. The cold spread over her chest, encasing her heart in ice.

Darion's head fell gently to the side, his hazel eyes clouded, scars seeming to have faded on his pale face.

She knew he was gone. Knew she could not help him, any more than she'd been able to help the injured Brownaes, or Morel, or any of the others lost in the cruel fight that had won them Gayrile.

She draped his tattered cloak over him and sat beside him in the wet sand. Listened to the sounds of battle as the Aces' forces crumpled. Felt the calm and darkness embrace her like the black waters of an icy sea.

Eventually, she felt herself stand and turn, moving back to the battle. She felt the heat of the fire as it flew, blast after blast, soldier after soldier. Felt the flames crackle into something new and twisted that she could not escape. Felt her blistered fingers grow cold as winter frost.

Her own red died away, and her fire blazed as white as the Ace-Lord's ice, spreading across the bloodstained beach, as the final howls of the Dal-kerri faded into silence.

29

A Fading Light

Fear.

When had it become such a frequent part of life? Every moment of peace Mel had managed to find since the war began seemed tainted. The happiness of his time with his family, the relief of hearing his mentor yet lived, the powerful promise spoken over him in the scribehouse—all had evaporated before the raw terror of the Ace's illusion, and the growing dread of the dryad's message.

At the dryad's words, Dandio had sprung into action, pulling Mel and Misty into the courtyard and shouting for a stable hand to bring Nella. Lord Andros' voice faded among the shouts of disbelief and dread of the many warriors who had heard the news.

Caer Sia was under attack. The Ace-Lord had never intended to attack Mata City, though he had laid the evidence so convincingly that even the best spies in the kingdom had believed it. Every attack, every battle, had only furthered his plot. The Red Dawn were spread throughout the land now, helping everywhere but where they were most needed, and many too far away to return to their home in time to help.

No, it was the perfect strategy, Mel thought bitterly.

The minutes passed in a blur. Dandio left briefly and returned with a few of the packs, and Mel helped Misty into Nella's saddle. Alder was there, briefly—Mel heard him bidding them a safe and swift flight.

Swift. That was the only thing that might save Sia's people.

It would be too late to prepare a counter attack. That much Dandio admitted, as he'd spurred Nella into the air and turned her north. By the time the Red Dawn was alerted, the Aces would be at their threshold, prepared to wreck the same destruction they'd inflicted during the quest for the Shards. Their best hope was to evacuate as many lives as they could to safety before the attack struck. The Aces had turned time against them.

Mel clung to Dandio's back, eyes squinted against the whipping wind. Despite the many questions, he was unable to speak. The lingering horror of the Ace's illusion, the agony in Aryion's voice, the terror of being trapped inside the shield with the deafening sound, seemed to have rendered him mute. Not even Misty ventured a word as they flew, gripping Mel's shoulders.

They stopped a little after moonrise when Nella had begun to tire. Dandio had her descend in a quiet meadow deep in the Magno Forest and drink from a stream. Once Nella was rested, they mounted up again and continued the ride.

Clouds covered the sky, concealing the comforting starlight. The moon stood pale and silent. Misty finally nodded off, her head resting against Mel's back. The nerves knotting in Mel's stomach banished any thoughts of sleep, and he clung to Dandio, listening to the distant sounds of night in the forest far below.

"Do you think… do you think the dryads came to Caer Sia, too?" he wondered finally, unable to stand the tense silence any longer. "Maybe they've been warned and have already prepared a counter attack."

"The dryads only learned this news today," Dandio answered quietly. "In which case, Caer Sia has the same amount of time to prepare as we do."

"Could the kragons help?" Mel asked.

"Lord Fireclaw cannot spare warriors—Tinkeeyo is still under siege. Our allies are spread thin—though I expect that is what the Ace-Lord planned." Dandio took a deep breath. His usual fiery determination seemed stifled by fear for his city and people. "No, in this instance, we would lose more lives by fighting."

Mel nodded numbly. He knew Dandio was right, but the thought of abandoning Caer Sia to the enemy wrenched his heart. First Wiverrun, then Appledale, and now Caer Sia. Doomed to destruction for the Ace-Lord's conquest.

Perhaps he could save the city with the Stone's power? Perhaps the song was the counter attack they desperately needed? But the thought sickened him with dread. The memory of that power had been polluted by the horror of the illusion. The once-comforting blue light caused the horrible scream to enter his mind again as if it had been planted there, a terror he could not shake away.

He squeezed his eyes shut, trying to steer his thoughts away from that. When he opened them, his gaze was drawn to movement in the forest below.

"Steady, Nella," Dandio whispered, pressing his heel against the gryphon's side to veer her left.

Mel looked down as they flew over, straining his eyes to see. Something was moving along the northern road like a black fog, swarming and stirring with activity. At last, he saw what it was.

Soldiers. More warriors than he'd ever seen, marching steadily toward Caer Sia. He glimpsed the bristling black fur of the Dal-kerri, enchanted soldiers of all races, and the mud-red scales of countless serpentines that flew just above the trees. Tens of thousands, moving in columns over the hills.

A low growl issued from Nella's throat. "Steady," Dandio murmured, and the gryphon grew quiet, flying onward.

They swept over the multitude of the Ace-army. Mel felt exposed, as if the Stone's light and the pounding of his own heart would give them away. The sheer masses overwhelmed him, and further convinced him it would be no good fighting, not against such numbers.

Nella sped onward, as if she too could sense the urgency. The Ace-army fell away behind them, but Mel's fear remained, knowing they were coming. He knew he should get some rest, knowing the real fight had not even begun. But his dreams tormented him, forbidding him to sleep. Aryion's scream echoed dimly in his mind over and over, along with the hissing taunts of the Ace-messenger. Images of friends long gone swam in his vision.

Crushing guilt settled on his shoulders. He'd gone to Tinkeeyo to help, to better understand his role as the New Blood, and yet he would return to Caer Sia more lost than ever. He suddenly felt very alone, suspended over the black forest as they flew toward the doomed city. Was this the High Light's plan? Caer Sia would fall, the Aces would overrun the north, and the Ace-Lord would claim a kingdom of darkness? Why couldn't the Stars send their armies and protect them? Better yet, why couldn't the High Light Himself enter the battle, destroy the Ace-Lord once and for all?

He took a deep breath, racking his thoughts for reassurance. He found none. Only growing despair as they flew north.

By the time Caer Sia's lights appeared below them, the sky flushed pale pink in the east. Mel was shivering with cold and his body ached from the grueling ride, but he barely noticed it as they swept down over the city.

Torches shone in the lantern-lit streets below them. Riders streamed through Caer Sia. Mel could not hear their voices, but he could guess what they were warning of. Crowds of people had already begun to gather near the harbor, their frightened voices drifting over the city.

"Looks as though the evacuation's begun," Dandio murmured, guiding Nella toward the castle.

"Where—where will they go?" Mel asked through chattering teeth.

"That will be a question for Jan. I assume our best move will be to evacuate the civilians to another Red Dawn stronghold."

"Like Fort Tinkeeyo," Mel guessed. "Is there anywhere else we could go?"

"I am not sure. East, perhaps," Dandio replied, swinging down from the saddle as Nella touched down in the castle courtyard. Mel nudged Misty awake and climbed down. She leaned heavily against him, still half asleep.

The courtyard of Castle Sia was a whirl of uncertain voices, hurrying soldiers, and riders galloping out into every corner of the sprawling capital, intent to warn every resident. The Hyenin general, Arrex, met them at the gates, his fox-like face drawn with concern. "Commander— the Aces are…"

"On their way," Dandio said, nodding. "The dryads alerted us yesterday afternoon. We've flown hard and fast from Tinkeeyo. When did you get the news?"

The deep voice that answered sent a stir of relief through Mel. "The dryads brought the message about six hours ago. It seems they were delayed in the Magno Forest by the Aces and their forces."

Mel turned. Wreathed in his black robes, his purple-red eyes filled with concern, was Iriam. His face was still pale from the serpentine's venom, and almost as gaunt as the Ace-Lord's. But seeing him up and about eased some of Mel's fear.

Dandio's expression relaxed as he saw the Neutral. "Iriam—thank the Light you are alive—we passed the Ace-army on our flight here. They have far too many numbers for us to effectively counter—I do not know..."

Iriam placed a hand on his shoulder, studying the Liznee's exhausted face. "Dandio. Do not trouble yourself with that. The High King has ordered an evacuation. How much time do you believe we have?"

Dandio let out a breath. "A day. Perhaps less."

"Then we will use that time well," Iriam told him. "Come."

Dandio seemed calmer at his words, and with a nod to Mel and Misty, led them inside the castle. Mel looked up at Iriam as they walked inside. "Are you..."

The ghost of a smile crossed Iriam's face. "I am well. I am glad to see you, Mel. The king told me of your quest to learn of the *Alené*."

"You knew?" Mel asked, startled. "About the Stones, and the song?"

"Partially," Iriam answered, as they entered the castle. "I was not as learned in that magic as Luet, but yes, I knew of the Song of the Stars. Were you successful in your search?"

"We found the song," Misty said, her voice bleary with sleep. "It made a shield—it saved Tinkeeyo."

Mel nodded, but could not tell the full story just yet.

Castle Sia had been bustling with noise nearly every moment of the war, but now, the voices were more urgent than hopeful. Couriers and court attendants rushed through the halls.

Familiar voices reached Mel's ears as they neared the council room. He recognized Jan's measured tone, and his parent's worried words.

Mrs. Smallbutton's voice rose, stubborn and frightened. "Sire, we can't leave, not yet. Not until they're back."

"I understand your concerns," Ĵan answered. His voice, though calm, was firm. "But you must leave soon. Your children may not return for several days. We have no way of knowing if the news has reached Tinkeeyo."

"Mom!" Misty cried, running forward as they entered the hall.

Both parents turned, relief on their faces. Mel stepped away from Dandio and Iriam and joined the reunion. The terror of the last few weeks faded slightly in his mother's embrace, but he didn't allow himself to stay there long.

"You're both all right? You're not hurt?" Elonie demanded, looking them both up and down.

"We heard Tinkeeyo was besieged," Joseph said. His normally cheery face was gray with concern. "Are you sure you two are all right?"

"We're okay," Misty said, nodding.

"We're fine," Mel assured them. "We weren't in the battle."

"And your quest?" his father asked, his expression changing from fearful to curious in a moment. "Did you find the scroll you were looking for?"

"We did," Mel said, looking at Ĵan. "We found Luet's writings."

"I am eager to hear your story, but now is not the time," Ĵan told him. He turned to the Smallbuttons. "Pack your belongings and head to the courtyard. General Leopold will escort you to a ship."

Mrs. Smallbutton nodded, took Misty's hand, and looked at Mel. Mel shook his head. "You guys go on—I'll be there soon."

From his mother's expression, he could tell she didn't believe him. But she said nothing, only turned away with sorrow and fear in her eyes. His father squeezed his shoulder lightly before he too walked away.

Ĵan clasped his brother's hand in brief greeting before leading them into the council room. "It is good to see you back safely. How fares Tinkeeyo?"

"The city is secured, at least," Dandio replied. "But they are still under siege. I doubt any of our allies will be able to reach us from there."

"I had feared as much," Ĵan said grimly. He paused beside the table. "Currently, our goal is to have the people gathered at the harbor. From there, we will evacuate to Lillary Bay. It is a small village, but only a few hour's sail, and the Red Dawn fort stationed there can protect them."

"We can't evacuate them all in a day," Dandio pointed out slowly. "Do you suppose there is any hope in defense? The people need more time."

"What about the Stones?" Mel asked hesitantly, looking at Ĵan. "Couldn't they protect Caer Sia?"

"That is not the purpose of the Stones," Iriam said. His tone was gentle, but held a note of finality. "In the same way the Jewel and Isilas were corrupted by turning them away from their true purpose, so this strategy could now corrupt the Blue Stone. It was not meant to shield the material, but mortal life."

"Even if it would *help* mortal life?" Mel asked, frustrated.

"Would it?" Ĵan asked quietly. "Corrupting the purpose of the last Star-Stone—do you believe that would truly be in the best interest of everyone?"

Mel let out a breath. Now that Ĵan put it that way, he understood. The Blue Stone was never meant to protect the physical kingdom—it had been given to guard the lives of the mortals. That power had saved the people of Tinkeeyo. Now, it must protect the people of Sia as they fled from the coming attack.

"But… what about Caer Sia?" he asked softly, looking at Jan. "I—I saw what the Aces did to Appledale."

Jan's gaze was distant, as though he could already see the destruction that was coming. "It is only a city," he said at last. "Brick and mortar can be rebuilt. Iriam is correct—the heart of Sia is its people, who we must now protect." He looked up at Iriam. "Nonetheless, Dandio is also right—we need more time. What would you have us do?"

The Neutral thought for a moment. "Your plan to evacuate is a sound one. Time is indeed your best ally now. Caer Sia was built to be protected by few; it is a difficult city to besiege. Few might protect it, if they are willing."

"The Aces are coming from the south," Dandio said thoughtfully, looking at his brother. "Jan—you and I can take a squadron of warriors and hold down the southern roads from the walls. We won't hold long, but it might be long enough for the people to escape."

Jan nodded, glancing at Iriam. "We can protect the outskirts and then retreat once the people are freed."

"The walls were not built to sustain a prolonged attack," Iriam said quietly. "Nor will there be a likelihood of your escape."

Mel looked at Jan worriedly, but the king only nodded. "If that is my fate, then I will accept it," he said softly. "The curse has long required my life—if my blood is to be spilled to save Sia, so be it."

"Your curse, sire, will not be broken in that way," Iriam replied. "You will better atone for it through life than through death."

"I understand," Jan said, glancing at Dandio. "But I refuse to flee until every living soul is out of Caer Sia. In the meantime, I must beg you to contact the Druids. If Sia is to fall, the north must be protected."

Iriam inclined his head slightly—Mel could see from his grim expression that he did not like Jan's plan, but clearly understood it to be necessary. "I shall send word to them. Hope that Sia may yet stand," he added, his purple-red eyes studying Jan's worn face. "The city shall survive as long as its people live."

Assuming we live, Mel couldn't resist adding mentally. Once the Aces destroyed Caer Sia, how long would the mortals last, realistically? The north would be lost. There was hardly a point in preserving the Star-Stones if there was no one left for them to protect.

"Await me in the war room," Jan told Dandio. "I must send a message to Badwater—they need to be aware of what has transpired."

Dandio nodded and turned to Mel. "Go with your family. You'll be safe in Lillary Bay."

Mel gave a short nod and headed out into the hall, listening to the fading sound of Jan's voice as the High King issued further orders. Dreary morning light filled the castle, and yet the world had never seemed darker. Fear and darkness. Was that all it had come to, after everything they'd fought for?

But he had no intention of fleeing. There was one thing that might stop the Aces from attacking, one thing he could offer to turn them away. They wanted the New Blood, and they wanted the Stone. Maybe, if he gave himself up, they'd stop their attack… and maybe he could bargain with them to free Aryion too.

He knew, in the back of his mind, that it was a bad decision, one Aryion would disapprove of. But the horror of the last few days blinded his judgment.

Resolved to this plan, he headed toward the stables.

"By your direction, I take it you are not going to the courtyard," came Iriam's quiet voice on the stairs behind him.

Mel stopped, staring ahead into the darkness of the hall, and let out a breath. "Iriam… I can't just leave. They're going to keep coming. The Aces are coming for me, aren't they?" he added, turning around. "Because I'm the last Wielder?"

"Perhaps, perhaps not," the Neutral answered, studying him carefully. "This conquest was in the making long before your time."

Mel turned away, about to continue onward, but he felt Iriam's eyes on his back. Frustration and desperation built to the surface, and he swung around sharply. "Then what am I supposed to do about it? Iriam—all these people are ready to die for the Stone, for the Prophecy, and I can't help them." He held up his hand, the lantern light shining on the scar the Blood Oath had left.

Iriam was silent for a moment. "Why did you swear the Oath, child?" he asked finally.

There was no accusation or reproach in his tone. He simply asked the question as calmly as if it were any other. Yet it seemed to pierce Mel's heart, as though aimed at every one of his doubts and fears, calling into question the motives he could no longer remember.

He hesitated, thinking through his answer. "I… I wanted to do the right thing," he stammered after a pause. "I wanted to help, to use the Stone the way it was meant to. And… I didn't want to be distracted by anything else."

"You gave up yourself," Iriam said quietly. "You gave up your fears, your cares, even your desire to free your mentor. You left it behind to pursue what you were called to do."

Mel closed his eyes. "I don't even know where I'm called anymore."

"Do you not?" A slight smile crossed the Neutral's face. "I believe the Prophecy was clear on that matter, if not on others. *When New Blood stands unbidden, Mortal guard what was united, Then the world shall yet survive."* He paused. "You are the New Blood. You have continued to guard the Stone, despite the darkness and trials the Aces have thrown upon you. You lean upon the High Light's power, as He intended."

"Then you think… you think the High Light is still in control?" Mel asked, suddenly feeling very small.

"I choose to believe it," Iriam replied. "I know if it were not so, the world would have fallen to darkness long ago." He placed a hand on Mel's shoulder, looking out the window. "And yet look. The dawn still shines. The world is dark, and it may grow darker still before this fight is over. But the light is still here, and it is the task of the New Blood to shine that light into the shadows."

Mel took a deep breath, staring out the window at the pale light of morning. The despair that had enveloped him fell away before the truths Iriam spoke.

He was not alone. His purpose had only just begun. His mission now lay with the people of Coonsia, to shine light and hope into these dark hours. He let his mind relax, returning to the comfort of the High Light's words in Tinkeeyo.

I am with you.

He did not hear the voice this time. But he felt the same peace settle over him like wings as he headed to the courtyard to join the evacuation.

30

Darkness

Allie did not remember the rest of the battle.

Her few memories were foggy and fragmented, grotesque shards of the gruesome fight. White fire launching from her hands, blistering her skin, striking down countless enchanted soldiers. A throbbing headache as her Essence tired. Blood, dried and sticky, on her hands, her face, her armor. The stench of it filled her nose.

She recalled, vaguely, someone pulling her away from the carnage on the beach—Jarus, maybe. She remembered questions, confused, worried, as doctors poked and pried at her, seeking for the source of the blood on her clothes. Her own calm voice answered, retelling the unexpected attack on Lieutenant Porto's group, the fight with the enchanted soldiers, and Redeyes appearing among the rocks.

From there, her memories became clear, every second preserved in her mind. Darion's last arrow taking down the serpentine that dove for her. Redeyes' claws ripping open the ranger's back. The cruel smile on the beast's face as he'd turned away, leaving the battle behind, having accomplished what he'd come for.

The Marks, reconciled. Paid by blood.

Redeyes was gone, according to the Coopers. Apparently he'd fled Gayrile with a handful of Rufa Brownaes. At first, Allie had felt a surge of fury that demanded she make them pay for all they'd done, all they'd killed. But her anger was soon replaced by a cold calm. Leaving Gayrile to pursue Redeyes and the surviving members of the Aces' forces might expose them to another attack. Now that Bridgeport had been reclaimed, they could not risk losing it again.

So she'd joined the Coopers as they returned to Bridgeport, where the Guardians tended their wounded, buried their dead, and celebrated the victory. The sounds of mourning and cheering alike grated in her ears. The festivities filling the streets below, the joyous cries of the liberated townsfolk, only served to accentuate the darkness lurking in her heart. They knew nothing of the price, of the deaths, of the blood that had been spilled for them. They would go about their lives just as they had done before the war.

It wasn't that simple. Even if, by some miracle, the Aces were defeated, she knew nothing would ever be the same. Known it from the moment the white fire had blazed from her hands.

She sat silently in the Guardians' barracks while a doctor tended the long gash on her arm. The blood and death of the day seemed to have become a part of her. Even in fresh clothes, with her skin scrubbed of the grime, the sickly scent clung to her.

No, there was no going forward after this. Her mind, torn between hope and fury, distracted by a quest for a cure that did not exist, was finally clear. Her next step was to kill the Ace-Lord, end this struggle before it went any further. She would return to Caer Sia, report to the Red Dawn as a soldier. She would do as she was ordered, pretend that nothing had changed. Pretend the world was still the same without the dead in it.

And then she would go to Ar-Salem. The Ace-Lord's Vessel would bring about his undoing. She would die along with him, leave this world of pain behind and see that the Ace-Lord was gone forever.

So she focused her mind on vengeance, allowed her grief to wear the guise of rage, and masked it all behind icy calm.

The days passed in a swirl of activity. Allie was not sure how long they spent in Bridgeport, overseeing the aftermath of the battle—four, five days perhaps. She joined the meetings with the Direns in the days following. Negotiations and details would be worked out after she left. On the fourth day after the battle, a messenger arrived with news about the siege in Tinkeeyo. The message was several days old, but at that time, the fort yet stood. Dandio, it seemed, was optimistic the Ace-army would be driven back.

There was no report about an attack on Mata City, as they'd feared. Allie wanted to believe that it had only been a rumor, but she doubted it.

"Our forces are prepared in Mata City," Jarus said, when Rygal voiced his concern at the news. "Lord Roan's already set the fleet to guard the canals nearest to the Strait. If the Aces try to attack from that way, we'll see them coming."

"Do you think the Aces will come back to Gayrile?" Porcini asked. His eyes were tired and sad, aging him beyond his years. Having lost both his father and his sister, the burden of leading the Chanterelle tribe had fallen on the young Brownae prince.

"The Guardians will be here to protect Gayrile," Rygal told him. "They'll also be on standby—if Mata City is attacked, we're the closest allies they have. Captain Pike will lead the men stationed here while I take a squadron back to the Mainland on the *Veritos* to report to the High King. I don't like dividing our forces, but I think it's necessary."

Allie glanced at him, startled to hear this. She'd assumed he would remain with the Guardians here, now that Gayrile was secured.

"You're going back to the Mainland, sir?" one of the Guardians asked.

Rygal shared a glance with Jarus. "Just until we're sure Mata City isn't under threat. We also need to report to the High King on what's happened here. I'll go to Caer Sia with the delegates, and return as soon as I can."

Allie felt his eyes turn to her, and sensed the concern in his gaze. He seemed to notice the darkness in her heart, even if he might not understand how deeply it went. She did not want to be pitied. It only added to her anger. Part of her wished he would stay in Gayrile with his warriors, so that he wouldn't see her when she embraced the darkness.

But a small part of her, that corner of her heart that still beat red and raw through the icy clutch, allowed a painful stab of relief that he would be with her.

Yet that relief threatened to break the numb shell around her heart, cause her to feel the pain. Friends, love… that meant very little now that she had resigned herself to the death awaiting her. Letting people come close to her would only hurt them in the long run, allowing the Ace-Lord's plan for her to be complete. So she pushed any relief from Rygal's company away. The darkness was comforting, guarding her from the pain.

She hadn't cried. Not for any of it. The tears were locked away behind the ice encasing her heart.

Only the memories could penetrate that shield, horrific images of the battle that entered her thoughts each night. Over and over she saw the enchanted soldiers close like fangs around the helpless Brownaes and felt the terror as her Essence was strengthened by a power that was not her own. Over and over, she saw Redeyes' claws strike Darion, saw him lying pale and gasping on the rocks, while his blood streamed beneath her fingers and his life slipped away. Again and again she saw her red fire pale to corrupted white, as the curse marred her heart beyond repair.

It would be another sleepless night.

Morning dawned foggy and humid, the haze mingling with the thick smoke of the factories. Dark clouds lurked to the east as she walked to the harbor. A storm awaited them in Caer Sia.

Jarus joined them onboard the *Veritos* as soon as he'd made sure the Cooper ships were ready. Allie could hear him and Rygal talking in lowered tones as the ship slipped out of the harbor and headed toward the Mainland. They would stop in Mata City to drop off the Coopers, then sail on and hopefully reach Caer Sia by the following morning.

A cool breeze blew over the water, refreshing her thoughts and turning her attention back to destroying the Ace-Lord. The entire war hinged upon his death—freeing the enchanted soldiers, stopping the attacks, ending the bloodshed—so she must figure out how to bring that about. Yet she could not see how. Iriam had once told her that Kahlifis had long ruled the Dark Realm as a warden chained to his kingdom. The Jewel's power had opened a gateway back into the mortal world after the Dividing War. While he'd been defeated in the first Ace-rise some thirty years ago, Safacon had found the Jewel, and caused the doorway to open again.

The Ace-Lord could not be killed, not in the same manner as his servants. To defeat him, the doorway must be closed and locked for good, trapping him in the dark kingdom he'd been made to rule.

Perhaps the Star-Stones could stop him, Allie wondered. But that didn't make sense—as she'd learned by now, the Stones themselves held no power, only channeled magic from one place to another.

"It is by his own magic that the Ace-Lord will be defeated, and in his own spells will he be snared." Cahadras' voice swam in Allie's mind again. Yes, the Ace-Lord might be defeated by his own magic. There might be a flaw in the Life-Blood Spell, as Rygal had mentioned all those weeks ago. But Allie no longer desired to find it. The resolve of death was the only thing grounding her tormented mind, keeping the darkness from dragging her down entirely. The only comfort she had would be taking the Ace-Lord down with her.

The *Veritos* did not anchor long in Mata City. Rygal went ashore with the Coopers to deliver a brief report to Lord Roan along with Jarus.

Allie stayed onboard, partly because of her own exhaustion, partly because she could not stand to hear more words of false comfort and hope. There had already been plenty of that in Gayrile, once the others had learned what had happened on the beach: *"There was nothing you could have done to stop it." "Don't worry, we'll avenge them." "Darion died to save you, don't blame yourself."*

She was sick of it. Sick of the lies her well-meaning companions told to comfort her. The truth was, she could have saved them—but instead, she'd allowed herself to be drawn into Redeyes' trap, and watched helplessly as they were slaughtered.

No, she didn't want to hear reassurances otherwise.

The Guardians, thankfully, understood that. Jarus wished her good-bye before leaving the ship, his eyes worried. Allie waited on the starboard deck, studying the lantern-lit city as the summer evening settled on the coast. There were no signs of active battle, though that didn't mean the city was safe. Cooper soldiers patrolled the streets, and they'd passed a perimeter of ships when they'd entered the harbor. At least the Coopers had taken action to protect their kingdom.

"How long will we stay here?" she asked the helmsman, a Dwarve with a bristling black beard.

He shook his head. "Not long, Miss. Once the Commander's made sure all's well here, we'll continue on to Caer Sia."

"Right," Allie murmured. As much as the Coopers would welcome them, they needed to bring the report of both the Diren alliance and the battle of Gayrile to Sia.

The Dwarve glanced at her with a wry grin. "Bet you're looking forward to getting home?"

Allie nodded slightly, but didn't say anything. Home? Home was just another word from a bygone time, before the curse had turned her into someone else. Not even the comfort of her family, which had usually been all she'd needed, could take away the darkness that filled her now.

Rygal returned after a few hours, looking relieved and ready to move. "No word of Aces on the Strait," he reported. "Lord Roan met us at the pier—Jarus'll give him the full report, but I wanted to check about any Ace activity nearby."

"Any word from the dryads?" Allie asked.

"Nothing new. Their last message came from Tinkeeyo three days ago about the siege," Rygal answered. "It sounds as though the Magno Forest is locked down tight."

The helmsman looked at him uneasily. "Tinkeeyo under siege? If the fort falls, the Aces will have a prime position in the south."

"That's what I'm concerned about," Rygal said. "There will be more news in Caer Sia, and the king will know how to proceed. So we'd better get going."

The *Veritos* continued on as night blanketed the waters. Allie remained above decks for a while, her back to the mizzenmast as she listened to the varying conversations of the sailors around her. Tinkeeyo besieged. Gayrile torn by war. Mata City under threat. Was anywhere truly safe now?

She knew the answer to that was a dark one.

Taking a breath, she headed below decks to her cabin.

. . . . . .

Captain Newgrange woke Rygal from troubled dreams—the Dwarve's low voice was worried. "Sorry, Commander. Sia's just been sighted, and we're worried something's amiss."

Rygal sat up blearily. It was still mostly dark, with only pale red light shining through the round window to signal the coming dawn. The voyage from Mata City had been a smooth one, free of the choppy waters that typically plagued the North Sea. He'd finally drifted off to sleep with his mind wondering over Mata City, over Gayrile, over Allie.

Now, the rustle of movement above decks and the unease in the helmsman's voice removed all other concerns from his mind. "Amiss?" he repeated. "Are we under attack?"

"No, sir," Captain Newgrange replied, starting for the stairs. "You'd best come see, all the same."

Rygal pulled on a fresh shirt and his leather armor—despite the helmsman's words, it would be best to be prepared for an attack. He buckled on his sword belt as he jogged up the steps.

The gentle breeze billowing the *Veritos'* sails, the cool of the early morning, and the lulling rocking of the waves held no signs of trouble. But his eyes were drawn to the coast, where the rising sun illuminated the craggy mountains embracing the valley of Sia. The familiar curve of the land, the city skyline outlined in the dawn, and the lanterns sparkling throughout the massive city greeted him at first sight, but as his eyes adjusted to the light, a prickle of unease ran down his back.

Ships filled Caer Sia's harbor, hundreds of them, more than he could ever remember seeing in one place. They moved in and out of the harbor—coasting in, docking briefly at piers, and then swinging slowly back out to sea in a methodical pattern.

"Bring up the signal flags," he said after a pause. "Let's call over one of the ships, see if someone can tell us what's going on."

"Aye, Commander," Captain Newgrange replied, striding to the helm and relaying this order to the crew.

Rygal placed his hands on the worn railing, trying to understand what was happening. Perhaps it was nothing. Perhaps the Red Dawn navy had simply been ordered elsewhere, and were mobilizing to aid one of their allies—Mata City, maybe.

Then again, if it was Mata City, the ships should be heading west—and from what he could tell from that swirl of movement, they were departing to the east.

Allie's low voice drew his attention back—she had emerged from her cabin, her brown hair hanging loose around her shoulders, her green eyes hollow from lack of sleep. "What's happening?"

For a moment Rygal debated softening the truth of his fears, but dismissed that idea and nodded toward the harbor. "We're trying to figure that out. Have you ever seen the Red Dawn do this before?"

Allie joined him at the railing, brow furrowed. "No, I—I've never seen all the ships called in like this. Maybe the city's under threat."

Captain Newgrange lowered his spy glass, his face grim. "Have a look, Commander. I don't think it's a minor threat."

Rygal peered through the glass, feeling his unease turn to real fear. Crowding the harbor roads, teeming by the masses, were thousands of civilians. People hurried for the piers, some laden with belongings, others carrying small children. Court attendants, civilians, farmers, and peasants alike crowded at the harbor, streaming onboard the ships in masses of fear and confusion. Red Dawn soldiers had formed a ring around the piers, organizing the exodus.

"They're… leaving," he said at last, shaking his head in disbelief as he passed the glass to Allie.

"We've signaled a ship, sir," the first mate called.

Waving several colorful flags with specific meanings, the sailors beckoned over a small sailboat. Judging by its size, it was a passenger vessel, used for transport across short distances. Even small crafts were being utilized.

Captain Newgrange cupped his hands around his mouth as the boat approached—despite his short stature, the Dwarve's voice echoed over the water as he called out. "Ho there! What's happening in Sia? Are we cleared to make port?"

An old Liznee captain called back. "Ho there, *Veritos*—make port if you will, but beware. The Aces have sent an attack force. The High King has ordered the city evacuated."

Evacuation. Rygal had suspected this by now, yet the words seemed to punch him in the chest. The Aces were coming—not to Mata City, as they'd feared, but to Caer Sia.

"Will we still make port, sir?" Newgrange asked slowly.

Rygal felt the eyes of the crew on him, waiting for his answer. He managed to nod, almost numb with shock. "Yes—get us to port, quickly. We'll see how we can help."

The *Veritos* swept into the harbor. As they drew nearer inland, Rygal could hear the rising, fearful voices echoing through the city. People shouted and cried out. Small children sobbed for their parents. Red Dawn soldiers barked commands, trying to keep everyone organized in groups. And yet there were so many—more people arrived with each moment from different parts of the capital.

"Must be a hundred thousand of them," he said aloud, staring at the growing crowd.

"Almost half a million according to the last census," Allie murmured beside him.

Rygal glanced at her. She looked utterly exhausted, voice dull and lifeless, her eyes vacant of her usual spark of determination and joy. The fight in Gayrile had taken more than her friends' lives. She watched the throng of helpless civilians with the vague indifference of a battle already lost.

"We'll help them," he ventured after a pause. "This won't be like last time, Allie—this time, we'll get the people out safely, before the Aces arrive."

"Help?" Allie repeated quietly, looking up at him. "Look at them. There's no counter attack, no attempt to fight—that means we are out of time. Jan would never surrender Sia otherwise." She folded her arms over her chest and let out a breath. "You're right. This isn't like last time."

She said it calmly, without a trace of sorrow or fear, yet Rygal read both in her expression. In her face he saw pain, carefully masked and hidden.

Neither of them had spoken of Darion yet, nor of any of the losses in Gayrile. The horror they shared seemed a subject neither could bring up, like a wall of ice forged between them. No words would breach the grief; Rygal knew that for a fact. Futile reassurances spoken by those who did not understand the pain meant nothing. *Can you blame her?* His mind inquired wryly. *You were hardly any better when you lost Norrin.*

No, he didn't blame her. Nor could he help her break that wall while the same barrier of grief still stood in his own heart.

The fleet of ships going in and out offered no room to dock in the harbor, so they lowered a rowboat into the restless waters. Captain Newgrange and three Guardians headed to shore with Rygal and Allie. Here, the cacophony of voices was almost deafening, overwhelming Rygal's mind with the fear and helplessness.

The Cagari general, Leopold, stood on the harbor's edge, calling orders to the frightened crowd. "Groups of fifty, please—groups of fifty. Please keep your children close."

His catlike eyes landed on the Guardians as they approached, and Rygal saw surprise cross his face as he saw them. "Heiress," he greeted Allie, sounding relieved. "It is very good to see you have returned safely."

"What's happening, General?" Allie asked. "Have the Aces..."

Leopold let out a breath. "They are on the way. The High King has ordered the evacuation." He looked at Rygal. "I am sorry to ask your men to risk it, but might you help?"

"Of course," Rygal said, still in a daze. "How... what can we do?"

The general nodded to the *Veritos*. "Your ship. Commander Ki has called for as many ships that are able to help, but there are only so many in the Red Dawn fleet, and it has already become a question of how many people we can evacuate to Lillary Bay before..." He trailed off abruptly.

"Right," Rygal said, straightening and turning to Newgrange. "Ah— can you signal them in, Captain?"

"Yes, sir," the Dwarve answered, moving briskly toward the pier.

Rygal looked at Leopold again. "Dandio's organized the evacuation? Where is he?"

"He has gone to the south wall—come, and I will give you the current plan," Leopold said, turning and leading them down the road.

"The south wall?" Allie asked. "Then do we plan to fight?"

"Not in a standard counter attack," Leopold replied quietly, shaking his head. "I do not like his strategy, but—frankly, there is no time. The Aces have sent an attack force, far more than the warriors stationed here can face. They have made certain our allies are either unable to help, or have been tied up in a conflict of their own." His golden eyes were solemn. "No… our best course of action is to get our people to a safe location."

"And you think Lillary Bay is safe?" Rygal asked slowly. He knew the village only by name—it was a military port on the opposite side of the mountains, small and populated mainly by Red Dawn officers, yet prepared with supply stores in case of siege.

"Perhaps not if it was under a full-scale attack," Leopold replied. "But the Aces will not be able to strike it without crossing the mountains, and it is but a two-hour voyage from Sia. Our ships are going there to unload their passengers and return to continue the evacuation."

Rygal nodded. It was a wise decision. Any other locations they might evacuate to were either too far away, or still torn by war. Assuming they could get the Sian civilians there, they'd be safe. Still, he hesitated before asking his next question. "How… much time do we have before the Aces arrive?"

"By now," Leopold said, "less than a day."

One day. One day to evacuate every citizen of Caer Sia and flee before the Aces attacked. This would be no occupation, Rygal knew, not like the Aces had done during the quest for the Shards. They didn't wish to claim Caer Sia. No, this would be total destruction.

He racked his mind for other ideas that might hold off the Aces, but hard as he tried, he knew there was nothing else they could do. Not with so little time to prepare a counter attack.

The downtown area of the capital was eerily silent as they walked. Rygal noticed overturned carts of goods, abandoned stalls, and shops whose doors hung open, their owners having fled in a hurry. As they climbed the slight hill to the castle, he could glimpse the many ships headed east, like a flock of birds fleeing a coming storm.

Standing inside the courtyard was Ajaha, clad in her courier uniform. With her was Iriam. The sight of the Neutral filled Rygal with relief—if there was ever a time they needed Iriam's advice, it was now.

Ajaha stepped forward with a relieved smile, giving Allie a light hug. "It is good to see you both alive," she said. Her voice betrayed her fear and weariness. "Light willing, you might give the king your report later. But tell me—is the north secured?"

"Gayrile's safe," Rygal replied. The mission felt like so long ago, far away and irrelevant. "A pack of Dal-kerri were led by an Ace to incite more fighting among the clans, but the Direns have allied against them, and we've driven the wolves out."

"That is good news," Ajaha said, looking relieved. Her eyes turned to look behind them, frowning slightly, as if she had missed something. Concern crossed her face as she turned to them again. "Darion...?"

Rygal took a breath to speak, but the words refused to come. He'd barely ever acknowledged how much he'd appreciated the ranger's presence, how their tentative friendship had forged into a deep bond during the hours spent in Castle Sia's library. The three of them had worked as a team for weeks now, planning together, protecting each other. No words would erase the pain of what had happened.

"It was Redeyes." Allie's voice was quiet and toneless.

Iriam's expression became grim, and Ajaha's face fell at her words. She put an arm around her daughter. Allie barely reacted to her touch, her expressionless gaze fixed on the cobblestone.

"Forgive me for interrupting," Leopold said in a low voice, "but we are running out of time."

"Indeed," Iriam said quietly. "Might you inform them of the plan?"

The Cagari general turned to the south, tracing a line on the horizon with his finger. "The Ace-army will strike from the southwest. The city districts on that side have been fully evacuated, though it will take at least another day before the city is completely emptied. The Aces will undoubtedly have arrived by then, so I would recommend you both head to Lillary Bay with the people," he said, looking at Ajaha and Allie. "You will be safe there."

"Wait," Allie interrupted, her eyes swinging over the empty courtyard. "Where's my father and Jan?"

Ajaha hesitated, and Rygal felt a stab of fear as he understood.

"They intend to hold the southwest walls," Iriam told them. "We need time to fully evacuate Caer Sia, time they intend to buy for us. It is time that we must use well."

"What?" Allie demanded, her voice rising.

"How are they getting out?" Rygal asked. He forced himself to speak calmly, but the same disbelief and fear that filled Allie's voice clutched his chest. "The south walls aren't equipped for battle, and they'll have no way to retreat."

"They have relocated several of our cannons," Ajaha replied. Her face was pale, yet she spoke steadily. "They may not hold long there, but that is not their intent. Once their position is overridden, they will retreat."

Once their position is overridden. The words echoed mockingly in Rygal's mind.

"You agreed to that?" Allie demanded, turning sharply to Iriam.

"I will not contradict the king," Iriam replied. "It may not be a wise strategy under ordinary circumstances, but I fear it is necessary as this extreme situation requires. They would not ask any others to take that risk, though General Arrex and his squadron have chosen to join them."

"Then I'm joining them too," Allie said firmly. Her voice trembled with helpless fury; Rygal could practically see the flames blazing in her eyes. "They've made their choice, but I'll make this one for myself. I'm staying, even if the city burns around us."

"No," Iriam said quietly. "In that I will contradict. There is a different risk entirely in regards to the Vessel. The Ace-Lord means to corrupt you. Your choice to stay would not be for the good of your people, but for yourself, and in that, you will help his plan succeed."

His words were low, yet Allie seemed to recoil before each one. Her jaw was set in a furious line, and for an instant Rygal could see the reckless fire battling with the desperate need to help her family. But she didn't say any more, only stood, silent and tense as a drawn bowstring.

"At least… let me stay and help," Rygal ventured after a pause, looking at Iriam. "The Guardians are here with me—the Red Dawn doesn't have to fight alone."

Already, he could see the answer in Iriam's face. "No," the Neutral repeated. "I do not doubt your skills, nor the bravery of your men. But the High King has made it clear that all others must go to Lillary Bay. Join the war council there, and give your report of Gayrile to General Leopold," he said, looking at the Cagari.

Rygal hesitated. Every fiber of his body wanted to argue otherwise, to insist that he join the desperate fight. Even if he were killed, surely it would be better than waiting in Lillary Bay, knowing that Jan and Dandio—men he had respected and admired for years—were facing down an innumerable host in a battle they could not hope to win.

But the expressions of those around him prevented him from arguing.

In General Leopold's eyes he saw the same helplessness, the same sorrow of being forced to leave his comrades.

Iriam's gaze was heavy, grim, and for the first time, Rygal saw a weariness in the Neutral's eyes, eyes that had watched the affairs of mortals for far longer than anyone truly knew. Weariness of a being who had seen more death than any of them here.

Ajaha's face was drawn, and despite her careful attempt to conceal it, Rygal saw tears glistening in her eyes, and could only imagine her fear for her husband.

Yet it was Allie's face that troubled him the most. No pain, no grief. Even the helpless rage seemed to have faded. The girl standing before him seemed a shell of herself, her fire replaced by shadows.

No longer was she determined to seek the cure for the curse that bound her. No longer did she seem to care. Allie was breaking, slowly yet surely, beneath the darkness that claimed her, a darkness Rygal could never help her overcome.

Not while the same shadows still lurked in his heart.

31

Task Assigned
Kamon. Two weeks earlier.

A warm breeze blew south from the Strait, rippling the pure white sails of the *Scarlet Consort* and sending waves lapping at the hull of the *Burman Marie*. Dawn touched golden rays upon the blossoming trees of Kamon, and Bryn could hear the cries of the tropical birds as she stood on the pier.

It was good to have a moment of rest. Her crew had been occupied with various jobs in West Coonsia, ferrying goods from one town to another, despite Richard's protests that it was below their pay grade. Her first mate was loyal to the end, Bryn knew. But he was still adjusting to the life of a simple privateer, so different from that of a Dricaster Ringmember.

Seven months had passed since she and Robin had helped defeat the outlaw Terrax, and abandoned their past lives as criminals. The Dricaster Crime Ring of Esile City had been overthrown through their efforts, and the southwestern coasts of Daffodalion were safer than they had been for decades.

Well, safer if you were a law-abiding civilian, she thought with a wry smile. She may have left bounty hunting behind her, but that didn't exactly erase the criminal records she and most of her crew still carried. The reputation, which clung to her name like tar, was not one that she could easily throw away.

Though her life had changed, the bounty hunter still lived inside the privateer. Her responsibilities had changed, away from the death that followed in her wake, and now centered on her crew—her family—protecting them, learning to captain, learning to make the right decisions to keep them out of danger. Difficult work at times. But she wouldn't trade it for anything.

For now, they were safe in Kamon. The island kingdom was far removed from the trouble in Esile and the conflict with the Aces. Thus, it was the perfect place for a group like theirs—two pirate crews who did not wish to involve themselves in the kingdom's war.

Bryn's crew had rejoined Robin's two days ago, and they'd decided to stay in Kamon for the remainder of the week. She felt a surge of satisfaction looking at the *Consort* and *Marie* anchored side by side. It was good to have everyone back together, and it was even better to be with Robin again.

The wind pulled at her dark hair, which fell unbound to her mid-back. She'd tied it back with a simple leather band across her brow. Robin had offered her one of his colorful bandannas shortly after she'd decided to join him on the seas, but she'd denied.

"It'd suit you," he'd insisted, though his sea-blue eyes had held a manic twinkle that told her he was teasing.

"I never said it didn't," Bryn had replied loftily. "I just think if either of us is to look a fool, it may as well be you."

Robin had only shrugged and smirked, an expression that used to infuriate her. Strange how life could change that way. She loved that cocky pirate more than she would have ever thought possible.

"Up early this morning?" Robin's voice came from behind her. He strode up the pier with a slight swagger. "Thought you'd gone to town with John and Oliver."

Bryn turned to face him, hiding her smile. "You know, most people just say, *Good morning, how are you today?*"

Robin kissed her, then nodded to the two ships. "Look at that breeze. Practically calling us back north. Remember that old superstition in Esile City about a northern wind bringing bad luck?"

"Mmm," Bryn murmured. She'd never paid much heed to sailor superstitions. There was enough bad luck without the wind bringing more. "Where've John and Oliver gone?" she asked, though she had a guess. Oliver turned thirteen today. The *Marie's* impetuous cabin boy had been clamoring to visit the shops as soon as they'd docked here.

"John's taken him to get a birthday present," Robin replied, confirming her assumption. "Oliver's got his heart set on one of those sea knives he saw in the market. John agreed to get him one on the condition that he'll only use it under supervision."

"Sounds like John," Bryn said with a slight smile. Leave it to the *Marie's* first mate to decide on that practicality. Despite John's strictness, he regarded Oliver like a younger brother, just as they all did.

Robin looked back at the ships. "Your crew plan to stay here for the week, then?"

"At least until we're repaired," Bryn answered.

He arched an eyebrow. "Repaired? What'd you do to my ship?"

"*Your* ship—oh, you're very funny. We both know Rich deferred captaining to me fair and square." Bryn shook her head, but his joking helped lighten her mood, which had returned to dismal thoughts of the *Consort.*

Since leaving Esile City, they'd seen remarkably few conflicts. As both she and Robin were still wanted criminals, she'd feared they might be hunted down by bounty hunters hired by any vengeful Dricaster associates.

But as the months passed in silence, Bryn had allowed herself to relax and believe that they were safely away.

It had been a bad decision. She'd become far too lax in precautions when they had made port ten days ago, in a small town on the coast of West Coonsia. They had headed ashore without scouting the area first. A Cagari bounty hunter had been waiting for them, having tracked them from Esile, and attacked as soon as the *Consort* left the harbor.

No one had been killed; Bryn supposed she should be grateful for that. But she couldn't forgive herself for the damage done to the *Scarlet Consort*. The Cagari ship only had four cannons to a side, but it had been enough. Two cannonballs had struck low on the *Consort* as they'd fled south, damaging the rudder.

She had stayed afloat, but could hardly sail without the rudder. Bryn still remembered that gut-wrenching crack when the shots had torn through the wood, splintering the ship she'd called home for the last several months. The *Consort's* guns had sent their attacker to the bottom of the sea, and they'd managed to limp the rest of the way to Kamon.

"We're not going anywhere with a busted rudder," she told Robin, shaking her head. "I'm hoping to patch her up while we're here."

Robin nodded, abandoning his teasing. He knew the pain and frustration of an injured ship. The *Marie* had suffered heavy damage during their mission to recover the compass; the scratches and scars still showed along her sides.

"Might as well get my boys to help your crew," he offered. "At least you haven't chosen a bad place to patch up a ship."

Oliver's voice came from the village behind them, dismayed. "Patch up a ship? We have to help?"

The cabin boy strode up the pier, carrying a new knife in a polished sheath. John walked behind him, looking slightly exasperated.

"Yes, you'll help," Robin told him matter-of-factly. "You'll do as your captain orders, Oliver, or it'll be five lashes for you."

"Or the brig," John put in, smoothing his well-trimmed mustache to hide a smile.

Oliver considered this, then looked at Robin again. "*I don't have to. It's my birthday. Right, Bryn?*" He looked imploringly to her.

"I'm not your captain," Bryn said with a shrug. "John's right—you had better listen, or Captain Trelawney will lock you in the brig."

"Brig's not bad," Oliver decided, trotting jauntily back to the *Marie*.

Robin shook his head. "That kid—absolutely no regard for authority."

"I wonder where he gets it, sir," John said, straight-faced.

Bryn interrupted before their bickering could continue, steering the conversation back. "Well—we're going to tow the *Consort* and moor her to shore. I was planning on hiring a few islanders to help us—Pao told me a few of their boys work for hire," she added. Pao had recently come aboard as the *Consort's* bosun.

Robin nodded. "That's wise. Talk to their harbormaster too—Harlin, Harris—something like that."

"Hasman, Captain," John informed him.

"Hasman, that's it," Robin said, looking at Bryn. "I need to borrow a couple charts—some of ours were lost in the storm last month."

Bryn nodded, following him back onto the *Scarlet Consort* as John walked to the *Marie*. While the time to rest was pleasant, having her ship out of action left her feeling trapped, as if she were marooned on Kamon.

The breeze carried the sweet floral scent of the trees as she stepped on board, and she managed a smile. Well, there were worse places to be marooned.

Richard, the *Consort's* first mate, was already busy, examining the damage from the pier. Bryn leaned over the stern rail to call down to him. "How's she looking, Rich?"

The burly sailor looked up, scratching a sideburned cheek. "Eh, not too bad, Cap'n. With luck it won't take long—we should be out of here in a week."

Bryn grinned slightly. "What, island life doesn't appeal to you?"

"Too muggy," Richard replied wryly, wiping the sweat from his brow. "Like breathing in molasses." He patted the *Consort's* side as he started toward the gangplank. "And it'll be good to get her seaworthy again. Never wise to assume you're safe in one place for long."

Bryn nodded. That was a lesson she'd learned many times over. Ringmember or not, life was far from safe, even in a place as peaceful and quiet as Kamon.

A raven fluttered across the deck and alighted on the rail near her hand. Bryn glanced at it, surprised at the bird's boldness, and shooed it. The raven did not move—it cocked its head and peered at her intently through a pair of brilliant green eyes.

"Look at that," Richard chuckled as he strode aboard. "Cocky little thing—looks like the one old Dakrind used to carry around."

Hawk Dakrind, the recently deposed Dricaster leader, had once had a tame crow. Bryn was convinced he'd only kept the bird around to train it to steal coins.

She raised her hand, intending the shoo the raven again. Yet something about it made her pause. Its scrutinizing gaze made her feel as though it could see right through her.

The raven opened its beak—and spoke.

"You're a difficult woman to find, Bryn Paya."

Bryn stepped back in shock, her hand flying to the knife at her belt. Richard swung around at the lilting voice, looking first at Bryn, then staring, wide-eyed, at the bird. "What in the blazes—Cap'n, did that—"

The raven ruffled its feathers, which seemed to recede into its body as its form grew and transformed before Bryn's eyes. Black feathers became smooth green scales, the beak vanished, and the green eyes peered out from a newt-like face. The scales around its eyes were a slightly darker shade than the rest of its body, resembling a bandit's mask.

Robin strode on deck, having heard the voice. His eyes landed immediately on the creature. "Good gravy," he sputtered, staring in absolute confusion.

"Wait," Bryn said quickly, as Richard reached cautiously for his pistol. Her initial surprise had faded, replaced by both suspicion and curiosity. The strange newcomer had made no move to harm them. A memory stirred in the back of her mind as she stared at the creature, but she couldn't place it.

The creature glanced at Richard. The voice had a lilting, musical quality to it, though it sounded rather weary. "Yes, please, let's have none of that," he said, nodding to the pistol. "Though your loyalty to your captain is admirable, I promise I mean her no harm."

Richard, seemingly convinced, peered at the newcomer with intense interest. "By the Crown—a Siren, aren't you? I've only ever heard stories— strange stories, to say the least."

"Indeed I am," the creature replied calmly. "And as for strange tales, well, I've heard many of my own."

"Who the blazes are you?" Robin demanded, striding up to stand beside Bryn.

The Siren turned to him. "That's not exactly your question to ask, but I'll tell you. I've come to find this lovely lady," he said, turning to Bryn. "My name is Lammar Skytooth."

The name was unfamiliar, but Bryn had heard of the Sirens, of their clever wit and their powers of shape-shifting. This Siren, apparently, had come to find her—though for what purpose, she had no idea. She'd made a name for herself as a bounty hunter, of course, but that had been under the name Bryn *Valetown*, and the Siren had called her by her maiden name…

"You're looking for me?" she asked slowly, completely confused.

The Siren gave her a crooked smile, showing his pointed teeth. "That I am, my lady. That is, if you are Bryn Paya?"

"Trelawney," Bryn corrected vaguely.

Lammar tilted his head slightly to one side, glancing between her and Robin. "Ah, well then! Congratulations to you both."

"Look, Green, you plan on telling us why you're here?" Robin demanded. "Who are you? Why are you looking for my wife?"

Lammar dropped down to the deck and looked up at them. "We'd better discuss that elsewhere. I'll tell you, at least, that this isn't about your past, ah, record."

Bryn saw the unease in Robin's face, but her concerns were not about the Crime Rings. This Siren wasn't here to arrest them—if he was, he would have already alerted Kamon's townguard. Nor, she thought, was he a bounty hunter—if the Siren had come to capture them, surely he would have taken a more formidable form.

No. She didn't understand why the Siren had come, but it seemed to be important.

"Get the men working on the repairs, Rich," she said, turning back to her puzzled first mate. "This won't take long." *Hopefully.*

She led the Siren to her cabin; Robin, still looking uncertain, followed. A simple round window allowed a blaze of golden sunlight to light the cot and small wooden desk, which she leaned against as she studied the Siren.

Lammar followed her inside and stretched stiffly, arching his back like a cat. "Quite a flight. Wings are exhausting. You wouldn't happen to have anything to eat, would you?" he added, glancing hopefully at Robin. "Your mention of gravy caught the attention of my stomach."

"Not till you've answered our questions," Bryn said firmly. "I don't think you're a threat, but I certainly don't trust you yet, not when you've turned up out of nowhere saying you're looking for me. How did you find us?"

Lammar turned to her, postponing the idea of food, and became serious. "Well, now. In answer to that question, that's a bit of a tale—it was certainly a search. I'll spare you the details. When you've been at this business as long as I have, you start to get quite good at knowing where people are."

"What business is that?" Robin asked warily.

The Siren waved a four-fingered hand dismissively. "Never mind that. Point is, I found you, though it did take me a while. My problem was, I was seeking for a Bryn Paya to be sailing with pirates on the *Burman Marie.* Wasn't till I got wind of a skilled archer taking down a Cagari pirate a few days ago that I realized I was seeking the captain of the *Scarlet Consort.*"

Bryn's hand drifted unconsciously to the smooth handle of the longbow resting across her desk. So Lammar did know her reputation, then. Knew the legacy of bloodshed and death that she would never be rid of.

"I take it this ship sustained damage in your recent exploits?" Lammar asked.

"A bit," Bryn replied shortly. "It'll take a little while until she's seaworthy, at least."

Lammar paused, thinking that over. "I suppose we'll figure that matter out later. In answer to your first question, someone else asked me to find you. I've traveled fast from Caer Sia."

A fresh prickle of unease ran down Bryn's spine. She had never gone to the Coonsian capital, but that mattered very little—what mattered was that they knew who she was, and who she had been. And it seemed they'd sent this Siren to find her.

"Caer Sia?" Robin repeated, moving closer to Bryn as if to shield her. "Haven't they got enough to worry about without tracking down a couple of pirates?"

"Oh, they do, mark my words," Lammar said grimly. "But as I told you—that's not why I'm here. What I've come to say relates more to the war you've managed to stay out of."

A guess entered Bryn's mind, and she looked at him suspiciously. "The war?" she repeated slowly. "If my brother's the one who sent you, he should have told you why we can't get involved. We're not warriors. We certainly have no intentions of fighting for Caer Sia."

Lammar turned his eyes to her. A strange foreboding twinged in Bryn's stomach at his glance, as though some sixth sense understood the truth even before the Siren spoke, his voice heavy.

"Aryion didn't send me. But it's for his sake that I've come to find you."

He held out a hand. Glimmering in his scaled palm was a small red pin, bearing the insignia of a snarling bear.

Bryn stared at the pin for a long moment as memories swarmed in her mind. Memories of everything she'd done, everyone she'd killed while wearing that badge. Memories, too, of the day she'd unclasped it as she'd cast that life aside, laying the pin in her brother's outstretched hand the day she'd left Esile City for good. Memories of a promise.

If ever you have need of me.

She raised her eyes to the Siren's, speaking slowly. "Aryion… where is Aryion?"

Lammar let out a breath. "That's why Mel sent me, Mrs. Trelawney. Aryion is a captive of the Aces."

32

Shattered

Days. Weeks. Time blurred away into the swirl of darkness and agony that had become his life.

Aryion knew there had once been a time before the darkness, a time when sunlight had warmed his skin and the wind had blown fresh in his face. Yet those memories were fading now, like a dream he could not fully recall, a life lived by another man entirely.

Time was irrelevant in the black, box-like prison, where the screams of friends long gone echoed over and over in the shadows. The pain was less in his body now—he'd become almost numb to physical hurt during the Deputy's tortures. Even the icy agony in his spine had lessened by now. Now, the pain was in his mind, greater than any he had ever endured, and one that threatened to break him.

The Ace-Deputy never interrogated him, never demanded information, never pressed for secrets. Every meeting was exactly the same. The Deputy would enter, purple-red eyes glinting in the ruined face.

"Tell me your name."

Aryion used to shout it in defiance, flinging his voice into the cell to prove his sanity and mind were still his own. By now, his voice had dwindled into a whisper.

"My name is Aryion Paya. I am the Hummingbird."

The Deputy never seemed fazed by this. "Will you serve?"

"Never."

And then the Ace would step close, which was the cue for the horrors to begin.

They were not seeking secrets. The Aces must know he had none to share, nothing that would have any real impact on their success in the war. They wanted to break him, to bring him to the point that he would swear the Oath and join their ranks as a mindless soldier.

The enchantment, Aryion knew, must be a choice. But that fact hadn't stopped the Deputy, or the ice that pierced his thoughts and dug claws into his mind. He felt the cold inside him constantly now, black and monstrous, a strength and rage previously foreign to his mortal body.

Perhaps they would simply kill him once they realized he would not serve. He had begun to hope so. Death was preferable to this pain and darkness, and the growing monster in his mind.

Silver light filtered into the cell, drawing his mind back to whatever present time it was, and he pressed his back against the wall as the Ace-Deputy entered. The self-satisfied glint in the purple-red eyes sickened him.

The Deputy waved a hand, causing the icy chains to haul him upright by his neck and arms.

"Tell me your name."

"Aryion Paya. Son of Aidronon." Cold seared his thoughts, and he choked. "The Hummingbird."

A wan smile creased the Deputy's ruined face. "Still resisting, I see. Will you serve?"

"No." He braced himself for the clawed hands, the blades piercing his mind, the feverish hours of agony. But the Deputy only studied him for a moment.

"You *are* stubborn, ranger," he said at last, shaking his head. "Let me ask a different question. Do you understand the purpose behind our meetings?"

Aryion did not answer, his aching mind caught off guard by this sudden change in routine.

The Deputy exhaled into the frigid cell. "You are here," he said at last, "to be broken. Only then may a new thing be built, as one must till a field before sowing. Your mind and life are already ours."

Despite himself, Aryion managed a hoarse laugh. "Really? It's taken you a long time to break me, in that case."

The Deputy shook his head again. "I admit I was hesitant to trust my master's plan. He has decided your future, and it was I who hesitated, fearful of simply destroying your mind entirely. But I have no doubt his suggestion will prove successful. There is weakness to be removed—pruned, as one might a young tree." He looked at Aryion. "You care for the New Blood, do you not?"

Aryion met his gaze, forcing his vision to focus. These questions were hypothetical; the Deputy could hardly care for what he had to say. But he flinched involuntarily as the Deputy stepped forward.

"Your mind," the Ace said in a conversational tone, "is stronger than your body. A mortal's body can be broken quite easily. Shatter the spine, sever the legs—there are many options that would render you incapacitated."

Fear chilled Aryion's heart, hard as he tried to hide it. The thought of never being able to walk again, or of bleeding out slowly in this black box, terrified him.

"But," the Deputy continued, taking Aryion's head in claw-like hands, "the mind is a more... resilient thing. The mortal mind can resist even the greatest pain inflicted to the body, yet it may be broken by fear or grief. Your loyalty and love for your apprentice is a weakness I cannot risk."

Aryion felt ice seeping into his thoughts. The darkness and shadows that had gripped him for weeks stirred to life like a ravenous beast as he strained against the chains. Memories of Mel, of their missions, of every conversation they'd ever had, stood out glistening white as the ice crystallized upon them, turning them brittle as frost... and he felt them breaking away, torn from his mind.

"No," he hissed, trying to pull back.

The ice turned sharp as knives, piercing his skull, and he gasped at the pain. The Deputy's grip tightened, nails digging into the ranger's head. "You know you only bring yourself more pain by this route," he said, sounding irritated. "You cannot resist, or you will be shattered."

"But I can resist you," Aryion rasped. "I can resist your ice and protect those memories—you can't destroy them unless I allow you."

"Can I not?" the Deputy inquired.

The ice splintered, shining white light behind his eyes. His entire body shook with the effort, but he fought, clinging desperately to the life he knew. His name. His role. His companions. Mel. The few pleasant memories that yet remained in his breaking mind.

"You are not the first to believe you could resist," the Deputy continued. "There have been many other prisoners. One of them was a ranger as well, in fact. His name, I believe, was Meadowlark."

Aryion faltered, gritting his teeth as he looked at the Ace.

"He was from Wiverrun, like so many others," the Deputy informed him. "I offered him something greater than the enchantment. The choice to ride with my vanguard, to join the ranks of the fiercest warriors we have gathered. My master was curious, you see," he said, his icy breath blowing in Aryion's face. "He wanted to know if a mortal's mind, once broken, might be rebuilt. It did not work on the Meadowlark—the sheer energy of resisting overwhelmed his old heart, and he perished."

For an instant, Aryion's focus slipped, startled by this new information. The Meadowlark had been Darion's mentor, the ranger of Wiverrun. He'd been captured by the Aces several weeks before they had discovered the ruins of Castle Droco. Before Mel had fallen into the void.

"Ah, I see you have heard of him," the Deputy said, and Aryion felt the icy grip tighten further. "Do not fear. You are younger and stronger than he was, and thus, I believe you will endure."

The blackness stirred in his heart, called to life by the illusions around him and turning the memories to anguish. Searing pain shot through his head as he resisted, and a cry of pain tore from his throat.

The Deputy's fingers burned like freezing brands against his face, the claws cutting into his skin. "If you continue this path, you will break," the Deputy warned, his usually smooth voice filled with sickening excitement. "How long do you think you can resist this? Why bring yourself such agony when all you must do is surrender? The power is already within you, you need only accept it."

White fog swirled in Aryion's mind, and his eyes blurred with tears. Sounds, sights, memories, seemed to have been washed away. He could hear his own throbbing heart, his own ragged gasps as the darkness embraced him in the black room.

The Deputy's voice hissed in his mind, becoming a part of him. *"Say the words. I have planted the power within you. Say the words, and it is all over."*

And, to his horror, he heard his own rasping voice respond. *"Warrior here… this Oath I…"*

"No!" Aryion flung his head back against the wall in a sudden burst of strength, tearing himself from the Deputy's grasp. He hung there, shaking, chest heaving as he gasped for breath. Black spots swam in his vision, and he felt himself fading into unconsciousness.

"Oh, we are not finished here."

The Deputy's frozen claws seized him right before the darkness engulfed him, dragging him back into consciousness. Icy fingers dug into Aryion's chest while the other gripped his forehead. The ruined face was practically frenzied with rage.

"Mortal fool," he hissed, inches from Aryion's face. "I *will* enjoy this."

White ice shone on his fingertips as the claws dug into Aryion's skin. Pain unlike any he had ever known racked his body as if the Deputy sought to rip his very heart from his chest. Ice seized and shredded the Essence from every muscle and vein, tearing and destroying the last of himself that remained.

The choked scream barely sounded like his own voice. He glimpsed the Deputy's smile of triumph and fought futilely to escape the deathly white. His body, exhausted from weeks of lesser torture, gave out, and he felt himself go limp as the cold encompassed him.

The chains loosened, sending him crashing to the floor onto his back. *Get up!* His mind screamed the command, but his body did not obey. The Deputy knelt, an armored knee pressed into his chest as his hands gripped Aryion's head again.

The ice entered his mind, and this time, he had no strength left to fight it.

"Embrace it," came the Deputy's voice, filling his thoughts. *"You are darkness. You will serve."*

With his last strength, Aryion thought of Mel, of talking with the boy on their journeys, of watching him learn and grow. Of all the memories from the quest of the Shards right up till the mission to Wiverrun. He had time to feel a pain far deeper than the agony that racked his body—grief.

I'm sorry, his thoughts wept.

Then the ice crystallized on the memories, and they shattered into fragments, gone forever.

The pain left him.

The Deputy straightened, waving a hand and drawing the prisoner upright with a clink of chains. The prisoner's gaze stared forward, his breathing slow and labored as a new strength slowly filled his body.

"Tell me your name," the Deputy commanded.

Slowly, voice low and rasping, the prisoner replied. "I have no name. None but what my master gives me."

"Will you serve?"

"I will serve."

The Deputy smiled. How very satisfying it was to be right.

"We are finished here," he informed the prisoner. "The illusions will next make clear what you are to do. Be prepared to ride with the vanguard."

He had to stop himself from calling the prisoner *Hummingbird.* That was not his name anymore. The thing in the chains was something new, something stronger, something without any burden of loyalty or love claiming his heart.

The Deputy turned and left the black cell, allowing darkness to engulf the room. Behind him, the prisoner sat against the wall, breathing slowly and deeply, dark eyes flecked with hollow, lifeless blue.

PART 3

The Wrath of the Sea

33

The Siren's Trick

Mata Strait

"With all due respect, Captain," John Tailor said uncertainly, "this plan is a wild one, even for you."

Bryn sighed as she glanced at the *Marie's* first mate. As much as she'd like to argue, he was right, as usual.

Four days had passed since Lammar had brought the news of Aryion's capture. Bryn had spent several hours debating over her next actions. Yes, she had promised to help whenever her brother needed it. She owed him that, after his help in Esile City and—more importantly—his choice not to report her or her companions to the Capital officers.

But she had been so careful to keep her crew away from the war, away from the danger that still followed her, and succeeded thus far. Bounty hunters and assassins were nothing to the Aces. Besides, they had next to no information about the Ace-Lord's fortress, as Lammar had admitted. Barely any knowledge of where Aryion would be—or even if he was still alive. Perhaps the Aces had already killed him.

But if not…

Bryn had lain awake long into the night, her thoughts a turmoil of doubts and fears, her fingers moving over the worn iron of the Dricaster pin. Sometime after moonrise, she finally came to a decision. She'd made her brother a promise. She owed it to him to try and save him.

By now, her hesitations had shifted away from whether or not she should act, and more for the plan itself.

With the *Scarlet Consort* still needing repairs, and since the *Burman Marie* was the smaller and faster of the two ships, they had embarked north with Robin's men. Most of Bryn's crew remained in Kamon with the *Consort*. They would follow her to the death; that much she knew. But she didn't want it to come to that. Only twenty of her men had joined her. Her newly recruited bosun, a Kamoni native named Pao Taki, had been among them.

Richard had come too, of course. Her first mate was fiercely loyal, albeit wary about challenging the Aces. He, more than any of the sailors, knew just what they were facing, thanks to the many legends and tales he'd heard while traveling all corners of Orlell. She could tell he was still uncertain about infiltrating Ar-Salem.

The two-day voyage had been plenty of time to strategize, yet Bryn's unease grew the further they went north. None of the men aboard the *Marie* were trained in combat, certainly not against the undead horrors Lammar had described. As she, Robin, and their respective first mates gathered in the cabin of the *Marie*, she could not deny the nagging thought that she'd made a terrible mistake.

John was right. It *was* a wild plan.

"From what I understand, your crew has completed missions with many such wild plans," Lammar commented, a hint of amusement in his lilting voice. The Siren sat next to Robin's desk, scaled tail coiled around himself, keen eyes studying the sailors. He alone seemed unworried by the task ahead—but then again, he was a shape-shifter. If the plan went sour, he'd have no problem escaping.

"If anyone doesn't like the plan, I don't blame you," Robin said, leaning his elbows on his desk. "But you all know we owe the Hummingbird. He's the only reason we weren't arrested after the whole fiasco in Esile City—the Capital would never have let us go if they'd known we were involved, even if we did take down the Crime Ring and give them Terrax like a birthday gift."

"Besides that, he's my brother," Bryn put in quietly, glancing at the sailors. "I promised to help him if he were ever in trouble. The Aces have no reason to expect us, and surprise is what counts most in a rescue mission."

"In your extensive experience," Robin added with a wry smile. He knew just as well as she did that she'd conducted very few rescue missions—those hadn't often come up in her past line of work. But there was one she recalled, when the *Marie's* crew had been captured by Hawk Dakrind. She'd managed to free Robin and his crew, and escape back to the Mainland.

"It's how I got you out of Drynrall," she replied with a shrug. She decided not to point out the fact that it had not been especially hard to fool Dakrind; he'd still considered her a loyal Dricaster bounty hunter at that time. Fooling the Ace-Lord, infiltrating Ar-Salem undetected, freeing Aryion, and escaping alive would be an entirely different matter.

She abandoned the pretense of confidence and looked at Lammar. "That said... we aren't skilled in rescue missions. What strategy would you suggest?"

Lammar inclined his head to her in acknowledgment and thought a moment. "Well, I won't sugarcoat it—we know next to nothing about Ar-Salem. No maps, no schematics, nothing. None of our spies have successfully scouted the castle, and none of our historical records account for its new and improved structure."

"Very helpful," Robin muttered. "What're you hoping to do, then?"

"I," Lammar said, his green eyes glinting, "am a Siren, and I fully intend to use my Light-given, ah, abilities."

Interest lit Robin's expression as he caught on. "Shape-shifting? What do you intend, turn into a crow and scout the place out for us?"

"Maybe," Lammar said. "I admit I'm still figuring that part out. From what I've heard, there's very little scouting one can do—Castle Salem is shrouded in darkness so dense no mortal eye can see inside. We'll be going in blind." He paused. "That said, I'll scout what I can, try to find an entrance and escape route—but not too soon before we go inside. If I'm seen, the Hummingbird will either be moved or killed."

Bryn let out a deep breath. "All right. In that case we'll attempt to enter tomorrow morning, right before dawn. If you think that's wise?" She knew that the early hours of morning were the ideal time for a strike—the dawn light brought a false promise of security, leaving the guards relaxed and sluggish.

Lammar nodded. "Morning might not affect the enchanted guards much, but it will the Aces. They all hate the daylight, and the coming dawn will make them nervous."

Bryn thought a moment. Lammar had told them about the enchanted soldiers. She'd only seen one such soldier—the young man in the blue-plumed hat who had given her and Robin their pay after they'd destroyed the compass. She remembered his empty expression and lifeless blue eyes shining with the strange new power that filled him. The enchanted soldiers no longer had mortal weaknesses—they shared the Ace-Lord's strength as his undying slaves.

She tried not to worry over them now. "The rest of our men will wait on the ship. They'll be standing by the guns, ready to get us out of here as soon as we've made it out with Aryion. The infiltration group should be small—no more than four or five."

She looked at the two first mates. "It's a risk, and it's one I won't ask of you unless you're willing. I'd prefer you both stay safely onboard the *Marie*, but the fact is, Robin and I need your help."

"I'm with you, Cap'n," Richard said with a slight salute.

"I am willing," John agreed, "though I would like to have a concrete strategy."

"The five of us, then," Robin said, nodding. "We'll anchor in the Strait, the same place we did the last time we had business with the Aces. We'll take the rowboat onshore and sneak inside the castle." He looked at Lammar. "Assuming you've found the best way in?"

"Oh, I'll figure something out," the Siren replied. "I'll head in this evening and see what I can learn."

"Very well," Bryn said. She studied the faces of the men before her, seeing their nervousness. Yes, the plan was an uncertain one. But there was a chance it might work.

She forced a smile, trying to hide her own fear and appear confident. She didn't worry over the plan itself. Years and years of risky missions had taught her to trust in her own strategy. But those strategies had only ever endangered one life—her own.

This mission placed the lives of everyone on board in danger.

. . . . . .

By dusk, they had reached Ar-Salem.

The last time Bryn had been here, it had been late at night, and the gradual rise of the hill concealed the Flats from view. She and Robin had walked over the slope and met the Aces' servant, an enchanted soldier who had given them their pay for the compass' destruction.

The darkness and fear she'd sensed last time hung heavy over the land, and this time, it seemed a visible thing. Hulking clouds lurked beyond the hill like billowing black smoke, melding with the night sky. The western horizon was still lined with the red of evening, as if the sun had left a warning of the bloodshed to come.

Lammar changed into a raven and fluttered away, disappearing over the hill and fading into the blackness. With luck, Bryn guessed, he'd return in a few hours, but there was no telling for certain. Seeing as there was nothing else they could do for now, most of the crew headed below decks to wait. Bryn remained above, staring tensely out at the shadowed slope. She figured she should attempt to get some rest, but the anxiety tightening her chest forbade any thoughts of sleep.

The soft sound of voices below reached her ears. Richard was telling a story.

"… and then the crystal faded away into the pool where it had been formed, and the young heir left the forest as the sun set, while the ghosts of her ancestors nodded their approval."

"*Ghosts of her ancestors?*" That was John's skeptical voice, which was clearly hiding amusement.

"Ghosts," Oliver echoed in delight. "D'you suppose ghosts are real, Rich?"

"If you believe in the legend of the *Red Canary*, then aye," Richard told him. "You know the song, lad—an otherworldly ship come to guide the lost through rough patches of sea. The lords of the Nøkken captain her, if the legends are to be believed."

A few muffled comments from the others, then Oliver's confident: "*I think that story's true—about crystals and Elves and all—perhaps in another world.*"

"Another world?" John sounded thoughtful. "Perhaps another civilization entirely, as some historians have theorized—a people before our time."

"Or it's just one of Richard's stories," one of the others suggested, and laughter rippled through the ship.

Bryn smiled to herself at the sound. It was good having them all together, though she wished it could have been under happier circumstances.

She could hear Oliver bickering with John over whether or not the "other worlds" were a logical theory. The cabin boy had been allowed to come only on the condition he would remain below. Bryn was beginning to wish she'd made him stay in Kamon. If they were attacked by the Aces, the group on the *Marie* would not be much safer than anyone caught on shore.

And there was the fear again, sharp and biting.

"You know," came Robin's voice behind her, "as fearless as you are, you sure tend to worry a lot."

Bryn sighed as she turned to him. "I don't like this. It'd have been better if you all had waited in Kamon, and Lammar and I could have handled this ourselves."

Robin arched an eyebrow, but his tone was not unkind. "So you could take all the risk on your own mighty shoulders, you mean?"

"It's more than a risk, Robin, you know that." She shook her head. "Even if we pull this off—rescue Aryion, and get out alive—what happens then? You know the Aces won't just let us go. Will we join the fight against them now?"

Robin thought for a few moments. "None of us are trained warriors, not for a war of this scale."

"Do you think the Ace-Lord will care?" Bryn pointed out. "Regardless of if we want to fight, this mission ensures we've joining the conflict. And I'm the one forcing our crews to risk it."

She nodded in the direction of the stairs. The cheerful voices still floated to her ears from below deck.

Robin was silent. "We aren't soldiers," he said at last. "But we can still help. If what the Siren said is true, this mission will help the New Blood with his purpose."

Bryn stared out over the water. He was right, she knew. There were more ways to help the cause than battle. Getting Aryion out would aid Mel's mission as the New Blood, and in turn, would help slow the Ace-Lord. They might act in the background, but they could act all the same.

"Speaking of the Siren, he's been gone too long," she said shortly, glaring at the dark clouds.

Robin squinted in the direction she indicated, unconcerned. "Eh, I'm sure he's fine."

Bryn swung her glare to him. "Are you just saying that to try to calm me down? Because it's not working."

Robin put a hand on hers gently, becoming serious. "He knows the risk. We all do. We've made our choice."

Bryn looked up, meeting his sea-blue eyes. So often his emotions were concealed behind an easy grin. Yet she could see past that, to the unease of the coming mission, and the love as he looked at her.

"I could order you to stay behind," she said with a weak attempt at a smile.

"You can't order me to do anything on *my* ship, madam," Robin answered smoothly.

Bryn closed the distance between them with a kiss, wishing that could erase the conflict in her mind. To sink into the moment and pretend the war and darkness were far away, and they could simply be husband and wife, alone and free on the high seas.

But the distant flutter of wings pulled her back to reality, and they both turned. The raven reappeared through the shadows, swooping around the mast before alighting on the deck.

"The good news is," Lammar said, flickering back into his usual shape, "I've found our way inside."

"Where?" Bryn demanded. "Were you able to get into the castle itself?"

"No," Lammar admitted. "I couldn't risk that, not with this cursed darkness. But I do know where the guards are stationed." He padded purposefully down the steps to reach them. "The bad news is, we need to go *now*. We can't wait till morning."

Bryn stared at him in disbelief. They'd only just settled on a plan, and night had barely fallen. "Now?" she repeated incredulously. "Why on Orlell would we do that?"

Lammar's expression was urgent. "Because the Ace-Lord is away. So's his deputy. I don't know how or why, but we need to take this opportunity while it lasts."

Bryn inhaled sharply. Rushing a mission was something she'd typically avoid. But if the Ace-Lord was gone, they couldn't miss the chance and wait until morning. The Ace-Lord might be back by then, and from all she'd heard, she highly doubted they could slip past him.

"I'll tell the crew," Robin said, heading for the hatch.

Bryn looked at Lammar again, trying to gather her thoughts. Her doubts seemed to have slunk back to the corners of her mind now that the time had come. There was no going back, and now, they would infiltrate the Ace-Lord's fortress. "How are we getting inside?" she asked, fetching her bow and quiver. "A side door—or a window, maybe?"

Lammar shook his head. "Oh no. We're going through the main gate."

Bryn stopped in her tracks, staring at him in disbelief. "The main gate—have you lost your mind? They'll kill us all before we can even see them."

"I think they will do nothing of the kind, Captain," Lammar replied. A mischievous light shone in his eyes as his shape changed and shifted again. His frame grew taller and darker. Not the black-armored warrior that Bryn had overheard him telling Richard about, nor any mortal being she'd yet seen—this was much larger, far more terrifying, a shadow with a half-decayed face and purple-red eyes.

"Your group," Lammar said, his voice now sly and cold as he grinned out of the ruined face, "will be presented as the prized prisoners of the Ace-Deputy."

34

The Black Box

Quickly, quietly, the four sailors left the *Marie* behind, paddling to shore.

Bryn stepped from the rowboat onto the damp sand onshore and set her oar inside. Despite her efforts, the wood clattered slightly, and she reached for her bow, peering up the hill for any signs they'd been noticed. It was so dark she could only just make out the gray outline of the *Marie* waiting back on the Strait. Thunderclouds lurked to the north, joining with the black fog ahead.

Richard and Robin hauled the boat up onto shore. The hull ground against the gravel, straining her already tense nerves. "Careful," she hissed, listening hard in the silence for any sounds. There were none. Aside from the monotonous lapping of saltwater against the rocks, the world they'd entered was desolate, silent as a grave.

She turned slowly to face Lammar—or, the thing that he'd become. He stood waiting, a tall shadow whose very gaze seemed to freeze her with fear. The Siren's newest form was, frankly, terrifying. He'd even managed to recreate the slightest dull shimmer of the Ace-Deputy's silver armor, adding to its ghostly aura. Bryn had to admit, it was a convincing disguise.

"Light above, that is disturbing," John murmured, slinging his rifle over his back. "Do you believe it will successfully fool the guards?"

The Deputy tilted his head slightly to the side in a very Lammar-type way, considering the question. "I've always prided myself on my theatrical skills," he said. "I'm sure I can convince them."

"Here's the shackles," Bryn said, producing the handcuffs and securing them around the wrists of her companions, then holding out her own wrists for Robin to cuff. He gave her a faint smile as he did so.

"Isn't this familiar."

Bryn managed to return his smile. Early into their mission to find the compass, she'd posed as a slaver, with Robin as her prisoner, to get past an enemy checkpoint. "It fooled the Rylanders," she pointed out. "Who knows, maybe it'll fool the Aces too."

"And we've got a very convincing captor," Robin pointed out, jerking his head at Lammar. "Good grief, I can't even look at—it. It's blasted creepy."

"As long as we do not encounter the real thing," John murmured nervously. "You are certain the Ace-Lord is away?"

"As certain as I could be," Lammar replied. "Enchanted soldiers aren't particularly talkative, you know."

Which did nothing to ease Bryn's concerns as they fell into a line, starting toward the black mass ahead. Wind tore across the Flats, pressing against them, as though forbidding them to go further. Lammar led them forward, his disguise never faltering.

"Why the Deputy?" Richard whispered as they started uphill. "Wouldn't the Ace-Lord be more frightening?"

"Undoubtedly," John told him. "But it wouldn't be practical. It is quite unlikely the Ace-Lord would concern himself with prisoners. The Deputy is the wiser choice for this operation."

"Keep it down," Bryn warned them. "We don't know if there are any scouts out here."

She strained her eyes through the murky darkness. The fog seemed a black pool, concealing everything within it. It swallowed them immediately, an embrace of freezing fear. The castle gradually appeared ahead, spires poking through the clouds like jagged bones, darker even than the shadows engulfing the Flats.

It had been rebuilt, Lammar had told them earlier. No longer did the castle stand a desolate ruin, a glimpse of a bygone age, a lost memory of the mortal world. Its black walls were wrought of a power far stronger than any of this world, and malice chilled the very air around it like a sickening scent warning her to flee while she had the chance. The darkness concealed any details, so that Castle Salem seemed a yawning pit that would close upon them the moment they entered its gates.

For one blind moment of panic, she wanted to abandon the mission while they were all still alive. But the thought was gone in an instant. They didn't have that choice anymore—and neither would Aryion. This was the only chance they'd get to rescue her brother.

"Easy does it," Lammar murmured as they crested the last rise, descending into the flat valley of Ar-Salem. It was uncanny hearing his words in that icy voice. "Remember, they can sense fear."

"Wouldn't we be afraid as prisoners, sir?" Richard asked quietly, his deep voice uncertain.

"I suppose that's a different sort of fear," Robin whispered back.

"Quiet," Bryn cautioned. Her pounding heart seemed to thunder in the silence around them. She tried to redirect her nervousness to something less suspicious, to play the role of a defeated and frightened prisoner. Yet her chained hands strayed subconsciously to her bow and quiver.

The dark gate loomed before them. High above, Bryn could make out the blurred silhouettes of the guards, their hollow blue eyes glowing faintly in the darkness. They opened the gate without a word from Lammar, their gazes following them inside the courtyard. She forced herself to keep her eyes ahead, but she could feel their dead eyes on her all the way through the castle entrance.

The courtyard was so dark she almost didn't see the four guards who stepped forward to meet them as they reached the doors. One of them—a captain, judging by his uniform and weapons—stepped forward. He bowed to the Deputy, but Bryn could hear the confusion in his voice. "Sir. We did not expect you to return so soon."

"Expect nothing, captain," Lammar snapped. "Do not believe yourself privy to my master's commands. If he will order me to return, then understand it is for a pressing reason."

If Bryn hadn't known otherwise, she would have fully believed the Deputy himself stood beside her. Lammar had perfectly captured the cold, demeaning tone and the reverence as he spoke of the Ace-Lord.

The captain seemed to believe it, too. "Apologies, sir. I understood your dealings with the Hummingbird were completed."

"You understood wrong," the Deputy answered icily. "There is one last matter I must attend to, and it involves these vagabonds," he gripped Robin by the back of the neck, hauling him forward, "Caer Sian spies who sought to infiltrate the palace."

The captain frowned slightly, peering at them. As he did, the dark clouds shifted slightly, allowing a faint beam of moonlight to fill the courtyard, lighting his pale face, hollow eyes, and a wide-brimmed hat with a blue plume.

Realization shot through Bryn's heart like a slap of cold water. This captain—this was the man who had met them with the payment for the compass. She remembered his courteous voice, his calm manner, his uncanny features.

Did Lammar know this? The slightest indication that he didn't, and the plan would fall to pieces. But there was no way to warn him now.

"Spies, my lord?" the captain asked slowly, looking back at the Deputy. "Are… these not the same pirates we hired to fetch the compass for our master?"

Lammar hesitated a split second; Bryn realized he had understood, far too late, that the guard knew who they were. But the Siren recovered quickly. "Why, I believe they are," he said shortly, as if it had just occurred to him. "It seems they refused to flee while they had the chance. I will undoubtedly learn more from them soon. Escort them to the Hummingbird's cell."

The captain paused a moment longer—Bryn could see him working over this information, catching the fatal flaw in the story. But the enchantment seemed to forbid him from questioning orders, and he turned to one of the guards. "Watch the gate while we take the prisoners. We will be back momentarily."

"Yes, Captain Fargrin," the man answered tonelessly.

The other two enchanted guards moved around the sailors, pressing them together. Bryn felt the chains bite into her wrists, and she forced herself to take a deep breath. One of the guards reached for her quiver, and she felt a flash of panic. If the man noticed the torch she'd stashed inside, then surely—

"Leave them their weapons," Lammar ordered briskly. "There is little good they can do."

"As you wish, sir," Captain Fargrin replied, pushing the four sailors inside. Bryn threw one last worried look at Lammar before they were separated, and she and her crew were swallowed by the shadows of Castle Salem.

It was pitch black. Her knee knocked against the corner of a stone wall, and she stumbled. A guard hauled her upright, dragging her forward. Muffled voices or the grunts and growls of beasts echoed from far away. Occasionally she managed to make out the vague, uncertain outlines of staircases or doorways, but then Fargrin turned them sharply to the right, down a dripping hallway that reeked of decay.

"What now?" Robin whispered, his mouth against her ear. "We hadn't planned on getting split up."

"Lammar will find us," Bryn murmured back, though she had no idea how. Even if the Siren managed to find them, how would they get back out? The ruse of captives and captor would only work on the way inside.

The guard shoved his crossbow against her back, and she fell silent. His weapon was hardly necessary; she couldn't even see, let alone concoct a strategy to attack. They couldn't hope to fight the enchanted soldiers—their best bet would be to find an escape route. Perhaps there was a back entrance or a side door. But even if there was, she could see nothing in the darkness.

They turned and continued downward until Bryn felt thoroughly lost. Castle Salem seemed a labyrinth of connecting corridors and stairways. She tripped on a step as they were marched straight downward, giving her the unpleasant sensation that they were descending down the throat of a massive snake. The air grew colder, and her boots skidded on frost slicking the stone.

Fargrin's voice broke the dead silence. "Halt."

The guards stopped. Bryn heard the low shuffles of her companions.

Robin was still beside her, and she was fairly sure both Richard and John remained behind her. That was good—it'd only complicate matters if they were separated. But Lammar had ordered them to be taken to Aryion's cell.

Assuming he's still alive, a nagging voice reminded her in her mind.

"I understood your dealings with the Hummingbird were completed," Fargrin had said at the gate. *Dealings,* Bryn thought anxiously, what sort of dealings? What had the Aces been doing to him?

Four clicks sounded in succession as a door was unlocked, and Bryn felt cold air on her face as a doorway opened before them, then she was shoved forward into blackness. Robin stumbled into her, and she staggered to keep her balance.

The door slammed closed. She heard the clicks as it locked again, and they were left alone in the cell.

Her heart raced in uncontrollable panic for an instant. She'd always hated small spaces, and she groped blindly in front of her as the shadows seemed to press inward. Her hands found empty air.

"Cap'n?" Richard's nervous whisper came from her right.

"I'm here," Bryn replied quietly. "Is everyone all right?"

"Just cold," Robin muttered. "Let's get these chains off us. And light the torch, John."

"Wait," Bryn whispered. The sound of the guards' footsteps came from far above. "Wait till we're sure they're gone."

She groped forward until her hand reached a cold wall. A metallic stench filled the room. The walls were coated in frost; she felt the cold bite into her fingers.

At last, the guards' footsteps died away. It was totally silent except for the ragged breathing of her companions.

"Aryion?" she whispered into the shadows.

Nothing.

"I believe they are gone," John ventured.

Bryn let out a breath. "All right. Just a little light—a match, not the torch."

There was a quiet rustling as John rummaged through his pockets. At least the guards hadn't searched them, Bryn thought, reaching into her pocket for the key and unlocking everyone's shackles. And they still had their weapons. That was very fortunate. Of course, their weapons would be little use if Lammar couldn't get the cell door open. Who knew how long it would take the Siren to find them? She tried not to worry about that now.

A tiny flicker of golden light sparked in John's hand as the sailor held the match aloft. The little flame was almost as bright as a lantern in this black cell, casting elongated shadows into the darkness.

Bryn squinted, peering forward in the dim light. The room they stood in was box-like, perfectly square and surprisingly large. The size played into the eerie, void-like emptiness of the cell—large, black, silent.

A figure hunched against the far wall.

Bryn's heart skipped a beat, and she moved forward. The other three followed her, letting the light reach the prisoner they'd come to find.

Blood streaked his filthy clothes, which were tattered and torn. His hair and beard were uncut and disheveled, dusted in white frost. His face was gaunt and pale as a skull's, patchworked with bruises and cuts. Yet Bryn recognized the face in an instant.

"Aryion," she whispered, dropping to her knees in front of her brother and putting her hands on his shoulders. "Aryion, wake up."

Aryion did not respond. His eyes were half-open, staring unfocused at nothing.

"Aryion," Bryn said again, as loud as she dared. "Aryion, come on—we don't have time—we're here to get you out, but you need to get up."

"What's the matter with him?" Robin whispered, kneeling next to her. "Is he…"

"He's alive," Bryn said slowly, though a sudden cold fear had stirred in her heart. "He's breathing. And he's awake—I think."

Robin waved a hand in front of the ranger's face, frowning. "Let's just get him moving—he needs to be ready to go when the Siren gets here. I'll pick the lock on his chains."

Bryn stood and took a step back, her eyes still on her brother's lifeless face. Alarm bells were jangling in her mind, but she didn't know why. There was something in his eyes—something hollow and dead—that chilled her to the core.

John lit another match as Robin set to work picking the lock around Aryion's neck. The skin was rubbed raw and bloody. The chains were wrought of the same black steel as the palace and seemed to emanate their own coldness.

"Any sign?" Bryn whispered to Richard, who stood facing the door.

"No—not that I can see a blasted thing," Richard answered. His voice was tense. "I don't like this, Cap'n. No guards at all… something's up."

"They would have little reason to guard this cell," John pointed out. "If the captain is to be believed, the Aces no longer desire information from the Hummingbird."

If they had required information from him in the first place, Bryn thought warily. From the guard's implication, the Deputy had been doing something else.

With a soft click, Robin undid the clasp around the ranger's neck and started on the chains around his wrists. Aryion turned his head slightly towards the light. She saw him blink, his gaze feverishly scanning the room.

The match went out.

"Light?" Robin asked shortly.

"Working on it, Captain," John replied. Elongated shadows stretched around the cell as he lit the torch, letting golden light illuminate the area around them, and allowing Bryn a better look at her brother.

His eyes. Something had changed in them. No longer the usual deep brown that they had in common, nor the hollow blue of the enchanted soldiers—something worse. The light gleaming in them was empty, and yet stronger than any natural strength.

Aryion turned his head back to Robin, his gaze focusing on the pirate.

"Robin…" Bryn started slowly.

The first cuff gave way.

Robin had just reached to start on the second when Aryion's pale hands locked around his throat.

The ranger's eyes glittered, flecked with lifeless blue as he drew himself to his full height, dragging Robin upright as if he weighed no more than a doll—Robin coughed, lashing out futilely with his fists. Bryn, already tense from a fear she couldn't understand, sprang forward, flinging herself upon her brother's back and hauling his head back by the hair.

Aryion didn't react, a brutish calm in his cold expression, his grip never faltering.

"Let go," Bryn ordered, as quietly as she could—any sounds of struggle, and the guards would be back. "Let him go now—it's us, we're here to help—"

Robin choked, clawing at the iron grip. Richard moved to help them as John gripped Aryion's other arm, trying to force his hold to release. Bryn reached to her belt, searching blindly for something to help—her hand traced over the hilt of her knife, but she could not bring herself to draw it against her brother. Her fingers found her water flask, and she snatched it up, uncorking and pouring it directly into Aryion's expressionless face.

Aryion reeled back, coughing, and dropped Robin. The ranger stumbled against the wall with a muted thud—the impact echoed through the room, and Bryn froze, listening for any signs of alarm in the hall.

"Watch it!" Richard warned as she did, and she swung around again. Aryion stepped forward, swinging a wide punch at her face—Bryn ducked out of the way just in time.

Richard stepped between them as the ranger lunged again, his wide-bladed saxe knife in his hand. Muffled sounds of activity came from far above. John raised his rifle, sights centered point-blank on Aryion's back.

"Don't!" Bryn ordered, fighting to keep her voice down. "Don't kill him—"

John hesitated—as Aryion leapt at Richard, the burly sailor dropped his shoulder, slamming into the ranger's chest. Aryion stumbled to the side, off balance for a moment. The muffled sounds transformed into the dreaded rhythm of someone walking down the stairs.

Bryn lunged at Aryion again, gripping his arm and dragging him to the floor. As she did, she felt his free hand lock on her arm, his fingers digging in like claws.

They struggled for an instant, kneeling on the floor. He was strong—unnaturally strong—she felt his grip tightening, crushing the muscles and tendons of her wrist, and she bit back a scream of pain.

John slammed the butt of his rifle into Aryion's ribs, throwing him to the side. Richard came from behind, his arm locking under Aryion's chin and tightening in a headlock. "Come on Hummingbird—snap out of it," he grunted.

Aryion writhed like a captive animal, slamming his head back into Richard's face so hard his grip loosened. Footsteps sounded in the corridor, then—to Bryn's horror—a series of clicks as the door was unlocked.

Aryion sprinted to the door as it swung open. An armored fist connected with his jaw as he reached it, sending him crashing back into John, who managed to catch the unconscious body.

Bryn's gaze swung to the door as the black-armored knight's shape flickered back into Lammar's. "What took you so long?" she hissed, the horror of the last few minutes blinding her reason.

Lammar shook his head slowly. "Enchanted soldiers aren't fools, so I had to evade them. But I could hear him battering you all halfway down the stairs." His green eyes took in the scene with deep concern—Robin, gasping for breath and holding his throat, Bryn holding her bruised wrist, and Richard bleeding heavily from the nose. "What's going on?"

"I don't know," Bryn said hoarsely, moving to Robin. His neck was red and bruising where the ranger's fingers had gripped it, but there did not seem to be permanent damage.

But if there had been… if the others hadn't been here to help… if Lammar hadn't come in the nick of time… there was no doubt that Aryion would have killed them all.

"Is he enchanted?" Lammar asked, as John lowered the body to the ground. "I've never heard of them being taken down by anything."

"I—don't think he's enchanted," Bryn replied haltingly. She could hear the fear and uncertainty in her voice, unable to put into words what had just happened. Her mind replayed that terrifying moment when Aryion had lifted Robin by the throat, that expressionless, brutish light in his eyes, and she felt sick.

Lammar looked at the ranger for a long moment; Bryn could see the concern and confusion on his face. But he shook his head. "We'll sort it out later. Right now we need to go."

Bryn nodded shortly, helping Robin to his feet and trying to gather herself. But the dread and dismay remained in her thoughts. Her fears had been all too true. The one they'd come to rescue was gone. What was left was a stranger with dead eyes who wore her brother's face like a mask.

35

Down Silent Stairs

Lammar made them douse the torch as they left the cell behind and headed back into the labyrinth of halls.

The Siren led them into the darkness, wearing the guise of the black-armored knight. His whispered voice beckoned them forward, and occasionally Bryn caught the glint of his green eyes behind the helmet. Robin leaned heavily on her shoulder as they marched blindly forward. His breath came rasping and painful, Aryion's deadly grip still marking his throat.

Bryn glanced back at Richard, who carried the limp body over his shoulder. Aryion. Her brother's name had always carried the weight of conflicting feelings. For years, they'd been estranged, he having gone to pursue a Blood Oath, and she headed south to join a Crime Ring. After unexpectedly reuniting during the search for the compass, they had put the past behind them, and it had been good to have her twin beside her again.

But the unconscious figure Richard carried was not her brother. She barely knew if he was human anymore.

He was not enchanted, of that much Bryn was certain. From the little she'd seen of the Ace-Lord's warriors, they all had the same hollow blue eyes and single-minded actions. They responded only to their master's wishes, relying on his orders to accomplish anything. The guards at the gate had certainly matched that description.

Aryion's dark eyes were flecked with the same lifeless blue as the enchanted soldiers, but there was something else there, too. Pain—tortured, tormented pain that had reduced him to this. As if he had struggled against himself and lost.

"Is it a curse?" she whispered, as Lammar made them pause. The total blackness of Castle Salem unnerved her. Then again, even if she'd been able to see, she doubted she would be able to find the way out of these winding corridors.

Lammar did not answer immediately. When he spoke, his voice was low and grim. "No, I don't believe it's a curse. I can't know anything for certain—I've never seen anything like it."

"Might it have been the shock?" John ventured quietly from the back of the group.

"Shock doesn't give you that kind of strength," Robin rasped. "You saw it, John—he lifted me off the floor like a ragdoll."

"Oh, I saw it," John murmured. "I am still having a difficult time *believing* it."

Lammar cautioned them to silence as they began descending down another flight of stairs. Bryn nearly slipped on the slick steps and put her hand against the wall for balance.

"Down?" she whispered uneasily. "We're going further down?"

"Far as I can tell," Lammar replied, "there's a cistern underneath the castle. That's our way out."

"A cistern?" Robin repeated, confused.

"Empty and abandoned," Lammar told him. "But the drainage canals should lead outside. If we follow them, we'll get outside, too."

"You're sure?" Bryn asked, still worried. The plan of descending back down into those dark tunnels seemed a risky one. She'd much prefer heading back up into the dim gray light, where at least they could see.

"I saw it on my fly-over. Trust me, Captain. It's our only shot," Lammar said. "That trick with the Deputy won't work twice. Our friend Captain Fargrin already seemed suspicious."

Bryn didn't argue that point, placing her hand on the hilt of her dagger as they moved blindly onward. Her longbow was her weapon of choice, but these tight confines made it cumbersome.

Down they walked. In the quiet blackness, the horrific moments in the cell flickered afresh into her thoughts: Aryion's tortured, maddened expression, his blank stare. Her wrist ached where he'd gripped it. But his eyes had scared her the most.

What had the Aces done to him? How long had he been a prisoner? Lammar had said he'd disappeared over two months ago—that meant two months in the black, box-like cell, subjected to whatever tortures the Aces had inflicted.

The Aces hadn't needed information from him, as far as they had guessed. Nor did Aryion bear signs of any typical methods of torture that Bryn had heard of. The blood staining his clothes was old and dried, so she doubted it had come from the Aces' questioning.

What *had* they done to him?

With a shudder, she pressed her hand to the damp wall and guided herself down. The muffled voices of activity in the rest of the castle faded away, until the only sounds were the shuffling of the hurried companions and the dull dripping damp of the tunnel.

Lammar's quiet voice came from ahead, his green eyes seeing slightly better in the dark than those of the humans. "The stairs end here— mind your footing."

Bryn traced the edge of the last step with her boot before carefully stepping to the floor. A puddle splashed under her boots as she did. "Can we risk a light?" she whispered. "We might stumble blindly into a trap at this rate."

A long pause as the Siren thought, then he sighed. "Very well. But watch your backs. You never know what unpleasant creatures might be attracted to the light."

"Light above," Robin rasped, edging closer to Bryn with a shudder. "You *had* to mention that idea."

They lit the torch, letting a comforting gold warmth fill the lower level of Castle Salem, and Bryn could see their surroundings for the first time.

The stairs ended in a long hallway with a high vaulted ceiling. Instead of the black and silver steel of the upper levels, the corridor was carved of ancient stone stained rusty red. Runes in a long-dead language were etched into the walls, along with simple, primitive carvings depicting strange figures.

John took a step nearer the wall, squinting at the markings with interest. "Fascinating… Captain, these carvings are likely millennia old, far older than any written history."

"This may be the original Castle Salem," Lammar mused, changing back into his usual shape and padding forward. "Come along—the cistern drains are this way."

John, after a longing look at the carvings, followed as the group started forward. Despite herself, Bryn could not help staring around in awe. The walls, as John had pointed out, were ancient, having stood long before the first Ace-rise—perhaps even before the Dividing War. The hieroglyphics depicted sketches of stories long past.

"Who built this castle?" she asked. "If it wasn't the Ace-Lord's while he was mortal, whose was it?"

"No one really knows," Lammar told her in a lowered voice. "Most think it was the domain of a human king, but no one knows who."

"There are many theories," John said, stopping to inspect another drawing. "The most popular is that of a lost civilization."

"Tell us about it when we've made it out," Robin ordered.

The arched hallway ended in another corridor. This one had been hollowed out by a regular stream of water. Now, though, it only contained puddles. Lammar moved into the passage first, raising his nose to the air as he scented for danger. Finding none, he turned to Richard. "Set him down. Let me see what's happened."

Richard slung Aryion's unconscious form from his shoulder, lowering him to the damp ground. Lammar bent over him carefully, frowning. He raised one of the ranger's eyelids lightly, peering at his eye.

"He's not enchanted," Bryn repeated. The words were monotonous, a futile attempt to reassure herself and everyone present that her brother was somehow still in there.

"Oh, you're right about that," Lammar murmured, looking up at her. "You said he gave no sign of recognizing any of you—he simply attacked?"

Bryn nodded tensely.

"Could they… alter his mind?" Richard asked slowly. "I've heard stories about the Aces affecting a man's thoughts."

"They can," Lammar said, but his face was uncertain. He finally shook his head. "He's waking up. Chain him for the time being, for his safety as much as ours. If he were to go running back into the tunnels, there's no telling if we'd ever find him again."

Aryion stirred as Richard clasped the cuffs over his wrists, his eyes fluttering open weakly. A bruise darkened his jaw, but he seemed unhurt beyond that. The wildness seemed to have passed. His expression was dull as he stumbled after them. It reminded Bryn, in a flash, of the Wavers, the cursed seafarers whose lust for the compass had brought them to a fixated madness.

She strode to the front of the group to the Siren, speaking quietly. "You know something about what's happened to him."

"I have a guess." Lammar said nothing more.

Bryn looked down at him. "Tell me. I need to know."

Lammar was quiet, his gaze fixed on the tunnel before them. "We received a report in Mata City a few months ago," he said finally. "The township of Wiverrun was taken by the Ace-Lord, the inhabitants captured or enchanted, or so we thought at first. Until we found the few civilians left."

He paused. "The Aces have ways of affecting the mind, like Richard suggested. Up until now, we've known that the enchantment placed on the soldiers is a choice each one must make. But we've been wondering for some time if the Ace-Lord will find a way around that—and it seems we were right."

"He's trying to force people to become enchanted?" Bryn asked slowly, puzzled.

"Yes, Captain. The few living recovered from Wiverrun were not enchanted, but neither were they themselves any longer. They've been called the Shattered—broken minds, destroyed memories. Even worse, while there's hope the enchanted soldiers will come to themselves again if the Ace-Lord's defeated, there is no turning back the Shattered."

Despair and defeat settled heavy in Bryn's heart. "You think that's what happened?" she asked quietly, glancing back at Aryion. His lifeless gaze stared ahead without a trace of the usual depth and clarity.

But Lammar was frowning. "I don't believe so. The Shattered—they don't react to anything whatsoever. Aryion certainly responded to your presence."

"His response wasn't exactly positive," Bryn said.

"But it was a response all the same," the Siren said. "I doubt his mind's been fully shattered. More likely it's been… altered." He thought for a moment. "Whatever his purpose, the Ace-Lord wanted Aryion a prisoner, and he wanted him kept alive. There's a reason behind these new 'gifts,' I'm sure. And I doubt it's a good one."

Bryn turned her eyes to the corridor ahead, her heart torn between helpless frustration and dull despair at Lammar's words. "So there's nothing we can do," she stated, hearing the finality in her voice.

"That I don't know either," Lammar said. "Parts of his mind are still intact. There may be enough to help him return to himself."

The group lapsed into silence as they continued down the drain passage, leaving Bryn to her thoughts. The sinister strength her brother had displayed in the cell showed just what he was now capable of, and she knew the Aces wouldn't have given him that power for nothing. What he had become was a weapon, and who knew what sort of havoc he would have wrecked if they hadn't come.

And yet… the brown remaining in his hollow eyes fed her meager hope that he could still be healed. Perhaps Lammar was right. Perhaps there was just enough of Aryion's mind left to help him return to himself.

Or perhaps her brother was truly gone forever.

That thought settled on her heart like a weight, but a heavier one had come with it. Mel. The boy would be waiting, hopeful they would return with his mentor.

When they did, it would be Bryn who crushed his hope, Bryn who must somehow explain to him that his mentor was gone. And she knew, without a doubt, that it would destroy him. The New Blood's resolve to defeat the Aces would crumble with it.

She brought her mind back to the present as they reached the end of the tunnel. The stone was replaced by rough hewn earth and rock, carved from the Flats. They stood on the top of a slight rise. Faint gray light pierced the darkness around them, and a cool draft wafted upwards.

"We've made it out," Richard murmured in relief.

"Not quite," Lammar replied, his face raised to the wind. "There are Dal-kerri below us—ten of them, I think." He frowned. "But only wolves… that's very odd."

"How so?" John asked, gripping his rifle uneasily.

"You don't find that strange?" Lammar asked, glancing at them. "Not a single patrol in the tunnels? Not a guard at any of the corridors? We know the Aces are here. The question is… why aren't they *here*, specifically?"

Bryn looked out into the night. Through the dark fog surrounding Castle Salem, the white of the Flats was just visible. The path to freedom opened wide before them. Lammar, she realized, with growing foreboding, was right. The only resistance they'd encountered had been the guards at the gate. While the upper levels had echoed with the faint sounds of voices and movement, it was nothing compared to the massive Ace-army Lammar had described. Surely the Aces would not be so careless, not when they were holding a valuable prisoner.

Unless…

"I assumed your dealings with the Hummingbird were completed."

The Deputy had finished with Aryion—either because Aryion had finally broken to his will, or because the Aces' focus had shifted elsewhere.

"Where would they be?" Robin whispered. "Do you suppose they've set a trap to spring once we set foot on the Flats?"

"Maybe, but it wouldn't require their entire army," Lammar replied. He took a few steps outside, peering around. Bryn waited tensely for an attack, but it never came. "The army isn't here," Lammar said finally. "Let's go—quickly. Watch out for Dal-kerri."

"Why haven't they stopped us?" Bryn stammered, totally lost. This strategy made no sense, nor did it match the conniving and clever scheme she'd been warned of.

"I expect because the loss of a prisoner doesn't trouble the Ace-Lord," Lammar answered. "He did something similar during the attack on Castle Droco a few months back. The heiress' efforts to free Mel and the High King were unhindered… because the Ace-Lord had moved on to a different part of his plan."

Bryn glanced at him as they jogged into the murky darkness. The uncertainty in the Sirens' green eyes had slowly evolved into dread— deep dread of something not even he could understand.

Dal-kerri stalked out of the fog, snarling and snapping fanged muzzles. Bryn set her stance and loosed an arrow at one. Robin drew his sword and cut down the next, while John caught another hound on the bayonet of his rifle before it could leap at Richard.

Bryn had already reached for another arrow, but by this point, Lammar had transformed again, his shape warping into a massive eagle-like beast whose huge wings sent the wolves reeling back.

Two more hounds bounded from the darkness. Bryn let an arrow fly, even as teeth snapped closed on her jerkin. A gunshot split the air, and the offending wolf fell to the ground as Robin lowered his pistol.

"The guards definitely heard that!" Bryn warned, turning sharply back toward the castle. For the first time, the low toll of a gong rumbled deep in Castle Salem's depths, ringing out the alarm.

"We're on the wrong side of the Flats!" Robin said, rounding on Lammar. "Did you mean to put the castle between us and the *Marie*?"

"Oh, Captain, I've never been *that* planned out," Lammar said with a sigh. His form flickered and twisted again, swelling massively in size, until a towering beast with plate-like gray scales and massive black wings reared its head over the Flats.

Bryn took a half step back in shock as the kragon beat its powerful wings, sending gray dust billowing around them.

"Hold tight!" Lammar's voice ordered. "Unless you'd rather fight your way back to the ship."

He sprang into the air, soaring down with talons extended. Bryn slung her longbow over her shoulder and looped her arm around a claw. Robin, looking both terrified and impressed, joined her, followed by the speechless John. The kragon's talons closed over Richard and Aryion, and in a beat of the huge wings, they were in the air.

The ground dropped away under Bryn's boots, and she felt as though her stomach had fallen with it. Clutching the claw, she looked back at Castle Salem as they swept through the foggy haze. Below in the darkness came the tolling gong, the shouts and cries of the alerted guards, and the rising howls of the frenzied hounds. The courtyard swarmed with bodies. A crossbow bolt whizzed past her face, and she tightened her grip.

"Can't you fly us away from the castle?" she yelled.

"Working on it!" Lammar snapped. The kragon's wings tilted unsteadily, caught by the wild winds of the Flats. He managed to veer around the castle to the left, heading over the moonlit Strait.

Bryn was never sure what made her glance back. She sensed, more than saw, the icy hatred of eyes behind her, and when she looked at the castle, a dark figure stood illuminated on the highest tower, ghostly robes billowing in the wind.

An Ace—its form far less solid than the Deputy's—raised its hands, white ice glimmering on its fingers.

"Lammar!" she shouted.

The bolt of ice flashed as it shot at them—the talons vanished in the same moment, and they were falling, tumbling downward. Lammar let himself drop beneath the white ice, which spun past him, fading harmlessly into the air beyond as Bryn hit the water.

The slap jarred the breath from her lungs. Sea water filled her nose. Kicking and thrashing, she struggled to the surface, gasping for air.

The *Burman Marie* cruised up the Strait. She glimpsed Robin and John swimming toward it. Richard surfaced just behind them, following.

Aryion. Where was Aryion?

She spun about in the salty water, peering through the darkness, her heart racing. A dark shape splashed a few feet from her, struggling weakly to stay afloat. She swam behind him, locking her arms under his shoulders and pulling his head above the water.

"Hang on," she panted, trying to ignore the surge of panic. If he turned on her now, they'd both drown, dragged into the depths of the Strait.

Aryion coughed, raising his face from the water with an effort. "North," he rasped.

His voice was unrecognizable, ragged and weak. But Bryn felt a surge of hope pierce her grim despair. "What?" she asked.

Aryion coughed again, his blue-flecked eyes fighting to stay conscious. "North… the kragon king can carry…" He trailed off, his face dipping back toward the water.

Green scaled hands lifted him as Lammar pulled them towards the *Marie*. Bryn gripped the lowered rope and hauled herself up the bulwark, arms shaking with exhaustion. Robin's hands took her arm and pulled her to the deck, where she dropped to her knees.

"Are you all right?" Robin asked anxiously—his face swam into focus in front of her. She nodded, falling into his arms as she caught her breath.

They were alive. Against all odds, they'd made it back.

"Too easy," Lammar muttered behind her, staring back at the castle. "Far too easy. I don't like it."

"Can't just be—glad it all worked, I suppose," Richard said, teeth chattering.

"Were you followed, Cap'n?" one of the sailors asked.

"No, I don't think so," Bryn answered faintly, getting to her feet. She could hardly believe the words any more than they could. "No… it worked. We're all right."

"I'll be convinced of that after we've reached Mata City," Lammar replied shortly.

"Right, then," Robin said. "Hard to starboard. We're going north—easy or not, I'd prefer we put a bit more distance between us and Castle Salem."

Aryion lay unmoving on the deck, his chest rising and falling as he breathed slowly. Lammar studied him a moment before looking up at Bryn. "Did he speak?"

"Briefly," Bryn replied. "Something about a kragon king going north."

A thoughtful light entered the Siren's eyes. "A kragon king… that's very interesting."

"How so?"

Lammar paused. "I expect Aryion's told you about the quest for the Shards almost a year ago. During that quest, the company was carried north to Caer Sia by the kragon king, Fireclaw. I believe that was the last time he encountered a kragon."

Bryn turned to the sailors. "Take him below—leave the chains on for now, but try and get him warm." She looked at Lammar again, hardly daring to trust the hope that had come alive inside her. "You think he remembered the quest for the Shards?"

"At least the parts regarding the kragon," Lammar said, padding toward the stern. "Perhaps certain things, if they were frequent occurrences in his life, might bring some of those memories back."

Bryn moved to the stern to stand beside Robin, her thoughts mulling over this new idea. Aryion's mind was not fully shattered. Maybe there was still a way to return her brother to himself.

Unless, she thought, as the fear entered her mind again, the Aces' plan still had him in their clutches. She was not sure what that plan was yet. But she couldn't flatter herself that their success was all due to her rescue strategy.

No, they had been allowed in and out of Castle Salem with minimal resistance, and the only logical reason was that the Ace-Lord's plan had centered elsewhere.

36

Arrival

By dawn, the Aces had reached the outskirts of Caer Sia, and Jan could practically feel time draining away.

Fear hung over the streets like the black smoke billowing around the walls. The evacuation had drawn on through the night as the civilians congregated in masses by the harbor, boarding the ships in agonizing slowness. The rising sun pierced through the hulking storm clouds, shining through the haze of smoke and casting orange-tinted light upon the attackers gathering behind the walls.

Jan stood on the wall overlooking the rolling forest stretching out to the southeast. This section of the wall had been leveled by the Aces when they'd claimed Caer Sia before, and only portions of it had since been repaired. Likely, the Aces were well aware of this, eager to strike against the unprotected capital. Yet the wall would now stand as the first line of defense against the Aces.

The Ace-army had appeared sometime around midnight, gathering in a black mass. Dal-kerri, serpentines, enchanted soldiers of numerous species, and other creatures Jan could not fully glimpse. They lurked in the shadows, waiting, gathering their strength after the journey and preparing for the attack.

Let them rest, Jan thought grimly. It would afford more time for the civilians to escape, time he and Dandio intended to prolong.

His hand closed over Drisilas' cold hilt. The Star-Stone was gone, of course—protected by Iriam for now. Strange how, though he well understood the Stone's corruption had been of his making, Isilas still seemed connected to him, as though a portion of its light was imbued in his Essence. He had failed in his task to protect it, yet he could not ignore the summoning call.

Was it still his call to answer? Surely it was too late to wonder that.

Jan closed his eyes a moment, wishing to blot out the teeming warriors on the edge of the city, the crimson flames casting shadows along the streets, and allowed his mind to fall back to another time. Luet's voice whispered in his thoughts, echoing words his father had once spoken.

"No king can bear the weight of a kingdom."

Did you mean this war, Luet? Jan wondered. *What am I meant to do without the Stone? Sia will soon be lost, and the war will be lost as well.*

The Star's voice cast golden light into the shadows of his mind, her words coming from a time long ago during the war against the tyrannical queen. *"The High Light is with you. Do not lose hope. You must seek the Druids."*

And then she had left Caer Sia for the last time. He had never had the chance to ask what she meant, nor the opportunity to follow her advice. She had perished on the seas in a plume of fire.

The trumpets sounded in warning to his right, and he focused his gaze again on the present. Red flames blazed from the pillars along the wall, crackling in a barrier at the base of the wall and spreading toward the homes and farms of the outskirts. Fire. The one thing the Aces feared. It would slow the Ace-army's advance and protect Sia's fleeing people even as it consumed the city.

The Ace-army surged forward in a wave of bodies. It took them several minutes before the flames were successfully doused, allowing the Dal-kerri to lunge against the wall.

"They have no need for strategy," Dandio said quietly to Jan's left. "They know we are outnumbered." A wry smile crossed his scarred face. "It's us who will rely on clever plots."

"I doubt we will have a chance to stall them through parlay," Jan told him. "How long would you expect the walls to hold?"

The walls shuddered as one of the Bruins slammed its shoulder against the stone. The carriage-sized bears towered over the howling wolves.

Dandio let out a breath. "An hour, perhaps—I doubt more than that. We'll retreat before the wall falls, draw them back into the city away from the harbor."

Thunder rumbled overhead. Jan glanced at his brother, sensing he understood the truth just as well as he did. There would be no escape from Caer Sia, no ships left to carry them to safety. This had been their choice, to stand and fight in the last hours of their kingdom. The Aces would have the capital, and the war must be won by another's efforts.

"We did not want the others to wait for us," he said quietly, meeting Dandio's eyes. "You know this."

"I do. I don't fear our enemies," Dandio added, his voice far away as he watched the masses of Dal-kerri below. "But Ajaha and Allie… they will be alone, and…" He trailed off abruptly, suddenly looking like a child who had lost his way in a world that sought to crush them both.

Jan tightened his grip on Drisilas' hilt. The Marks claimed his life—he had considered this reason enough for his own sacrifice. But to ask that of Dandio and his men? Knowing that these warriors, his brother included, were willing to make that sacrifice as well, filled Ĵan's heart with an emotion he had not anticipated—a stubborn determination to survive. Cahadras and Iriam had both told him his death was no longer required. Perhaps this fight could yet be won.

Fire stirred in his Essence as he looked at his brother. "They will be all right," he said softly. "Both of them. And I do not intend to die today."

Dandio looked at him with a tired smile. "Really? Well, I hope you've come up with some way for us to avoid it."

"I am not sure that is up to us," Ĵan murmured, studying the gradually lightening sky above. Lit by the fires and the smoke-choked sun, the towering redwoods of the Magno Forest seemed to glow.

Seek the Druids.

The Druids alone might aid them now, so he must trust Iriam to reach them. It was time he abandoned his own will for this battle. Time to surrender it to another power. To no longer seek reconciliation by death, but instead, salvation through life.

Lightning crackled in the distance, joining the fires scraping the sky and the rolling blasts of cannon fire as the last stand of the Red Dawn began.

· · · · · ·

The smoke-tinted sunlight illuminated the *Burman Marie* as they approached Sia's coast.

Following their narrow escape from Castle Salem, Bryn had ridden high on the giddy excitement of their successful mission. No matter if the Ace-Lord had allowed them—the fact was, she and her companions had successfully slipped in and out of Castle Salem alive. Since her brother's mumbled, confused words during his rescue, she'd hoped fragments of his memory were still intact, and might return.

The following days saw the return of the grim truth. Lammar clearly sensed something was amiss, and though he told Bryn very little, his dread had begun to enter her own heart. At the Siren's request, the *Marie* anchored in Mata City and he went ashore to get the latest information. Bryn had been hesitant to anchor here—they were all wanted men in Mata City—but Lammar had promised no harm would come, and had only needed to show an insignia to the guard at the dock before being admitted ashore.

He'd returned an hour or so later, confused and troubled. All was well in Mata City. The Coopers were prepared in case of battle, and yet no battle had come. The latest news had come last night. There had been a battle in Gayrile, and the Aces' forces were defeated. The leader of the Guardians of Gayrile had arrived in Mata City yesterday, and left shortly after to escort the Caer Sian delegates back to the capital. There was no sign of impending attack on Mata City.

"We can take our time going east, in that case," Robin had commented as they'd gathered in the *Marie's* cabin. "If all's well, the crew can have a breather."

"Don't be so sure, Captain," Lammar said warily. His green-scaled face was tense, far cry from his usual easy-going manner. "Our informants are good—very good. We received news that the Aces intend to attack the north, and we were certain Mata City, as a pivotal location, would be their target."

"Yes, but there's obviously no trouble there, Lammar," Bryn ventured, trying to both reassure him and find a reason behind the confusing situation. "Maybe the news your informants found meant trouble in Gayrile—there was a battle there, right?"

"None of the reports ever mentioned Gayrile as a possibility," Lammar replied irritably. "All signs pointed to a Mainland kingdom in the north, and my informants are rarely wrong. I don't like this. The Aces have us blinded—none of our spies have learned the truth of what they are planning."

"And... what is it you think they are planning?" John asked slowly. The first mate's brow was furrowed; Bryn knew he was seeking a logical explanation for the Aces' lack of action. "Surely there is some reason they allowed us to free the Hummingbird."

"Oh, I'm certain there's a reason, Mr. Tailor," Lammar answered grimly. "Thing is, I've been tracking you lot for the last three weeks—I'm a bit out of the loop, as it were."

"Well, at least the Coopers aren't in danger," Robin said. "Try not to worry. We'll get to Caer Sia, drop off the Hummingbird, and you can get caught up on news."

Lammar managed a slight grin, but his scaled face was shadowed with worry.

Bryn wished she could agree with Robin, that all was well and there was nothing to worry about. But the Aces were up to something. Allowing them to escape so easily with the prisoner they had worked hard to keep confined convinced her of that. She'd hoped that Aryion could somehow explain what had happened when he came to himself.

That hope was dashed with each day that passed as they sailed to Caer Sia.

Aryion showed no improvement on the voyage. He did not speak, his empty blue-flecked eyes staring at nothing as he sat chained to the wall in the storage room that had once been Bryn's cabin on the *Marie*. By day he was silent, unresponsive to any offers of food or water. By night, he screamed and thrashed as if battling unseen opponents, straining against the chains, unhearing any attempts to calm him.

The ship's doctor, Harry, treated the ranger's injuries. Several old wounds had healed poorly and were red-rimmed with infection. But there was little he could do for the damage to his mind.

"I've never seen anything like it," he admitted the evening they left Mata City, rubbing his bald head uncertainly. "Sanity can be affected by extreme stress, you know—someone can be brought to madness if the tortures were severe enough."

"Is there any way to help him?" Robin asked, frowning.

"Not that I know of, Cap'n," Harry said heavily, looking at Bryn. "But—don't give up just yet. You said he regained a part of his memory—maybe it'll continue to come back to him slowly."

Bryn nodded, hiding her anxious frustration. Slowly. How long would it take? Months of torture might take years to heal fully.

She tried to shake the fears away, turning her gaze toward land as they approached Caer Sia.

Smoke filled the air, and the sun glowed orange through the gathering storm clouds. The capital city was swathed in the haze, and the tips of tall, elegant buildings were silhouetted through the fog. The castle was just visible before them. Lammar had ordered them to make for the near side of the city, in a secluded port away from the main harbor so that the pirate ship's appearance would go unnoticed.

"They'll be glad to see you, no doubt," he assured Robin as the *Marie* glided closer. "Just, ah, know that some of the generals might not."

"Eh, can't really blame them," Robin said lightly. "I'm still a wanted criminal here for good reason. One time, when I'd first got the *Marie*, Matthew and I—" John elbowed him before he could finish.

"Well, you'll be safe enough for now," Lammar told him with a crooked smile. "Whatever your criminal records, you're here by request of the New Blood. I'll vouch for you myself if needed."

Bryn gave him a grateful smile, studying the city as the *Marie* approached. High rocky cliffs and lush evergreens greeted her gaze, and she inhaled the sharp pine scent mingled with smoke. It had been so long since she'd been in country like this. It was a shame the smoke polluted the otherwise picturesque scene.

"This is quite unusual," John murmured, squinting at the shore through his spyglass. "There are no guards on the walls."

"Might be out of view," Robin said. "The hill sort of hides the castle from sight." He turned to Bryn. "Did you ever come to Sia when you lived in Elimar?"

"No, my father didn't allow it," Bryn replied vaguely, still studying the city. The buildings and slant of the hills blocked the main harbor from view. Something felt off to her, but she couldn't place it. Several ships coasted through the sea, heading west, as the *Marie* swept inland.

Lammar scented the breeze, which blew from the sea. "I can't smell any trouble—but there's so much smoke over the Mainland it's hard to tell."

"That seems concerning," John said uneasily.

"I can't tell where the smoke's coming from," Lammar replied. "But this time of year there are often wildfires in the Magno Forest. I expect that's the reason for this haze." His brow furrowed as he looked at the castle again. "All the same, I'd have expected the watchmen to have sounded the horn for our arrival by now."

"Well, we aren't headed for the main harbor," Robin pointed out.

Oliver stood by the tiller, peering toward the city in excitement. "Can I come ashore too, Cap'n?" he asked hopefully, turning eager eyes to Robin.

"What, to snag a sip of the king's wine? Absolutely not," Robin said flatly.

"I don't even *like* wine," Oliver told him. "I'll behave—and I want to say hello to Mel again."

Robin glanced at Bryn for help; she gave him a slight shrug to say *"he's your problem."*

"Oh, very well," Robin said wearily, looking at the cabin boy again. "But stay close to John. If he tells me you've been any sort of trouble, it'll be seven lashes."

Oliver beamed, completely unconcerned by Robin's typical baseless threat, and bounded to John's side. The first mate heaved a sigh, but handed the boy his spyglass. "I suppose that means I'll be coming ashore as well, Captain?" he asked.

"Oh, you're required to come ashore, John," Robin told him with a grin. "You're the only one who will actually *enjoy* all the protocol we're in for."

"Won't be much protocol, I expect," Lammar said, studying the city. "Sia seems quiet today. We should get to the castle with relative ease."

A quiet cove lay on the eastern side of the castle, where a weathered pier jutted forward into the small harbor. Windswept cedars whispered a greeting as the *Marie* drew broadside.

Robin turned to Matthew. "Take her back around into the main harbor to pick us up after we've sorted everything out, it's closer to the castle. We shouldn't be long."

"Aye, sir," the second mate agreed.

Richard brought Aryion up from the berth. The ranger's silence and his expressionless face sent a fresh pulse of dread through Bryn as she thought of Mel. The boy would be waiting for them, hopeful and eager to be reunited with his mentor, and their arrival would only crush his hopes.

She shook the thought from her head. Right now, she should at least be grateful that the ordeal was over. The *Marie* had safely reached Caer Sia.

37

∽ ∽ ∽ ∽ ∽ ∽ ∽ ∽ ∽ ∽

Smoke and Snakes

All was silent as the seven companions left the hidden harbor and entered the smoky streets of Caer Sia.

This part of the capital, Bryn guessed, must be inhabited by some of the richest souls on the Mainland. The mansions and manor-homes were taller even than the huge factories of Esile City, and much more extravagant. Built from silvery stone, they seemed to reach to the cloudy sky, windows polished and allowing an occasional glimpse into the well-furnished rooms within.

But no voices came from the buildings. As they continued onward into the downtown district, the silence began to grate on Bryn's nerves.

"Where is everyone?" Robin murmured, an edge of unease in his voice. "I'd have expected the city to be crawling with soldiers, with all that's going on."

"You don't suppose the Aces attacked here?" Richard suggested, concerned.

"I suppose there would be more signs of that," John told him, but he looked worried.

Bryn glanced back at Aryion, who walked quietly next to Richard, hands chained before him, expression dull as he stared at the ground. Part of her had hoped he'd regain some memory by simply returning to Caer Sia; from what he'd once told her, he and Mel had spent quite

430

a bit of time here. Yet there was no change in his manner. He was as unresponsive as ever.

Lammar padded a little ahead of the group, his green eyes rapidly scanning the desolate streets, face raised to the smoky air as he sought urgently for some clue as to what was going on.

As they reached another empty marketplace, he turned back to the group. "Forget going to the castle. I can scent people near the harbor—quite a lot of them. We need to find out what the blazes is going on."

"D'you think the people have all run away?" Oliver asked, clearly trying to hide his fear.

"I doubt it. Caer Sia would defend itself," Lammar answered grimly. "Keep your weapons ready. And keep Aryion close," he added to Richard. "I don't know if he'll turn on you again, and we can't risk that."

Richard nodded, gripping the ranger's shoulder and holding tighter to the chain in his other hand. Aryion glanced around the street with a sort of vague interest at the change in scenery, but nothing about their surroundings roused a change in him.

Bryn slipped her bow off her shoulder and held an arrow loosely on the string, peering around them for signs of activity. Nothing. Caer Sia's people, as Oliver had noted, seemed to have vanished. But why? This was the strongest city in the north. If it had been attacked, the people would have been safer barricaded within.

"If there was an attack," Robin ventured after a pause, seeming to guess her thoughts, "wouldn't we have heard about it in Mata City?"

"Maybe," Lammar said, "but it can take days for news to reach Mata City. There's always the chance something happened in the time it took us to get here."

"An attack seems unlikely," John said, studying the deserted streets as they walked on. "A force large enough to threaten the Red Dawn would move slowly—it would take them several days to arrive, and the news of their coming would spread. If it were a surprise attack, the Aces would need something to distract from it."

"Like a false report," Lammar murmured, his eyes widening as he finally understood. "Light above. All the signs were there—we misread them completely—"

Foreboding gripped Bryn's heart. In the same moment, the wind shifted, coiling around them from the southwest and carrying faint yet horribly familiar howls. She turned sharply, straining her eyes to look south. As the wind stirred the foggy haze and cleared the air, she could at last see the ominous red glow engulfing the city outskirts, and hear the distant clamor of battle.

An attack to a Mainland kingdom, her mind realized slowly. Mata City had never been the target. It had been Caer Sia all along, Caer Sia that had allowed her forces to be spread and separated across the Mainland in defense of her allies.

Lammar's face was drawn with bitter defeat as he realized, at last, the truth of what was happening. "Get back to the ship," he ordered at last, his shape flickering and changing into a raven. "Go back to Mata City, and don't wait for me."

With that, he flew off, speeding toward the distant fight.

"Let's go!" Robin ordered, turning to lead them back to the *Marie*.

Bryn moved to follow, but a blur of movement caught the corner of her eye. Her bow came up in a flash, her arrow slamming into the chest of an orc in the same instant its sword cut for Robin's neck.

The orc staggered back under the impact, looked down at the arrow with mild surprise, then snapped the shaft in half and started forward again, its eyes glowing hollow blue. Six others came behind it, cutlasses and crossbows pointed at the sailors.

"The harbor!" Bryn shouted as she loosed another arrow. She could hear the raw fear in her own voice, the panic of the trap they'd just fallen into. *You fool,* her mind berated her, *you knew there was something wrong, and you still let them come ashore.* She gritted her teeth and ran after the others down the road. Aryion would hardly be able to fight, Oliver was just a child, and the rest of them would stand no more chance than she would against the enchanted soldiers.

Another group of orcs appeared from around the street corner, their expressionless gaze fixed on the fleeing sailors. John raised his rifle and fired—the orc reeled back, but the wound in its skull healed in another moment, and it continued onward. Robin led them forward blindly—he didn't know this city anymore than she did, and now they were caught in a grid of unfamiliar streets as the undying warriors pursued them.

Bryn felt her mind spiraling into panic. She would not lose her crew. She'd brought them into this mess and she had to get them out.

Think, Bryn! What would you do if this was your mission and it'd gone sour?

Her eyes landed on a flat-roofed taphouse twenty paces ahead.

As a bounty hunter, whenever something had gone wrong during a mission, Bryn had always relied on one skill—climbing. Scaling the buildings of Esile City and gaining higher ground to flee her pursuers. It had worked time and time again, and it must work now.

"Robin!" she called, pointing sharply to the roof of the building. Thankfully he understood, turning to the right. A stack of barrels stood along the wall outside. Robin climbed first, slowly but smoothly. Oliver stepped up after him, just shy of reaching the rooftop. Richard lifted the boy from behind like a toddler, hoisting him the rest of the way, then reached for Aryion.

For the first time all day, the ranger reacted, wrenching himself away from Richard's grip. John moved to stop him—Aryion kicked him in the chest and staggered back against the building, his eyes wild and haunted.

"Not now," Bryn muttered desperately, bringing her longbow to full draw. For half a second, she debated sending an arrow through her brother's leg, at least to debilitate him for now. But the thought was banished in an instant. She might miss and cripple him for life. Besides, it would be much harder getting him out of Sia if he couldn't walk.

"I'll get him!" she called to John and Richard. "Get up on the roof."

The sailors hesitated but obeyed. Aryion tripped on the trailing chain and fell behind the barrels, straining against his bonds like a captive animal. The orcs, clearly seeing he was not a threat, advanced on Bryn. She sent an arrow through the foot of the nearest, pinning his boot to the street, but the others kept coming, blood gleaming on their blades.

"Bryn!" Robin cried, reaching for her.

Bryn climbed onto the barrel, reaching for the roof, but her eyes landed on Aryion. *Leave him*, her thoughts ordered, but her heart demanded otherwise. He wouldn't stand a chance, chained and confused as he was. The orcs would kill him and their entire mission would be for nothing.

"Bryn!" Robin warned again, his voice rising.

Bryn sighed and looked up at him. "Meet us by the harbor—I'll be there soon."

Robin's face twisted in fear. "Are you mad?" he demanded. "You can't—"

"Just get them to the *Marie*, Robin!" Bryn ordered, jumping down to the street again. Her heart pounded in her throat as she faced the orcs. There was no way she could defeat them all—that much was certain.

She loosed another arrow and dropped quickly down next to Aryion, who flinched away. "It's me!" she hissed, tone sharpened by adrenaline. "Do you want to be killed by orcs or do you want to get out of here?"

Her hands shook as she found the key in her pocket. *Oh, this is a horrible idea.* She unlocked the manacle on his right wrist—his other hand gripped her arm, unfamiliar hatred blazing in his eyes.

"Mel wanted us to find you!" Bryn cried, in one last desperate attempt to reach him. "Mel sent us—Aryion, wake up!"

For the first time, she sensed her words had gotten through. The wildness faded for an instant, and he frowned, confused, as if seeking to remember something. His iron grip loosened slightly.

An axe shattered the barrel in front of them, spraying her face in alcohol. Bryn grabbed her brother's arm and ran down the short alley between the taphouse and the next block of buildings. The orcs followed them, leaving Robin and the others behind. Good. They might escape to the harbor, flee back to sea on the *Marie*.

"Come on," she murmured, though she doubted Aryion registered her voice. He still gripped her arm, though not as tightly as before.

Dal-kerri howled around them. Bryn looked around the shops, unsure of where to go. The orcs still followed them in a careful and calculated advance. They had no real reason to hurry—Bryn would wear out long before they did, and then they'd kill both her and her brother.

Aryion turned suddenly to the right, nearly hauling her off balance and drawing her down a different road. Bryn, about to pull herself free, followed instead as a glimmer of hope entered her mind. Aryion led her down the desolate streets, turning sharply down various alleys, weaving around the buildings as he hurried forward. The grid of roads and towering buildings blurred in Bryn's mind until she was thoroughly lost. She was unsure if Aryion understood what he was doing, less sure if she could trust him.

But in another moment, they turned down a road, and the harbor came into view downhill.

"Good," Bryn breathed, relieved. "Come on—we're almost out of here."

She edged down the road. The view of the harbor was blocked behind buildings, but now at least, she had a sense of direction. Aryion let go of her arm, following silently, but his eyes seemed slightly more alert, scanning the side streets as they jogged onward.

The road joined with another. A street sign pointed left, guiding them to the harbor. Bryn picked up her pace.

She had barely reached the crossroads when Aryion slammed into her from behind, knocking her to the ground.

Bryn got to her knees, already prepared to fend off her brother's mindless attack, but saw in an instant that something far worse had come.

Bat-like wings beat the air as a hideous beast with mud-red scales settled on the ground before her, letting out a hissing snarl of satisfaction.

Bryn had heard Mel tell Oliver all about the serpentines, but even the boy's stories had failed to capture the sheer horror of the monster. Its bulbous white eyes fixed on Bryn as it bared curved fangs dripping with venom. One bite, that was what Mel had warned Oliver—one bite was all it took, and the venom would kill you.

Aryion dragged himself to his knees, clutching his head. Bryn ignored him, her attention solely on the beast before them. She brought her bow to full draw and sent the arrow at the beast's neck. The snake swayed out of the way; Bryn heard the clatter as her arrow landed harmlessly in the street beyond.

The snake hissed in fury and sprang. Its claws gripped her shoulders as it flung her to the ground. Bryn squirmed, raising her arms over her face as the snake's teeth snapped. Her armguard protected her forearm from the fangs—her other hand groped desperately for the dagger in her boot, pinned just out of reach.

Aryion knelt four paces away, writhing as if in agony. His hands gripped his head, white-knuckled.

Bryn kicked the serpentine in the belly, shoving it off her enough to draw her dagger. The snake sprang out of the blade's reach, circling slowly. Movement drew Bryn's gaze to the right—the orcs had reached them, eyes shining in anticipation as they marched forward.

"Aryion!" she shouted, her voice shrill. "Snap out of it—I need your help, please—"

The serpentine sprang again. Bryn dropped beneath it, plunging her dagger between the scales to the soft flesh beneath. The winged snake collapsed with one final hiss.

She staggered to her feet as the enchanted soldiers reached them, parrying the first sword across the blade of her dagger. Blinding pain flared from her left side as a sword glanced across her ribs. Gasping, Bryn swung her bow like a quarterstaff into the side of the orc's head.

The enchanted soldier stumbled back, stunned for an instant, his sword clattering to the cobblestone.

"Aryion!" Bryn screamed again. Sobbing for breath, she dodged another blow, slashing at the orc's face. An iron-shod boot connected with the side of her knee, and she crumpled to the ground, raising her hand in one last futile attempt to defend herself.

The thought swam dully into her head how pointless this all was—the mission to Ar-Salem had meant nothing, her hopes that Aryion would be healed meant nothing—because in the end, they'd both be killed here.

It was such a meaningless way to die.

. . . . . .

Darkness swirled in his head, a blurred nightmare of gray fog.

He felt the cold stone of the cobbled street under his hands and knees as he was shoved from behind, hurtling into the woman who seemed oddly familiar. Wings beat the air behind him, and he glanced back as the creature alighted on the street. A bizarre cross between a snake and a bat, fangs dripping venom, eyes alight with malice.

Serpentine. It was a serpentine.

What's it doing in Caer Sia? his tired mind inquired.

The icy voice that lived inside him replied briskly. *"That doesn't matter. None of this matters. It's all a dream, remember?"*

And yet, strangely enough, he could not stop himself from thinking about it more and more. Caer Sia. Why was that word so familiar? Oh, yes, of course—he'd been here many times before. But there had been someone with him, someone with a cheerful voice and bright eyes.

"Do not think on that," the voice ordered, and pain flared behind his eyes. *"Remember this? Remember what comes of such thinking? Do not question the dream."*

He gritted his teeth, clutching his head in his hands. The pain seemed to come from the memories, memories from a time before he had awakened in the black box with nothing in his mind but ice. The black box… how had he come to be there?

"You have only known darkness. You were born in the darkness."

But I wasn't, his thoughts argued back. *Because if I've only known darkness… then why is the light so familiar?*

Ice seared his skull, and he heard himself groan in pain as he shrunk down against the stone road. Stone. There was no stone in the black box either, only cold and shadows and the smooth voice whispering in his mind.

What came before that? he asked the void. *What am I—who am I, and what is the importance of Caer Sia?*

The voice grew livid, and fear clenched his heart. His body reacted involuntarily to the anger, for when the voice grew angry, only agony would follow. But this time, he forced himself to ignore it and pressed deeper into the strange dark nothingness. Shattered memories littered his thoughts, fragments of images, confused and out of place.

"There was nothing before the shadow, fool," the voice snarled, and freezing pain gripped him. *"There is nothing but the darkness."*

There's light here, his mind persisted, though the pain was almost unbearable. With a great effort, he opened his eyes. Sunlight pierced his vision, and he inhaled the sharp, acrid scent of sea and smoke.

Smoke—smoke from a fire—yes, fire was familiar, as hot and wrathful as the anger in his chest. He was furious—furious, and he had no idea why. Furious, yet so filled with grief it seemed to rob his body of breath.

"Aryion! Snap out of it—I need your help, please!"

Why was the woman's voice so familiar? Why had she stayed to help him? And why had the name she'd mentioned by the barrels completely gripped his mind for an instant, as though she'd stopped time with one word?

What was the name? he pleaded through the haze of pain. *Come on, Aryion, remember...*

Aryion—that was another name he knew, though he did not know why.

The woman's voice shone a ray of light into his tangled thoughts. An image swam in his mind—a small girl, with messy dark hair and a cheerful face so like his own it was almost like looking in a mirror—

"Come on, Aryion, I found mice in the field!" The little voice was similar to the woman's, though now her voice was shrill with fear.

Brynlee. Pain gripped his thoughts again, but he fought past it, desperately fending off the icy darkness that threatened to envelop him again. He gulped breaths of the smoke-filled air. The name—the name she'd said by the barrels—the name was—

"Aryion!" she cried out again.

His vision focused as she was knocked down. Blood dripped from a cut along her side as she raised her hands in futile defense against the press of orcs.

Orcs.

The scene electrified his mind like a bolt of lightning, connecting every moment of the life before the darkness.

In a split second, he knelt in the ruin of a burning house with this woman—his sister—beside the bodies of their parents as the orcs were driven from Valetown—

Warrior here this Oath I swear.

The world spun, and he fell to the ground, retching as the onrush of memories overwhelmed his senses. His hand fell against something sharp and cold, and he felt warm blood running beneath his fingers. A sword—dropped by one of the enchanted orcs—blood running from his hand, red against the blade—

May no dark night or mortal fear.

He heard his own voice, much younger and filled with fear and grief, speaking the words. His hand closed around the fallen hilt.

How familiar that was, the feel of a sword in his hand, the weight, the grip—how familiar, and how many horrible things associated with it.

With a grunt, he got to his feet. The orcs, seconds from striking the woman down, paused, looking at him with confused surprise. The present seemed to flicker away, and in a moment, he stared into the eyes of another orc, one who looked down on him with contempt.

Hagshrub, smiling in malice as he stepped forward.

Aryion felt his sword come up, felt the practiced movements flow smooth and fluid. He struck again and again, though the wounds he inflicted healed in moments. The cold was driven slowly from his numbed mind, and he felt strength returning—a new kind of strength, an unnatural strength that caused his muscles to tremble so that he nearly fell.

But with every blow, every slash, every parry, there came a new scene, flashing before his eyes.

Hagshrub, slaying his father.

His sister, left alone and lost in the empty house.

Ringmembers, falling dead as he completed the task assigned to him.

The Forest of Light, frozen and lifeless before his eyes.

A gauntleted fist connected with the side of his head, and he staggered sideways. Dimly, he saw Bryn getting slowly to her feet, saw the enchanted soldiers hesitating for the first time as if uneasy.

He tightened his grip on the sword, stepping forward, but new memories filled his mind, sharp and painful like blades of ice, as the shattered fragments pieced themselves back into the horrors they were.

A quest. A battle. Orcs streaming from the woods. A wizard falling dead at the feet of the Ace-Messenger. River water filling his mouth and nose as he swam, struggling to save someone whose face remained just out of sight.

May nothing cause this Oath to break.

The enchanted orcs lunged, and he parried the blows, gasping for breath, the blood roaring in his veins. He saw the scenes from events long gone, though he could not recall what they were. Shards, joined and glowing blue. A knife in his ribs, then a comforting blue light.

Then, ships. Pirates. Ringmembers—he'd returned to Esile City, and yet the unknown companion was with him. He knew it, though it had been purged from his mind.

His focus returned for an instant to the present, seeing only the enchanted soldiers swarming around him, fending off their blades with a skill and strength entirely new to him. The onslaught of memories from a life he no longer recalled seemed to have ended, gone after the mission to Esile City.

And then at last he remembered Mel.

Mel.

The name flickered like fire in his mind, searing the icy darkness. The memories connected to it had been shattered, gone forever, and yet his heart did not forget.

A charge to protect. An apprentice. Had he trained the boy? He thought he might have offered to at some point. Yet as hard as he fought, he could recall nothing besides the boy's name and the emotion carried with it. Agony ached in his mind, and he stumbled, crying out. Bryn's voice came from somewhere nearby, but he hardly heard.

Gone, his thoughts whispered, confused, scared. *It's all gone... what happened to him?*

The cold, sneering voice replied. *"Would you like me to show you?"*

For the first time, the boy's face came clearly into his memory, lit by a brilliant crackle of lightning in a storm-torn sky. He felt Mel's hand slip from his and saw him fall, saw his tear-filled eyes as he vanished into the infinite darkness of the void beneath the marble bridge.

"He is dead, Hummingbird."

Aryion crumpled to his knees, feeling as if the words were a chain around his neck, tightening and hauling him downward into the earth. "No," he choked, and for the first time heard his own rasping, ragged voice.

The cold voice was filled with cruel pleasure, whispering triumphant in his mind, hard as he tried to fight it. *"He is dead, because you failed to protect him."*

Darkness, unstoppable darkness, reached for his thoughts again, and he felt himself slipping back into it.

"No!" he shouted, leaping to his feet and clashing with the last enchanted soldier. His blade flashed through the smoky air as he struck again and again, pressing the startled warrior back until at last the soldier lost his footing and fell backward downhill.

The world came sharply into focus again, too bright, too loud. His head throbbed. Cold claws seemed to have closed around his skull. His one victory of regaining those few fragmented memories paled before the agonizing truth.

This promise sworn, his thoughts finished mechanically, as at last, the montage of tortured memories ended. *This Oath I make.*

His apprentice was gone.

38

The Deputy's Wrath

Bryn stood painfully. Blood ran from a cut along her side, and pain shot through her as she moved, but she barely noticed it. Her eyes were fixed solely on Aryion.

Her brother clashed with the last enchanted orc, the stolen sword a blur in his hand. The warrior seemed baffled by the speed and intensity of the attack, and she noticed in disbelief that Aryion's blows caused wounds that did not immediately fade away. He might not be able to kill the enchanted soldiers, but whatever new strength the Deputy had bestowed in him made him a far deadlier opponent than he'd been before.

Aryion's blue-flecked eyes blazed with hatred as he slashed, pressing the orc back. The steep road, slick with ash and blood, made footing unsteady, and Aryion moved on mercilessly, until the soldier's feet went out from under him and he fell awkwardly, stumbling away from the fight in confused defeat.

Aryion dropped to his knees, chest heaving, his expression lost and confused.

"Aryion?" Bryn whispered, hardly daring to hope.

Her brother did not respond, staring at the ground, murmuring softly. "Dead… I lost…"

"Aryion?" Bryn repeated, touching his shoulder lightly.

He jumped at her touch, looking up sharply. His gaze fixed on her face, and he frowned slightly. "Lee?" he rasped. "What… how…" He looked down at the chain, still manacled to his left wrist.

"You're all right," Bryn said, crouching beside him and undoing the lock. She could hardly contain the relief of hearing his voice, seeing the animal-like madness had vanished. "It's all right. We're in Caer Sia, but we need to get back to the *Burman Marie*."

Aryion looked at her blearily, his tormented mind fighting to make sense of the words. "Caer Sia… why? What's happening?"

"I think it's on fire," Bryn said slowly, pulling him to his feet.

"What… what's the *Burman Marie*?" he asked after a pause.

"Our ship. Well, Robin's ship. It's our way out of here," Bryn told him with a prickle of unease. Exactly how much of his memory was still intact? At least he remembered her—and he seemed to remember Caer Sia.

They leaned on one another as they moved down the road. Aryion's disoriented gaze settled on the serpentine's body. "Where did that come from?"

"Your guess is as good as mine," Bryn answered. She realized in a heartbeat that he was not fully well. His mind had pieced together just enough to help him remember some important details, though the effort had nearly spent him of his strange new strength. He clearly remembered nothing of their voyage here.

Dal-kerri howled in the distance. The rumble of cannonfire from the far side of the city told her the fight must still be happening, and she wondered if Lammar had joined it.

The rhythm of iron-shod feet came from ahead, and she pulled Aryion into the shadow of a building as a group of orcs jogged past, headed back toward the castle. There would be time to worry for Lammar later. Right now, they needed to get out of here.

Pain stabbed her side as she continued, and she stumbled. Aryion slipped his arm under hers, supporting her forward. His face was pale, eyes clouded by the overwhelming return of the fragmented memories. Slowly, they headed downhill, past block after block of empty shops and apartments. The buildings had not been damaged, Bryn noticed, though she assumed the battle was only now reaching this side of the city.

"What happened?" Aryion rasped after a long silence. "I can't remember… any of it."

"I—I can tell you once we're out," Bryn panted. "Lammar sent us to free you—I expect you won't remember anything that happened in Ar-Salem."

A shadow passed over her brother's face at the name, like a nightmare he could not fully recall. "I can remember parts of it. Nothing about you being there, though."

"I've only been around for the last week or so," Bryn answered. "Lammar was worried the Aces would attack Mata City, but they came to Sia instead. By the time we found that out, we were already here."

She shook her head tiredly. There was so much to tell him, so much horror to explain. She hoped they'd have time to unpack it all later— not that she would have many answers to his questions. Most of those answers could hopefully come from Mel, assuming the boy had escaped the city before the attack.

The hum of hundreds of fearful voices reached her ears as they approached the harbor. A ring of soldiers formed a protective barrier around a large crowd of civilians who were slowly boarding the waiting vessels. Ships of all sizes had been utilized in the evacuation, and yet there were still so many civilians. Despite knowing nothing of these people, Bryn felt a stab of fear for them. Time had run out. The Ace-army was mere minutes from reaching them.

A familiar voice rose above the crowd. "Blast your rules, that's *my ship* in the harbor! My wife needs my help, and if you intend to stop me—"

"Captain, please—"

Bryn felt a surge of relief as she recognized Robin and John's voices. Robin was arguing with a tall Hyenin soldier who wore the armor and colors of a Red Dawn general. John was attempting to intercede, but it sounded as though the discussion was over. Richard and Oliver stood uncertainly in the background, both unhurt.

"This harbor has been locked down for evacuation use only, Captain," the Hyenin informed him. "Whether or not the ship is yours, you cannot dock here."

"It *is* my blasted ship!" Robin snapped, throwing his hands up as if to implore the heavens for help. "We don't have time for this—we didn't know about the evacuation, but once we dock we'll be out of your way, don't you understand!"

"Robin!" Bryn called, stumbling forward through the perimeter of soldiers.

His eyes landed on her, and his frustration evaporated into relief. He ran to her, taking her gently into his arms. "Bryn—you're all right—are you all right?" he demanded, his voice tight with fear. His gaze lingered on the blood on her side.

"I'm fine. Just a scratch," Bryn replied, ignoring the pain that argued otherwise.

Robin's gaze swung to Aryion, who stood uneasily beside them. "I take it he's…"

Aryion's mind seemed to return to the present as he turned to Robin. "Ah… Captain Trelawney, glad you are here."

"Oh, I'm here and quite fine," Robin murmured, clearly still uneasy after Aryion's attack in Ar-Salem. But he shook Aryion's hand with genuine warmth. "Good to have you back, ranger."

The general's startled voice came from behind them. "Light above— Master Hummingbird."

Aryion turned to him, his brow furrowed, mind working desperately to recall the name. "General Arrex," he said finally, nodding slightly.

General Arrex shook his fox-like head slowly, looking stunned. "We had thought you lost—we thought the Aces had…"

"We'll figure this out later," Robin put in. "General, now that you *see* the importance of our mission, may we please disembark on my ship?"

General Arrex sighed in resignation. "Yes, I understand. But I must ask your help." He nodded to the crowd of frightened civilians.

Bryn hesitated. Escorting civilians was not what they had signed up for, war or no. Not when many of these people would turn her crew in to local law officials under regular circumstances. But then, that hardly mattered with the city under attack.

Robin seemed to come to the same conclusion, but he frowned slightly. "We… can't take many of them," he said slowly.

"I understand that. But even the few you can carry will be lives saved," the general said quietly. "Please. Our resources are stretched thin."

"I take it you were unaware this attack was coming?" John asked.

"Quite," Arrex said heavily. "The High King and the Commander are fighting to gain us time, but I fear it will not be long enough." He looked at Robin. "How many do you think you can take?"

Robin thought a moment, arms folded over his chest. "I'd say thirty, maybe thirty-five," he said at last. "But we don't have enough supplies to get that many to Mata City."

"Then forget Mata City for now," Arrex said. "We are evacuating to Lillary Bay. It is a military port with plenty of provisions. You and your crew will be safe there."

Robin nodded. "Very well. Thank you, General," he added as an afterthought.

Together, the companions moved down the crowded piers as Robin signaled to the *Marie*. The majority of Caer Sia's people, Bryn guessed, would have been moved to safety by now. Yet there were still far too many waiting by the harbor. Their attire showed different ranks and classes—rich and poor, all were desperate to flee. The majority left were those who had dwelt on the city outskirts; farmers and peasants abandoning their simple homes, lords and ladies who'd left their fine manors.

"We learned the battle is along the southern wall, though the Aces are swiftly advancing past it," John said as the *Marie* drew alongside the pier. "It seems the High King himself is among the defenders."

"I didn't know kings had to fight in battles like this," Oliver said.

"Jan would," Aryion said softly. His gaze was distant, taking in the panicked civilians as his mind came in and out of the present.

Matthew joined them on the pier, and Robin filled him in on the evacuation plan. None of the sailors argued with their captain's orders. Everyone could sense the gravity of the day. Once the *Marie* was prepared, General Arrex ushered a small group of townsfolk their way. A few looked uneasy about boarding a pirate ship, but no one voiced a protest.

"It'll be tight," John commented to them, "but you will all fit." He smiled wryly to Bryn. "I suppose it is a blessing we are not carrying cargo."

The group had just begun to board the *Marie* when the Dal-kerri arrived.

Bryn never saw where the wolves came from exactly. Likely, they had been prowling in the shadows of the buildings, waiting for the order. They bounded forward in a huge pack of bristling fur and snarling teeth, charging for the crowd of helpless civilians, who cried out in terror and rushed for the overloaded ships.

The soldiers saw them too, closing in a protective perimeter, fending off the wolves left and right as they poured forth. A small pack broke through their defenses, springing upon their prey.

Aryion swept past Bryn before she could stop him, gripping his stolen sword as he ran back to the battle.

"Get them on board!" Robin shouted, jogging after Aryion, already raising his pistol.

"Captain, wait—we need a plan—" John yelled, starting to follow.

"Stop—hold on, just—oh, for the love of it all," Bryn groaned, looking at Richard. "Get whoever we can carry on board—we have to help."

"Aye, Cap'n," Richard replied, and his booming voice echoed over the pier, calling the panicked civilians towards him.

Bryn ran after John. A fresh jolt of pain shot through her side, and she winced, placing a hand against the cut.

John slowed his pace, looking at her pale face in concern. "Captain—

it may be best for you to wait on the *Marie*."

"It probably would," Bryn agreed, "but I'm not letting them get themselves killed."

She drew an arrow from her quiver as they reached the frantic battle at the harbor road. Her side throbbed as she raised her bow, but she held it steady, loosing the arrow into a hound that leapt at a small child.

The citizens, already fearful of the coming attack, were panicking now, running in all directions, some swarming onto the full ships in the harbor, others seeking to run back up the streets. Bryn could hear General Arrex shouting desperately for order, but his voice was lost in the swarm of terror.

John raised his rifle, setting his stance beside Bryn as he shot down a Dal-kerri. Bryn had already drawn another arrow. She saw Aryion fighting in a blur of slashing steel, saw Robin nearby, his pistol in one hand and his curved sword in the other.

"Come on!" she yelled at the townsfolk nearest her. "Go down that pier—get on the ship, hurry!" It was no good trying to organize them into groups, not now that death had come. They would take as many as they could carry. Civilians ran past her and John, headed for the ships.

More hounds came from the smoke-filled city, their eerie howls echoing over Caer Sia. Serpentines reeled in the sky, diving down upon the unprotected crowd. Bryn's arrow felled one—she saw another's teeth make contact with a soldier, who collapsed to the street.

"Robin!" she shouted. The din of clashing metal, howling wolves, and screaming people drowned out her voice. A mass of bodies blocked Robin and Aryion from view—she turned in time to see an orc's cudgel connect with Robin's shoulder. A wolf lunged at her as she stepped forward—John shot it cleanly through the head, and it collapsed at Bryn's feet.

Shouts and screams rang over the water. There was nothing they could do, Bryn thought in horror. There were simply not enough ships. Several people were swimming, clinging to the sides of the vessels like rats. A few captains had thrown any unneeded supplies overboard to make more room.

"Retreat!" General Arrex ordered, his voice carrying over the harbor. "Go now—there is no time—you must—"

A plume of white ice flared behind his body, cutting off his voice. Bryn saw his golden eyes register brief surprise before his body collapsed lifeless to the street.

She stepped back in horror.

Cantering to the pier was a skeletal horse with a single jagged horn set in its head. Its hollow eyes flashed blue as it screamed a haunting whinny.

Riding on its back was the Ace-Deputy.

Lammar had captured the Aces' appearance fairly well, enough for her to immediately recognize the apparition before her—but the real thing was another horror entirely. The half-skull face twisted in a triumphant smile as General Arrex fell, purple-red eyes flashing over the panicking civilians.

Almost lazily, he raised his hands, launching white ice across the pier. His voice was not especially loud, yet it rang out over the screams of the people in the harbor.

"This, mortal fools," he chided, "this is what becomes of those who resist the Ace-Lord's power. Caer Sia has fallen. Your punishment has come."

White ice flashed, again and again, at the loyal soldiers. Bryn saw their bodies fall, unable to escape the Deputy's wrath.

Choking back a helpless scream, she started forward, reaching for an arrow. John's hand stopped her. "Bryn—hurry, Robin is hurt."

Bryn swung around, her heart pounding. The wolves had bounded away, snarling in victory as they moved to join the Ace-Deputy. Aryion stood frozen over Robin, the sword sliding from his grasp as he stared at the Deputy. Robin lay unmoving, a dark bruise forming over his temple.

John and Bryn pulled the unconscious captain upright, bracing him between them. "Aryion—come on," Bryn ordered, her voice raw with fear.

Aryion did not move, as if rooted to the spot. His eyes were fixed on the Deputy, his face a mask of shock, horror, and hatred.

The Deputy reeled the Dal-kerri horse about, a wicked mirth on his face as he rode down to the harbor toward the surviving soldiers.

Directly toward the *Marie*.

"Aryion!" Bryn yelled.

At last her brother moved, stumbling after them down the pier towards the *Marie*. Behind them, Bryn heard screams, the ominous crackle of white ice, the cantering hooves as the Deputy drew closer. She hurried on, gasping at the pain in her side, hauling Robin's limp form down the pier.

Richard lingered on the gangplank, helping the last passenger on board.

"Get aboard!" John shouted at him. "Get aboard, now!"

Richard sprang to the decks. Aryion reached the rail and collapsed onboard, his strength spent. Bryn and John stumbled after him, supporting Robin between them.

"Oars!" John yelled, nearly tripping on the gangplank. "Hard to starboard—get us—"

Out of the corner of her eye, Bryn saw the white ice flash, so close she felt the freezing cold on her face. John's voice cut out abruptly, and she fell forward to the *Marie's* deck, pulled down by Robin's weight.

The *Marie* swung away from Sia's piers. Bryn rolled onto her side, glimpsing the last satisfied smile on the Deputy's ruined face before he turned back to the helpless crowd.

"West, boys!" Richard bellowed. "Now!"

Bryn drew herself to her hands and knees. Pain shot afresh through her side, but she ignored it, staring at Robin. His chest moved slowly as he breathed. Unconscious, but alive.

"John? John?"

Oliver's voice, rising with panic, reached her ears. White ice.

Realization, dull and heavy as a brick, settled in her heart as she looked over.

Oliver knelt, struggling to raise John from the deck. The first mate's eyes were half-open, reflecting the auburn sunlight. A few sailors gathered around him, staring in numb silence.

Bryn crawled forward, guilt and grief clenching her heart. Gently, she felt beneath the cold jaw, feeling for a pulse she already knew was not there.

"He won't wake up—he won't wake up, Bryn," Oliver stammered, his voice choked, tears streaming down his dirty face.

The Deputy's wrath. Leveled upon them for stealing away his prized prisoner.

"I'm not letting them get themselves killed." Her own words from minutes ago rang mockingly in her ears. It was she who had drawn the crew into this struggle, this war that was not theirs to fight.

She closed her eyes a moment, trying to replace the sight of the cold, still face with John as she'd known him—watching birds through his spyglass, bantering with Richard, looking out for Oliver. Yet she could not escape the present.

Silently, she took Oliver in her arms as he sobbed, while the *Burman Marie* cut through the waters to the west.

39

Tempest

Two hours from Caer Sia, if the sea allowed and the wind was willing, stood Lillary Bay.

Allie had visited the small port several times as a child, when her father would come to inspect the garrison. Less than a hundred civilian residents lived here; the barracks housed most of the naval officers. Fort Lillary stood above the crescent-shaped bay, hewn from gray stone. Several generals lived in the upper parts of the fort, settled in the shadow of the purple-gray crags of the mountains.

Any memories of happier visits were gone now, as the fearful voices of the thousands upon thousands of refugees flooded the village.

The *Veritos* had left Allie, Rygal, and a handful of officials in Lillary Bay that morning before returning to Caer Sia. Allie had glimpsed the Garilian ship a few times during the day, moving with the flow of vessels going in and out of Lillary Bay. So many people, yet there were still not enough ships to evacuate Caer Sia in time.

Evening was falling, and she could see the ships filling the harbor and the edge of the refugee camp to the left of the fort. Caer Sia's civilians moved from the docks in droves, lost, frightened, and grieving as they were ushered to the camp.

Storm clouds roiled to the west, and the low roll of thunder warned of a coming storm. She could smell it in the air as the wind whistled through the window. The tempest would soon make the North Sea far too treacherous to sail. Anyone left in Caer Sia would be trapped there to be killed by the Aces.

Jan and Dandio would be trapped.

Not even that fact could break the shield of ice clutching her heart. She wanted to feel grief, sorrow, or—if that was too much to wish for— anger, the kind of fury that had brought the inferno blazing from her veins in Gayrile. But her anger did not blaze, only sat cold with the icy wall in her chest.

The Vessel had taken over now. Her own actions had seen the Ace-Lord's plan to fruition, the blood on her hands and the white fire in her Essence a testament to his power.

There was nothing left for it. No hope of breaking the curse. No bright future she could foolishly believe in. The Ace-Lord must die, and the Vessel, now corrupted by his darkness, would die with him. It was all she had left to hope for.

She let out a breath and turned away from the window, wishing to block out the sounds of grieving and frightened voices outside. Everyone, it seemed, had lost a parent, a sibling, a child. Cries and sobs filled the port.

Rygal's hesitant voice spoke behind her. "Allie?"

She looked up. The young warrior stood uncertainly in the hall, one hand resting on his sword hilt. He looked so tired—he probably hadn't slept any more than she had the last few days.

"What is it?" she asked. Her voice hardly sounded like her own, dull and quiet.

Rygal nodded down the hall. "They, ah, they want to talk to you. General Leopold's called a council."

Another meeting. Councils, discussions over plans, futile words of hope—that was all they were. As if the horrors of war could be repaired by a meeting.

She managed a slight nod and moved down the hall. Rygal's gray-blue eyes glanced out the window, then turned back to her. "We're working to help them," he said, clearly seeking some words of reassurance. "The civilians. They'll be settled in the field camp, and Mel's gone to heal the critically wounded."

Allie didn't reply as they walked down the hall. She could sense the sorrow and worry in his gaze, and felt a fresh stir of anger in her ice-clad heart. *Stop pitying me*, she wanted to snap. *Stop feeling sorry for me. It won't help anything, and it's only making things worse.*

Fort Lillary's council hall was filled with people, waiting in grim silence. Ajaha stood, her face drawn with fear, grief, and exhaustion. She squeezed her daughter's hand lightly before sitting down across the table. Two Liznee generals waited at the table, along with the Dwarve captain, Newgrange, who had become Rygal's second-in-command.

General Leopold, who'd overseen the beginning of the evacuation, stood at the table, his panther-like face drawn with weariness. As general and steward of Sia, he must now oversee matters of war and government. "Thank you for coming," he said, as the door closed behind Rygal and Allie. "Please, sit. There is much news to discuss."

Allie sat down next to Glentree. The burly warrior's face was stony, and one hand traced the edge of his battle axe, showing his desire to return to the desperate defense. But he managed a slight smile as Rygal and Allie entered. "Good to see you both 'ere. We've heard nothing but bad news from Gayrile over the last few weeks."

"Well, the good news is, the Dal-kerri have been driven out of Gayrile," Rygal told him.

"I am glad to hear that," Leopold said. "The Direns will protect the Northern Isles, and the Coopers may aid the defense as well."

"And… do you think they could help us drive the Aces from Sia?" Rygal asked.

The Cagari shook his head. "No, we do not believe the Aces intend to occupy Sia as they did before. From what we have gathered, they mean to lay the city waste and halt our war efforts with one blow."

"Not as if there will be much of a war effort after this," one of the generals muttered.

"An' how's that helpful?" Glentree growled. "There's nothing we can do. None of us saw this comin', not even Iriam."

"Where is Iriam?" Rygal ventured.

"If I knew the answer to that question, I would have postponed this meeting until he returns," Leopold sighed. "Currently, we know very little, only that the High King requested that Iriam try to make contact with the Druids."

"The Druids?" Glentree repeated, a light coming back to his eyes. "If the legends are true, they'll raise the trees and the sea to fight."

"Legends won't stop the Aces," Allie said flatly. Iriam's mission made very little sense to her. From the little she'd heard of the horrors in Tinkeeyo, not even the dryads were safe from the Aces.

"A grim outlook, but a logical one, highness," Leopold agreed wearily. "We were led astray, falling for every false report the Aces fed us. But Glentree is right. There is nothing we can do to change it now; in fact, I am not sure what we ought to do at all."

He paused, studying everyone assembled. "The last of Lady Ajaha's courier teams reached Lillary an hour ago with a report. The southern walls have fallen. As of this point, the Ace-army has conquered Caer Sia."

Conquered.

The word rang in Allie's ears like the toll of a distant bell. Sia was lost. Those who had stayed—the Red Dawn knights, Jan, her father—they were all gone.

"What of the defenders?" Captain Newgrange asked hesitantly.

"We do not know," Ajaha replied softly. "Dandio—Commander Ki's plan was to light fires along the perimeter of the city and retreat gradually, hoping to slow the Aces' advance. But I do not know where they intended to retreat."

"Couldn't someone sail back to help them?" Rygal asked. "If the evacuation's finished, surely one or two of our ships could return."

"Even if we were to risk entering Sia's harbor," Leopold said, "the winds and tides have turned against Lillary Bay. We can go nowhere until this storm has let up—not even our warships could survive the tempest."

Allie stared at the table top, a faint ringing in her ears. Cold spread through her veins until her entire body seemed numb. They were dead. Dead, like so many others. *Say something,* her mind screamed. *Cry, shout, let the inferno rise again. Why don't you care?* Yet her heart could not even react to the news, desensitized by the fear and horror after everything that had happened.

Glentree spoke, slowly and hesitantly. "What... what of Dessian? What about the *Blue Moon*?"

Allie glanced at him, confused by the change in topic. The *Blue Moon* was captained by Admiral Dessian, the leader of the Red Dawn's navy and one of the finest seamen alive. But Admiral Dessian had been gone for months, headed to Kasabren with Dusty to rally the Wildkid Clans.

Leopold frowned slightly. "Admiral Dessian... he is due to return soon. He may attempt to enter Caer Sia, with no way of knowing what has transpired."

"Unless the dryads have got word to him," Rygal pointed out. "If the *Blue Moon* could sail through the storm, they might be able to get in and out of Caer Sia."

"They'd be on their way back now," Glentree pressed. "If anyone's fool enough to risk a tempest like this, you know it'd be Dessian."

Leopold sighed. "Oh, that I do not doubt. But even if you are right, we have no way to get word to them. Our best hope to reach them, I believe, would lie with the dryads, but we have no contact to reach them."

"We might," Ajaha said quietly. A new light shone in her eyes.

Allie looked at her mother, not sure what she meant. Leopold frowned slightly. "I take it you know of some way to contact the dryads?"

"Potentially," Ajaha answered, speaking slowly. "Few know the ways of the dryads as well as the Druids, and I admit I am only a little learned in those old ways. However, Luet was my friend as well as the king's. She told us that a mortal may speak to the dryads, and they would listen, if the mortal asked in the name of the Light."

"You think they would fight for us?" Rygal asked. "They've been hesitant to join us in battle this whole time."

"No, but they might carry my warning to Admiral Dessian," Ajaha replied. "I do not believe my words go alone. Iriam has gone to contact the Druids at the request of the High King. They may join the dryads and rescue the defenders who remain in Sia."

"Those are a lot of 'mights,' ma'am," Captain Newgrange pointed out uneasily. "Especially if the defenders are already lost."

"You think so?" Glentree asked bluntly, folding his burly arms over his chest. "Even if that's the case, I'll believe it when I see it. They're out there facin' the Aces. I say we try whatever we can to bring 'em home."

The Dwarve captain spread his hands in surrender. "I hope they're alive as much as anyone. But it might not be worth risking more lives."

"They'd take the chance for us," Rygal said crisply.

"Gentlemen," Leopold interjected tiredly, motioning for silence. He looked at Ajaha. "I admit I know very little of the ways of the dryads. Lillary Bay is locked down by order of the High King; no one may leave the city for any purpose."

"I need not go far," Ajaha said. "This forest is the same that borders the valley of Sia. I shall appeal to the trees and see if they choose to hear my words."

"I do not doubt you," Leopold replied. "That said, the lockdown is still in effect, and you know as well as I that only an order from the Crown may overrule it. I cannot sanction such a mission."

"You're the steward of Sia," Glentree pressed. "Without the king, it's your permission she needs."

"General, please," Rygal pleaded. "Even if the dryads won't listen, we have to at least try."

"As I have said," Leopold said, looking at Glentree and Rygal, "my role as steward cannot overrule the lockdown command. Lady Ki's mission must be sanctioned by the queen."

In the dead silence that followed, Allie sensed every eye turn to her.

The queen of Caer Sia. The title had never felt more wrong.

Was this what the Ace-Lord had planned? Kill Ĵan, and allow the Vessel to ascend to the throne while darkness engulfed her heart and ice flowed in her veins? Whether or not he'd intended this, it would serve him well. Somehow, in the mere span of hours, it was her authority that mattered, her choice that placed lives in the balance, her command that even her own mother must obey.

She felt Ajaha's steady gaze on her. Her mother's expression was calm as ever, but her eyes betrayed the agony of not knowing whether or not those she loved yet lived.

"You know they might already be dead," Allie said at last. The words came from far away, the voice no longer her own, trying to crush that stubborn hope in her heart. She saw Rygal's face fall, his eyes pleading with hers.

Ajaha closed her eyes and nodded slightly. "They may, my dear. But we also may yet help to save them."

Allie let out a breath, looking down. Her mother was right. She hated the uncertainty of it all, wished in the depths of her icy heart that they were already dead, if only so that the fear would be gone and she would be untouchable, emotionless, having lost anything preventing her from what must be done. She could focus entirely on killing the Ace-Lord, focus on her quest for death, focus on the end looming before her.

But she looked up at her mother again. "Fine. If you think it's worth it, I won't stop you."

Ajaha nodded to her daughter. "I will not be long. My team will accompany me into the hills. I hope the storm has not driven the dryads into their trees."

"Very well," Leopold answered. "May the Light guard your path, and may you be successful."

Ajaha left the room. Allie could already hear rain pelting against the fort and wind ripping through the forest outside as though to tear every living thing from the face of the world.

There was a pause before Leopold spoke again. "We cannot delay our actions for long. There are enough supplies to sustain the civilians in Lillary Bay, but we must determine our next strategy soon. The Blue Stone will not be safe here forever. We must use this time wisely, despite the uncertainty."

"Time?" Allie repeated. "What does time have to do with it? We're completely out of time now. It doesn't matter where we run and hide. What matters is killing the Ace-Lord."

The others looked at her in disbelief.

"What? That's the only thing that's going to end the war," Allie stated, meeting their gazes. "No matter how long we fight, no matter how many of us die—that's the only way to stop this. And yet we haven't put a single thought to that, have we?"

Her words were sharp and cold, and she knew they were out of line, even if she was queen. The snide tone and icy accusation was far cry from how Jan had trained her to speak in a council like this. But Jan hadn't finished that training, and he never would.

"We… have not planned for that yet, your highness," Leopold answered at last. "Our priority has been for our people's well-being… and for your own life. If you wish us to strategize such a mission, we may do so."

Allie nodded shortly and said nothing more. She heard him assigning tasks to the warriors in the room, and heard the slight shuffles as they left one by one. She remained seated, her vision fractured, her heart numb and cold. General Leopold said something quietly to her before he left—some words of hope and bravery. His voice echoed with the many others who'd spoken the same things to her over the last few days.

Hope. Hope was fickle. It swept away at the slightest shadow, leaving her in darkness. The Prophecy's words had never held hope for her—the little it spoke of the Vessel was a warning of death and doom: *If mortal heart remains unmarred; The spell that bound leaves deeper scars; Than the shadow that awakened.*

Her heart was long past marred. The Ace-Lord had filled it with darkness and broken it into pieces so that she felt nothing besides the icy chains.

Someone sat in the chair to her right. She hadn't realized Rygal was still in the room.

"I'm assuming you have a plan to beat the Ace-Lord, for you to ask that?" he asked gently.

Allie picked at the tabletop. "No, I don't. Not at all."

Rygal was silent a moment. "We can talk to Iriam when he gets back. We might even be able to ask the Druids. They might know about the Life-Blood Spell and how to break it."

"Break it?" Her voice cracked with a wry laugh. "Rygal, there's no breaking it. I'm done pretending otherwise. You can't just undo a curse like this."

"So… what are you planning to do?"

There was the question she still didn't have an answer for. Any strategy, any idea that might come to her, was muddled by the storm of emotions crowding her mind. She raised her chin slightly, facing him. "I'm going to kill the Ace-Lord. That's how his scheme for the Vessel will backfire on him. I'll kill him and end the war."

"You'll kill him?" Rygal repeated, raising his eyebrows. "And the Life-Blood Spell?"

"Will break when I do it," Allie said, standing so abruptly her chair fell over behind her. "We knew that was always how it would end, even with everything we read—nothing you or I or Darion would ever—"

She stopped. The name seemed to have stuck in her throat like a barb.

"I'm sorry," Rygal said quietly, standing. "I—I know that doesn't…"

"Don't," Allie interrupted hoarsely. "Don't apologize, don't tell me it's all going to be fine—you don't understand, you can't understand."

She turned toward the door. Rygal's voice stopped her before she could leave. "If the Life-Blood Spell can't be broken, wouldn't the Prophecy tell us that?"

Allie stopped, staring at the polished wood of the door. "I don't know. It doesn't matter. That's what's going to happen."

"Because the Ace-Lord told you that," Rygal guessed slowly. "He said… none of your choices would matter?"

"Yes. No. I—why are you asking me all this?" Allie snapped, turning to him. "It's not like this matters. Nothing in the Prophecy tells us what we're supposed to do. If I'm going to die, I don't want some false hope to cling to otherwise."

"That's the Ace-Lord talking, not you," Rygal said.

"And if it is?" Allie demanded, her voice rising. The blood was roaring in her ears. Her heart was pounding so hard she thought it might shatter. Pale fire crackled on her clenched knuckles. "Stop telling me there's hope in the Prophecy—stop telling me everything's going to be all right—because it isn't, it never was. Don't tell me there's some storybook ending to this war. It will *never* be all right, Rygal, because they're *dead*—my father, and Jan, and Darion, and Morel, and all those soldiers—they're dead because I couldn't help them."

Her voice broke, and she paused, her back pressed against the door. Her chest ached. The fear and anger overpowered her, and she felt the fire snuff out, leaving her with the cold and blackness.

"Don't tell me there's light," she whispered. "Not when I feel *so close* to the darkness."

She closed her eyes against the tempest of pain as the wind howled outside. The shadows in her heart wrapped around her in freezing claws that threatened to pull her apart.

Until Rygal spoke. His voice sounded as though it came from far away, calling to life a time he had buried. "I've never... told you about Norrin, have I."

Allie opened her eyes. Rygal stood in front of her, his gaze roaming around the room as though to find some comfort there. "He died on the quest for the Shards. I couldn't save him. I watched the Aces kill him."

He took a shaky breath, as if each word came with an effort, drawn from the depths of agonizing memories. "I just wanted to kill them. For weeks, that was all I could think about. Couldn't eat, couldn't sleep—it was exhausting. Eventually, I think my heart was so worn out that the anger just disappeared... and then it *hurt*, like no pain I've ever felt in my life."

Somewhere inside Allie, a tiny crack split the ice encasing her heart. A deep pressure was building inside her chest.

"I can never get rid of that pain," Rygal said softly. "It's still there, every day. I hated hearing that it would get better because it... it never really does."

He met her gaze, his eyes shining with tears. "I'm not going to tell you anything," he said hoarsely. "But I do know where you are because I've been there too... and I'm here with you now."

The cold shield cracked in two, and Allie finally felt the agony the shadows had hidden. The anger was quenched by tears and she knew it as grief—grief so strong it seemed to drag her into the depths of the world.

She buried her face in her blistered hands and sank to her knees on the hard floor, breaking beneath the anguish. But strong arms caught her, holding her tightly. She pressed her face into Rygal's chest as she wept, feeling again as if she were suspended in the void, torn between worlds, in a struggle seeking to rip her to pieces.

Except Rygal was with her. Holding her as if he would never let go. Holding her shattered heart intact. She felt the rhythm of his heart beat as she leaned into his embrace and the storm roared outside.

The pain did not leave. But the cold had gone, replaced by the soft crackle of the fire in her heart. Her own fire. Her own Essence. In the midst of the darkness, she felt the ember of light growing brighter.

40

∽ ∽ ∽ ∽ ∽ ∽ ∽ ∽ ∽

The End of the Dream

Sounds of grief filled Lillary Bay as the *Burman Marie* anchored at the pier.

Thunder clouds gathered overhead, casting somber shadows over the small village, and wind tore through the trees. Days of endless heat might have made the coming rain a welcome sight to Bryn, yet now, the overcast weather only added to the heaviness and sorrow filling the town.

The *Marie* was one of hundreds of ships packing the harbor. Many of Caer Sia's citizens waited near the water, desperately hoping their loved ones would be on one of those ships. Already, though, the news of the bloody attack had reached Lillary, and Bryn could hear the cries of those whose loved ones had been among the fallen.

The voyage to Lillary had been brief, but it had been one of the worst in her life. Comforting Oliver as he cried for the man who'd been like a brother. Supervising as the men gently wrapped John's body in his hammock and laid him in a quiet corner below decks. Trying to offer answers for the thirty-seven civilians who'd watched their friends and neighbors perish at the hands of the Ace-Deputy. And, when Robin awoke, it was she who had to deliver the news of his best friend's death.

She sat in the cabin for a while with Robin, offering whatever comfort she could. His concussion was serious enough that Harry ordered him to rest for the next few days. Robin had argued, as Bryn had known he would, determined to join his surviving crewmates.

"The best thing you can do is avoid making your injury worse," Bryn had told him gently. "We need you. Don't push it to something more severe."

He'd finally agreed, and had fallen asleep on his cot, his head resting in Bryn's lap, the tears dried on his face.

Bryn left quietly, heading back on deck as the ship reached Lillary. Richard and Matthew waited beside the ship's wheel. Aryion was there too, his back against the mast, his face gray with weariness and pain.

"How many do you suppose they were able to evacuate?" Richard asked softly, studying the masses in the harbor.

"Looks like the majority," Matthew answered. His lilting voice was heavy. In the matter of minutes, the role of first mate had fallen to him, and it had been his task to organize his grieving crewmates. "Then again, there were a lot still trapped on the piers."

Bryn closed her eyes a moment, wishing she could be rid of that scene forever. But the horror of their last few moments in Caer Sia plagued her mind. The terrified screams of the helpless townspeople as they'd been attacked still rang in her ears.

She forced her mind back to the present. They were not safe yet. "When we get ashore, don't go too far from the ship. We're technically still wanted criminals in Coonsia, and the Siren isn't here to vouch for us."

"Aye, Cap'n," Richard agreed, though he sounded so tired Bryn doubted he wanted to disembark at all.

They drew alongside the pier and lowered the gangplank. A few Red Dawn soldiers stood with the crowds in the harbor, but no one stopped to question the *Marie*. Fort Lillary, a square wooden building that looked too small to be a military base, stood to their right. The rain drizzled on a large cluster of tents nearby, which seemed to stand as a refugee camp.

The passengers disembarked in silence, stumbling to shore. A few of them thanked Bryn as they passed, but most seemed shell-shocked by the day, their expressions lifeless, eyes dull with fear.

Harry appeared from below, a few spots of blood staining his apron. The *Marie's* doctor had been busy for the last few hours tending the civilians who'd been bitten by Dal-kerri. "We need more medical supplies," he told Bryn as he came on deck. "And the captain needs more than what I can give him—that was a nasty knock on the head."

Bryn nodded. She could never remember feeling so tired. "All right. You can come ashore with Aryion and me."

Her brother glanced up blearily at his name. Since coming to himself in Caer Sia, he'd shown some improvement, the brutish madness having left him. But his memories still seemed broken and out of place. His face was grim and shadowed with exhaustion, but he adamantly refused Harry's offer to take a sedative for rest.

"You will want to make contact with whoever is in charge here," he rasped, pulling himself painfully to his feet. "I would expect it to be one of the generals."

Bryn nodded again. Add it to her list of things to take care of. "Keep an eye on Robin," she told Richard. "If he wakes up, let him know where we've gone."

She headed down the gangplank with Harry and Aryion close behind. Voices filled the windswept forest around Lillary Bay. She glimpsed a few of their passengers heading to join the crowds, and hoped at least some of them would be reunited with their loved ones.

Aryion spoke quietly behind her, his strange blue-flecked eyes scanning the crowds. "Bryn… do you know if… if Mel…"

He trailed off after the name, as if it hurt him to say. Bryn glanced back at him. She didn't know what to say. If Mel had been in Caer Sia during the attack, he would have likely made it onboard a ship—he was important to the Liznee cause, that much she knew. But what if he'd joined the defense with the High King? What if he'd been slain by the Deputy, like so many others?

"I don't know," she admitted. "I just don't know."

. . . . . .

Not even the Kamon battle had prepared Mel for the overwhelming grief he saw in Lillary Bay.

His family had settled into a small room in the fort, which probably typically housed a general. It barely fit all four of them, but considering most people were either sharing rooms with other families or sleeping out in the tents, it was something to be grateful for. Still, there was much to do, so he'd only rested for a few hours before heading outside, leaving Misty reading a few scrolls they'd salvaged from Castle Sia's library and his parents talking in hushed voices.

News had come from Caer Sia, leaking in fearful fragments through the fort. Jan and Dandio were trapped in the city, and with the storm breaking over the sea and churning it to a froth, no ships could attempt a rescue. The peace and calm he'd felt just before leaving Caer Sia faltered as he headed to the refugee camp. So many dead—men and women, old and young. Dal-kerri had attacked at the harbor, the report stated, massacring those who were left.

Mel wanted to cover his ears to their pain and just rest safely with his family in the fort. But his heart ordered otherwise. The Blue Stone glowed warm in his pocket, as if urging him forward.

A field hospital had been set up beside the lines of tents. Frightened, sorrowful voices filled the air along with the urgent calls of nurses and doctors. The sheer quantity of wounded overwhelmed the few resources.

Mel stepped inside a tent that seemed to be acting as a sort of command central and smiled at an exhausted looking orderly. "Hi—can I help?"

The man frowned slightly, but his eyes widened in understanding as he noticed the glowing blue Stone. "Oh, New Blood," he breathed. "Are you certain you wish to—"

"Please," Mel pressed. "I can help—just tell me who needs it the most."

The doctor nodded. "Very well. Come with me."

He led Mel down the rows of tents to one near the end. People lay inside, bearing serious injuries. "Most of these were bitten by serpentines," the doctor explained. "We do not have enough antivenom to help them all, nor enough fireflower poultice, which is the most effective cure. But if you believe you can help…"

Mel paused. "The Stone can at least heal their wounds. I'm not sure if it can remove the venom, but it'll slow down the effects," he added, recalling what he'd learned when Iriam had been bitten.

The doctor nodded gratefully. "Yes—yes, please do. Any help you can give is appreciated."

Mel ducked inside the tent. The warm air was heavy with the metallic stench of blood. Several people had been bitten or clawed by Dal-kerri, but others lay pale and still from serpentine venom. One woman nursed a cruel slash under her arm from an enchanted orc's blade.

The first two men he treated had been bitten by Dal-kerri. Painful wounds, and they had lost a lot of blood, but the Stone's power stopped the bleeding and sent them into restful sleep. The next patient was an elderly woman, semi-conscious and delirious. A serpentine had bit into her ankle.

Mel knelt beside her, letting the Stone glow blue, trying to turn his mind to the High Light. The despair around him seemed to weigh down his thoughts. Iriam believed there was still hope and light, but it was growing harder to believe that.

He closed his eyes a moment. The mind-numbing horror of the Ace-messenger's words back in Tinkeeyo overwhelmed the peace he sought to cling to. He felt lost and fearful, and so alone it hurt. Aryion's agonized scream filled his thoughts with every waking moment.

Where was his mentor? Was he still alive? Or was the pain-filled illusion in Tinkeeyo the last time Mel would ever hear his voice?

He took a breath as the Stone's light faded, and turned his attention to the next patient. This wouldn't do. He could hardly center his mind on the High Light with the nagging dread for his mentor plaguing his thoughts.

It took him a while to finish with the injured in the tent. By the time he stepped outside to find the orderly again, rain pattered down on the camp, filling the air with its sweet scent. The roiling wind had faded to a gentle breeze, and Mel breathed the fresh air deeply.

"'Scuze me... lad?"

Mel glanced over at the sound of the voice. A portly man with a bald head and an apron spotted in blood stood before him, studying him intently. He was familiar—Mel was certain he'd met this man before—but he could not think of where.

The man's face showed both surprise and relief. "Oh, thank the Light—Cap'n hoped you'd have made it out, but none of us were sure…" He stepped forward and clasped Mel's hand as warmly as if they had known each other all their lives.

Mel's tired mind finally connected the face. He had met this man—on a ship, sailing for Esile City. This was one of the many sailors he'd been introduced to on the *Burman Marie*. Henry—no, Harry, that was it.

What on Orlell was he doing here?

"It's—good to see you," he stammered. "Sorry, I didn't—recognize you."

"Not to worry, lad," Harry said, shaking his head rapidly. "It's mighty good to see you're all right. We worried you might have—but never mind that, come, quickly now."

He placed a hand on Mel's shoulder, weaving through the crowds and leading him forward. Mel allowed himself to be led through the lines of tents, past the weary civilians, toward the docks. His mind could not make sense of what was happening. The *Burman Marie* was in Lillary Bay—they hadn't joined the war, as far as he knew—apparently the sailors were looking for him.

What if…

Hope, fluttering in his stomach like wings, came to life inside him, sending chills down his limbs. No, he thought, terrified he was wrong. No, that was impossible.

And yet… hadn't he always hoped the Dricaster pin would be of use?

Aryion stood, back against a tree, as the rain shimmered down around him.

A few droplets of summer rain fell on his face. He hadn't realized how much he'd missed this during those dark days of captivity, darkness he couldn't fully recall. Then again, maybe that was a good thing.

Every muscle in his body felt as though it had been pulled apart and then pieced together again. The blinding speed, the unexplainable new strength—gifts courtesy of his time with the Aces. But the Deputy hadn't counted on him managing to remember—Aryion had Bryn to thank for that. His new skills were impressive, but his body had yet to catch up to them. The fight in Caer Sia had fully drained him.

In addition to his physical exhaustion, there was the constant mental strain, making his head ache. The few memories he'd managed to recall were jumbled and disorganized, sights and sounds from a life that seemed to have been lived by someone else. He knew who he was, knew some of the people around him, but any memory connected to them had been severed. His only memory of Mel was the scene at the marble bridge, a moment he would have liked to forget forever. Yet if it was all he had of his apprentice, he would cling to the image even though it hurt.

Was he dead, then? Fallen to his death in the void long ago, as the Deputy's hissing voice claimed? Aryion did not know. But if his apprentice was still alive, where was he now?

He was afraid to ask Bryn that question, afraid the answer would bring the darkness back, plunge him back into the horrific dream. The agony he'd endured had weakened his mind to a point that he did not know if he could bear to feel that much grief again.

So he waited in silence. Bryn talked quietly with the harbor master, a Red Dawn captain who was trying to organize the many ships crowding Lillary's harbor. The *Burman Marie*, it seemed, would be allowed to stay while they tended their wounded and buried their dead. Where the *Marie* would go afterwards would be decided later.

Where *he* would go afterwards, he had no idea. Stay and fight in the war? He barely remembered the purpose behind the conflict now. His singular role in the war had revolved around Mel—guard the New Blood, protect him on the quest, protect him while he guarded the Stone. Without Mel, and with his mind and memory broken, he no longer understood his own role.

Harry's excited voice came to the left, near the wide circle of tents. "Cap'n!"

Odd. The *Marie's* doctor had only been gone a few minutes. Surely he hadn't gathered the supplies they'd needed so quickly, not with all these crowds.

Then another voice spoke.

"Aryion?"

His heart stopped. How many times had he heard that voice, turning his name into a question, hesitant, tense with fear, as though afraid the joy that trembled there might be shattered in a moment?

Slowly, he turned, his eyes resting on the figure standing behind Harry. Blue light illuminated the young face, drawn with fear but so familiar.

"Aryion?" The voice cracked with emotion.

He was dreaming. He had to be dreaming again, trapped in the void in his mind. The scene before him could not be real.

Vaguely, he heard Bryn speaking hesitantly, as though trying to explain something terrible in the gentlest way she knew—but he did not hear her words. His voice, torn and rasping from weeks of torture, could only whisper his apprentice's name. "Mel…"

And the next moment, Mel had run into his arms, and Aryion held the boy tightly as tears of joy and relief flowed down his battered face. The dream—the nightmare—faded away as he held the apprentice he had feared forever lost, and Mel clung to his mentor who had, at last, been found.

41

Omens

North Sea. About two leagues from the coast of Sia.

Restless wind whipped over the *Blue Moon*, bringing the scent of distant smoke as Dusty stood on deck.

Around her, the warship had only just begun to waken with the activity of the sailors. The soft lapping of the waves filled the stillness in the hours of the dawn, and the skyline was slowly lightening behind them. Stars still spread overhead in a glimmering tapestry, shining through the haze. Ahead, there was only darkness, storm clouds hulking on the horizon and blotting out the fading stars.

The coastline of Coonsia greeted Dusty's gaze, like a voice reassuring her that the long journey was nearly over. Her squadron of Wildkids had joined with Admiral Dessian's men almost three months ago, sailing back to Kasabren to rally the Clans. The voyage, though long, had been surprisingly uneventful. They'd encountered a storm off the northeastern coast of Daffodalion, and had a brief skirmish with Jenna raiders down the Durbin Strait. But at last, they had reached Kasabren.

She moved toward the tiller, nodding to the bosun and smiling to her younger brother Nellioh, who stood on watch. As dangerous as the times were, she was glad to have her siblings on the journey. Even Graysil, who was only fourteen, had insisted on returning with her to the Mainland. If it were Dusty's choice, she would have ordered them to remain in Kasabren, where the lush jungles and tangled wilds might shield them from the Aces.

But in her heart, she knew better. The time had passed for hiding. Two hundred Wildkid warriors from three of the five Clans had embarked with them on the *Blue Moon,* prepared for the war awaiting them. The rest of the Clan army would be a week or so behind them, still gathering their forces. But they would come. Dusty's mission to rally the Wildkid Clans, some two years in the making, was at last drawing to completion.

Admiral Dessian stood at the tiller. The Liznee was loathe to allow anyone else at the *Blue Moon's* helm, and the voyage had proven his skill several times. His keen blue eyes scanned the water before them, one hand stroking his small pointed beard. "I assume you can smell the smoke," he said as Dusty approached.

"Easily. You can practically taste it," Dusty replied.

A wry grin crossed his face. After months of travel, the Liznee soldiers and the Wildkid warriors had come to rely upon each other in a way that might have been impossible years ago. Each leaned upon the other, protecting one another as if they were one family.

Upon reaching Kasabren, Admiral Dessian and a few of his officers had accompanied the Wildkids to the encampment of the Mara-N'Tell. Here, Dusty had given her report of the Aces' actions, enhanced by the notes Darion Blackbird had given her regarding the voids in Wiverrun. She had been unsure how her father might react—though a fierce warrior, he was very protective of the Clan, and hesitant to send his people to war.

But his children's reports had persuaded him. The N'Tell had held a council with two other Clans, where at last, the decision to join the

Ace-war had been made. The Wildkid warriors had embarked to the west again less than two weeks after their arrival. Once they reached Caer Sia, their focus would turn to preparations of war as they joined with the Red Dawn against the Ace-Lord.

She turned her eyes back toward the coast, where a slight indent in the land and the rise of the mountains marked Sia's harbor. The sight of the coming storm and the growing stench of smoke worried her in a way she could not explain.

"Can't see a blasted thing in this light," Dessian muttered, lowering the spyglass. "The storm is blowing all this smoke inland."

"Do you think there's trouble in Sia?" Dusty asked slowly, trying to ignore the prickle of fear. The mission to Kasabren had taken them months—who knew what had transpired in their absence. Perhaps the Ace-Lord was already... She shook her head, refusing to finish that suggestion.

Dessian thought for a moment, studying the roiling clouds overhead. "The storm we can handle," he said at last. "But this smoke concerns me." He turned to his lieutenant waiting beside him. "Rouse the men. Out oars and await my command."

"Aye, Admiral," the lieutenant replied.

Joesp appeared from below, the wind tousling his black fur as he moved to his older sister. "Smell that smoke?" he asked quietly. "Is it coming from Caer Sia?"

"Near as we can tell," Dusty told him. It was a struggle to keep her voice calm, to give orders without revealing her growing fear. "Wake the others. Smoke or no, the warriors may want to be prepared when we sail into that." She nodded to the churning clouds.

Joesp's face fell as he noticed the storm. He, along with most Wildkids, were unaccustomed to being at sea for long periods of time. It was just their luck they'd be caught in a storm so close to their destination.

"There may be a wildfire in the hills," Dessian mused, his hands running over the smooth wood of the ship's wheel. "That has happened before, especially at this time of year."

"This smoke doesn't smell like a forest fire," Dusty replied, scenting the acrid wind again. "If the fire was just burning trees, the smoke would smell different—fresher, cleaner. This smells…" she thought a moment, trying to think how to describe it. "Bitter. Sour, almost."

"Well, I will take your word for it," the admiral replied.

The crew of the *Blue Moon* had come awake by now, the orders of the officers ringing over the deck as the sailors moved to their tasks. Wind tore at the sails, and waves rocked the warship as though she were a canoe. The storm's pull would guide them into Caer Sia, Dusty guessed, but with the sails down and oars out, they could retain some control and balance.

Trying to ignore her unease of the storm, she turned her eyes back to the darkened valley before them. The scene only added to her fear. "There are no lights," she told Dessian quietly. "From here we'd at least be able to see the lanterns in the streets and castle walls."

Dessian looked at her, concerned. "Can you see any signs of fire?" he asked, keeping his voice lowered. Despite the clamor of voices around them, he clearly knew as well as she did that they didn't want to worry the crew.

Dusty squinted through the shadows. Wildkid senses were far superior to most other mortals', but through the smoke and haunting darkness, she felt utterly blind. "No," she admitted after a long pause. "The thickest smoke seems to be on the far side of the city."

The admiral frowned deeply. "The southern walls? Those are well-fortified and designed to protect the city from fire in case of siege." He paused. "Unless, of course, the fire began inside the city…"

Graysil's hesitant voice came from behind them. "What's happening?"

Dusty turned as her younger sister came up the stairs, holding tightly to the rail. Newuel stood behind her. The ash-gray patterns on their fur could have sold them as twins, despite the four years between them.

"We're approaching Caer Sia," Dusty answered, trying to sound unworried. Nothing had truly been proven a danger yet, she reminded herself. The uncertain light might only be playing tricks on her tense mind. "We will have to sail through the storm, though, so you might want to wait below."

Graysil shivered in the wind, but shook her head. Dusty didn't argue, seeing as there was no real reason for her two siblings to wait in the stuffy confines of the berth. Both had braved worse things than the weather.

A wave split against the *Moon's* prow, spraying her with salt water, and she clutched the rail tighter. Sailing, she thought bitterly. Why Rygal enjoyed being at sea so much was beyond her.

"How long till we reach the harbor?" she asked.

"That depends on the waves and wind," Dessian replied, holding the wheel steady. "You can't simply plow straight through a storm like this. You must skirt it, dance around it, like a raven scolding a hawk."

Another wave broke over the rail, dousing the three Wildkids. Dusty shook her ears clear of water and looked at the admiral wearily. "Ravens and hawks? Really?"

"I am only saying, it's easier said than done," Dessian said, an amused light in his blue eyes. "Tell me again, why do your Clans not choose to see more of the world when it has so much to offer? If one braves the sea, there is an entirely new side of the map to explore."

Dusty managed a grin. "Well, Admiral, I'm glad you enjoy the sea. But my people and I might be inclined to disagree with you."

She focused on the wind again, trying to pick out individual scents. Her troubled thoughts made it difficult. A memory returned to her mind from a winter evening long past, standing in Elimar when she was barely eleven, trying to find Rygal and Dandio in the dark night. She'd been afraid, her senses muffled by fear. She still remembered the Elf Linwy speaking to her calmly, bringing her thoughts back to the present. Helping her focus on finding the scents that led to her friends.

No matter how many years had passed, no matter how many missions she'd endured, she could still be distracted so easily by the fear of what could go wrong.

But she pushed that away, inhaled deeply, pressing through the confused blur of smells and reading what the wind told her. Smoke, acrid and stinging, black like tar. Perhaps from a house or building. Another stench mingled with it, growing stronger every moment, though she couldn't place what it was.

"We might turn back for Lillary Bay, sir!" the bosun called. "It may be wiser to wait out the storm."

"No, keep her forward!" Dessian shouted back. "We are following a west wind—if we leave it behind, we will be trapped on the wrong side of the border until the storm lets up."

The tangled scents grew sharper with each moment as the wind and waves propelled them forward, and now she identified them. Dal-kerri. Many of them, more than she'd ever smelled in one place. Enchanted soldiers too, carrying the distinctive artificial smell. But rising over both came the sickening reek of death.

Dusty peered through the lashing rain to see the vague silhouette of the city. Darkness and haze blanketed Caer Sia, but there was one other scent she had only ever smelled once before—something cold, so cold it seemed to sting her nose as she inhaled, like a breath of frostbite.

"Aces," she whispered, and this time, she could not keep the fear from her voice. "Admiral—there are Aces in Caer Sia—Aces and Dal-kerri."

Dessian's eyes widened in disbelief and horror. "Aces? How many?" He peered futilely through his spyglass a moment, then lowered it with a muttered curse.

"Should we still try to make port, sir?" the lieutenant asked quietly.

Dessian's jaw set in a rigid line as he studied the coastline across the waves. "Is there anyone in the city?" he asked finally, looking at Dusty. "Can you scent or hear any survivors?"

Dusty breathed deeply for several moments, seeking through the blurred scents for something—anything—that might give hope. It was impossible. The stench of the Ace-army overwhelmed all else. "I—can't tell," she admitted at last. "I'd probably be able to tell if we were closer to the harbor," she offered, knowing that was a risky suggestion. If the Aces had taken over Caer Sia, they would undoubtedly spot the *Blue Moon* the moment she entered the harbor.

Dessian looked up at the clouds, his face rigid as rain lashed the decks of the *Moon*. "I cannot risk it," he said at last, defeated. "If we are to sail through this storm, we must at least have a safe harbor on the other side. We'll make for Badwater instead, see if they know what has happened in Sia, and determine a new strategy."

"Sir!" The lookout's urgent cry came from above. Dusty had glimpsed what he'd seen a moment before, though she could not understand what she was looking at. Fluttering over the water from the harbor, buffeted by the gales but headed steadily towards them, was a catlike shape whose feathered wings carried it forward.

"A gryphon," Dessian breathed, brow furrowed.

"Is it Commander Ki?" the lieutenant asked, peering through the rain.

Dusty watched as the gryphon approached. She'd initially hoped, like the lieutenant, that it was Dandio, on the back of the gryphon he'd trained and rode during the quest for Drisilas. But she sensed at once that this guess was wrong. There was no rider. And there was something strange about the creature's flight—lopsided, uncertain.

Almost unnatural.

"What's the matter with it?" Newuel murmured beside the rail.

"It might be enchanted," Dusty said slowly. She reached for her quiver, though she doubted her arrow would fly true in this wind.

"Guns, up!" Dessian ordered. Five soldiers stepped forward, rifles raised as the beast drew closer.

Through the sheeting rain, Dusty saw the gryphon raise its head, saw the glitter of its eyes—not the hollow blue of the Dal-kerri, but green. In another instant, the gryphon's shape vanished before them, replaced by a raven, fighting through the winds that fought to force it back.

Dusty lowered her bow, hurrying toward the prow with a surge of recognition. "A Siren—it's Lammar!"

"Lower your guns!" Dessian shouted, moving to follow. "Help him aboard!"

The raven battled against the winds, wings torn sideways by the gale, dropping dangerously low to the choppy waves. At Dessian's command, the soldiers rushed to the prow as the Siren approached. Dusty ran with them, skidding on the wet deck, stumbling forward as Lammar dropped out of sight beneath the bulwarks.

Joesp shouted from the prow—he had hold of the raven's wing, lifting him to the deck as Dusty and Dessian reached him.

The raven's form flickered, soaked feathers replaced by scales streaked with mud and blood. Lammar lay on the deck, gasping for breath, and for a moment Dusty feared he would sink into unconsciousness before explaining anything. But then he raised himself, meeting Dessian's gaze and managing to rasp out words.

"Admiral—the king—the Commander—they're in the city—trapped to the south—"

Fear gripped Dusty's heart, and for a moment her mind could not process the message. Jan and Dandio were still in Caer Sia.

"Hard to starboard, now!" Dessian ordered. "Bring us into the harbor." He knelt by the Siren, his face drawn. "What has happened here?"

"Aces—attacked," Lammar panted. He struggled to stand, but his limbs simply gave out. Dusty put a hand on his shoulder to steady him. "Two days ago—the civilians were evacuated to Lillary—the king wanted to stay behind—buy us time."

"Take him below," Dessian told one of the sailors, who carefully lifted the Siren's battered form. Lammar protested weakly, but in his current state he could not do much about it. The fight through the storm, and the battle he had come from, had left him utterly drained.

Dusty straightened, forcing herself to be calm. Now was not the time to panic. "Tell the warriors to prepare to head ashore," she told Joesp. "Graysil, go with them."

Her younger sister didn't argue—her face was tight with fear.

Dusty looked at Dessian as the *Blue Moon* swung inland, unsure what the admiral planned. Not even the best strategy in the world would change the fact that they would be highly outnumbered and uncertain what they'd find, and she could tell from one look at his weathered face that he knew it.

"We've the favor of the tide," Dessian told her, gripping the ship's wheel.

"That's good, right?" Dusty asked. Any advantage was something to be grateful for.

But that spark of hope was doused by Dessian's grim expression. "It's quite good for the moment," he answered. "But it also means getting *into* Sia will be far easier than getting *out*."

42

Specters

Wind whipped in Dusty's hair and hauled on the sails as the *Blue Moon* swept inland. Waves churned on the seaward edge of harbor, as if held back by an invisible wall. As Admiral Dessian had noted earlier, the direction of the wind and the rushing of the sea guided them steadily inland. But the same wind and current would be against them if they had to flee.

Dusty took a deep breath, holding tightly to the port rail. Darkness shrouded Caer Sia, filling the city like black liquid, and not even the distant light of dawn could reach within. A few buildings were vaguely outlined through the fog, and if she squinted southward, she could make out a faint reddish glow.

The fires, they had begun to guess, had been lit by the Red Dawn, in a desperate attempt to slow the Aces' progress. The Aces hated and feared fire. Dusty recalled the race to Mata City and the way the Dal-kerri had fled before the flames—perhaps that strategy would work again here.

This thought vanished as the harbor bank came into view, and her stomach twisted with horror.

A wide stretch of road circled the harbor, a place where passengers might gather and wait for a vessel or watch for incoming ships. Littering the roads were bodies of townsfolk. There were at least a hundred, though the dim light and the stench dulling her senses made it hard to count. They had fallen by the buildings, on the piers, on the rocks where some had attempted to flee into the sea as a last resort.

Civilians and soldiers alike. Slaughtered by the Aces.

The senseless brutality sickened her, yet she looked on, allowing the scene to ingrain in her thoughts. This was why they had come. This was what the Aces had in store for Kasabren too. The Ace-Lord's conquest would not stop here. Far too many had already died trying to stop him.

But perhaps they might yet save Jan and Dandio.

"Bring her about," Dessian ordered quietly. The bosun echoed the command, and the sailors moved to obey. Dusty felt the slow turn as the *Moon* angled slightly to the left, drifting on the rolling waves but coming no closer to the piers.

"Aren't we headed ashore?" she asked.

"We cannot risk docking here," Dessian replied, buckling on his sword belt. "It will be far easier for us to slip in and out in a dinghy than a warship."

"Us?" Joesp repeated, glancing over.

"My men and I may know the sea, young Wildkid," Dessian said with a faint grin, "but our skills of tracking are nothing compared to the N'Tell. If we are to find the High King and the Commander quickly, we will need your aid. How many of your warriors can you spare?" he added, looking at Dusty.

Dusty managed a smile. "As many as you need, Admiral—though I do think a smaller party would be wiser."

"Very well. Choose ten of your finest, and I will take a squad of soldiers to guard our backs," Dessian answered. He turned to the bosun. "Do not drift closer to the piers. We must beware of any devilry the Aces may have set here. Be prepared to pick us up at King's Cove."

"You're sure that port won't be overrun?" Dusty asked him. "It's much closer to the castle."

"I have no way of knowing anything for certain, but I can safely guess it will be a wiser choice than anchoring in the main harbor," Dessian replied. He looked at her curiously. "How do you even know about King's Cove? It's a private port—only Red Dawn officers are authorized to anchor there."

"I didn't know that," Dusty said. "It's the same place we docked at before the battle with Kado, on my first visit here. Dandio had us enter Caer Sia from that side." How well she remembered that day, sailing on the *Sun's Crest* into the forested harbor and riding like the wind into the capital, while Hazes and orcs had swarmed behind them.

Dessian raised his eyebrows, impressed. "Well, let us hope it will serve us as well today as it did then."

Two dinghies were lowered into the toiling waves. A squadron each of Red Dawn soldiers and Wildkids climbed aboard. Dusty glimpsed Graysil's worried face amid the watchers on the *Blue Moon's* decks before the rowboats entered the gray haze, hiding the ship from view.

She turned her attention before her again, flexing her fingers over the smooth handle of her bow. The boats reached the shore, and the passengers jumped onto the bloodstained piers. The castle spires poked through the smoke to their right. The buildings along the harbor, Dusty noticed, had been ransacked, windows smashed, doors kicked in. White ice glittered in patches on the road.

"Where to, Admiral?" one of the soldiers asked in a hushed whisper.

Dusty raised her head, seeking a scent. The reek of death and burning stung her nose, but there was another scent too, far away—the warm smell of living bodies.

She turned to Dessian. "South—there's a very faint scent of life coming due south of us."

"Southward, then," Dessian ordered, turning down a road. "Make haste, men."

The soldiers formed tight ranks and followed at a quick march. Dusty jogged with him as rain shimmered down upon them, occasionally raising her head and seeking for the scents. Wind blurred the faint traces she'd caught, confusing and muddling the signs. She felt as though she were stumbling blindly toward a great chasm, and her breath came in short gasps.

Steady, she ordered herself. *Calm and steady. Nerves won't help anyone.*

In the same instant, the wind whispered on her skin as she sensed the watchers.

Dusty could not tell where the sensation came from. Some sixth sense, innate to every woodland creature, had flickered to life. She felt their eyes from every corner of the city, as the wind sighed words in a language she did not understand and the very rain seemed to crackle with expectancy.

"Wait," she called quietly.

Dessian raised a hand and the Red Dawn soldiers stopped. The other Wildkids had sensed it too, their ears pricked up in both confusion and unease, their eyes scanning the area around them, trying to find the source.

"What is it?" Dessian whispered.

"There's..." Dusty hesitated, completely at a loss for how to describe the sensation to him. "The wind... there's something else here. It's watching us."

Several soldiers reached for their weapons, glancing warily into the fog. "An enemy?" Dessian asked.

"No… not that I can tell," Dusty replied, hoping she was right. The sensation was not one of danger. It felt as though she had been in a room full of darkness and suddenly, inexplicably, someone had shone a light. Even stranger—it was familiar. She'd felt this before, the prickle down her spine that stood her fur on end and filled her heart with longing—but when? Where?

"It's all around us," Nellioh said, gripping his spear tighter. His rust-red fur had risen in hackles like that of a fearful wolf.

"I don't think it's dangerous," Joesp told him, though he sounded uncertain. "The voices—can you hear them? They sound as though they are trying to calm us."

"Or warn us," Newuel pointed out, glancing worriedly at his older siblings.

Dusty closed her eyes, shutting out the fearful faces of the others and focusing fully on the wind as it whistled around her. The unseen speakers—hundreds of them, as far as she could tell—called out in their strange languages, sounding over the ruined city and rising over the forested hills. At last the words came clear.

Come. Quickly. A daughter of Sia requested us to come, to save the one she loves. Follow where we guide.

"The forest," Dusty breathed, finally understanding. "There are *dryads* in Caer Sia."

Dessian looked around, his expression less of fear and more of awe. "Are you certain?"

Dusty listened a moment longer, feeling the dryads' urgency. "They're here to guide us—we have to trust them."

Dessian inhaled deeply, sought for an answer, then let out his breath again with a weak shrug. "Oh... very well then. Come along, men."

Rain pattered on the burned buildings as the group headed down the deserted roads. The wind carried the urgent voices of the trees. Here and there Dusty could catch words.

"They are coming... they are coming to help..."

"Beware the white ice... it breaks and kills..."

"Quickly—quickly—"

Dryads in Caer Sia. Allie had mentioned something about meeting a dryad on the way to Wiverrun, and Dusty had heard stories about the old alliance between the mortals and dryads long ago. But who had wakened the dryads? Who had brought them here? And why did the rain seem to shimmer silver and the water shift and rise around them as if tugged by invisible fingers?

A word swam into her memory, one murmured by the ancient storyteller of the N'Tell. *Druid.* The magic filling the air around her was Druid.

Shouts and clatters came from ahead. The street sloped gently downhill, and as they reached the crest, Dusty finally saw the desperate battle.

Thirty Liznee knights stood below them, raising a continuous wall of crackling crimson flame before them. Clashing against the fiery shield in hideous droves were Dal-kerri—hundreds of them—piling upon each other in snapping waves. The fires held, sputtering in the sheeting rain, but Dusty could sense the defenders tiring. Many already bore severe injuries. Beyond the wolves, moving resolutely forward, came enchanted soldiers, their hollow eyes fixed upon their exhausted quarry.

Dusty did not see Jan or Dandio among the defenders.

"Forward, now!" Dessian barked, jarring them out of the shocked pause. "Strengthen the fires!"

Red flame sparking in their hands, the soldiers ran forward with their admiral, joining their comrades. Dusty led her warriors forward—not to the battle, as there was not much they could do to aid the fiery shield. Instead she moved to the bloodied knights, taking a man by the arm and guiding him away from the fray. "Come with us, toward the castle—there's a port there—the *Blue Moon* is waiting."

The Red Dawn knight pulled away, his face streaked in soot and blood. She could see his weary mind struggling to make sense of what was happening.

"Go!" Dusty ordered again. "Newuel—lead them to the port." Slowly, surely, the exhausted Liznee knights began to retreat, stumbling back up the muddy road, following the young Wildkid toward the distant safety of King's Cove. Dusty wiped the rain from her eyes, squinting down the line as the fires blazed. Armored bodies lay spread along the road behind.

"Where is the king?" Dessian shouted. He and his knights had raised a wall of fire, flames surging from their hands and forming a shield before them.

Dusty grabbed the arm of another retreating Liznee. "Sir—where is the High King and the Commander?"

The soldier looked at her, the grief in his face stabbing Dusty's heart with dread. "Trapped," he rasped, nodding downhill. "That building— they held that position to try and give us a chance to get out, but they're cut off—no way back out."

Dusty followed his eyes. A brick building stood a mere arrowshot away, surrounded by a sea of wolves. Its roof had been torn to pieces, and she could see Dal-kerri and serpentines scaling the walls, leaping downward, attacking someone inside. Through the broken windows came a weak flash of red fire.

"Admiral!" she cried, pointing.

Dessian's face tightened as his gaze traveled down the road. Dusty could tell his mind was working desperately to find some strategy that might help. The wisest choice was to retreat, to go back to the *Moon* and escape with their lives. To press forward, into that mindless fray, would only end in death—first Ĵan and Dandio's, then their own.

Dessian stood for a long moment, conflict on his face. At last he turned to her. "Go with your brothers," he said quietly. "Help the wounded. Wait for us if you will, but I will not ask any others to risk their lives with me."

Dusty hesitated, knowing better than to argue his orders. But the idea of simply fleeing went against her entire reason for coming here. "They're still alive," she said firmly. "We might have a chance to help them if we're all together."

A sad smile appeared on Dessian's face. "Dusty. Not even the whole Red Dawn would defeat a force of that size, but I must make certain I have tried." He nodded toward the twisted frenzy of Dal-kerri and serpentines. "Take your men to Lillary Bay, it is the nearest haven. Fight another day."

Dusty looked at the battered building, at the few flashes of fire from within. Ĵan and Dandio had bought enough time for their soldiers to escape—and they would likely pay for it with their lives. Her heart ached at the truth in Dessian's words, and it took all her effort to turn away from the battle.

Thunder rumbled overhead, and as if on cue, rain poured from the heavens as though a floodgate had opened. Dusty paused at the admiral's side, squinting through the sudden torrent.

"Pull back!" Dessian ordered. The red flames flickered as his knights moved away. The wind forced the fire back into the Liznees' faces, causing their shield to falter. The Dal-kerri pressed forward, snarling and howling in triumph.

"The wind is against us, Admiral!" one of the soldiers cried fearfully.

"Do the Aces now command the rain and wind?" Dessian muttered through gritted teeth, sending a weak blast of flame toward the Dal-kerri.

Dusty looked up into the thundering clouds, unsure what she was looking for, less sure if anything could help them now.

But what she saw was the rain shining silver, twisting and joining the wind, hanging suspended in the air. The strange sensation, that sixth sense, filled her again as she sensed the dryads—no, not dryads, but a power like them—a force wilder, stronger.

Fiercer.

The Dal-kerri hesitated, muzzles raised to the air, growling warily as they too sensed the threat.

In a split second, the rain came alive.

Dusty saw warriors moving like shadows through the darkness, nearly transparent, eyes flashing white. They rose from the sea, riding on the rain-strewn wind. Ghosts of the water, lords of the sea.

The Nøkken. She had heard their name in many a tale, yet never imagined them to rise before her.

They swept forward in a swirl of breeze reminiscent of the dryads, but the sea came with a vengeance the forest did not know. The Nøkken rose as an army, strengthened by the pouring rain, taller than she could have believed, silvery tridents glinting in their sea-spray hands as they attacked.

Dessian's voice cracked as he shouted for the soldiers to advance—Dusty could not even form words as she ran with him through the breach the Nøkken had opened. The spirits of the sea swept around them, cold and fierce as the gale. Perhaps they had been summoned by the Druids—perhaps the High Light Himself had roused them. She could only stare in shock and awe at the army that had risen from the waters.

They reached the broken building. A few wolves lunged as they came—Dessian's fire blasted the first, and Dusty's arrow took down the next. She swung her bow upward, just in time to shoot the serpentine that lunged. In the same moment, the door was kicked open from the inside, and a Liznee fell to his knees in the mud.

Dusty dropped down beside him. His face was almost unrecognizable beneath the layer of blood and grime, but he still wore his crown and familiar half-smile.

"I take it… you were successful," Jan breathed.

Dusty felt herself smile, so relieved to see the king alive. "Yes, sire—we're here to get you out. Where's…"

A second Liznee stumbled from the building as she spoke, bracing himself against the broken wall. Parts of his armor had been torn off, and blood streaked his cheekbone and lip from a gash of a Dal-kerri claw. The silvery light of the Nøkken lit the black scar creasing his exhausted face.

"Help the king," Dessian ordered, moving to Dandio.

Dandio leaned heavily on his shoulder, spitting out a mouthful of blood. "Took you long enough," he panted to Dessian, but relief had filled his green eyes at the sight of his friend. "The others…"

"They are awaiting you on the *Blue Moon*, sir," Dessian told him. "Now, we must hurry."

Dusty helped Ĵan to his feet, supporting him as they moved down the street. As far as she could tell, his weakness came less from his injuries and more from his exhausted state. The soldiers flanked them as they stumbled for the castle.

The Nøkken ghosted through the rain, striking the Dal-kerri. Ĵan's gaze followed them in awe. "I… always thought… the Druids would wake the dryads," he whispered hoarsely, stunned. "I had… forgotten about the Nøkken."

"Are the Druids here?" Dusty asked him as they stumbled up the road. The wolves had drawn back, fleeing the sea spirits, but she could scent several packs still prowling the streets, and kept her hand on her dagger hilt.

"I do not know," Ĵan answered. "I sent Iriam to find them… to implore them to help Sia… but I have not seen them. Perhaps it is they who woke the Nøkken."

They passed the castle, moving steadily for the sea. Dal-kerri howled behind them.

"Not far now," Dessian called, his voice tense.

They hurried on. A new smell joined the scents in the wind—the cold, dry scent of Aces. It chilled the air like coming snow.

The tiny harbor came into view. The dinghy waited at the pier, and Dusty saw a second riding the choppy waves toward the waiting *Blue Moon*. Joesp and Nellioh stood on the dock, aiding the desperate retreat. Joy and relief lit their faces as the exhausted warriors reached them.

Ĵan stumbled in weariness as Dusty helped him into the boat. Dandio fell in beside him, raising himself slightly to peer back toward the castle. A sound reached Dusty's ears, but for a moment she could not tell what it was. The rhythm from some hooved creature, growing steadily louder and filling her heart with dread.

"There's a horse coming," she told Dessian. "Or—something that sounds like it."

Dessian paused. The drumming of hoofbeats approached, headed towards them. For a brief moment, Dusty hoped it was the Druids—but the chill that froze the air around them warned otherwise.

"Aces," she whispered, mouth dry with fear.

"Cast off!" Dessian ordered, climbing onboard. "Row, men—hurry—"

Even as the last syllable left his mouth, the two riders came into view.

The horses they rode looked as though they had died long ago and dragged themselves back from the Dark Realm. Their skull-like heads were far too long, their eyes flashing blue. A jagged horn rose from the center of their heads, rimmed with blood. Their ragged manes and tails were caked with the muck of the day.

The Aces drove them forward, riding toward the harbor. The leader spurred his mount onward, and Dusty could see triumph shining on the ruined face—half skull, half flesh.

Caught. After all they had fought through, they would all be killed. There was nowhere to run, nowhere to hide. The Deputy raised his hands, white ice shining on his fingertips, and Dusty closed her eyes, feeling the last bitter sensation of defeat.

And opened them again as, in a thunderclap of indigo light, three figures rose from the darkness between them and the Deputy.

At first Dusty thought the newcomers were Aces, but the deep blue ice that rose in a protective shield and the light flashing from their purple-red eyes was far different. Two of them bore strange silver markings over their skin, their robes deep green like the forest around them. The third stood tall, black cloak billowing, as indigo light glowed around him.

The Neutrals. Rising from the shadows. Revealing themselves at last.

The Deputy drew up short as his deadly white blast was intercepted by Iriam's blue ice, his face dissolving in shock and disbelief.

"Leave this place," Iriam commanded, his voice holding an authority Dusty had only seen glimpses of before. "The price has been paid. Leave lest you bear a heavier curse than your master."

The Deputy hissed, lashing out again. The two Druids raised their hands again, standing firm on the pier as the white and blue clashed in a blinding flash.

"This is not over, Neutral," the Deputy snarled to Iriam, his voice carrying in the wind. "The tempest shall claim all who attempt to escape."

He took a step back and struck the weathered dock, shattering the wood, yet the Druids only shimmered away in a trail of silver.

Waves clawed at the *Moon's* bulwarks, rocking her violently from side to side as the dinghy reached her. Dusty's hands shook from weariness and adrenaline as the sailors hauled them to the decks. It was Graysil who caught her as she fell to the deck. Through the rain and salty spray, she glimpsed the sailors bringing Jan and Dandio aboard, and saw Iriam reach them in a shimmer of deep blue light.

"East," Dessian choked, stumbling to the tiller. "East, men."

Wind howled in Dusty's face. The strength and might of the Nøkken, so welcome on the steady ground of land, turned against them as they fled the harbor and the wrath of the sea embraced them. The storm howled like the Dal-kerri they'd recently escaped. Waves broke over the deck as if to drag them down. Through the gray darkness, Dusty could not even make out the horizon.

"The storm's against us, sir!" the bosun warned. "It's dragging us back to Sia!"

Dessian's voice was lost in the howling wind. Another wave poured over the rail where Dusty and Graysil huddled, drenching them to the bone. Dusty's heart seemed numb with terror. All they had faced today, the horror and bloodshed, all paled before the sheer fury of the wild sea.

The sailors were shouting, confused, frightened. The *Moon* keeled sideways as waves threatened to claim them. The tempest roared like a living thing. Dessian bellowed orders from the tiller, fighting to hold the wheel steady.

Dusty held Graysil close, unable to do anything but huddle down in terror and wait for the sea to swallow them. The wind that had once carried a promise of alliance was now hostile. She could hear the wild voices of the Nøkken all around them, yet now they seemed taunting and twisted, gleeful of the mortal lives they would soon claim.

Then, through the waves and darkness on the horizon, she saw a glimmer of gold.

She blinked, certain she was imagining it, that the fear had driven her mad. But the vision stayed.

Far ahead, gliding unhindered through the storm, was a ship that glittered gold.

"Admiral!" she panted, pointing toward the apparition.

Dessian followed her gaze—his eyes widened in disbelief. Several sailors saw it too, their shouts fading away as they stared at the distant ship. The wind hauled on the *Blue Moon's* sails, yet this time, Dusty could feel it spurring them, like unseen hands guiding them to the path.

"Hard to starboard," Dessian ordered. "Follow that ship." The sailors did as he ordered as if in a daze, staring at the ghostly ship on the horizon.

"Stay here," Dusty told Graysil. Shakily, she got to her feet and made her way to the tiller. The glimmering golden ship seemed to be made of pure sunlight, shifting and uncertain through the haze, leading them forward through the tempest. "Admiral—what is that?" she asked at last.

Dessian stared at the ship, shaking his head slowly. "I have heard stories," he answered quietly. "All seamen know the tales. It's another legend come to life before us today."

Dusty did not ask what he meant. She'd heard of this ship too, though the Wildkids called it by another name, and she had dismissed it simply as myth. Mythology, like the Ace-Lord that waged war against them. Mythology, like the Nøkken who had risen from the sea and the Druids who had saved them.

Mythology, like a ship sprung from a pirate's song that guided them onward.

She glanced at Iriam, who stood beside Dessian. His eyes studied the distant ship while a slight smile played on his dark features.

The wind howled around them, the waves wrenched and rolled as if to tear the *Blue Moon* apart, yet they passed through the tempest unharmed, following the ghostly golden ship back into the light of day.

Only then did the *Red Canary* fade away into the sunlight, like a dream before the dawn.

43

The Queen's Decision

Dawn light filtered through the rain-soaked trees of Lillary Bay, warming Allie's face as she looked out the window toward the harbor. Heavy clouds lingered on the edge of the horizon, but the fury of the storm had passed. Despite the early hour, she felt rested. Rested, and strangely calm.

The grief and hurt had not gone. She still felt their weight upon her shoulders. But her mind was clear, as though the High Light had at last illuminated the path before her, guiding her forward despite the curse's darkness.

Ajaha had returned to the fort late last night, exhausted and uncertain. There had been no update regarding Caer Sia, nor was there any way to know if the dryads had heard Ajaha's words. They had been there, Ajaha had said—that much she was sure of. But if they'd agreed to help, no one yet knew.

Ajaha and Allie had waited together through the night, finding comfort sitting together as the tempest passed. Not even the darkness of the Life-Blood Spell could disrupt the comfort Allie found in her mother's presence. She did not go into detail about what had happened in Gayrile, or the truth of her future, or the blackness of the curse. The tears came easier now.

Yet she could only allow so much time for tears. Now was the time for action, and though her heart hoped that Jan and her father still lived, the role of High Queen had fallen to her for the present.

She moved away from the window, ignoring the throbbing ache from the patchwork of bruises and cuts she'd accumulated over the last week. Somewhere in the dark night, the inkling of a plan had entered her mind, one that she needed Mel's input on. The boy would probably be with Aryion, Allie thought, feeling a slight smile cross her face. That was one small glimmer of light yesterday. Aryion was alive and determined to keep his apprentice safe despite his exhausted state.

But Lillary Bay would not be safe for the Blue Stone. Allie couldn't deny that, not after seeing the Aces tear through Caer Sia—the most fortified city in the north—as though it were made of straw. The Aces might attack again—they still wanted the last uncorrupted Star-Stone, and if they came here, battle would again involve Sia's helpless refugees.

It was time to get moving again.

The door opened, and Ajaha looked at her in surprise. "I thought you were still asleep. Did you rest well?"

"Yes," Allie said, embracing her mother. "And you? Tell me you managed to get some rest, at least."

"Enough," Ajaha replied, a faint smile touching her tired face. "You sound far too much like your father." Her smile faded at the words.

"Is there any news this morning?" Allie asked slowly.

Ajaha shook her head, her face grim. "No. I believe General Leopold intends to hold a meeting later with the generals. Oh—and Aryion informed me he believes Lammar was in Caer Sia as well."

"Lammar?" Allie echoed, mildly surprised.

"He was with the crew of the *Burman Marie* when they freed Aryion. It seems they returned to Caer Sia in the midst of the battle. Aryion was unsure exactly what happened—his mind is still fragmented," Ajaha replied.

Allie thought a moment. The fact that the Siren had been in Caer Sia both confused her and added to the steadily growing hope in her heart that Ĵan and her father were still alive. Foolish hope, maybe—yet it seemed so certain, as if her family's heartstrings were intertwined.

"I'll ask Aryion about it," she said instead, buckling on her sword belt. "Either way, we can't just wait around for news to arrive."

"Indeed." Ajaha studied her, her eyes lingering on the rips in her daughter's armor and the bandage around her arm. "Have you a plan for the meantime, then?"

"Not yet." Allie hesitated, trying to organize her thoughts. "I think it'd be best to move the Blue Stone, try to keep battle away from the civilians as much as we can. But I don't know where... and I want to... I want to do what Ĵan would do," she finished haltingly. Emotion choked her voice as the grief and uncertainty crept to the surface. She was not her uncle. Nothing could change that.

The light touch of her mother's hand on her arm drew her eyes up. "That is quite a burden to place upon yourself," Ajaha said gently. "Your uncle... he does not carry his responsibilities alone. In times such as these, Ĵan chooses to rely upon the support and advice of others."

Allie let out a breath, hearing the truth in the words. Some of the uncertainty lessened as she looked at her mother. "All right. Then... I need to call a council."

Ajaha did not argue, following her daughter out into the hall. "That seems a sound choice. About what, might I inquire?"

"About the Stone." Allie paused, thinking, as they walked down the corridor. "I don't know if the Aces would attack here, but if they did...

if they do, we need to get the Blue Stone—and Mel—somewhere else. And I feel I should go with him—protecting the New Blood seems to be the one thing the Ace-Lord can't use against me." The Ace-Lord's strategy of corruption had been most successful whenever she'd been in battle. It would be wise to remove herself from such situations, at least until the turmoil in her spirit had settled.

Ajaha nodded thoughtfully. "You are likely correct. Who would you like me to gather for you?"

"General Leopold and Glentree," Allie replied, drawing from Jan's usual group of advisors. "Mel and Aryion. And you should be there—and any of your team who you think might help." She faltered. Considering she'd only ever observed Jan's councils, organizing one herself felt completely foreign. "I'm allowed to do this, right?" she added hesitantly.

"You are acting as High Queen," Ajaha told her with a small smile. "Yes, you may. I will see to fetching the generals, if you will speak with Mel and Aryion. I assume you will wish Rygal there as well?"

Allie nodded, unsure why her face warmed at the mention of his name. The conversation last night, heavy and tearful as it had been, seemed to have drawn them closer together.

They headed downstairs. Ajaha gave her shoulder a gentle squeeze before moving gracefully away. Muted conversations filled the lower levels of Fort Lillary. Allie glanced out the window, where the slight hill allowed a clear view out at the harbor and the ships clustered at the piers. Nearly the entirety of the Red Dawn navy was gathered in a forest of masts and rigging.

Aryion sat at a table in a quiet corner of the mess hall, his blue-flecked eyes scanning the room. Shadows lingered on his gaunt and battered face, but his hair and beard had been trimmed so that he'd begun to look like his usual self. He gave her a nod as she approached. "Good morning, Heiress."

"Morning. How are you feeling?" Allie asked.

Mel's voice interrupted before Aryion could reply. "The doctors said he's supposed to get more rest."

The apprentice strode over, carrying a mug of steaming tea. Rygal was with him, his dark hair tousled and damp from the morning rain, and Allie could not explain why her heart seemed to come alive at the sight of him.

"Good morning Allie," Mel said cheerfully. The fear that had plagued his young face for weeks was gone, and light shone again in his eyes as he turned to his mentor. "Here," he said as he set the mug on the table, "the doctors say it'll help your lungs."

"Mel," Aryion said patiently, "if I wished for someone to play nursemaid for me—"

"I brought your sword too," Mel continued, undaunted, as he unslung the sword from his shoulder and set it on the table. "Rygal said the blade's getting rusty and I should have cleaned it—but I think it's just dirt, so—"

Aryion's gaze swung to Rygal, exasperated. "Did you really tell him that? As if the New Blood has nothing better to do than sharpen my sword?"

"If I had an apprentice," Rygal said, shrugging slightly, "I'd hope he'd keep my sword sharp no matter what titles people call him."

"*If* you ever had an apprentice," Aryion said, taking a sip of the tea, "you would do better to have him as a barber."

Rygal grinned and ran a hand through his unruly hair, then looked at Allie. "I, ah, brought you tea as well. It's quite pleasant on a chilly morning like this—and Mel's right about it being good for you, too."

"Thanks," Allie said, accepting the warm mug. Their hands brushed lightly as she took it, and her heart fluttered unexpectedly in her chest.

Thankfully Mel drew her mind back to the present. "Robin and Bryn are heading out today," he told his mentor. "I was hoping to see them off."

"As was I," Aryion agreed, nodding thoughtfully. "I suppose there's nothing besides our thanks to offer them?"

"I could talk to General Leopold," Allie offered slowly. "Maybe we could make them privateers under the Red Dawn."

"I don't think Robin would agree to that," Mel said doubtfully.

"Well, we should give them something," Allie decided, then returned to her original purpose for the conversation. "We're calling a meeting this morning—I was hoping you all could come. Unless the *Burman Marie* is leaving now," she added, glancing at Mel.

"No, Bryn said they'd leave later this morning," Mel replied, looking at her curiously. "A meeting? What about?"

"A plan. At least—the start of one," Allie told him, wishing for Ĵan's steady confidence in these matters. But the others didn't press, only followed to the council hall looking interested.

Rygal paused at the door, meeting her eyes. "A plan?" he asked quietly. "Have we heard if there's been any change in Caer Sia?"

"No," Allie told him, keeping her voice down. "I'm not sure… at least, we don't know yet if anyone made it out of the city. I'm concerned about what General Leopold mentioned yesterday, about moving the Stone somewhere more secure. Anywhere the Blue Stone is could become a battlefield now—that puts everyone else in danger."

She nodded toward the window, where the distant voices of the multitude drifted inward. They'd barely settled in Lillary, and yet the relative safety was already hanging by a thread.

"Can't argue with that," Rygal murmured grimly. "And there's bound to be somewhere. The Ace-Lord hasn't claimed the world yet, after all."

"Thanks," Allie said with a wry smile. "This is the first war council I've called, you know."

"Well, we're all behind you, Highness," Rygal replied, the familiar crooked grin flickering over his face and lighting his gray-blue eyes. She could see concern and care glimmering there, and felt her heart flutter like a flickering flame.

Don't do this, her mind warned. *Don't turn this into anything more than a friendship. Not when you've only got a few months left to live.*

The Life-Blood Spell would not just go away. She was still marked for death, and it would be easier if her companions accepted that with her. Distance was the wisest choice.

Ajaha and two couriers were already inside, along with General Leopold and Glentree. Allie felt all eyes turn to her expectantly as she entered, and again wished for Ĵan's experience and guidance here. But Ĵan was not here—and someone must take charge in his absence. Someone who had been trained for this time.

She sat at the head of the table, drawing from her uncle's teaching. "Thank you for coming, everyone. I would like to hear your advice and counsel, but first," she looked at her mother, "could you fill everyone in on the latest news?"

Defer to a courier, Ĵan's voice floated into her mind. *That is why they are here. Let them speak while you gather your thoughts.* She could see his face in her mind, the concealed smile shining in his eyes.

Ajaha gave her a slight nod of approval before she began. "Indeed. The most recent message came from Mata City only this morning. The Cooper kingdom is well-defended, and is prepared to defend the north. They have also confirmed that the Aces have not advanced past the mountains. It seems they remain in the valley of Sia, with no immediate intent to attack Lillary."

Relief reflected on every face in the room. Time, Allie realized, was their most important ally, and she was glad they had a moment to determine their next move.

"Thank you," she told her mother before looking at the others. "My concern is about the Blue Stone. As the last uncorrupted Star-Stone, we know the Ace-Lord will come after it eventually—even if he doesn't plan to attack us now, I worry he will soon. It'd be wiser to get both it and Mel in a more secure place."

"Where would you have him go?" Aryion asked quietly. The ranger's voice was still a shadow of his old firm tone, rasping and weak. "If the Aces have claimed Sia, there is nowhere else as secure."

Allie could understand the weariness in his voice. The last few weeks had been so full of battle or frantic movement that, now they'd settled for a moment in Lillary Bay, they had all realized just how tired they were.

"Mel?" she asked, looking at the young apprentice. "You know the Blue Stone's magic better than any of us here. Is there anywhere we could go?"

Mel was frowning, but not in doubt—he looked like he was thinking hard. "Actually… yes," he said finally, sounding almost surprised with himself. He looked at Rygal. "Remember on the quest for Drisilas, when we went to the hama-dryads?"

Rygal's face cleared in understanding. "The hama-dryads… I almost forgot about them. They're not far from here—a few hour's ride, maybe less."

"And the Stone would be safe there?" Aryion asked.

"The hama-dryads guarded the Stone Isilas for centuries after the Dividing War," Ajaha reminded him. "Not only that, their village is guarded by the same pure and powerful magic as the Druids."

"Munben-Lia is one of the Druids' scribes," Mel put in. "His tribe's already offered to help. We could send him a message and ask if they could protect the Stone."

Allie nodded, feeling a surge of relief replace the uncertainty. "All right. Ah—could you send them a message?" she added to her mother.

"Their village is deeply concealed," Ajaha answered slowly, "but we will do what we can to reach them."

"There are some among your father's regiment who know the location, Highness," General Leopold put in. "We were there to defend the hama-dryads years ago, and I can tell you the way."

"Thank you, General," Allie said, deeply grateful. She held his gaze as she said it, offering appreciation as an apology for her attitude yesterday.

Leopold inclined his panther-like head to her, understanding and accepting the olive branch. "Of course, Highness. In the meantime, I suggest you prepare to leave."

"Right," Allie agreed, looking back at the others. "Then Mel and I will go to the hama-dryads. Aryion, you should join us as well," she said, looking at the ranger. "I would ask you to protect Mel, but I know you'll do that without my command," she added.

"It may be wise for a Red Dawn squadron to join you," Ajaha said. "The tribe of Lia can offer security once you have reached them, but these are perilous times for travel."

"We may be able to spare you a squadron of warriors," Leopold said, though he sounded uncertain. Allie pictured the swirl of movement in the harbor, the many injured townsfolk, the hundreds of thousands still displaced…

"I'd rather your men stay here to protect the civilians," she said slowly. "Your men haven't had a rest for the last several weeks."

"None of us have," Rygal said with a tired smile. "Still, I could gather some Guardians and go with you. I doubt any of them will object to a few weeks of quiet with the hama-dryads."

"That—would be great," Allie replied, her heart skipping a beat. "Thank you." She shook the surge of giddiness away—this was a war council, after all. "I place command of Lillary Bay with General Leopold while we're gone—if anything changes, send us a message by way of the dryads."

She stood, prepared to call the meeting to conclusion as she'd seen Jan do. But before she did, the door opened, and a weary, lilting voice reached her ears.

"Terribly sorry for interrupting."

"Lammar!" Rygal exclaimed in shock, moving forward.

The Siren padded slowly into the room. His green scales were caked in grime and clouded in bruises, but the look in his eyes sent a surge of hope through Allie's heart.

"Good news," Lammar said, a smile gradually lighting his exhausted face as he looked at everyone assembled. "It's good news. The High King and the Commander are alive. Admiral Dessian is coming to Lillary as we speak."

They were alive. Allie had braced herself for the worst, and now the unbelievable truth seemed to steal her breath.

Glentree gave a roar of joy and pounded his fist on the table. "Light be praised, I knew they'd manage!" He was the only one who managed to speak—the others seemed struck only by wordless relief. Ajaha pressed her folded hands against her face, tears slipping beneath her closed eyes in a silent prayer of thanks.

"They're alive," Lammar continued, "but the king sent me ahead. He thinks it's wise you move the Stone somewhere safe. Munben-Lia has offered shelter, if the New Blood wishes to take refuge with the tribe of Lia."

Jan wanted us to do that? Allie's thoughts echoed. After all the uncertainty of the morning, to know she had acted rightly brought sudden tears to her eyes. Relief, so sharp it hurt, gripped her heart. Against all likelihood, Jan and her father had lived through the night to the brilliant dawn beyond.

44

The Ranger's Promise

The sun sparkled on the resting sea as Mel and Aryion walked to the harbor.

The storm clouds had dispersed into the distance, lining the horizon in indigo gray. Without the roiling tempest, Mel hoped the *Burman Marie* would have a safe, easy sail to wherever she was headed.

He'd stopped on his way out of the fort to tell his family about their new plan, and the joyful news Lammar had brought. The Smallbuttons would remain in Lillary Bay, protected by the Red Dawn. While he was hesitant to part with them, he knew it was the best choice. Here, his family could remain away from the conflict and safe, for the time being.

"Do you believe the Wildkid warriors will come with the *Blue Moon*?" Aryion asked.

"Hopefully," Mel answered. "At least—that was Dusty's mission. If they're back, I hope she's brought some warriors with her."

"Good," Aryion murmured. They paused on the road, peering west. No sign of the *Blue Moon* yet, Mel noted with disappointment, but through the haze of fog and lingering smoke, it was difficult to tell.

At last Aryion turned. "Well, come along. Bryn's waiting for us."

They walked down the road along the crowded dock. The slender pirate frigate was dwarfed by the large warships of the Red Dawn, but Mel glimpsed her flagless mast.

He noticed it took *Aryion* a moment to identify the ship. Every hour that passed seemed to slowly return more of his old self, but his dark eyes were still flecked with lifeless blue. Every now and then Mel would see the lively spark leave them altogether, leaving his mentor still and silent.

"Tell me again," Aryion began hesitantly, after a pause, "how did you contact Bryn?"

Mel glanced at him. He'd told his mentor the story yesterday. Bryn had filled in the gaps here and there too, explaining Lammar's strategy to get into Castle Salem. But Mel noticed she'd seemed to skip over parts here and there regarding Aryion's rescue. She had only said that when they had found him, he had not been himself.

"The Dricaster pin," he replied. "Lammar found Bryn by tracking her through the Crime Ring networks—all he had to do was show it to a pirate or outlaw to get information. It did take him a while, though."

"I can imagine," Aryion said, nodding to himself as they walked. "And… you were in Tinkeeyo, while that occurred?"

"Yeah—Jan wanted me to learn more about the Blue Stone. There was a new form of power I hadn't heard of before," Mel answered, sidestepping a mud puddle as they moved down the narrow road.

"Really? What was it?"

"It's called the Song of the Stars," Mel said, hesitating a moment. He wished he could speak proudly of the new power he'd learned of, of the peace that had settled over him, of the sheer thrill of feeling the High Light's presence.

Yet the Aces had tainted that. His heart refused to settle on the peace, unable to think of *Allá Alené* without the jarring memories of the Ace-Messenger's words, of the keening screams of the dying dryads, of the ear-splitting cry of agony that had filled his mind.

That had been no illusion, he realized, with a look at his mentor. Aryion's broken memories, the hollow blue light in his eyes, the unnatural new strength that seemed to only weaken his body were the proof. The pure power of the Blue Stone had brought forth a completely new darkness to challenge the good, a darkness Mel feared more than he wanted to admit.

Aryion seemed to notice his hesitation, but didn't ask any more as they reached the pier and the two figures waiting for them.

Bryn stood in her dark woolen cloak, her hair tied back by a colorful bandanna. Next to her stood Robin. The captain moved in evident pain, a bandage wrapped around his head. Their faces reflected both exhaustion and grief; Mel knew what the mission to Ar-Salem had cost them. But they smiled warmly as the two rangers approached.

"Good to see you on your feet again, Captain," Aryion said to Robin, clasping his hand.

"I've taken worse," Robin answered, with a glimmer of his usual swagger.

"You've never fully healed from those, either," Bryn said dryly, looking at Aryion. "Neither have you, for that matter. Harry wanted me to give you these," she said, placing a neatly wrapped bundle in her brother's hand. "Herbs and medicines to help your injuries—it'll build up your strength."

"Strength," Aryion echoed wryly. "Of which variety?"

"It won't get rid of the Ace's… effects," Bryn said slowly. "But it should help your body adjust to normal life again."

Aryion nodded, pocketing the bundle. "Well, thank you. And thank you for everything," he added, looking between the two of them. "I owe you both my life."

"The heiress wanted us to give you this," Mel said, pulling a folded page from his pocket. "It's a more official thanks."

He passed it to Robin, watching the pirate's eyes scan the page before looking up in disbelief. "A pardon?"

"Not exactly," Aryion said with a slight smile. "The heiress can't officially pardon a person with your record without the support of the other ten Coonsian lords. But that letter will ensure your safety in Coonsia for the next twelve months, at least enough for you to rest and recover without being arrested."

"And," Mel added, looking at Bryn, "it's the least we can do after everything you've done."

He paused, not sure if what he wished to offer was something he could realistically do. But he felt it was the right thing to do.

He looked between Bryn and Robin a moment. "I'm not sure where this all will end," he said slowly. "But if I'm still... if I can ever..." he trailed off, fighting to find the right words.

The shadow of a smile crossed Robin's face. "Don't worry about favors, Mel. If you're keeping track, this is payback for your help in Esile City."

"Maybe, but this mission was more than that," Mel said, meeting his eyes. "I know what it's like to fight a war that isn't yours, and I know your crew paid a heavy price." He took a deep breath. "If there's ever anything you need—no matter what, no matter where you are—come find us," he said, glancing at Aryion. Considering how little they knew of their future, he wasn't sure his mentor would approve of this. There was no guarantee either of them would survive to the end of this war, which could make the entire offer baseless.

But Aryion was nodding. "Yes. You have our word."

Robin looked down. Bryn glanced between Aryion and Mel for a moment before she spoke, her voice quiet. "Very well. A pledge for a pledge. Thank you."

Mel embraced them, his heart filled with gratitude for them both. "Where are you headed next?" he asked.

Robin shrugged slightly. "Well, we'll return to Kamon to pick up the *Consort* and the rest of the crew. After that, wherever the wind leads, I suppose. Perhaps south again, towards the Durbin Strait."

"Travel safely," Aryion told them. "You may have clemency in Coonsia for now, but I doubt that extends to the Randuins."

"We'll be all right," Bryn reassured him. She smiled at Mel and nodded toward her brother. "Take care of him, will you."

"I will," Mel said. It was the least he could do, after the countless times his mentor had saved his life. If Mel could help him now, he would.

They watched as the *Burman Marie* sailed from Lillary Bay. The pirate frigate had scarcely vanished over the horizon when a warship appeared, sails torn from her long voyage, limping steadily for Lillary Bay.

The *Blue Moon* glided over the waves, finally reaching the safety of the harbor.

· · · · · ·

Reunion. Despite all the darkness, the death, the horror that had transpired, the joy and relief of the *Blue Moon's* return momentarily banished all else from Allie's mind.

The scenes painted themselves forever in her memory. The cheers of the crowds as the last of the defenders returned. Admiral Dessian, caked in mud and grime but raising his hands in victory. Dusty and her siblings, fur damp and ragged, tired faces shining with smiles as they set foot in Lillary.

And at last, leaning upon each other, bruised and battered, came Jan and Dandio.

Alive.

She felt a choked sob of relief tear from her throat as she moved to meet them. Even after Lammar's words, some part of her had still feared the worst. But here they were, by a miracle she could scarcely believe.

Iriam followed behind them as they disembarked. Wherever the Neutral had been, whatever sources he'd reached, Allie would ask later. For now, she moved away from Rygal and ran forward into her father's embrace.

His armor was filthy, and fresh blood leaked from half a dozen wounds, but he took her in his arms and held her so tightly Allie didn't notice. She felt Jan's arms wrap around her, felt the tears build in her chest. For a moment, the crushing pain and darkness was lifted from her shoulders, and she could rest in their embrace.

"Are you all right?" Dandio asked, pulling away at last.

"Yes—are you?" Allie began hesitantly, noting the blood staining their clothes.

"We are fine," Jan assured her. "We have Admiral Dessian to thank for that."

"Very little was my doing, sire," Dessian said behind him, shaking his head in wonder. "You will not believe our story."

Then Ajaha was there, her eyes shining in the golden sunlight. Dandio strode forward, unhindered by his injuries as he took his wife in his arms and kissed her for a long time.

The Wildkids disembarked as the watching crowd cheered, both in joy that they too had survived Caer Sia, and in gratitude that they had come to aid in the war. Dusty stepped forward with a wide smile as she saw Rygal and Allie. "Glad to see you're both still alive," she commented as they both hugged her. Her shining eyes turned to Aryion, standing next to Mel, and relief and wonder crossed her face. "Lammar mentioned—I couldn't believe it—I suppose I'll have to wait to hear everything that's happened to all of you."

"Get some rest first," Rygal told her. "You look about ready to fall asleep where you stand."

"Not yet," Dusty replied wryly. "We've arranged for my squadron to come with you to the hama-dryads. The High King requested I meet with their chieftain about our clans' alliance, and my warriors can offer protection."

"Indeed," came Iriam's deep voice behind them. "I am sorry to interrupt these reunions," he said gently, looking at Jan, "but there are many pressing matters we must attend to, and I fear it may be wise for some of us to be off."

Jan nodded, looking at Allie. "Lammar brought my message?"

"Yes—we're ready to head out," Allie answered. "Mel and I figured the Blue Stone would need to be somewhere safer, but I wasn't sure what to do about Isilas."

"No, no, you did exactly as you ought." Jan squeezed her shoulder lightly, a smile on his battered face, which caused the last of her doubts to fade away.

She followed them all back to the fort, where horses waited for their departure. Despite the ride ahead, she didn't feel weary. The hope filling her seemed a steady and sure light, hope that caused the shadows to pale. Not even the darkness of the Life-Blood Spell could dim its glow.

Cursed light. It blazed through the smoky air in the ruins of Castle Sia, glaring off the water and into the Ace-Deputy's eyes.

The deaths filling the last day and night, the triumph of the destruction they had inflicted, even the satisfaction that his plot for the Hummingbird was coming about quite nicely… it seemed burned away by the horrific truth he had just witnessed. He stood before the ruined pier of the small cove near the castle, staring across the water, where the Liznee warship had vanished mere hours ago.

They were within his grasp—*blazes*, it was maddening. He'd tasted their fear so strongly as he'd launched the blast—and then the figures had appeared, deflecting his blow, rising out of the shadows he had come to trust.

He had forgotten that others commanded those shadows. His master's brethren, forgotten for centuries. Surely the Deputy couldn't have known they would come—he had never fought the Druids, only heard of them, when his master had first imbued the eleven Aces with his icy magic and taught them the ways of the darkness. Druids. Prophets from a bygone age, back when the mortals used to seek the Light with greater faith, and skepticism was not such a common weakness.

No, it was maddening that they had chosen this moment to return.

The low, hollow voice of an enchanted orc drew him from his angry and fearful musings. "You have been summoned."

The Deputy rounded on him irritably. "By whom? Don't tell me that brute Redeyes has chosen now to rejoin this conquest."

He doubted that. Redeyes, the Rufa Brownaes, and the rest of his master's forces that had survived the battle in Gayrile would still be on a ship, forced to sail the long way around West Coonsia to reach Ar-Salem from the south. Thanks to the Cooper's blockade, they would lose days—maybe weeks—of time. Perhaps they should have done as the false reports had suggested, and attacked Mata City after all.

But the enchanted orc shook his head. "No. My lord has summoned you."

Unease chilled the Deputy's heart, as much as he tried to ignore it. He turned away from the broken dock, settling himself as he strode down the road to where a darker shadow waited.

The Ace-Lord's purple-red eyes swept over Castle Sia. The enchanted soldiers and mercenaries had made easy work of raiding and plundering the palace, but the Dal-kerri had inflicted more damage—doors knocked in, windows broken, elegant halls stained by their foul paws.

"You seem troubled, Deputy," the Ace-Lord commented quietly.

The Deputy paused, glancing around the castle. "No… my lord. I did not expect you so soon."

"I heard a rumor of a troubling matter," the Ace-Lord replied. "I came to know your report. Tell me. Who caused this?"

He swept a black-clawed hand downward, gesturing to a silver trident embedded in a Dal-kerri hound. Behind it, a cherry tree had wrenched its roots from the ground like a beast woken from slumber. Teeth and blades had hacked off its limbs, but its roots were still twisted and locked around the throat of the Bruin it had strangled before its fall.

The forest and the sea. Two enemies long forgotten.

The Deputy faltered, knowing there was no easy way to break the news. "They…were here, my lord," he said at last. "The ones you have told us of…the ones believed gone. Ones with ice and shadows like us, but fighting alongside the mortals." He hesitated a moment longer. "The ones who call themselves the Druids."

The Ace-Lord was completely silent. Beneath the hood, the Deputy could see his eyes glittering—not in interest, not in rage. A strange sort of surprise and excitement that a new challenger had entered his game.

"So," he mused after a long pause. "The Druids have returned, have they? How very interesting. I did not expect their involvement in the least."

"They roused the sea," the Deputy continued, faltering. "The trees we can counter—I do not know about the Nøkken. If the Druids have joined the mortals..." He trailed off, unable to conceal his uncertainty.

"Is that fear I sense in your voice, Deputy?" the Ace-Lord asked, his voice low. "Do you not know that even the Druids fell before me in the Dividing War? Yes, this is very unexpected... but it is not something to fear, only a sign that my vision is soon to come to completion." He turned, taking a step toward the twisted tree. "As for the spirits of Orlell, what are they but wood and water? Even the sea is subdued beneath the ice."

White ice spread up the tree trunk, shattering it into crystallized fragments. The Ace-Lord faced the Deputy. "The Druids wish a war with us. Their fate is sealed." He nodded toward Castle Sia. "As for the mortals, let them drown in their despair. The destruction of this city shall be a testament to what is to come."

The Deputy nodded. The brief moment of unease had passed. He was again confident in his master's plan, and watched in both satisfaction and awe as the white ice that had long ago consumed his mortal village crept up Castle Sia's towers.

45

The Wielder's Task

Evening had just begun to fall as the riders reached the lands of the hama-dryads.

Mel had only spent a few days with the tribe of Lia during the quest for Drisilas. He recalled the exhaustion and fear he'd felt then, desperate to find help for an injured Dandio.

The quiet forest still seemed much the same as the group rode through the trees and the dirt path became a well-trodden road. Willows swayed above a rippling creek, and a soft breeze danced through the cattails and reeds.

He turned his eyes back to the travelers. Twenty Wildkid warriors had accompanied them. Though weary from their long voyage and the sudden fight in Caer Sia, they had agreed to join the group without hesitation. Rygal and Allie rode with them; Mel could hear them talking quietly with Dusty, explaining all that had transpired over the last several months.

"The guards are coming to meet us," Aryion called softly to Dusty, drawing Mel's attention to the left. His mentor sat in the saddle, blue-flecked eyes scanning the shadowed woods. In the evening twilight, Mel couldn't see anyone.

"They are?" he asked, puzzled. "I—don't see them."

Aryion nodded without a trace of doubt. "Five of them. They carry spears."

Dusty motioned for the group to halt. A few moments later, the guards came into view, moving through the trees without a sound and forming up on the road. But they waved the riders onward. "Our chieftain is expecting you," one explained. "The dryads informed us of your coming."

They thanked him and rode on into the village. Clusters of dome-like huts filled the grove, their walls made of the silvery willow bark. Firelight lit them within, casting a golden glow through the trees. The dense trees rose up before the entrance, yet the branches drew back as if pulled by a powerful wind, admitting them forward. The strange, ever-present whisper Mel remembered from the Druids' cavern hung in the air.

Rygal looked around the shadowed woods with interest. "I think you mentioned dryads the last time we were here," Mel heard him comment to Dusty. "Can you see them?"

"I hear them," Dusty replied. "They speak the Diné tongue, but I can only catch a few words."

Mel looked up at the boughs of the willows as they passed underneath. As with the Druids, he didn't feel afraid, only strangely invasive. The words he heard and the breeze whispering over his face did not seem meant for mortal ears. It reminded him of the High Light's voice—powerful, quiet, calling every fiber in his body to life—but in a different way. Then again, the dryad's magic had come from the High Light also—pure magic from the beginning of the world.

Munben-Lia met them as they dismounted in the glade. The wizened chieftain stood clad in the same simple gray robes. Beside him stood another hama-dryad, younger, who carried a bow and quiver slung on his back. As his eyes rested on Mel, his pale blue face spread in a welcoming smile.

"It is good to see you again, child," he said as Mel swung down from the saddle. "When we last met, your quest was to return the High King's sword. I understand that quest was successful."

Mel clasped the warrior's hand as he recognized him. "Kalos-Lia— good to see you too. Drisilas is safe, and so is the Stone," he added, looking at Munben.

The aged chieftain inclined his head in approval, then moved to meet the other companions. Rygal and Dusty had both been here before, and greeted Kalos cheerfully before introducing the others.

"Your lodgings have been arranged for however long you have need of them," Munben said. "The High King has sent word that he will arrive in several days, once matters in Lillary have been attended to. He urges you to rest in the meantime."

"Thank you, sir," Allie said, but Mel could see the uncertainty on her face. "We appreciate your hospitality, but—we don't want to bring the Aces here."

Munben smiled slightly. "Your concern is noted, but unnecessary, Heiress. Rest assured that the tribe of Lia long guarded the Star-Stone after the Dividing War, and we are prepared to guard you along with it."

His gentle words helped ease Mel's own fears. The rippling creek, the rustle of the breeze, assured him of the refuge and rest to be found here. He pushed the uncertain questions away for now, allowing his mind to settle, like he had in the Magno Forest all those weeks ago while stars had spread above.

Several hama-dryad soldiers directed them to the stables for the horses. Others showed them to the huts where they could rest. The huts each held four beds. Two of Dusty's brothers had already claimed theirs. Mel set his belongings on the third bed and considered staying to sleep—he'd slept fleetingly the last few nights, wrapped up in thoughts and worries for one thing or another. Having Aryion back eased his heart, but he couldn't help fearing his mentor would never fully recover.

He glanced over at Aryion again. Seeing the guards through the shadows, even before the Wildkids had sensed them, was proof of the strange new abilities the Aces had given him. Mel wasn't sure why yet… but knowing the Ace-Deputy, it meant nothing good.

He pushed that concern away for now, looking around the village. "This reminds me of Kamon," he commented to his mentor. The tropical village might not resemble the willows and oaks of the forest, but the hospitality of the Kamoni and hama-dryads was a shared trait.

Aryion's brow was furrowed as he looked around, taking everything in as if trying to recall it. "You've been here before?" he asked finally.

"Yep, during the quest for Drisilas," Mel answered. "We weren't here very long. But Dandio had been bitten by a serpentine, so we had to stop and find help."

Aryion nodded slowly. He still seemed lost. Escaping the Ace-Lord's clutches had plunged him immediately back into a reality he struggled to understand.

"What can you… remember?" Mel asked hesitantly.

Aryion let out a breath. "I am not sure. The information is all still there, I think—images, sounds, names, faces. But none of them make sense—there's no meaning attached to them. They seem clouded."

"Bryn worried maybe you'd been shattered," Mel ventured. She'd mentioned this during her recounting of the mission to Ar-Salem. The possibility had been so dark Mel didn't even want to think of that. "We know that didn't happen though—because you can remember things."

"No. That's… that's not what happened," Aryion said. "The Deputy… wanted to find out if the enchantment—if one could be forced to swear it. So he gave me a part of his own strength to resist it… as far as I recall."

His face had darkened, eyes glimmering hollow blue in the evening light. A haunted look had come over his expression again like a thundercloud.

"You're back now," Mel said, trying to steer the conversation away from the dark memories. "You're here. It's over."

"I think so," Aryion answered quietly. There was a long pause, then he shook his head. "Hang it all, I—I need it to make sense. Could you… remind me of some things?"

"Sure," Mel said, nodding rapidly.

Aryion thought a moment. "All right… I have been training you for two years?"

"One," Mel corrected. "After the quest for the Shards."

"One, yes," Aryion said, nodding. "And our first mission was to Esile City, which is when we met the crew of the *Marie*."

"Yep," Mel verified.

"But meeting them wasn't our mission…" Aryion murmured, frowning.

"No, we were hunting Terrax."

"And we were successful." Aryion looked at him uncertainly. "Right?"

"Yep," Mel said again, forcing a smile. "Last I heard, he's still in prison, and he'll probably be there for a long time."

"Good. Good." Aryion's face had cleared, the haunted shadows slowly fading away again. "When did you swear the Oath?"

Mel tightened his fist over the scar on his palm. "After you were taken, I…I swore it to protect the Stone and keep it from corruption.

Cahadras said that was the best promise I could make. I had to give up my own plans—trust the Druids to rescue you instead."

"So you redeemed the Blood Oath," Aryion said thoughtfully. "You swore it for something selfless—that's hardly ever happened in history, as far as I can recall."

"Really?" Mel asked, his heart lifting. He had been so afraid of Aryion's reaction to this decision. Swearing a Blood Oath was one matter—it was something else entirely when that Oath barred Mel from helping with Aryion's rescue. He had feared his mentor might resent him for it.

But Aryion nodded, and a smile flickered over his features. "Yes, Mel, it's a good thing. I'm very proud of you."

Mel glanced away, his face warming at the praise. "Thanks. I—I just hope I'm still able to do something to help the fight."

"How do you mean?"

Mel let out a breath. The words of the song drifted through his mind. Learning about the *Alené* had been encouraging, but he was unsure if he'd ever be able to bring himself to use that power again. Not when the Ace's voice might hiss in his mind, clouding over the comfort of the Light. The horrific illusions cast inside the shield still snarled in his thoughts, darkening his dreams.

"I learned about the Song," he said at last. "I was able to use the Stone in Tinkeeyo to help the soldiers, but after that... after that, the Aces were able to... they cast an illusion inside it. I'm—I don't know if I can do it again."

"Inside the shield?" Aryion frowned, looking deeply concerned. "I thought the Stone protects you from the Aces' illusions."

"It normally does. I think the *Alené* spell makes you more vulnerable," Mel said slowly. He wasn't sure about this, but he recalled Iriam warning about something like that once. "But I know I have to try again. The spell worked, once I stopped trying so hard and just let it happen. And I heard the High Light's voice—well, not heard exactly. More like sensed."

He frowned, seeking the right word. Nothing accurately described the voice that had spoken over him in the scribehouse, calming his fears, girding him with a strength far greater than anything he could have on his own. Remembering that soothed his lingering frustration and fear of the Ace-Messenger's illusions.

"The High Light," Aryion echoed. For a moment, the flecks of blue faded in his eyes, and his battered face relaxed in thoughtful peace. "I remember the High Light too. Those memories don't seem affected. In an odd way, I don't suppose I ever forgot."

"I don't think the Aces can take Him away," Mel said.

Aryion nodded slowly, looking at his apprentice again. "Mel, do you remember what Cahadras told you in Kamon—about the Light still commanding the world, even with the Ace-Lord in it?"

The tone of his voice had changed to one he often used while teaching Mel something during long days on the trail. Mel felt himself smile, both at the familiarity, and at the fact that his mentor had recalled this detail without the slightest prompting. "Yeah. I guess it's less scary remembering that."

"Yes," Aryion agreed, studying him. "I understand your hesitation to use the Stone again. I don't blame you for your fear. But that has been your calling. The Light will protect you in your mission—and so will I."

Mel met his gaze. There were still flecks of blue in his dark eyes, still bruises on his face, still a shadow dampening his mind. And yet Mel could see that slowly, he was beginning to heal.

"Thanks," he said softly, feeling as though the High Light's voice had whispered behind his mentor's words, moving like the wind through the willow trees.

. . . . . .

It was Iriam's quiet voice that drew Ĵan out of reading reports.

Several days had passed in Lillary Bay, allowing his body to rest and the injuries sustained from the battle to heal. All the same, there was little time to sit and rest. Dandio was already at work organizing the Red Dawn, assessing all that had been lost in Caer Sia and making certain the citizens were well-protected. He was clearly determined to remain in the thick of the action, prepared to decide the next strategy in the war.

Despite this, Ĵan could tell Dandio was growing as weary of the war as everyone else. For too long, they had been fighting, sustaining heavy losses, losing many lives. The bloodshed, the grief, the anger of all that had been taken, had begun to wear on the mortals, and Ĵan could not stop the nagging doubt creeping into his mind. How long would they last? The Ace-Lord had planted seeds of fear and corruption in every mortal heart, and he could afford to drag the conflict out as long as was needed until the mortals either surrendered or were destroyed.

And yet the end had begun to glimmer in the distance. He had talked with Iriam, wanting the Neutral's advice for the plan growing in his mind. With Caer Sia fallen, the Aces would attempt to lengthen the war farther, letting despair crush any resistance. The best move for them now was to strike back quickly.

And so Ĵan had begun planning a full-out attack on Ar-Salem.

Specific strategy and details would be decided soon. First, he would need both Iriam's advice and the support of the other nine Coonsian

Lords. Many had already sworn to join with the Liznees—Lord Roan of the Coopers, Lord Fireclaw of the kragons, Lord Andros of Tinkeeyo, and Lord Casper of the Direns, to name a few. The most recent ally had been Dusty's father, Chief Sorrel of the N'Tell. But others had thus far remained out of direct battle, such as the Hyenins and the other kingdoms of West Coonsia, who aided the supply lines but had not yet entered the conflict.

Though their kingdoms were allied, asking them to join an offensive strike was not a request Jan could make lightly. An assault of this nature against the Aces would end in one of two ways—death to the Ace-Lord, or death to every mortal that joined the charge. There would be no second chance. This battle would end the war.

Five willing dryads had gone out from Lillary across Coonsia, and two had already returned with answering letters. The messages, which were from Lord Ter-Li of the Cagari and Lord Ceral of Arkran, had contained good news. Their kingdoms, despite the danger, both swore to join the Liznees in the attack.

Once he heard from the others, they would arrange a war council. Ajaha had left that morning, headed to Mata City. The Cooper kingdom was now the last northern stronghold for the mortals, and it would also be the best place to begin the march to reach Ar-Salem.

Jan had just sat down at the table in Lillary's small meeting hall, intending to compose his response to the two lords. Iriam's deep voice reached him, drawing him out of his thoughts about the coming battle. "Forgive me for interrupting you, sire."

Jan looked up, shaking his head slightly with a smile. It was good to have the Neutral back to his usual self, now that he was recovered. Jan was incredibly grateful he was here. "Not to worry, Iriam. What is it?"

Iriam's purple-red eyes scanned briefly over the letters, then met Jan's gaze. "I understand some of the lords have replied?"

"Two of them, and they both agree to join us," Jan answered, setting the papers and inkwell aside. "Do you believe... do you believe this is our best course of action?"

Many things had changed over his years as king, but his reliance on Iriam's advice had stayed constant. It did not matter how many times Jan reassured himself—without the Neutral's guidance, he would feel lost. It was Iriam who had helped him understand the High Light's guiding more often than anyone else.

"I do not doubt its necessity," Iriam answered. "The only uncertainty, I fear, is in the outcome."

Jan let out a breath. Yes, that was the question. If attacking the Aces was what they were meant to do by the High Light, that was one thing. But if they were all meant to die... was that something he could ask of his people? Was that what the war led to?

Iriam spoke before Jan could voice that grim question. "If you have a moment, then come. There is someone who wishes to speak to you."

Jan stood stiffly—his body still ached from the desperate battle in Caer Sia. But Iriam's words distracted him from the pain with a new interest. He arched an eyebrow curiously as the Neutral led him from the meeting room and up the stairs to the upper bulwarks of the fort. "The dryads, I expect?" he asked. "Which messengers have returned?"

But he trailed off abruptly as Iriam led him onto the walls of Fort Lillary, where a figure gleaming gold stood waiting. She turned to him as he approached, flashing blue eyes meeting his inquiring gaze.

"I am glad to see you, High King," Cahadras said, as Jan bowed to her. "The Stars have seen the losses in Caer Sia, and many feared you lost."

"My lady," Jan said, startled to see the Star again. Since the battle with the Bruin, he had neither seen nor heard from the Stars. Everything that had happened since had caused them to slip to the back of his mind. Yet here stood Cahadras before him. "I am pleasantly surprised to see you. For what do I owe the pleasure of your visit?"

Cahadras studied him a moment. "Have you Isilas, son of Galaruel?"

Jan paused, startled by this question. "Yes, my lady." He reached into his breast pocket, producing the shining gold case. *Guard it well,* Cahadras had charged him. He still remembered the way she had pulled the pale, corrupted Stone from Drisilas' hilt before encasing it with liquid gold.

When Sia had been attacked, he had entrusted the Stone to Iriam; if he and Dandio were slain, they could not risk letting Isilas fall into the Ace-Lord's hands. Yet they had survived, and Iriam had returned it to him upon reaching Lillary.

He offered it to Cahadras, who held it in her palm and looked up at him again. "Tell me, High King, do you recall what I told you of the Stone's corruption?"

Jan bowed his head. "Yes, my lady—that is why I gave it up, so that it may be redeemed again. It cannot exist as a weapon of war—nor do I have any right to Wield it any longer."

"Indeed," Cahadras said quietly. "You speak true in that it must only be used for its true purpose. No longer must it be a weapon of war, for thus it was corrupted. Yet the time has come for it to be Wielded again."

The golden case turned molten, receding into the fiery light surrounding her, until she held the Star-Stone out before him.

Jan stared at her in disbelief as white light shone over Fort Lillary.

For the last several months, he had expected a new Wielder would be chosen to take up Isilas and somehow undo the corruption. Surely Cahadras did not mean that role for *him*, not after his actions were the very reason the Stone's purpose had been warped.

"Is it not—am I not—" he stammered at last, glancing over at Iriam, whose dark face gave nothing away. At last he faced Cahadras again. "I am the reason the Stone is corrupted. Surely my hands will only worsen that."

"You speak rightly," Cahadras answered levelly. "But as your hands corrupted it, thus your hands must see about its restoration. You have done wrongly with the Stone, High King. Now, you must choose to do right."

She still held Isilas before her. Ĵan could see his own reflection in the glassy surface, his face worn and weary, confusion and surprise in his eyes. The white light blazed in his face, and he felt the Essence stir in his heart as though answering to a call.

Restoration. He had known it must happen from the moment Redeyes' claws had torn the Marks on his chest, the price of twisting the Stone's magic. The wrong had been atoned for, but the matter of Isilas had yet to be made right. He could never have imagined that it would be by his own hands.

Slowly, he took the white Stone from the Star Queen, feeling the familiar weight and the cool against his fingers. Far colder than it had been when he'd first taken it up, back when the hama-dryads had returned it to the Liznees as a token of gratitude and plea for protection.

Protection. The original purpose of the Star-Stone. A purpose Mel had learned far better than he ever had. Yet now he had the chance to make it right.

Jan raised his eyes to the Star Queen's gaze. "So I choose. If there is anything I may do to restore the corrupted Stone, know that I will do it."

The trace of a smile crossed Cahadras' face, and she nodded. "Very well. Be wise in your actions, High King. Trust in the Light."

For a moment, her words echoed those of a softer voice from another time, quiet and gentle. The task of Wielder, one he believed he must abandon, now called to him again. He closed his eyes a moment to conceal the unexpected tears, and Luet's face swam in his mind.

When he opened his eyes again, Cahadras had vanished, leaving only a glittering trail of golden sparks. But Isilas remained in his palm, casting white light over the walls as dusk fell.

46

The Dryad's Dance

Time passed peacefully among the tribe of Lia, and Allie could not recall when she had been more grateful for so many days of rest.

The hama-dryad village seemed far away from the rest of the world, detached from the war. Still, the subtle signs of the conflict were constant. The dryads brought news each day to Munben-Lia, warnings of battle or troubles elsewhere in the world. Their reports helped keep Allie's focus on what was coming, kept her from falling back into the darkness that had nearly consumed her.

Jan arrived on their seventh morning among the Lia, with the Star-Stone Isilas. He recounted, to his captivated audience, how he had again taken up the task of Wielder. Not by his own design or power, he had told them, but as the Light willed, giving him the opportunity to undo the wrongs he had caused.

"Cahadras said something like that after we escaped Castle Droco," Allie told him hesitantly as they sat around the fire. "She said the atoning would lie less in your past, and more in what you'd do in the present. I wonder if this is what she meant."

"Perhaps," Jan mused, one hand playing lightly over the Star-Stone. While Mel usually kept the Blue Stone in his pocket, Jan had requested a simple chain and case for Isilas, keeping it near him at all times. The hama-dryads had crafted it with ease—though, Allie remembered, it was they who had first forged Drisilas with the Stone in the hilt.

She was glad Jan was here. With both her parents engaged in the war, her uncle was a welcome comfort as he'd been many times past. She didn't ask about plans of war, or details about the battle he'd alluded they were preparing for.

No—for the first time since the war had begun, she forced herself to rest and enjoy the silence. The peaceful village, nestled deep in the forest, was a welcome distraction from the darkness. She could talk with her friends, and be with Rygal, as much as the days allowed.

Still, reality asserted itself constantly in her mind. The end was coming, as surely as the early signs of autumn had begun to tinge the trees of the wood. The war would end, and with it the curse, which dug its teeth into her heart and threatened to take her with it.

She no longer fought against that fate. No longer ignored the words of the Prophecy. If she were to die, it would be in the High Light's plan—not as the Ace-Lord willed. The final strike Jan had mentioned would end the war one way or another, and she knew without an ounce of doubt that she would have her chance then to face the Ace-Lord. The Vessel would kill him. The Willing Warrior's sacrifice would be fulfilled.

No, her fear no longer lay in her own death, though the weight of it threatened to crush her to pieces. Rather, it was the nagging concern for how her companions would react to the fact.

Her mind knew the wisest choice would be distance. Her loved ones had already suffered enough grief and loss, and she hated to think that her death would further their pain. Jan alone could understand this— for years, he'd been certain his Marks must be atoned by his death, causing him to hide the truth from everyone. He feared for her, she knew that. His stubborn heart would never allow him to accept the horrible truth. Yet when it happened, Allie knew he would understand her reasoning and would accept it in time.

Mel worried for her too—but he had Aryion now, and Allie doubted anything would shake his newfound joy now that his mentor was free. Aryion was recovering more each day, and strangely, Allie found the ranger the easiest to talk to. They had both lost a piece of themselves to the Aces forever, and they both had been given powers they did not understand. The truth of the Life-Blood Spell troubled him as much as the others, but he agreed that killing the Ace-Lord would be Allie's best course of action.

It was easier to distance herself from them. All of them but Rygal, who seemed neither to accept nor deny the inevitable ending ahead for her. He was simply there with her despite it, and however her mind demanded that she push him away—for his own sake, more than hers— she could not find it within her. Not when his eyes lit up when he was with her and her heart would fill with warmth at his every glance.

Hasn't he lost enough? Her thoughts would warn when she felt that flutter in her heart. *You'll draw him in to distract yourself from the future, and the ending will break his heart.*

But he knew how it would end and cared for her all the same, and she loved him the more for it.

Weeks passed. The days were warm and muggy, but the mornings and evenings carried a chill in the wind that promised the end of summer. The companions had been welcomed in among the tribe of Lia, and they helped to harvest the crops, gather water from the stream, and repair the rounded domes of the huts when the weather beat on them. Dusty and the other Wildkids joined the warriors in training and preparing for battle. Aryion and Mel went hunting with Kalos-Lia and the other young men of the village almost daily. Ĵan was often speaking with Munben, learning much from the aged chieftain whose people had long protected the Star-Stone.

So Allie was often with Rygal. They never spoke of the Life-Blood Spell or the war, rarely of the grief that lingered. The time was enough to enjoy an illusion of safety, a vision of what could have been.

They had been with the hama-dryads for around two weeks when the news reached them from the dryads. Allie joined Mel, Ĵan, Aryion, Rygal, and Dusty in Munben-Lia's large meeting hut as evening fell. The nine lords had all answered Ĵan's call, promising to join the coming fight.

"So what's going to happen next?" Mel asked curiously.

Ĵan took a sip of his tea, thinking a moment. "There is to be a council in Mata City in four days' time," he said at last. "We had thought to wait a few more weeks, to allow time to hone our strategy and gather more warriors. However, it is of the Druids' advice—and my own judgment— that we must strike soon."

"Why?" Dusty asked slowly. Her voice was calm, but Allie could hear her hesitation.

Munben-Lia answered, his voice filled with steady determination. "Because, young one, our time is running short. The Ace-Lord seeks to draw the struggle out as much as he can. What has happened to Caer Sia may happen to many other kingdoms, until he has worn the mortals down and our fear destroys our remaining resolve."

"And we cannot allow that to happen," Ĵan said grimly. "A war council must be held. We have already gathered many warriors—if we take too long to gather others, there may not be a kingdom to fight for by the time we feel prepared."

"So we're leaving?" Allie asked, trying to hide her disappointment. She'd known they would eventually. Return to the war, face the darkness again.

"The day after tomorrow," Jan replied, giving her a slight smile. "I shall return to Lillary Bay this evening to meet with Dandio and Iriam, to review our strategy. From there, we will set sail to Mata City once you have joined us. Enjoy the time. Let yourself rest, but be ready."

Two days. Hardly enough time to wrap her mind around what was coming. But leave she must. Her final mission awaited.

The hut was strangely silent that night without Jan to talk to. Not that there was much to speak about—she didn't wish to burden him with her thoughts, not with so much already troubling his mind. She slept haltingly, visions of the Ace-Lord's cruel smile and the swirling black gateway reaching into her dreams.

Morning dawned bright and sunny, the trees glittering with dew. Birds called in the forest, joining the conversation and noise in the hama-dryad village.

Activity greeted Allie's eyes as she left her hut. Hama-dryads moved busily throughout the village, carrying baskets or firewood, while others minded cookpots.

Mel emerged from the woods with Aryion, each carrying an armload of firewood. At the direction of Kalos-Lia, they deposited it on a growing pile in the center of the cleared space. Rygal was helping trim the overhanging branches of the willow above them. Curious, Allie pulled on her cloak and moved to join them.

"The day does not look like rain," Kalos was saying cheerfully as the rangers set down the wood. "It will be a fine evening for the festivities tonight." His gaze landed on Allie, and he smiled and nodded to her.

"Good morning, Heiress."

"Morning," Allie answered, glancing at her companions. "What's going on? Don't tell me this is some sort of farewell party for us."

Kalos chuckled and shook his head. "Indeed not, I regret. Tonight is the *Onalia*—a celebration of summer's end, where my people gather and enjoy a night of food and song. Despite the darkness without, our tradition will proceed, and we hope you will join us."

"Jan told us to relax," Mel pointed out with a grin. "This isn't a bad way to do it."

"Oh, there is very little relaxing," Dusty told him. She and Joesp walked out of one of the huts with an armload of vines. "If this is anything like the *Onalias* we have in Kasabren, most of the night is spent dancing and singing and all sorts of merry making. You're absolutely exhausted by the end and it's wonderful."

"Dancing?" Rygal repeated, clipping the branch Kalos indicated.

"I don't know how," Mel said immediately.

"That is the fun of it," Joesp told him with a grin.

"As much fun as I believe it will be," Aryion said, a wry smile crossing his face, "the chieftain still wishes a ring of guards patrolling the edge of the village."

"If we rotate shifts, there will still be time for everyone to enjoy themselves," Dusty said. "And you'll regret it if you don't join in," she added, looking pointedly at Rygal. He shrugged nonchalantly.

"*I* never said I wouldn't join in. Nellioh said the food is the main part of it, anyway."

Allie hid a smile as she turned away. A festival, she thought, her heart lifting. That was just what she needed today. One last night of happiness before they returned to matters of war.

As Kalos had explained, the food was indeed a central part of the *Onalia*. The sun had barely lightened the sky before the sounds and smells of cooking filled the air. The aroma of roasting meat and steaming harvest drifted through the village as Allie and Dusty set to work loading the wagons.

"I hope you're excited," Dusty commented with a grin, setting a bundle beside the packs. "I doubt it's common for anyone outside of the tribe to be included in the festivities."

"Do the Wildkids have a celebration like this too?" Allie asked, examining her sword blade. She'd made sure to keep it sharp and clean during the weeks in Lia, but it would be good to sharpen it again before they left to Mata City.

"Sort of," Dusty said. "At least—we have an *Onalia* at the summer solstice. It's one of the only times all five Clans agree to gather in peace, no matter how much fighting has happened before." She nodded back toward the village. "This, I think, will be a little different."

"I hope the hama-dryads sing some of the same songs," Graysil said, looking hopefully at her older sister.

"I'm not sure," Dusty said with a shrug. "Perhaps you could talk with the musicians beforehand to find out." She looked at Allie again. "What about you? I'm sure there are plenty of parties in Caer Sia."

"Oh, yes," Allie said with a laugh. "There's an event practically every weekend, and we have balls at the castle every few months. Lords and ladies and knights come and the dancing will go on all night. Once I wore right through a pair of shoes from all the dances."

She still remembered the way the entire sole of the shoe had fallen out as she'd climbed up the stairs. It was the hardest she'd ever seen Jan laugh.

But those memories were tinged with sadness now. It only reminded her of Caer Sia and what was lost. The only home she'd ever known was gone—though she didn't have to think about returning. The war would end with her.

She shook that thought away, noticing Dusty's careful gaze. The Wildkid's face showed the same sorrow and concern as the rest of her friends. Once, it would have made Allie frustrated, but now, her pride had faded enough to accept the sympathy.

Thankfully Dusty didn't bring that topic up, adjusting her expression to a smile again. "Well—I imagine this'll feel different than a Caer Sian ball, but I'm certain we'll enjoy it all the same."

Allie nodded, turning her attention back to the wagon as they loaded the gear for tomorrow's ride. One last night. She tried not to dwell on any other thoughts.

Night approached, and the lanterns throughout the village seemed to light the entire forest with a golden glow. Wind blew through the trees as Allie, Dusty, and Graysil moved toward the center of the village. The breeze tugged at Allie's hair and clothes, and for a moment, she thought she could catch the whispered voices of the dryads. But perhaps that was just her imagination.

Other voices rose into the evening sky. The village shone with life and firelight. A great bonfire blazed in the center of the village, and the hama-dryads moved eagerly around it, talking and calling out to each other. To Allie's right, a long wooden table bore earthen platters of food where a woodland feast awaited them.

Munben's voice filled the air as they entered. "Welcome, friends. Tonight, lay aside your cares and fears, and let us thank the Light for all we have. Whatever dark troubles lay outside of Lia, let this be a place of joy this evening." Allie glimpsed his twinkling blue eyes through the eager crowds as he gestured toward the tables. "And let us enjoy our feast."

Cheering and talking, groups of hama-dryads moved toward the food. Allie followed Dusty, but was caught by the crowd in their eager rush to the table. She attempted to weave her way back out, and a platter of roasted meat, squash, and greens was pressed into her hands by a matronly hama-dryad. She managed to break away from the lines of waiting dancers, carrying the plate and moving back toward the group of Wildkids. Music started up behind her—the thrumming of several stringed instruments, accented by the pounding of a drum while the cheery notes of a flute lifted high.

"Ah, this is exactly the tune to start with," Joesp said, nodding in satisfaction. He and Graysil sat cross-legged on the ground with plates of food in their laps next to Aryion and Mel.

"I think I've heard it somewhere before," Allie said, sitting down beside them. Warm aromas drifted up from her plate, and she realized how hungry she was. The seasoned venison, slightly tangy vegetables, and the fresh watercress were quickly gone.

Songs and conversations filled the village. As people finished their supper, they moved toward the bonfire, joining hands in dance. There was no propriety or show, no flourishing movements or stiff steps. The dances were fluid and smooth, simple yet free as the wind that swirled with the dancers. Once or twice Allie glimpsed a dryad on the edge of the village, watching the celebration or twirling in the air just out of reach of the firelight.

Nellioh and Newuel appeared through the trees. "Better have left us some," Nellioh commented shortly to Dusty.

"Can't vouch for that when the food is this good," Dusty replied through a mouthful.

"Well, we've been on guard the last hour," her brother shot back. "You better plan to *feed* your guards."

Munben's amused voice came from behind Allie, interrupting the Wildkids' bantering. "Do not fret, there is plenty for everyone." The chieftain stood by the willow trees, watching the dancers with a smile. "This is a fine evening," he mused. "In an age of darkness, it does one's heart well to rejoice in what we have."

"Perimeter is secure, Grandfather," Kalos said, appearing from the tables with his own plate. "We are rotating positions every four songs or so."

"Aren't you joining in?" Aryion asked him.

The young captain gave a slight shrug. "Oh, certainly for the meal. But I'm afraid my duties come first. I'd hope to see you all out there enjoying yourselves." He nodded toward the circles of dancers, who had paused to cheer for the musicians as the song ended.

"Aryion can't dance," Rygal said, taking a sip of cider.

"Nor can you," Aryion informed him with a glare, but his blue-flecked eyes were glimmering with a hidden smile.

"If you can walk, you can dance," Dusty said firmly, getting to her feet. Behind her, the two mandolins had begun strumming a rhythmic jig. She hesitated a split second; Allie saw her face color slightly, but then she squared her shoulders determinedly and extended a hand. "If you're willing, Hummingbird?"

Rygal choked on his drink. Aryion blinked in shock, then, seeming too stunned to argue, rose and followed her toward the circles.

Allie shook her head with a laugh and looked at Kalos. "I can take over watch for the next few dances, Captain," she offered. "You deserve a break as much as we do." She could tell the young hama-dryad was itching to join the dance.

"If you will, Heiress," Kalos said, looking grateful. "Commander, you two might watch the western road?"

You two, Allie's mind echoed, enjoying the sound of it.

Rygal, who had begun to take another sip of cider, stopped. "Oh—ah—of course." He stood and offered a hand to Allie.

Allie took it as he pulled her to her feet. His fingers were warm on her skin, and she let go quickly, moving to the tree where she'd propped her sword. *Settle yourself,* her mind warned. They were tasked with guarding the Lia village so these people could enjoy their celebration in blissful protection from the war. It would not do to be distracted with anything else.

They passed a second group of guards on the road. The wagon would carry them this way tomorrow, back to Lillary and the waiting warship, back to the battle. The thought cast a shadow over the cheery ring of firelight where the dancers swirled.

"Have there been any signs of trouble yet?" she asked as she and Rygal took their positions on either side of the path. Ahead, the trees had twisted in a protective wall across the road, effectively barring all but the hama-dryads from entry into the village.

"No," Rygal told her. "Then again, setting guard is more of a precaution. The tribe's stayed hidden for years."

And they would be leaving that safety tomorrow, Allie's mind added.

"I wanted to talk to you about something," Rygal began after a pause.

Her heart was immediately racing. She glanced at him as casually as she could, hoping the dim light hid the color that had flared to her face.

But Rygal's words were not what she had anticipated. "The Life-Blood Spell... the original use of it. Morel told me that it appeared in Brownae legends, but I wanted to ask Munben-Lia about it too." He hesitated. "A lot of it is similar to the *Alené*—calling on the High Light's power."

"But the Ace-Lord twisted it," Allie said slowly, "right?"

"Yes." His face was grim, a deep sorrow lingering in his blue eyes. "I've been trying to learn the spell—to see if someone could bind the Ace-Lord, drawing on the High Light's power, since we know it's stronger than the Ace-Lord's."

"You have?" Allie asked, interested. She'd seen how he had learned Essence channeling from Norrin's writings, as well Iriam's teaching. The unique magic of a Guardian seemed to have accelerated his learning. But his face was so grim that she sensed his findings about this topic had been less successful. "Have you… managed it?"

"No. Well, maybe—I haven't tested it yet, obviously." Rygal let out a breath. "The issue is, even using the original spell wouldn't just overrule the curse. So you'd still… the Ace-Lord would still…" He trailed off, knuckles whitening on his sword hilt, face shadowed by the coming night.

Blood alone. Allie had assumed as much, after all they'd learned of the enchantment. The death she had resolved herself to still awaited, and not even the spell in its original power would change that.

"What if *I* learned the spell?" she asked after a pause. "You could teach me the basics. The High Light's power is stronger than the Ace-Lord's—maybe I could learn the spell and bind him instead."

"But you'd still be bound," Rygal said doubtfully.

"Yes… but the Ace-Lord would be, too. That might be the key I've been looking for—the only way to truly ensure he'll die with me." She could tell from Rygal's face that he didn't like it. "Please, Rygal—even if it doesn't work, it can hardly make anything worse. If I'm to die, the best I can do is take the Ace-Lord down too. Please teach me."

Rygal was silent a long moment, but finally he nodded. "All right. If it's what you want."

"Thanks," Allie said quietly, turning back to face the trees.

The song ended behind them, and the dancers cheered. Allie sought for a change in topic, something less dark and grim, something that might continue the illusion of peace and happiness that she'd found here among the tribe of Lia. She'd just drawn breath to speak when the soft thrum of a harp filled the air behind her, plucking the melody of a gentle waltz and flooding her mind with memories.

"Oh, this is a good song," she breathed, feeling a smile cross her face despite herself. How often had she danced this waltz with her father, or with Jan, when she was very small? It sounded far different out in the forest, without the wide ballroom of Castle Sia to amplify the music. But the wind carried the song to her, bringing the memories of twirling and swaying with hundreds of other dancers.

Rygal had his head tilted slightly to the side, listening to the melody. "I think I've heard it before. Maybe at one of those parties in Caer Sia?"

Allie nodded, her body itching to begin the familiar motions. "It's always been my favorite. I haven't danced it in a while, but I can still remember the steps."

"Could you show me?"

Her heart fluttered in her chest. *No, Asescia—distance is best,* her mind ordered. *Especially after you've made him promise he'll help with your death.* But the lonesome, lovely melody of the flutes and harps drowned out the dark reality and made all else fade away.

"I suppose… if we keep an eye on the road," she said, moving closer.

Rygal nodded. "Yes, of course—um…" He hesitated, hands hovering uncertainly before him, far cry from his usual brash confidence.

"Ah—take my hand here, and yours goes here," Allie said, placing his hand on her waist and taking his other in hers. Shivers ran down her back, and she listened again to the song. "And we go to the right—your left… on three…"

Slowly, making sure he could keep up, they stepped to the right two steps, then three back. Allie stepped away, keeping a hold of his hand, twirling and then moving back so that his arms were around her as they moved forward. Three steps forward, another twirl away, and they were face to face again.

"And now again," she whispered, waiting for the next beat of the song.

When it came, it was he who guided her in the steps, while she quietly reminded him of the directions. Rygal learned quickly, his balance measured and easy after years of swordplay. His gray-blue eyes remained fixed on her face, lit by the distant light of the fire, as he listened intently to her words.

Right, back, forward again.

The mandolins joined the harp and flute. To Allie, the entire forest seemed to swell in song, the distant hum of conversation fading away until she seemed suspended in the air, turning and spinning, stepping out of his arms but never out of his grasp, his hand holding hers.

Fears lurked on the edges of her mind, but could not reach her here. Even if it all ended in death, she would cling to these few remaining moments where she felt truly alive. The fire of her Essence crackled in an entirely new way, as though their hearts beat in time with the song.

Forward for the last time.

Her leather jerkin and tunic twisted around her frame as she twirled. It was far cry from the elegant gowns she'd worn before, in that other life. Yet this was not a dance between partners in a ball, surrounded by finery and pomp. This was a moment between two souls, clad in armor, swords at their sides, weary of battle. Pretending, for the moment, that the world was theirs to cherish, their lives intertwined with the other for as long as they lived.

A final twirl, a final strum of the harp, and she returned, chest to chest, his brow against hers. His dark hair brushed her cheek, and she could feel the steady beat of his heart.

For one wild instant, she wished to close the distance between their lips, to stay in this imaginary world without a war, where all she had was his arms around her and their hearts beating together.

The song ended, and with it, the illusion.

Rygal stepped back, still holding her hand lightly. Allie's eyes moved to the shadowed woods as the wind faded away around them. It was over now, this brief time of peace, where her body had rested and her heart had become irreversibly intertwined with his, despite the future looming before her.

She kept her hand in his, as though with that simple gesture, they could hold onto this moment and freeze time just a little longer. But the moment had already passed, fleeting away with the chilly wind.

Tomorrow there would be war.

PART 4

The Rise of the Shadow

47

∽ ∽ ∽ ∽ ∽ ∽ ∽ ∽ ∽ ∽

An Offer of Deceit

Dandio's voice roused Allie, calling to the crew above decks as the *Gryphon* sailed west.

She had barely slept the night before, her mind overfilled with many conflicting emotions. In some thoughts, resolve for what lay ahead and determination to see her mission through. In others, grief for all she would lose, as well as deep fear for her companions. Still, too, were the remnants of peace she'd gained among the hama-dryads, and with it, love so sharp and fierce it almost hurt. Rygal's gray-blue eyes filled her mind as she dozed in and out of dreams, and when she woke, she could still feel his arms around her as they had been when they'd danced, his face illuminated by light as golden as the flames that he'd learned to summon.

Dusty had shaken her awake a few hours before dawn, drawing her away from solitude and rest and back to the fight awaiting them. Allie had joined her companions and left the village, riding back to Lillary Bay. From there, they had boarded the *Gryphon* with Jan, Dandio, and Iriam and began the two-day voyage to Mata City.

The early hour and the gentle rocking of the ship had helped Allie to doze off again below decks. The clatter of rapid footsteps and her father's muffled words above pulled her from half-sleep.

Wearily, she got up, rubbing sleep from her eyes as she walked

556

through the berth to reach the stairs. The morning light reflected on the rolling waves, shining through a bank of white clouds and illuminating the coast to the left.

The sailors had gathered on the starboard rail, studying the coast. For a moment she could not understand what was going on. They couldn't have reached Mata City yet.

Then she saw the familiar outline of Sia's coast, and her heart twisted in her chest.

Fire had spread throughout the entire eastern district, swallowing up city and forest alike before it had been doused by the Nøkken's rain. The gentle rolling hills, once filled with elegant buildings, shops, houses, and crowded streets, were bleak and barren, blackened by the fires from the Red Dawn's desperate escape. The harbor had been spared from the blaze, but many of its piers had been broken, shattered by white ice.

Yet Allie's eyes were drawn to Castle Sia.

Her home had been leveled. It was too far away to see details, but she could see the walls had been broken to pieces like fragile pottery. The courtyard had been rent in two by pale ice. The seaward side of the castle had been crushed inward, leaving only the skeletal towers.

"Light above," Glentree rumbled quietly behind her. "They've made it the spittin' image of Castle Droco."

Allie closed her eyes for a moment, wishing to see Castle Sia as she had known it for so long. But the only image her mind could see now were the blanched walls and broken towers of the white ruin of Droco, where countless had died. Where Mel had fallen. Where she had been cursed. The two ruins were nearly identical. The Ace-Lord's sick attempt at irony.

Dandio stood at the stern beside the helmsman, his face grim. At last, he turned back to the sea before him. "Bear west," he ordered shortly. Slowly, hesitantly, the sailors obeyed. They too had lost homes, friends, and family, and beheld the destruction with grief and despair.

"I don't see any Dal-kerri," Mel said hesitantly at Allie's left. "It—it looks like the Aces are gone."

"They have little reason to remain in the city," Aryion added quietly, glancing at her. "Once the war is over, it will not take long to rebuild, Allie."

He so rarely called her by that name. She could hear the desperate attempt at optimism in his and Mel's voices and managed a slight nod. "It's only a city. What matters is that most of the people survived."

She could tell from their troubled faces that neither believed her ruse of calm. But they didn't say any more. Aryion moved down the rail to speak to Jan. The High King's face was steady as he studied the city, but Allie could see the pain in his expression.

A hand touched her shoulder lightly, and she looked up into Rygal's eyes. "I don't think they destroyed it for the reason they'd originally planned," he said softly. "The Ace-Lord wouldn't have spent all the time making the castle look like that. He was angry, Allie—angry we slipped out of his grasp."

Allie looked at the ruins again, realizing Rygal was right. The destruction was not enough to hide the furious strikes, the reckless anger written in the Aces' wild attack. Though the city had burned, though the castle had fallen, though lives had been lost, the mortals had survived, and the Ace-Lord was furious.

Caer Sia could rebuild. There would be a home for the survivors of the war, so long as they fought on. It added another motive to her mission of killing the Ace-Lord. Fighting for a future for the ones who survived.

She took a deep breath and turned back to Rygal. "I think you're right. Still, I don't think we can count on escaping the Aces anymore."

He glanced at her. "You have a plan?"

"The start of one," Allie replied. She hesitated a moment longer, wishing she had a more concrete strategy to share, but then decided he might be able to offer advice. "My first idea was about the gateway void—the one in Castle Salem. I think it's the last void left. I don't know if this would work…but I don't think the Ace-Lord has any other way to go in and out of the Dark Realm, now that the Jewel's power is gone. If we could close the void with him inside, he'd be trapped again."

"Trapped without a key," Rygal mused, folding his arms over his chest as he thought. "It's not a bad idea, but how would you get him into the void in the first place?"

There was the flaw in her plan. The Ace-Lord had thousands of years of experience in strategy; he'd know his own vulnerability inside the voids. He'd likely see her plan coming a mile away. But Allie finally thought she had an answer for that problem.

"That's where the spell comes in," she explained. "If I'm able to cast the Life-Blood Spell, the Ace-Lord's bound to me. I can draw the fighting into the void—I'm able to be inside it without the illusions attacking me."

She'd learned that when she'd rescued Jan and Mel. Her powers as the Vessel allowed her to traverse the voids unhindered. If the Ace-Lord was cursed too, he could not harm Allie—he would have to remove the curse if he wished to kill her, or sacrifice a large portion of his own magic.

Hopefully, the sheer unexpectedness of Allie's attack—assuming she learned the spell properly—would give her the upper hand. Not for long, but perhaps long enough to draw the Ace-Lord into the black gateway with her.

"And then?" Rygal prompted.

"And then someone closes the door behind us," Allie finished.

How simple it sounded aloud. The truth sent shivers of dread down her spine. Trapped inside that cold, empty, lifeless world of shadows and death with the Ace-Lord for the last meager moments of life. It was a horrible, lonely way to die.

Does that really matter? She reminded herself dryly. *You're going to die anyway. But you have a mission to complete before that.*

Rygal's face was drawn. "Someone," he repeated at last, voice low. "You think…my fire might close the void too?"

"Only one way to find out," Allie replied, managing a weak smile. "Only if you're willing…"

"I'm willing. I just…I'd hate to…" He trailed off abruptly, jaw tightening. At last, he nodded. "I'm with you."

"Thanks," she replied quietly. Her heart swelled in gratitude and love again, but the weight of the curse dampened their warmth, and she focused again on the grim topic. "About the spell… what do I need to know?"

Rygal thought for a moment, staring out across the waves as Caer Sia faded away behind them. "The most important piece is your focus," he said at last. "Figure out where your mind is—center yourself on the Light. Draw from that power, not anything else. At least…that's how it works with Essence channeling."

Allie nodded slowly. It took quite an effort to settle her restless thoughts. The darkness in her heart fought against her, hissing thoughts of death and vengeance instead of hope and light. "Are…are the words the same?" she asked after a pause.

"Yes. You remember them?"

How could she forget. She had heard them every sleepless night since that moment in Castle Droco, and they played again in her thoughts. *Aranac, co vey devarris, dovannon.* Her lips moved around the words, but she didn't voice them aloud, almost afraid to.

Perhaps it would not work at all. Perhaps the darkness planted in her heart would overcome her efforts to focus on the light. No matter her motives, this spell had been claimed by the same darkness that filled her—what would keep that from consuming her the moment she spoke the words?

But she had no alternative. The Ace-Lord must be snared by his own dark magic. So, she would call on the Light, seeking true power behind the spell, and cling to that with her last breath.

. . . . . .

The *Gryphon* anchored in Badwater that evening, and through the sulfur-scented haze, Mel could make out the multi-colored rocks near the river mouth.

He'd never been to Badwater, but this trip did not allow much time for sightseeing. They'd only stopped to pick up a group of couriers who were also bound for the council in Mata City. Mel knew the couriers had been busier than usual these last few weeks, gathering as much information they could about Ar-Salem before the attack took place. He couldn't help wondering about the many mysterious trips they had risked and what all they had learned.

"What information are they looking for?" he wondered quietly to Aryion as they waited on the *Gryphon's* stern for the passengers to arrive. "I mean... we know where the Aces are, and we know a lot about their army, too."

"We do," his mentor answered, nodding slightly. "But from what I've heard, there are very few details regarding Castle Salem itself. It's completely surrounded by the Aces' fog. Bryn and Lammar both said it was so dark inside that they can't tell us what was where."

He leaned against the mast, studying Badwater. The bruises had faded on his face, and clad in his typical leather armor with his sword at his side, he was beginning to look more like himself. But the hollow blue light lingering in his eyes still gave him the appearance of a stranger.

"Do you remember anything about the castle?" Mel asked hesitantly. "I—I know you were kept in a cell, but…"

He trailed off. The shadows darkened on his mentor's face, and his gaze suddenly seemed far away, reliving memories too horrible for Mel to know.

"No," Aryion said after a pause. "No, I… I don't recall the inside of Castle Salem. Only the black box."

Mel nodded, growing quiet again. He'd told Aryion as much as he could remember after he'd fallen from the marble bridge, but that wasn't much. As Dandio had pointed out before, the Aces seemed to have erased that time from Mel's mind—Mel guessed it was to keep their dark fortress secret for as long as possible.

But he had yet to ask Aryion about his time as prisoner. His mentor's memories had been altered, but he had not forgotten his time in the cell—the black box, as they referred to it. Whatever had happened to him, Mel did not want to stir up. Nor did he want to think about his growing unease about why the Aces had allowed his mentor to be rescued at all.

He pushed the thoughts away as five couriers boarded the *Gryphon*. They bowed to Jan and thanked the helmsman and Dandio for giving them a ride east.

"It's no trouble," Dandio replied with a smile, shaking hands with each of them. "After all, we'll need your reports in Mata City."

"Well, thanks for the lift all the same," a familiar voice said cheerfully. Mel started up and moved to the gangplank. Half-hidden by the tall Liznee couriers was an otter-like shape with dark fur.

"Jarus!" he called, hurrying forward.

Jarus, hearing his voice, wove through the crowd to meet him. "Mel— I'm so glad you're all right—I heard you'd been captured by the Aces, and then besieged in Tinkeeyo—and *then* evacuated from Caer Sia—it's good to see you're alive," he finished at last. He smiled, but his blue eyes were worried.

"I'm fine—I'm here," Mel reassured him.

Jarus turned to Aryion, looking equally relieved. "You're back, too? I'd heard—"

"Yes, Jarus," Aryion told him, a rare smile crossing his weary face as he clasped the Cooper's furry paw. "How have things been in Mata City?"

"Dark," Jarus said grimly, "as one would expect in these times." He turned to Jan. "I've come with news for you, sire, and I'd like to know what the rest of you make of it."

Curious, Mel followed Jarus, Jan, and Iriam below decks. They were soon joined by Dandio, Rygal, and Allie, all of whom looked equally interested to hear the news the Cooper had brought.

"Have you heard from Lammar?" was the first thing Jarus asked Rygal.

Rygal shook his head. "Not since we got to the hama-dryads—two, three weeks ago now, I'd guess."

"Don't tell me there's another fight in Gayrile," Allie said worriedly.

Mel could only imagine the catastrophe that would be—if the Diren factions began fighting now, of all times, the north would be weakened further, and the attack on Castle Salem would be called off.

"No, thankfully," Jarus assured her. "Gayrile's secure. But Lammar received a message a few days ago, and he asked me to pass it on—a message from the Aces."

Mel sensed the entire room tense at the words. He looked at Jarus in shock. Jan's brow furrowed. "A message from the Aces?" he repeated at length. "Of what sort?"

"That's what we're not sure about," Jarus replied slowly. "It was a request for parlay."

The High King's expression was still calm, but Mel could see the confusion in his green eyes. Dandio's face was dark, and Aryion had moved a hand to his sword hilt.

"Parlay?" Allie echoed, her voice filled with suspicion. "The Aces would never settle for a treaty, not after everything that's happened. There's no way we could negotiate the end of the war."

"That's what I thought, too," Jarus said, glancing between Jan and Iriam. "I've never heard of the Aces offering anyone a chance to settle."

"It is likely a trap," Dandio said, looking at his brother. "They employed similar tactics in Gayrile—gathering all the leaders in one place for a mass execution."

"But why use that strategy again?" Rygal asked, frowning deeply. Mel could see he was fighting to make sense of the news. "It didn't work for them then, and we'd be expecting it now."

"He's right," Aryion said. His rasping voice was filled with the same suspicion and unease Mel felt. "Why attempt a parlay at all, much less at this time?"

"I wonder," Iriam said, his slow, deep voice filling the small cabin, "if this is a trap of a different nature. I believe they may intend to put forth a bargain."

Bargain. There was only one thing the Ace-Lord would wish to bargain for. Mel's hand slipped subconsciously to his pocket, feeling the familiar warmth of the Blue Stone.

Jan reached for Isilas, his face grim as he looked at Iriam. "We cannot risk such a meeting. Either they intend to bargain for the Stones or they will take them by force."

"Certainly not," Iriam agreed, but his face was troubled. "But you must act wisely in this choice, sire. Should we outright refuse to meet them, they will undoubtedly twist it to try to prove that the Liznees are the sole cause for the continued war. Several of our more recent allies believed this conflict was of Caer Sia's making, and it took great loss to convince them otherwise. If the Aces spread the lie that we refused their offer of peace, it may shatter those fragile alliances."

Mel looked at Jan, seeing the concern on the king's face. He remembered the tedious process to get Elimar to join the war, and the tenuous alliance with the Diren clans. Under any other circumstance, a discussion was a wise choice—a chance to settle the conflict without more bloodshed and hopefully come to a resolution of peace.

But these weren't normal circumstances. This was the Ace-Lord, trapping the mortals in an impossible choice.

Jan looked at the Cooper. "When do the Aces request this meeting to take place?"

"Two days from now," Jarus replied, his furry face worried. "Lammar says he thinks they planned that date on purpose, to make us less sure of our choices during the war council."

"He is likely correct," Jan agreed grimly. "The Ace-Lord is a master of seeding doubt. And he knows if we refuse him, our allies will turn against us, and every alliance will be for nothing."

Mel gripped the Blue Stone, feeling it dig into his scarred palm. Jan was right, but he couldn't see any solution to the problem. The Ace-Lord had played this card at the opportune time, enjoying the doubt and confusion it would cause. He would make nervousness and uncertainty infiltrate the upcoming war council, letting it affect the actions and choices of the fearful mortals.

"We cannot refuse them," Jan said after another pause, looking up at Iriam. "Let us write a return message. We will agree to meet with them."

Mel stared at him in disbelief. Of all plans, he'd expected this one the least. Iriam studied the High King, his expression giving nothing away. "And what would you like to include in this message, sire?"

"We agree to meet for parlay in two days' time on the Flats," Jan said, leaning back in his chair as he spoke. "We will hear their bargain, but we will not bring the Star-Stones."

Dandio folded his arms over his chest, looking at his brother carefully. "And… what's stopping them from simply tearing your Essence out of your chest the moment they realize you refuse their demands?"

"Because," Jan said slowly, "I do not believe they *can*. The Prophecy does not speak of a treaty ending the war, and I highly doubt it will. But it does warn us to hearken to the call and to not lose hope. The Ace-Lord is bound by the Prophecy's words—he cannot simply disregard it and kill us all, or else he would have already done so."

"Like how the Deputy wanted to loose the Bruin into the world," Allie said slowly. A glimmer of understanding shone in her eyes. "And the Stars came to stop it because that wasn't within the Prophecy—do you think the Stars may come again?"

"The Stars are not the only ones who guard the Prophecy's words," Iriam reminded her. "The Druids will also make certain the Ace-Lord does not cast off its bonds." He nodded thoughtfully. "Yes, I believe it to be a wise choice of action, sire. Nonetheless, it is based entirely upon your trust in the Prophecy, and in the High Light. The Aces will sense any doubt."

"It's not the Prophecy I doubt," Dandio put in slowly. "Its promises secure our victory; in that we have been assured. But it doesn't secure which of us live to see it."

"Which is why I will not go alone," Jan said with a faint smile. "You will accompany me, and Iriam, and Asescia, if she is willing."

"Me?" Allie asked, looking confused. "I mean—I was hoping I'd be able to come," she added, "but why do you want me there?"

"To show that the Vessel yet stands," Jan told her. "The Ace-Lord has not corrupted you as he may believe. You still fight for the Light despite it all. So does the New Blood," he added, looking at Mel. "If you are willing to accompany us, let the Aces see you remain unhindered despite all that has been cast upon you."

Mel nodded quickly. Interest drowned out the chill of fear that had filled his heart. Meeting the Aces for a parlay that would undoubtedly end dangerously was typically not a wise strategy. But showing the Aces he was undeterred by the darkness allowed him to strike back in a different way.

"Dandio will guard the High King, and Rygal stands to guard the Vessel," Iriam said, his eyes sweeping over the assembled companions until they rested on Aryion. "Hummingbird, you have long protected the New Blood. But I am unsure if you should accompany us. The Deputy will undoubtedly seek to trouble your mind."

Mel glanced back at his mentor worriedly. The glitter of blue in his eyes, the shadows on his face, seemed stronger in the darkness of the cabin. He had recovered slowly over the last few weeks, but the Deputy had a way of getting in one's head and shattering any confidence. Mel still remembered the sly words that had led him to surrender himself on the marble bridge.

But Aryion shook his head. "I go with Mel. His safety is more important than my own well-being. Besides that," he added, glancing away, "I will have to face the Deputy again eventually."

Mel could tell Iriam was still unsure, but he did not argue, only nodded slightly. "Very well. You will guard the New Blood."

"I am hesitant to ask any to carry our message back," Jan said. "Both Lammar and the dryads have risked enough thus far." He glanced at Iriam, seeming almost hesitant to voice the idea. "There is another force in Orlell that hates the Aces as well, though I am not sure how one would reach them. They aided us in Caer Sia, and they may aid us now."

Iriam nodded thoughtfully. "Indeed they may. I will do what I can."

Mel wasn't sure what they were talking about. But a light of understanding and interest had lit Dandio's eyes. Wind whistled above deck, and Mel could hear the salty spray lapping at the *Gryphon's* sides like watery hands, as though the beings Jan had alluded to had stirred to life again at his voice.

48

The Council of Mata

Mata City's wide harbor swarmed with movement as the *Gryphon* moved toward shore.

To Allie's eyes, it seemed each ship had come from a different corner of Orlell. The vast majority were Cooper ships, small and slender, with their two distinctive triangular sails extended like a bird's wings. Others were from the desert kingdoms, curved hulls arching out of the water with brilliantly colored banners hanging from their prows.

The Red Dawn warships were here too, dwarfing the other vessels, colors soaring in the wind and guns gleaming on their decks. The bulk of the Red Dawn's navy, as her father had explained last night, was still occupied in keeping the northern seas safe. But many of the warships had come to Mata City to join the approaching battle. Crowds moved in a steady stream to Castle Mata, comprised of many different species, and she could see the massive outlines of three kragons soaring over the cliffs.

It had been centuries since the kingdoms of Coonsia had gathered thus. But the times required it. Today, they would discuss their strike back against the Aces.

"That's a lot of ships," Mel murmured beside her. The apprentice's eyes were wide as he stared at the bustling harbor.

"How many of these representatives were at the council of Flora?"

Allie asked him. Jan had told her about the meeting in Flora when the Aces had first reappeared, before the quest for the Shards had begun.

"A lot—I don't remember them all," Mel admitted. "The Coopers were there, and some desert-dwellers, I think."

"And the Guardians," Rygal said, moving to stand beside Allie as the ship approached the pier.

"Oh, right, and the Guardians," Mel said, nodding rapidly. "I don't remember the kragons being there."

Aryion's low voice came from behind them. "No, the kragons were occupied in the Magno Forest." The ranger walked to the rail with Jarus padding behind him. "It's good they are here today," he observed. "Though I can't help wondering where they will sit."

"Not to worry," Jarus said with a chuckle. "There's an outside meeting hall the Coopers built specifically to include the kragons. We don't often use it because of the weather, but it'll work perfectly today." He squinted up at the brilliant blue sky.

"Look at them all," Rygal murmured, sounding impressed as he watched the many different species headed to the castle. He looked at Jan as the High King strode on deck. "I knew you had sent a call for aid, but there must be twenty different kingdoms represented here."

"Closer to thirty, in fact," Jan told him with a smile. "The warriors of Lia will arrive the day after tomorrow, but the rest will be here today. Lord Casper informed me the Chanterelle Brownaes will accompany the Direns as well."

"Good," Rygal said, but Allie saw the shadow that crossed his face at the mention of the Brownaes. It seemed with every new arrival of delegates came a different set of painful memories. The last time she'd been in Mata City was right after she'd learned of her new dark powers, and Drisilas had blazed white fire. She still remembered the desperate battle, the heat on her face, Darion's worried voice warning her to run.

A familiar cold grief settled in her chest, threatening to crush her heart. But she took a deep breath and pushed it away, touching Rygal's hand lightly. Both of them had experienced the same horror. He understood and appreciated her quiet support, and a slight smile flickered over his face. "Morel always hated these kinds of meetings," he said softly. "Preferred to just jump into the fight without taking hours debating strategies."

"So do you," Allie pointed out.

"Fair enough," Rygal conceded, shaking his head. Pain still lingered in his face, but the smile that lit his blue eyes was genuine.

And there was her heart, breaking every rule she'd tried to set up around it to ease the pain of her future.

She let go of his hand as they followed Jarus up the road, trailing behind the crowds of delegates heading to Castle Mata. The rugged stone fortress overlooked the northern seas as it had for centuries, visible from almost any part of the city.

Voices echoed off the stone walls of the courtyard. Castle Mata itself was not especially large, but this outdoor meeting area could easily accommodate the gathering while still being secure. The sea breeze rippled Allie's hair as she entered through the archway. A large round table dominated most of the courtyard, where several groups of delegates had already seated themselves.

Ajaha stood inside the archway with Lord Roan. The Cooper lord's eyes twinkled kindly in his furry face, which was just beginning to show signs of gray. "Welcome, High King," he said with a bow to Jan. "I trust all appears in order here?"

"Yes, Lord Roan, thank you," Jan replied, clasping the Cooper's paw.

Ajaha embraced Dandio and Allie. Her calm, determined expression showed none of the weariness she surely felt after weeks of preparation. "You had best find your seats," she told them. "This will be quite a crowded council."

Allie nodded, a little dazed by the blur of noise and movement. Dusty and her siblings moved past her to join their father and the rest of the N'Tell delegates, who had only arrived in Mata City a few days ago. The Wildkid warriors drew many wondering stares—it had been centuries since any of their people had gathered here.

Lammar moved toward the archway as they entered. He threw them a smile, but his green eyes were worried as he moved to Iriam. "I take it Jarus brought the message?" he asked, lowering his voice. "I'd have delivered it myself if duties allowed, though I doubt I could have made it make any more sense."

Iriam nodded. "The High King has chosen what is to be done. You need not trouble yourself with the Aces' message."

Lammar shrugged slightly, a crooked grin on his face. "Well, as you like it. I suppose I'll have to find out what that means later."

Lord Roan rapped on the tabletop, letting them know the council was about to begin. Allie sat between Rygal and Mel just to the right of Jan's place. The warriors stood in distinct groups behind their respective leaders—humans, Elves, Hyenins, Cagari, Wildkids, Dwarves, Direns, Brownaes. She recognized Porcini seated with the Chanterelle warriors; the young Brownae would be representing his people at this meeting. He noticed her and grinned across the table. Next to him was Quinn Fireleaf, with his father Lord Andros of Tinkeeyo. Settled at the end of the table to Allie's left, casting massive shadows over the other delegates, were Lord Fireclaw and two kragon warriors.

"Far more than there were in Flora," Aryion murmured. He stood just behind Mel's chair, his dark eyes scanning the crowd.

"Well, that seems good," Rygal whispered back to him. "If the council of Flora started our battle efforts, maybe this one will determine our final attack."

Allie glanced at the assembled crowd again. Lords and kings had come with their finest warriors—some whose names she knew only from legend. Others she had fought alongside. And here she sat, with far less experience and knowledge than they. Seated between the New Blood and the Commander of the Guardians of Gayrile. The Vessel's only role here was the one the Ace-Lord had given her—but hopefully she could soon change that.

A second brisk rap on the table quieted the muted conversations. Lord Roan sat in his place, looking over the large assembly with a welcoming smile on his furry face. "Thank you for coming here," he began. Despite the distant thunder of the sea, his voice echoed off the stone walls of the courtyard. "Each of you represent kingdoms, cities, and tribes across Orlell. But more than that, you represent your people— lives you have thus far guarded from the Ace-Lord's hand.

"We have little time for formalities," the Cooper lord continued. "We cannot speak of minor affairs—this is a council of war. On this, the High King will speak."

Jan stood. The High King's dark suit was still stained by travel, and his golden crown had been scuffed at some point—perhaps during his capture in Caer Droco. Despite it, Allie looked at her uncle with more admiration than she had ever felt before. All that had happened—the loss of his kingdom, the burden of the Star-Stone, the fear for his companions—none showed in his green eyes, which glittered with steady determination.

His voice was not especially loud, but the words called everyone to rapt attention. "My friends. In three days, as the High Light wills, the Red Dawn will march against the Aces."

Ripples of shock, fear, and excitement spread through the crowd like a stone tossed into a pool. Allie had already known this was a possibility—Jan had been planning it for weeks, while Dandio and his generals had strategized and Iriam had advised them. But hearing it out loud solidified it as truth.

"Our reasons for this," Jan continued, once the surprise had quieted, "all stem from one simple yet crucial fact: we are running out of time. The Ace-Lord intends to lengthen this war as long as he sees fit. His forces will continue to attack us, destroy our homes, besiege our fortresses, and kill those we love. In doing so, they gradually crush our spirits, corrupting us with dark despair while their strength grows. Already, my lords, many of your warriors have lost their lives in this war. With every drop of mortal blood, we draw no closer to victory, though the Aces grow more powerful each day."

"What can we do against them, sire?" one of the Elven lords inquired uneasily. "Defense has been our only hope up thus far. If battle is futile, why will this attack be any different?"

"Because this strike will end the war, one way or another," Jan stated levelly.

Again, a murmur of startled and fearful voices whispered through the courtyard. Allie saw the kragons tilt their huge heads in disbelief.

"I will not soften the fact," Jan said. "I will not hide the gravity of what we request. In only a few day's time, we will appear before the Aces to deliver our terms of ultimatum, and show them we are united against their dark regime. Today, my lords, you must choose. You may remain as you have been, fending off the Aces' attacks as they strike again and again. Or, if you refuse as I do to continue playing the Ace-Lord's game, stand with us and fight."

"To our deaths?" the Hyenin lord asked bitterly.

"If that is the High Light's will," Jan replied calmly. "But I believe the Prophecy's words that promise victory." He paused, studying the crowd. "It is a weighty choice, the highest price I could ask of you. But the alternative is months—years, perhaps—of a war we cannot hope to survive. The choice is yours to make. If you will leave this council, the time is now, and I will not hold it against you. By remaining, you join our fight."

The words faded into the muted roll of the sea. Allie sat in silence, looking around at the delegates, wondering who would stay. What Jan described promised more loss, more grief, more pain. Those who rode to war with the Red Dawn would still be outnumbered by the Ace-army. So many of their allies had hesitated to join them—surely others would refuse to risk their lives to such a strategy.

And yet the answering silence told her otherwise.

Not a soul stirred around the table. At last, Lord Fireclaw spoke, his rasping, croaking voice filling the courtyard. "The kragons are vith you, High King. So ve pledge."

"So pledges Arkran," the human king said, clasping a gauntleted hand to his broad chest.

"And the Cagari," Lord Ter-Li added, golden eyes flashing.

One by one, each of the lords gave their pledge, each voice adding to the growing fire in Allie's heart. As at last Chief Sorrel pledged the N'Tell Wildkids to the fight, a surge of excitement and determination replaced the worried murmurs. There were no cheers, no shouts, but

Allie could sense the resolve and camaraderie that had taken root. The many species and kingdoms had united as one army against the Ace-Lord.

Ĵan inclined his head to them; Allie saw the relief and gratitude on his face. "Thank you, my friends. Your willingness, your sacrifice, and your bravery will not be forgotten." He turned to Dandio. "Now, let us tell you of our strategy."

Dandio stood and squared his shoulders, studying the waiting crowd. "Well—I shall keep this brief. The Ace-Lord has chosen a strategic position in Ar-Salem—while we can access it fairly easily from the Mata Strait, the space between the waters and the castle would leave any approaching force completely exposed. Not only that, we have learned that Castle Salem is shrouded by an impenetrable darkness, making it nearly impossible to reach." He looked at Lammar.

"Not just darkness," Lammar said. His lilting voice was tinged with a fear that sent chills down Allie's spine. "Since the release of the Hummingbird, we have learned the Aces have doubled security measures. We have reason to believe there are all manners of illusions protecting Castle Salem, which will make it much more difficult for a mortal to get in or out. At least… most mortals," he added, glancing at Allie.

Allie hesitated, sensing all eyes turn upon her. She had entered Castle Salem when she'd freed Ĵan and Mel, though the castle had looked much different then. But at Ĵan's slight nod of encouragement, she stood. "I was in Castle Salem once, but only for a short time," she began slowly. "It wasn't dark then, but I think the Ace-Lord can make it appear however he wants. There was a large void in the lower levels of the castle, connected to the void in Castle Droco. But I think that gateway has been destroyed, now that Castle Droco is gone."

"It was gone when I was there," Lammar confirmed, "as far as I could make out, that is."

"It is logical," Iriam said. "The gateways, as we have observed, are faulty creations. While the Patches only lead to different parts of the mortal world, the gateways lead outside of it—into the middleworld between time and space, perhaps even into the Dark Realm itself. This makes them highly unstable, and they must draw a great deal of the Ace-Lord's power for them to function. It is reasonable to assume the Ace-Lord would have closed the larger gateway, once it had served its purpose."

"Then the Ace-Lord no longer has a way to access the Dark Realm?" Quinn asked hopefully.

"There's still one way," Allie said softly. "One last gateway in the highest tower of Castle Salem—it's where we managed to escape last time."

The tower gateway had seemed like a sort of private entrance for the Ace-Lord alone. Instead of a direct passageway to another place, as the other voids had been, this had resembled a long, windswept hall, gray and blurred around her, with different doorways leading to unknown places. She had reached the end of the hall with an effort, finding the gateway back into Castle Droco had been destroyed by the Bruin. When she'd tried to pass through, she had ended up suspended between worlds, unable to escape as the clutching shadows had dragged her, Jan, and Mel back into the corridor.

The terror of it still filled her nightmares, and she shuddered involuntarily at the memory.

"If it is the last gateway, sire," Lord Andros said, looking at Jan, "how might we go about closing it?"

Jan paused, a flicker of uncertainty crossing his face. "That is a question we have not yet learned the answer to. Fire weakens the voids—Asescia's fire in particular managed to destroy a Patch near Appledale. However, the power holding the gateways open is maintained by the Ace-Lord's strength."

"As are the enchanted soldiers," Lord Casper put in grimly. "We have learned of the choice the Ace-army must make, though as of now there is no undoing that choice. The Direns who turned away from the Aces in Gayrile informed us that blood alone will break the curse. The Ace-Lord must then be defeated if there is to be any hope of freeing them."

Blood alone, Allie's mind echoed, seeing Jan's gaze turn briefly to her. The barely concealed pain in his and Dandio's eyes cut to her heart. Yet she did not feel afraid this time. No longer would she cower like a child before a nightmare. She would stand firmly in the midst of the shadows that sought to crush her.

Taking a deep breath, she straightened as those around the table lapsed into uncertain silence. "I have a plan to defeat the Ace-Lord… though I don't know if it will work."

Everyone looked at her, but she kept her eyes on Jan and her parents, noting the concern on their faces. But none silenced her. Jan gave her a slight nod, encouraging her to continue.

And so she went on, speaking the truth she had hidden from for so long. She sensed the icy chains of the Life-Blood Spell tightening futilely around her, but not even that would stop her now. "The Ace-Lord cursed me several months ago. It's known as the Life-Blood Spell—a way for the Ace-Lord to create a mortal Vessel. A portion of his power fills me—it's allowed me to kill the enchanted soldiers and enter the voids, as some of you have heard. But only because he wished me to, as his plan was to use me to corrupt the people around me."

No one spoke. The crowd listened in utter silence.

Allie went on. "The Ace-Lord wanted me to embrace that corruption, to join the darkness, to join him. And—I nearly did, for a time." She glanced briefly at Rygal; the light in his gray-blue eyes urged her onward. "Now I've found the Light's leading again. I understand what I need to do. The Life-Blood Spell means that I'll share in the Ace-Lord's fall. I've learned the true origins of the spell—that it once drew on the High Light's pure magic, not the Ace-Lord's darkness. I think, if I can bind the Ace-Lord with that power, I'll ensure he follows me into death. I have to be the one to kill him."

Dandio closed his eyes briefly. Allie glimpsed grief and pain cross her mother's face for a split second before her carefully disciplined expression covered it. Jan's face was unchanged, concealing the pain and uncertainty she knew he felt. He only met her eyes and nodded slightly, accepting her plan.

"How do you intend to do that, Heiress?" That was Jarus. The Cooper's voice was edged in sorrow.

Allie paused. With all she had thought of, all the variables she'd worked through, she was still uncertain of her strategy. As if any plan could thwart the Lord of Death. She turned to Iriam, seeking the answers in his dark face. "Iriam… you once told me that the Ace-Lord isn't the ruler of the Dark Realm like he thinks—that he is death's warden, serving the High Light's plan even though he resists it?"

The Neutral inclined his head in confirmation. "Indeed. Lord Kahlifis, as he was once known, must still abide by the rules and laws the High Light set in place at the beginning of time. For centuries after the Dividing War, the Ace-Lord remained locked securely in the Dark Realm, though he wished to spread his darkness into the mortal world.

It was only through the corrupted Star-Stone he had claimed—the Jewel of Power, and Safacon's meddling with it—that he returned."

Allie nodded slowly. She remembered studying that in Caer Sia, in another life. "Yes. I think, with the Life-Blood Spell, I can lock the Ace-Lord in the Dark Realm. The spell's own rules would require it. I can't kill him—I don't know if anything truly can. But if I was able to enter the gateway and draw the Ace-Lord inside with me… someone might close the door behind us."

Her eyes drifted back to Rygal.

"Someone?" Dandio asked, frowning slightly. "I thought you were the only one who can close the voids."

"I might be," Allie admitted. "And I know the gateways are more powerful than the Patches. But Rygal's mastered Essence channeling in just a short time, and I think he can do it."

A brief and grateful smile spread over Rygal's face. She smiled back, fighting to keep herself from blushing. Strange how her heart behaved so, even in a council of war where she spoke of her coming death.

"What Allie's explained to me," Rygal said, looking at the others, "is that, essentially, all I would be doing is closing the door. She can draw the Ace-Lord inside the void, and my fire could destroy the gateway behind her."

He spoke calmly, but Allie saw the pain on his face as he spoke.

Jan looked thoughtful, but frowned slightly. "It is not a bad strategy. However, I do not know if trapping the Ace-Lord inside will hinder his power. He might be able to open the gateway again after it is closed."

"Perhaps, perhaps not," Iriam said. "The only way the Ace-Lord managed to open the gateways before was due to the Jewel of Power— the Vana Jydra, the Stone that opened paths between worlds. A portion of that power also filled the compass," he added, with a glance at Mel. "With the last remnants of the Jewel's magic destroyed, there is no power to open the gateways again."

"But the Ace-Lord wouldn't die," Mel pointed out hesitantly. "He'd just be stuck in the Dark Realm."

"I don't think killing him our goal," Allie answered softly. "He'll only turn vengeance against us… I understand that now. Trapping him in the shadows he came from is our best hope."

How easily the words came to her. How different than the last time she'd suggested her plan in Mata City. Back then she'd stumbled over her words and risen angrily to any counterarguments. Now, she felt calm, level-headed, answering their hesitant questions with answers that came without searching. She could almost sense the High Light leading her, His words becoming hers.

This was her path. She would no longer shrink before fear or blaze in fury. The fire that stirred her heart was her own again, Essence sparked by the Light's call. The words of the Prophecy whispered in her mind, reinforcing her resolve.

When Lord of Death brings life to all, The spell that bound leaves deeper scars, Than the shadow that awakened.

She was bound by death. But through her choice, she might bring life to everyone left.

49

Ultimatum

The dull gray sand of the Salem Flats spread in a colorless carpet, dusting the horses' hooves as the companions rode. The pale white caused the hulking darkness of Ar-Salem to stand out all the more, seeming to Allie to grow blacker as they rode forward.

Two days had passed since the war council of Mata City. Hope and excitement had warmed her heart up till now, but nothing would distract from what was coming. The allied forces of the mortal kingdoms had begun to gather for battle.

She glanced behind her. A ridge marked the edge of the Flats, where they had come from. Their army waited there—hundreds of thousands of warriors prepared to fight back against the Ace-Lord. The tips of the nearest clusters of tents were just visible as they rode into the valley of the Flats before the hillside hid them from view. Ajaha would be waiting there, along with Jarus and Lammar and the rest of the delegates and lords. Waiting to hear the outcome of this conversation.

She tightened her grip on the reins, calming the surge of adrenaline that shot through her all over again as the reality of what they were doing settled in. It seemed a reckless strategy. But as Iriam had assured them, it might be the wisest for this moment. Not only would the negotiation confirm their trust in the Prophecy's words, it would also buy more time for the armies to be in place for the offensive.

"We will wait here," came Jan's voice, drawing Allie's attention away from the ridge. Together, the seven companions drew their horses to a stop. Allie's horse pawed the ground anxiously, clearly sensing her tension, and she patted his mane to calm him. The black bulk of Castle Salem stood before them to the right. Still a few miles away, Allie guessed, yet she could sense the darkness from here.

She let out another breath. The fear and uncertainty seemed a palpable thing, as real as the wind hissing over the empty landscape. What Jan had said before was true. The Ace-Lord's offer of parlay was a double-edged sword, sharper than the one at her belt. Refuse, and their new allies would forever blame them—accept, and they put everyone at risk.

Jan alone seemed confident in the plan, his fingers working over the paper he held. Allie wasn't sure why he had bothered to write up terms for the Aces' surrender. Surely the Aces would never accept them.

"Can't see a thing," Rygal murmured to her left. He squinted at the distant shadowy bulk of Castle Salem.

"Doubt we'd be able to see much, even without the darkness," she commented. "It's still a ways off."

"Probably not," Rygal agreed, "but it's still too close for comfort."

Allie managed a weak smile. She had never seen him so unsettled. Then again, meeting the Aces face-to-face was not something one looked forward to.

"I still think we might have brought a squadron with us," Dandio said quietly to Jan. One hand tightened restlessly on the hilt of his sword, and his silver-maned mare stood poised, ready for battle.

"I would not risk their lives," Jan replied. "You know the Aces would have turned their presence against us somehow. I am already unsure whether allowing you all to come was the right move."

"It's just as risky for you as it is for us," Mel pointed out with a nonchalant shrug. "The Aces can't do anything that's outside the Prophecy's words, remember."

He seemed the only one confident in that sentiment. Allie knew he was right, but it was difficult to make herself believe that. She could tell from Dandio and Rygal's faces that they were still nervous.

"Mel is correct," came Iriam's deep voice. The Neutral stood beside Jan. "We are prepared to defend ourselves. In this, we must trust in the Light. Do not be afraid."

Allie nodded shortly, deciding not to voice the fears filling her mind. She figured she would be safe—the Aces would not harm their master's Vessel. But her companions? Jan and Mel were both Wielders, and thus targets. Dandio and Aryion could hardly do anything to protect them if the Ace-Lord demanded their deaths.

She took a breath to steady herself, squaring her shoulders, and glanced at the others. Iriam and Jan waited at the front of the group. Both seemed calm, though she could tell from the tight set of her uncle's stance that he shared her nervousness. Dandio rode on Jan's other side, an inch or two taller than his brother, shifting slightly in the saddle as though prepared to launch into battle at any moment. Allie felt better with her father here. There was no one she trusted more to protect them if the meeting went poorly.

To her right rode Mel, with Aryion waiting silently behind him. The ranger's blue-flecked eyes studied the distant castle, as though the shadows were calling him back. Not enchanted, nor fully shattered. Something else entirely.

Rygal rode right beside Allie, so close she could almost feel his warmth. His presence settled her anxious heart, allowed her memories to drift back to the glade in the hama-dryad's forest, as she'd rested in his embrace while the music swelled around them.

Had that only been a few days ago? It felt like a lifetime. There was so much left unsaid, so much that could never be.

Distance, Asescia. The words of the Life-Blood Spell drifted into her mind, calling her focus back to the mission before her. Bind the Ace-Lord. Call upon the pure magic the spell had once drawn from, and use it to lock him back in the domain of darkness.

Aranac, co vey devarris, dovannon. She knew the words quite well by now, though it still took an effort to center her heart on the Light. She forced her heart there now, letting the High Light's peace settle her nerves.

"You think they'll bring soldiers?" Mel ventured hesitantly.

"I doubt it," Jan told him quietly, "but we can never be sure. That is why the Druids are here."

Allie didn't see the Druids at all, but Iriam had assured them they would come. There was still a chance the Aces would attempt an assault. In that case, the Druids would aid their hurried retreat. Assuming the Druids would come, that is…

"The Ace-Lord will not go back on his word," Iriam stated. "His Deputy is cunning and treacherous, but if the Ace-Lord intends to deceive us, he will doubtless do it by another, more clever way. I do not believe he plans to slaughter us here."

"Speak of the devil," Dandio said, nodding forward. "Here they come."

Allie looked up sharply. The shapes had appeared in the valley before them, moving steadily forward. A rider, seated on a skeletal horse with a jagged horn, driving forward with ominous rhythm. The sun glinted off the Deputy's tarnished armor, and she could make out his satisfied smile. Matching the devilish horse's pace was a hulking feline shape.

Redeyes. She hadn't seen him since the battle on Gayrile's beach. Not since he'd torn Darion's life from his body with one blow.

Her stomach turned, and she felt sick with a fresh wave of rage and grief. Rygal's gentle hand on her arm steadied her at her involuntary gasp. "I'm here. Don't worry."

"Dal-kerri horses?" Mel whispered, staring at the rider.

"They had them in Caer Sia as well," Dandio told him. His jaw was set, and he tightened his grip on his sword.

The horses snorted uneasily as the two figures approached. Redeyes prowled before them, tail lashing the air. The light in his eyes betrayed his eager desire to attack everyone present, but the Ace-Lord's orders clearly restrained him.

The Deputy drew his devilish horse to a halt, a twisted smirk on his ruined face. His sly voice broke the tense silence, ringing over the Flats like a whip. "So you *have* come, after all."

Aryion flinched as though he'd been struck, his face white and drawn. Mel looked back at him, startled and confused—Allie heard him ask something softly.

The Deputy's smile widened as his eyes found the ranger. "Well, look who is here," he mused to Redeyes. "The nameless slave has crawled back to his master's voice. It looks as though he has resumed his task of protecting the boy."

"Not as though he has succeeded as well as he thinks," Redeyes replied in amusement.

"We have not come to banter words," Jan interrupted. "You called us here for a negotiation, and it is a negotiation I expect to hear, not petty insults."

"Have you?" the Deputy asked disdainfully. "My master believes otherwise. Surely you will not agree to the terms we have laid before you."

"What are those terms, exactly?" Iriam inquired. "We are prepared to hear them. Or were you sent here intending to fight?"

For an instant, the self-satisfied smile vanished, and hatred flashed in the Deputy's eyes. "My master warned me of your treacherous nature, Neutral," he snapped. "You and your company of misfits—serving the Light, you claim, while all are rotten to the heart with darkness. You, a betrayer of your race, keeping company with a Marked one," he jabbed a finger at Jan, "a cursed Vessel," his eyes flashed to Allie, "and a man bound twice over by the Blood Oath." He let out a short bark of laughter as he regarded Aryion. "How very good it is to see you again, Hummingbird—though that is not your name anymore. Do you remember your time with us? Have you told them of the black cell? Or need I remind you what you are?"

Aryion didn't move, but Allie could see his entire frame was trembling—whether from rage, fear, or the sheer will of restraint, she couldn't tell.

"Enough of this," Jan said. "What are the terms, Deputy?"

"Surrender, High King," the Deputy answered, his eyes flicking back to Jan. The Dal-kerri horse snorted and stamped, its hideous teeth bared. "Surrender and end this pointless war. Give up the Star-Stones, lay your weapons down, and bow to the Ace-Lord. These are the terms I was tasked to bring—refuse, and every mortal shall be annihilated."

The last word hissed into the silence.

Jan looked at him, his face unchanged. "Those," he answered at last, voice level, "are not proper terms. What of my people? What of those who do not bear arms? I believe you neglected to include their fate."

"That is not for me to say," the Deputy replied slyly. "My master shall determine their future. Should they join him willingly, they shall live."

"Live as an enchanted slave, I assume," Jan said slowly.

The Deputy's smile vanished. His voice was rising in anger. "This is my message, Liznee. This chance will not come a second time. If you will not accept these terms, the blood of the mortals shall be on your hands. Give me the Star-Stones you are fool enough to guard."

"That I will not do," Jan replied, unfolding the paper. Allie was amazed he was still so composed. The Deputy's anger, the death he spoke of, had filled her with both rage and fear. "What I will do is offer counter-terms, as is custom for a parlay of this kind, and you will answer. Though, I suppose, you do not recall the mortal customs."

The subtle jibe was the last straw. Ice crusted the Deputy's hands. His voice sank to a dangerous hiss. "Mortal customs? Bandy words with me, High King, and watch as I kill your companions one by one. Who shall be first? The New Blood? Or your guard dog of a brother?"

Allie clenched her fists, trying to temper the rising fire. Redeyes snarled in anticipation. Dandio had half raised his sword, red fire playing in his fingers.

Jan raised a hand. "That was not the agreement," he stated. "Your terms for this meeting assured us there will be no battle."

"No battle, perhaps," the Deputy spat. "And no harm to your person, High King—not yet. But this is *far* too sweet an opportunity to miss."

White ice flashed from his hand, directly at Dandio's chest—but the blast never reached him. A ray of indigo ice came from the left, slicing the Deputy's bolt in half and scattering shards across the ground.

Allie looked at Iriam in disbelief—there was no way the Neutral could have reacted so quickly. But the blast had not come from his direction at all.

Materializing from the shadows several paces away, nearly invisible in their deep green and blue robes, were three silent watchers. Their purple-red eyes were fixed intently on the Deputy, the silvery markings on their faces still glowing slightly.

It was the first time Allie had seen the Druids. Even from a distance, their presence filled her with hope and awe. They said nothing, only watched.

"As I was saying," Ĵan said—he had not even flinched, looking back at the page in his hands, "those are threats, not a proper parlay. By our customs, we have brought our own terms as well."

The Deputy lowered his hands, his face livid. "Where are the Stones, Liznee?" he spat.

"Oh, the Stones are safe," Ĵan answered, glancing up at him. "Far from here, of course. As you pointed out, presenting them here would be foolish."

"Coward," Redeyes growled, claws raking the packed ground.

"If you would like to call it that. Now, our terms. I assume you will report my exact words to your master?"

"If you wish," the Deputy snapped. His eyes darted between the Druids and Ĵan—Allie could tell he was judging if he could strike faster than the Druids could parry. He seemed to decide against it—the lightning-fast blast that had saved Dandio's life could very easily claim his head next.

"Very well, then," Ĵan continued. "Terms of surrender. One: the Ace-Lord shall disassemble his forces at once, removing the enchantment from affected souls and releasing the rest from service. Two: the Aces shall leave Orlell and close the remaining voids behind them. Three: the Ace-Lord shall remove the Life-Blood Spell from the Vessel and release her from his bond." He looked up. "I trust you will remember all that?"

"Vividly," the Deputy hissed.

Allie exchanged an awed glance with Rygal. She had never heard anyone insult the Ace-Deputy—Ĵan least of all. His words were measured, delivering the quick, subtle insults interwoven with the terms. He almost looked like he was *enjoying* this.

"Very well," Ĵan said again, folding the page and returning it to his breast pocket. "We shall expect your master's answer by tomorrow morning. The Nøkken will carry his message."

The Deputy glared at him, clearly scrambling for a scathing reply. The mention of the Nøkken had angered him all the more, throwing him off guard.

But it was a low, cold voice that spoke, and in a flash, Allie's calm was gone. "There is no need for that, High King. I shall give you my answer now."

A shadow flickered into view before Allie's eyes in a gathering stream of black, standing just in front of the Deputy. In another moment, the Ace-Lord stood before them, towering over Ĵan, his purple-red eyes regarding them levelly.

For an instant no one moved. Allie felt as though she was frozen in place, chills flowing through her body.

The Ace-Lord was silent for a moment, his black robes rippling like liquid shadows around him. The illusion he often wore was cast aside, leaving him in his true form—a decayed, long-dead wraith who reveled in the fear and death to come.

"Terms, High King?" he breathed, chilling the air around them. "Terms are nothing without action behind them. Do you believe you can command me to leave your world? To remove the enchantment binding my warriors? To loose the Vessel?" His gaze rested on Allie. She tried to stare back defiantly, but her resolve faltered.

"Those are our terms," Jan said shortly, recovering himself. "You would do well to agree to them."

The Ace-Lord turned to him. "That, mortal, is impossible. My conquest is already set into motion, and the events of the Prophecy—nay, the events of time itself—will not be stopped by your desires. Our worlds are interlocked, interwoven as a tapestry. I cannot break the rules of time any more than you can stop the change of the seasons. Does not your Prophecy tell you so?"

"The Prophecy speaks of hope," Jan said firmly. "It speaks of life, of victory, of the endurance of the mortals. It ensures your downfall."

The Ace-Lord did not answer, only closed his eyes and inhaled deeply. "Your fear… it is sweet," he breathed at last, ice crackling on the rocks around him. "Stronger than the mightiest draught. Mortal fear rots the core of Orlell, and so my kingdom rises."

"If you refuse our terms, then war is the only recourse," Iriam said quietly.

"So be it," the Ace-Lord replied. Allie's heart seemed to sink into the ground. "War you will have, mortals. But know, when the battle has finished and the survivors gather in bloodied ranks for mercy, no mercy shall be given. All who follow will be judged as those who led them to their deaths."

The black clouds over Castle Salem clawed at the sky. Thunder rumbled in the distance.

"Read well the signs," the Ace-Lord said, gesturing shortly for the Deputy and Redeyes to go. "Look to the sky and see the fate of Orlell. You have chosen this game, and you shall see the final stages."

With that, he turned, and in a blur of shadows he vanished, streaking across the darkening sky back toward Castle Salem.

"Blast it," Dandio muttered, sliding his sword back into the scabbard as he turned to Jan. "I can't say I expected otherwise—but I suppose there is nothing we can do. Battle would have come regardless."

Jan let out a breath and nodded, but said nothing.

"Do not believe his lies of the Prophecy," Iriam told them. "He misinterprets its words and reshapes them to fit his intents. The truth will persevere."

"Iriam?"

Mel's hesitant voice caused Allie to turn. In the same moment, she realized how the midday light had suddenly begun to fade, as though the world had sunk into dusk in a matter of seconds.

Her gaze moved to the sky.

Like the shroud of shadows that had filled the gateway, or the clawed hand of some massive being, darkness engulfed the sun, blotting out the light and dousing the world in shadows. The sky faded to gray, black clouds churning overhead as a frigid breeze swept over the land.

When sun and stars are darkened; To the call you must still hearken.

The shadow had risen. The last battle for Orlell had begun.

50

The Last Dusk

Shadows followed the riders back to the ridge.

Mel recalled the darkness that had filled Caer Sia when the Aces had occupied it, the foggy gray clouding the streets and limiting his vision. But that was nothing compared to the total darkness that blanketed the world now, or the way the sun had completely vanished behind it.

There was little conversation as they rode uphill. Pinpricks of light marked the slope where the mortal armies had made their camps. The world had been plunged into twilight by the Ace-Lord, and Mel could not help fearing they would never see the sun rise again.

He stayed close to Aryion as the horses trotted back to camp—both for the comfort of his mentor's protective presence and to make sure Aryion was all right. Something had changed in the ranger's grim face, his blue-flecked eyes distant and troubled. But Mel didn't dare venture a question. He'd seen how Aryion had flinched at the Deputy's sneering voice, which had brought him so much pain in Ar-Salem.

Mel didn't know what the Aces had done to his mentor. But there had been some catalyst to reduce him to this state—the hollow blue, the shattered memories, the unnatural strength that threatened to tear his body apart. Hard as he tried to convince himself otherwise, he was certain that the Deputy had wanted Aryion here today, satisfied to destroy the little of himself that he had regained.

Mel shook his head to clear it, looking around the camp. Aryion was talking quietly with Iriam, his voice hoarse and quiet. "When do you expect the attack to begin?"

"That will soon be determined," the Neutral answered. "I anticipate us to strike in the next few days. We cannot afford to waste time."

Mel turned back to him, unable to stop his doubts. "Iriam, do you think we should have… I mean, was this the right thing for us…"

He trailed off, but Iriam seemed to guess his thoughts. "This was our best choice," he replied quietly. "Disregarding the Aces' message entirely would have had far worse consequences. We acted rightly. Even this darkness was foretold by the Prophecy."

Mel let out a breath, knowing he was right. The Prophecy had written of this very moment: *When sun and stars are darkened; To the call you must still hearken.*

Darkness had come as foretold. Now was the time for action.

Lights from thousands of torches and campfires lit the area as they entered the camp. Many of the armies were already settled, turning the desolate land into a small city. Mel could hear uneasy voices among the tents.

A command post had been set up at the center of the Red Dawn forces. Ajaha, Lammar, and three couriers met them there; Mel could hear Jan explaining what had transpired and giving orders. "Send word throughout Coonsia," the king said in a low voice. "Let it be known that we still breathe. I will not have the Aces spread some rumor that we have already been slain."

"Shall I summon the generals?" Ajaha asked.

"Shortly," Jan replied. "First, we must discuss a different part of our strategy."

His gaze turned back to Mel as he said this, and Mel wondered what he meant. He wasn't sure how much of the mission he could help with, especially with the Oath. Then again, the Blood Oath could hardly hold precedence, now that the end of the world had come. If he were to take up the Blue Stone again, he doubted it would be to hide and wait the war out.

Dusty and Jarus met them at the command tent. Jan and Iriam left with Lord Roan and Lammar to meet with the other lords, and Dandio went to speak with General Leopold. The others waited outside the tent, allowing the grooms to take the horses.

"I'm guessing the Aces didn't accept our terms?" Jarus asked, as Mel swung down from the saddle.

"No," Mel answered. "But I doubted they ever would have surrendered."

"This meeting was more for our benefit than theirs," Allie said behind him. She stood next to Rygal—rather close, Mel couldn't help noticing. "If we had refused, the Ace-Lord would have weaponized it against our allies."

"It was risky, all the same," Dusty remarked. "I'm glad you're all here safe. How'd the king's message go over?"

"You should have *seen* it," Rygal broke in, a grin stretching over his face. "I've never seen anyone call the Ace-Deputy a fool in three different ways and get away with it."

"Jan did what?" Jarus repeated in disbelief.

"It was unbelievable," Allie put in, shaking her head with an incredulous smile. "I wish I remembered it all—oh, how'd he put it?"

"*'I trust you'll remember all that,'*" Rygal quoted, in a decent imitation of Jan's elegant accent, which brought laughter from Allie and Jarus and even caused a smile to cross Aryion's battered face.

"I can't believe it," Dusty said, shaking her head, "but he *is* the High King, and the Deputy hardly deserves any less. What's the plan now? Dandio told me to wait here for another meeting."

"I'd expect it's about our strategy," Allie told her. Mel noticed her face became grim at the words. "I don't know what details, though."

"Let us discuss that, then," came Jan's voice. He had returned with Iriam and Dandio. "Now that you are all here, we can speak about your mission."

Mel looked up at him, puzzled, as they entered the command tent. "Now? I thought we had to talk to the other lords, too."

"We certainly will," the High King replied. "The rest of our forces will be organized tomorrow morning. But this part of the strategy is something we believe best to keep among as few ears as possible."

Curious now, Mel slipped inside, standing beside Aryion and Jarus. A round table filled the command tent, depicting a map of the Salem Flats. Carved figurines of foot soldiers and riders had already been arrayed on the edges, as well as a realistic miniature of the castle itself.

"I appreciate your restraint during today's discussion," Jan told them, once they had all entered. "I believe the Ace-Deputy intended to goad us into battle early, which would have undoubtedly led to our destruction. Now," he continued, looking at the table, "there is a specific mission, one with a role I must ask each of you to play."

Mel glanced at the others, sensing the nervous interest spreading among them. Rygal and Allie were the only two who did not seem surprised, clearly already knowing their part in the plan. But the others looked startled.

"All of us?" Dusty echoed. "I don't mean to argue, sire—my warriors are all prepared to fight. But I don't know how much help we can offer against Aces."

"All of you," Jan answered with a nod. "You would not have been summoned otherwise. First, Dandio might explain what has been established thus far."

Dandio studied the waiting companions. "In two days' time, the Red Dawn and our allies will launch a direct attack upon Castle Salem, seeking to draw the Ace-army out and keep the battle contained in the valley. During our attack," his eyes drifted to Allie, "a small strike force will enter Castle Salem with the purpose of destroying the Ace-Lord."

Mel looked at Allie. She stood straight and calm, her expression determined. The willing warrior, he realized, changed from the fiery and reckless girl he'd once known. Her fate was sealed by the Prophecy, and she was clearly resolved to what was before her. A stab of sorrow pierced his chest as he thought of it.

"That strike force will number around thirty warriors," Dandio continued. "You will escort Allie to Castle Salem, eliminating any opposition that may arise—and I do not doubt there will be a fight. You will enter from the westward side, from the Mata Strait. Maya Puddlepaw and her team have crafted a vessel for this mission, a small, swift ship that can wait undetected among the shoals of the Strait."

A flash of pride crossed Jarus' furry face at the mention of Maya's contribution.

"The strike force must be swift and silent," Jan said, looking at Dusty. "Of all the soldiers assembled, none are as skilled in silent movement as those of the N'Tell. Thus, I request you to choose among your warriors and select those who are willing to join this mission."

Dusty nodded. Though her expression still bore traces of fear, she accepted the directive with the fierce determination Mel remembered of her.

"Your goal is to reach Castle Salem's gates and hold them," Dandio said. "The main part of the fighting, I hope, will be on the Flats. But I expect the Ace-Lord to have devised some manner of devilry to stop you. There is no telling what lies within that accursed fog around the castle."

"That is where the next piece of your mission comes in," Jan added. For the first time, he sounded unsure of his words. "The illusions of the fog, I fear, will be more dangerous than the Dal-kerri. As we have observed before, the one thing that can break through the Aces' illusions are the Star-Stones. I had intended to accompany you myself, but I fear my presence will draw more opposition to your path."

His gaze turned to Mel.

The realization finally clicked into place in Mel's mind. The New Blood's task. Only the Blue Stone could protect the warriors from whatever illusions the Aces would cast. Only the power of the *Alené* could shield and guide them.

"Mel, I do not know the rules of the Blood Oath," Dandio admitted, as Mel hesitated. "If it were my choice, I would have you remain safely in camp. But Jan is right—we need the Stone, and what you have learned in Tinkeeyo may protect many lives here."

Mel took a breath, looking down at the healed scar on his palm. The Blood Oath had kept him from the conflict thus far… but wasn't that mostly because of his own feelings? He hadn't sworn an Oath against fighting—he'd sworn the Oath to give up his own desires, to put protecting the Stone above all else. Now, with the world on the brink of destruction, the New Blood must return to his call.

"I don't… I don't think it's about the Blood Oath anymore," he said at last, looking between the Liznee brothers. "Not in the same way I've been fulfilling it, I mean. If the Stone helps save Orlell—if *I* can do something to save it—I'm still fulfilling my promise."

He glanced at Iriam, and was glad to see approval on the Neutral's face. "You surrendered your own wishes when you swore the Oath," he said thoughtfully. "Now, you must surrender all to see this fight through."

Brief fear chilled Mel's heart again at the thought of facing the Aces, but he nodded. Every event in his life seemed to flash before his eyes in a moment, every second that had led him here. He was ready.

"And I will ask you once again to protect him, Hummingbird," Dandio said, turning to Aryion. "Your apprentice is the key to this mission's success. Keep him safe."

Aryion nodded silently. Blue light still shone in his dark eyes, but his face was clear and steady.

"Jarus Puddlepaw will go also," Jan said, with a slight smile at the Cooper's surprised and eager expression. "The skills you displayed during the quest for the Shards are not forgotten, and you will join Aryion in keeping Mel safe."

"I will, sire," Jarus agreed, looking both excited and frightened.

"Stay with Dusty's squadron," Dandio said. "You will hold the gates while Rygal and Allie enter the castle." He looked to his daughter. "As for your task—I do not know what may await you inside the gates, and I believe this goes without saying—it is absolutely imperative that you find the Ace-Lord as swiftly as possible. Only with his defeat can this war end. Let us hope Rygal's fire can close the gateway behind you, after you have drawn the Ace-Lord into the void."

He spoke as calmly as though it were any other strategy, but Mel saw the pain in his face.

Mel steered the conversation away from that painful thought. There were still questions to be answered. "So—we'll reach the gates, and then what?" he asked, looking at Dandio. "What are we going to do while Rygal and Allie are inside?"

Dandio nodded slightly, returning to the topic at hand. "What I would recommend you do," he said, looking at Dusty, "is to set your warriors at the westward gates with the castle at your backs. Let Mel use the Blue Stone from without, while Aryion and Jarus protect him from attacks."

Use the Blue Stone, Mel's mind echoed dully, feeling the familiar doubt dig its claws into his heart. There was a time that calling the Stone's magic forth had been easy—now, even the once-comforting light served to remind him of the horrors in Tinkeeyo. The Stone might protect him from some attacks, but how would that stop the illusions the Aces could cast inside his mind?

But there was nothing he could do about that. Better to focus on the little he could control. His path had led him here. The pain, the losses, the Blood Oath—all faded away, replaced by the mission the High Light had bestowed upon him. So he would fight, while the Stone's light shone before him and the Song rose around him.

. . . . . .

Allie had never realized just how much she'd appreciated the natural light of day until she awoke without a dawn. Dull gray light filled the small tent she shared with her family, and she realized that sometime in the restless night she had finally drifted off to sleep.

Stiffly, she rolled up her bedmat. The fight itself, Dandio had said last night, would not truly begin for two more days, but the strike team must be in position before that. Today, she and her companions would board the small frigate and begin the tense wait on the Mata Strait. There they would stay until the Red Dawn was prepared and the attack had begun, summoning them to Castle Salem.

The end had come.

The thought clenched her heart with fear. So much at stake. Her father and Jan would be leading the charge—Jan hoped the corrupted Star-Stone would goad the Ace-army out into the open. It was a terrible risk, but it was one they were all taking. They needed the Aces in the same place.

Well, all but the Ace-Lord. He would be waiting in the tower, waiting for the Vessel.

Allie took a deep breath, shaking the last thoughts of sleep away. Time to go.

The finality of it all hung over every moment of the morning. She'd managed to avoid the thought last night, even as she bid Jan and Dandio farewell. Now, the grim reality hissed behind every small moment. Last time among the Red Dawn. Last time to pack her bag. Last time to hear the quiet rustle of the waking camp as the soldiers prepared for war.

Footsteps crunched on the packed earth outside the tent. Dusty had probably come to fetch her. "I'm coming," Allie called.

"Good morning to you too," came Ajaha's quiet voice.

Allie looked up. Her mother stood framed in the tent entrance, dressed in her courier uniform. She smiled gently, but the grief in her eyes was something Allie couldn't ease.

"Morning," she answered, trying to find something else to say. To speak some futile hope to her mother, ease the agonizing pain of losing her child. Of all farewells, this seemed the most difficult. Her father, Jan, her friends… they feared for her the same. But this was her mother. Strong as steel and yet delicate as a flower. Unbroken by the cares of the world and yet crushed by this loss. The pain didn't show on her face. Only her eyes betrayed it.

Ajaha stepped inside and glanced at Allie's pack. "I assume you have packed everything you will need? You will spend a brief time on the ship before you venture inland again."

"I know—I think I've got it all," Allie said. There wasn't much to remember. The Wildkids would pack all basic supplies. "Have there been any updates on the Ace-army?" she asked after a pause.

"They have begun to mobilize," Ajaha answered. "Your father believes they plan to attack Mata City."

"Mata City?" Allie repeated worriedly.

"I do not think it will happen," Ajaha reassured her. "Once the Red Dawn and their allies are in their position, the Aces will be stopped in the Flats."

The slightest tremor of fear in her voice cut to Allie's heart, and for the first time, her resolve faltered. She did not want to go through with this mission. Did not want to face the Ace-Lord. Did not want to fall with him into the eternal darkness of the gateway.

She did not want to die. She wanted to stay here, hide behind her mother's tall frame as she'd done when she was very small. Let the horror pass her by.

But the Prophecy demanded otherwise.

Allie swallowed hard, heart suddenly in her throat. "I… I don't know if…"

Her mother's cool hand rested on her cheek, raising her eyes. "Asescia. Do not doubt your path. Wherever it may lead, the Light guides you."

Allie took a shaking breath. "I know. I'm… worried for you, and everyone else. What if I…"

"That is your fear speaking," Ajaha said gently, as she trailed off. "Your plan is sound. We'll be all right. And," she paused for a moment, "it may do you well to consider the chance that *you* may be all right, too."

Allie looked up at her, confused. "What do you mean? The Prophecy says..."

"The Prophecy calls for a willing warrior to perish with the dawn," Ajaha said quietly. "That may be you, Asescia. But I have wondered, and Iriam has theorized... if the willing warrior applies to someone else, considering the thousands of selfless knights who even now prepare for battle. In the same way that the title New Blood could have applied to Hagshrub—or even Jarus, for that matter—perhaps the role of the willing warrior could be filled by another as well."

Allie stared at her in shock, suddenly breathless. Her mother's words echoed Darion's all those weeks ago—in everything that had occurred since, she'd completely pushed the unlikely thought aside. Yet now, this suggestion flooded her heart with both uncertainty and relief. "But... but I thought..." she stammered finally, hardly able to speak.

Ajaha sighed. "Iriam was wary to suggest an alternative, especially when your actions were nearer to the Vessel's than the Warrior's. He didn't want you to doubt the Prophecy—and neither do I. But I am only suggesting the alternative possibility, as we have often misinterpreted the heart of the High Light's words and promises."

Allie shook her head slowly, dumbfounded. This possibility was at once so unlikely and so breathtakingly wonderful she could hardly gather her thoughts.

"I do not know whether we are correct," Ajaha said. "Whatever the Light wills will happen. But I want to make certain of one thing." She placed her hands on her daughter's shoulders. "I want to be certain that you do not go into this fight *intending* to die. Your life is in the High Light's hand, and if your death is His will, then surrender you must. But whatever the outcome, I want you to promise me that you will give the Ace-Lord a fight to remember."

Allie looked into her eyes, seeing the fire blazing there. Her own flame crackled in response in her chest. The hope in her mother's words had filled her with fresh energy, drowning out the gloomy thoughts. Her throat was tight with emotion as she nodded firmly. "I will, Mum."

She hugged Ajaha tightly, blinking back the tears. There was no telling the outcome of the fight. But she'd been so resolved to dying over the last few weeks, she was practically prepared to stroll up to the Ace-Lord without a sword.

The Prophecy did not call for that. Hope was no soft, fragile thing, but a battered warrior dragging herself up to continue fighting.

Rygal met her outside the tent, carrying a torch and leading their horses. "Feeling ready?" he asked, managing a smile.

"Very," Allie replied, startled to realize she meant it. She was ready to fight, to end the war—by her own death if needed, but only if the High Light guided her thus. "Where are we meeting the Wildkids?"

"At the Strait," Rygal replied. "We'll ride there with the rangers—the ship's waiting for us."

Allie nodded and swung into the saddle. Dull gray light covered the Flats. From their position on the rise, she could make out the black mass that marked Castle Salem. They would come from the far side—both to avoid the bulk of the fighting, and because Lammar had better intel from the seaward direction. That said, the seaward side also left them with far more distance to cross in order to reach the castle.

"Are we sure it's worth coming from the Strait?" she wondered. "The Ace-Lord's probably expecting us from every direction. We could try to set up at a closer location."

"See, that's what I told Lammar," Rygal replied, tightening the saddle bags. "But have you ever tried telling a Siren he's over-planning?"

"I haven't, but I'll take your word for it."

He shook his head, but a small grin had made its way through the worry on his face. "You seem to be in a good mood."

Allie shrugged, but he wasn't wrong. The conversation with her mother, the new hope that had sprung to life, filled her with renewed determination and an almost hesitant joy. "I suppose I am. The war is going to end one way or another—that's almost comforting—and we have a plan to move forward with."

"Fair enough," Rygal said, patting his horse's neck and staring out across the gray plains. There was a moment of silence before he spoke again. "It's strange to think about—that it could all be over soon. What if… what if this works? What if we win?"

Allie looked at him. The same hesitant hope shone in his blue eyes. She hadn't given much thought to imagine some impossible future where the war was over and she was still alive. But if her strategy worked, if by some miracle they both lived, if the war ended… what would become of her? Of them? Her heart fluttered, and she fought for the words, not wanting to crush the light in his eyes nor offer false hope.

"If we win?" she echoed after a pause. "If we win… promise me you'll learn that waltz?"

"Only if you're there to dance it with me," he replied quietly, eyes lingering on her face.

She met his gaze, wishing to forget the curse, the war, the death to come, and pause here. Remember the warmth of his arms around her, his teasing grins during their sparring matches, their conversations and jokes. Try to pin down when exactly in their friendship she had fallen so in love. To return to another time.

But the clatter of hooves brought the brief moment to an end, and Aryion and Mel appeared. The Blue Stone cast a soft halo of light around them before Mel slipped it into his vest pocket. "Ready?" he asked eagerly.

Allie nodded, turning her horse to follow the others down the steep path, which led north for a short distance before dropping down toward the Strait. Through the dim light, she could make out the vague outline of a ship's mast, almost invisible among the rocky cliff edge. As they drew closer, she realized it was not one sail but three. The fore and stern sails were turned at opposite angles, spread to opposite sides of the ship like a bird's wings, while the central mast was positioned to catch the wind in the center.

A group of the Mara-N'Tell's finest warriors waited silently for them. Allie dismounted, pulling on her pack as she walked toward the strange little craft.

"Looks like the Jenna ships," Aryion murmured, interested.

"Jan said it's one of Maya's designs," Rygal replied. "I wonder if she took some inspiration?"

"Just a little," came a familiar voice to their right. Maya appeared through the shadowy haze, the slight breeze ruffling her blonde fur. She smiled as she saw them. "I know it's not a very big ship—she's actually only a prototype."

"It's perfect, Maya," Rygal told her with a smile. "I didn't know you'd be here to see us off."

"Only to be sure the ship will do—my team and I sailed her here this morning," Maya told him. "I can't stay long. Ella's with Jarus' parents—she woke up to wish her father goodbye and fell asleep pretty quick afterwards." Her smile faded at the words, and her gaze drifted to Jarus, who was talking cheerfully with one of the Wildkids. Allie could only guess the fears plaguing her mind for her husband. But Maya shook her head. "Well—you'd better be going. Lammar said the sooner you're off the better."

She padded after them as they moved to the crowd waiting on shore. Lammar appeared through the Wildkids, smiling in approval at the blonde Cooper. "Not bad, Maya. Not only will it get them there quick, but any scouts of the Aces won't recognize that sort of sail rig."

"I hope so," Maya replied, though her voice was tinged with fear.

Aryion and Mel moved to talk to one of Dusty's brothers. Rygal shouldered his pack and shifted his shield to his other shoulder. "I think we're all set, Lammar," he said. "I'll check with Dusty though—she's technically leading this operation."

"I'll meet you onboard," Allie told him. But her eyes lingered on him as he headed toward the ship. When she turned back to the Siren, his gaze was flicking between her and Rygal.

"So that's the way the wind blows."

"*Honestly*, Lammar," Maya said, but Allie saw her smile as she moved toward Jarus.

Allie decided against rising to the challenge, avoiding the topic of a pleasant future that might not exist. Instead, she steered the conversation back to the mission. "Is there anything else I need to know about Castle Salem, Lammar? What's our best way in?"

The Siren nodded, serious in an instant. "That's a tricky one, Heiress. I'd expect that the Aces will be ready to fight as soon as you walk through the gates. You might try sneaking in through the old well system, the same way Bryn and I got Aryion out." He hesitated. "But that'll only put you that much farther from the tower."

Allie frowned. It was a difficult choice. Sneaking in through a back entrance might get them inside undetected, but once inside, they'd have more ground to cover. Besides, considering they'd likely be detected either way, it might be smarter to choose the most direct route.

"What's the fastest way in, then?" she asked.

"Well, the main gate," Lammar said reluctantly. "I imagine it to be the most direct way. But it'll be risky."

"So's the whole mission," Allie said, managing a slight smile. "Thanks for the advice, all the same."

"Aye. Good luck, Heiress," Lammar added quietly, but his lilting voice betrayed deep concern as Allie walked to the ship.

51

∽ ∽ ∽ ∽ ∽ ∽ ∽ ∽ ∽

Nightfall

Firelight filled the camp as the kragons arrived.

Jan stood, studying the murky darkness in the valley before him. Behind him, the hundreds of campfires burned along the ridge, illuminating the countless tents. The rest of their allies, he hoped, would arrive tonight, joining the mortal lines and preparing for battle. The ridge allowed a wide view of the Flats and the shadow-shrouded castle, some miles from their position here.

He had heard stories of Castle Salem. No one, not even the Druids, knew its exact origins. He could see the vague outline of its towers above the clouds in the valley, shifting in and out of focus like a mirage. Perhaps the illusion encircling it was one of many. Perhaps the castle itself was an illusion maintained by the Ace-Lord, like the silvery guise he sometimes wore.

Jan could recall very little of the inside of the castle during his time as a prisoner—the moments after Asescia had found and rescued him were blurry with pain and uncertainty. Illusions and sounds thundered in his mind, making it difficult to know what had actually happened. He remembered climbing stairs, clashing briefly with Redeyes, and finding Mel unconscious. Then they had retreated through a black gateway in the highest tower, while voices of those long lost screamed in his mind and the darkest pains he had known were summoned from his memories.

No, he did not often think back to those moments. Now, though, he scoured those memories, seeking for something—anything that might aid Allie's mission. Surely there was some weakness, some flaw in the Ace-Lord's voids that might be turned against him.

The one thing he recalled was the fact that the Aces had a difficult time maintaining their illusions if one resisted them. The Deputy, for example, had swiftly abandoned his illusions during the fight on the marble bridge. Jan had reminded Allie of this, but he doubted it would be much help to her. With luck, all the Aces would be on the battlefield, and the Ace-Lord did not share that weakness.

Her mission, he had come to realize, was not something he could help. He must trust Allie and Rygal and the others, let go of his concerns, and focus on his own fight.

Isilas hung on its chain inside his jacket, cold and pale. If his plan worked, the Star-Stone's presence would draw the Ace-army out from their concealment in the fog and goad them into battle. He was unsure, at first, about bringing the Stone into the fight. But Cahadras had told him his actions—his alone—may undo the corruption of Isilas. So he would protect it with his life, despite the danger.

Five kragons flew overhead, drawing his attention back to the present. Lord Fireclaw's warriors had been busy all night, surveying the Flats and keeping watch on the distant castle. Now, Jan recognized the vast wingspan of the kragon lord himself a moment before Fireclaw settled on the hillock nearby.

"High King," Fireclaw rasped, inclining his head briefly in greeting before reporting briskly in his accented growl. "De vind blows hard from de south. De Vingship is in position now, and the Dal-kerri cannot scent them."

Jan peered toward the distant Strait. The Wingship, as the kragons had taken to calling Maya's design, had left with Allie and her companions yesterday, and would be waiting on the Strait. Hard as he tried, he could not see them from here—though he knew that was a good thing.

"The wind is on our side, then," he said to Fireclaw. "The Coopers should be in position on the Strait." Battle plans ran through his mind, recalling where and when the different forces would attack. His concerns for Allie only muddled his thoughts. "Has there been any movement from the castle?" he asked, looking at the kragon again. "We received a report this morning that their army is preparing, but nothing since then."

Fireclaw raised his massive head, the breeze rippling through the feathers along his back. "De vind carries death, High King," he snarled after a pause. "Volves, orcs, Aces, men who do not die… they begin to march."

Dread and excitement surged in Jan's heart in equal amounts, and he looked at the kragon sharply. "The Ace-army? They are marching… now?" He peered down into the valley of the Flats, but could make out nothing in the uncertain darkness. They had assumed the Aces would mobilize quickly following their ultimatum, but to know they were on the move now fueled the restless fire of his Essence.

"Soon," Fireclaw said, still scenting the restless wind. "By night, they vill be in position. I go to ready my warriors." He spread his wings again, speeding over the ridge toward the kragons.

Jan turned on his heel, striding to the command tent. Dandio, General Leopold, and Lord Roan stood inside, studying the map as he entered. The latter two made to bow; Jan waved it aside briskly. "Never mind that—Lord Fireclaw has just informed me the Ace-army has begun to march. He believes they will be in position by nightfall."

"Nightfall?" Leopold echoed dryly, catlike eyes glancing out at the shadowed world. "We are *living* in nightfall, sire."

"How many?" Dandio asked.

"I would expect the full force," Jan replied, ignoring the fear that chilled his own heart. The full force—not even the attack of Caer Sia had seen that many warriors, and that had been weeks ago. By now, the Ace-Lord would have amassed all the more to his conquest.

"We're prepared for it," Dandio said, one hand gripping his sword hilt. His voice was firm and fierce, yet Jan could read the uncertainty in his face. The dents and scratches in his armor were more defined in the dim light, and the scar on his face seemed darker. So many battles. So much bloodshed. Jan was exhausted of it. But this battle would be like none before—a fight they must see through to the end, if there was to be any future for the mortals.

Dandio turned to Leopold. "Would you mind fetching Iriam—I will need his advice."

"Of course, Commander," Leopold replied, hesitating a moment. "Might you know where I can find him?"

"He will be with the Druids," Jan said. "They are at the edge of the forest, near the hama-dryad command post."

The Cagari general bowed slightly and left the tent. Lord Roan looked up at Jan, furry face both concerned and determined. "Have we received word from the dryads?"

"No, but we have learned before that they are unable to reach Castle Salem at all," Jan said, glancing at Dandio. This was concerning. Along with their worry for Allie and the others, there was the fact that if anything went wrong, the two groups would be unable to contact each other. Should the Aces lay some sort of trap for the Red Dawn, or lure Allie's group into an illusion, there was no way to warn the other party.

Dandio's jaw tightened. "I'd worried about that. That's partly what I intended to ask Iriam about, though." Jan frowned slightly, and he elaborated. "The Aces have set their perimeter here." He traced a wide circle around Castle Salem. "Anyone who seeks to reach the castle will have to go through the fog first. Whatever illusions they've cast within will make it incredibly difficult for a force to infiltrate."

"That perimeter may falter once Allie begins her attack," Jan reminded him. Iriam had explained that the Ace-Lord was expending a great amount of his strength to maintain his many traps: the gateway, the enchanted soldiers, the illusions. Once Allie engaged him in battle, the perimeter would hopefully be the first to weaken.

"I hope it will," Dandio said. "But we can't be certain. We know that once Allie's group attacks him, he'll have to focus on them, which means some of his defenses will have to go. He cannot close the voids, as he still needs the Dark Realm's power, and of course he needs the enchanted soldiers."

"Those soldiers may grow stronger once the illusion falls," Lord Roan pointed out hesitantly. "Sire, if the Ace-Lord draws back the perimeter, that magic will only be re-dispersed. He will not need all of it to fight the Vessel, but he will need to strengthen his forces to compensate for the lost shield."

Jan let out a breath. The Cooper Lord was likely correct. The Ace-Lord was too clever a strategist to take such a risk. "We will deal with that when it comes," he said, dismissing this concern for now and looking at Dandio. "What else did you wish to ask Iriam?"

Dandio turned his focus back to the map, moving a small cluster of figurines closer to the castle. "When and if the Ace-Lord's perimeter falls, a troop of Red Dawn knights may infiltrate that weakness, reaching the castle gates and aiding the Wildkids' defenses. That way, we can both maintain contact with their group and aid Allie's mission."

Jan nodded thoughtfully. It was a wise strategy. "And you intend to ask Iriam to lead that force?"

"With the exception of you or I, there's no one I'd trust more for it," Dandio answered with a wry smile. "I hope he'll agree to it."

"Shall my warriors join that strike, Commander?" Lord Roan inquired. "If the Ace-Lord's perimeter falls, we might attack from the Strait and further weaken the castle."

Dandio shook his head. "No—I appreciate your willingness, but the distance between the Strait and the castle would leave you completely exposed for too long. Stay on the seaward side guarding the west. We cannot allow any Dal-kerri to slink away into the wilds."

"As you wish," the Cooper replied.

Voices stirred outside, the rising swell of readying warriors. Horse hooves clattered on the parched ground, forming up near the slope down to the Flats.

The desolate wilds had transformed into a battlefield, awaiting the blood to come.

. . . . . .

Aryion's eyes had quickly adjusted to the gray darkness surrounding him, but that did not comfort his heart in the least.

A chill wind whipped down the Mata Strait, over the decks of the slender little ship as the second night settled on the Salem Flats. The cold was preferable to the stuffy confines below decks, which reminded him all too well of the darkness that had gripped him in Castle Salem.

His fragmented memories had begun to heal. Though he still barely recalled any missions with Mel, he clung to the few recollections fiercely, gathering the shards of his past and piecing them together like broken pottery.

Yet along with the pleasant memories had come something else, a darkness that had become a part of him. The cold voice still hissed in his mind. He'd all but ignored it till now—the shadows had been so overwhelmed by the light and relief of being reunited with his apprentice and companions.

But the darkness hadn't just gone away. The Deputy had called it back to life with his sly, sneering words only a few days ago.

"Need I remind you what you are?"

No, his thoughts argued back furiously, though the fear and pain had flooded his mind as if the claw-like hands still gripped it, filling his head with white ice. *No, you have no claim over me anymore. I've found the light again. You can't lie to me that darkness is all I know.*

And yet he could not stop the memories of the black box—horrific memories—flooding his mind in agonizing fragments. He had no idea how many of them were real, but they tormented him as he tried to piece together the truth.

Bryn had explained a few things to him, after he'd come back to himself in Lillary Bay. She'd said he had been comatose when they found him, unresponsive at first, violent at other moments. She had not gone into detail, and he had not asked, afraid to hear what he'd done. The scars where the chains had dug into his wrists and neck seemed to tell the story of another person altogether.

Even in returning to the light and company of the ones he cared for, there was still the darkness, lurking like a beast prepared to attack. He hadn't dared lift his sword since leaving Caer Sia, afraid the very feel of the hilt in his hand would plunge him back into the nightmare, where his actions barely felt like his own and an unnatural strength flowed through him.

The Deputy had taken his strengths and weaknesses and shattered both with the white ice. Had twisted him into something dark that stirred to life at his sneering voice, something that barely felt human. Had wrought something new from the agony and the shadows.

The sword at his belt, its leather hilt worn smooth from years of use, would have to be drawn eventually. Battle was coming, one that would end the Ace-War one way or another.

So what then? He could not simply hide this new power, so maybe he could attempt to use it against the Aces? That was what Asescia had chosen to do—to use the powers vested in her to fight the Ace-Lord. But Asescia's curse, as he understood, had been a calculated choice of the Ace-Lord, turning the Heiress into his own Vessel.

What the Deputy had done… this was more brutal, more violent. Breaking the mind, clearing it of all memories, of all light, of all fears, and in their place, implanting a darkness that stirred to life the nearer they got to Castle Salem.

Movement to his right made him flinch involuntarily.

"Sorry—I didn't mean to startle you," Asescia said as he straightened. "I didn't see you."

Aryion shook his head, settling his tense nerves. "No matter. Is everything all right?" He glanced toward the hatch. The faint voices of the Wildkids drifted to his ears, and he could make out Mel's among them.

"Everything's fine," Asescia reassured him. "I just came up to get some air." She moved a few paces aft, studying the distant shoreline, her cloak wrapped around her slim frame. Aryion could see her squinting through the shadows, as though trying to glimpse the Red Dawn encampment on the far hills.

"They are in position, as far as I can tell," he told her, glancing in the same direction. "I can see their fires on the hill."

Allie looked at him, hope lighting her face. "You can see them? Can you tell where the Red Dawn is camped?"

Aryion stood stiffly, moving to the rail. His muscles felt raw and tight. No matter if he could now wield a sword better than ever before—the new strength took a heavy toll on his still-mortal body.

He peered through the darkness for a moment. The dim light cast a gray hue over everything, the color washing out, so that he could only see the outlines of shapes. Certainly no details that would tell him more. "I can't tell where exactly they are," he said after a pause. "By your father's strategy, I would assume they are camped on the east side."

Allie nodded slightly but didn't say any more, standing tensely by the rail. Her thoughts clearly dwelt on the gathering forces, prepared to launch their attack tomorrow. Her fears, as far as he could tell, did not lay in her own fate—she seemed calm, resolved to what was to come.

But she looked up at him again. "Could I… ask you a question?"

"Just one, highness."

"I don't mean to pry," Allie continued. "But… in Castle Salem… do you know what sort of spell it was that…" she trailed off, gesturing vaguely.

Broken memories of excruciating pain swam through his thoughts as he sought an answer. "I… don't believe it was a spell. The Deputy wanted to see if I could be made into… if someone might be enchanted without choosing it."

"I thought that caused the shattering," Allie said hesitantly. "At least… that's what Darion thought."

Grief crossed her face before she concealed it again. The name was another reminder of the struggle he had been unable to help with during his captivity.

"And he was right, to a point," he told her quietly. "The Deputy attempted to remove all memories that attached the person to who they'd been. There are different sorts of enchanted soldiers—some that share his powers, similar to what the Ace-Lord has done with his spell."

Allie's gaze lingered searchingly on his face, seeming to study the blue flecks left in his eyes.

"Is there a reason for your questions?" he asked after a pause, a slight smile twisting his face.

Allie glanced away, hesitating again. "Not exactly. I'm just trying to understand what the Aces—what their different strategies are. Every spell of theirs has been different—the illusions, the enchantment, the shattering, the Life-Blood Spell."

Aryion nodded slowly. Different, yes, and yet they all shared the same darkness. "The Life-Blood Spell… were you offered the choice to claim it?" he asked.

A shadow crossed the Liznee girl's face. "No. Cahadras told me that's often how it is. The mortal is often unwilling when bound—like the Prophecy says. But we learned that it wasn't always a curse. It used to draw on the High Light's power—the Ace-Lord only corrupted it and turned it to evil."

"Like the Jewel of Power?" Aryion asked, interested.

"I think so." Allie took a breath. "It's the only piece in this plan I'm not sure about—binding the Ace-Lord. The spell is corrupted—so is my fire."

There was the uncertainty again, which she tried so hard to hide. Her newfound confidence faltered under the massive burden she carried, so weighty for someone still so young. Now, her plan would determine the fate of the world.

"Your strategy seems sound," he told her after a pause. "And I doubt the Ace-Lord will expect it. Using the Spell in that way, drawing on the Light's strength—that's not something he can counter, not with the darkest magic."

"I think you're right," Allie said quietly. "Still… I suppose we won't know until it happens."

In the gray darkness, her face was still troubled, worn with fears and grief. But Aryion could see a determined spark shining in her eyes again.

He rested a hand on his sword hilt. The darkness still whispered in his thoughts. But he could feel a new strength filling him, a fresh energy flowing through his veins like fire.

52

❧ ❧ ❧ ❧ ❧ ❧ ❧ ❧ ❧

Into the Mist

"There they are," Dandio said grimly.

Dawn had arrived at last, bringing only a slight change in lighting. To Jan, the world seemed plunged in a dense fog, impenetrable except by the strongest fire. From their vantage point above the valley, he could see fog swirling around the far side of the Flats, concealing Castle Salem and most of the west from view. There lay the Ace-Lord's defensive perimeter, effectively keeping the Red Dawn and the mortals back. Allie's team would infiltrate from that direction as soon as the signal was given.

The mortal allies spread along the ridge, banners fluttering in the icy breeze. Thousands of horses snorted and stamped among the cavalry charge, sensing the tense expectation of their riders. Among them waited the footsoldiers, holding weapons at the ready. Four kragons soared in the sky to Jan's left, hovering over the thin line of trees where the hama-dryad forces waited.

Lord Fireclaw's prediction of the Ace-army's progress had proven correct. The shadows of night had hidden them from view, and there were no campfires to reveal their positions. Of course, the Ace-Lord's forces had no dealings with fire.

But now, as night gave way to gray dawn, Jan could see them.

The Ace-army appeared as a black mass settled before them, spreading across the Flats like a living void of darkness, surging and teeming like rats in the mist. He could hear the eager howls of the Dal-kerri hounds, the gurgling rumbles of the massive Bruins, and the occasional hiss of a serpentine. The enchanted soldiers were lost amid the blurred tangle of bodies, so that it was impossible to distinguish man from beast. Jan knew they were there—the Rufa Brownaes, orc and goblin tribes, Black Dwarves, and many others who'd sworn allegiance to the Ace-Lord.

Countless warriors, stripped of any individuality, transformed into a faceless monster of gargantuan proportions.

His horse snorted uneasily, and he put a hand on the stallion's neck to steady him. The acrid stench of Dal-kerri filled the air around them. Dandio's black mare stood calmly, but her ears flicked uneasily, clearly sensing the battle to come.

"There's no way to know if that is all of them," Dandio murmured, studying the teeming bodies in the fog.

"No," Jan agreed. This was a crucial point. While the fog did not fully hide the Ace-army, the limited visibility meant the Red Dawn might charge directly into a trap. Thus, they must draw the force out of hiding first. "We will likely see the full force soon," he added. "With any luck, they shall take the bait we offer."

"There's little luck in war," Dandio said.

"Now you sound like Iriam," Jan remarked with a wry smile, but he nodded. "Still, I trust that your plan is sound. The Ace-Lord may be difficult to deceive, but the Deputy will be easier to flatter."

He turned his eyes back to the valley. Torches lit the ridge, casting elongated shadows downhill.

"We have the better position," Dandio pointed out after a pause, rubbing his chin with a gauntleted hand. "They will have to forge uphill to reach our lines."

"True."

Dandio let out a breath and looked at his brother. "Our one advantage is keeping to the high ground, you know—leaving that goes against everything I would typically recommend. A lone strike, a retreat after two feints, exposing our one asset so early… nothing about this makes sense."

Ĵan turned his eyes to the gray sky, where the eclipsed sun cast dim light upon the army of the Lord of Death. For a moment, his mind drifted back many years, and they were simply two brothers battling creatures that had risen from their imaginations. Now, those very monsters had come to life before them.

"I agree," he said quietly. "Very little makes sense now." He drew Isilas forth, feeling the familiar smooth sides of the Stone, and met his brother's eyes. "Do you trust me?"

"With my life," Dandio answered without hesitation, and a wry smile crossed his scarred face. They clasped hands briefly—the wordless pledge of king and commander, and the promise of brothers.

The black mare pawed the ground eagerly, and Ĵan's stallion tossed his head.

Dandio turned to Leopold, who waited on his left. "Hold the line. Wait until the Dal-kerri have reached the first marker before you order the battalion forward." He turned back to Ĵan, a familiar fire in his eyes. "Right, then. Let's draw these thrice-cursed Aces out of their little hole."

Ĵan gripped the reins, fixed his eyes on the fog below, then spurred his horse forward. He and Dandio cantered downhill toward the black mass. Behind him, he heard the rising notes of Leopold's horn giving the first signal. Their army stirred in readiness, but they did not charge—not yet.

He gripped Isilas before him, letting the Stone cast pale rays through the fog. Already, he saw the illusions crumbling—the mist nearest him was swept away as though by a powerful wind.

Light blazed from Isilas' core, crackling like fire, as though linked to his own Essence. Even in its corrupted state, the true source of the Stone's power shone brighter than the shadows without. The light pierced the illusions, scattering the fog as Ĵan and Dandio galloped along the valley's edge.

But the Stone's light affected more than the illusions.

As the nearest mist was swept aside, a shriek of rage rose from the waiting Dal-kerri. Howling and snarling, they lunged forward as one, abandoning their ranks in a frenzied rush to attack the hated light. As they did, white ice crystallized the ground. Ĵan turned his stallion's head just in time, shouting a warning to Dandio. His brother galloped close beside him, fire blazing from his hands as he deflected two blasts of ice.

"We have their attention," Ĵan called, keeping his head down. Isilas shone brilliantly, growing hotter by the moment. The pale light lit the oncoming force—thousands, perhaps tens of thousands, of enchanted soldiers. Even more numerous were the Dal-kerri, who lunged at the two riders, teeth snapping. Serpentines rose behind them in a flurry of bat-like wings.

"Head right," Dandio warned, deflecting another blast of ice. "We haven't seen the Aces, they're still inside that blasted fog—have to draw them out—"

Ĵan clipped his heels to the stallion's sides, galloping at an angle for the surging army. In a rhythm of countless boots, paws, and hooves, the Ace-army broke from their ranks, maddened by the Stone's light as they charged for the Red Dawn. Despite himself, Ĵan felt a smile cross his face. Dandio's plan had worked perfectly. The Ace-army had seized upon the bait with claws of steel.

"Move behind me!" he called to his brother. He heard Dandio shout something in reply, but his words were drowned out as Leopold's battalion charged to meet the onslaught. Even with their skilled knights, they would be outnumbered ten to one, and an unwelcome dread chilled his heart.

Isilas blazed in his hand, hotter and hotter until it seared his palm. *Unworthy,* the pain told him, echoing his own doubts. *It was your doing to corrupt it, and your hand is no longer worthy to wield this power.*

But this time he had no argument, nothing to counter. Only a prayer for forgiveness as the screams and clashes of battle erupted around him. *I was never worthy,* he answered in his heart, *and this power was never mine to wield. But I must ask for it once more—not for myself, but for these people—please, let the Light shine forth!*

White ice flashed past him, grazing his cheek, and he felt blood running down his neck. Isilas' pale light seemed to falter as three Aces appeared before him, black robes billowing in the wind, their skull-like faces grinning in anticipation.

Jan turned his horse back, straight for the line of woods as deadly ice sliced the air behind him. Dandio's red fire deflected one with a splitting crack—Jan heard him cry out in warning, and saw the fatal bolt fly at his face from the corner of his eye.

But a blaze of light flashed from Isilas' core, shattering the ice before it touched him.

He looked down at the Star-Stone, gripped in his blistered fingers. The light had darkened—no, not darkened, but no longer the blinding white of corruption. A flame of blue shone in its core, growing brighter and hotter by the moment.

"Left!" Dandio shouted behind him. "Back for the ridge—we have them where we want them!"

They turned, galloping back for the hills as the Ace-army swarmed behind them. The three Aces faltered before the brilliant blue; Jan glimpsed the surprise and unease on their ruined faces.

He looked left as they raced for the trees. General Leopold's horn sounded the second signal. Already, he saw Lord Fireclaw's warriors diving from the sky, claws flashing as they attacked.

. . . . . .

"A peculiar strategy," the Ace-Lord mused quietly, standing before the window in the high tower of Castle Salem.

The Deputy looked at him, hate and rage twisting his face. "The Stone, my lord," he stammered at last. "Its corruption has been—halted."

"I observed as much, my Deputy," the Ace-Lord replied calmly, his gaze remaining on the battle outside.

They had both watched as the scene unfolded. Watched as the High King and the Commander had charged, goading the Dal-kerri to attack and exposing the position of the three Aces on the front lines. Watched as their ordered ranks had been broken, despite the captains' efforts to control the beasts. Watched as the pale light of the Star-Stone had gradually faded blue again.

Outnumbered as the mortals were, they would prefer to see all their opponents at once to better assess their actions. In one wildly reckless move, the High King had brought the Ace-army into the open.

Sometimes the Ace-Lord enjoyed being surprised. He had almost feared the war would end quickly, as the sheer numbers of his force overwhelmed the mortal army. The High King's opening move promised a much more interesting game.

"You are dismissed," he told the Deputy. "Join our forces and reorganize them. And alert Redeyes to begin his task."

"As you wish, my lord," the Deputy answered, his jaw still tense with anger. "I—I trust you understand this is a trap?"

"Of course it is a trap, Deputy," the Ace-Lord answered, his voice still measured. "The mortals will not win this conflict without resorting to deception and ploys."

"Then you expected they would draw our warriors out?" the Deputy asked, sounding both impressed and puzzled.

"Indeed. It is a wise strategy in these circumstances," the Ace-Lord answered. "I did not expect them to do it in such a way. But the losses we can afford. Thus, for now, we shall play their little game. Fear is made sweeter if hope is at its ripest, and we have our own traps to spring." He turned back to the window, a smile playing over his decayed face as he watched the distant swirl of fighting. "Now, go. When you have finished organizing the force, join the vanguard at the castle gates. I believe we shall shortly see whether or not your work with your prisoner was successful."

"As you wish," the Deputy said again, but this time, his voice was calm, understanding what his master intended and eager to see the plot play out.

· · · · · ·

"That's our signal," Dusty called, as the second horn blast split the foggy air above the Strait.

Allie had waited tensely at the starboard rail for the last twenty minutes. At the Wildkid's voice, she moved promptly to the waiting rowboat, her heart pounding against her ribs. They had waited in gray darkness, settled on the little ship while the fog of the Nøkken concealed them from watching eyes, waiting for that very signal.

They had heard the sounds of movement on the shadowed Flats last night, and knew the Ace-army would be marching into position. The sounds had not told Allie much, not as much as they told Jarus or the Wildkids, with their ears better attuned to picking up the sounds. The one thing she had gathered was the sheer size of the army, far bigger than the force that had attacked Caer Sia.

Minutes before, the first trumpet blast had sent chills of adrenaline through her limbs. That meant Jan and her father had already launched their risky strategy to draw the Ace-army out of hiding. Whether or not it had worked, there was no way of knowing—and she had very little time to worry about it now.

The decks of the Wingship came alive at Dusty's voice, and the Wild-kid warriors and Cooper sailors lowered the rowboats to the water. Fog hovered over the Strait, hiding the distant banks from view. Allie could just see the outline of distant hills, and nearer, to her left, the top spire of Castle Salem.

There it was, waiting for the Vessel to enter its black halls.

"How much time do we have?" Aryion asked, looking at Dusty. He stood by the rail, peering into the foggy darkness.

"About an hour by Dandio's reckoning," Dusty answered. Her warriors had already boarded the boats. "We don't have a very large distance to cross, but the problem will be the illusions."

"I can help you there," Mel said as he climbed into the boat.

"That's great," Dusty said, "but you know that's what the Aces are expecting."

"That's why I'm here," Jarus said cheerfully, sliding his knife into its scabbard.

"Why we're both here," Aryion agreed, joining his apprentice in the boat.

Allie took a deep breath, resting her hand lightly on her sword hilt. She didn't feel afraid. Her mind felt calm and clear. The fire crackled readily in her veins.

Rygal cast their boat off from the ship, his armor glinting in the lantern light as he sat on the bench beside Allie.

"I'd say you look tense," she said quietly, "but I can't really blame you."

A slight smile flickered over his worried face. "Didn't I always say that—"

"When we'd spar, yes. All the time." Allie met his eyes, abandoning her attempt at humor. "It's going to be all right."

Rygal nodded, brow furrowed slightly. "Oddly enough… I think you're right."

"When we reach the shore," Aryion said, interrupting their quiet conversation, "keep your minds calm. The Aces can sense fear—your thoughts will betray you."

"I think they already know we're coming," Jarus answered. He raised his face to the wind, scenting the foggy air.

"They probably do," Allie agreed. "But Aryion's right. Our reaction to the illusions will reveal our position through our fear."

That knowledge chilled her more than anything else. She'd resolved herself to what awaited her in the tower. But the approach to that, toiling through mist while the illusions screamed in her mind… She hadn't had to worry about that during her last mission, protected by the Ace-Lord's curse. She doubted he would grant her the same immunity now. If the Ace-Lord could terrify her into the role of the Vessel, she had no doubt he would try.

"The Stone can get rid of those illusions," Mel ventured hesitantly. "When I sang the song in Tinkeeyo, it made a shield. I'm going to try that here, too."

"Which will help," Aryion told him, "but when you do, you will be vulnerable. It's your choice, but my advice is to wait until it is absolutely necessary before you use that power."

"I think so too," Rygal added, looking at Mel. "Both for the danger, and because a glowing Star-Stone and a song will definitely reveal our position."

"Better quiet down," Jarus cautioned in a low voice. "We're here."

Allie could barely see the hills through the fog—it was far thicker than the shroud that had concealed them on the Strait. This mist seemed a coiling wall of gray. She didn't see the shoreline until the rowboat ground against it, and the soft lapping of the water on the rocks drifted to her ears.

They had arrived.

Aryion and Rygal dragged their boat onto shore as the other boats reached them. The Wildkid warriors crouched in the shadows, ears twitching, curved daggers and spears in their hands, arrows on their bowstrings.

Dusty came last, stashing the last boat with Joesp and joining the semi-circle of waiting warriors. "The castle is directly before us," she told them softly. "About a half mile, I would guess. I can't tell if there's anything between us and them."

"I smell Dal-kerri," Jarus said softly, his furry face furrowed. "But I can't tell where—the fog distorts their scent."

"I can't hear the fighting anymore," Mel murmured, glancing in the direction of the battlefield.

"I can't hear *anything* anymore," Rygal observed slowly. "Anyone else?"

Allie strained her ears for a moment before realizing he was right. Aside from their muted voices and the dull shuffle of their motions, the world around them was soundless. The mist engulfed them in a void of pale gray. The distant clamor of battle, the lapping water, the whispering wind over the Flats—all had gone. It was silent as a grave.

"Let's go," Dusty said after a pause. "Our hour begins now."

"What happens in an hour?" one of the younger Wildkids whispered.

"The next signal," Joesp reminded him. "The Red Dawn will pull back and draw the Ace-army after them, but there is a chance the Aces may return to the castle. If we are not at the gates by then, we'll be cut off."

They moved forward in formation, Wildkids surrounding Allie on either side. Rygal walked behind her, and Mel was ahead, the Stone glimmering faintly through the cloth of his vest pocket. She could make out Aryion's tall form next to him, but the mist blurred his features. Occasionally, the fog shifted so she could see Jarus next to Aryion, the Cooper's dark fur standing out in the white mist.

She flexed her fingers on her sword, realizing she'd subconsciously been gripping the hilt white-knuckled. She breathed in deeply, forcing herself to relax. Though her mind felt at ease, that didn't stop the adrenaline surging through her body. The unnatural stillness surrounding them did nothing to calm her.

And then she heard them. Voices, muttering in the air around her.

Allie paused, listening. The voices murmured in her ears, blurred and indistinct at first, but then gradually growing louder, until they screamed around her. Filled with pain and horrifically familiar.

"Too many—there are too many, fall back—"

"Dandio, they are on the right—hurry—"

"Fall back—fall back, men!"

"Dad," Allie choked, covering her ears to block out the sounds. Her hands were shaking, and her heart pounded so hard it hurt. The

Wildkids had stopped, each staggering back before sounds or sights only they could sense. But she heard nothing besides the voices—her father's, then Jan's, intermingled with the sounds of battle and the screams of the dead or dying. Rising with them was Redeyes' victorious roar.

Mel's voice cut through the terrible sounds. "It's an illusion! It's not real—it's the Aces—"

Gasping at the effort, Allie fought to block out the cries and raised her eyes, focusing on her companions. Mel had his hand in his pocket, already pulling the Stone out.

"No—don't use the Stone, Mel," she managed to pant.

Mel looked at her in disbelief. "It'll stop the illusions!"

"I know," Allie stammered. "But these illusions—the Aces set them up to catch us—they don't know where exactly we are—the Stone will give us away." Gritting her teeth, she hauled her mind back to the present, her body trembling from the fear and pain.

"We'll have to fight past it," Jarus said breathlessly. The Cooper had both paws clasped over his ears, but he seemed to have come to the same conclusion as Allie. "Whatever you do—don't follow the sounds, no matter what happens—that's how they'll catch us."

Dusty shook her head to clear it, face pale. "Very well—stay close, everyone."

Allie blinked away the tears and looked around. Their orderly ranks had broken—several of the Wildkids had staggered a few paces into the fog, following the illusions. Rygal knelt, his face drawn, leaning heavily on his sword. Allie took his hand and pulled him to his feet.

"Can you hear them too?" he asked. "You said—last time—the illusions didn't affect you."

"I think that was because the Ace-Lord wanted me there," Allie answered. Her voice sounded as though it came from far away. Though the voices had faded into the fog, the fear remained in her heart. The worst of it, she knew, was how *plausible* that scene had been. Perhaps it was happening right now—the Red Dawn scattered—her father slain—Redeyes killing Jan—

No. She could not afford to think like that. What they must do was continue on, no matter what happened.

Aryion had fallen to his hands and knees. As Mel helped him up, Allie saw an unfamiliar light in his blue-flecked eyes. "They wanted me here," he whispered hoarsely, shaking his head hard. "Mel… the Deputy… made me into something… something that I cannot control."

Foreboding gripped Allie's chest. Mel's face filled with concern, but he took his mentor's hand. "Just stay close to me—maybe the Stone can help if you're near it."

"Form up around the New Blood," Dusty ordered. "He's right—the Stone's presence has helped stop the illusions before."

The Wildkids grouped around them again, gripping their weapons as they started forward.

Utter silence filled the air around them. The illusions had slipped away like a large predator tormenting its helpless prey. It didn't matter that the sounds weren't real, Allie thought dully—in the moment, with her nerves already on edge, the illusions could serve to break her resolve. Though, that was likely what the Ace-Lord intended.

They walked on. Voices swam in and out of the air, but not as loud or painful as the first illusions. These came as snatches of memory. Jenna voices, harsh and echoing. Her parent's voices layering urgently over the other, just loud enough for her to recognize but not clear enough for her to tell what they were saying. She heard her companions' voices, too, though if they were real or not she couldn't tell. The world within the mist had a dreamlike quality, impossible to decipher from reality.

Rygal walked on her left, his jaw tightening with each step forward. Allie slipped her hand into his. His fingers interlocked with hers, but his face was still pale.

Several tense minutes passed before Aryion stopped. The ranger stood, hands clenched into fists at his sides, his eyes closed as he gasped for breath as though struggling against himself.

"Aryion?" Mel whispered anxiously.

Aryion's frame trembled before some great effort. At last he opened his eyes, his voice strangled. "My hands... tie my hands," he rasped. "Now—I can't stop it."

"No," Mel said firmly. "You're all right—we don't have to—" He broke off, wincing as some sound filled his mind.

Rygal hesitated, but fetched a length of rope from his pack and moved to the ranger uneasily. "You're sure...?"

Aryion gritted his teeth, speaking with an effort. "Can't you see... I can't stop this, it's what the Deputy wanted—turn me against—the rest of you." He jerked his head at the others, who waited uncertainly. "Do it, Rygal."

Rygal hesitated a second longer before securing the ranger's arms behind his back. "If you say so..."

"Tie them tighter," Aryion ordered shortly. "I can break those." Rygal gave a slight shrug and tightened the knots—Allie saw Aryion grimace as the cord bit into his skin.

"You're sure we can't just use the Stone?" Jarus asked.

"Not yet," Dusty said, shaking her head. "We're still too far from the castle. The Stone's light will give us away." She looked at Aryion a long moment, her expression troubled. "I—don't mean to be rude, but… is there anything you might do that we should be prepared for?"

Aryion let out a breath and shook his head. "I—don't know. I'll be fine once we're out of this blasted fog. Take my sword just in case," he added.

Mel did as he asked, sliding his mentor's sword into a loop on his pack. Allie was about to voice some reassurance, but the inhuman gleam lurking in Aryion's eyes withered any such effort. Whatever the Deputy had done to him seemed to have come to life again upon entering the mist.

"Let's pick up the pace," Dusty said. "We're probably halfway."

They started forward at a brisk march. Rygal kept a hand on Aryion's arm, ensuring the ranger did not break away. Allie walked next to them, trying to ignore the chills of foreboding running down her spine. She took Rygal's free hand in hers again, needing something to hold her in reality as the sounds started again.

Screams, shouts, cries of the past filled her mind. She heard snatches of distant battle, the chilling crackle of ice, the panting and snapping of Dal-kerri, the howling and icy torrent of the wind that had dragged her back into the Ace-Lord's gateway, freezing her in time and space.

"It's not real," she whispered, barely feeling the words that had come from her lips. They were a mindless chant, the only thing grounding her to reality. "It's not real. It's just an illusion… it's not real."

The sounds faded as she moved on. New voices replaced them, but drifted farther away as her mind fought against the mist.

She kept her hand in Rygal's, hearing him whispering the same words beside her. Saying it aloud seemed to help. Aryion stumbled ahead of them, straining now and then against the ropes while hollow light shone in his eyes. Dark veins stood out on his neck as he struggled with some unseen demon in his mind.

The black outline of Castle Salem had just come into focus before them when Allie heard a new combination of sounds, sounds she recognized instantly.

Waves lapping against the coast. Brownae warriors crying out in pain. The clash of swords. The hiss of serpentines above her.

And this time, the sounds were not alone.

The scene replayed itself before her eyes, painted from the mist itself. She saw the dead scattered across the rocky beach, the enchanted soldiers surrounding her, the blood on their swords lit by her red fire as it flared again and again. She felt the ache of the cut on her shoulder, felt the inferno rising uncontrollably in her chest.

No. Not this day. Anything but this day.

She squeezed her eyes shut to block it out, but the scene was drawn from her memory, and she could not escape it. She watched, from a far closer angle than she had lived, in far too much detail, as Redeyes loomed up behind Darion even as the ranger raised his arrow in her defense.

"No!" she gasped, gripping her head in both hands. *No,* her thoughts screamed, *turn around, don't let that shot fly, turn around, he's going to—*

She felt herself stagger forward, engulfed in the illusion, Redeyes before her, snarling in triumph. Fire crackled from her hands—too late, she knew—too late to stop the past. But the renewed horror of this battle had broken the little control she had left.

Red fire blazed from her fingertips—she saw Redeyes' claws rake again down Darion's back, shredding the life from him in a single blow.

Her knees slammed against the parched ground of the Flats, and she knelt there, gasping.

Red flames flickered on the ground before her, blindingly bright in the gray nothingness. They flared for an instant before fading away.

Rygal was beside her, trying to raise her. "Allie—Allie, it's not real—wake up—"

Her vision blurred, and she felt sick. Dusty's voice, rising in tension, echoed in her ears, at last drawing her back to reality. "I scent something—form up, quickly."

A collection of cluttered and frightened voices followed this announcement.

"No enchanted soldiers—a few Dal-kerri, I think, but I can't tell…" That was Jarus' voice, filled with fear.

"I don't see them," came Mel's hesitant words. "Are you sure they're not an illusion?"

"No, we couldn't scent an illusion," one of the Wildkids snapped, his fear sharpening his tone.

"It's not an illusion," Dusty answered, though she sounded uneasy. "I can't tell exactly what it is, but there seem to be Dal-kerri."

Allie struggled to her feet—her limbs seemed to have turned to jelly, and she fell into Rygal's arms again.

"How many?" Rygal asked.

"A whole pack, maybe more," one of the other Wildkids answered, her voice trembling with fear. "They're coming from the castle—they saw the fire."

"You *had* to shoot fire at it, Heiress," another Wildkid said bitterly.

"This isn't her fault," Rygal snapped immediately. "Settle your tone before I make you."

Allie's gaze finally focused on the present, and she put a hand on his shoulder as a much more urgent fear presented itself. "Rygal—Rygal, help Aryion—"

Rygal's gaze followed hers, and he sprang forward.

Aryion had dropped to his knees, writhing as he fought the restraints, his pale face twisted in a brutish frenzy. In one swift movement, he broke the ropes securing him as though they were made of straw, then lunged at Mel and the Star-Stone. His apprentice staggered back, eyes wide in disbelief and horror as he clutched the Blue Stone close.

Rygal intercepted him just in time, tackling the ranger to the ground and locking an arm around his throat. Aryion thrashed in his grip, fighting blindly.

"Aryion—it's me," Mel stammered, his voice raw with fear. His face cleared as he raised the Blue Stone above him.

"They'll know—Mel, stop!" Allie ordered, stumbling forward. Aryion choked, clawing at Rygal's arm. A haunted light shone in his eyes, a darkness planted by the Deputy weeks before for this very purpose.

"They already know!" Mel yelled back. "They're coming—this is the closest we're going to get." With that, he allowed the blue light to shine forth.

Allie sensed, as well as saw, the illusions fade away. The fog pulled back, and with it, the strange silence shrouding this part of the Flats. She was instantly aware of the clamor of battle less than a mile away—the rumble of cannonfire, the clashing steel, the flashing fire.

But her attention was drawn to the left. Receding with the fog were the shadows surrounding Castle Salem. The companions stood just over a hundred yards from it, close enough to see the veins of silver inlaying the black walls and the stained glass windows of the high towers.

The massive black gates facing them had been flung open. Streaming across the Flats toward the small group, howling in excitement, were hundreds of Dal-kerri.

53

Flames of Red and Blue

In every battle and slaughter the Ace-Deputy had brought about in servitude to his master, one thing was consistent. He had always enjoyed it.

The Red Dawn's first charge had broken before the utter strength of the Ace-army, driven back up the rise. Bodies carpeted the Flats, and the stench of death filled the air. But that charge had dealt a blow to the Ace-army, too. The High King had seen to it that the Ace-army were caught in one place when the first attack had struck them, and destroyed the illusions concealing them. The Dal-kerri had charged forward in frenzied excitement, and the three Aces, who had been ordered to remain hidden until the chosen time, had nonetheless fallen for the Liznee king's trick and revealed themselves far too early.

Stubborn mortals, and infuriatingly clever at times, too.

The Deputy turned his mount's head back toward the battle lines, letting the skeletal horse-like beast gallop freely over the bloodstained battlefield. The Ace-Lord's forces had been reorganized quickly enough. The enchanted soldiers followed orders without question, as did the mercenaries, though they responded slower. The beasts were harder to control—goaded into excitement by the scent of blood, itching for a fight.

Redeyes was no different, the Deputy thought in disgust. He hadn't seen the massive cat since the charge had begun. Either the brute had been slain—which, though preferable, was highly unlikely—or he'd gone to gorge himself on the spoils of war.

Dark clouds roiled overhead, and the wind was rich with the promise of coming snow. Captain Fargrin waited before the front lines, saluting as the Deputy rode over. "Sir—the serpentines are gathered and have been prepared."

"What are our casualties?" the Deputy asked shortly, studying the warriors. The enchantment kept their forces from death, but irritatingly, the spell had still been cast on mortal bodies. Several of their squadrons had been caught in the line of fire of the Red Dawn's cannons, sustaining injuries so severe they would take hours to regenerate. That would cost time—valuable time, which the Ace-Lord would not count lightly.

"About thirty of my regiment have been removed from the battle," Fargrin answered. "As for the others, I am not sure. I believe Redeyes may have more information—he has gone to the north side of the force."

"The north?" the Deputy repeated, feeling a flash of anger. "I ordered him to organize the next charge."

Captain Fargrin did not reply. Foolish Redeyes. Foolish, prideful cat, so insistent that the only orders he followed came from the Ace-Lord directly. He paid little heed to anyone else, not even the Deputy, though the Deputy's orders were nearly as powerful as the Ace-Lord's on the battlefield.

He inhaled deeply, cooling the anger that had risen in him. "No matter. Captain, join my vanguard and await your next orders. We have a new assignment."

Fargrin hesitated a moment. "We are leaving the battlefield?"

"Only this area of it. We are to guard the main gates," the Deputy replied. "Now go."

The enchanted captain bowed slightly and moved to join the waiting squadron.

Of all the squadrons in the Ace-army, none gave the Deputy such pride as his own vanguard. It consisted mostly of orcs—tall and burly, the finest warriors of their people, made the more so after the Deputy had finished fashioning them. The enchantment bound the vanguard, but the Deputy had added to it, imbuing them with his strength, turning them into something no longer fully mortal. Beast-like strength, animal mindlessness, able to withstand the deepest pain.

It was this fate that he had intended for the Hummingbird, though the ranger's mind had broken before he could complete the process. The stubborn prisoner had been left with only a portion of the power that could have been his, a strength he could not fully control. But the illusions would have drawn it out of him by now, the Deputy knew. The stronger the illusions, the more powerful the vanguard grew, as he had intended for them. Once exposed to the fog placed on the perimeter, the ranger would not be able to resist the effects.

A low, skeptical snarl drew him from his thoughts. "The gates? What do you mean by this?"

The Deputy turned to face Redeyes. The great cat's black fur was covered in blood, none of it his own. His claws and teeth were stained by it. The light in his soulless eyes still glimmered with the enjoyment of the killing he had done.

"And where have you been?" the Deputy demanded. "I ordered you to wait with the serpentines."

Redeyes met his gaze with the same contempt and dislike in the Deputy's voice. "I was brought forth to kill," he said shortly. "Not to organize your war. That is my task, and until my master gives me another, that is what I shall continue to do. Those who have been Marked must be reckoned with."

"*Our* master," the Deputy said delicately, "has given command of this defense to me. Thus, you are under my orders."

"I will agree to that only after my task is finished," Redeyes replied.

The Deputy shook his head in resignation. Fine. Let the Ace-Lord deal with Redeyes later. He did not have time to argue with the insufferable beast now. "As you wish. There is but one Marked One left, though I do not have the faintest guess of where the High King is now."

"He was wounded," Redeyes told him, an eager light in his face. "I scented his blood on the arrows of the field. It shall not be a difficult fight."

The Deputy nodded, satisfied. "Very well. When you have finished that task, join my squadron at the main gates. We will likely have need of you."

"Why the gates?" Redeyes asked again. "No mortal would be fool enough to infiltrate there."

"Clearly, you have not met *these* mortals in particular," the Deputy snapped back. "Go back to your mission. Enjoy the kill. I will see you shortly."

Redeyes turned and prowled back down the lines of warriors, raising his massive head to the breeze. The Deputy watched him go, hating every self-satisfied step the beast took. Redeyes knew very well who had command over them both, as much as the Deputy might hold some authority over the army. The Messenger must see to it that the Marked

Ones were reckoned with, as the Ace-Lord had ordered.

Once that task was finished, the Deputy hoped greatly that he might be the one that would send the prideful beast back to the land of the dead.

He swung his mount's head to the right and cantered toward the waiting vanguard.

．．．．．．

"Archers, forward! Now!"

Dusty's sharp command split the tense pause that hovered over the company as the fog receded before the Stone's light. Allie shielded her eyes from the blinding blue as the illusions were swept aside, her gaze fixed on the oncoming Dal-kerri.

Hundreds of them, as the Wildkids had scented earlier, almost as large as the group that had attacked in Gayrile. Except then, there had been far more warriors to help them—here, caught out in the open and still reeling from the illusions' effects, the Wildkids' infiltration group might be easily overwhelmed.

Allie tore her eyes away from the hounds and rushed to Rygal, who had fallen to the ground with Aryion. The ranger had gone limp at the flash of blue; he lay unmoving on the parched earth, gasping for air, his blue-flecked eyes hollow and expressionless. The brutish madness had passed, leaving him unresponsive.

"Aryion—Aryion, please—" Mel's voice was tight with fear as he knelt by his mentor, pressing the Blue Stone into his cold hand.

Rygal stood, dragging Aryion upright. "We need to get to the gates."

"We'll carry him," Joesp said, moving forward with Nellioh. "Just keep us covered from the Dal-kerri."

Allie nodded, letting fire play at her fingertips. The surging inferno brought forth by the illusion had faded, and her thoughts were heavy with shame. *Fool,* her mind berated her furiously, *the Wildkids were right—your fire revealed our position.*

"It wasn't your fault, Allie," Rygal told her firmly, clearly guessing her line of thought. "Any of us would have fallen for it, and the Aces would have figured out where we were eventually."

"Right," Allie said, shaking her head to clear it. It didn't matter whose fault it was—what mattered now was reaching those gates. The Dal-kerri were nearly upon them, prowling forward across the Flats. She turned to Dusty. "Where do you want us?"

Dusty gave her a weak smile. "Well, I've got a terrible plan, but I think it will work."

"We've had a lot of bad plans that ended up working," Rygal said.

"All right: we're not going to form up for a fight here. We're going to charge right through the Dal-kerri and keep running until we reach the gate."

Allie looked at her in disbelief—this was far cry from Dusty's usual careful strategy. Rygal raised his eyebrows. "I—suppose we'd keep the momentum of the charge—it might work."

"I can create a shield for us, too," Mel said. His voice was still shaky, but his pale face was set in determination.

"Arrowhead formation," Dusty ordered. "Archers on the edge. Rygal and Allie, take the lead with me—your fires can help drive the warriors back. Jarus, stay close to Mel."

Jarus nodded—he had already moved to Mel's side, saxe knife gripped in his paw.

Allie stepped to the front of the group, raising her sword and letting fire flicker in the fingers of her other hand. Golden light warmed her face at her right as Rygal raised his sword and shield, and she threw him a slight smile. "Ready?"

Rygal grinned, firelight reflecting in his blue eyes and illuminating that crooked smile that had captured her heart. "Whenever you are, princess."

"Steady!" Dusty ordered behind them. The archers had their bows at the ready. The Blue Stone shone behind Allie, casting her shadow across the ground before her.

The Dal-kerri had almost reached them—Allie could see the leaders quickening their pace, hackles bristling, teeth bared in anticipation.

"Now!" Dusty shouted.

A volley of arrows leapt away as the companions surged forward. The closest hounds, startled by the sudden advance, were far too near to avoid the deadly blades that raised to meet them. Some skidded on the loose shale as the Wildkids raced past them—screaming with rage, they regained their footing and bounded toward their fleeing quarry.

Allie raised her hand and spread crimson flames across the ground before her. Rygal's golden fire shot along the blade of his sword, joining her blast as they drove a fiery wedge through the Dal-kerri charge. She heard Dusty's voice calling commands to the others, heard the deep thrums of the answering bows. Her boots pounded the ground as she ran, eyes fixed on the outline of Castle Salem directly ahead. Hounds sprang endlessly before her. She slashed and stabbed, never stopping long enough to see if the blows had landed, keeping her pace as they pressed for the castle.

Then, over Dusty's shouts and the howls of the Dal-kerri, she heard Mel begin the song.

The boy's voice came clear as he ran, raising the words in the old Liznaeic tongue, loud and strong over the cacophony of battle. Allie saw the Dal-kerri hesitate a moment before a ray of brilliant blue light shot from the Stone's core. Veins of blue fire spread before, behind, and beside them as they ran, until it seemed to Allie that every one of her companions were cloaked in blue flames.

"Keep going!" Dusty shouted.

"Keep singing, Mel!" came Jarus' excited voice, and she heard the Cooper pick up the words of the song. He missed a few words here and there, but that did not seem to matter. The Song of the Stars rose into the air over the Salem Flats, accompanied by the multi-colored flames.

The Dal-kerri had drawn back, shrinking away before the fire, clawing at their ears as though the song burned them. The Wildkids drove forward unhindered.

Castle Salem loomed before them.

It was the first time Allie had seen it up close. She'd been inside before, but only for a moment, and her memories of that time were blurry with her fears for Jan and Mel. But now, she beheld Castle Salem in its full dark glory. Black walls and beams wrought by unnatural power stood over the desolate valley, gleaming with silver veins. Five glossy towers rose high into stormy sky, black against the roiling gray clouds, so that the silhouette looked like a great horned crown. Instead of the ancient yet haunting might that had filled the air around Castle Droco, Castle Salem cast an ominous foreboding, frigid cold as Ace-ice, cruel as its master, beckoning her forward.

She caught a wolf across her sword blade and kept running. The Wildkids formed up before the great gates, a new volley of arrows leaping from their bows. Now that Allie was up close, she could see the top of a high wall surrounding Castle Salem, at least thirty feet tall. No guards stood on the bulwarks, nor in the courtyard beyond—as her father had predicted, the bulk of the Ace-army would be on the Flats, focus fixed on the trap the Red Dawn had laid for them.

But even as she had the thought, a lone sentry seemed to materialize from the shadows, ghosting forward. White ice glittered on its fingertips as its purple-red eyes fixed on Mel.

Mel, still holding the Stone above his head, faltered as the ice crackled in the air.

"Get back!" Allie cried breathlessly, her voice breaking in terror as she sprinted forward.

It all happened in an instant, so fast Allie barely registered it—Rygal stepped in front of Mel, golden fire spreading along his shield as the white ice flew from the Ace's hands. The ice struck his shield, sending him toppling backward into Mel. In the same breath, Allie's red fire struck the Ace in the shoulder. She heard its furious hiss as it raised its hands again, a second blast already sparkling in its fingers.

She barely had a second to think, seeing only the white ice, hearing Dusty's warning cry. White fire blazed again in her hands, crackling with an intensity she could no longer control, as she stepped forward, sending two blasts in quick succession. The first shattered the bolt of ice—the second cleaved the Ace's head cleanly from its shoulders. The black robes hung suspended for an instant before they crumpled to the ground.

Allie fell to her knees, gasping for air, trying to steady her pounding heart. The inferno surged to life in her chest, blazing around her. Someone gripped her shoulders, steadying her—Rygal. Ash streaked his face, and his shield still gleamed with white frost. But he was unharmed. "Allie—Allie, are you all right?"

"Yes," she managed to pant. "I'm… not hurt." Her eyes swept over the scene around her. Mel knelt where Rygal had shielded him, still holding the Star-Stone aloft and allowing blue fire to spread in a shield around him. In front of her, pale fire gradually engulfed the Ace's body.

"You just—did you see what you just did?" Rygal asked incredulously, managing an unsteady smile.

Allie took a deep breath, turning away from the burning body. The aggression and heat hadn't been her own. She had not felt the inferno since Gayrile, when her heart had been encased in ice and her flames had blazed white like the corrupted Star-Stone. But the horror of the last hour—the illusions, Aryion's sudden attack, the wolves, and that heart-stopping terror when the Ace had emerged—had fed into the fear.

Fear that the Ace-Lord had used well. Fear that fed his own power, imbued in the Vessel.

"I'm all right," she answered softly. "But—I don't think I should use that power again."

"Gates are secured," Dusty reported, helping draw Allie out of her churning thoughts. The Wildkids had gathered in two semi-circles around the gates, arrows on their bowstrings, blades drawn and ready. Aryion stood with them—the ranger's expression was still glazed and distant, and hollow blue light lurked in his eyes.

But Allie had no time to worry for him as she turned slowly to face the castle. The path lay open before her. Through the courtyard, up the stairs, into the high tower to the gateway that awaited.

No time to think twice. No time to say goodbye to the others. The time for fear had passed.

She looked at Rygal, seeing both unease and determination in his eyes. He nodded steadily and tightened his grip on his sword.

Allie turned to Dusty—the Wildkid's gaze flicked between the two of them, filled with sorrow and worry. But she managed a slight smile. "We'll hold the gates. Good luck."

"You too," Allie told her. She paused a moment longer and glanced down at her bloodied sword. At last, she wiped the blade clean on her sleeve and slid it back into the scabbard. She would hardly need it inside the tower—the Ace-Lord would not be killed by mortal weapons. Thus, she must rely on the fire—not the white flames, though they would tempt her when the horror and rage overwhelmed her. No, that power was not the one she needed to trust in.

Trust in the High Light, came her mother's words. She looked up at the sky. For just an instant, the black clouds parted, and she glimpsed the stars shimmering high above, illuminating the path as the Light guided her onward.

With Rygal beside her, Allie turned and strode through the gates of Castle Salem as the first snowflakes began to fall upon the blood-stained Flats.

54

❧ ❧ ❧ ❧ ❧ ❧ ❧ ❧ ❧

Debt Atoned

Blood. It filled his nostrils as he breathed, streaked the ground around him, shone on the blackened blade of Drisilas.

Jan took another deep breath, forcing fresh air into his bruised lungs, and leaned heavily upon the sword as he studied the battlefield. Thus far, Dandio's plan had worked perfectly. The Ace-army had surged forward, closing iron jaws upon the trap the Red Dawn had laid for them. General Leopold's battalion had fought valiantly before falling back, feigning defeat, and drawing the Dal-kerri away from Castle Salem and into the kragons' waiting claws.

Lord Fireclaw had charged then, his warriors raining fire and talons upon the backs of the wolves. They had killed nearly the entire pack before the enemy leaders had regained control, drawing the frenzied hounds back. As Leopold had sounded the third signal, Jan and Dandio had spurred their mounts back down into the fray again.

From there it had been nothing but steel and fire and blood for what seemed like hours. The gray light gave no indication of how much time passed. Snow had begun to fall by the time the Ace-army started to pull back, as though wearied. The mortal allies had followed, pressing them back into the valley.

It was then that the Ace-Lord had sprung his own trap.

A massive host of enchanted soldiers had struck from their concealment

650

in the shadows, hitting the unprotected right flank. The kragons, circling above, had seen the danger first, diving down in a desperate attempt to warn their allies—but not swift enough. Ĵan had been in the center of the charge—at first, he hadn't understood the kragons' reactions, the thunder of battle and galloping horses drowning out their warning.

But Dandio's shouts had finally reached his ears, ordering the charge left, away from the sudden onslaught. Arrows and fire hissed through the air, and gunshots crackled behind them as they fought to flee the deadly attack. The stench of gunpowder and death filled the valley as the mortals had fled for the thin line of trees, where the hama-dryad archers could protect them.

Ĵan's horse had been shot out from under him by a crossbow bolt as he'd galloped back toward Dandio. He had hit the ground hard, crashing into the muck, narrowly avoiding being pinned beneath the body of his loyal stallion. Battle raged around him as he fended off the hounds. There he had stood, voice hoarse as he shouted for the wounded to withdraw, letting Isilas shine a beacon out of the bloodbath and guide the wounded to the safety of the trees.

That light had undoubtedly revealed his position to the enemy archers.

Where the arrows had come from, he hadn't seen—only felt them strike, one after another, one stabbing his ribs and the other slamming into his shoulder with enough force to heave him backward. He had fallen to his knees, barely even registering the pain as he gripped the Star-Stone. *Take it from here*, his mind had ordered. *You must get the Stone away, or they will take it!*

Through the haze of pain, the dark mass of the oncoming charge swam before his eyes, but then the figures rose up between them, clad in deep greens and blues. Startled cries rose from the Ace-army as indigo ice crusted the soil, protecting the retreating wounded. Through a blur of pain he realized, in relief, that the Druids had arrived.

A hand had pulled him upright, supporting him as he staggered to the tree line, where his knees gave out and he fell to the ground again.

"Be still," came Iriam's deep voice from above. "Have you the Stone?"

"Yes," Jan answered, barely recognizing his own rasping voice. Pain flared in his shoulder as Iriam removed the arrow, and he clenched his teeth to keep from crying out. "Where… where is Dandio? Have you seen him?"

The Neutral did not immediately answer, and cold fear clutched Jan's heart. "No, I have not. I intend to find him—the strategy to attack the Ace-Lord's fortress may need adjusting."

Jan looked up at him. "Allie's attack?" he rasped. "Why?"

Iriam paused, looking back towards the castle. "The perimeter has fallen. However, many Dal-kerri guard Castle Salem, and we have received word that the Deputy himself has gone to aid their defense." He pressed a cloth to the wound on Jan's ribs.

"When—will you join Allie's group?" Jan panted, shaking his head to clear it. The next part of the plan—Iriam must lead a force to strengthen the Wildkids guarding the gates, while the Red Dawn continued to battle the Ace-army here.

"I will go now, if it is your order," Iriam replied. "But I too fear for Dandio. His battalion attacked the front lines, and they may have been cut off from retreat." The uncertainty in his usually steady voice heightened Jan's growing fear. Yet dangerous as Dandio's plight would be, nothing must hinder Allie's mission. Iriam's presence was more needed at the gates of Castle Salem.

With an effort, he stood, gripping Drisilas and holding the Star-Stone to his chest with the other hand. "I will find Dandio. You must help Asescia and the Wildkids—if they aren't inside Castle Salem by now, they may be in peril."

Iriam inclined his head slightly to him, concern still on his face. "Very well, sire. See to it that you go to the medical tent first." He headed down the tree line, where the shadowy green concealed the Druids.

Jan leaned on Drisilas, staring down at the churning mass of bodies in the valley below as he gathered his strength. The smell of gunpowder, steel, and blood carried on the wind. The Strait traced a silver line to his left, and through the dim light he could make out the lanterns onboard the Cooper ships. Swarms of Dal-kerri had attacked the Coopers on the beach; he could see the tangle of battle from here. The archers of Elimar, their green and golden uniforms occasionally visible in the darkness, held their positions at the base of the hill, protecting the camp at their backs. Kragons swept over the battlefield, occasionally diving down to strike. Flares of white ice retaliated, and twice Jan saw it hit its mark, saw a kragon plummet lifeless into the chaos.

Where was Dandio?

Painfully, he turned, not toward the medical tent, but toward the command post. Five Red Dawn officers had joined the hama-dryads in the trees. Munben-Lia stood listening to their report, but all stopped as the High King limped up to them.

"Sire…" one of the generals began, concern on his face.

Jan studied the group, feeling his heart sink. Dandio was not here. "Where is the Commander?" he asked, looking from one to another.

Admiral Dessian shook his head uncertainly, blood staining his silver skin. "We don't know, sire. He and Glentree led the last charge. When the second attack came, we lost sight of him."

That division of the Ace-army, Jan knew, was mainly Dal-kerri hounds. Surely there were no beasts among them that would delay Dandio and Glentree for long—and if they had been outnumbered, they would have retreated. Dandio was a smart enough strategist to know to do that. The only beast in the Ace-army that would match him would be an Ace itself—but Jan had not seen any in that area.

Or...

Fear, icy cold, chilled his heart, as though claws had raked over his chest. "What area was he last seen?" he asked at last, taking another painful breath.

"The left flank, we believe," one of the generals replied slowly.

"You are wounded, sire," Munben said, his deep voice measured but troubled. "Allow us to seek the Commander. You must go to the healers."

Jan shook his head. "No—this I must know. I alone may be able to help him." He met Dessian's uneasy gaze. "Tell me—do we know who commanded that section of the Ace-Lord's forces? His Deputy, or another Ace?"

"That update came from the dryads," Dessian answered, glancing at Munben. "Who commands the left flank?"

The hama-dryad chieftain placed a gnarled hand on the ashen bark of the tree beside him, closing his eyes a moment as if straining to hear a voice. Wind stirred the branches, carrying the screams and cries of the battle beyond.

"There is no commander of the left flank," Munben said at last, brow furrowed. "Only hounds and snakes. But the dead trees in that valley bear the scars of the Messenger."

Jan lowered his eyes. Redeyes, the Messenger of the dead. The Marks on his chest seemed to flare again in pain, like a whisper reminding him of the fate before him.

At last he looked at Dessian. "Continue to the next phase of the plan. Do not wait for us."

"Allow my warriors to accompany you," the admiral insisted. "Sire, please—if Redeyes has attacked Dandio, he surely intends to draw you to him as well."

"I don't doubt that," Jan agreed quietly. "But the outcome of this battle is more important than what Redeyes desires. I may turn his plot against him."

He turned, striding back through the trees, passing crowds of wounded warriors as he went. Snow speckled the dead on the Salem Flats. Blood trailed down his left arm and wet his side as he placed the Star-Stone safely in its case.

There was no uncertainty about where he had to go, what he must do. Redeyes was a brutally predictable creature. There would be no subterfuge or trickery in his trap. He must have the blood of the Marked One, as the curse required, and Jan must face him, as he had long anticipated.

No, Jan thought, as he stumbled through the snowy trees, his unease had now settled solely on dread for his brother.

. . . . . .

Dandio dragged himself to his feet and watched as the last hound fell dead, fire smoldering on its chest.

A trap. He should have expected it, but there was not much he could do now. What mattered was that the Red Dawn knights and their allies had managed to regroup quickly, driving forward against the Aces' lines while the wounded had retreated. Fire had blazed among the Dal-kerri, searing the serpentines, and lit the left flank in brilliant red light.

Dandio had not seen where Redeyes had come from. The great cat seemed to have emerged from the shadows themselves, just as Glentree had left to aid the retreating soldiers. Redeyes had waited for Dandio to dismount, waited for him to pursue a small pack of Dal-kerri into the tree line, then came from behind and struck. His claws had shredded the back of Dandio's armor as though it were made of paper, but the steel had saved his life, leaving only broken edges that dug into his skin.

Dandio had spun about, fire blazing in his hand, realizing in an instant that he had miscalculated. The Dal-kerri lunged upon him, teeth snapping at his throat, rancid breath on his face. He had no idea how long the fight took—it felt like mere seconds, fire blazing from his fingers, sword a blur in his other hand. Motions so terribly familiar they had become second nature.

Finally the last hound fell, and he faced Redeyes. The beast made no move to attack, only crouched before him, tail lashing the underbrush with the satisfaction of a cat watching a mouse.

Dandio waited a moment, catching his breath, every muscle in his body tense as he waited for the beast to spring. "Come on, then," he snapped at last, fire crackling in his fingers.

Redeyes regarded him with contempt. "If I am to enjoy killing you, it will be as I choose it," he growled. "The Dal-kerri did not take you long to defeat."

"Fearful, aren't you," Dandio mused, pacing slowly to the side. "I suppose you should be. After all, I was the one who sent you to the land of the dead in the first place—and I have no qualms about doing so again."

The growl rose in Redeyes' chest. "It will not be so this time. There is only one other death that shall bring me more pleasure than yours, Liznee."

A trumpet blast split the air beyond, the signal for the next charge.

What charge was this? The fourth? His mind, distracted by the unexpected meeting with Redeyes, struggled to remember for a moment. Yes, it was the fourth. The time for Leopold—if Leopold was still alive to command—to lead the attack in a wide sweep, striking each side of the Ace-army. Someone had hopefully commanded the Druids to go join the Wildkids at the gates—likely Jan.

Good, Dandio thought fervently, *stay with the command post, Jan, don't try to come help me here—it's you Redeyes wants, not me.*

He understood the true nature of Redeyes' plan now. If Jan were to hear of his plight here, he would come to help—and walk right into Redeyes' claws. Redeyes had timed his attack very well—drawing Dandio here, to the edge of the battle, knowing Jan would come.

Dandio waited a moment, analyzing the situation. Attempting to escape would be fatal. Waiting for his brother to come help him would be far worse. He was alone, and if Redeyes wished to kill him, the best he could do was prevent him from killing any others.

Only one choice left, then.

Dandio took a deep breath, bracing himself for the pain to come, then lunged forward, fire flashing in one fist while he raised his sword.

Redeyes reacted at once, his claws catching Dandio's sword and hauling his arm sideways. Red fire burned the beast's fur, and Redeyes snarled in pain. Dandio wrenched his sword back, but the blade remained pinned beneath Redeyes' claws. He raised his other arm, shoving fire into the beast's face.

Redeyes' teeth closed on his forearm, crushing muscle and bone. A choked cry of pain tore from Dandio's throat—he let go of his sword, slamming his fist into the cat's face. Blinded by red flames, Redeyes twisted his head sharply to the side, throwing Dandio across the ice-packed clearing.

Dandio struggled to his knees, cradling his left arm. Agonizing pain radiated from beneath his mangled armguard, and he knew in an instant the bone had been broken.

Redeyes growled in triumph, pacing closer. Dandio crouched, fire flickering in his good hand, waiting for the cat to spring. Redeyes' next pounce would claim his life, he knew dimly. But a blast down the beast's throat, even as the claws claimed him, would at least keep the brute from killing any others, and bring them down to the grave together.

But a flare of flame struck Redeyes in the side before he sprang, throwing him off balance. Dandio turned to the trees, already knowing who had come, feeling a simultaneous surge of relief and dread. Of all the times he had hoped to be wrong—this had to be the worst.

. . . . . .

Jan stumbled into the glade, watching as the red sparks died on Redeyes' black fur. He had hurried through the stunted trees, listening to the distant thunder of battle as snow fell around him, but barely registered the sounds. He had seen the flare of Dandio's red fire, and, seconds later, heard his brother's strangled cry of pain that seemed to stop his heart. He had watched, too far away to help, as Redeyes had flung his brother across the glade. But he had been close enough to prevent the beast from striking a second time.

His first blast struck Redeyes in the ribs, flinging him sideways before he could leap. Dandio, hunched over his bleeding arm, looked over swiftly as Ĵan stumbled through the underbrush to reach him. The look on his face was a mixture of relief and horror. "He… wanted you to come here," he gasped, making a motion as if to push Ĵan back. "Go—get out—"

Redeyes prowled around them. Smoke trailed from the burns on his side, but the fire had angered him more than hurt him. "High King," he hissed, a hideous smile spreading over his face. "I expected you sooner."

Ĵan leaned on Drisilas, placing himself between Redeyes and Dandio. Pain radiated from the arrow wounds, and he felt the blood trailing down his side, but he gripped his sword tightly. The Star-Stone pressed against his chest, and he could feel its warmth with each heartbeat. This fight had waited before him for years, a fight he had dreaded above all others, a fate he had hidden from. Now, his trepidation had faded.

Nonetheless, he knew he could not defeat Redeyes alone. Not injured as he was.

He hesitated, glancing back at his brother. His immediate thought had been to order Dandio to flee, but knew he would never agree to leave him. Dandio had already dragged himself to his feet, injured arm pressed into his tattered cloak, fire flickering in his hand.

"Are you able to take my right?" Ĵan asked quietly.

Dandio gave a short, hoarse laugh. "I'll manage. Got a plan?"

"Partially," Ĵan said, watching as Redeyes paced before them, his pitiless eyes watching eagerly. "Mind his claws. And he fears fire—use it as much as possible."

"You understand," Dandio murmured, with a touch of wry humor, "I have defeated him before."

"I don't doubt that," Ĵan answered. "But it is me he wants, not you."

They stood there, shoulder to shoulder. Redeyes' gaze swung between the two of them, hateful and eager, and he gave a low growl of pleasure. "Your blade is cold today, High King. Where then is the fire you wished to summon?"

Jan did not answer, though the same thought had already crossed his mind. Drisilas blazed no more, cold and blackened, streaked in blood. The familiar heat, the warmth, the security the flames had brought, were gone as well.

Redeyes pounced, sharp claws flashing as he struck at Jan—Jan stepped back, the claws glancing off Drisilas' blade with a ringing screech. He sent fire crackling from his other hand; Redeyes dropped beneath the blast and slashed at the king again as Dandio fired a bolt from Jan's right. This time the flames made contact, singing the black fur. Redeyes snarled in fury and sprang at Dandio, who generated a shield of fire just in time.

Jan stepped forward as the beast slashed against Dandio's shield, sending another crackling blast into the burns they'd just inflicted. Redeyes stumbled, turning his blazing eyes to Jan. The fire, Jan realized, would not be enough to kill him. The beast was toying with them, drawing out their already weakened strength—once that strength was spent, they would both be dead.

He brought Drisilas up as Redeyes leapt upon him, slashing at the great cat's throat as he fell onto his back. Blood splattered across his face as he hit the ground, the air punched from his lungs. The great cat's claws sank into his injured shoulder, pinning his sword arm to the ground and opening the arrow wound afresh. Redeyes' teeth tore at his jerkin, seeking the Star-Stone.

Fire glanced over the cat's back before his teeth could tear deeper. Blindly, Jan wrested his hands free, flames crackling up his forearms as he shielded his face. He felt Redeyes' claws retract as the beast sprang off him. Blood streamed from a gash below Redeyes' jaw, and his breaths came rasping. Drisilas had finally dealt a more serious wound—though still not enough to stop him.

Jan rolled to his knees, gasping for air. Across the glade, Dandio launched two swift blasts at Redeyes before snatching up his fallen sword. Redeyes prowled toward him, bloodied teeth bared.

"Get back!" Jan ordered, fire flickering in his hand. His vision fragmented for a moment as he did. The Essence he'd spent only further weakened his exhausted body, but he launched the fire all the same, a desperate blast as Redeyes prowled towards his brother.

Dandio retreated slowly, his sword held before him. Redeyes ignored Jan's fire, looming before Dandio. The contempt and excitement in his eyes chilled Jan to the core. He would kill Dandio, revel in it, and then kill Jan as the grief crushed him.

Light help me.

Pain shot from his ribs as he stumbled forward, drawing breath to cry out in futile warning.

Dandio raised his injured hand, sending a wild blast of flame directly into the beast's face as Redeyes sprang. The cat's claws locked on Dandio's shoulders, slamming him down to the ground and knocking the sword from his grip. His teeth glinted to receive Dandio's throat.

Not him, Jan's thoughts screamed, *he's not the one who bears the Marks—he's not the one who deserves to die.*

The last fire of his Essence blazed in his chest, spread through his veins, channeled through his hands as he raised Drisilas. The little he had learned of channeling echoed in his mind as his thoughts cried out a desperate prayer.

All happened in a split second. Dandio plunged his good hand into Redeyes' open mouth, flames blazing in his fist, even as the cat's claws rent his breastplate in two. As he did, Ĵan brought Drisilas straight down, red flames crackling down the blade as his Essence channeled in a brief fiery blast and the sword pierced Redeyes' heart.

For an instant they hung there, suspended by blades and teeth and claws.

Redeyes let out a low, gurgling growl and slumped forward, claws still dug into Dandio's chest and plunging deeper by the moment.

Ĵan fell forward over Redeyes' side, still clutching Drisilas' hilt. Black spots swam in his vision, but he held on. "Let him go," he rasped, fire flickering weakly over his knuckles. "Let him go, you devil."

Redeyes snarled, but at last his claws loosened and he slumped to the frozen ground. Ĵan's grip on his hilt finally gave out as he collapsed beside the beast. Drisilas' hilt glimmered between Redeyes' shoulder blades, and smoke drifted from his seared throat.

Ĵan lay there, feeling his blood stream into the snow, his face inches from Redeyes' as darkness slowly engulfed him. For an instant, the great cat's eyes locked on his, twin flames blazing with hatred and pain.

Then the fire went out as Redeyes died.

55

Shadow Recalled

Through the thunder of clashing steel, Dal-kerri howls, and the battle cries of the Wildkid warriors, the icy voice was hissing again in Aryion's mind.

"Welcome," it snarled, hard as he tried to resist it. *"Did you believe you were rid of this? Do you not know that I am a part of you now, living in your thoughts forever?"*

Aryion closed his eyes, gripping his sword hilt. His legs were unsteady, muscles left trembling from the agony within the enchanted fog. It had been as if he were back in the black cell of Castle Salem, where his mind had filled with darkness and his body was controlled by another power.

While the others had heard voices and sounds in the illusions the fog created, to Aryion, the mist had been silent, icy hands searing his head and drawing forth the uncontrollable darkness the Deputy had planted in him. And, hard as he had tried to fight it, the blind violence and madness had taken him like the talons of a great beast. He was not exactly sure what had happened. The bleeding cuts on his arms where he had broken the ropes, the white dust covering his clothes where he had fallen, the hissing voice in his mind—those were the only clues, shadows of a dark nightmare he'd fallen back into.

But then he'd heard Mel's voice, rising high in the song of the *Alené,* and the shadows receded before it, bringing the return of present reality.

With great effort Aryion drowned out the hissing voice with truth and the resolve of his mission. *Protect him. Protect him.* That was why he had come here—not to writhe beneath the unseen demons in his mind, but to protect the boy he had come to love as a son.

Splitting pain gripped his mind as he set his stance, his back to the gates, and surveyed the battle around him. The frantic race to Castle Salem had not been in vain—Rygal and Allie had made it inside. Before him, Dal-kerri bounded over the pale flatlands towards the gates, leaping upon the outnumbered Wildkids in a wave of teeth and claws. The archers formed a protective ring around the castle gates—Mel stood and sang in the middle, the Stone above his head, casting brilliant blue light over the defenders.

His apprentice had described the mighty power of the *Alené*, but words could not do it justice. To Aryion, it seemed living vines had uncoiled from the Stone, spreading tendrils of coiling blue light around the warriors. Light spread down his body, too, comforting as the warmth of a fire upon his face. A shiver went down his spine, more of awe than of fear, as he beheld the High Light's power, channeled through the Star-Stone, held aloft in the New Blood's hand.

New strength, not the dark power the Deputy had given him, but true power borne of the same pure magic filling the air around him surged through his body as he stepped forward to join the battle. Jarus stood next to Mel, knife in paw, cutting down any wolves that broke through the archers' barrier, but he was tiring. Two hounds sprang at him at once—Jarus killed the first, but stumbled back as the second pounced upon him.

Aryion's sword slashed through the Dal-kerri's throat before its teeth made contact with the Cooper's neck. The blade swung smooth and fluid in his hand, familiar and trusted, returning some fragments of who he had been.

Jarus caught his breath and looked up gratefully. "Thanks for that. You all right?" His face was conflicted—Aryion could only guess what he had witnessed of him in the mist.

"I am now," he replied shortly. "Stay close to Mel. I can defend your place here."

He stood beside the Wildkid archers, slashing and stabbing everything that lunged at him. The blood roared in his ears, his heart hammering in rhythm with his strikes. His vision focused solely on his opponents, a new purpose crying a mantra in his mind. A purpose given to him—not by the Deputy, but by the High Light—a purpose to fight and defend his companions. The light of the *Alené* covered him as he fought, stronger than the voice whispering in his mind.

Dusty's voice drew him out of the motions, and he sensed the attacks fading away. "Hold! They're drawing back."

The archers lowered their bows. Dead Dal-kerri covered the plain before them. The survivors, as Dusty had just observed, had retreated, snarling, back toward the lines of the enemy army.

Mel's voice faltered, and he coughed, swaying in place. "Sorry—had to catch my breath," he panted.

"Take a minute, Mel," Dusty told him. "We'll regroup before the next pack arrives." She turned to Aryion, studying him carefully. Blood streaked her face from a cut just under her cheekbone, and her dark fur was matted by dust and grime, but she was mostly uninjured. "Are you…"

"Better now," Aryion told her, not wishing to dwell on the darkness in his mind. "I don't believe it will happen again," he added, sensing her unease. "Now that we are out of the fog, that is."

"Right," Dusty agreed, looking relieved.

Aryion moved back to Mel, who sat on the ground, his shoulders sagging in weariness. He glanced up at his mentor, and Aryion saw a trace of fear there that tore at his heart. "Are you all right?" he asked quietly.

Mel nodded rapidly. "Yeah—just had to catch my breath."

"That is not entirely what I meant," Aryion said slowly, scouring his memories for details of the last moments within the mist. The seconds were blurred and uncertain. Rygal had tackled him to the ground—he remembered the impact—but something had come before that. He looked at Mel, sickened. "I… attacked you, didn't I?"

"You tried to," Mel said hesitantly. "At least—I think you tried to attack the Stone. But it's okay," he added quickly. "You're here now. And the Stone can keep the illusions at bay."

Aryion nodded, unable to speak of the horror and guilt. The hissing voice, the unnatural strength, had overpowered him to the point that he had attacked his own apprentice. If Rygal hadn't—

He shook his head sharply, refusing to finish that thought. "I'm sorry," he said, and walked back to the archers.

Most of the Wildkids had suffered injuries. Four had been killed—their bodies lay across the plain.

Aryion moved to Jarus, who sat cleaning his knife blade. "I believe Mel is right about the Stone protecting us," he said quietly. "But I am not sure how far that protection extends."

Jarus looked up at him. "You're not sure that you're… safe, you mean?"

"I do not want to risk it," Aryion answered. "I can still protect him, but I would prefer not to be too close, in case… in case it were to happen again."

Dal-kerri blood stained his hands, and he wiped them uselessly on his trousers. So much blood. No telling if he were to break again, if the umber blood on his skin might be replaced by that of one of his companions…

Feeling ill, he looked at Jarus. "Stay close to Mel and keep him safe. I'll stay with the archers and try to prevent anything from breaking through to you."

"I can do that," Jarus agreed, nodding. "And Aryion—we know it wasn't your fault," he added.

Aryion paused as snow swirled around him, considering the Cooper's words. In the back of his mind, he could appreciate Jarus' sentiment, understand and agree with the fact that very little had been his fault. But that did not mean it was any less his responsibility.

"I know it wasn't my fault," he said after a pause, "but I need to gain control of it before I do something that is."

. . . . . .

The Stone warmed Mel's fingers as he sat on the cold ground next to Jarus, breathing deeply to calm his tired voice. His throat felt raw, and weariness filled his body at the sheer thought of another fight like that. This conflict, he thought, was undoubtedly the most difficult battle he'd ever endured, taxing both his heart and his body.

"Something is coming," one of the Wildkids announced nervously, raising his face to the wind. "I do not recognize the scent."

"I do," Jarus said, his eyes lighting up. "It's Iriam—with some others that match his scent," he added, sounding perplexed.

"The Druids," Mel breathed, a surge of excitement replacing the weariness. "I didn't know when they were coming to help us."

"Iriam was coming," Dusty corrected him. Her voice held a note of unease. "It's good they're coming, but it's odd the Druids would choose to involve themselves here."

Aryion, standing with the archers to Mel's left, glanced at her, clearly sensing her line of thought. "You believe there's something we must prepare for? Something serious enough for us to need the Druids' aid?"

"Let's hope not," Dusty said. "I can't smell anything—but we have never been able to scent the enchanted soldiers from a distance." She looked at the archers, coming to a decision. "Form up and be ready. I don't know why the Druids are coming to help, but we'll find out soon."

Mel got to his feet, trying to hide the nervousness that had suddenly flooded him. Perhaps the Druids were simply coming with Iriam to make sure Allie's plan had worked. But for them to leave their position on the battlefield either meant some plan had changed, or there was trouble headed this way.

Most likely both, he thought.

He looked down at the Blue Stone, which glimmered in the eerie darkness. A gleaming crease running down the middle was the only indicator that it had once been two Shards. Memories of that struggle filled his mind for a moment—facing the Ace-Lord in the throne room in Castle Sia, flung in and out of the illusions even as he'd fought to join the Shards.

The Stone could protect him from visual illusions. The only tricks that could penetrate his shield would be the sounds, which he feared no less than the others. Hearing the screams and cries of his loved ones as he'd journeyed through the fog had exhausted him.

"There's another group coming," Joesp said slowly. The black-furred Wildkid stood to Mel's right, his face raised to the breeze. "From the direction of the battlefield—their scent bears resemblance to the enchanted soldiers, but there is something... different."

"I smell it too," Jarus said. The Cooper's ears flicked back uneasily. "Quite a lot of them, though I can't tell how many—I can't even tell *what* they are."

A chill ran down Mel's spine. "What do you mean? Aren't they just enchanted soldiers?"

"This scent's different," Jarus said, the dread in his eyes heightening Mel's fear. "Sharper, stronger—orcs, I think, but—there's something horrible about them."

At these words, Aryion turned to them. Even in the dim light, Mel could see his face pale.

"What is it?" he asked hesitantly.

"Iriam's here," Dusty said, interrupting the fearful conversation.

Shifting through the shadows, clad in robes of forest green or indigo blue, came the nine Druids. The silvery markings on their skin shone through the snowy wind.

Iriam strode among them. "It is good to see you all standing," he said, as Mel moved forward to meet him. "How fares your mission?"

"Well enough," Dusty told him. "Rygal and Allie have made it inside, and we've secured the gates for now."

"Good. That is very good," Iriam said, but his face was grim. "I fear we bring both reinforcements and fell news. A force marches upon you here, and the dryads have warned us that it is led by the Ace-Deputy himself."

"Enchanted soldiers?" Dusty asked.

"No."

All eyes turned to Aryion at the ranger's low voice. His face was drawn, studying the distant plain as though seeking a different answer. But at last he continued. "They are not enchanted soldiers. Not like the others. I—I have heard of these warriors. The Deputy's vanguard. They swore the enchantment, but they were gifted... other powers... as well."

Far across the plain, Mel saw the first riders appearing, cantering on undead mounts toward the gates.

"What sort of powers?" Dusty asked uneasily.

"Unnatural strength," Aryion replied. "Complete invulnerability. Heightened skill in battle." He looked down at his hands, stained by Dal-kerri blood, and Mel's heart sank as he understood.

"Is that... why..." he started hesitantly.

"It is what the Deputy intended for me," Aryion replied shortly. He took a breath, looking at Iriam. "I may not be able to undo what he did. But I may be able to match the vanguard in strength."

"You are not invulnerable as they are," Iriam reminded him mildly.

"Perhaps not. But I was changed by the same darkness," Aryion answered, turning to Dusty. "Move your archers closer to the gates. Your arrows won't stop them."

"We will form a barrier," Iriam said at last. "Our presence should keep the Ace-Deputy at bay. He fears and despises the Druids."

Mel looked between Iriam and Aryion in disbelief. The idea of hiding in the shadow of the gates, watching as the battle against immortal warriors unfolded, was more than he could bear. "We can't just fall back!" he protested. "And the Stone—"

"The Stone must be protected," Iriam reminded him gently. "You will better serve us here."

Mel knew he was right, knew all strategy—and his own Oath—demanded that the Stone be kept safe. But he could not accept the idea of Aryion facing the vanguard; even with his new strength, he would be outmatched and killed. It seemed he had only just got his mentor back—now, he might lose him for good.

"Move back as he says," Dusty ordered her warriors, motioning them toward the gates. "Encircle the New Blood, and keep your arrows at the ready."

Mel pressed past them to reach Aryion, grabbing his mentor's arm. "You're punishing yourself."

Aryion looked down at him and shook his head. "No. I'm doing what I must to keep you safe, as I promised. Your own oath keeps you guarding the Stone."

"I know," Mel answered, shaking his head. "I know you think it's your fault—what happened in the fog—but that's what the Deputy wants." His mentor hesitated, and he pressed on. "I know I have to guard the Stone. I can't help you on the battlefield, but I might be able to help another way."

Aryion arched an eyebrow. "You have a plan?"

Mel looked down at the Stone. Singing the song again would leave him vulnerable, especially with the Deputy involved. But he had to try. "I think so. Just stay where I can see you."

"I will try. Stay safe—please."

"Jarus'll keep me safe," Mel assured him.

"I daresay he'd better," Aryion replied with a tired smile, and with that, he moved to join the Druids as the vanguard galloped closer.

The Wildkid archers blocked the oncoming riders from Mel's sight, so that he could only hear the pounding of hooves as the demon horses drew close. He climbed onto a boulder beside the wall, catching glimpses of the steeds—sleek black hides, dagger-like horns, gaunt faces with broken teeth.

Aryion stood, stance set, sword in hand as he watched the riders circle. He had discarded his cloak, and seemed small and unprotected beside the towering Druids.

A rider wheeled his mount around, and Mel got his first glimpse of the vanguard. They seemed enchanted upon first sight, eyes shining hollow blue. But he could sense what was different about them, what Jarus had been unable to explain. There was an icy darkness about them, an evil that shrouded them, and an utterly wicked light on their frozen faces. Most were orcs, as far as Mel could tell, tall and muscular, their mortal strength enhanced and crafted into something unnaturally powerful.

These were no innocent mortals, tricked or bribed into servitude. These warriors had sworn the Oath with pride, and claimed the darkness the Deputy imbued them with eagerly. Theirs was a brotherhood forged of ice, wrought of darkness, and they embraced it without hesitation.

"Steady," Dusty said in a low voice—two or three of her archers had half-raised their bows. She glanced back at Mel, and Mel could see the same fear he felt reflected in her eyes.

Mel looked at Aryion, standing completely still beside the Druids, waiting for the right moment.

As one, the vanguard drew up sharply, their horses stamping and snorting, facing the semi-circle of defenders. Eleven figures—Iriam, Aryion, and the nine Druids—stood before them. Mel saw their hollow eyes scanning the tiny group with a bloodthirsty eagerness, like a starved wolf spotting prey.

All was still for a split second, aside from the swirling snow.

Then, in the same moment the vanguard charged, Aryion stepped forward.

Mel saw his mentor's sword come up, catching the upper leg of the first Dal-kerri steed, spraying the Flats with umber blood. The beast gave a scream of pain and rage as it fell forward, its rider thrown from the saddle. Aryion spun, clashing with the next warrior—their blades locked in place for an instant before he kicked the orc backward, directly into the hooves of another charging steed.

The Druids had responded too—ice the color of the night sky spread before them in blades, piercing the few steeds who did not turn aside fast enough. The remaining riders drew their mounts back, but Mel barely noticed them—his eyes were solely on his mentor.

He'd seen glimpses of Aryion's new powers before. This was something else entirely. Aryion caught every blow with ease, his blade a blur as he cut and slashed and parried. Five orcs encircled him, yet they were forced back. His natural strength enhanced, Mel thought dimly—if that were so, it meant the Deputy had taken one of the best swordsmen Mel had ever known and transformed him into a master.

But he was not invincible. Every one of his blows found a target, yet the warriors did not falter. No blood spilled from their wounds, no hesitation crossed their brutish faces.

The vanguard who had been thrown from their horses attacked the Druids. Mel saw ice pierce several of them, stopping the orcs in their tracks for a moment, but three made it through, and Mel saw them clashing with the ancient sorcerers.

"The Stone, Mel!" Jarus' shout drew him out of his frozen horror.

"Right!" he yelled back, taking a deep breath. "Do you see any Aces?"

"No, not yet!" Jarus replied. He stood tensely, ears laid back, hackles up along his back as he waited. Mel could tell he was nervous—neither of them would stand a chance against those massive warriors.

But their protection came from a higher power. Raising the Stone, he began the words of the song again.

As if from far away, he heard the sounds of battle, the screams, the clashing, the roars. He sensed, too, that his voice was joined by others. The Wildkids had caught onto the song's words, joining in here and there. Jarus knew the song by now too, his clear Cooper voice rising with Mel's. The Blue Stone glowed warm, shedding blue light over the battlefield.

But Mel's thoughts were not on the world around him, turning instead to the power that had guided him here. *Please*, his heart pleaded as he sang, *please help us. You've guided us this far—You've brought me here—please help us now!*

His eyes were open, fixed on the indistinct blur that was his mentor. His mind did not beg the Stone for power—it was only a conduit, as he was. A vessel for the High Light's power. The Essence in his heart sang the words of the song, harmonizing with the blue light. Brilliant fire spread around him, and he sensed the Presence with him, looking down on the battle.

Fire crackled down his body like a cloak. Fire licked across the plain, swirled around Aryion's sword as he spun in the blue sparks. Fire formed a shield before them, and for the first time, Mel saw the vanguard hesitate, squinting in the sudden flare of pure light.

He had just drawn breath to sing on when the sneering voice entered his mind, and in a moment, the peace was gone.

"How very nice of you to join us, New Blood."

Mel choked on the words, terror filling him. *No,* his mind screamed back, *no, go away, you have no power here.* He sang on, but the Ace's voice continued.

"You have been away for quite some time. Reading books, hiding in libraries—how frivolous. Have you not seen how many have died? Do you want me to show you how much blood has been spilled in this futile defense already?"

"Jarus," Mel gasped, squeezing his eyes shut, "Jarus, keep singing—I can't—"

He felt the Cooper's paws cover his hands, saw the Stone grow brightly, and tried desperately to hear the Light's voice again. But all that filled his mind was fear—terror that gripped him in icy claws, terror that had pierced his shield, terror he could not fight.

"I suppose such scenes have little effect. No, there is a different story I wish to reacquaint you with—your brief stay with us in Castle Droco. I understand you have forgotten it."

"No," Mel said through gritted teeth—but the sounds had already begun, and with them, the return of the horrific tortures the Aces had purged from his mind. He felt freezing hands locked on his head again, felt the cold embrace of a void, and his own screams thundered in his ears.

The Ace's voice was edged in triumph. *"Oh, you would have helped us a great deal, if you were not so stubborn. Still, your pain was quite enjoyable."*

Pain shot through his head, and a cry tore from his throat. He forced his eyes open with an effort. The shield was flickering. In the fray of battle he saw a blade glance over Aryion's shoulder, knocking him sideways.

"Where are you?" Mel shouted, searching desperately across the plain. They had to be nearby. The Aces could never cast illusions without being in the general vicinity. But he saw nothing in the murky darkness.

"So much fear surrounding your mentor. Do you know what will become of him? Should the Deputy fall, so shall he—dead and cold, life stripped from his body. His Essence is sustained by us now."

Mel strained his eyes in the gray darkness. *Find them,* his mind ordered, *find them, get them to stop, or everyone's dead—*

And at last, he saw them. Two Aces, watching the battle with satisfaction.

He had expected the Messenger—the sly voice was unmistakable, though the Ace had died long ago. He appeared as a shadow now, slipping soundlessly across the dimly lit plain, skirting the battlefield and casting sounds and illusions amid the swirl of warriors.

But through the hulking bodies of the vanguard Mel saw the second Ace, the gleam of his tarnished armor, the smile on his half-decayed face.

Mel hadn't seen him in months, not since the battle on the marble bridge. The fear of that day filled his heart afresh, knowing now what had become of him in the Ace-Lord's clutches, and he could not speak.

"Where are they?" That was Aryion's voice, filled with a fire Mel had never heard. He glimpsed his mentor through the Druids' icy shield, eyes wide and fierce, fixed on Mel's tortured face.

"Aryion…" he managed to choke, clutching the Stone as he pointed across the Flats. The chaos of battle drowned out his voice. But Aryion saw him, blue-flecked eyes flashing as he followed Mel's gesture, seeking through the darkness for his apprentice's invisible attackers.

At last his gaze found the Deputy.

56

The Nameless

Aryion heard Mel's voice shouting, but the thunder of battle drowned out the words. His focus centered on the warriors of the vanguard, striking left and right as the strength flowed through him and the blue fire shielded him. Adrenaline pumped through his veins. His sword felt weightless in his hand, blocking blades, striking again and again.

Mel's scream caused him to falter.

A blade caught him across the shoulders, throwing him to the side. Iriam's dark blue ice flung the warrior back before the orc could strike again. Aryion turned to see Mel clutching his head, the fiery shield flickering uncertainly.

"Where are you?" Mel cried, swinging his gaze wildly over the battlefield.

"Mel!" Aryion shouted. An iron-shod boot connected with his chest, kicking him down. Winded for an instant, he deflected the next blow and stumbled back, turning his eyes back to his apprentice. "Mel—what's happening?"

"An illusion," Iriam warned from above. The Neutral stood among the Druids, raising a shield of deep blue ice and pressing the vanguard warriors back. "There is an illusion within the Stone's reach—the *Alené* spell will fail if he is not helped."

Aryion got to his feet, the agony in Mel's voice tightening his chest so that his breath came in short gasps. He barely registered the Neutral's last statement, barely noticed that the fiery blue shield embracing them had begun to fade. His mind was fixed only on Mel, every fiber in his body screaming for him to help his apprentice. "Where are they?" he shouted.

Mel's eyes turned to him, wide and fearful, and he pointed. The darkness concealed everything beyond the battlefield, but Aryion turned his gaze north, over the heads of the vanguard, over the bodies of the Dal-kerri, toward a small rise in the distance.

And he saw them.

Two Aces. The first was shadowy, a ghost of its former self, who swept forward wraith-like to join the vanguard to Aryion's left. Yet Aryion barely registered him—his focus had been drawn solely to the Deputy.

He looked the same, standing alone on the rise. Silver armor, purple-red eyes glinting in satisfaction and hate, smiling the cold smile that had haunted Aryion's dreams for months.

Every moment, every pain-filled horror he had endured in the black box, flooded his mind again—yet the rage that filled him came entirely from the fact that the Ace had dared to harm his apprentice.

"I see them." His voice sounded eerily calm as he raised his sword. "The Deputy and another Ace."

Iriam followed his gaze. "The Messenger," he murmured, surprised. "I had thought the illusions seemed familiar."

"Shall we engage him?" one of the Druids inquired, ice flashing from her palms as she pressed back a warrior.

"Keep him from reaching the walls," Iriam replied. "He is barely a shadow, a ghost—the only harm he might do is through the illusions."

Aryion's eyes were still on the Deputy, fighting to control the flood of fury and pain that filled his mind. Gripping his sword, he stepped forward. "I'll take him."

Iriam only nodded slightly, unsurprised. "I shall be glad to assist you."

Together, they moved forward. Vanguard soldiers lunged at them—Aryion deflected the blows, though the force nearly knocked him down. Iriam's ice pressed the others back, though even then the warriors continued to fight against the shield, clawing like beasts to reach their prey.

Aryion ignored them, his focus fixed on the Deputy, as though he were peering down a long black tunnel with an ending darker still. Shadowy fog surrounded the Ace, and he could see the withered lips moving softly, continuing to cast the illusions that tormented Mel. He ran on, leaping over the Dal-kerri carcasses on the ground and sprinting up the slight hill.

Fury and momentum carried him forward as he reached the hilltop. His sword slashed at the Deputy's throat as he sprang up the rise.

The Deputy turned in the same moment, swaying out of the blade's reach, white ice flashing in his hands. Aryion's sword connected with his armored shoulder, and the deadly bolt flew awry. Snow and muck slid beneath Aryion's boots, but he kept his balance as he faced the Ace-Deputy.

The Deputy straightened, face twisted in a mocking smile. "I expected you would come," he said at last. "Vengeance is your way, and there is much we have to reckon for."

Aryion circled him, gripping his sword. His entire body seemed to shiver with expectancy, the pent-up wrath called to the surface by the

Deputy's voice. His head throbbed as though it would split in two—some lingering effect of the Ace's curse on his memories. But he pushed the pain and rage away.

"I am not here for vengeance," he answered. "But I am going to kill you."

The Deputy laughed softly, drawing an ancient broadsword from its scabbard. He twirled it lightly in his hands, an eager gleam in his eyes, then lunged.

. . . . . .

As the illusion's sounds vanished, Mel knew in a flash Aryion had attacked the Deputy. He peered futilely through the dim light toward the place where he had seen the Aces, but could see nothing. Fear, icy cold, gripped his heart, overwhelming him for a moment.

"Mel!" Jarus' shout drew him back to present reality. The Cooper's fur was streaked in Dal-kerri blood, and several cuts scored his forearms. "The wolves are breaking through—can you sing the song again?"

"I can try," Mel said shakily, taking a deep breath and raising the Stone. But the words stuck in his tired throat. Terror seemed to have robbed him of strength.

A pack of hounds broke through the Druids' defenses, springing upon the Wildkid archers. Dusty's voice shouted orders, but Mel could not see her in the wild rush. The archers felled several of the hounds, but four prowled forward, eyes fixed on Mel and Jarus.

Jarus edged back, holding his knife, but his limbs trembled. The brutal battle over the last hour had begun to take its toll. He'd never fight them off, wearied as he was.

"Here," Mel panted, drawing his own blade and pressing the Star-Stone into Jarus' paw. "Take the Stone—get behind me."

Jarus looked at him in disbelief. "Does that—"

"As long as the Stone's safe, that's all that matters!" Mel reminded him firmly. "Sing, Jarus—Luet said the *Alené* can be used by anyone, that's why the song has power—you don't have to be powerful to call on the Light."

He gripped his dagger, watching as the wolves approached. Four. Too many for just one.

If you're expecting to lose, you've already lost. Aryion's teaching floated into his thoughts, and he stood firm as the first Dal-kerri charged, sinking his blade into the wolf's fur. Dark blood spurted from the wound, and the hound fell forward with a howl, sending Mel staggering beneath its weight.

Jarus had begun the song behind him, his voice shaky and uncertain. Mel's memories spun back to Tinkeeyo for a moment, seeking the calm and peace he had found there. He heard Misty's voice in his mind, as though she were here singing the song with them. His thoughts recalled the meaning behind the old Liznaeic words:

"O here, through darkness deep,

Shine light that life yet keeps."

Light flared from the Stone's core, a brilliant blaze that caused the hounds to hesitate. "Louder," Mel called. The wolves sprang—Mel slashed at the first, but felt the teeth of another tear down his arm. He let out a cry at the sharp flash of pain, stumbling. Jarus' knife plunged into the Dal-kerri's chest.

The Stone flashed blue light over the field. The fourth hound hesitated, snarling in hatred.

Gasping for breath, choking back a sob of pain, Mel sang as loud as he could.

"Hear now my mortal tongue,

Fire wrought, atoned by—"

The Dal-kerri lunged before he could finish, flinging him onto his back on the ground. Winded, Mel raised his dagger, striking blindly upward. Teeth snapped in his face. He became aware, dimly, that the fiery shield had begun to falter again.

"Keep going!" he screamed in Jarus' direction. The Dal-kerri pinned him down, and he kicked and squirmed desperately. His voice cracked as he screamed the words of the song. The hound snarled, snapping for his neck—Mel brought his dagger up, sinking it into its chest. The wolf sagged on top of him, dead.

"Mel!" Jarus' voice was shrill with fear.

Mel kicked the hound's body off him, coughing and retching from the terror of the fight. The heat of the monster's breath, the pain of its claws and teeth, filled his mind again, highlighting just how close he had come to death. For an instant he could not think straight, gasping for air. The glimmer of blue light came from his right—far weaker than before.

He turned. The Druids had formed an icy barrier, fending off the vanguard, and the Wildkid archers stood firm in their place.

Jarus stood, knife fallen from his grasp, his eyes wide and fearful. Mel swung around, trying to see what the Cooper feared, but saw nothing. "What?" he choked.

And then the voices began again.

Misty's first. Her screams thundered in Mel's mind, deafeningly loud. Then Dandio's, raw with pain, and finally Aryion's, seeming to stop Mel's heart with terror.

He doubled over, clutching his head, eyes squeezed shut. *It's just an illusion*, he wanted to shout, but his voice was gone. The roar of agony filling his mind was all he was aware of.

. . . . . .

The force behind the Deputy's blow jarred Aryion's arm, sending a fresh stab of pain into his skull. But he parried, slashed again, and blocked the next strike just in time. Cold surrounded the Ace, colder even than the snow-strewn wind, threatening to freeze his heart. The fragments of darkness the Deputy had imbued in him grew stronger the closer he came to the Ace, further hindering him in the fight.

He dove beneath the Deputy's blow, rolling to his feet in time to strike. Again, his blade was intercepted. Any advantages he'd had before were as nothing now—no blade could penetrate the Ace's armor, and Aryion could not get close enough for a successful blow. Not when the biting cold gripped his thoughts so easily, like chains hauling him down.

"Weak," the Deputy's voice hissed in his mind. *"And to think I once thought you worthy of joining the vanguard's ranks."*

Pain flared behind Aryion's eyes—he slashed blindly at the Deputy. Ice flashed, connecting with his chest and flinging him backwards into the filthy hands of the vanguard. Three warriors held him in place with grips of steel. He thrashed in their hold, but the orcs held him fast, far stronger than the ropes he had recently broken free of.

A blast of indigo ice flashed between them, sinking a blade through the first orc's thigh. The warriors' grip on Aryion's arms faltered as Iriam appeared. Hatred flashed in the Deputy's eyes as he saw the Neutral, but he did not attack, only barked a command to the vanguard. The orcs flung Aryion aside and surged for the Neutral.

Iriam met Aryion's eyes, and nodded slightly, serious and steady. He could hold the vanguard back while the Deputy was dealt with.

Aryion set his stance again, ignoring the pounding headache and the shivering strength filling his muscles as he lunged forward. The Deputy parried his blow easily and struck at his neck—Aryion managed to deflect it, but a blast of ice came at him in the same instant, pale white and deadly. He flung himself out of the way, feeling the chill as it passed him by.

"Yes, flee," the Deputy mocked, as Aryion straightened. "Flee if you wish. This is your end, you nameless servant—the end of a wretched slave who would not serve."

Aryion took a steadying breath, his mind racing for a strategy. The ice, and the blinding pain, ensured he could not get close enough to land a blow without being killed. Even then, the Deputy's armor would protect him. There were no weak points in the silver armor, nothing he could—

The Deputy raised his hands again, sweeping ice across the ground in crystallized blades. Aryion leapt over the blast, a plan coming to him as he sprang forward. The problem was the blasts of ice—that needed to be removed from the equation—

He charged straight for the Deputy, sword raised. Surprise crossed the ruined face before the Deputy raised his hands, likely out of instinct more than anything else. His hand locked on Aryion's neck, stopping him—biting cold filled Aryion's head, searing his mind. Vision blurring with pain, he swept his blade down upon the clawed hand and felt it finally connect with flesh.

The Deputy shrieked and reeled back, shoving Aryion away. Violet blood darker even than that of the Dal-kerri stained the snow around

them as the Deputy clutched the bloodied stump of his arm. His left
hand had been severed by Aryion's blade.

Aryion stumbled in the snow, gasping at the icy pain in his head.
Madness flashed in the Deputy's eyes as he faced him again, and his
voice snarled in Aryion's mind.

"Take my power, will you? Then I shall reclaim what is mine!"

Aryion, still catching his breath, saw the bolt coming, knew it would
be too late to try to dodge, and could only raise his sword in futile
defense. The ice slammed into him like a battering ram, flinging him off
his feet. His head slammed against the hard ground.

The energy, the fire, the power he had grown accustomed to, was
stripped from his limbs in a moment.

. . . . . .

Mel felt Jarus' trembling paw grip his arm, and the faint glimmer of blue
pierced his eyelids. He forced his eyes open. Jarus' mouth moved as he spoke,
but the cacophony of agonized screams drowned out the Cooper's words.

"I can't—I can't—" he choked, unable to speak. The voices—Misty,
his parents, Aryion, Dandio, all filled with an anguish he could not
help—made it impossible to think clearly or hear anything else. He was
trapped again, frozen in place by the fear.

"It's an illusion!" Jarus' voice was tight with pain, but his words broke
through the sounds. "It's not real, Mel—we have to fight it—the shield
needs to stand."

Mel clenched his teeth and forced himself upright again. The cries
faded slightly, and he was again aware of the clashing and clatter of
battle around him. An illusion—it was all an illusion. But it had not
been cast by the Deputy—there had been another Ace with him, one
Mel had glimpsed briefly in Tinkeeyo, one he'd not seen in years.

His eyes scanned the blur of movement past the lines of battle, and at last he saw the source. A shadow crept along the edge of the gate, ghosting through the Druids' shield and past the ring of archers.

A memory swam into Mel's mind, a memory of waiting for a carriage in Carna, seeing a smoky slither beneath the awning of a building, just out of reach of the sunlight.

The shadow straightened before them and came slowly into focus.

An Ace. Ghostlike, robes seemingly made of smoke, partially transparent, adding to the uncertainty of its appearance. A nightmare rising from the ground before them. A being drawn from an evil memory.

"Is that… it can't…" Jarus began shakily.

The Ace-Messenger rose before them, its face concealed by its cowl, except for the glimmer of its purple-red eyes.

Mel stared at the apparition before them, every horror this wraith had brought about filling his aching mind afresh. This was the same Ace that had first mentioned the role of New Blood to him. Had drawn him and Jarus away from the fighting. Had killed Norrin.

But the Ace-Messenger looked much different now. Aside from the sly voice in his mind, Mel didn't think it could physically speak at all. It was incomplete, broken, ghostly. No white ice glittered in its hands. The only power it had lay in the illusions and the fear it inspired. Already, he could see the Wildkid archers faltering, affected by sounds only they could hear, sent into their minds at the Ace's hands.

Such fear—the horror of the voices, the pain of resisting—how many times had it infected Mel's thoughts, defeating him again and again, causing him to close his eyes to the light.

He could no longer afford such defeat.

Though his mind screamed at him to surrender, though the tortured echoes still filled his thoughts, his heart ordered him to fight on.

Taking a deep breath, Mel put his hand on top of the Stone, pressing it into Jarus' paw. The warmth of the blue fire spread through their joined hands, filling Mel's veins as they held the Stone together.

"Keep singing," he rasped. "We're going to keep singing."

Jarus nodded wordlessly, and they lifted the song again.

As they did, the Messenger's ghostly form twisted, fury flashing in the red eyes as it turned to them.

"I gave you a chance to surrender, boy."

The screams began again, so loud Mel thought for certain everyone could hear them. They drowned out the battle, swept away his own weak voice as he struggled to continue the song.

But Jarus was there too, and though the Cooper's voice was as fearful as his own, Mel heard the same fierce determination there, the stubborn perseverance they each shared.

The Stone glimmered. Blue fire spread from its core, wreathing Mel and Jarus, cloaking them in light so bright it burned away the scenes before them.

But the Ace fought on, his voice filling Mel's mind. *"Coward—selfish coward—do you not hear their pain? Do you not wish to stop it? Even now your friends fall lifeless. Their blood shall be on your hands, as it was for all the others."*

Scenes replayed in Mel's mind, scenes he had long sought to forget. Llyrion's death. Dandio, lying bleeding beside the serpentine. Norrin, chest glittering white. Aryion, bleeding out in the throne room of Sia. And so many others—friends, family, laying down their lives to save him. He saw their faces twisted in agony, frozen in death.

The guilt he had fought so long to move past pierced his chest like a blade, and he could not speak. The words of the song died away on his lips.

"See what has come about? Do you not recall the lost?"

"I do!" Mel cried aloud. The words were torn from the darkest corners of his heart. "Every day—every night—I remember, and I wish I could have helped them, but I couldn't—I couldn't stop it. And I'll never forget that. But—I know—there's forgiveness—and healing—and truth in the Light."

The blue fire plumed stronger around him. Through the shining light he saw the Messenger hesitate.

His voice cracked in weariness, and he could only whisper the rest. "I'm done running from the pain. I'm done trying to forget. You can't use it against me any more."

Jarus' voice rose beside him in the song. Blue fire spread across the ground, blazing around the Wildkids, rising over Mel's bleeding shoulders like wings. The voices of the illusions faded away before it, labeled false, named a lie by the one they sought to torment.

The Messenger raised a hand, fighting against the brilliant blaze. *"You are ours, child,"* he hissed, but his voice was weakening. *"A cursed child, a mortal chosen for our number—that is who you are. Your guilt names you as ours. What other name have you to challenge the claim we have upon you?"*

Mel raised his head. The Song of the Stars soared around him, and fire burned across the ground. The Essence of his heart blazed with it as he answered, claiming the call and the name the High Light had given him.

"I'm the New Blood."

Fire roiled in the air, twisting, blazing. It engulfed the ghostly apparition before them, swallowed the Messenger up as though he were nothing more than a passing shadow. In another moment, the darkness was gone, the illusions faded, and Mel and Jarus stood in the circle of the archers while blue fire spread in a shield to the heavens.

. . . . . .

Aryion could not move.

His vision blurred into blackness, and the ringing in his ears and the pounding of his heart was all he was aware of. *Get up,* his thoughts screamed, *get up and fight!* Yet his body refused to obey. He lay on the cold ground, shaking uncontrollably as pain racked his body.

"*Mortal fool,*" the voice hissed, piercing his brain like a dagger. "*I know your weakness. I have seen all you are. Did you believe you could escape that?*"

"Aryion!" Iriam's deep voice came from far away. Had the Neutral rejoined the fight, fending off both the Deputy and his vanguard? He could not stand against them all for long. Aryion had no way of knowing—all that swam before his eyes was gray darkness, as if a veil had been pulled before his vision.

"*Feel the pain. Know you could have been powerful.*"

The voice grew triumphant. Aryion's head pounded as though it would explode. Gasping, he fought to get up again, to keep fighting, but the blast seemed to have drained him of his strength.

With great effort, he rolled over, chest down in the snow. His arms shook as he tried to raise himself. The world around him was a faded gray, much dimmer than his previous state had allowed him to see. He could still make out uncertain shapes. Flashes of ice—one deep indigo, the other white—flickered nearby as two tall figures circled each other. The vanguard stood beyond, waiting and watching the fight.

The world was plunged into twilight, the moonlight doused by black clouds. Blinking rapidly, his gaze fixed on the Deputy, surrounded by the silvery light cast by his armor. Iriam, his face invisible in the blackness, deflected the deadly blasts. One connected with Iriam's shoulder as Aryion watched, and the Neutral faltered.

Get up, his brain shouted again. His entire body felt as though it had been crushed beneath a stone wall, and his head ached so much tears sprang to his eyes. Limbs trembling, he dragged himself up to his knees, then sat up.

Two vanguard soldiers moved toward him, ugly smiles stretched over their faces as they raised their blades. Aryion lifted his sword—the blade felt as though it weighed a ton. With shaking arms, he managed to parry the brutal blows. The vanguard warriors struck again, looming over him as he stumbled back.

He couldn't defeat them. He knew that in a heartbeat. The vanguard were sustained by the Deputy's Essence—not even the Druids had managed to kill any of them.

Forget the vanguard. They would die with the Deputy—thus, his priority must be joining that fight.

He risked a glance to the battling ice-wielders. Despite the loss of his hand, the Deputy was fighting viciously. Iriam moved carefully, analyzing the best point of attack. He'd likely come to the same conclusion as Aryion—there was no breaking through the armor, not without being killed by the white ice.

Taking a deep breath, Aryion ducked beneath the vanguard's blades and ran, lunging toward the fight. Iriam was fighting calmly, but violet blood streaked his face from a blow on the jaw. The anger and madness in the Deputy's eyes told Aryion that the Ace clearly intended to bring them both down with him.

The Deputy swung to face him as Aryion stumbled forward. Dark blood stained the ground around him. His left side would be unprotected. Yet his severed hand had only served to anger him further. Every blast launching from his remaining hand crackled pure white.

Aryion dodged a wild blast. Iriam struck from behind at the same instant, his indigo ice opening a gap in the silver armor. With a snarl, the Deputy rounded on the Neutral, screaming a command to the waiting vanguard. The hulking soldiers jogged toward them. Iriam, seeing it, raised his hands, spreading a circular protective barrier of dark blue ice between them and the orcs. He raised his hands slowly, lifting the icy wall taller in a swift and desperate attempt to shield them from the deathless warriors.

White ice glittered in the Deputy's fingers as he rounded on the unprotected Neutral.

Aryion saw the readied blast, knew it would strip the life from Iriam in an instant. Without a second thought, barely registering his aching head or trembling muscles, he lunged forward, throwing himself against the Deputy. His shoulder connected with the armored chest as they crashed into the muck.

Bitter coldness seared Aryion's head, seeming to pierce his mind with icy blades. His sword slipped from his grasp.

The Deputy's clawlike hand locked on his head. White light flared behind his eyes, and he heard his own strangled scream tear from his throat. He dug his fingers into the withered wrist, fighting vainly to break the grip, but his strength gave out and he fell to the side.

The Deputy's armored knee pressed against his throat, hand locked on his brow, shoving his head down into the bloodied ground.

Blindly, Aryion groped through the mud and slush for his sword. He glimpsed blue ice striking the Deputy from behind again, heard the crack as it widened the gap in the tarnished armor. The Ace gave a snarl of fury, letting go of Aryion's head and firing a blast of white at the Neutral. The ice slammed into Iriam's quickly raised barrier, shattering it into pieces. The vanguard swarmed forward again, reaching for the Neutral as though to tear him apart.

Aryion gasped and choked desperately for air, the Deputy's knee driving into his throat. Mud filled his ears and engulfed his head. Stars swam in his vision.

Through the fog of pain, his desperately searching fingers found the hilt of his sword.

Summoning every ounce of strength remaining to him, Aryion hauled his sword free of the mud and slashed across the Deputy's exposed neck.

The Ace-Deputy gave a short gasp, his head snapping to the side as he choked on his own dark blood, but his grip did not falter. White ice flickered on his fingers before Aryion's eyes.

In the same instant he did so, a blade of indigo ice pierced him through from behind.

Aryion hadn't realized Iriam had a clear shot at the Deputy or the strength to wield his ice, surrounded as he was by the teeming vanguard. He had stepped forward, encircled by orcs nearly as tall as he was, raising his hands for one final blast and sending the ice through the tear in the armor, straight through the Deputy's black heart.

The vanguard crumpled lifeless, a mere hairbreadth from reaching the Neutral.

The Deputy slumped forward, his half-decayed face registering hate, surprise, and pain in one last emotion. White ice shimmered on his fingers before he fell to the side, crashing into the bloodied snow.

Aryion felt himself inhale, felt his sword slip from his hand again, felt a brief surge of relief a moment before darkness engulfed his vision, and there was nothing besides the shadows.

57

The Ace-Lord's Vision

Utter silence filled the black halls of Castle Salem as Allie and Rygal slipped inside.

The silver-veined walls seemed to swallow the echoes of the closing doors, as well as the distant cacophony of battle beyond the courtyard. Allie allowed a flame of red to light on her palm, illuminating the room before them. For a moment, she was reminded of the strange, whispering middleworld, a world detached from all else.

As far as she could tell, they were still in the mortal world, though Castle Salem hardly seemed to fit in a mortal reality.

As Lammar had described, Castle Salem was filled with darkness, though not the same black fog as surrounded it outside. The true depth of darkness came from the castle itself. The black walls were wrought of an iron-like material. The red fire in Allie's hands reflected off of their surface and glinted in the veins of silver woven within them, giving the castle an otherworldly glow.

She could see about ten paces ahead of them. The doors led them into a short hall, which ended in four staircases—two leading up, two winding down. Down, Allie recalled, would probably take them to the cistern where she'd discovered Jan. But she had no way to know for certain. Castle Salem held a dreamlike quality—she felt no one place would appear the same way twice. She might be able to find the place where she'd rescued Jan, maybe search out the black, box-like prison where Aryion had been kept. But she felt if they were to seek those places, they would be lost, doomed to wander the winding corridors and ancient stairs for hours.

No. The path inside Castle Salem was one the Ace-Lord must prepare for all who entered it. Last time, he'd guided her to find Jan and Mel and retreat back through the gateway.

Did he *want* her to come to him?

"No sign of guards," Rygal observed quietly. He stood beside her, holding his sword loosely, golden sparks still shining on the blade.

Allie raised her hand, letting red light fill the hall. He was right, she realized. Just as it had been on her last visit here, the halls of Castle Salem were devoid of activity. But the last time she'd at least heard the voices and movement of the Ace-army elsewhere in the palace. This time, the only sound was her own nervous breathing.

"I guess they're all fighting on the Flats," she whispered at last, though prickles of fear spread down her spine. While it would make their journey easier if the Ace-Lord was guiding them, why would he *want* to be found? Surely he knew she'd come to kill him. Maybe he planned one last ploy to deceive the Vessel, sway her to his side. But she felt that was unlikely.

Slowly, she and Rygal walked down the hall to the staircases. Her red fire glinted off a stained glass window on the back wall. Fragmented glass in shades of red, blue, and gold depicted a scene of Lord Kahlifis as he had been before he had claimed the title Ace-Lord. Hundreds of mortals bowed before the silver-clad lord. The castle in the picture looked eerily like Castle Sia, but twisted and black.

"Allie, look," Rygal said, pointing at the corner of the picture. "Those are Liznees bowing—and Direns." He frowned deeply. "You don't suppose… he knew? Knew we'd join forces with the Direns?"

"And the Elves?" Allie whispered. Her eyes had moved to the opposite corner, where the details of the Elven armor depicted warriors of both Tinkeeyo and Elimar.

Fear chilled her heart, and she turned slowly to Rygal. "The Elven alliance was something we never dared to hope for—yet he *knew* it was going to happen."

"Knew or guessed?" Rygal mused. "He doesn't know the future."

"He knew this future," Allie answered softly. She moved up the stairs on the right, her mind puzzling over the stained glass mural. Surely it was a coincidence, a twisted dream the Ace-Lord hoped for the future. But then… how often had the Ace-Lord pointed out the predictability of mortals?

Those alliances had encouraged Allie that the Ace-Lord's scheme would fail, with the mortals joining together. And yet he had expected them, seeing it as nothing more than proof that the mortals would join beneath him.

"All the same," Rygal began slowly, "we know the Ace-Lord doesn't control time."

Allie paused, thinking it through. Rygal was right. The High Light had brought them here, guiding them all this way. Even the Ace-Lord must follow His plan, though he might seek to twist his own purpose, strive for a power that had never been his. She did not understand it, doubted she ever would fully. But thinking of the High Light eased the fear slightly.

"I think it's this way," she said, continuing upward. "I'd expect the Ace-Lord would be in the tower."

Rygal followed. "You've been here before, right?"

"I remember where the tower was," Allie replied. "But the palace—it looks completely different now, Rygal. I can't explain how." She gestured around them vaguely.

"You mean it's… harder to see?" Rygal asked.

"Well, yes—but the stairs have moved," Allie answered, shaking her head. "Either I came in at a different level, or this entire castle has changed. Nothing about it is the same. They moved *walls*."

Rygal did not pursue this, only followed her up the stairs. Allie thought in silence, trying to come up with an answer that explained why the palace had changed. She eventually gave up. The interior of Castle Salem made no sense—staircases winding into nothingness, voids of darkness gaping in doorways, echoes of voices long past whispering in the halls.

A dream. Detached from the nightmare without.

The stairs marched them up to another level. This place was slightly better lit, faint tinted light filtering through another stained glass window on the wall before them. Two more staircases spread upward in opposite directions. Between them waited four Dal-kerri hounds, who sprang to their feet with snarls.

Fire flared in Allie's hands as she stepped forward. The red blaze consumed two wolves as they sprang for her, and Rygal's sword took down the others. He spun the blade thoughtfully in his hand, studying the hounds. "Not much in the way of guards," he commented, "but I suppose they're here to keep us on our toes."

"Or to make sure we're going the right way," Allie said softly. She pointed wordlessly up the staircase on the right side. Waiting silently in the shadows were more wolves, hundreds of them, their eyes reflecting the firelight. To the left, the staircase was empty, the railing shimmering slightly with white ice.

The hounds watched, a few growling softly, but they made no move as Allie and Rygal stepped toward the stained glass window. The image it depicted sent all of Allie's fears flooding back.

The picture showed her face.

She stood, wreathed in white fire, swirling in the inferno as Dal-kerri and enchanted soldiers lay dead at her feet. The Ace-Lord stood on her right, clad in gleaming silver. A Druid with pale markings was depicted on her left. Her white flames swirled amid the Druid's deep blue ice, joining the silver light shining from the Ace-Lord's hand.

"What does that mean?" she asked, confused and troubled. "Does he think—does he think I'm going to help him defeat the Druids?"

"I'm not sure," Rygal said, staring at the picture for several moments. "Maybe... well, I don't know."

"What?"

"Well... you know how the Ace-Lord has his own interpretation of the Prophecy?" Rygal nodded at the fractured image. "I wonder if this is how it ends in his mind. Look at the Druid's eyes."

Allie turned her gaze back. The Druid's glassy eyes were made of hollow blue.

Enchantment. Silent, voiceless servitude for all eternity. That was exactly what the Ace-Lord intended for the mortals, why he had selected the Vessel. This was what she would help him bring about, in this future he had foreseen for her.

She felt sick. Tearing her eyes away from the window, she started up the left-hand stairs.

"That's not going to happen, Allie," Rygal said quietly, following. "You know that's not how this will end."

"How it ends?" Allie echoed softly, staring ahead into the shadows. "How it ends is death. I know it's strange to hope for that, but any other way, then that's my future." She nodded back at the stained glass. "I tried—for a moment—to believe otherwise. That the Prophecy was wrong. That the Ace-Lord was wrong too. But if that's my mindset… I'm letting more people die."

She shook her head slightly, sensing the ominous truth. Blood alone will break the curse. The words entered her mind again, and now she understood. "The Prophecy calls for a sacrifice," she said at last, looking back at Rygal again. "The willing warrior dies at the dawn, and I think the night is ending."

They walked in silence for a little while, up and up the arching staircase while darkness filled the levels below them. Allie searched her mind for something, anything, that might ease the brutal truth of her words. Something to soften the grief she knew was soon to grip so many of her loved ones.

Rygal didn't ask for comfort, though. He only walked with her into the darkness, silent in his support.

She could sense it, sense the end coming, like sand shimmering through an hourglass. Time ticking down. A heartbeat slipping away.

She took his hand as they walked on, needing something to ground her to the present. To slow the relentless passing of the seconds, stop time for a moment, allow her to imagine what might have been. The warmth of his fingers, interwoven with hers, sent her thoughts back to their dance in the forest. She could hear the rhythm of the song in their footsteps as they climbed the stairs.

Then the stairs ended. A set of double doors stood before them, rimmed in white ice.

He was waiting for her in there, the Ace-Lord. The Lord of Death awaiting the Vessel in a tower at the end of the world.

Allie paused before the doors, took a deep breath. Took the fear in her mind captive and let her crimson fire crackle in her heart.

"He's in there," she whispered, still holding Rygal's hand.

Rygal let out a breath. "All right. Are you… ready?"

Out of time.

She let the fire fade from her hand as she turned to face him. There was no longer time to hesitate, or find the right words. The last nagging thoughts demanding distance died away as she stepped close, slipping her hand behind his head as she drew his lips to hers. Warmth spread through her, as though the fires of their Essence had intertwined. His dark hair brushed her cheek, and she felt the steady rhythm of his heart beat with her own.

It was only a moment, that last glimmer of what might have been, before the mission caused her to pull away.

She took a half step back, lit the passage with red fire again, and looked up at Rygal. His face showed a mixture of joy, love, and a deep sorrow that cut to her heart.

"I'm ready," she said finally, and he nodded.

Allie opened the door.

The tower room looked exactly as she remembered it, despite the fact she'd come by a different way before. There was a short table in the center, made of dark wood. A stained glass window on her right, smaller than the two in the halls, overlooked the Flats, and she could make out the distant blur of battle far across the plain.

The gateway void stood directly before her, wrought of silvery metal, blackness swirling in its depths. Beside it, robes drifting like shadows around his wraith-like frame, hands clasped behind his back as he stared out the window, stood the Ace-Lord.

"I am pleased you have arrived so promptly, Vessel," he said without turning. "I take it your pathway was quite clear?"

"Clear enough," Allie answered shortly, rattled by his manner. Every nerve in her body had been tensed for an attack that had not come—the Ace-Lord seemed completely unperturbed. Then again, he did not fear death, not by mortal weapons. His defeat must come about another way. Her eyes darted to the swirling void, the words of the binding spell on the tip of her tongue. But the Ace-Lord spoke again.

"Well then. Now that you have arrived, we may begin." He turned to study them. "You need not stand so anxious, however sweet your fear is to me. Sit and rest a moment."

Allie didn't move. Alarm bells were jangling in her mind, but she had no idea why. Surely the Ace-Lord knew why they'd come...

The Ace-Lord glanced out the window again. "You should know that your forces yet live, though they have drawn back. The war is yet to be won by either side. I am quite pleased with the outcome. This game has played out exactly as I have foreseen it."

"Then you know why we've come," Allie said bluntly, eyeing the ghostly lord before her. "Why are you stalling? You must know I'm here to kill you."

Rygal threw her an uneasy glance, but said nothing.

The shadow of a smile crossed the Ace-Lord's face. "Oh yes, I know the nature of your mission. By killing me, you intend to break the curse binding you, and follow me into death even as you hope to end this war.

Yes," he mused, nodding thoughtfully, "it is a wise strategy. However, in the outcome, you are mistaken."

"How so?" Allie asked. Fire played on her fingers, but she allowed it to fade. The Ace-Lord did not seem to be stalling. He'd expected she would come and he seemed to wish to speak to her—though she couldn't guess the reason.

The Ace-Lord waved a hand to the table. "If you will not sit, then let us speak all the same. There is something I must ask of you."

"I'll save you the time. I'll never join you," Allie snapped. The fire crackled to life again as she braced herself for the fight to begin, for the Ace-Lord to fling a blast of white ice at her or Rygal, but he didn't. He only looked at her with a mixture of scorn and impatience.

"I understand that, Vessel, and I never ask for the same thing twice. No, what I propose is an exchange. An answer to the questions we each seek, one that we each may provide the other."

Allie stared at him, totally confused by this. Answers? Answers, while a battle raged beyond? Friends, family, were out there fighting and dying while she bandied words with the Lord of Death. But then… if she refused, she might miss something vitally important. Worse, she might die for nothing.

She shared a brief glance with Rygal before replying. "Very well. Answer mine first. How do you think this will end? You know the mortals will never agree to serve you."

Satisfaction flickered over the Ace-Lord's face. "Ah, a strategic question. You are indeed quite like your father." He looked out the window, where the blazes of fires and the rumble of cannons engulfed the Flats.

"I have long dealt in the matters of mortals," he said after a pause. "Centuries of death, before your ancestors were ever conceived. Yet I have observed two facts that remain consistent."

He paced slowly away from the window and placed a hand on the side of the gateway. "The first is that mortals are stubborn creatures. You cannot be swayed in any matter unless you persuade yourself that it was your choice. Take away that choice, and you ensure they shall fight against you forever. But present servitude as gifts, present bondage as paradise, present the darkest sins as the purest light, and a mortal shall follow as willingly as a sheep, as loyally as a blind dog."

Fire flared far across the Flats. The Red Dawn must have charged again. Snow swept against the stained glass window.

"And the second?" Rygal asked, studying the Ace-Lord carefully.

"The second," the Ace-Lord answered, "is that mortals are, at their core, selfish. However they may argue otherwise, you need only observe the events of the world to see it. Rulers have sold their people for the smallest convenience of mortal comfort. Tyrants have leveled cities in the pursuit of power. Men fall back before the darkness and let it consume their comrades, if only to buy them a few more meager years of life."

"You're wrong," Allie said quietly. "Some mortals are like that, yes. Everyone's made choices they regret. But I've seen mortals do more—joining together to help each other. Just like now." She gestured out the snow-strewn window.

"An astute observation, but an incomplete one," the Ace-Lord replied. "You know, as well as I, that selfishness is as common in a mortal's heart as fear. And, just as fear is unique to each heart, so also are their desires." His eyes flicked between the two of them, a slight smile touching his gaunt face. "You may speak of sacrificing all to save your people, but were the tables turned, do you believe you would allow another to make the same choice?"

Allie hesitated. The Ace-Lord seemed to have looked into her heart, seeing her doubts and calling them forth one by one. She was prepared to die. But what if more than that was required to defeat him? What if the lives of her friends, her father, Jan, so many others—what if their blood must also be spilled to bring about victory? Could she truly convince herself that she'd let that happen for the greater good?

"What do you want to know from me?" she asked at last, trying to keep her voice level.

The Ace-Lord inclined his head to her. "It is a simple matter, certainly not as weighty as your own question. What I wish to know relates to the Prophecy, the final stanza. The Willing Warrior. Tell me your interpretation of it."

Allie stared at him, trying to figure out why in Orlell he wanted to know that. She hadn't studied that stanza in particular, no more than the rest of the Prophecy. There seemed to be no harm in telling him. "The… the Willing Warrior. The way I see it, a mortal's life will become one with the Ace-Lord's—your life. Bound together. It's about me, and the Life-Blood Spell."

"Indeed," the Ace-Lord breathed thoughtfully. He seemed both perplexed and intrigued by her answer, which Allie couldn't understand. "So you believe the unwilling, as written in the third stanza, must now become willing. But how, precisely, shall such a change of heart come about?"

Allie exchanged a swift glance with Rygal, seeing the same unease and distrust in his eyes. Her mind, so prepared for battle and resolved to death, left her unprepared for the Ace-Lord's questions. "I—I am willing," she answered at last, raising her chin and meeting his eyes with as much fire as she could muster. "I'm willing."

"Is there a reason for your questions, Ace-Lord?" Rygal asked tensely, tightening his grip on his sword. "We didn't come here to discuss the war or the Prophecy with you—I trust you know that."

"No. And you would not still breathe were it not for my interest in such matters," the Ace-Lord informed him crisply. "If the Vessel still wishes to save the mortal lives she cares for, there is a bargain I would make, if you will hear it."

Allie let out a pent-up breath. She didn't have much of a choice but to hear him out. The Ace-Lord had guessed their strategy—worse, he'd prepared for it. "All right," she said after a pause. "What do you propose?"

The Ace-Lord nodded slightly, looking pleased. "I shall withdraw my forces. The war shall cease at this moment. My armies shall return to the Dark Realm, as shall I, and so also shall you, Vessel."

Into the Dark Realm. The thought, however long she'd tried to steel herself for it, chilled her heart. Yet that had been her plan—albeit with far less fighting than she'd expected. It would at least keep everyone else alive. Rygal would close the door behind them and she and the Ace-Lord would be trapped in the Dark Realm forever.

The faces of all who had been lost swam in her mind, all those she had been unable to save. This, at least, could be her choice. Not in the way she'd hoped. But maybe it would work.

"Very well," she whispered at last, almost afraid to speak out loud. "I agree." Rygal looked at her in disbelief, but she continued. "First tell me this. You told me that I had no choice in the matter back in Appledale. If that's true, then why haven't you been able to control what I've been doing this whole time? I've never chosen your side, and I never will."

"Indeed?" A cold smile glittered in the Ace-Lord's eyes. "Are you still so ignorant of your own actions, Vessel? The horrors you have brought about? The corruption of the Star-Stone. The blood of the mindless soldiers. The deaths you have reveled in." He laughed softly. "No, you have never truly had a choice. From the moment the Life-Blood Spell was spoken over you, you have acted *exactly* as I intended. So too have I foreseen your future."

"Future?" Allie repeated, dread closing around her heart.

"Did you not observe the depictions in the halls as you arrived?" the Ace-Lord inquired. "Surely you have understood the fate that awaits you."

The stained glass scenes re-entered Allie's mind, and this time, it seemed her own reflection reached out and dragged her forward to a fate she could not resist. The glassy eyes shone with pale, triumphant light.

Helpless anger filled her heart, destroying the remnants of calm and clarity. Fire flickered in her fingers as she took a step forward. "That fate isn't in the Prophecy," she stated, though the gradually paling fire told her otherwise. "And my only future lies in killing you."

She lunged, hardly realizing what she was doing. Rygal moved forward as she did, golden fire already blazing along his sword and shield rim.

The Ace-Lord swept a blast of ice that shoved Rygal back toward the door, then deflected the blast of red that crackled from Allie's hand. Allie drew her sword—a pale blade of ice flashed from the Ace-Lord's palm as he knocked her blow aside with ease. She saw his smile, saw the disdain and satisfaction in his face, and her fire blazed hotter.

With a cry, she slashed again, this time for the Ace-Lord's throat. He stepped back calmly out of the reach of the blade, catching the tip of her sword across his armguard. Allie stumbled, off balance for an instant, drawing breath to speak the spell. Before she could, the Ace-Lord's hand gripped the back of her jerkin as he turned and hauled her inside the gaping void.

Leaving Rygal standing alone in the tower.

58

The Warrior's Choice

Alone.

Rygal had waited, tense and filled with a rising dread, since they'd entered the tower, listening to the Ace-Lord's low words and Allie's voice growing gradually more fearful. In one swift motion, the Ace-Lord had thrown her into the swirling darkness of the gateway before vanishing after her.

He'd taken her.

"Allie!" he shouted, stepping closer to the void. He knew she was gone. Knew she could no longer hear him from whatever dark place the Ace-Lord had taken her. Her name was torn from him all the same, his desperate heart unable to accept the truth.

Shaking, he stared into the gateway. The only sound came from the whispering shadows, stirred by a strange wind from another world. The sudden, utter silence was jarring.

Keep to the plan, Allie's voice reminded him in his mind.

But their plan—their plan hadn't worked. The Ace-Lord had expected them—had *wanted* them to come here. He still needed the Vessel, and there was nothing Allie could do about it. Hard as she would fight, the Ace-Lord had her in his grip, her Essence chained to his. She'd fight and she would die.

Wasn't that what she was planning to do in the first place?

Yes, he argued back mentally—but they hadn't expected the Ace-Lord to plan for that.

Choking back a cry of both fury and grief, he let the flames crackle down the blade of his sword and shield rim. She was gone. She was gone, and she was counting on him to close the door behind them.

But...

Who was to say that would accomplish anything? The Ace-Lord was right. Since Allie had accepted his bargain, the Ace-army would fall back and return to the Dark Realm. The war would simply stop, with neither side having won—just as the Aces had retreated after the first Ace-rise over thirty years ago.

Except the Ace-Lord had time. He did not need to enter the mortal world to have control, not with a Vessel. He'd puppeted Safacon, controlled the Darkness. Unless this gateway was destroyed, he'd return Allie to the mortal world—a new Deputy of shadow—and through her, he'd gain the Star-Stones and open the doorways again, orchestrating yet another war.

And there would be absolutely nothing standing in his way. Not with the mortal forces weakened after this conflict. Not with despair crushing every heart. Not with fear gripping the world like a plague.

So what to do?

"Help me!" he shouted into the black palace. "What do I do? How do we beat him?"

He didn't know if his ragged prayer was heard. It was certainly less elegant than the song that Mel had used to commune with the High Light. Certainly shorter than the prayers he remembered from Norrin. But he felt the Presence, as surely as he had felt it in a winter glade all those years ago, when he had lain awake and feared the Hazes.

There was no awesome light, no thundering voice as he'd heard of. Only the sense that some almighty Being had placed hands upon his shoulders, strengthening his panicked heart.

Rygal took a deep breath, touched the tip of his sword to the gateway. The darkness seemed to recoil from the light and heat, but the void stifled the flames, unhindered. His fire had no affect on the gateway—the Ace-Lord had probably counted on that, too. Their entire plan was falling to pieces.

"No—he wants this to happen," Rygal murmured to himself, trying to sort out his frantic thoughts. "The Ace-Lord wanted Allie here… he wanted her to go into the void with him… he still wants her alive…" He swallowed hard, horror and grief threatening to engulf him. Allie. Lost. His heart felt cold and lifeless without her, as if a portion of her own fiery Essence had filled him at her touch. The memory of her hand in his, her reckless determination so like his own, the soft press of her lips against his in the darkness minutes ago—the memories had no warmth. He'd lost her, just as he'd always feared.

He shook his head to clear it. No—no, there'd be time to grieve later, assuming he lived through this black night.

The Ace-Lord had predicted everything up till this point, and by all logic, his predictions for Allie's future would occur too. The Willing Warrior, gone with the dawn. Stolen without a single chance to fulfill her true role in the Prophecy.

That couldn't be how it ended. The Ace-Lord may have anticipated it—but the High Light was over this story, was He not? Norrin had always told him so, and Rygal had seen the truth of it again and again.

Gripping his sword, he peered into the shifting shadows, which seemed to beckon him forward.

Sounds and illusions until you're lost. Allie had described it that way, when she'd recounted her journey through the voids to him. Except Rygal didn't have the Life-Blood Spell protecting him from the illusions, as Allie'd had. He'd simply be swept away, dragged down by the voices and illusions of the past. The Ace-Lord would reclaim the power vested in Allie before killing her himself, and all would be lost.

But the Ace-Lord's plan had counted on one crucial element. He had expected Allie to come alone.

Rygal spun the sword in his hand, tracing the point through the blackness. The flames sputtered, as if affected by some moisture in the gateway. *Protect her.* That was his task this whole mission, wasn't it? Even if he had never truly been charged thus, the order to keep Allie safe seemed to have been engraved upon his heart.

"Light help me," he whispered, and stepped into the archway.

. . . . . .

Searing cold shot through Allie's head, causing the pale fire sputtering in her hands to falter. The Ace-Lord's hand was locked around the back of her neck, piercing her mind with ice.

The swirling darkness of the void engulfed her, and she fought blindly. A great wind tore around her as she was dragged forward. The Ace-Lord's broken nails dug into her skin, colder than any natural thing, and she cried out in pain and fear. Her voice was lost to the void around them. Any moment now, her thoughts echoed, any moment, the white ice would shatter her Essence to pieces. Any moment now it would all be over.

The Ace-Lord flung her forward—she fell though the howling winds before crashing down on something solid. Gasping for air, Allie got to her hands and knees, feeling the cold stone beneath her.

Where was she?

Shaking from both pain and from the biting cold, Allie looked around. White lights twinkled and swirled below and above, lighting the area around her. She crouched in the ruin of a great stone fortress, suspended in the nothingness of the void. Three towers rose up around her, the tallest in the center, giving the outline of a massive horned crown.

The middleworld, she realized vaguely—but not the arching bridge she'd encountered before. At least she had not been hauled directly into the Dark Realm as she had feared. She crawled to the edge of the ruin, peering cautiously beyond the broken walls. The twisting swirl of freezing air and snow wafted upward from the fathomless depths below.

She leapt to her feet, pale fire flashing in her hands, as the Ace-Lord descended behind her, suspended by his own silvery light. His appearance flickered to the illusion of the lord he had once been as he landed, changing before her eyes. Silver armor gleamed, purple-red eyes glinted from a gaunt face that still appeared skeletal, white hair fell over his chest plate. The wind sent his tattered robes billowing as he stood before her.

"I hope," Kahlifis said, rich voice echoing over the gray stones, "that your ill-conceived attack is no indication that you intend to complicate our bargain."

"Our bargain's fulfilled," Allie snapped back. "I'm here, like you wanted. But the future you intend for me will not be mine."

"So much you have heard and still understand nothing," the Ace-Lord said, irritation in his voice. "Our futures are one, as is written in the Prophecy. In all you pretend to know, you have missed the fatal flaw in

its words. The paradox of the Prophecy lies in the Willing Warrior—
that is a role you can never fulfill."

Allie looked down at her hands. The fire had paled—not quite the
white of the inferno, but no longer her own red, either. Corrupted. She
could almost sense the Life-Blood Spell darkening her heart with every
passing moment, now that she'd chosen this fate.

The path the Ace-Lord had laid to guide her here was strikingly clear.
The stained glass in the hall filled her thoughts again—the image of
herself, wreathed in pale flames, of the enchanted Druid beside her,
of the Ace-Lord watching in satisfaction. Claimed by death, as she
had always feared, but in a far more twisted way than she had first
imagined.

Helpless rage filled her as the fire flared in her hands, and she leapt
forward. The Ace-Lord flung a ray of ice that caught her across the
knees, sending her falling hard to the stone—she sprang to her feet,
firing two rapid blasts. The Ace-Lord deflected the fire, extinguishing
it on his icy palms, and as he did, hot pain shot up Allie's fingers and
arms.

She gasped, shaking her hands, feeling the skin blistering. Her fire.
The Ace-Lord had turned it against her yet again.

"You shall tire long before I, Vessel," the Ace-Lord informed her. "I
cautioned you against complicating our bargain."

Allie met his eyes and took a calming breath. Searing pain radiated
over her palms, yet it also brought clarity in the midst of her angry attack.
All that Iriam had taught her of the Words of Old, all her mother had
ever told her of the High Light's grace and mercy, joined together in a
peace that soothed her helpless fury.

"If I am to die," she said quietly, "I'll do it to end you and this war, not because of a curse you claim over me. Even with the Life-Blood Spell, even with all you've led me to do—that power isn't yours, either. The High Light has guided me here, just as He gave you charge over death. You're bound by that role, just as I am."

For the first time, the calm vanished, and the Ace-Lord's face turned livid. "Fool," he hissed, raising his hands. White ice locked Allie in place, freezing her where she stood. "Think you that I do not know you have long abandoned the light you claim to follow? Your own transgressions bar you from such redemption. Yes, blood alone may break the curse—and your own flows black and marred."

Allie fired down at the icy restraints, breaking free. She raised her hands, the words of the Life-Blood Spell filling her thoughts in one desperate attempt to gain the upper hand. "*Aranac—co vey—*" Another icy blast caught her across the chest midway through the words, punching the air from her lungs and flinging her back against the stone wall.

She heard the Ace-Lord laugh. "Ah, another curious strategy. Do you believe binding me will reverse the claim the darkness holds over you?"

"You corrupted the Spell," Allie panted. "That magic was never yours to claim." Arms trembling, she let two more fiery blasts fly, feeling the heat sear her face and neck. The Ace-Lord's ice flung her back again, slamming her against the wall so hard she tasted blood in her mouth.

"Your life is mine," the Ace-Lord intoned, stepping forward. "If you intend to bring yourself such pain, know that it does not affect my own power."

"I know," Allie whispered through blistered lips. "I know I can't kill you. But I can take myself out of this game… ensure you'll never have me."

Painfully, she called the fire forth, let it wind in a spinning, crackling blaze around her before she let it fly. The Ace-Lord deflected it with a ray of ice, but not before the fire struck his chest, blackening his silver armor. The bolt felt as though a red-hot blade pierced Allie in the heart, and she swayed in place, gasping at the frigid air.

She sensed the Ace-Lord falter for a moment, and realized her last blow had been somewhat successful. But the Ace-Lord recovered far swifter than she could. Icy chains wrapped around her body before she could fight them, hauling her forward. The Ace-Lord's claw-like hand closed on her neck, and through blurred vision she saw his eyes blazing.

"Your plan, yet again, holds a fatal flaw," he hissed, so close she could feel his icy breath on her face. "I did not wish to kill you; it would have been far easier if you had descended into the Dark Realm of your own accord. But now I *shall* kill you, send you into the shadows by my power. Death does not stop fate, Vessel. When you are returned to the mortal world, your mind and heart shall know nothing beyond your servitude."

White ice flared in his hand, connecting to Allie's head and chest. Through blinding pain, she heard him whisper the words, reclaiming the dark power of the curse within her as his own. She felt the icy chains withdraw with the Life-Blood Spell in her last seconds of life.

. . . . . .

Rygal fell.

Darkness deeper than any he had ever known engulfed him in the void. In contrast to the chilling silence of the fog outside Castle Salem, it was thunderously loud inside the gateway. Howling wind clawed at his face, threatening to snuff out the flames sputtering along his sword and shield. He seemed suspended in midair, staggering forward into nothingness.

Voices sounded all around him—screams, cries, shouts from every moment of his life. Every horror he had seen, every monster he had confronted, loomed before his eyes, grotesquely twisted, larger than life as they reached for him. He saw the shifting forms of the Hazes, felt the metallic grip of the Serventiri hauling him backward.

Rygal slashed blindly at the invisible restraints. The cold took his breath away, as if his Essence had been torn from him by an Ace's white ice. Uncontrollable fear seized him.

"Why come you here, mortal?"

The voice thundered over the cries of the illusions, roaring in his mind. Whether it was the Ace-Lord, the Deputy, or some other dark guardian, he had no idea. But the venom in it left no doubt that it was utterly evil.

"This is the domain of Kahlifis. None shall pass but they who seek death."

The shadowy forms of a hundred Hazes loomed before him, blades shining in the darkness, and Rygal felt the ache of the old injury in his shoulder from years before. He stumbled, lifting his sword with an effort, squinting against the howling wind.

"Let me through," he shouted, his voice strained in terror. "I come for the Ace-Lord—let me through!"

He sensed rippling laughter all around him. The masses of Hazes transformed before his eyes, gathering into the towering figure of the Darkness. White ice crystallized on its four hands as it struck. Rygal tried to dodge, found he could no longer move, and instead plummeted straight downward. The unseen guard laughed again, glee in its wicked voice.

"This is no place for a mortal. Enter the shadows if you dare. Your mind and your Essence shall be ours to claim."

His yellow fire snuffed out in the void, and he felt himself slam onto something cold. Complete blackness surrounded him, and for an instant he feared he had been struck blind. Fear unlike any he had ever felt froze his heart, and he huddled in the shadows, gripping his sword as the screams of the illusions echoed around him.

Then, in his mind, a face appeared like a blaze of sunlight—Norrin's.

"Get up, boy. Get up before it is too late."

Rygal took a deep breath, inhaling the frigid air. Shaking, he pressed his shield against the ground and hauled himself upright. The wind nearly shoved him down again, but he held steady. He felt the cold, the fear, the throbbing of his heart. Recalled all he had learned and centered his thoughts on the Light.

"You have the blood of a Guardian, so act wisely."

The illusions howled louder, but he sensed the High Light's presence, greater than the darkness around him. He felt the blood flowing through his veins like fire.

Flames flickered down his sword again, piercing the darkness surrounding him. "I am here for the Ace-Lord," he stated, voice echoing through the wind. "By the sacred name of the Light, let me pass!"

A low hiss came from the shadows, but the illusions died away, and he felt himself being pressed forward, carried by the wind. Abruptly, his boots connected with stone, and he fell to his knees in the courtyard of a gray ruin. Pale stars spun away into nothingness beyond, illuminating the stones around him.

Shaking, his strength nearly spent, he looked up in the same instant that the white ice locked on Allie's chest.

The Ace-Lord held her by the throat just ten paces away. Burns seared his black skin and stood out on Allie's face and neck. They stood in the center of the ruins, broken stone walls rising around them.

The white ice gleamed, crackling in the stillness.

Allie.

He whispered her name, but it was the Ace-Lord's triumphant voice that filled the void as he spoke the words of a spell. In a brilliant flash of cold light, Rygal saw the Life-Blood Spell leave Allie's body, saw the magic return to the Ace-Lord like a powerful draught of strength.

Allie sagged weakly in the Ace-Lord's grasp, the first tinges of red entering the ice as her Essence was torn from her body.

Rygal sprang to his feet, sprinting across the stone, sliding on the ice-slicked rocks. Words—words he had studied again and again with Allie as they'd sought for a cure to the curse months before—came readily to his mind, and this time, the power they drew from split the void's darkness with the High Light's golden fire.

His blazing sword flashed over the Ace-Lord's armored shoulder as he struck. *"Aranac—co vey—devarris—"*

The Ace-Lord whipped around, Allie's still body falling from his grasp, as he fired a blast of white into the hated light. Rygal raised his shield just in time—the ice rent the shield into pieces, sending shards of iron clattering to the stone. The Ace-Lord's pale blade sliced at his throat—Rygal parried, his blade shuddering beneath the weight of the blow, but the crackling flames did not falter. Gasping, he stepped forward, seizing the Ace-Lord's face as he cried out the last word. *"Dovannon—"*

The fire flashed briefly before the ice overcame it, and his sword was cold again. The Ace-Lord's frigid skin seared his hand—Rygal let go and stepped back. Before he could regain his balance, the Ace-Lord's icy blade rammed through his chest.

For an instant Rygal felt nothing, only the air forced from his lungs and the freezing wind coiling around him. Only when the Ace-Lord withdrew the blade, causing him to collapse to his knees, did he feel the pain radiating from the fatal wound.

. . . . . .

The Ace-Lord had dropped Allie so suddenly her head slammed against the cold stone. Blackness claimed her vision briefly, so that for a moment, she was certain it was all over. She had never been sure what death would feel like.

But the sudden flash of golden fire, the familiar heat warming her blistered face, drew her back to the reality that she still breathed. At first, she could not understand what she heard, certain she was dreaming. Impossible. Rygal was supposed to be in the tower room back in the mortal world, closing the gateway. He couldn't have passed through the void, unless by some magic.

Yet she knew his voice, raw with fear and pain, shouting words she recognized—though the pure light blazing with them was far different than the blackness the curse had been turned into.

She felt herself inhale, breath filling her lungs, and struggled to rise, but her muscles refused to obey. Her vision slowly focused on two blurred figures—the Ace-Lord, black robes swirling wildly around him, and Rygal, wreathed in brilliant flames as he shouted the last word of the Life-Blood Spell, channeling the Light's power.

"*Dovannon—*"

She saw him draw breath again as he gripped the Ace-Lord's face, then fell back against the wall—in one swift motion, the Ace-Lord plunged his sword straight through Rygal's chest.

No, her mind whispered, and she felt her heart shatter into pieces.

Rygal choked, looking down as if in surprise at the icy blade—the Ace-Lord wrenched the sword free, causing him to crumple to his knees.

No, her heart screamed again. She struggled to rise, but the grief and horror seemed a physical weight, crushing her down.

The Ace-Lord took a step back, inhaling deeply, satisfaction in his eyes. "And so it is finished," he breathed, raising his head to look up into the darkness. "The war has ended. The game is won. The Vessel shall enter the Dark Realm."

He raised his hands, white ice gleaming again on his fingertips—but the blast did not come. Allie dragged herself to her knees, watching in disbelief.

The Ace-Lord's white ice had receded back into his fingers like snow melting before a hearth. As he stared at his hand in shock, the illusions fell away, revealing the wraith-like lord whose dark blood had already begun to leak through the gaps in the armor.

When Willing Warrior be gone at dawn; Ace-Lord, mortal, together one.

Rygal raised his head, blood trailing down his chin as he gave a short, fierce grin.

Victory.

"Impossible," the Ace-Lord whispered, looking down at his own blood. "Certainly it cannot be so… no mortal has…" He trailed off, looking at Rygal in a mixture of hatred, pain, and something almost like respect.

Rygal did not answer, only lowered his head wearily as his life drained away.

The Ace-Lord hissed, making to strike him again—as he did, a ray of golden fire split the darkness of the void, consuming the swirling nothingness, and began to engulf the ancient ruin. Unseen forces of light barred him from breaking what had been foretold, just as with the Bruin.

Allie crawled to Rygal as he slumped onto his back. Victory. Her mind knew it had come, in a way no one had foreseen. Written in the Prophecy. Understood, at the last moment, by Rygal.

A sacrifice. A mortal, willingly taking part in the curse.

She reached him, tears stinging as they ran down her blistered face, and though her mind knew it, her heart could not accept it. "Why… why… you weren't supposed…" Her throat tightened as she touched his pale face. His eyes met hers, filled with pain and love, and her heart broke from both. "It wasn't… it was supposed to be me."

He smiled, shook his head weakly as he answered in a rasping whisper. "No… it never was."

The golden fire swirled in the howling wind, spreading downward to reach them—yet it would not be enough to close the gateway.

Shaking, Allie raised herself, summoning the last amount of strength within her into a blast that finally burned pure red. Crimson flames spread into the wind around her before she collapsed again, clutching Rygal close. His hand brushed her hair back, whispering in her ear. "It's okay… it's okay… don't…"

"I'm here," she choked. "I won't leave you. I won't leave you."

Brilliant fire engulfed the stone walls, and their surroundings began to fade into white. Allie heard the Ace-Lord's voice calling furious, futile spells as he fought the collapsing void, heard the crackle of his ice spreading desperately over the walls as his own strength drained away. Dying a second time. Dying slowly, painfully, by the spell he had sought to corrupt.

The white ice finally melted away, and the Ace-Lord lowered his hands, tattered robes torn in the wind, armor glinting in the fire-light. His purple-red eyes flashed as he stared at the two mortals who had bested him, and for an instant Allie thought he would fling himself upon them, kill them both with the last strength remaining to him.

But the Ace-Lord only smiled his skull-like smile as the Lord of Death returned to his own realm. "Wise move, son of Gayrile," he whispered, as the gold and red flames swirled around him and his wraith-like frame faded away into the shadows.

. . . . . .

Light shone brightly in Rygal's eyes.

He no longer felt pain, nor the fear and grief that had gripped him for so long. Only the warmth of the golden fire as it engulfed the void and the Ace-Lord, and Allie's tears on his face. Only triumph and joy in his weakening heart.

The soft warmth of the flames, the steady breath of the wind, the gradually lightening of the world around him eased the last of his fears, settled his ragged breaths into a quiet rhythm. He felt as though he were drifting in a sea of light, as if time had turned back to the day he had been swept from the fishing vessel to the Mainland, the day it had all begun.

He felt himself drifting, felt the waves around him again, yet this time, the sea was calm. Deep, quiet waters illuminated by unseen fire.

Death was not the dark thing he had always heard it to be… instead, it felt as though his spirit were embraced by the peaceful flames.

Allie's face swam above him through his blurred vision. So beautiful. He had never told her how much he loved her; the words had simply never come.

Her face eventually faded away to be replaced by another, one both unfamiliar and yet one he knew at the same time. Perhaps it was Norrin's. Perhaps it was his father's.

Perhaps it was another, One in whom he had just learned to trust.

He felt the last throb of his heart as the void melted away.

The fight was finally finished.

59

Stars and Snow

Breath. It came slow and painful as Jan lay in the snow. Darkness reached for him to draw him away from life, to pull him into whatever waited beyond the dawn. Yet his mind did not focus on the pain, the fear, the grief.

He had not expected to still be breathing, with Drisilas plunged into Redeyes' heart and his Essence completely exhausted. Isilas flickered faint light under his torn jerkin, cold against the old scars on his chest. The Marks ensured his death, and so death he waited for.

And yet… death did not come.

Through the black night roared a wind, so strong it ripped through the shadows and the fog on the Flats, carrying sounds he did not understand. To the watchers on the battlefield, a great light flared from the highest tower of Castle Salem—only for an instant, leaving the mortal forces standing in confusion and awe, while the Ace-army crumbled into chaos.

Jan took another breath, forcing his eyes open and turning his head toward the distant battlefield. He could see nothing through the underbrush. The sounds did not tell him what was happening. Nor could he understand why he was still here, living and breathing as the darkness over Ar-Salem seemed rent in two and the last illusions were swept away.

Perhaps…

The word entered his mind, bringing with it a plethora of emotions. Hope. Grief. Disbelief. The words of the Prophecy swam through his thoughts.

When willing warrior be gone at dawn.

"Jan?"

Dandio's voice cut through the half-consciousness, drawing him back to life. Vaguely, he sensed his brother above him, seeking to slow the flow of blood. Somewhere in his heart, he knew Asescia's mission had succeeded, and felt a pain so deep and dark it threatened to overcome his weary body.

But perhaps…

Perhaps the Prophecy yet held hope. Perhaps the High Light still promised a future for the broken, the ones bound by fear, the ones Marked by death.

With an effort, he drew his focus to the unexpected present. Voices—frightened, confused, questioning—drifted from the Flats as the hounds fled, the enchanted soldiers shouted in confusion, and the last wraiths dissolved into the snow-filled air.

Redeyes lay dead beside him. Jan had always expected to die with the beast, almost hoped for it at times. For so long it had seemed the only way to truly redeem himself, to atone for the wrongs that had caused him to be Marked.

Yet perhaps redemption was brighter in life than in death.

Perhaps that was why the Light yet shone upon him.

Dandio gripped his hand, drawing him upright. Blood trickled from the wound on Jan's side, and streaked the snow around him as he sat up. It speckled Dandio's broken armor, too, as he held his wounded arm close. His brother's face was drawn with concern, but he gave an almost incredulous smile, as though he was as stunned as Jan that they had survived the night. "Can you hear them?" he asked hoarsely. "The voices… listen."

Jan turned, looking toward the Flats. He could make out the black masses of Dal-kerri fleeing into the fading shadows, and the throngs of enchanted soldiers standing confused and disoriented. Mortal voices reached them, too far away for them to understand. The distance was too great for him to see any details or clues as to what on Orlell had occurred. Yet, as his mind finally cleared, his thoughts centered hesitantly yet hopefully on the unbelievable truth.

"I hear them," Jan replied hoarsely. His voice was ragged, his Essence nearly completely drained by the brutal fight, but the hope filled him with a fresh strength.

They leaned upon each other as they stood. Dandio peered around them in disbelief. "The light," he murmured at last. "The darkness—it is fading. What do you think has happened?"

"I think," Jan said slowly, still hardly daring to believe it himself, "I think this fight is finally over."

They turned their eyes to the south, where the dark clouds had been swept away and Castle Salem stood silhouetted in the pale light. But they could not yet know what had transpired, only make their way back to the battlefield in fearful yet expectant silence.

· · · · · ·

Mel and Jarus had stood side by side, the Blue Stone shining in their combined grip as they fended off Dal-kerri, for what had felt like hours. The fiery power of the *Alené* had lit the battle at the castle gates. They had sang on, even as the ghost of the Ace-Messenger dissolved into blue flames, as the vanguard crumpled suddenly like wooden dolls, leaving the Wildkids and Druids to turn their defense to the enchanted soldiers.

Mel had stumbled over the words for a moment, squinting through the vivid blue light to see if he was mistaken. He wasn't. The vanguard were dead—all of them, falling as if the strings holding them up had been cut.

He turned his eyes toward the slight rise where Aryion had gone, but could see nothing through the fiery shield.

Captain Fargrin's voice had intermingled with Dusty's as each shouted orders to their forces. The enchanted soldiers had faltered in confusion when the vanguard collapsed, and the Wildkids pressed against them, forcing them back.

At the same moment they did, a blinding flash of golden light blazed from the castle behind him, lighting the Flats with the strength of a thousand fires—and then it was gone, dazzling Mel's eyes.

He did not understand what he saw as his vision cleared. Only watched in stunned silence as the fog receded, the darkness faded away, and the last snowflakes settled quietly upon the land.

At the flash, the enchanted soldiers fell to their knees, clutching their heads or crying out in pain. They were immediately encircled by the Wildkids, who advanced upon them slowly, hesitantly, fearing some trick. Yet the soldiers made no move to fight. They had simply crumpled, some gasping at the frigid air, others staring dully up at the sky, and still others cursing and flinching as they blinked around them in bewilderment.

Mel turned back to the palace.

The hulking storm clouds, which had shrouded Castle Salem for months and darkened the entire land, were gone, leaving only the dull gray sky above. Mel beheld an ancient ruin built on the rocky hills, crumbling with age, lonely and silent, snow dusting its towers.

Victory.

The word entered his mind in a whisper, and his heart suddenly beat in wild hope.

"They did it," he rasped.

"Hold," Dusty ordered her troops. Her voice, though tense and exhausted from the long night of battle, held the same hesitant hope that Mel felt. "Don't hurt them." She had lowered her spear at Captain Fargrin's chest, but did not strike. Fargrin's face was bent to the ground as he knelt, gasping for breath, yet Mel saw the moment the last traces of hollow blue faded, leaving hazel eyes that seemed oddly familiar.

"The enchantment," Jarus murmured, raising his face to scent the wind. "It's gone. At least—the soldiers smell like mortals now."

Gone.

Gone was the weight that had settled on Mel's shoulders from the moment he'd entered this fight. Gone were the shadows that had plagued his mind and heart for so long. Gone was the guilt, which he had at last come to peace with.

His mind seemed unable to accept the truth, so impossible it seemed. But the sight of the ruin behind him and the hundreds of enchanted soldiers kneeling before him affirmed it.

The war, over. The spell, broken.

Knees trembling, he broke through the circle of Wildkids, stumbling for the slight hill. The bodies of the vanguard littered the ground—sustained by the Deputy's essence, bound by a darker Oath than the enchantment.

Iriam stood on the opposite side of the slope, flanked by two Druids. Though streaked in blood and mud, they appeared unhurt, only exhausted. Their eyes were fixed on Castle Salem, wonder on their faces.

Mel barely noticed them. Fear gripped his heart as his eyes searched vainly through the carnage on the hilltop. His gaze was drawn to a black mass in the mud to his right. Tattered rags and tarnished armor, that was all that remained. Or were shadows simply less frightening after the night had passed?

"Aryion," he whispered, his voice trembling as he looked through the bodies. The mud disfigured the faces of many dead. Aryion's sword gleamed beside the Deputy's lifeless body, but Mel did not see his mentor.

Then a muddied hand clutched his arm, and he looked into Aryion's eyes.

"Are you all right? Are you hurt?" Aryion's voice was nearly as hoarse as Mel's. He knelt in the filthy slush, so covered in mud and blood that Mel barely recognized him, except for his eyes.

Brown. No trace of the hollow blue, of the madness or anguish that had gripped him.

"No—I'm fine," Mel managed to choke. The relief seemed to rob him of his voice, the truth finally settling upon him and filling his heart with so much emotion he could not speak.

The war was over. The Aces were gone.

Aryion's face was still concerned, mistaking the tears welling in Mel's eyes for something else, seeking the source of the blood on his apprentice's arm. Worry filled the eyes that had seemed so long to belong to another man entirely. "You're sure? Mel, what—"

"I'm fine," Mel said again, feeling the tears running down his cheeks. "It's over… Aryion, it's over."

The reality of his own words seemed impossible, a far away future that they would never see. Yet the snow had ceased, the war had ended, the Aces were gone. The last shadows faded away as he hugged his mentor tightly, buried his face in his shoulder, and wept tears of joy.

60

Mortal Heart

Snow fell silently upon the ruined walls, dusted the gray stones, and gradually blanketed the skeletal ruin of Castle Salem around Allie.

She blinked the snowflakes from her eyelashes. Light. It was all around her, pale and cold but gradually growing brighter as the thunderclouds faded away into the dawn sky above. She could *see*—she hadn't realized just how much the Life-Blood Spell had darkened her natural senses. She saw vivid colors, smelled the wet ash on the rocks, felt the cold wind filling her lungs with life, and the steady beat of her heart.

The burns on her face stung from the remains of tears, and as she sat up, she felt the blisters across her collarbone and neck. But her Liznee fire that had blazed forth in the last moments, closing the gateway, was red again, far removed from the Ace-Lord's grasp.

Free. The icy chains that had bound her heart were shattered.

Allie closed her eyes a moment, feeling fresh tears run down her cheeks. The mortal heart—her heart—had been marred by the Life-Blood Spell. The Ace-Lord had chosen her as his Vessel, ensuring she would never be anything but his pawn. Hers was not the blood that would break her chains. For that, another sacrifice was required—the Willing Warrior.

Gratitude and grief melded together so sharply she could hardly breathe. She settled against the broken wall, pulling her knees to her chest as she struggled to gather her thoughts.

What now?

Allie glanced over her shoulder, where the great stained glass window had once stood. There was no sign of it now, nor any sign of the elegance and horror that had been Castle Salem. The Ace-Lord, the gateway, Rygal… all had been lost into the final swirl of conquering fire when the void had closed. The palace was a ruin once again, blackened stones and crumbling walls, and the only shadows within it were cast by the natural light.

She could just make out the battlefield beyond the walls, half-shrouded by the thin veil of morning mist rising from the Strait. Who had survived? Who else had fallen?

She hadn't expected to feel this fear. The potential that she would live to see her family and friends again, after the Ace-Lord was defeated, was one she had long abandoned, resolving herself to her own death.

But that fate had never been hers.

Rygal's face, drawn with pain and streaked in blood, entered her mind again, and she buried her face in her hands.

Those last horrific moments in the void replayed in her mind—the Ace-Lord's white ice tearing her Essence from her body as he removed the curse; Rygal's voice breaking the blinding pain; the Ace-Lord's blade plunging through Rygal's chest; the golden and red flames engulfing the void, closing the doorway forever.

She was so grateful. And she was so filled with grief it felt as though her heart would break.

A short sob broke from her throat, yet her body felt too exhausted even for tears. She raised her eyes to the sky, watching as the clouds faded. Stars glimmered in the lightening sky.

"Was this how it was supposed to be?" she whispered, not sure if her confused prayer was heard. "Why… why not me? I—I know I deserve it."

She could not explain what she heard. The voice that answered was not especially loud, a gentle whisper in her tormented mind. The Light called her redeemed. No matter the curse that had claimed her, no matter the blood on her hands, not even the Lord of Death could change that. And she felt, as surely as though it were written in the Prophecy, that even the darkness she had endured had served to guide her back to a faith and peace she had long forgotten.

Golden fire blazed to her right, and when she looked up, a tall figure in gleaming garb stood before her.

"Do you understand what he has done, child?"

Allie stared at Cahadras a moment. At one point, she had loathed the Star Queen's cryptic words, frustrated she would not speak plainly. And yet, seeing how everything had worked out, she now believed that the Stars had expected this future no more than the mortals had.

"He saved Orlell," she answered softly, after a pause. "Rygal… Rygal saved everyone."

Cahadras nodded thoughtfully, something not unlike surprise still lingering in her eyes. "So he did," she mused. Her usually proud voice was quiet as she cast her eyes over the ruin of Castle Salem. At last she looked at Allie. "Might we speak together, if you have the strength?"

Allie nodded slightly and stood stiffly, leaning against the wall.

Cahadras glanced out at the snow-dusted battlefield, seeming almost hesitant to speak. "I admit I have long judged the mortals, in my heart," she said at last. "Many of our race do. We have watched since the beginning of time, seeing every meaningless battle, every dark plot, every life that was lost in pursuit of selfish gain. Despite the words of peace and hope the High Light offered, few held to the truths of the Words of Old."

Allie nodded again. She had no argument. The Ace-Lord's words before had held a grain of truth. The selfishness of the mortals was a weakness he had counted on, one he had exploited time and time again. No wonder he had never predicted the Life-Blood Spell being turned against him. That would call for willing sacrifice, a selfless act.

"Long have we watched the mortals," Cahadras continued, her voice distant. "We obey the High Light's orders often with doubt in our hearts, despite the fact that it is His plan directing all. I admit to you that I had begun to fear the mortals' efforts would fail," she added, looking at Allie. "Orlell would be lost, and Kahlifis would reign over those who yet remained."

"But he didn't," Allie said hoarsely. She cleared her throat, taking a breath before speaking. "I… I can't blame you for thinking like that. I used to think so, too. And I thought the Prophecy was nothing more than some confusing old scroll—and the only way to win was to just keep fighting, no matter what the Prophecy said." She shook her head, recalling that determined belligerence she'd clung to for so long. "I suppose… I suppose I always thought my life had no real impact on what was going to happen. I believed the Ace-Lord's words, that I was marked for death."

"Perhaps," Cahadras murmured. "And yet you live, and the Prophecy has come to pass as foretold."

Allie looked down at her blistered hands, the words of the seventh stanza entering her mind.

When nameless New Blood knows their call,
If Mortal's heart remains unmarred,

When Lord of Death brings life to all,

The spell that bound leaves deeper scars

Than the shadow that awakened.

The Ace-Lord had sought to mar the mortals. Had come very close to victory, in fact. And yet despite it all, the mortals still lived, and dawn had come.

"Selfishness may remain a common weakness, just as fear is," Cahadras mused. "Had this story been told another way, I fear that weakness would have been your ruin. The price of peace, the fight of guarding one's heart, the weight of one's call… that is a burden few can bear."

"Maybe it's not meant to be borne alone," Allie answered softly. "Maybe that burden is something we bear together—fighting for each other, holding our hope." Hadn't she once read something like that in the Words of Old?

"Well said," Cahadras agreed, her severe features softening for a moment. There was a long silence. The valley beyond appeared less shadowed to Allie, dusted in glittering snow so that the Salem Flats sparkled like a thousand Star-Stones.

"There is one other matter we must speak of," Cahadras said after a pause, turning to Allie. "The truth of the Life-Blood Spell, its origin, its corruption, is something I did not inform you of when you were first cursed. You must forgive me in this matter. The chance of it becoming relevant seemed so unlikely that I did not wish to trouble you with it."

Allie frowned, confused. "What do you mean?"

Cahadras folded her hands before her, her face thoughtful. "The Life-Blood Spell was once pure magic, as you have learned," she said. "A powerful covenant, entwining one's Essence with the High Light as the *Alené* allowed. Kahlifis twisted it, corrupting it to draw from his own power, and using it to subjugate the mortals to his will. He used the curse sparingly, well aware that there is always a price to pay for corrupting magic. All dark magic has a flaw. In corrupting the Life-Blood Spell, Kahlifis made certain that there was only one weakness—one flaw, nearly impossible to exploit, so that it left the curse virtually without consequence."

Wind blew gently over the land, like a whisper of unknown hope. Allie stared at her, unsure why her heart was suddenly racing. "We… read about a flaw," she whispered. "I didn't think…" she trailed off.

"That flaw," Cahadras continued, "states that if a mortal willingly takes the curse of the Life-Blood Spell, death shall release them, while the Ace who corrupted that magic shall fall. The mortal shall be freed— not by their blood, but by their heart. A heart that chooses sacrifice cannot be marred by a corrupted curse."

If mortal heart remains unmarred.

Allie could not speak, her heart suddenly racing. At last she managed to answer, voice unsteady. "What… what are you saying? That death shall… it will release…" She stopped, suddenly unable to continue.

Golden fire flickered in the air beside Cahadras, spreading down a shape that gradually came into focus. Allie thought, for a moment, that another Star was appearing before her. Yet the form was different, not just stepping through the flames, but wrought by them, formed out of the fire as the High Light returned his life.

She watched, as though in a dream, as Rygal's face came into focus through the fire.

"His choice was made," Cahadras said quietly. "The mortal, willingly bound. The Lord of Death has no claim over him, not in such a way."

The flames vanished, and Rygal fell to his knees with a gasp, as though emerging from frigid water. Allie caught him as he did, arms wrapped around him, feeling the warmth of his body. He was here—truly here, not a ghost, not some last cruel illusion, but here in her arms as though he had never gone. A sob broke from her throat as she clung to him.

"Allie?" His voice was puzzled, rasping—he wiped the tears from her face, fingers lingering in concern on the burns, yet Allie could not stop the tears.

He was here. He lived—he lived—

"H-how?" she finally stammered, pulling back and placing a hand on his chest. His armor was still rent and twisted, and a dark scar marred his skin where the Ace-Lord's terrible sword had plunged through his body. Yet the blood was gone, and she could feel his heart beating against her fingers.

Rygal looked around the ruined castle, still gathering his breath. His eyes landed on Cahadras, and Allie saw wonder and confusion, then fear, cross his face. "The Ace-Lord?" he asked anxiously. "Is..."

"The Ace-Lord shall not return in such a way," Cahadras answered with a slight nod of reassurance. "In corrupting the Life-Blood Spell, his own magic ensnared him. Your choice was made, son of Maran—an act so wholly against a mortal's natural desires. You knew not of the flaw of the Spell to ensure your survival, yet you willingly chose death to save the few left. By such an action, the Ace-Lord is bound by the twisted rules of his own curse, which he cannot go back on."

Rygal looked down at his broken armor, at Allie, then back to Cahadras. "The flaw... I never thought about the flaw," he said shakily. "Only that... that the Ace-Lord might be bound by the High Light's power...

once he'd released you from the curse," he added, looking at Allie again.

"And thus your choice was selfless," Cahadras said, nodding. "The warrior, willing, as the Prophecy foretold."

Allie wrapped her arms around him as the tears came again. The fear and grief were drowned out by wonder and joy. He held her tightly, as though he would never let go.

Golden fire flickered a third time, spreading from Cahadras' crown and joining with the vivid light of the rising sun. Her fierce eyes met Allie's a moment, and a smile flickered briefly over her face. "Be at peace, mortals. The night has ended."

The Star Queen faded away in a flare of fire, as sunlight sparkled over the snow and the first joyous voices of victory rose over the Salem Flats.

61

After the Dawn

Allie was not certain how long the battle had lasted. Every minute seemed alive now, intermingled with both darkness and light, hope and grief, joy and mourning.

The moments were preserved crystal-clear in her mind. Emerging through the ruined gates of Castle Salem into the embraces of their companions beyond—Mel, Jarus, Dusty, Aryion, and the other Wildkid warriors. Seeing Iriam's rare smile of approval as he stood among the Druids. Hearing the many questions and exclamations from the friends who had feared she would never return through those gates. Rygal remained beside her, neither of them fully able to explain the events that had taken place within the tower.

The critically wounded were hurried back to the Wingship, which still waited on the Strait. They would be taken back to Mata City, receiving better treatment than the Red Dawn's overloaded field hospitals could provide. Among them was Joesp. The young Wildkid had fearlessly defended his younger brothers from the vanguard. Two arrows had struck him before he had fallen, while his brothers shielded him until the spell was broken.

"He may yet live," Aryion told Dusty quietly, seeing her worried face. The ranger had helped to tend the wounded with the few supplies they had. "Don't give up on him yet."

Dusty had boarded the Wingship with the other Wildkids only after seeing that the enchanted soldiers were well-secured. Allie quickly understood that the matter of the enchanted soldiers would not be a simple one. The enchantment broken, the soldiers had returned to themselves in the middle of a battlefield, most with no recollection of how they had gotten there. They seemed to remember only their choice to serve the Aces, and nothing after that.

Most of the enemy soldiers at the gates—over a hundred in all—seemed to come from the Magno regions, yet not all of them were the unfortunate, deceived peasants she had expected. Many of them were experienced warriors, mercenaries, who were dismayed they had lost the war. Others, though, were simple farmers and fishermen, baffled and frightened to awaken with bloodied swords in their hands.

Iriam and the Druids saw to it that the warriors were relieved of their weapons and restrained, but not harmed. "Even if the choice was their own," he told Jarus, when the Cooper worried over taking the captives, "they must be given the chance to choose life again, now that the Aces are gone."

The formerly enchanted soldiers made no effort to resist their captors. A few shouted or cursed as they were bound, but most were silent, their faces lost and vacant. The nine Druids flanked them as they were marched over the hill and into the valley.

The rising sun melted the dusting of snow and illuminated the horrors of the long night of battle. The group marched along the edge of the ridge, so that the carnage in the valley below was spread before them. So many dead. The stench churned Allie's stomach and filled her heart with fear.

The remaining forces of the Ace-army had been rounded up, the soldiers brought to their knees and restrained. Allie could see the Red Dawn generals giving orders to the guards as the captives were gathered.

What could they possibly do for them? What could be done?

A troop of Elven and Alfona warriors met them at the entrance to the camp, led by Quinn and Wolfsbane. Though filthy and bearing several wounds, they smiled widely as they saw Allie and her companions.

"It is very good to see you have returned," Quinn said, clasping hands with Iriam with wonder in his eyes. "I—I take it the mission succeeded?"

"Indeed," Iriam told him, his purple-red eyes flicking briefly to Allie and Rygal before returning to Quinn. "How fare your forces?"

"Better than many," the elf said gravely. The tribesman's face was streaked in Dal-kerri blood. "The dead are still to be tended; the wounded, all the more so."

"What of the High King?" Iriam inquired.

"Among the injured, as is the Commander," Wolfsbane answered. "But we have been assured they are both alive."

Allie let out a breath of relief. Suddenly, all she wanted was to see her father.

The first friend she recognized among the fallen was when a group of hama-dryads bore a body bound in gray linen past them with reverence and sorrow. Kalos-Lia had fought until his last strength among his archers, beset on all sides by Dal-kerri and serpentines. Allie had not known him well, but she felt a deep grief knowing he would not return to join another celebration beneath the summer trees, knowing such joy had always been dearer to him than the honor of the bow in his hand.

She hesitated as the hama-dryads passed them by, not sure where to go. Death and grief seemed to grip the encampment in cold claws, the voices and cries of the injured echoing around them. There were countless wounded—the kragons swept over the battlefield, helping to transport them to safety, but even they seemed overwhelmed. Mel, carrying the Blue Stone, headed to the nearest field hospital, with Aryion accompanying him. She heard Jarus say something about going to the Cooper encampment.

Rygal left after making sure she was all right, going to find any surviving Guardians. It was strange without him beside her. She'd become so used to his near-constant presence as they'd protected each other through the long dark night. Now that dawn had come, she barely recognized what the light shone on, barely knew who she'd become.

Iriam's hand rested gently on her shoulder. "Come. Let us attend to those who most need to see you alive."

He guided her through the camp until they reached the scarlet and silver tents of the Red Dawn. Ajaha appeared at the doorway of one; disbelief, joy, and relief crossed her face in succession as she swept forward to meet them. Allie embraced her mother tightly, tears welling in her eyes.

"The spell?" Ajaha whispered, her voice tense. "Did… was it…"

"It was broken," Allie replied, feeling the truth of the words settle upon her heart. "The spell, the Ace-Lord… it's all gone."

And for that moment, that was all that mattered. The discussions, the meetings, the answers to the thousands of questions in her mind… that could wait for now.

They entered the tent, which only held two cots. The soft light of the lantern illuminated the figures in each, as the nurses worked above them.

Jan lay in one, eyes closed, his face so pale and still that for one horrible instant Allie thought he was already dead. But the steady rise and fall of his chest reassured her otherwise.

The second figure sat upright slowly as they entered. One arm was bound in a sling, and a cruel bruise marked his neck. But he paid the wounds no heed, stunned relief filling his scarred face.

"Asescia?" Dandio asked hoarsely, as though unsure whether or not the figure before him was an illusion.

Allie knelt beside her father's cot, taking his hand in hers. "I'm here," she said, voice choked with emotion.

Dandio hugged her with his uninjured arm, and she buried her face in his shoulder, so indescribably relieved that he was alive, and that she was here with him. Fresh tears sprang to her eyes at the familiar embrace. How often had he held her just like this, shielding her from a thunderstorm, comforting her after a nightmare?

"Are you…" she began hesitantly, looking worriedly at his bloodied bandages, then at her uncle's unmoving form on the other cot.

"They will both live," one of the medics reassured her. "The High King's injuries were serious, but he shall recover."

Allie nodded, some of her fear fading as she studied Jan's face. Though pale and bruised, there was something in his sleeping features she had not seen for a very long time. Peace. Redeyes was finally gone, and though much healing was yet to be done, the Marks no longer bound him.

She sat with her parents in the tent, preferring the stuffy darkness over the grief and uncertainty waiting outside. Dandio told her of the battle from his perspective, about the danger they had faced and the blood that had been spilled. The losses were still being assessed. Many men had been lost in the chaos just before the spell had been broken, as if the Ace-army had been whipped into one last frenzied rage. Glentree was heading up the search for the living; despite the giant's own injuries, he was determined to help. General Leopold had also survived, though narrowly, and he and Admiral Dessian were now organizing the transport of the wounded.

"Our forces on the west of the battlefield took the heaviest losses, as far as I can tell," Dandio said, shaking his head in both weariness and sorrow. "There was an unexpected attack that separated Ĵan and I, and led us to fight Redeyes alone. The Red Dawn was completely cut off, trapped beside the Strait. Lord Roan led a battalion of Coopers into the fray to aid our forces—never underestimate a Cooper whose allies are in danger." A slight, sad smile crossed his face. "They fought bravely, with no fear of the cost. Lord Roan saved those men with his last breath."

Allie closed her eyes a moment, stricken by the loss. Remembering the Cooper lord's steady leadership and the hope in which he had always believed, hurt more than she would have expected.

After the spell had been broken, Dandio said, he and Ĵan had hardly understood what was happening at first. They had stumbled back to their men on the battlefield as the crowds of enchanted soldiers were restrained. The surviving Dal-kerri, it seemed, had scattered, some dying to the swords of the outriders, others managing to flee into the tangled wilderness of the Magno Forest. But the Aces had all perished upon the Ace-Lord's death.

"The vanguard were like that too," Allie told him, remembering Mel's report of the Deputy's hulking warriors. "They died with the Ace-Deputy."

"Their Essence was sustained by his, I believe," Ajaha said thoughtfully. "The Aces' lives were bound to their master, just as their wills."

Like mine was, Allie's thoughts added, recalling the icy chains that had bound her heart. Yet she was here. Living and breathing and so strangely lost, now that the fight was over.

Ajaha returned to the couriers, who were now working to spread the news of the victory throughout the rest of the kingdom. Allie remained in the tent with her father. She didn't feel tired, but when a medic brought another cot for her and offered to treat her burns, she agreed without complaint, and eventually drifted off.

Even in sleep, the uncertainty and fear lingered over her. She heard the Ace-Lord's voice, saw his skull-like smile even as the flames consumed him, saw the icy blade plunge into Rygal's chest over and over.

The battle was over, but the struggle was still before her. She doubted it would ever truly be finished.

. . . . . .

The following morning, Allie returned to Mata City.

While the work had only just begun, there was little she could do to help. Dandio eventually convinced her to leave; despite his broken arm, he was determined to resume the tasks of Commander. While just as weary as everyone else, a hesitant hope shone again in his eyes. Rygal stayed with him, helping along with the surviving Guardians of Gayrile.

Ajaha accompanied her on the voyage north, along with Jan. Though slowly recovering, his wounds required more medical attention than the field doctors could administer. Mel and Aryion came too, along with Jarus. The loss of Lord Roan weighed heavily on the normally cheerful Cooper.

Iriam remained with the Druids, saying there was a matter that he needed to attend to. Allie was not sure what he meant—the Neutral seemed graver than usual, sorrowful, as if anticipating some parting. He did not explain more, and she felt too tired to press him for more.

It was Jan to whom Allie ended up recounting the full story of the Ace-Lord's defeat. He did not interrupt once, only listened with intense interest as she told him of the discussion in the tower room, the void of darkness she'd been dragged into, and the black future the Ace-Lord had intended for her.

She had to pause a moment before continuing. The parts surrounding Rygal's sacrifice were still fresh with pain. She could hardly understand why he'd acted as he did. But that part of her story was the most important, especially as she'd never expected to return from the void.

She could tell Jan grew more and more intrigued as she spoke, explaining Rygal's successful effort to bind the Ace-Lord with the Life-Blood Spell and how the Ace-Lord had brought his own defeat through Rygal's death. She was then left to explain what Cahadras had told her—about the fatal flaw in the spell, which returned Rygal to the mortal world.

"Cahadras said… the Ace-Lord can't claim a life in that way," she finished haltingly, swallowing the lump in her throat. "I didn't know why. None of it makes sense to me, especially when… when I was sure I was the one who deserved death more." She glanced down at her bandaged hands.

"It is strange," Jan agreed quietly. "I would never have supposed that to be our key to victory, and yet it fits the Prophecy's words to the letter." He paused. "As for whether or not one deserves death, I don't believe that is for us to decide. If another chooses to give themselves up for us, what choice have we but to live as redeemed?"

Allie let out a breath, hearing the truth in her uncle's words, but did not speak anymore.

Clouds shrouded the sun as they reached Mata City that afternoon, and the frigid air from the last few days had been replaced by a gentle breeze carrying the last warmth of the season. The rocky hills and firelit city seemed somehow quieter than before, despite the small crowd of joyful townsfolk that met them at the harbor.

Maya, accompanied by three of her fellow shipbuilders and little Ella, waited for them. The other Coopers parted to allow Maya forward—Ella bounded past them all to reach Jarus. Allie saw some of the Cooper's grief lessen as he embraced his family.

She stayed with her mother as they walked to Castle Mata. Hushed voices filled Mata City. Theirs was not the first ship that had returned, carrying news and survivors. War was over. The sun shone again. And yet the light had been paid for with a heavy cost.

The High King, despite his injuries, joined the couriers as they worked with the delegates of the many different kingdoms, doing what they could. A council would decide details eventually, Allie was certain, though she wasn't sure what that would entail. In all that she had ever read of war, very little dealt in the aftermath—that strange vacant period of grief and rest while the dark shadows lingered in her mind.

She waited in the courier suite, watching out the window as the canals swarmed with ships and the streets gradually filled with soldiers and townsfolk alike.

The end of the war. She'd hoped for victory since the war had begun all those months ago now, but she'd never once stopped to wonder about what it would look like. She herself had only been involved in the last few battles, yet that short time seemed enough to erase every other aspect of her being. Who had she been before this fight? Before the Life-Blood Spell? Before she'd seen blood on her sword blade and felt her own fire burn her skin?

In recent times, she hadn't given her future much thought. Aside from hoping for the war to end, a time after it was never one she'd expected to experience. Up until two days ago, she was going to die. Now, the purpose that had bound her life and the death she'd resolved for herself were gone, leaving an unknown future spread before her.

And she was terrified.

Taking a deep breath, she pressed her face against the glass, watching the ships in the harbor as more and more warriors returned from the battlefield. The last stanza of the Prophecy whispered in her thoughts, and her mind responded to each line with the truth that had transpired.

When nameless New Blood knows their call.

Mel's face filled her thoughts, lit by the light of the Blue Stone as he raised his voice in the song of the *Alené* and called upon the High Light's power.

If Mortal heart remains unmarred.

How often that line had haunted her. But this time, it was not her face she saw, but Rygal's. The light in his blue eyes. The lines that grief had left on his face. His steady voice drawing her out of the dark agony and back into the light.

When Lord of Death brings life to all; The spell that bound leaves deeper scars; Than the Shadow that awakened.

Bound. The chains, broken. The Lord of Death returned to his realm, defeated by his own power.

Allie unwrapped the bandages from her hands, the burns still shining red and raw. Eventually the blisters would heal, though the scars would always be there. Far less deep than the scars that would have marred her heart if she had chosen the Ace-Lord's destiny for her.

And yet, what was to become of a warrior when there was no longer a war to fight?

Spells and Stones, mortal roles, hold your hope

Lest the Ace-Lord take your bones.

She no longer doubted the power of hope. It had become as palpable a magic as the Ace-Lord's dark spells or the brilliant light of the Star-Stones.

Yet what was the future she must now hope for?

The Last Council

Two weeks passed in Mata City, as the ships continued their comings and goings and news drifted in and out as steady as the tide. Messages were passed throughout the kingdoms, carrying both triumphant news and a call for aid now that the war was over.

Allie stayed with Jan most days. Though still recovering from his injuries, the High King had set to work managing the many matters and questions of the war-torn kingdom, as well as the aftermath of the battle itself. Ajaha's courier teams brought in new reports daily. More groups of previously enchanted soldiers had been captured and brought to Mata City, joining the Ace-Lord's surviving force. They formed a crowd of lost, confused, angry mortals, some with next to no knowledge of how they'd arrived, others with no recollection of who they had been before the curse.

"They will be tended to," Jan had assured her, but Allie could see the same concern in his face as she felt. Helping the enchanted soldiers would be no simple task, especially the decision for their fate considering their actions.

Jarus joined the king's council occasionally, though he had many duties of his own. The Coopers had begun the difficult deliberations over who would be chosen as the next lord of Mata City.

At last, the morning brought the *Gryphon's* return to Mata harbor, with Dandio and Glentree bringing the last warriors from the battlefield. With them came Rygal and the Guardians, and though Allie's heart seemed to grow warmer in his presence, she felt unsure of herself around him now, almost nervous. The moments before they'd entered the Ace-Lord's tower, the love she had finally admitted to herself, seemed far away, as if lived by a different person. In a way, they had.

Now that her life was no longer suspended on a timeframe, and the light shone upon her uncertain future, she had no idea how to act around him. No words to say. It seemed Rygal felt the same—he said very little to her, only took her hand briefly as he greeted her before moving away.

Allie forced herself not to think of her feelings now. There were more pressing matters to attend to.

The group that gathered in Castle Mata's council room was small, yet it was encouraging to have so many of her companions there. In addition to her parents and Jan, Iriam organized the meeting, and Aryion, Mel, Dusty, and Rygal joined them.

It reminded Allie of the meeting they'd held in Caer Sia shortly after their return from Wiverrun, though that discussion had only added to the fear and uncertainty in her mind. In contrast, this council promised hope that, slowly but surely, healing had begun. Rain pattered softly on the stone roof, and the roaring fire in the hearth filled the room with warmth and light.

The report Dandio gave was heavy yet hopeful. The armies had at last returned, having tended to the injured and the dead. Still, hundreds of soldiers were yet to be accounted for, some bodies unidentified, others missing entirely. The valley of Ar-Salem now stood as a burial ground for the multitude whose lives had been lost in the brutal fight.

"You have done everything you could for them," Jan told his brother gently. "And I am very grateful for your efforts."

"I understand that," Dandio agreed, letting out a tired sigh before he continued. "Lord Fireclaw and his forces have returned to the Magno Forest; the kragons believe the Dal-kerri may have fled back toward Caer Droco."

"Yes, I received his message a few days ago," Jan replied, nodding. "His supposition may be correct—the Magno Forest is an easy place for the Dal-kerri to disappear. I fear it may take us months before they are all accounted for."

"They can't cause much trouble without the Ace-Lord though, right?" Mel asked worriedly, echoing the concerns in Allie's mind. This war had only just drawn to a close. The thought of another conflict exhausted her.

"You need not fear them," Iriam assured him. "The Dal-kerri no longer have a leader to command them, and though fierce, they hold no more power than any other beast of the wood. They shall wander, disorganized, into the Magno Forest, and likely remain hidden."

"Lord Fireclaw will alert us if there's trouble from the Dal-kerri," Jan added. "I also intend to alert Lord Andros, and be certain the Elves are on their guard as well. With the new alliance between Tinkeeyo and the Alfona, the Magno Forest shall be well-protected."

"And Elimar?" Ajaha asked, a tinge of worry in her voice. "They have recently sent warning of orcs gathering in the far northeast."

"Tinkeeyo's warriors shall aid Elimar as well," Jan said. "Coonsia is left vulnerable after the Aces—I fear all our enemies know it." He straightened painfully in the wooden chair, one hand pressing to his wounded side as he looked at Aryion. "You know the Elimar area quite well. As of now there is no direct threat from the orcs, but once we have a plan and you both have rested, might you and Mel join the Elimar guard?"

Aryion nodded. "We have contacts in Daffodalion as well," he said, with a glance at his apprentice. "If the orcs are up to trouble in the Anozira again, perhaps the Randuins can aid our defense."

"Good. Well, I shall give you a more detailed report if such a mission is necessary," Jan told him, straightening the stack of reports before looking at Dandio. "How fare the Red Dawn?"

"Well enough, and improving over the last few days," Dandio said with a faint smile. "Admiral Dessian and the fleet have returned to the northern blockade, and General Leopold and Glentree mentioned meeting with the Guardians," he added, looking inquiringly at Rygal.

Rygal nodded. "Lammar's already headed back to Gayrile, actually. Something about a new arrangement that would allow the Guardians and the Red Dawn to protect each other's kingdoms mutually. It'll need the support of the Garilian lords, of course, but we're stronger together. Besides—it might help prevent another Safacon from taking control during all this unrest."

"That is true," Jan agreed, nodding in approval. "I look forward to hearing more about it in the next few weeks. I assume it will take some time for the diplomats to come to an agreement, though."

"Wouldn't surprise me," Rygal replied dryly. "Once we've finished everything here, I'll head back to Gayrile with the Guardians and help with the discussions."

Allie studied the pages on the table before her, hoping her face did not show the emotions that had flooded her mind at his words. *Back to Gayrile.* She'd known it was coming, known it was a good thing to hope for. Rygal would go home, to the role he'd learned to fill and the kingdom that was finally free. It was good news. So why did it come like a knife to her heart?

She pushed the feelings away, bringing her attention back to the present as Ajaha spoke. "My teams are currently working with Lammar's informants. Lord Menrah of the Hyenins warned us that remnants of the Ace-army may have fled across the Strait into the Lago Desert, and his forces have already caught a squadron of formerly enchanted soldiers."

"What *will* be done with the enchanted soldiers?" Dandio asked slowly, glancing at his brother. "We cannot allow them to remain unpunished—willing or not, their choices brought about many deaths. Some of our allies are already calling for their executions."

"I know," Jan said quietly, "and I cannot blame them for that. But that said, the enchantment is gone, and many of those warriors have regained control of their thoughts and minds. They have no desire to return to the darkness that bound them."

"You know this is a difficult matter," Iriam told him gravely. "Those who chose the enchantment willingly have long stood as opponents to the kingdom. Those who served for other reasons are now left with a shadow of who they were. The pieces of their minds they have regained may not be enough to help them live their lives."

Allie knew his bleak words were all too true. She'd seen the reactions of the enchanted soldiers that they'd escorted back from the battlefield—many had looked more angry than confused, angry and dismayed that they had lost. The twisted gifts of the enchantment had been something they'd enjoyed, as they fought for the Ace-Lord out of their own volition.

Yet she'd seen others, too. Hundreds of faces who simply looked lost and frightened, returning to themselves with blades in their grasp and blood on their hands. How many had been simple peasants and farmers, peaceful people pressed into the Ace-Lord's deadly service?

Darion's face entered her thoughts, and she recalled his words, his determination to help the lost, no matter what they had done. His mission was one Allie had promised help—seeking a cure for the enchantment. A mission she had failed time and time again. She owed it to Darion's memory to advocate for them, at the very least.

"They must still be given a choice," she said at last, glancing around the table. "I—I know some of them won't care whether or not we want to help them. Some were criminals long before they joined the Ace-Lord. But even if they did choose his side, they might be having second thoughts now." She looked down at the scars on her hands and forearms. "I can tell you, if the Ace-Lord gave you power like that, you don't have much control of your own mind."

"That much I can second," Aryion said quietly.

Allie looked at the ranger, then at Iriam, noting the approval in the Neutral's eyes. At last she turned her gaze to Ĵan, waiting for the king's verdict.

"What I intend to do," Ĵan said at last, "is determine which of the enchanted soldiers chose their service in full understanding. We know many sided with the Aces in rebellion—such as the Rufa Brownaes, as well as the orc and Dwarve tribes. Those who did so shall be given the choice of banishment or imprisonment."

"And for the unwilling?" Dusty asked, her ears pricked forward in interest.

"For the unwilling, I believe we are called to mercy," Jan stated. "Despite what they have done, many have already come forward expressing regret. Extending forgiveness may not be what some would call fair, but I am firm in my decision that it is the right thing to do." Allie noticed his hand lingered on Isilas for a moment, as the Star-Stone glimmered softly.

"It is the right choice," Iriam told him, nodding thoughtfully. "Even those who demand vengeance will understand it in time."

"The Stones might be able to help, too," Mel put in. "The Blue Stone can heal, and its light was able to break the illusions."

"Could the Druids help them as well?" Rygal wondered, looking at Iriam. "Everything I've heard of them says they know the ways of the mind."

"They may," Iriam said, "but that is not their calling at present, I fear. They will not remain here long."

They all looked at him in surprise. "They're leaving?" Mel asked, startled. "When?"

Iriam paused, looking at Jan, who alone seemed unsurprised to hear this news. At last, the Neutral continued. "There are certain parameters for the living beings of Orlell," he said, speaking slowly. "Beings who were created for this mortal world, whose path and calling lies here. Yet there are others whose calling has always led elsewhere. The Druids are such beings. The Neutrals have never truly belonged to Orlell—we came here under Kahlifis' rule, then resisted when he turned against the High Light. Yet after the Dividing War, we remained, some aiding the mortals or others remaining in exile, as the Light directed."

He glanced around at his interested audience. "The Druids used those years to turn away from the darkness that had corrupted their magic. They used their power for Orlell, drawing from the natural and pure magic of the High Light as their people were meant to do. It was always known that when the time came to battle Kahlifis, they would join that fight, and so they have done."

"And… now that that time's over… what happens?" Dusty asked haltingly, her brow furrowed.

"Now, the mission of the Druids is complete," Iriam told her. "Their purpose here has been fulfilled. Now, we must follow the High Light's guiding elsewhere."

Allie stared at him, a dull ache of realization filling her chest. "You're… you're leaving too?"

The same dismay filled the faces of Mel, Rygal, and Dusty, and they looked in disbelief at the Neutral who had guided them for so long they had almost taken his advice for granted.

A slight, sad smile crossed Iriam's face. "For a time, child," he answered. "I do not share the same purpose as the Druid Council. However, I have a duty to my people and the few of us who are left. Whatever place they must reach, wherever they are now called, must be known to me, as the last guardian of our race. When that task is completed, know that I shall return."

"But we need you," Mel stammered. "The fight's over, but there's so much we still need to do—so much we don't know."

Iriam shook his head. "The time has passed where I can guide you. The Prophecy is fulfilled. The war is over. Your choices must be without my guidance—I am bound by the same rules as the Stars, and I cannot interfere unless commanded thus."

He laid a gentle hand on Allie's shoulder, drawing her eyes up to meet his. She could see the sorrow written on his face, a face that had always seemed older than time itself. "My part in your studies is over for now," he told her. "But that does not mean there is any less for you to learn and accomplish. Each of you." His purple-red eyes scanned the faces around the table. "You have done as I have taught, and know that I am truly, deeply proud of each of you. Through every dark night you fought on, and learned to seek the Light as the Words of Old teach. I do not doubt you will continue in that."

Allie looked away, feeling tears of both gratitude and sadness fill her eyes. Remembering her lessons with Iriam, every word of advice he had ever given her, even the harsh chastising she had once resented... though she might not have appreciated it in the moment, she knew without a doubt that his wisdom would stay with her.

"We shall depart two evenings from now," Iriam said. "Where I go, it is not for me to know yet. Nor do I know how long the time will be. But you have my word, I will return."

"I will ask your advice once more, then," Ĵan said, "though I cannot imagine how I will manage without it in the future."

Iriam laughed—something Allie had hardly ever heard him do—and shook his head again. "You have managed the matters of mortals without me more than you realize," he told Ĵan. "I have gone away to meet with the Druids quite often, though it was not for you to know then. The rule of Safacon, the rebellion of Drona, the return of the Darkness... all have prepared you for this time." He cast his gaze around the others in the room before turning back to Jan. "Nonetheless I will answer your question."

Jan took a breath, exchanging a look with Dandio. For a moment, Allie caught a glimpse of the young and uncertain princes who had long been under Iriam's tutelage. Yet the men in their place were the High King and the Commander, bruised and battered, care and wisdom lining their silver-skinned faces. *Perhaps I've changed too,* she thought to herself. If Iriam had imparted the same wisdom to Jan as he had taught her, perhaps one day, she could become wise and strong like her uncle. A ruler who sought the safety of the people over her own gain, who remained in steady faith of the High Light.

"It is the matter of the Star-Stones," Jan said, his gaze meeting Iriam's again. "I would like to know your advice. Isilas' corruption," he drew it forth carefully, allowing pale blue light to illuminate the tabletop, "has been halted by the grace of the Light, and both it and the Blue Stone are no longer in immediate danger. But I am still uncertain."

"The Aces are gone," Dandio told him. "Any other threat can't compare much to them."

"All the same," Jan answered, "Isilas was not corrupted by the Aces, but by mortal hand. I fear the Stones will never truly be safe if we continue to keep them. Besides that, I believe that in the same way the time of the Druids has passed, so has the time of the Stones." He looked at Mel. "Would you agree?"

Mel nodded slowly, his brow furrowed as he thought. "I can't really explain it, but I feel the same. Like it'd be almost... wrong... to keep the Stones now that the Aces are gone. The power they hold, the secret of the *Alené*—it was all for that time, just like the Prophecy." He looked down at the Star-Stone, the blue light shining on his face.

"We have guarded them," Jan continued. "I am concerned that, if we continued to keep them, our reasons would turn selfish, and our goals for them would become little different than the Ace-Lord's. That said… I do not know what would be the wisest course of action."

Iriam's face was thoughtful. "The time of the Star-Stones has passed," he stated finally. "I am glad both Wielders are in agreement of that." He was quiet a moment. At last he looked between Jan and Mel. "I advise you to seek the Light's guidance, not mine, in this matter. The correct choice will present itself in time."

63

A Path and a Promise

Weeks passed by in Mata City following the Druid's departure.

Mel never asked where they were going or how they would get there. Their ships simply rose out of the sea itself, silvery vessels tall and slender like swans. There was no sign of their crews, but Mel thought he glimpsed watery hands raising the ships above the waves.

And so they departed, the nine Druids and Iriam with them. Mel felt a deep sorrow at the Neutral's leaving, as well as an intense curiosity for when he would return and what might prompt him to do so.

It was not the only parting. The Wildkids were preparing to return to Kasabren, escorted again by Admiral Dessian and the crew of the *Blue Moon*. A crowd gathered in the harbor to see them off. Mel hugged Dusty and her brothers goodbye, knowing it would likely be a long while before he would see them again.

"You'll come visit soon?" he asked her hopefully. "Once everything's settled?"

"I hope so," Dusty answered, with a glance at Aryion. "Or… perhaps you could come to Kasabren. It's been some time since any human has visited our island, and I think… I think the time has come for that to change."

"Then farewell, for now," Aryion said, the shadow of a smile crossing his face.

The same evening the *Blue Moon* departed from Mata Bay, a small Caer Sian sailboat arrived from Lillary, anchoring at the pier where Mel and Aryion stood. In another moment, Mel's father had wrapped his arms around him, his mother was kissing his cheek, and Misty was hugging him so tight it almost hurt.

He didn't complain. There had been so many moments in the dark fight where he had feared he'd never see them again, and he rested in their embrace with joy.

"I thought you guys would wait in Lillary Bay," he said, once they had all returned to the Puddlepaws' house. Jarus had been called away by the Cooper delegates, but Maya said he would return soon. There was a look in her blue eyes Mel didn't exactly understand—a sort of hesitant, nervous anticipation, and he noticed she kept glancing at the door.

"We had planned to stay there," Joseph answered, nodding. "But now that the refugees have begun to return home, we decided we had better come get you before going back to Caer Sia."

"Caer Sia?" Mel repeated, surprised.

"It was the High King's command," Aryion told him. "Now that the Aces are gone, it is safe for the civilians to return to Sia."

"There's… much to be rebuilt," Joseph said hesitantly, "and the city will be slow to heal. But the people are eager to be home."

"The word came that the war was over two weeks ago," Elonie put in. "Some had feared it would never end."

"It was so dark," Misty murmured with a shudder. "And cold. Was that what the Prophecy talked about? *When the sun and stars are darkened?*"

"I think so," Mel agreed softly. How often he had studied those stanzas, wondering over the lines, puzzling over the words. At times he'd doubted everything about it, doubted what would become of the New Blood. At one point he'd believed his life would be forfeit.

Yet here he was. Living to the end of another day to sit around the table with his family and the mentor he had feared lost.

"What are we going to do now, Mom?" Misty asked, looking hesitantly at her mother. "Where are we going to live?"

"We could live in Caer Sia," Mel said before either parents answered. "We know it'll be safe."

"And so many of our friends live there too," Misty added, nodding eagerly.

"We have friends in Appledale as well," Joseph reminded her gently. "There are a lot of people there who need our help to find the Light again, now that the shadow is past."

"But... our house," Mel began haltingly, glancing at Misty. Images of the devastation in Appledale filled his mind again, the crushing pain of seeing their ruined home. "And... I might be leaving again soon. If we're going to Elimar," he added, looking at Aryion.

"That might not be for some time yet," Aryion reminded him. His features were still gaunt, shadows under his eyes, and Mel sensed he was as weary from the fighting as Mel was. The idea of resting for a while—settling down, helping the people of Caer Sia and Appledale recover and rebuild, and leaving the question of the future for someone else to decide—was suddenly quite appealing.

The Stone hung heavy in his pocket like a weight, and he remembered thinking the very same thing when he'd first taken the Shard. So afraid of what the future would hold, longing greatly for life as it had been.

Life would never go back to that time. He knew enough now to understand that. Still, that did not mean he could not hope for a better tomorrow, where his family could again be settled in safety and he could enjoy his life as a ranger.

"We'll discuss living arrangements later," Elonie said, placing her hand on her husband's arm. She turned toward the kitchen, seeming to change the subject. "Maya, dear, might I help with anything?"

"Oh, that's all right, thank you," Maya called back. There was the slosh of sudsy water before the Cooper appeared, her blonde fur damp around her forearms. "You might call it crazy, but after everything that's been going on, there's nothing more satisfying than some simple chores around the house. Ella, come *here*."

The last sentence was directed to her daughter, who had bounded up to the door and was reaching futilely for the knob.

"Jarus said they're determining the election today?" Aryion asked as Maya moved toward the determined toddler.

"Yes," Maya answered, with the same nervous energy Mel had noticed before. "Our political system is a little different here in Mata City—the crown doesn't always defer to the heir of the previous lord. The people vote for who they want as leader." She pulled Ella away from the door.

"Bet they'll choose Jarus," Mel murmured to Aryion.

"They might, though it would be unusual," his mentor replied quietly. "Still, with his ties to Gayrile, he might be a solid candidate."

"Maybe we could live in Mata City," Misty mused, looking at her father. "I bet the Coopers need a book binder. Is there a library here?"

"Several," Maya answered with a smile. "If you like, Ella and I can show you our favorite one tomorrow."

Misty nodded eagerly. "Yes please—I need to finish my essays. I missed most of summer term, so I'm having to catch up."

Mel shook his head in her direction, but he felt himself smile. "Maybe

I'll come too. I need to write a message to Bryn, and let her know how everything's ended up." He looked at Aryion with a slight frown. "Though I'm not sure how we'd get that message to her."

"I am sure Lammar can handle it," Aryion answered.

The door opened suddenly, admitting first Dandio, then Jarus, who looked up at them with a mixture of bewilderment and disbelief.

"Me," he said after a beat, shaking his head slowly. "They... the delegates want *me* as the next lord of Mata City."

Any other words he said were drowned out by the excited cheers of Joseph, Mel, and Misty. Maya hugged Jarus tightly, her eyes shining with pride and joy.

"A unanimous vote," Dandio said, nodding in satisfaction. "Light above, that might be the first time I've seen that many stuffy delegates all agree on *anything*."

"Well done," Aryion told Jarus with a smile.

"That's amazing, Jarus!" Mel said with a grin, clapping the Cooper's shoulder enthusiastically. "You're going to do great."

"I hope so," Jarus murmured fervently, shaking his head slowly, but a smile had crossed his face. "I don't know why—they'd choose me, but..."

"You'll do wonderfully," Maya told him, taking his paw in hers. "I— you had mentioned Lammar wanted to nominate you, but—oh, Jarus, it's so wonderful!"

"I don't know how much I can blame Lammar at all," Jarus said with an incredulous laugh. "He mentioned it, sure, but they were all in agreement. It will be official after the election, of course—the people still get a voice in it."

"If they've any sense, they'll choose you," Joseph chuckled. "Well done!"

The evening lapsed into comfortable conversation, cheerful, hopeful conversation that promised no ghost of the shadows. Mel's fears had slipped away. The guilt and pain of the past were gone. Even the questions of the future seemed to have faded to the back of his mind, no longer crowding his thoughts, but waiting patiently. The day was done, and the falling rain carried the sweet scent of coming autumn.

The war was over, and Mel's heart could finally rest.

． ． ． ． ． ．

Home. How little Allie had expected to see it again.

A week after the election of the new lord of Mata City, her family's discussions steered away from politics and treaties and returned instead to the fate of the city awaiting them. Civilians had begun to return, Jan said. Thanks to the efforts of the Red Dawn and the aid of the Nøkken, the city itself had suffered far less damage than the Aces might have caused. Buildings had been broken down, houses had been burned, the castle had been torn apart, but the capital city would recover.

She and her family bade the Puddlepaws farewell. Aryion and Mel would come to Caer Sia in a few weeks, choosing to stay in Mata City a little longer.

Rygal accompanied them back on the *Gryphon*, arranging for the Guardians to meet him in Sia. The short voyage did not afford much time for Allie to talk with him. They both seemed hesitant around each other, as if afraid any conversation might suddenly turn into another discussion entirely, a topic Allie still wasn't sure of talking about.

The emotions in her heart refused to be compressed into simple words. They lingered instead on the fringes of her mind, wandering into her dreams. The memory of his lips against hers in the darkness, even as she'd prepared herself for death, still filled her stomach with butterflies. Her dreams were tangled and confused—horrific memories intertwining with the hope and love she was still hesitant to acknowledge.

By morning, the *Gryphon* entered Sia's harbor.

The city shimmered with last night's rain, and the noisy bustle of activity filled the streets. Ash still stained the buildings, rubble sat in piles beside the houses, but the people had begun the work. Carriages moved people and supplies from one part of the city to another, and as they bumped up the familiar roads, Allie felt a glimmer of hope making its way through the uncertainty and darkness in her heart.

Castle Sia's walls stood quiet and lonesome. Two of its towers had fallen in on themselves, and the destruction had been made to mimic the ruin of Castle Droco. Yet Allie saw no sign of that blanched fortress before her. No matter the broken walls, the rubble filling the courtyard, the debris scattered across the streets. She only saw her home, one that had always been waiting for her.

She placed a hand on the door frame of the main entrance to the palace. The doors had been broken inwards, wrenched from their hinges. She remembered how many times she'd entered through here, hurrying to her studies after a sparring session with Rygal, or running to tell Jan something before his next meeting began.

How she had missed this place.

"We will rebuild," came her mother's quiet voice behind her, and she felt Ajaha's hand on her back. "It may be broken now, but it can be raised again, stronger than ever."

"I'm starting to feel that will be better," Allie murmured, not sure how she could put her thoughts into words. There were joyful memories here of happy days long gone. But darkness too. Rumors of shadows and bloodshed. Scars on the library walls and ice that had split the courtyard stones in two.

They would rebuild, without a sign of the Aces or the darkness that had tried to claim them. Raising a new thing from the broken stones.

Her family settled at an inn that night, resting comfortably in the familiar city. Allie lay awake long into the night, thinking over many things. The uncertainty, the fear of the unexpected future before her... it was beginning to fade, replaced with nervous excitement that filled her before the start of a new journey. Whether or not she'd expected it didn't matter—it was a gift. Time granted to her by the High Light. A life she would live to the fullest.

The path before her was still half-hidden in shadow. But it was a path all the same. Her steps would be guided by the Light. All Iriam had taught her of the Words of Old had prepared her for this.

No... there was only one uncertainty still in her mind, one she could no longer push aside.

The *Ignis Veritos* entered Caer Sia's harbor the following morning. Allie saw its familiar sails among those of the Red Dawn ships, which were still ferrying soldiers and civilians from all across Coonsia. So many partings and goings still filled the days... and yet the one before her hurt in a different way.

She stayed with Rygal for most of the day, knowing this would be the last before his departure. There was a short meeting with the High King and his counselors, discussing an upcoming alliance between the tribes of Gayrile and Caer Sia. Several tribes were still unsure whether or not the new arrangement would benefit them.

"I think they'll agree to it eventually," Rygal mused. "The Ace attack on Gayrile, and the battle of Bridgeport, showed them that we're stronger allied together."

"I believe you are right," Jan answered. "Still, we will wait for the matters in Mata City to stabilize before we begin negotiations. I would hate to have our new Lord Puddlepaw overworked within his first month in office."

"By the time he's ready, we'll probably have just decided on a date," Rygal said dryly, shaking his head as he looked at Allie. "Think about how long it took the delegates to settle on a day for the peace negotiations back in Gayrile."

"Let's hope it's not as bad as that," Allie said with a smile. "But just let me know if you need another Caer Sian delegate to join in."

He returned the smile, but there was another light in his blue eyes, too, one she hoped she wasn't imagining.

Evening fell in Caer Sia, and a fiery sunset painted the incoming rain clouds. A cool breeze blew gently from the south. The leaves of the cherry trees lining Caer Sia's streets had begun to show hints of red and yellow as Rygal and Allie walked to the harbor.

"Do you have a plan to contact the other Garilian lords?" she asked.

"Lammar's working on it," Rygal answered. "To be honest, I'm not sure how much the Guardians will need to handle. It's all politics now, which is not our area of expertise." He shook his head in mock dismay.

"*War is politics*," Allie said, in a fairly good impression of Jan's voice, which made Rygal laugh. "That will be a relief though," she added. "You should enjoy the quiet while it lasts."

"Says the one who wanted to join the fight so bad she got herself captured in Wiverrun?"

"That's not relevant," Allie retaliated. "Also, that wasn't *my* plan."

"I know," Rygal said, smiling. "Still, I think that's when I realized… what I thought of you."

A shiver ran down Allie's spine, and she felt her face warm. Why did her words simply refuse to come? She'd thought out everything she'd wanted to say last night, but it all seemed flat and empty in the light of day. Nothing could truly capture what she wanted him to know.

"I… I wanted to remind you," she began finally. "You still owe me that dance. You said you'd learn it once the war was over." *And if we were both still alive,* her mind finished. At that time, the promise had seemed so futile. A painful reminder of something that would never be.

And now? Now that the future spread before them both and their paths joined for this last day together… what would come then?

"I did promise that, didn't I?" A smile crossed his face again as he studied the waiting *Veritos.* The sunset sparkled on the waves, reflecting in his eyes. "Well, you never know. Maybe there will be some sort of banquet, or celebration later, and… and I could fulfill that promise."

"Maybe," Allie agreed, wishing very much that would be the case. "Could the Guardians spare you for that time?"

"I hope so," he murmured, turning to face her. His face held the same confusing blend of uncertainty and happiness as Allie felt. For a moment he hesitated, seeking the right words. "I'm… no good at this," he said at last, shaking his head. "But I want you to know… I love you, Asescia. I have for some time—though it's taken me a while to fully realize how much."

Joy, fierce and bright as the flames in her heart, spread through her veins, choking out her voice for a moment. The fear that had devoured her, the darkness that had nearly claimed her, seemed far away, distant as a dream.

"I love you too," she finally managed to reply, startled to feel tears burning behind her vision. "And I want—I hope—I don't know what will happen now, with everything that still needs to be done… I can't claim the Commander of the Guardians until it's settled, I think."

"Nor I the Heiress of Sia," Rygal replied with a smile. "Still, I did talk to your father about—well, this. He seemed almost pleased, which I'm mildly afraid of." Allie laughed, despite the tears. Rygal brushed them away gently, turning her eyes to his again. "But I will come back, if you'll have me then. That much I can promise you."

"You'll promise?" Allie whispered.

For answer, he pulled her close and kissed her, as the winds rippled over the harbor and waves rocked the waiting ships like a summons of the next mission.

Epilogue
Two months later

Silence.

It filled the frost-dusted trees as the five riders entered the forest.

Signs of autumn shone on the woods past the border, where red-tinted leaves clung stubbornly to the branches of sleeping trees. If Rygal strained his ears, or peered just right into the tangled brush that framed the trail as the companions rode northeast, he was certain he could hear whispered words in a wild tongue, or glimpse the watching eyes of the dryads.

Or perhaps he was only imagining it. The dryads were quieter now, now that there were no dire messages to bring, nor reports of battle and bloodshed to warrant their help.

The trees slept. The wind was still. But he could sense their presence, like a warm breeze calling a weary traveler home.

"We're nearly there," Aryion said from up ahead.

Rygal raised his eyes, scanning the woods surrounding them. Aryion and Mel rode ahead, guiding their horses down the trail. Mel's face glowed with interest and excitement as he glanced back at Rygal. "How long's it been since you were here?"

"Years," Rygal answered, shaking his head. "I haven't been here since the rise of Kado."

He'd been a child then, even younger than Mel. Still unsure of his place in the world, of who he was, who he would become. It seemed a lifetime past, yet was as fresh in his mind as yesterday.

Dusty had told him of the legend of the Forest of Light then, how the

High Light had created it to be a sanctuary of peace after the Dividing War. Perhaps that was why the Ace-Lord had chosen to destroy it first in his conquest.

"That is more recently than some," Jan said behind him, a quiet note of amusement in his voice. The High King's keen green eyes scanned the glade. "It has been many years since I walked this path, yet it still seems the same." He frowned thoughtfully, as though unable to put it into words.

"I've only heard tales of the Forest," Allie murmured. She rode beside Rygal, wrapped in her cloak. A few strands of brown hair drifted across her face, which still bore the pale scars from the white flames.

The trail wound up a slight hill, bringing them to a glade as gray and dark as a void. The cold and shadow that had previously gripped it were gone now, Rygal knew. But he still felt a shiver as if from some last remnant of the Ace-Lord's magic as they entered what had once been the Forest of Light.

All was still, much as it had been when he had come here all those years ago. The only noise came from the soft babble of the stream running from the center of the clearing. Frost crusted the ground, glittering on the wilted grass. The silver trees encircling the glade seemed drained of their color, standing bare and lifeless. Drops of dew sparkled on their withered boughs.

Scars and shadows, that was all the Aces had left behind. It was the task of the mortals to move onward despite it.

The companions paused, looking around the desolate glade. "Is this the right place?" Allie asked finally, her face uncertain as she glanced at Jan.

The High King studied the wood a moment. Rygal could see him struggling to find some glimmer of the pure magic that had once filled the wood. But the only light came from his own hand as he drew the Star-Stone from its place and looked at Mel. "I believe it is. What do you think?"

Mel's eyes scanned the dead forest before he nodded. "Yeah… yeah, it's time."

The group dismounted, gathering around the stream. Frost crunched under Rygal's boots as he did. Allie moved to his side, and he put an arm around her, holding her close in a quiet promise. His heart seemed to beat faster at her presence, beating against the dark scar on his chest that would never fade.

They watched wordlessly as the two Wielders moved forward together to the spring, the Star-Stones illuminating their faces. One, worn with years of care and trouble, the other far younger, both having lived through similar horrors. Yet Rygal saw in their eyes the same surety and calm that he felt, now that the Aces were gone.

Slowly, the Wielders knelt and laid the Stones gently in the crystal-clear water.

There were no words spoken, no great flash of light, no thundering druidic voice. All Rygal saw were the two Star-Stones, spreading pure blue light into the water, until the spring itself seemed to glow with their power.

Not a false power. Not the darkness that the Ace-Lord had used to bring about so much ruin and that promised only death for all who claimed it. This was something stronger. A power that shone a brilliant light into the darkness, loosing the icy chains of the strongest curse. A power that whispered in the words of the Prophecy, shone in the lyrics of the song, and filled the breath of every living creature of Orlell.

A power stronger than the forces of death.

In one final glimmer, the Star-Stones faded away, dissolving into the stream as if their power might flow into the very core of the mortal world. Healing and shielding and making all things new. The chilly breeze blew gently around them, sighing in the boughs of the trees as Jan and Mel stood.

Tomorrow they would return to Caer Sia. Back to the uncertain times and the partings that remained. There was so much left to rebuild. So much work to be done. So much darkness that still lurked in the hearts of the mortals.

Yet Rygal felt hope, too, burning like a fire that could not be snuffed out by the coldest ice. Hope that there was more still to come. Hope that even the darkest days would pass.

Even as the thought crossed his mind, the faintest glint of fresh green reached his eyes beside the stream as they mounted up again.

"Allie," he murmured, touching her hand and drawing her eyes back to the spring. They watched, in silent wonder, as two seedlings broke from the barren ground where the Stones had vanished.

Two fire-flowers twinkled golden light over the frosty grass, twin beacons of flame in the gray wood.

The curse was broken. The evening would fall and the dawn would come again as the days continued in the song of time while the High Light wrote the story.

Winter was coming, whispered by the breeze soaring through the Forest of Light, and Orlell rested in peace.

End of the Orlell Chronicles

Glossary/Pronunciation Guide

Ace-Deputy
leader of the Ace-army, cunning and sly

Ajaha Ki (ah-ZHA-ha KEE)
Dandio's wife; a skilled courier

Alfona (al-FO-nah)
tribe of native Cantrians in the Magno Forest

Allá Alené (ah-LAH all-leh-NAY)
ancient spell of the Star-Stones

Arrex (AIR-rex)
Hyenin general in the Red Dawn

Aryion Paya (AR-ree-on PY-ah)
ranger known as the Hummingbird

Asescia Ki (ah-SESS-see-ah KEE)
heiress to the crown of Caer Sia. Also known as Allie

Brownae (BROWN-ee)
race of 4-feet tall, furry forest dwellers

Bryn Trelawney
pirate captain of the Scarlet Consort, Aryion's sister

Caer Sia (care-SEE-uh)
the capital city of Coonsia

Cahadras (cah-HAD-drass)
queen of the Stars

Cantrians (CAN-tree-ins)
most common type of Essence-filled being; includes humans and elves

Dal-kerri (dahl-KARE-ee)
wolf-like beasts in the Ace-army

Dandio Ki (dan-DYE-oh KEE)
commander of Caer Sian army, brother of the High King

Darion (DARE-ee-in)
young ranger of Wiverrun

Dessian (DESS-ee-in)
Liznee admiral of the Red Dawn

Dusty
fiery and skilled Wildkid warrior

Fargrin (FAR-grin)
enchanted captain in the Ace-army

Fyrocrians (FY-roh-CREE-ins)
Essence-filled individual whose power manifests as fire, includes Liznees

Glentree
giant, loyal warrior, Dandio's deputy

Iriam (EER-ree-ahm)
Neutral, advisor to the High King

Jan Ki (ZHAN KEE)
High King of the Liznees

Jarus Puddlepaw (JARE-is)
Cooper diplomat, Maya's husband

Kahlifis (KAHL-eh-fis)
rebel Netrocrian king; now known as the Ace-Lord

Lammar (la-MARR)
Siren informant

Maya Puddlepaw
Cooper shipwright, Jarus' wife

Mel Smallbutton
young ranger apprentice, the New Blood

Munben-Lia (MOON-ben LEE-ah)
hama-dryad chieftain

Morel Inmana
fierce leader of the Chanterelle Brownae tribe

Netrocrians (net-tro-CREE-ins)
Essence-filled being whose power manifests as ice and darkness

Neutral
race of Netrocrians who remained loyal to the Light in the Dividing War

Nøkken (NIH-kin)
sea-spirits

Porcini Inmana
Brownae diplomat, Morel's brother

Redeyes
black tiger-like beast serving the Ace-Lord

Robin Trelawney
pirate captain of the Burman Marie

Rygal (RYE-gull)
young warrior and leader of the Guardians of Gayrile

Acknowledgements

If you have read all the way to this point, it is to be hoped that you have read (and enjoyed) the last 770 pages of this finale. For that, I can only say thank you. An author is nothing without their readers, and I'm blessed to have some of the best.

Shoutout to Union Block Coffeehouse and Crossroads Cafe for supplying at least 250 hours of great coffee and excellent writing environments over the last two years of writing and editing SotS.

Thanks to my two main editors—Rebekah Smith and my mom Leslie. You guys make even the most tedious line editing fun with your notes and ideas. Rebekah, thanks for making me laugh with your reactions to some scenes. Mom, you've been there since day one. I could not have done this without you, in more ways than one, and I'm overwhelmed by your love for this series.

Lots of love to the Orlell Team of family and friends for supporting this series' journey since it began: Amanda, Meagan, Alexis, the Eells family, the Writer's Group of Calvary McMinnville, and the entire Bjornstedt clan. There's a reason companions and family are major themes in this book.

To my Launchers, you guys are the best. Thanks for helping market this book, and I've loved every email convo we've shared.

Huge thanks to Emilie with EAH Creative for designing a seriously epic cover image, and making the whole design process so fun! I'm still gushing over it as I write this.

To the true Light of the World, thank You for bringing me out of the darkness.

Lastly, to my husband Levi. Thanks for making every exhausting day, every late-night brainstorm session, every long outlining conversation worth it. This story would not be the same without you. You've encouraged me, pushed me past my comfort zone, and helped me out of more plot holes than I could count. I can't wait for our next adventure.

So friends, farewell for now, and as the High King would urge,

Seek the Light!

www.ingramcontent.com/pod-product-compliance
Lightning Source LLC
Chambersburg PA
CBHW011510010826
48973CB00015B/2887